100
CREEPY
LITTLE
CREATURES

100 CREEPY LITTLE CREATURES

EDITED BY

STEFAN R. DZIEMIANOWICZ,

ROBERT WEINBERG

& MARTIN H. GREENBERG

BARNES
&NOBLE
BOOKS
NEW YORK

This edition published by Barnes & Noble, Inc.,
by arrangement with Martin H. Greenberg

1994 Barnes & Noble Books

ISBN 1-56619-919-0

Book design by Mario A. Moreno

Printed and bound in the United States of America

M 9 8 7 6 5 4 3 2

Acknowledgements

Grateful acknowledgment is made to the following for permission to reprint their copyrighted materials:

"The Amulet of Hell" by Robert Leonard Russell; "The Avenging Hand" by Roy Wallace Davis; "The Beast of the Yungas" by Willis Knapp Jones; "The Beetle" by Garnett Radcliffe; "A Birthday Present for Tommy" by Charles King; "The Cactus" by Mildred Johnson; "The Edge of the Shadow" by R. Ernest Dupuy; "Exhibit A" by Anne Harris Hadley; "Fairy Gossamer" by Harry Harrison Kroll; "Father's Vampire" by Alvin Taylor and Len J. Moffatt; "The Fisherman's Special" by H. L. Thomson; "The Frog" by Granville S. Hoss; "Ghouls of the Sea" by J.B.S. Fullilove; "The Green-and-Gold Bug" by J. M. Alvey; "I'll Be Glad When I'm Dead" by Charles King; "The Inn" by Rex Ernest; "The Keen Eyes and Ears of Kara Kedi" by Claude Farrère; "Left by the Tide" by Edward E. Schiff; "The Marmot" by Allison V. Harding; "Mummy" by Kelsey Percival Kitchel; "The Phantom Drug" by A. W. Kapfer; "The Place of Hairy Death" by Anthony M. Rud; "The Plant-Thing" by R. G. Macready; "The Power of the Dog" by G. G. Pendarves; "A Problem of the Dark" by Frances Arthur; "Seven Drops of Blood" by H. F. Jamison; "The Silver Knife" by Ralph Allen Lang; "Smoke Fantasy" by Thomas R. Jordan; "There Was Soot on the Cat" by Suzanne Pickett; "The Throwback" by Orlin Frederick; "The Toad Idol" by Kirk W. Mashburn; "Tzo-Lin's Nightingales" by Ben Belitt; "The Werewolf Howls" by Clifford Ball; "The Werewolf's Howl" by Brooke Byrne; "The White Dog" by Feodor Sologub.

All of the above copyright © 1924 by Rural Publishing Co.; copyright © 1924–38 by Popular Fiction Publishing Co.; copyright © 1938–53 by Weird Tales. Reprinted by permission of Weird Tales Ltd.

"Baynter's Imp" by August Derleth—Copyright © 1943 by Weird Tales. Reprinted by permission of the Scott Meredith Literary Agency, Inc., 845 Third Ave., New York, NY 10022.

"Call First" by Ramsey Campbell—Copyright © 1975 by Kirby McCauley for NIGHT CHILLS. Reprinted by permission of the author.

"Dagon" by H. P. Lovecraft—Copyright © 1923 by Rural Publishing Co. for WEIRD TALES. Reprinted by permission of the Scott Meredith Literary Agency, Inc., 845 Third Ave., New York, NY 10022.

"Dark Brother" by Donald R. Burleson—Copyright © 1993 by Donald R. Burleson. First published in LEMON DROPS AND OTHER HORRORS. Reprinted by permission of the author.

Contents

Introduction   XVII

After Dark in the Playing Fields   1
M. R. James

The Amulet of Hell   4
Robert Leonard Russell

The American's Tale   10
Arthur Conan Doyle

Amina   16
Edward Lucas White

The Avenging Hand   26
Roy Wallace Davis

The Basilisk   32
R. Murray Gilchrist

Baynter's Imp   38
August Derleth

The Beast of the Yungas   44
Willis Knapp Jones

The Beetle   51
Garnett Radcliffe

A Birthday Present for Tommy   57
Charles King

The Cactus   65
Mildred Johnson

Call First   74
Ramsey Campbell

Caterpillars   78
E. F. Benson

Dagon   86
H. P. LOVECRAFT

The Damned Thing   91
AMBROSE BIERCE

Dark Brother   99
DONALD R. BURLESON

Deep Wood   103
STEPHEN M. RAINEY

Demons of the Sea   111
WILLIAM HOPE HODGSON

The Deserted Garden   120
AUGUST DERLETH

The Devil of the Marsh   125
H. B. MARRIOTT-WATSON

The Devilish Rat   129
ALBERT PAGE MITCHELL

Dog, Cat, and Baby   137
JOE R. LANSDALE

Dummy   139
SIMON MacCULLOCH

The Dump   145
JOE R. LANSDALE

The Edge of the Shadow   150
R. ERNEST DUPUY

Exhibit A   154
ANNE HARRIS HADLEY

Fairy Gossamer   160
HARRY HARRISON KROLL

Familiar Face   165
ROBERT M. PRICE

FATHER'S VAMPIRE 174
ALVIN TAYLOR AND LEN J. MOFFATT

THE FEATHER PILLOW 181
HORACIO QUIROGA

THE FISHERMAN'S SPECIAL 184
H. L. THOMSON

THE FROG 188
GRANVILLE S. HOSS

FROGFATHER 193
MANLY WADE WELLMAN

THE GARGOYLE SACRIFICE 198
TINA L. JENS

GHOULS OF THE SEA 204
J.B.S. FULLILOVE

THE GRAY WOLF 208
GEORGE MACDONALD

THE GREEN-AND-GOLD BUG 213
J. M. ALVEY

THE HOUSE ON THE RYNEK 217
DERMOT CHESSON SPENCE

I'LL BE GLAD WHEN I'M DEAD 226
CHARLES KING

INDIGESTION 231
BARRY N. MALZBERG

THE INN 238
REX ERNEST

ITCHING FOR ACTION 243
CHARLES GAROFALO

JIKININKI 250
LAFCADIO HEARN

JOHN MORTONSON'S FUNERAL 254
AMBROSE BIERCE

THE KEEN EYES AND EARS OF KARA KEDI 255
CLAUDE FARRÈRE

THE KELPIE 260
MANLY WADE WELLMAN

LADIES IN WAITING 266
HUGH B. CAVE

LAURA 274
SAKI

LEFT BY THE TIDE 279
EDWARD E. SCHIFF

THE LESSER BRETHREN MOURN 282
SEABURY QUINN

THE MARMOT 290
ALLISON V. HARDING

METZENGERSTEIN 298
EDGAR ALLAN POE

MIMIC 305
DONALD A. WOLLHEIM

MIVE 311
CARL JACOBI

THE MOON-SLAVE 317
BARRY PAIN

MONSTERS IN THE NIGHT 321
CLARK ASHTON SMITH

THE MOTHER OF MONSTERS 324
GUY DE MAUPASSANT

MOTHER OF TOADS 328
CLARK ASHTON SMITH

MUMMY 335
KELSEY PERCIVAL KITCHEL

MY FATHER, THE CAT 341
HENRY SLESAR

THE NECROMANCER 348
ARTHUR GRAY

NIGHT SHAPES 354
ROBERT WEINBERG

THE OWL ON THE MOOR 357
MARC SCHORER AND AUGUST DERLETH

THE PHANTOM DRUG 361
A. W. KAPFER

THE PLACE OF HAIRY DEATH 368
ANTHONY M. RUD

THE PLANT-THING 376
R. G. MACREADY

THE POWER OF THE DOG 381
G. G. PENDARVES

A PROBLEM OF THE DARK 388
FRANCES ARTHUR

PROFESSOR JONKIN'S CANNIBAL PLANT 395
HOWARD R. GARIS

THE QUARE GANDER 403
J. SHERIDAN LE FANU

THE REAL WOLF 411
THOMAS LIGOTTI

THE SACRIFICE 415
MIROSLAW LIPINSKI

THE SEEDS FROM OUTSIDE 421
EDMOND HAMILTON

SEEING THE WORLD 426
RAMSEY CAMPBELL

SEVEN DROPS OF BLOOD 432
H. F. JAMISON

SHORT AND NASTY 439
DARRELL SCHWEITZER

THE SILVER KNIFE 448
RALPH ALLEN LANG

THE SKY GARDEN 453
PETER CANNON

SMOKE FANTASY 461
THOMAS R. JORDAN

SMUDGE MAKES A NEW BEST FRIEND 463
PETER CANNON

SNAIL GHOST 469
WILL MURRAY

SOMETHING NASTY 473
WILLIAM F. NOLAN

THE SPECTER SPIDERS 481
WILLIAM J. WINTLE

THE SPIDER OF GUYANA 489
EMILE ERCKMANN AND ALEXANDRE CHATRIAN

SPIDERTALK 498
STEVE RASNIC TEM

THE TABERNACLE 504
HENRY S. WHITEHEAD

TAKE ME, FOR INSTANCE 509
HUGH B. CAVE

THAT ONLY A MOTHER COULD LOVE 516
MOLLIE L. BURLESON

THERE WAS SOOT ON THE CAT 520
SUZANNE PICKETT

THERE'S NO SUCH THING AS MONSTERS 526
STEVE RASNIC TEM

THE THROWBACK 528
ORLIN FREDERICK

THE TOAD IDOL 530
KIRK W. MASHBURN

TZO-LIN'S NIGHTINGALES 535
BEN BELITT

THE UNNAMABLE 541
H. P. LOVECRAFT

THE VAMPIRE MAID 548
HUME NISBET

THE WEREWOLF HOWLS 553
CLIFFORD BALL

THE WEREWOLF'S HOWL 560
BROOKE BYRNE

THE WEREWOLF SNARLS 567
MANLY WADE WELLMAN

THE WHITE DOG 572
FEODOR SOLOGUB

THE WHITE WYRAK 577
STEFAN GRABINSKI (TRANSLATED BY MIROSLAW LIPINSKI)

INTRODUCTION

There's an old saying that what you can't see can't hurt you. For centuries, horror writers have acknowledged this by populating their stories with a menagerie of creatures who give visible shape to the unknown and the indescribable.

The entities you will encounter in *100 Creepy Little Creatures* are representative of the wide variety of animals and entities who comprise the horrific bestiary. Some, such as the goose of J. Sheridan Le Fanu's "The Quare Gander," the horse of Edgar Allan Poe's "Metzengerstein," the cat of Peter Cannon's "Smudge Makes a New Best Friend," the butterflies of Carl Jacobi's "Mive," and the honeybees of Henry S. Whitehead's "The Tabernacle," are unlikely agents of supernatural dread. Others, including the spiders of Anthony Rud's "The Place of Hairy Death" and William J. Wintle's "The Spectre Spiders," the eponymous animal of Albert Page Mitchell's "The Devilish Rat," and the vermin of Charles Garofalo's "Itching for Action," are by their nature associated with the disgusting and disquieting.

Many of these creatures have become staples of supernatural fiction. The vampires of Hume Nisbet's "The Vampire Maid" and Alvin Taylor and Len J. Moffatt's "Father's Vampire," the werewolves of Thomas Ligotti's "The Real Wolf" and Barry Pain's "The Moon Slave," the ghouls of Edward Lucas White's "Amina" and Barry Malzberg's "Indigestion," the sea monsters of William Hope Hodgson's "Demons of the Sea" and J.B.S. Fullilove's "Ghouls of the Sea," the demons of August Derleth's "Baynter's Imp" and H. B. Marriott-Watson's "The Devil of the Marsh," the reanimated corpse of Ramsey Campbell's "Call First," the little people of Mollie Burleson's "That Only a Mother Could Love," and Kelsey Percival Kitchel's "Mummy" will be familiar to readers who have even a nodding acquaintance with fantastic literature. Somewhat less familiar are the creatures that embody myths and legends of particular times and cultures: the beast of classical antiquity in F. Murray Gilchrist's "The Basilisk," the creature of American folklore in Manly Wade Wellman's "Frogfather," the thing of Japanese legend who goes by the name that Lafacadio Hearn translates as "Jikininki," and the animal of Asian magic in Alison V. Harding's "The Marmot." Even less familiar are those creatures whom the authors have created specifically to serve the needs of their stories: the manifestations of childhood fancy in Robert Weinberg's "Night Shapes" and Charles King's "A Birthday Present for Tommy," the monster who inhabits chimneys and preys on unsuspecting sweeps in Stefan Grabinski's "The White Wyrak," the unseen visitors in Hugh B. Cave's "Take Me, for Instance," the evolutionary anomaly of Donald Wollheim's "Mimic," the cosmic traveler of Will Murray's "Snail Ghost," and the creature whose impending arrival foreshadows death in Darrell Schweitzer's "Short and Nasty."

Almost as varied as the species these creatures represent are the uses to which the authors put them. The benevolence of the creatures in Seabury Quinn's "The Lesser Brethren Mourn" and Henry Slesar's "My Father, the Cat" is counterbalanced by the malevolence of those in Arthur Gray's "The Necromancer" and Robert Leonard Russell's "The Amulet." Robert M. Price in "Familiar-Face" and Stephen Mark Rainey in "Deep Wood" make their subjects the agents of supernatural retribution. By contrast Horacio Quiroga in "The Feather Pillow," Donald R. Burleson in "Dark Brother," and Joe R. Lansdale in "Dog, Cat, and Baby" evoke terror simply by allowing their creatures to follow their animal instincts. Where the nonhuman beings in Edmond Hamilton's "The Seeds from Outside" and Howard R. Garis's "Professor Jonkin's Cannibal Plant" are symbols of man's spirit of scientific inquiry, the creatures liberated in Tina Jens's "The Gargoyle Sacrifice" and Clark Ashton Smith's "Monsters in the Night" reflect the worst of mankind's fears and superstitions. The creatures of H. P. Lovecraft's "Dagon" and E. F. Benson's "Caterpillars" are meant to express concepts that defy human understanding, while those that creep through Simon MacCulloch's "Dummy," Miroslaw Lipinski's "The Sacrifice," and Steve Rasnic Tem's "There's No Such Thing as Monsters" reveal truths about human nature we would just as soon not acknowledge.

Regardless of what these creatures are and what they represent, the stories in which they appear extend horror's hallowed tradition of displacing that which we fear onto the alien and the "other." By their brevity, these stories concentrate the unease we feel when contemplating ideas that fall outside the pale of understanding. And in their rendering of what we think of as "unhuman," they hold a mirror up to the very concerns that make us human.

—Stefan Dziemianowicz

After Dark in the Playing Fields

M. R. James

The hour was late and the night was fair. I had halted not far from Sheeps' Bridge and was thinking about the stillness, only broken by the sound of the weir, when a loud tremulous hoot just above me made me jump. It is always annoying to be startled, but I have a kindness for owls. This one was evidently very near: I looked about for it. There it was, sitting plumply on a branch about twelve feet up. I pointed my stick at it and said, "Was that you?" "Drop it," said the owl. "I know it ain't only a stick, but I don't like it. Yes, of course it was me: who do you suppose it would be if it warn't?"

We will take as read the sentences about my surprise. I lowered the stick. "Well," said the owl, "what about it? If you will come out here of a Midsummer evening like what this is, what do you expect?" "I beg your pardon," I said, "I should have remembered. May I say that I think myself very lucky to have met you tonight? I hope you have time for a little talk?" "Well," said the owl ungraciously, "I don't know as it matters so particular tonight. I've had me supper as it happens, and if you ain't too long over it—ah-h-h!" Suddenly it broke into a loud scream, flapped its wings furiously, bent forward and clutched its perch tightly, continuing to scream. Plainly something was pulling hard at it from behind. The strain relaxed abruptly, the owl nearly fell over, and then whipped round, ruffling up all over, and made a vicious dab at something unseen by me. "Oh, I *am* sorry," said a small clear voice in a solicitous tone. "I made sure it was loose. I do hope I didn't hurt you." "Didn't 'urt me?" said the owl bitterly. "Of course you 'urt me, and well you know it, you young infidel. That feather was no more loose than—oh, if I could git at you! Now I shouldn't wonder but what you've throwed me all out of balance. Why can't you let a person set quiet for two minutes at a time without you must come creepin' up and—well, you've done it this time, anyway. I shall go straight to 'eadquarters and"—finding it was now addressing the empty air—"why, where have you got to now? Oh, it is too bad, that it is!"

"Dear me!" I said, "I'm afraid this isn't the first time you've been annoyed in this way. May I ask exactly what happened?"

"Yes, you may ask," said the owl, still looking narrowly about as it spoke, "but it 'ud take me till the latter end of next week to tell you. Fancy coming and pulling out anyone's tail feather! 'Urt me something crool, it did. And what for, I should like to know? Answer me that! Where's the *reason* of it?"

All that occurred to me was to murmur, "The clamorous owl that nightly hoots and wonders at our quaint spirits." I hardly thought the point would be taken, but the owl said sharply: "What's that? Yes, you needn't to repeat it. I 'eard. And I'll tell you what's at the bottom of it, and you mark my words." It bent toward me and whispered, with many nods of its round head: "Pride! stand-offishness! that's what it is! *Come not near our fairy queen*" (this in a tone of bitter contempt). "Oh, dear no! we ain't good enough for the likes of them. Us that's been noted time out of mind for the best singers in the Fields: now, ain't that so?"

"Well," I said, doubtfully enough, "*I* like to hear you very much: but, you know, some people think a lot of the thrushes and nightingales and so on; you must have heard of that, haven't you? And then, perhaps—of course I don't know—perhaps your style of singing isn't exactly what they think suitable to accompany their dancing, eh?"

"I should kindly 'ope not," said the owl, drawing itself up. "Our family's never give in to dancing, nor never won't neither. Why, whatever are you thinkin' of!" it went on with rising temper. "A pretty thing it would be for me to set there hiccuppin' at them"—it stopped and looked cautiously all round it and up and down and then continued in a louder voice—"them little ladies and gentlemen. If it ain't sootable for them, I'm very sure it ain't sootable for me. And" (temper rising again) "if they expect me never to say a word just because they're dancin' and carryin' on with their foolishness, they're very much mistook, and so I tell 'em."

From what had passed before I was afraid this was an imprudent line to take, and I was right. Hardly had the owl given its last emphatic nod when four small slim forms dropped from a bough above, and in a twinkling some sort of grass rope was thrown round the body of the unhappy bird, and it was borne off through the air, loudly protesting, in the direction of Fellows' Pond. Splashes and gurgles and shrieks of unfeeling laughter were heard as I hurried up. Something darted away over my head, and as I stood peering over the bank of the pond, which was all in commotion, a very angry and disheveled owl scrambled heavily up the bank, and stopping near my feet shook itself and flapped and

2

hissed for several minutes without saying anything I should care to repeat.

Glaring at me, it eventually said—and the grim suppressed rage in its voice was such that I hastily drew back a step or two—" 'Ear that? Said they was very sorry, but they'd mistook me for a duck. Oh, if it ain't enough to make anyone go reg'lar distracted in their mind and tear everythink to flinders for miles round." So carried away was it by passion, that it began the process at once by rooting up a large beakful of grass, which alas! got into its throat; and the choking that resulted made me really afraid that it would break a vessel. But the paroxysm was mastered, and the owl sat up, winking and breathless but intact.

Some expression of sympathy seemed to be required; yet I was chary of offering it, for in its present state of mind I felt that the bird might interpret the best-meant phrase as a fresh insult. So we stood looking at each other without speech for a very awkward minute, and then came a diversion. First the thin voice of the pavilion clock, then the deeper sound from the Castle quadrangle, then Lupton's Tower, drowning the Curfew Tower by its nearness.

"What's that?" said the owl, suddenly and hoarsely. "Midnight, I should think," said I, and had recourse to my watch. "Midnight?" cried the owl, evidently much startled, "and me too wet to fly a yard! Here, you pick me up and put me in the tree; don't, I'll climb up your leg, and you won't ask me to do that twice. Quick now!" I obeyed. "Which tree do you want?" "Why, my tree, to be sure! Over there!" It nodded toward the Wall. "All right. Bad-calx tree do you mean?" I said, beginning to run in that direction. " 'Ow should I know what silly names you call it? The one what 'as like a door in it. Go faster! They'll be coming in another minute." "Who? What's the matter?" I asked as I ran, clutching the wet creature, and much afraid of stumbling and coming over with it in the long grass. *"You'll* see fast enough," said this selfish bird. "You just let me git on the tree, *I* shall be all right."

And I suppose it was, for it scrabbled very quickly up the trunk with its wings spread and disappeared in a hollow without a word of thanks. I looked round, not very comfortably. The Curfew Tower was still playing St. David's tune and the little chime that follows, for the third and last time, but the other bells had finished what they had to say, and now there was silence, and again the "restless changing weir" was the only thing that broke—no, that emphasized it.

Why had the owl been so anxious to get into hiding? That of course was what now exercised me. Whatever and whoever was coming, I was sure that this was no time for me to cross the open field: I should do best

3

to dissemble my presence by staying on the darker side of the tree. And that is what I did.

All this took place some years ago, before summertime came in. I do sometimes go into the Playing Fields at night still, but I come in before true midnight. And I find I do not like a crowd after dark—for example at the Fourth of July fireworks. You see—no, you do not, but I see—such curious faces: and the people to whom they belong flit about so oddly, often at your elbow when you least expect it, and looking close into your face, as if they were searching for someone—who may be thankful, I think, if they do not find him. "Where do they come from?" Why, some, I think, out of the water, and some out of the ground. They look like that. But I am sure it is best to take no notice of them, and not to touch them.

Yes, I certainly prefer the daylight population of the Playing Fields to that which comes there after dark.

THE AMULET OF HELL

ROBERT LEONARD RUSSELL

I had been walking in the drizzling rain for some time when I first came to the dingy little curio shop whose faded sign announced: "G. Kodopolis—Curios." It was on a narrow, dirty street in a part of town with which I was totally unfamiliar.

The hour was well toward midnight, but a light was burning in the shop and, although the place had a queerly alien aspect, I felt a sudden, inexplicable urge to enter it. So I pushed open the door and went in.

Once inside, I scarcely noticed the merchandise lining the grimy walls, for my eyes fell immediately upon the only other person in the place, and he was indeed singular enough to claim my whole attention. The man was tall, skeleton-thin in his strangely dark and baggy garments, and the portion of his face that showed above the tangled beard was like nothing more than yellowed parchment stretched over a skull.

But his eyes drew me most; large, jet black, they seemed to gaze into my innermost being, and from them emanated a peculiar force of their own.

I started to speak, but words would not come; I tried to move, but my muscles refused to obey my brain. I could only stare into those eyes and lose myself in their depths. A wave of blackness swept over me and I recall nothing else that happened until I stumbled out into the street some time later, clutching some small, hard object tightly in one hand.

I walked along dazedly for a time; then I found myself quite unexpectedly at the door of my apartment house. I climbed the stairs to my rooms, threw myself fully dressed across the bed, and immediately fell asleep.

It was late next morning when I awoke with a listless feeling and a slight pain at my throat. I was stiff and cramped from sleeping in my clothes, and a small hard something was boring into the middle of my back. I rolled over, found the object, and held it up to the light.

It was an amulet, a rosary of black beads hung with an inverted crucifix bearing the form of an obscene satyr in place of the pendent Christ. It was evidently the thing I had carried from the curio shop, and it puzzled me quite as much as did the strange incidents of the past night.

I stayed in my room all that day, for a strange lethargy possessed me. It was accompanied by a peculiar depression of spirits that increased almost to melancholia as the day wore on and darkness approached. Several times I tried to lose myself in some book or other, but the printed pages had no appeal for me, and ever and anon something came in between my eyes and the words before me—it was the face of the old man in the curio shop, G. Kodopolis.

I went early to bed, but sleep evaded me. I tossed fitfully on my bed for hours before slumber at last claimed me. And slumber brought horrid dreams to plague me.

I was sitting on my bed in the black nothingness of interstellar space, and a hissing *thing* came to gnaw at my throat, a thing with the face of G. Kodopolis, the shopkeeper. Then I plunged down into a black well that had no bottom, and the scene vanished, leaving only his eyes. So the dream ended.

I awoke next morning with the same feeling of apathy that I had experienced before. I called in Doctor McGee, an unimaginative, stolid individual, who examined me mechanically and gave his diagnosis.

"Looks like anemia, Mr. Trellan," he said when he had finished, "but

5

I can't be certain as yet. Just rest for a few days and then we can tell more about it."

The doctor had hardly gone when Pietro Jachini, an Italian friend of mine from across the hall, came in to see me. He gave me one careful look and his eyes widened in horror.

"*Dio*, Jim," he gasped, "it is devil's work!"

He insisted on examining my neck. Then he brought a mirror and showed me what he had found: two tiny punctures in the skin over my jugular vein. With a shock, the dreams of the past night came back to me.

"Jim," Jachini began in what seemed rather ludicrous earnestness, "something has happened. What is it? You must tell me of anything out of the way that has happened to you recently. I want to help you, and God knows you'll need help."

So I told him of my queer experience in the little old shop in the fog. When I came to a description of G. Kodopolis, my friend's olive face blanched and he muttered something, ending with:

"It is even worse than I thought from your wan appearance and the marks on your throat. You have heard of vampires, have you not, Jim?"

"Of course, Pietro," I began, "but you surely don't think *he* is a vampire? Why, such things exist only in outworn superstitions, and—" I broke off at the look he gave me.

"No, not a vampire," Jachini said; "that is what I thought at first, but your description of him . . . tell me, Jim, did he *give* you anything?"

I nodded, found the amulet among the papers and books on my table and handed it to him. He gave the thing one look, crossed himself and dropped it back on the table.

Excusing himself hurriedly, Pietro rushed across the hall to his own room. I lay back, staring at the ceiling and wondering what it was all about. My meeting with Kodopolis, my hideous dreams, the punctures on my neck, Pietro's queer actions and his mention of the old superstition of vampires—what could it all mean?

In a few minutes Jachini was back, carrying a small, black-bound volume. Without a word, he sat down and began to turn through it. I caught a momentary glimpse of the title page: the name of the book was *Vampyrs*. At length Pietro found the section he had sought, and he began to read the queer sentences aloud.

"The *vrykolokas* of Greek superstition," he read in his rich, scarcely accented voice, "is the undead body of some exceedingly vicious mortal. It lives not, yet is not dead, existing on fresh blood of hapless men.

Unlike the true vampire, it is not shut within a coffin by day, but is then listless and inactive, especially if it has fed the night previous. Not like other vampires, the *vrykolokas* eats of the bodies of its victims when all blood is exhausted.

"The creature is unaffected by sacred tokens, excepting the image of our Lord on His tree. The stake, the knife, and the silver bullet are alike useless against the monster, as are all mortal weapons. Only fire may destroy a *vrykolokas*. Yet he binds himself to a victim by some link such as an amulet or a witch-mark, and the victim is freed if the link be in some manner broken."

I started at the mention of an amulet. Did all this have some hidden significance to me? I would have interrupted Jachini, but he motioned me to silence and read on:

"The *vrykolokas* may be distinguished by its odd skin like old papyrus, its hypnotic eyes, by abnormal hair-growings upon its visage, and its emaciation. It is—"

Then I screamed. Jachini must have dropped the book and stared at me, but I was unaware of anything save that the description of the *vrykolokas* in the old book would have served equally well to describe G. Kodopolis. An icy trickle ran down my spine as the awful truth forced itself upon me—Kodopolis was a *vrykolokas* and I was his victim.

"So you see it, too, Jim," said Jachini understandingly.

"Yes, yes," I gasped, "I see it all now. Pietro, the amulet, *destroy it*—it must be the link, and the book says—"

Jachini picked up the blasphemous rosary, crossed to the fireplace, and tossed the thing into the midst of the glowing embers. It landed upright, stuck, and the little flames licked around it. Yet it remained unblemished by the radiance, and slowly the fire began to recede until the dread token was left on a tiny heap of dead coals in the center of the fire. Jachini shrugged, then dragged the thing from the fire onto the hearthstone.

"I feared as much," he said, "but there is yet another way. I shall weight the thing with a stone and drop it off the Park Street bridge—once in the river it will be gone forever."

He took the thing and left. In a little while he came back to tell me that it was done. So, with that hellish trinket gone, I felt certain that my troubles were over. I spent the rest of the day in greater peace of mind, and went to bed directly after dinner, to fall asleep almost at once.

I slept soundly for an hour or so, when I was awakened by a knock at my door. I answered it, to find a messenger boy with a parcel for me. I took it, tossed it on the table unopened, and went back to sleep.

I slept this time until the sun, streaming in my window next morning, woke me, but my sleep was haunted by dreams in which old Kodopolis crept again into my room to sink his fangs into my throat.

When I got up next day, I opened the package that had been delivered to me. A hand of ice gripped my spine as I saw what it contained. In the box was the hideous little amulet that Pietro Jachini had thrown into the river and, in that moment, I knew that my dreadful dreams of the night just past were no dreams at all but hideous reality.

I passed the whole of that day in a horror of anticipation, for I knew that with the coming of night, the monster that called itself Kodopolis would again visit me.

Doctor McGee called again during the day. If he but knew the true cause of my ailment it might shock him out of his stolid composure. But he would only think me a madman if I should tell him the truth.

Jachini spent much of the time with me. He sat by my bed while I told him of the return of the amulet and of my *dreams*. He insisted on remaining with me that night, but I refused, for a plan was taking form in my mind; yet if it failed I feared that I might draw my friend, too, into the toils of the monster, Kodopolis. So as night drew on he reluctantly took his leave and I was left alone.

I lay on my bed in the darkness for a long time. I felt that the end was not far off, for I could not stand many more visits by the *vrykolokas*, and if my plan failed all my blood would soon be gone and the thing would come again—to *eat*.

I looked toward a window at the far end of the room. There, lit by the glow of nearby street lamps, was a face I knew only too well. That yellow, bearded skull and those evil eyes could belong to no other than the monstrous G. Kodopolis himself.

A sort of hypnosis began to creep over me, my eyelids drooped, my tense muscles relaxed. I had no will to struggle, though I felt the weight of the *vrykolokas* on my chest, felt his sharp teeth at my throat. Then, as the very blood of life commenced to drain from my body, I lapsed into complete unconsciousness. . . .

Slowly I fought my way back to sensibility. The monster had feasted and fled again into the darkness; yet I could still feel the terrible power of him about me. I knew I must act at once, for I was so weak that Kodopolis's next visitation must certainly be his last, and I could visualize those rending fangs and talons at work. . . .

I pushed back the covers and got to my feet. I was weak and giddy, but I knew what I must do. I dressed in a few minutes, slipped downstairs into the dark street, and began to walk. The influence of Kodopolis drew me to his lair as a magnet draws steel; yet I cannot to this day retrace my steps to the street where I came at last to the ancient shop.

The door was unlocked, and I pushed my way into the dusty old place. I went straight back to the curtains that shut off the rear of the shop, and through them into the room beyond.

On a long couch in the center of the room lay the *vrykolokas* himself, his evil yellow face passive, his dark eyes mercifully closed.

I withdrew quickly from the monster's chamber, my mind all alert now. I must hasten to my task before the creature sensed something amiss. The old book Jachini had read to me had said: *"Only fire may totally destroy a vrykolokas."* And Kodopolis's shop was a veritable tinder-box. A match dropped in one of the stacks of old books that littered the place would start a blaze that would soon spread to the dry, ancient wood of the walls. The result would be a holocaust.

I swept a stack of the old volumes to the floor and touched a match to their crumbling pages. The flames licked over them hungrily, and I fed the blaze with more books, then with wooden sections from the shelves. The fire spread rapidly.

So intent was I upon my work that I all but missed the slight sound as the curtains behind me parted. But I heard in time and turned to see G. Kodopolis standing in the entrance to the back room. He stared dazedly at the fire; then his dark eyes blazed with ferocity as he saw me. With an animal snarl he leaped forward.

The flames were roaring up the walls now, painting the whole grim scene a hellish red. Desperately I seized a burning brand from the fire and hurled it into the monster's leering face. Fire licked at his flowing beard, caught in his dark garments. He shrieked once, horribly, and toppled back into the fire.

As Kodopolis disappeared in the roaring inferno, I jerked open the door, threw myself out into the darkness, and ran. I ran until I was near exhaustion; then I fell. My head met something hard and I became unconscious.

I came to in a hospital bed, my head bandaged and strangely light. I called a nurse and questioned her. She told me that I had been found lying unconscious in the street early that morning and I had been brought to the hospital with a deep head wound and a slight concussion.

I was allowed no visitors that day, but the next afternoon Pietro Jachini came to see me. I told him the conclusion of the affair and he sat quiet through my recital, nodding a bit now and then at some incident.

When Pietro returned, the following day, he brought some newspapers, including every issue of the past few days. We looked through each of them with utmost care, but there was no mention of the fire in the curio shop. Yet the conflagration was so fierce that no power on earth, or even those of hell that were at Kodopolis's command, could have saved the old shop from complete destruction.

So the tale ends, but sometimes, even now, I dream and doubt for a time that G. Kodopolis's horrid undead existence is at an end. Still, the creature must have been destroyed in the fire; for though I still have his hellish amulet, the link between us, he has never again come to me.

THE AMERICAN'S TALE

ARTHUR CONAN DOYLE

It air strange, it air," he was saying as I opened the door of the room where our social little semiliterary society met; "but I could tell you queerer things than that 'ere—almighty queer things. You can't learn everything out of books, sirs, nohow. You see it ain't the men as can string English together and as has had good eddications as finds themselves in the queer places I've been in. They're mostly rough men, sirs, as can scarce speak aright, far less tell with pen and ink the things they've seen; but if they could they'd make some of your European's har riz with astonishment. They would, sirs, you bet!"

His name was Jefferson Adams, I believe; I know his initials were J. A., for you may see them yet deeply whittled on the right-hand upper panel of our smoking-room door. He left us this legacy, and also some artistic patterns done in tobacco juice upon our Turkey carpet; but beyond these reminiscences our American storyteller has vanished from our ken. He gleamed across our ordinary quiet conviviality like some brilliant meteor, and then was lost in the outer darkness. That night, however, our Nevada friend was in full swing; and I quietly lit my pipe and dropped into the nearest chair, anxious not to interrupt his story.

"Mind you," he continued, "I hain't got no grudge against your men of science. I likes and respects a chap as can match every beast and plant, from a huckleberry to a grizzly with a jaw-breakin' name; but if you wants real interestin' facts, something a bit juicy, you go to your whalers and your frontiersmen, and your scouts and Hudson Bay men, chaps who mostly can scarce sign their names."

There was a pause here, as Mr. Jefferson Adams produced a long cheroot and lit it. We preserved a strict silence in the room, for we had already learned that on the slightest interruption our Yankee drew himself into his shell again. He glanced round with a self-satisfied smile as he remarked our expectant looks, and continued through a halo of smoke.

"Now which of you gentlemen has ever been in Arizona? None, I'll warrant. And of all English or Americans as can put pen to paper, how many has been in Arizona? Precious few, I calc'late. I've been there, sirs, lived there for years; and when I think of what I've seen there, why, I can scarce get myself to believe it now.

"Ah, there's a country! I was one of Walker's filibusters, as they chose to call us; and after we'd busted up, and the chief was shot, some of us made tracks and located down there. A reg'lar English and American colony, we was, with our wives and children, and all complete. I reckon there's some of the old folk there yet, and that they hain't forgotten what I'm agoing to tell you. No, I warrant they hain't, never on this side of the grave, sirs.

"I was talking about the country, though; and I guess I could astonish you considerable if I spoke of nothing else. To think of such a land being built for a few 'Greasers' and half-breeds! It's a misusing of the gifts of Providence, that's what I calls it. Grass as hung over a chap's head as he rode through it, and trees so thick that you couldn't catch a glimpse of blue sky for leagues and leagues, and orchids like umbrellas! Maybe some of you has seen a plant as they calls the 'fly-catcher,' in some parts of the States?"

"*Dionaea muscipula,*" murmured Dawson, our scientific man par excellence.

"Ah, 'Die near a municipal,' that's him! You'll see a fly stand on that 'ere plant, and then you'll see the two sides of a leaf snap up together and catch it between them, and grind it up and mash it to bits, for all the world like some great sea squid with its beak; and hours after, if you open the leaf, you'll see the body lying half-digested, and in bits. Well, I've seen those flytraps in Arizona with leaves eight and ten feet long, and thorns or teeth a foot or more; why, they could—But darn it, I'm going too fast!

"It's about the death of Joe Hawkins I was going to tell you; 'bout as

11

queer a thing, I reckon, as ever you heard tell on. There wasn't nobody in Montana as didn't know of Joe Hawkins—'Alabama' Joe, as he was called there. A reg'lar out and outer, he was, 'bout the darndest skunk as ever man clapt eyes on. He was a good chap enough, mind ye, as long as you stroked him the right way; but rile him anyhow, and he were worse nor a wildcat. I've seen him empty his six-shooter into a crowd as chanced to jostle him agoing into Simpson's bar when there was a dance on; and he bowied Tom Hooper 'cause he spilt his liquor over his weskit by mistake. No, he didn't stick at murder, Joe didn't; and he weren't a man to be trusted further nor you could see him.

"Now at the time I tell on, when Joe Hawkins was swaggerin' about the town and layin' down the law with his shootin'-irons, there was an Englishman there of the name of Scott—Tom Scott, if I rec'lects aright. This chap Scott was a thorough Britisher (beggin' the present company's pardon), and yet he didn't freeze much to the British set there, or they didn't freeze much to him. He was a quiet simple man, Scott was—rather too quiet for a rough set like that; sneakin' they called him, but he weren't that. He kept hisself mostly apart, an' didn't interfere with nobody so long as he were left alone. Some said as how he'd been kinder ill-treated at home—been a Chartist, or something of that sort, and had to up stick and run; but he never spoke of it hisself, an' never complained. Bad luck or good, that chap kept a stiff lip on him.

"This chap Scott was a sort o' butt among the men about Montana, for he was so quiet an' simple-like. There was no party either to take up his grievances; for, as I've been saying, the Britishers hardly counted him one of them, and many a rough joke they played on him. He never cut up rough, but was polite to all hisself. I think the boys got to think he hadn't much grit in him till he showed 'em their mistake.

"It was in Simpson's bar as the row got up, an' that led to the queer thing I was going to tell you of. Alabama Joe and one or two other rowdies were dead on the Britishers in those days, and they spoke their opinions pretty free, though I warned them as there'd be an almighty muss. That partic'lar night Joe was nigh half drunk, an' he swaggered about the town with his six-shooter, lookin' out for a quarrel. Then he turned into the bar where he know'd he'd find some o' the English as ready for one as he was hisself. Sure enough, there was half a dozen lounging about, an' Tom Scott standin' alone before the stove. Joe sat down by the table, and put his revolver and bowie down in front of him. 'Them's my arguments, Jeff,' he says to me, 'if any white-livered Britisher dares give me the lie.' I tried to stop him, sirs; but he weren't a man as you could easily turn, an' he began to speak in a way as no chap could stand. Why, even a 'Greaser' would flare up if you said as much of Greaserland! There was a commotion at the bar, an' every man laid his hands on his wepin's; but afore they could draw we heard a quiet voice from the stove: 'Say your prayers, Joe Hawkins; for, by Heaven, you're a dead man!' Joe turned round and looked like grabbin' at his iron; but it weren't no manner of use. Tom Scott was standing up, covering him with his Derringer; a smile on his white face, but the very devil shining in his eye. 'It ain't that the old country has used me overwell,' he says, 'but no man shall speak agin it afore me, and live.' For a second or two I could see his finger tighten round the trigger, an' then he gave a laugh, an' threw the pistol on the floor. 'No,' he says, 'I can't shoot a half-drunk man. Take your dirty life, Joe, an' use it better nor you have done. You've been nearer the grave this night than you will be agin until your time comes. You'd best make tracks now, I guess. Nay, never look black at me, man; I'm not afeard at your shootin'-iron. A bully's nigh always a coward.' And he swung contemptuously round, and relit his half-smoked pipe from the stove; while Alabama slunk out o' the bar, with the laughs of the Britishers ringing in his ears. I saw his face as he passed me, and on it I saw murder, sirs—murder, as plain as ever I seed anything in my life.

"I stayed in the bar after the row, and watched Tom Scott as he shook hands with the men about. It seemed kinder queer to me to see him smilin' and cheerful-like; for I knew Joe's bloodthirsty mind, and that the Englishman had small chance of ever seeing the morning. He lived in an out-of-the-way sort of place, you see, clean off the trail, and had to pass through the Flytrap Gulch to get to it. This here gulch was a marshy gloomy place, lonely enough during the day even; for it were always a creepy sort o' thing to see the great eight- and ten-foot leaves snapping up if aught touched them; but at night there were never a soul near. Some parts of the marsh, too, were soft and deep, and a body thrown in would be gone by the morning. I could see Alabama Joe crouchin' under the leaves of the great Flytrap in the darkest part of the gulch, with a scowl on his face and a revolver in his hand; I could see it, sirs, as plain as with my two eyes.

" 'Bout midnight Simpson shuts up his bar, so out we had to go. Tom Scott started off for his three-mile walk at a slashing pace. I just dropped him a hint as he passed me, for I kinder liked the chap. 'Keep your Derringer loose in your belt, sir,' I says, 'for you might chance to need it.' He looked round at me with his quiet smile, and then I lost sight of him in the gloom. I never thought to see him again. He'd hardly gone afore Simpson comes up to me and says, 'There'll be a nice job in the Flytrap Gulch tonight, Jeff; the boys say that Hawkins started half an hour ago to wait for Scott and shoot him on sight. I calc'late the coroner'll be wanted tomorrow.'

"What passed in the gulch that night? It were a question as were asked pretty free next morning. A half-breed was in Ferguson's store after daybreak, and he said as he'd chanced to be near the gulch 'bout one in the morning. It warn't easy to get at his story, he seemed so uncommon scared; but he told us, at last, as he'd heard the fearfulest screams in the stillness of the night. There weren't no shots, he said, but scream after scream, kinder muffled, like a man with a serapé over his head, an' in mortal pain. Abner Brandon and me, and a few more, was in the store at the time; so we mounted and rode out to Scott's house, passing through the gulch on the way. There weren't nothing partic'lar to be seen there—no blood nor marks of a fight, nor nothing; and when we gets up to Scott's house, out he comes to meet us as fresh as a lark. 'Hullo, Jeff!' says he, 'no need for the pistols after all. Come in an' have a cocktail, boys.' 'Did ye see or hear nothing as ye came home last night?' says I. 'No,' says he; 'all was quiet enough. An owl kinder moaning in the Flytrap Gulch—that was all. Come, jump off and have a glass.' 'Thank ye,' said Abner. So off we gets, and Tom Scott rode into the settlement with us when we went back.

"An all-fired commotion was on in Main Street as we rode into it. The 'Merican party seemed to have gone clean crazed. Alabama Joe was gone, not a darned particle of him left. Since he went out to the gulch nary eye had seen him. As we got off our horses there was a considerable crowd in front of Simpson's, and some ugly looks at Tom Scott, I can tell you. There was a clickin' of pistols, and I saw as Scott had his hand in his bosom too. There weren't a single English face about. 'Stand aside, Jeff Adams,' says Zebb Humphrey, as great a scoundrel as ever lived, 'you hain't got no hand in this game. Say, boys, are we, free Americans, to be murdered by any darned Britisher?' It was the quickest thing as ever I seed. There was a rush an' a crack; Zebb was down, with Scott's ball in his thigh, and Scott hisself was on the ground with a dozen men holding him. It weren't no use struggling, so he lay quiet. They seemed a bit uncertain what to do with him at first, but then one of Alabama's special chums put them up to it. 'Joe's gone,' he said; 'nothing ain't surer nor that, an' there lies the man as killed him. Some on you knows as Joe went on business to the gulch last night; he never came back. That 'ere Britisher passed through after he'd gone; they'd had a row, screams is heard 'mong the great flytraps. I say agin he has played poor Joe some o' his sneakin' tricks, an' thrown him into the swamp. It

14

ain't no wonder as the body is gone. But air we to stan' by and see English murderin' our own chums? I guess not. Let Judge Lynch try him, that's what I say.' 'Lynch him!'' shouted a hundred angry voices— for all the rag-tag an' bobtail o' the settlement was round us by this time. "Here, boys, fetch a rope, and swing him up. Up with him over Simpson's door!' 'See here though,' says another, coming forrards; 'let's hang him by the great flytrap in the gulch. Let Joe see as he's revenged, if so be as he's buried 'bout theer.' There was a shout for this, an' away they went, with Scott tied on his mustang in the middle, and a mounted guard, with cocked revolvers, round him; for we knew as there was a score or so Britishers about, as didn't seem to recognise Judge Lynch, and was dead on a free fight.

"I went out with them, my heart bleedin' for Scott, though he didn't seem a cent put out, he didn't. He were game to the backbone. Seems kinder queer, sirs, hangin' a man to a flytrap; but our'n were a reg'lar tree, and the leaves like a brace of boats with a hinge between 'em and thorns at the bottom.

"We passed down the gulch to the place where the great one grows, and there we seed it with the leaves, some open, some shut. But we seed something worse nor that. Standin' round the tree was some thirty men, Britishers all, an' armed to the teeth. They was waitin' for us evidently, an' had a businesslike look about 'em, as if they'd come for something and meant to have it. There was the raw material there for about as warm a scrimmidge as ever I seed. As we rode up, a great red-bearded Scotch-man—Cameron were his name—stood out afore the rest, his revolver cocked in his hand. 'See here, boys,' he says, 'you've got no call to hurt a hair of that man's head. You hain't proved as Joe is dead yet; and if you had, you hain't proved as Scott killed him. Anyhow, it were in self-defence; for you all know as he was lying in wait for Scott, to shoot him on sight; so I say agin, you hain't got no call to hurt that man; and what's more, I've got thirty six-barrelled arguments against your doin' it.' 'It's an interestin' pint, and worth arguin' out,' said the man as was Alabama Joe's special chum. There was a clickin' of pistols, and a loosenin' of knives, and the two parties began to draw up to one another, an' it looked like a rise in the mortality of Montana. Scott was standing behind with a pistol at his ear if he stirred, lookin' quiet and composed as having no money on the table, when sudden he gives a start an' a shout as rang in our ears like a trumpet. 'Joe!' he cried, 'Joe! Look at him! In the flytrap!' We all turned an' looked where he was pointin'. Jerusalem! I think we won't get that picter out of our minds agin. One of the great leaves of the flytrap, that had been shut and touchin' the

15

ground as it lay, was slowly rolling back upon its hinges. There, lying like a child in its cradle, was Alabama Joe in the hollow of the leaf. The great thorns had been slowly driven through his heart as it shut upon him. We could see as he'd tried to cut his way out, for there was a slit in the thick fleshy leaf, an' his bowie was in his hand; but it had smothered him first. He'd lain down on it likely to keep the damp off while he were awaitin' for Scott, and it had closed on him as you've seen your little hothouse ones do on a fly; an' there he were as we found him, torn and crushed into pulp by the great jagged teeth of the man-eatin' plant. There, sirs, I think you'll own as that's a curious story."

"And what became of Scott?" asked Jack Sinclair.

"Why, we carried him back on our shoulders, we did, to Simpson's bar, and he stood us liquors round. Made a speech too—a darned fine speech—from the counter. Somethin' about the British lion an' the 'Merican eagle walkin' arm in arm for ever an' a day. And now, sirs, that yarn was long, and my cheroot's out, so I reckon I'll make tracks afore it's later"; and with a "Good-night!" he left the room.

"A most extraordinary narrative!" said Dawson. "Who would have thought a *Dionaea* had such power!"

"Deuced rum yarn!" said young Sinclair.

"Evidently a matter-of-fact truthful man," said the doctor.

"Or the most original liar that ever lived," said I.

I wonder which he was.

AMINA

EDWARD LUCAS WHITE

Waldo, brought face to face with the actuality of the unbelievable—as he himself would have worded it—was completely dazed. In silence he suffered the consul to lead him from the tepid gloom of the interior, through the ruinous doorway, out into the hot, stunning brilliance of the desert landscape. Hassan followed, with never a look behind him. With-

16

out any word he had taken Waldo's gun from his nerveless hand and carried it, with his own and the consul's.

The consul strode across the gravelly sand, some fifty paces from the southwest corner of the tomb, to a bit of not wholly ruined wall from which there was a clear view of the doorway side of the tomb and of the side with the larger crevice.

"Hassan," he commanded, "watch here."

Hassan said something in Persian.

"How many cubs were there?" the consul asked Waldo.

Waldo stared mute.

"How many young ones did you see?" the consul asked again.

"Twenty or more," Waldo made answer.

"That's impossible," snapped the consul.

"There seemed to be sixteen or eighteen," Waldo asserted. Hassan smiled and grunted. The consul took from him two guns, handed Waldo his, and they walked around the tomb to a point about equally distant from the opposite corner. There was another bit of ruin, and in front of it, on the side toward the tomb, was a block of stone mostly in the shadow of the wall.

"Convenient," said the consul. "Sit on that stone and lean against the wall, make yourself comfortable. You are a bit shaken, but you will be all right in a moment. You should have something to eat, but we have nothing. Anyhow, take a good swallow of this."

He stood by him as Waldo gasped over the raw brandy.

"Hassan will bring you his water-bottle before he goes," the consul went on; "drink plenty, for you must stay here for some time. And now, pay attention to me. We must extirpate these vermin. The male, I judge, is absent. If he had been anywhere about, you would not now be alive. The young cannot be as many as you say, but, I take it, we have to deal with ten, a full litter. We must smoke them out. Hassan will go back to camp after fuel and the guard. Meanwhile, you and I must see that none escape."

He took Waldo's gun, opened the breech, shut it, examined the magazine and handed it back to him.

"Now watch me closely," he said. He paced off, looking to his left past the tomb. Presently he stopped and gathered several stones together.

"You see these?" he called.

Waldo shouted an affirmation.

The consul came back, passed on in the same line, looking to his right

17

past the tomb, and presently, at a similar distance, put up another tiny cairn, shouted again and was again answered. Again he returned.

"Now you are sure you cannot mistake those two marks I have made?"

"Very sure indeed," said Waldo.

"It is important," warned the consul. "I am going back to where I left Hassan, to watch there while he is gone. You will watch here. You may pace as often as you like to either of those stone heaps. From either you can see me on my beat. Do not diverge from the line from one to the other. For as soon as Hassan is out of sight I shall shoot any moving thing I see nearer. Sit here till you see me set up similar limits for my sentry-go on the farther side, then shoot any moving thing not on my line of patrol. Keep a lookout all around you. There is one chance in a million that the male might return in daylight—mostly they are nocturnal, but this lair is evidently exceptional. Keep a bright lookout.

"And now listen to me. You must not feel any foolish sentimentalism about any fancied resemblance of these vermin to human beings. Shoot, and shoot to kill. Not only is it our duty, in general, to abolish them, but it will be very dangerous for us if we do not. There is little or no solidarity in Mohammedan communities, but on the comparatively few points upon which public opinion exists it acts with amazing promptitude and vigor. One matter as to which there is no disagreement is that it is incumbent upon every man to assist in eradicating these creatures. The good old Biblical custom of stoning to death is the mode of lynching indigenous hereabouts. These modern Asiatics are quite capable of applying it to anyone believed derelict against any of these inimical monsters. If we let one escape and the rumor of it gets about, we may precipitate an outburst of racial prejudice difficult to cope with. Shoot, I say, without hesitation or mercy."

"I understand," said Waldo.

"I don't care whether you understand or not," said the consul, "I want you to act. Shoot if needful, and shoot straight." And he tramped off.

Hassan presently appeared, and Waldo drank from his water-bottle as nearly all of its contents as Hassan would permit. After his departure Waldo's first alertness soon gave place to mere endurance of the monotony of watching and the intensity of the heat. His discomfort became suffering, and what with the fury of the dry glare, the pangs of thirst and his bewilderment of mind, Waldo was moving in a waking dream by the time Hassan returned with two donkeys and a mule laden with brushwood. Behind the beasts straggled the guard.

Waldo's trance became a nightmare when the smoke took effect and the battle began. He was, however, not only not required to join in the killing, but was enjoined to keep back. He did keep very much in the background, seeing only so much of the slaughter as his curiosity would not let him refrain from viewing. Yet he felt all a murderer as he gazed at the ten small carcasses laid out arow, and the memory of his vigil and its end, indeed of the whole day, though it was the day of his most marvelous adventure, remains to him as the broken recollections of a phantasmagoria.

On the morning of his memorable peril Waldo had waked early. The experiences of his sea-voyage, the sights at Gibraltar, at Port Said, in the canal, at Suez, at Aden, at Muscat, and at Basrah had formed an altogether inadequate transition from the decorous regularity of house and school life in New England to the breathless wonder of the desert immensities.

Everything seemed unreal, and yet the reality of its strangeness so besieged him that he could not feel at home in it, he could not sleep heavily in a tent. After composing himself to sleep, he lay long conscious and awakened early, as on this morning, just at the beginning of the false dawn.

The consul was fast asleep, snoring loudly. Waldo dressed quietly and went out; mechanically, without any purpose or forethought, taking his gun. Outside he found Hassan, seated, his gun across his knees, his head sunk forward, as fast asleep as the consul. Ali and Ibrahim had left the camp the day before for supplies. Waldo was the only waking creature about; for the guards, camped some little distance off, were but logs about the ashes of their fire. Meaning merely to enjoy, under the white glow of the false dawn, the magical reappearance of the constellations and the short last glory of the star-laden firmament, that brief coolness which compensated a trifle for the hot morning, the fiery day and the warmish night, he seated himself on a rock, some paces from the tent and twice as far from the guards. Turning his gun in his hands he felt an irresistible temptation to wander off by himself, to stroll alone through the fascinating emptiness of the arid landscape.

When he had begun camp life he had expected to find the consul, that combination of sportsman, explorer and archaeologist, a particularly easygoing guardian. He had looked forward to absolutely untrameled liberty in the spacious expanse of the limitless wastes. The reality he had found exactly the reverse of his preconceptions. The consul's first injunction was:

"Never let yourself get out of sight of me or of Hassan unless he or I send you off with Ali or Ibrahim. Let nothing tempt you to roam about alone. Even a ramble is dangerous. You might lose sight of the camp before you knew it."

At first Waldo acquiesced, later he protested. "I have a good pocket compass. I know how to use it. I never lost my way in the Maine woods."

"No Kourds in the Maine woods," said the consul.

Yet before long Waldo noticed that the few Kourds they encountered seemed simple-hearted, peaceful folk. No semblance of danger or even of adventure had appeared. Their armed guard of a dozen greasy tatter-demalions had passed their time in uneasy loafing.

Likewise Waldo noticed that the consul seemed indifferent to the ruins they passed by or encamped among, that his feeling for sites and topography was cooler than lukewarm, that he showed no ardor in the pursuit of the scanty and uninteresting game. He had picked up enough of several dialects to hear repeated conversations about "them." "Have you heard of any about here?" "Has one been killed?" "Any traces of them in this district?" And such queries he could make out in the various talks with the natives they met, as to what "they" were he received no enlightenment.

Then he had questioned Hassan as to why he was so restricted in his movements. Hassan spoke some English and regaled him with tales of Afrits, ghouls, specters and other uncanny legendary presences; of the jinn of the waste, appearing in human shape, talking all languages, ever on the alert to ensnare infidels; of the woman whose feet turned the wrong way at the ankles, luring the unwary to a pool and there drowning her victims; of the malignant ghosts of dead brigands, more terrible than their living fellows; of the spirit in the shape of a wild ass, or of a gazelle, enticing its pursuers to the brink of a precipice and itself seeming to run ahead upon an expanse of sand, a mere mirage, dissolving as the victim passed the brink and fell to death; of the sprite in the semblance of a hare feigning a limp, or of a ground bird feigning a broken wing, drawing its pursuer after it till he met death in an unseen pit or well shaft.

Ali and Ibrahim spoke no English. As far as Waldo could understand their long harangues, they told similar stories or hinted at dangers equally vague and imaginary. These childish bogy-tales merely whetted Waldo's craving for independence.

Now, as he sat on a rock, longing to enjoy the perfect sky, the clear, early air, the wide, lonely landscape, along with the sense of having it to himself, it seemed to him that the consul was merely innately cautious, overcautious. There was no danger. He would have a fine leisurely stroll, kill something perhaps, and certainly be back in camp before the sun grew hot. He stood up.

Some hours later he was seated on a fallen coping stone in the shadow of a ruined tomb. All the country they had been traversing is full of tombs and remains of tombs, prehistoric, Bactrian, old Persian, Parthian, Sassanian, or Mohammedan, scattered everywhere in groups or solitary. Vanished utterly are the faintest traces of the cities, towns, and villages, ephemeral houses or temporary huts, in which had lived the countless generations of mourners who had reared these tombs.

The tombs, built more durably than mere dwellings of the living, remained. Complete or ruinous, or reduced to mere fragments, they were everywhere. In that district they were all of one type. Each was domed and below was square, its one door facing eastward and opening into a large empty room, behind which were the mortuary chambers.

In the shadow of such a tomb Waldo sat. He had shot nothing, had lost his way, had no idea of the direction of the camp, was tired, warm, and thirsty. He had forgotten his water-bottle.

He swept his gaze over the vast, desolate prospect, the unvaried turquoise of the sky arched above the rolling desert. Far reddish hills along the skyline hooped in the less distant brown hillocks which, without diversifying it, hummocked the yellow landscape. Sand and rocks with a lean, starved bush or two made up the nearer view, broken here and there by dazzling white or streaked, grayish, crumbling ruins. The sun had not been long above the horizon, yet the whole surface of the desert was quivering with heat.

As Waldo sat viewing the outlook a woman came round the corner of the tomb. All the village women Waldo had seen had worn yashmaks or some other form of face covering or veil. This woman was bareheaded and unveiled. She wore some sort of yellowish-brown garment which enveloped her from neck to ankles, showing no waist line. Her feet, in defiance of the blistering sands, were bare.

At sight of Waldo she stopped and stared at him as he at her. He remarked the un-European posture of her feet, not at all turned out, but with the inner lines parallel. She wore no anklets, he observed, no bracelets, no necklace or earrings. Her bare arms he thought the most muscular he had ever seen on a human being. Her nails were pointed and long, both on her hands and feet. Her hair was black, short, and tousled, yet she did not look wild or uncomely. Her eyes smiled and her lips had the effect of smiling, though they did not part ever so little, not showing at all the teeth behind them.

21

"What a pity," said Waldo aloud, "that she does not speak English."

"I do speak English," said the woman, and Waldo noticed that as she spoke, her lips did not perceptibly open. "What does the gentleman want?"

"You speak English!" Waldo exclaimed, jumping to his feet. "What luck! Where did you learn it?"

"At the mission school," she replied, an amused smile playing about the corners of her rather wide, unopening mouth. "What can be done for you?" She spoke with scarcely any foreign accent, but very slowly and with a sort of growl running along from syllable to syllable.

"I am thirsty," said Waldo, "and I have lost my way."

"Is the gentleman living in a brown tent, shaped like half a melon?" she inquired, the queer, rumbling note drawling from one word to the next, her lips barely separated.

"Yes, that is our camp," said Waldo.

"I could guide the gentleman that way," she droned; "but it is far, and there is no water on that side."

"I want water first," said Waldo, "or milk."

"If you mean cow's milk, we have none. But we have goat's milk. There is to drink where I dwell," she said, sing-songing the words. "It is not far. It is the other way."

"Show me," said he.

She began to walk, Waldo, his gun under his arm, beside her. She trod noiselessly and fast. Waldo could scarcely keep up with her. As they walked he often fell behind and noted how her swathing garments clung to a lithe, shapely back, neat waist, and firm hips. Each time he hurried and caught up with her, he scanned her with intermittent glances, puzzled that her waist, so well-marked at the spine, showed no particular definition in front; that the outline of her from neck to knees, perfectly shapeless under her wrappings, was without any waistline or suggestion of firmness or undulation. Likewise he remarked the amused flicker in her eyes and the compressed line of her red, her too-red lips.

"How long were you in the mission school?" he inquired.

"Four years," she replied.

"Are you a Christian?" he asked.

"The Free-folk do not submit to baptism," she stated simply, but with rather more of the droning growl between her words.

He felt a queer shiver as he watched the scarcely moved lips through which the syllables edged their way.

"But you are not veiled," he could not resist saying.

"The Free-folk," she rejoined, "are never veiled."

"Then you are not a Mohammedan?" he ventured.

"The Free-folk are not Moslems."

"Who are the Free-folk?" he blurted out incautiously.

She shot one baleful glance at him. Waldo remembered that he had to do with an Asiatic. He recalled the three permitted questions.

"What is your name?" he inquired.

"Amina," she told him.

"That is a name from the 'Arabian Nights'," he hazarded.

"From the foolish tales of the believers," she sneered. "The Free-folk know nothing of such follies." The unvarying shutness of her speaking lips, the drawly burr between the syllables, struck him all the more as her lips curled but did not open.

"You utter your words in a strange way," he said.

"Your language is not mine," she replied.

"How is it that you learned my language at the mission school and are not a Christian?"

"They teach all at the mission school," she said, "and the maidens of the Free-folk are like the other maidens they teach, though the Free-folk when grown are not as town-dwellers are. Therefore they taught me as any town-bred girl, not knowing me for what I am."

"They taught you well," he commented.

"I have the gift of tongues," she uttered enigmatically, with an odd note of triumph burring the words through her unmoving lips.

Waldo felt a horrid shudder all over him, not only at her uncanny words, but also from mere faintness.

"Is it far to your home?" he breathed.

"It is there," she said, pointing to the doorway of a large tomb just before them.

The wholly open arch admitted them into a fairly spacious interior, cool with the abiding temperature of thick masonry. There was no rubbish on the floor. Waldo, relieved to escape the blistering glare outside, seated himself on a block of stone midway between the door and the inner partition wall, resting his gun butt on the floor. For the moment he was blinded by the change from the insistent brilliance of the desert morning to the blurred gray light of the interior.

When his sight cleared he looked about and remarked, opposite the door, the ragged hole which laid open the desecrated mausoleum. As his eyes grew accustomed to the dimness he was so startled that he stood up. It seemed to him that from its four corners the room swarmed with naked children. To his inexperienced conjecture they seemed about two years old, but they moved with the assurance of boys of eight or ten.

23

"Whose are these children?" he exclaimed.

"Mine," she said.

"All yours?" he protested.

"All mine," she replied, a curious suppressed boisterousness in her demeanor.

"But there are twenty of them," he cried.

"You count badly in the dark," she told him. "There are fewer."

"There certainly are a dozen," he maintained, spinning round as they danced and scampered about.

"The Free-people have large families," she said.

"But they are all of one age," Waldo exclaimed, his tongue dry against the roof of his mouth.

She laughed, an unpleasant, mocking laugh, clapping her hands. She was between him and the doorway, and as most of the light came from it he could not see her lips.

"Is not that like a man! No woman would have made that mistake."

Waldo was confuted and sat down again. The children circulated around him, chattering, laughing, giggling, snickering, making noises indicative of glee.

"Please get me something cool to drink," said Waldo, and his tongue was not only dry but big in his mouth.

"We shall have to drink shortly," she said, "but it will be warm."

Waldo began to feel uneasy. The children pranced around him, jabbering strange, guttural noises, licking their lips, pointing at him, their eyes fixed on him, with now and then a glance at their mother.

"Where is the water?"

The woman stood silent, her arms hanging at her sides, and it seemed to Waldo she was shorter than she had been.

"Where is the water?" he repeated.

"Patience, patience," she growled, and came a step near to him.

The sunlight struck upon her back and made a sort of halo about her hips. She seemed still shorter than before. There was a something furtive in her bearing, and the little ones sniggered evilly.

At that instant two rifle shots rang out almost as one. The woman fell face downward on the floor. The babies shrieked in a shrill chorus. Then she leapt up from all fours with an explosive suddenness, staggered in a hurled, lurching rush toward the hole in the wall, and, with a frightful yell, threw up her arms and whirled backward to the ground, doubled and contorted like a dying fish, stiffened, shuddered and was still. Waldo, his horrified eyes fixed on her face, even in his amazement noted that her lips did not open.

24

The children, squealing faint cries of dismay, scrambled through the hole in the inner wall, vanishing into the inky void beyond. The last had hardly gone when the consul appeared in the doorway, his smoking gun in his hand.

"Not a second too soon, my boy," he ejaculated. "She was just going to spring."

He cocked his gun and prodded the body with the muzzle.

"Good and dead," he commented. "What luck! Generally it takes three or four bullets to finish one. I've known one with two bullets through her lungs to kill a man."

"Did you murder this woman?" Waldo demanded fiercely.

"Murder?" the consul snorted. "Murder! Look at that."

He knelt down and pulled open the full, close lips, disclosing not human teeth, but small incisors, cusped grinders, wide-spaced; and long, keen, overlapping canines, like those of a greyhound: a fierce, deadly, carnivorous dentition, menacing and combative.

Waldo felt a qualm, yet the face and form still swayed his horrified sympathy for their humanness.

"Do you shoot women because they have long teeth?" Waldo insisted, revolted at the horrid death he had watched.

"You are hard to convince," said the consul sternly. "Do you call that a woman?"

He stripped the clothing from the carcass.

Waldo sickened all over. What he saw was not the front of a woman, but more like the underside of an old fox-terrier with puppies, or of a white sow, with her second litter; from collarbone to groin ten lolloping udders, two rows, mauled, stringy, and flaccid.

"What kind of a creature is it?" he asked faintly.

"A Ghoul, my boy," the consul answered solemnly, almost in a whisper.

"I thought they did not exist," Waldo babbled. "I thought they were mythical; I thought there were none."

"I can very well believe that there are none in Rhode Island," the consul said gravely. "This is in Persia, and Persia is in Asia."

25

The Avenging Hand

Roy Wallace Davis

I had been on the island of Corda less than three days when there came to me the ominous feeling that all was not well. Being thousands of miles from home in the jungled hills of the remotest of the South Sea islands was in nowise an inviting predicament for a youth of seventeen. Only four white men inhabited the place: myself, my elder brother, Louis, who had worked here for years in the service of a forestry company; and two young scientists, who had spent months on the island endeavoring to obtain from the natives the formula for a great healing medicine, which contained a certain sap substance from a rare plant found no other place in the world. By chance these men had heard of the medical feat of the brown-skin Cordans, and had sought every possible means of getting a sample of the medicine or of learning its ingredients, that they might startle the medical world by contributing the medicine to the surgical profession. Yet, despite every inducement of brilliant and colorful jewels and unreasonable promises, the little men of the semisavage tribes had demurred, looking on the pale-face men with suspicion, and concealing their great discovery for their own use.

But my interest was in none of these projects. Another problem confronted every human being on the island, myself more than anyone else, I thought, for it loomed before me as an incomprehensible and horrible mystery, suggesting itself to me only through the exotic actions of the island's populace. Conversations of the white men in low tones that increased day by day, and ceased when I came near, combined with the furtive actions of the natives, filled me with suspicion and brought over my life an inauspicious fear.

Then on a dull and gloomy September afternoon it was that the reason for the surreptitious performances of all was revealed to me. My brother called me to his side, and in a concise story related to me the situation before us—that which had kept him in a constant state of uneasiness since my arrival on the island. In this story he divulged the

26

facts that haunted my soul. His words were the turning point of my life as I sat there listening, spellbound.

Some months before, the story ran, my brother had encountered a family of beings, manlike in form, yet larger than men ever grew, covered with a thin, ugly growth of dark brown hair, and having teeth resembling fangs rather than those of men. On being attacked by the monsters, he had killed the entire group except the father. Then his ammunition was gone, and he escaped from the island in his boat only to be followed by the angered thing to Corda. Once here he had replenished his supply of shots and wounded the beast, he thought fatally. Several weeks later it was found out he had not rid the island of the great terror. Lingering in the dense jungles of the island between life and death for some time, it had again come forth with revenge in its heart and with the determination to rule or ruin.

Now the mind of the sturdy young forester was confronted with a problem that terrorized his very soul day and night—one of the two must die! Not only did he consider the loss of himself, provided he must yield to the great giant, but the young scientists and I would become the victims of its wrath. We could all leave; they could abandon the long-worked projects, but Louis was born of a spirit unlike this. He had brought on the enmity, and he would fight the battle against the appeal of all of us.

The appearance of the brute on the island had apparently affected the lives of the natives even more than those of the white men. They regarded the huge creature as a forest devil possessing divine power, and believed that it had been sent among them to destroy all life on the island to atone for the wrong done its kind. In their crude signs they predicted evil of the most diabolical nature to Louis's life for killing the monsters. Though they dreaded the beast, they dared not take any action toward killing it, because of their religious belief that when the last of a group is wiped out its spirit will come back to keep alive the memory of the group, and thus torment them. Again and again they had cautioned Louis, telling him the significance the death of the beast would have. But their predictions were in vain. It had come to his hut many nights in its attempted attacks, and he would not delay the battle a night longer. The next time he would accept the challenge.

"Tonight," Louis told me in a hesitating but determined voice, "I may die. You may die too then, and if so, the same fate will likely befall the scientists. If you are spared, go back home, and remember I died like a man."

❋ ❋ ❋

The dreadful reality that I had heard of the hideous being on the island brought over me a horripilation that tormented my mind incessantly until I even wished the end would not be prolonged. The afternoon had worn away quietly, and night was closing over us, bringing with it the feeling that it would be my last. A clear, full moon lighted Corda as the tower lamp illuminates the city square, but like the shadows of the great skyscrapers, the tall pines of the little island threw a gloom here and there over the stunted underbrush that clothed the rocky hills around our cabin. It was in these shadows that a huge figure lurked, now and then zigzagging its way from one clump to the next, evidently believing itself to be unobserved. There was no alternative — our hut was its destination, and the hour of its long-planned stroke of vengeance was at hand.

My mind was suddenly obsessed with a feeling of terror I had never known before, and my sensations became indescribably horrible as that huge, giantlike beast-man came undaunted, fearlessly on, nearer and nearer to the hut. I was unnerved, weak, for my brother's life and my own were in his hands, and I realized that I was helpless.

The wretched silence of waiting for death, which seemed hours rather than minutes, was broken by Louis. I turned my eyes, which had been fixed to and following the beast, to my brother. There was no time to pity him, and moreover neither of us owed pity to the other, for this brute, that came with vengeance in its heart, came not with any human scruples; we should both die alike, falling in the clutches of that powerful figure to be paralyzed, torn to pieces, and devoured.

I had only time to breathe a short, hurried prayer, and I believe I asked for strength for my brother against this mighty manlike animal that came to crush him.

Louis's hand intuitively gripped the revolver that had hung to his side since the presence of the giant on the island. His conclusion had been to meet the brute in the open, for there he would have more chance in battle than in the small space of the hut. He reached for the dirk knife in the wall and felt its razorlike edge, which he had recently whetted for the purpose it was to serve tonight. He would not await the attack, but would meet his assailant halfway.

As Louis stepped from the shadow of the cabin into the bright rays of the moon the awful realization of my plight came over me like a new discovery and rendered me even more helpless than before. Suddenly, as if rising from out of the earth, a grotesque, humanlike figure emerged from a clump of pines not fifty feet from where I stood pinned to the ground, and, crouching low, rushed on the man it meant to destroy. Like a flash the most gruesome picture I had ever seen filled my gaze for a second, and then all became blank. I remember the incident as a haunting nightmare. A huge figure like a man and yet like a beast moved swiftly past me, rising as it came to its full height of some seven feet. The flashing eyes and hairy face and body stamped indelibly on my memory the picture I can never forget. With the long, clawlike fingers of its enormous, hairy hands clenched tight, and a hideous, unshapely face that expressed vengeance, the mighty being sprang toward its intended victim. Two shots rang out in the stillness of the night, followed by an unearthly scream that chilled the blood in my veins.

In the light of the moon I saw that awful being cringe in pain, clench its jaws in a fit of agony, and grasp the man in its powerful arms. I thought I could hear every bone in his body being crushed under the grip of the brute, and felt that I should leap upon it to die with him, but I could not move from the spot where I stood cringing and trying, but in vain, to turn my eyes away. Agonizing screams of pain now came from a familiar yet different voice. Louis was dying the most horrible death imaginable before my eyes, while I stood helpless. I was rooted to the ground, and cold drops of sweat exuded from and stood on my forehead.

Then came a furious scramble in which the interlocked forms clutched and rolled over and over on the ground. The man of the woods had not given way to the mighty strength of the beast, and the forceful, yet comparatively weak, struggle that he made to hold off death as long as possible was tearing my heart. Once he freed himself from the clutches of those huge, ugly arms and leaped away only to be overpowered again and borne to the ground. A bright steel object flashed in the moonlight, and shrieks of pain filled the still night air. The mighty figure whirled frantically in every direction now, with its foe clinging about its shoulders. The tide of battle had evidently turned; the strength of the beast was being matched by the skill of man. Horrifying cries now came incessantly from both; the suspense, which at last was filled with hope, was brain-racking. Suddenly a heavy object fell at my feet. The mighty beast-man lunged forward with a force that sent Louis in a heap several yards away. A bloody stub of an arm waved in the air as the great form reeled with a deafening groan and dropped at my feet, dead.

The battle was over. I ran to the motionless body of my brother, leaned over him and listened. His body was covered with blood that spurted from his right arm. I attempted turning him over, to make a closer examination, but the sight that met my eyes made my heart sink. His arm below the elbow clung to his body only by a small piece of skin.

Deathly sick at heart, I fairly flew over the hills of the little island, spurred on by one desperate purpose. Then the little village of the natives, not far from our hut, came into view. The natives and their healing medicine had been my first thought, I having remembered what the scientists had told me of the almost magic power of the sap properties in the medicine. I dashed into the midst of the grass-covered huts, made a desperate effort to speak, and fell in a dead faint.

Three days later I opened my eyes to find myself lying on a small bed in the rear of our hut. This was the awaking from a long, unconscious sleep that had begun when I fell exhausted in the village of the natives. One of the natives of the island stood beside the bed, half naked and grinning broadly. In his own tongue he chattered something that was incomprehensible to me, and opening the door to the adjoining room, beckoned to me to enter. In my weakened condition I raised myself from the bed and walked unsteadily to where he stood, still grinning and chattering. Then the sight met my eyes that recalled all the horrible memories of the dreadful struggle, and drove me almost to distraction. Louis was on the bed in the corner of the room and beside him lay the huge, hairy arm that had fallen near me during the fight—it was now a part of my brother.

I could see it all now. The great healing power of the medicine had not been exaggerated. The evidence of that was before me. Also I now clearly understood the smile of the natives that stood about the room. The spirit of the mighty forest-devil could not come back to hover over them and pour out its wrath upon them, for there yet remained life in the arm of the beast that had been grafted by their skill and medicine on the stub of my brother's arm. In their minds they had appeased the wrath of the beast-man by preserving some of its life. Now, they thought, if there was any resentment of the beast remaining it would be directed toward the man that had taken its life. Thus, by the operation, they had preserved some of the life of the forest-devil and at the same time made friends, they thought, with this divine monster by torturing its slayer forever with the presence of the hand that would be a horror to his life.

Louis was convalescing rapidly under the special care of the natives, who knew that his death would mean the cessation of life in the arm of the divine devil, and bring back the spirit of the beast to torment them. In less than five weeks after the killing of his dreaded foe he was up and walking about the hut. The medical men were now striving more than ever in their efforts to produce the correct formula for the wonderful medicine, which the natives continually refused to give out. The little brown-skin islanders had retired again to their own village, happy over the success of the operation. To me they were a group of arrogant and insidious beings to be despised. As a result of their actions, I had to turn in horror from the person that meant everything to my happiness.

In the days that followed, the odious organ became more and more obnoxious to my brother. It was inimical to his rest and peace, and it refused to function at his command. At night the arm jerked wildly, until within two months after the grafting, his brain seemed to have no power over it.

One night I was awakened by a quick movement as if someone had attempted shoving me from the bed. I turned to look at Louis, who slept with me now, and then with a scream that deafened me, I landed with a single leap in the corner of the room. Collecting my senses, I lighted the lantern. Lying on his back, Louis was struggling with his clenched knees and left arm to loose the giant hand that clutched his throat. Beating down a fear that held me back, I sprang on him, and with all my strength, loosed the hold. The arm moved slowly down to his side as if subdued.

My brain felt paralyzed. The most unearthly problem that ever faced man was before me now. The spirit of revenge instilled in a bodily organ other than the brain was impossible, I thought; yet there was the evidence. One solution came to my mind, and I set myself to immediate action. With a strong rope I tied the arm at the wrist to the heavy log bed-frame. The pale and livid form of my brother was sickening to see as he lay there terror-stricken and exhausted. On the morrow I would have the repulsive organ amputated and hurled into the sea to its master, while in the meantime I would sleep in the adjoining room. I had touched that thing my last time.

Weary and tired from fear and restlessness I soon fell into a troubled sleep once more. How long I slept I can not remember, but the awakening shortly after midnight remains yet stamped in my mind as the most horrible feeling I have ever known. In the silence of the dark night I strained my ears for the sound which I prayed had been only imaginary. Then the terrible realization that I had not been mistaken came over me and bound me in weakness to the bed. Again and again I heard it, plainer now than ever. My auditory faculties became more and more sentient until to me it roared like thunder. The straining of the powerful arm against the rope that bound it grated louder and louder. Then came the whining of the man in his struggle against the calamity that was inevitable. The whines rose to cries as minutes lengthened to hours. The rope could not stand the strain much longer—it was parting now, strand by strand. The break was like the explosion of a cannon to me. Screams of terror rang in my ears, followed by a hurried bustle, then a gasping for breath. The gasps became longer and less audible, weakening until they could scarcely be heard.

For a moment I had become insensible. Then I remembered my brother and listened, but the stillness of the night had closed over the hut once more, and the struggle that had broken the peace and quiet of the little island of Corda had ceased forever. My brother had been strangled by the avenging hand of the man-beast.

THE BASILISK

R. MURRAY GILCHRIST

Marina gave no sign that she heard my protestation. The embroidery of Venus's hands in her silk picture of the Judgment of Paris was seemingly of greater import to her than the love which almost tore my soul and body asunder. In absolute despair I sat until she had replenished her needle seven times. Then impassioned nature cried aloud:

"You do not love me!"

She looked up somewhat wearily, as one debarred from rest. "Listen," she said. "There is a creature called a Basilisk, which turns men and women into stone. In my girlhood I saw the Basilisk—I am stone!"

And, rising from her chair, she departed the room, leaving me in amazed doubt as to whether I had heard aright. I had always known of some curious secret in her life: a secret which permitted her to speak of and to understand things to which no other woman had dared to lift her thoughts. But alas! it was a secret whose influence ever thrust her back from the attaining of happiness. She would warm, then freeze instantly; discuss the purest wisdom, then cease with contemptuous lips and eyes. Doubtless this strangeness had been the first thing to awaken my passion. Her beauty was not of the kind that smites men with sudden craving: it was pale and reposeful, the loveliness of a marble image. Yet, as time went on, so wondrous became her fascination that even the murmur of her swaying garments sickened me with longing. Not more than a year had passed since our first meeting, when I had found her laden with flaming tendrils in the thinned woods of my heritage. A very Dryad, robed in grass color, she was chanting to the sylvan deities. The invisible web took me, and I became her slave.

Her house lay two leagues from mine. It was a low-built mansion lying in a concave park. The thatch was gaudy with stonecrop and lichen. Among the central chimneys a foreign bird sat on a nest of twigs. The long windows blazed with heraldic devices, and paintings of kings and queens and nobles hung in the dim chambers. Here she dwelt with a retinue of aged servants, fantastic women and men half imbecile, who *salaamed* before her with eastern humility and yet addressed her in such terms as gossips use. Had she given them life they could not have obeyed with more reverence. Quaint things the women wrought for her —pomanders and cushions of thistle-down; and the men were never happier than when they could tell her of the first thrush's egg in the thornbush or a sighting of the bitterns that haunted the marsh. She was their goddess and their daughter. Each day had its own routine. In the morning she rode and sang and played; at noon she read in the dusty library, drinking to the full of the dramatists and the platonists. Her own life was such a tragedy as an Elizabethan would have adored. None save her people knew her history, but there were wonderful stories of how she had bowed to tradition, and concentrated in herself the characteristics of a thousand wizard fathers. In the blossom of her youth she had sought strange knowledge, and had tasted thereof, and rued.

The morning after my declaration she rode across her park to the meditating walk I always paced till noon. She was alone, dressed in a habit of white with a loose girdle of blue. As her mare reached the yew hedge, she dismounted, and came to me with more lightness than I had ever beheld in her. At her waist hung a black glass mirror, and her half-bare arms were adorned with cabalistic jewels.

When I knelt to kiss her hand, she sighed heavily. "Ask me nothing," she said. "Life itself is too joyless to be more embittered by explanations. Let all rest between us as now. I will love coldly, you warmly, with no nearer approaching." Her voice rang full of a wistful expectancy, as if she knew that I should combat her half-explained decision. She read me well, for almost ere she had done I cried out loudly against it: "It can never be so—I cannot breathe—I shall die."

She sank to the low moss-covered wall. "Must the sacrifice be made?" she asked, half to herself. "Must I tell him all?" Silence prevailed a while, then turning away her face she said, "From the first I loved you, but last night in the darkness, when I could not sleep for thinking of your words, love sprang into desire."

I was forbidden to speak.

"And desire seemed to burst the cords that bound me. In that moment's strength I felt that I could give all for the joy of being once utterly yours."

I longed to clasp her to my heart. But her eyes were stern, and a frown crossed her brow.

"At morning light," she said, "desire died, but in my ecstasy I had sworn to give what must be given for that short bliss, and to lie in your arms and pant against you before another midnight. So I have come to bid you fare with me to the place where the spell may be loosed, and happiness bought."

She called the mare; it came whinnying, and pawed the ground until she had stroked its neck. She mounted, setting in my hand a tiny, satin-shod foot that seemed rather child's than woman's. "Let us go together to my house," she said. "I have orders to give and duties to fulfil. I will not keep you there long, for we must start soon on our errand." I walked exultantly at her side, but, the grange in view, I entreated her to speak explicitly of our mysterious journey. She stooped and patted my head. " 'Tis but a matter of buying and selling," she answered.

When she had arranged her household affairs, she came to the library and bade me follow her. Then, with the mirror still swinging against her knees, she led me through the garden and the wilderness down to a misty wood. It being autumn, the trees were tinted gloriously in dusky bars of coloring. The rowan, with his amber leaves and scarlet berries, stood before the brown black-spotted sycamore; the silver beech flaunted his golden coins against my poverty; firs, green and fawn-hued, slumbered in hazy gossamer. No bird caroled, although the sun was hot. Marina noted the absence of sound, and without prelude of any kind began to sing from the ballad of the Witch Mother: about the nine enchanted knots, and the trouble-comb in the lady's knotted hair, and the master-kid that ran beneath her couch. Every drop of my blood froze in dread, for whilst she sang her face took on the majesty of one who traffics with infernal powers. As the shade of the trees fell over her, and we passed intermittently out of the light, I saw that her eyes glittered like rings of sapphires. Believing now that the ordeal she must undergo would be too frightful, I begged her to return. Supplicating on my knees—"Let me face the evil alone!" I said, "I will entreat the loosening of the bonds. I will compel and accept any penalty." She grew calm. "Nay," she said, very gently, "if aught can conquer, it is my love alone. In the fervor of my last wish I can dare everything."

By now, at the end of a sloping alley, we had reached the shores of a vast marsh. Some unknown quality in the sparkling water had stained its whole bed a bright yellow. Green leaves, of such a sour brightness as almost poisoned to behold, floated on the surface of the rush-girdled pools. Weeds like tempting veils of mossy velvet grew beneath in vivid contrast with the soil. Alders and willows hung over the margin. From where we stood a half-submerged path of rough stones, threaded by deep swift channels, crossed to the very center. Marina put her foot upon the first step. "I must go first," she said. "Only once before have I gone this way, yet I know its pitfalls better than any living creature."

Before I could hinder her she was leaping from stone to stone like a hunted animal. I followed hastily, seeking, but vainly, to lessen the space between us. She was gasping for breath, and her heartbeats sounded like the ticking of a clock. When we reached a great pool, itself almost a lake, that was covered with lavender scum, the path turned abruptly to the right, where stood an isolated grove of wasted elms. As Marina beheld this, her pace slackened, and she paused in momentary indecision; but, at my first word of pleading that she should go no further, she went on, dragging her silken mud-bespattered skirts. We climbed the slippery shores of the island (for island it was, being raised much above the level of the marsh), and Marina led the way over lush grass to an open glade. A great marble tank lay there, supported on two thick pillars. Decayed boughs rested on the crust of stagnancy within, and frogs, bloated and almost blue, rolled off at our approach. To the left stood the columns of a temple, a round, domed building, with a closed door of bronze. Wild vines had grown athwart the portal; rank, clinging herbs had sprung from the over-teeming soil; astrological figures were chiseled on the broad stairs.

Here Marina stopped. "I shall blindfold you," she said, taking off her loose sash, "and you must vow obedience to all I tell you. The least error will betray us." I promised, and submitted to the bandage. With a pressure of the hand, and bidding me neither move nor speak, she left me and went to the door of the temple. Thrice her hand struck the dull metal. At the last stroke a hissing shriek came from within, and the massive hinges creaked loudly. A breath like an icy tongue leaped out and touched me, and in the terror my hand sprang to the kerchief. Marina's voice, filled with agony, gave me instant pause. *"Oh, why am I thus torn between the man and the fiend? The mesh that holds life in will be ripped from end to end! Is there no mercy?"*

My hand fell impotent. Every muscle shrank. I felt myself turn to stone. After a while came a sweet scent of smouldering wood: such an Oriental fragrance as is offered to Indian gods. Then the door swung to, and I heard Marina's voice, dim and wordless, but raised in wild deprecation. Hour after hour passed so, and still I waited. Not until the sash grew crimson with the rays of the sinking sun did the door open.

"Come to me!" Marina whispered. "Do not take off your blindfold. Quick—we must not stay here long. He is glutted with my sacrifice."

Newborn joy rang in her tones. I stumbled across and was caught in her arms. Shafts of delight pierced my heart at the first contact with her warm breasts. She turned me round, and bidding me look straight in front, with one swift touch untied the knot. The first thing my dazed eyes fell upon was the mirror of black glass which had hung from her waist. She held it so that I might gaze into its depths. And there, with a cry of amazement and fear, *I saw the shadow of the Basilisk.*

The Thing was lying prone on the floor, the presentiment of a sleeping horror. Vivid scarlet and sable feathers covered its gold-crowned cock's head, and its leathern dragon wings were folded. Its sinuous tail, capped with a snake's eyes and mouth, was curved in luxurious and delighted satiety. A prodigious evil leaped in its atmosphere. But even as I looked a mist crowded over the surface of the mirror; the shadow faded, leaving only an indistinct and wavering shape. Marina breathed upon it, and, as I peered and pored, the gloom went off the plate and left, where the Thing had lain, the prostrate figure of a man. He was young and stalwart, a dark outline with a white face, and short black curls that fell in tangles over a shapely forehead, and eyelids languorous and red. His aspect was that of a wearied demon god.

When Marina looked sideways and saw my wonderment, she laughed delightedly in one rippling running tune that should have quickened the dead entrails of the marsh. "I have conquered!" she cried. "I have purchased the fullness of joy!" And with one outstretched arm she closed the door before I could turn to look; with the other she encircled my neck, and, bringing down my head, pressed my mouth to hers. The mirror fell from her hand, and with her foot she crushed its shards into the dank mold.

The sun had sunk behind the trees now, and glittered through the intricate leafage like a charcoal-burner's fire. All the nymphs of the pools arose and danced, gray and cold, exulting at the absence of the divine light. So thickly gathered the vapors that the path grew perilous. "Stay, love," I said. "Let me take you in my arms and carry you. It is no longer safe for you to walk alone." She made no reply, but, a flush arising to her pale cheeks, she stood and let me lift her to my bosom. She rested a hand on either shoulder, and gave no sign of fear as I bounded from stone to stone. The way lengthened deliciously, and by the time we reached the plantation the moon was rising over the further hills. Hope and fear fought in my heart; soon both were set at rest. When I set her on the dry ground she stood a-tiptoe, and murmured with exquisite shame: "Tonight, then, dearest. My home is yours now."

So, in a rapture too subtle for words, we walked together, arm-enfolded, to her house. Preparations for a banquet were going on within: the windows were ablaze, and figures passed behind them bowed with heavy dishes. At the threshold of the hall we were met by a triumphant crash of melody. In the musicians' gallery bald-pated veterans played with flute and harp and viol-de-gamba. In two long rows the antic retainers stood, and bowed, and cried merrily: "Joy and health to the bride and groom!" And they kissed Marina's hands and mine, and, with the players sending forth that half-forgotten tenderness which threads through ancient songbooks, we passed to the feast, seating ourselves on the dais, whilst the servants filled the tables below. But we made little feint of appetite. As the last dish of confections was removed a weird pageant swept across the further end of the banqueting-room: Oberon and Titania with Robin Goodfellow and the rest, attired in silks and satins gorgeous of hue, and bedizened with such late flowers as were still with us. I leaned forward to commend, and saw that each face was brown and wizened and thin-haired, so that their motions and their wedding paean felt goblin and discomforting; nor could I smile till they departed by the further door. Then the tables were cleared away, and Marina, taking my fingertips in hers, opened a stately dance. The servants followed, and in the second maze, a shrill and joyful laughter proclaimed that the bride had sought her chamber. . . .

Ere the dawn I wakened from a troubled sleep. My dream had been of despair: I had been persecuted by a host of devils, thieves of a priceless jewel. So I leaned over the pillow for Marina's consolation; my lips sought hers, my hand crept beneath her head. My heart gave one mad bound—then stopped.

Baynter's Imp

AUGUST DERLETH

Cyril Baynter was one of the more obnoxious men about town. He liked to think of himself as an elegant dandy, but, thanks to a hearty appetite and the wherewithal to gratify it, his dream version of himself was several degrees removed from reality. He was a great hand with the ladies, naturally, what with his car and the money he had inherited from his grandfather, a lumber baron from the middle west who had made his pile by the simple expedient of devastating the forests—on his own ten-acre pieces as well as on all the acreage surrounding them and belonging to absentee owners.

Cyril had some of the old man's rapacity, but lacked his energy.

He liked to think that it was his lack of energy which was responsible for the lukewarm way in which Belle Fassett treated him. This was woeful self-deception, but then, Cyril was a master of that. His friends wagered persistently that money and/or women would ultimately get Cyril into trouble.

However, it was neither. It was his curiosity.

Cyril loved to gratify his curiosity, just as long as it did not involve too much effort on his part. He had once, in an idle moment, dreamed of being a sort of keyhole reporter for Chicago, a la Winchell, but this, like so many other dreams Cyril had had, never materialized. He satisfied his curiosity in various ways; he dug up choice morsels about his friends and exhibited them at awkward moments—which was not calculated to endear him; he rummaged around in old newspaper files, but there he usually became so interested in the comics that he soon forgot his purpose; and he bought up sealed trunks and boxes at auctions.

At one of these he became the possessor of a trunk which had in it nothing whatever but a single bottle, of old glass, packed with as much care as if it were destined to be shipped on a trip around the world and its owner was taking no chances on its breaking.

It was rather a carafe than a bottle, of dark blue glass, and, when held up to the light, did not seem to contain anything. Nonetheless, it was sealed very firmly, not with a cork but with a lead stopper that was kept down by other lead melted over the stopper and the entire upper neck of the bottle. Moreover, on all this there had been inscribed a great many cabalistic designs, including many a warning in Latin, Greek, and a language Cyril could not read, that the bottle must not be opened on pain of the punishment of seven hells and the like.

Naturally, Cyril opened it at once.

If he expected a manifestation of some kind, he was disappointed. The bottle was empty. Much to his disgust it did not even contain a smell. He put it on the mantel of his studio—for he made a pretense at being an artist and, since he could do nothing else, having neither sense of form nor of color, splashed paint on canvases and called himself a Surrealist. Occasionally a gullible critic who knew no more about what he was doing than Cyril did let out vague hints that perhaps Baynter had something—this was just to be on the safe side, in case he had; but on the whole there were not many people stupid enough to be taken in by what Cyril called his "art."

There the bottle rested for two days without any further thought being given to it. As a matter of fact, Cyril did not enter his studio for two days thereafter, and when he did enter it, he was in a cold rage because it looked very much as if Bert Trayle was going to cut him out with Belle. He had long suspected that Belle preferred Bert, even if Bert did not have money or social position, but it was becoming plainer now that Belle had broken an engagement and left him to think that he had been thrust aside in favor of Bert.

Candidly, it was enough to put anyone in a temper, even someone less vain than Cyril. He came into his studio, plumped himself into a chair, and sulked.

Out of this sulk he was abruptly aroused by a not-unpleasant voice inquiring, "Can I be of any assistance?"

He looked up, he looked around, he saw no one.

"Right over here, Fish-eyes."

The voice came from the mantel. Cyril looked in that direction and away again; then he looked back. Was it smoke or a fog on his glasses that made the top of the blue bottle seem clouded? He got up and went over to the mantel.

It was not fog.

It was a quite reasonably distinct miniature of a man, about a foot high, unclothed, but wearing a pair of horns and a forked tail.

"Good God!" exclaimed Cyril involuntarily, whereupon the creature grimaced.

"There's no need to be offensive," he said.

"Where did you come from?"

"Out of the bottle. I'm the imp who lived in it. Spent nine hundred years there until you let me out the other day. Why, it took two whole days to materialize again—I was so much out of practice."

Cyril blinked, closed his eyes, rubbed his hands over them; in short, he did all the conventional things, but when he looked again, the imp was still very much there, save only for the faintly disturbing circumstance that he could be seen through. Indeed, he was really not more than half visible.

"I asked you before whether I could be of any help?"

Cyril replied that he did not think so. Nothing could change Belle's mind. But if something were to happen to Trayle—! Now, there was an idea! It struck him amidships and he turned to the imp to expound it, but the imp had gone.

A little shakily, Cyril returned to his chair to brood about his sanity. Like most hypochondriacs, he had the habit of looking at every disturbing symptom in its worst possible light. There was nothing the matter with the bottle at all. He made a note to have the stopper repaired, so that he might use it, if occasion demanded, and went to take an aspirin. What a thing to happen him! What a hallucination! Fortunately, there was no one else in the room, or he might have been hard put to it to offer a suitable explanation.

During the night he thought someone whispered into his ear that the matter had been attended to. He sat up and looked blearily around, but he was much too tired to investigate what must certainly have been a dream, and went to sleep again.

He slept until noon. Then he had breakfast in bed.

In the course of breakfast, he learned via the morning paper that Herbert Trayle had been fished out of the Chicago River; he had apparently driven over the open Michigan Avenue Bridge. No one had any explanation of how it had happened; Trayle had had a drink or two, but was certainly not in any sense of the word high.

Cyril was not so obtuse as to think this a coincidence. He went directly to his studio and over to the bottle on the mantel.

"Imp!" he said, somewhat uncertainly.

He heard someone yawning; it seemed to come out of the bottle. There was an imprecation for people who interrupted the sleep of others. And then the imp appeared, flowing up out of the bottle like a faint haze of smoke and taking shape. He sat there with his legs crossed and contemplated his long, thin fingers.

"Did you do this?" asked Cyril, pointing to the story in the paper.

The imp smiled. "A little awkward—but I managed," he said modestly.

Cyril was not unaware of the implications and possibilities presented by the imp. In fact, there came into being at once within his thoughts a vast panorama of events that might take place; he began to feel like a hard-pressed general to whom a new and enormously potent weapon had been granted.

Belle was, of course, the first problem.

He had no hope that the imp could change Belle's mind by direct action, but there was that kind of indirection like the elimination of the opposition that might work very well indeed. Now that Trayle was out of the way, there remained only Belle's father; the old man had opposed him, not very determinedly, to be sure, but just enough to strengthen Belle. If something were to happen to him—!

He looked speculatively at the imp, who sat with his legs crossed and his head tilted to one side, looking at him as curiously as Cyril now gazed at the inhabitant of the bottle. Cyril discovered that the imp had no difficulty reading his mind.

"Why all this bother about a woman?" inquired the imp scornfully.

Cyril tried to explain that Belle was exceptional, but the imp interrupted rudely to point out that every lovesick swain felt precisely the same way, and it was simply against the law of averages for so many exceptional women to exist. It was that way nine hundred years ago and it was the same today.

"Nevertheless, if her old man were out of the way," grumbled Cyril.

With a sound very much like a Bronx cheer, the imp vanished.

Cyril settled down to plan his future, looking through rose-colored glasses.

He never had a pang of conscience about the unfortunate accident that had removed Belle's father so soon after Trayle's death. Of course, to Belle he oozed sympathy; if he had really felt it, he would have been hard put to it to show anything of it; but since it was simply an act, there was nothing to it. He was delicate in that he did not force himself on Belle for at least a month after her father's death, taking time out only long enough to send her a little something for remembrance from time to time.

In the second month, he began to pay her the most assiduous attention he had ever paid her in their entire acquaintance. Cyril was not without charm when he was not sulking; and now, with the importance of his money having increased since her father's death, Belle was inclined to overlook many of his obnoxious points.

In short, Belle began to look upon him with considerably more favor.

Cyril was transported. He knew that the battle was not yet won, but the first round was very definitely his. The whole thing went to his head in a very disagreeable fashion; Cyril was one of those people who believe that any stroke of luck is by nature an outgrowth of his own personality; and he went around preening and priding himself on his ability to charm so attractive a feminine morsel as Belle Fassett.

He might have forgotten all about the imp, had he not seen the bottle from time to time. The imp was far less given to visibility; he appeared very rarely; he seemed to prefer sleeping, explaining that he had got into the habit. After all, nine centuries in a bottle had left him with very little aptitude for anything else to do. On one unforgettable occasion Cyril had come upon him reading a first edition of a book by Horatio Alger (paper covers), chuckling heartily over the Alger formula, and setting forth in no uncertain terms the thesis that the people in Mr. Alger's stories had quite obviously no awareness of genuine evil.

For some reason, Cyril was disagreeably affected by this incident.

He began to think in terms of a lifetime with the imp. He would have a hard time explaining the imp and his bottle to Belle. And what would Belle think if she were to come upon the imp without warning? The more he thought about this, the more troubled he became. In the first place, it would be impossible to explain the imp to Belle; she would simply not believe it. In the second, if she were forced to believe it, she would come to the not altogether unjustified conclusion that Cyril was leagued with the forces of darkness. In the third, the whole business might frighten her far too much for his good; and finally, if she did actually see the imp, she would probably pack up and leave him instantly.

These cogitations and reflections took Cyril an entire week, but at the end of that time, he had come to a conclusion.

The imp must go.

After all, he had served his purpose, and it was time for him to be returned to the bottle and put away in a good safe place. Very likely the original owner had had good reasons for taking this course with the imp. He was not only disconcerting, but there was always that ghastly uncertainty; Cyril might very easily some day cradle the wrong kind of wish in his thoughts, and before he could stop it, the imp would have gone out and converted the wish into the fact.

No, it would never do to keep the imp.

Very slyly, Cyril had a new stopper made, and one evening he walked unconcernedly up to the bottle, with the idea of stopping it up and sealing it before the imp could escape. The plan was sound, but he had no sooner come up to the bottle than he was possessed by doubts. Was the imp in the bottle?

"Imp!" he called.

"Now what?" The voice came from the bottle.

Excellent, thought Cyril, and put the stopper into the bottle.

He should not have awakened the imp, for, once awake, the imp was instantly aware of what Cyril intended to do, and he was out of the bottle before the stopper closed his egress.

Naturally, he was outraged. He had been an obedient imp within his obvious limitations, and he had given Cyril no cause for anger.

"One thing I can't stand is ingratitude," he said.

Cyril whirled around.

It was the imp, all right.

But Cyril had very little time to think about it. Something was happening to him. It was not an unpleasant sensation, but an extremely curious one; he seemed to be shrinking in size, diminishing with breathless rapidity. Then he felt himself picked up unceremoniously and poured—that was the word; he thought of it—into the bottle. And in a flash, the stopper was in, and the creature outside was sealing it.

The creature outside had a disturbing resemblance to Cyril.

As a matter of fact, in all but spirit, it was Cyril. The imp had simply appropriated Cyril's earthly possessions, including his body, and had put Cyril in his place.

If Cyril had any doubts about his future, they were resolved very quickly. The imp in Cyril's body took the bottle outside and buried it deep in the garden.

That was the end of Cyril Baynter.

The imp, however, saw no reason why he should not live Cyril's life. He followed the Alger formula by extension, married Belle, and had a modestly successful life, with three children, born fortunately in Cyril's image and not in his—for nothing short of a miracle would have offered suitable explanation of horns and tails.

THE BEAST OF THE YUNGAS

WILLIS KNAPP JONES

Fear?" the explorer repeated, pushing back his sherbet glass with a quick, nervous hand. "Oh, I suppose I've hung back as often as the next man, but in time one gets calloused to fear, I imagine."

Several of the dinner guests expressed polite interest, but Grace Demming, debutante daughter of the hostess, looked at the guest of honor with an expression in her wide-set gray eyes like one regarding a super-creature. "Haven't you ever been afraid, Mr. Winslow?" Her rich contralto voice was very lovely.

"If you mean fear as those fiction writers describe it, when a man's soul is turned to water, I can't say I've ever experienced it, nor come in contact with it except—perhaps—" He paused awkwardly, glanced at the ladies around the table, then finished hurriedly: "No, never."

Mrs. Mason, the dowager next to him, caught him up quickly as though scenting a choice bit of gossip. "Was it something terrible?" she inquired. "You needn't be afraid to tell us. It couldn't be nearly so unprintable as many things we read every day in the papers."

"Well," the explorer began, "it isn't scandalous. I didn't mean to give that impression. In fact—to tell the truth, it's something I've been trying to drive out of my mind, but it persists in coming back without bringing an explanation with it."

Miss Demming's gray eyes seemed to plead with him, too. He had been especially conscious all evening of the way they held him, seeming to draw him out.

And now there was a strange aloofness in that girl as though she were curtained off from the world. His explorer instinct made him want to know more about her. He had gone into Afghanistan once just because he had read that a certain temple in Mangfu had a curtain screening off a mystery that not more than two people then alive had seen. He wanted to pierce the veil.

"I'm afraid you won't be satisfied," Winslow began. "I don't know what caused the fear. I can't tell you any of the details, but the thing that seared my soul was a look of fright in the eyes of another man." He made a gesture as though to repel the host of memories crowding in upon him. "It's not a pretty story. After all, I believe I'd better not tell it."

If that were meant for a refusal, its only effect was to make the guests more interested. All of them urged him to continue — all but Miss Demming; yet her half-parted lips and that inscrutable something in her eyes made him go on.

"It was in Bolivia that it happened — Bolivia, that unexplored country where anything might be true. I was in La Paz concluding some Inca investigation. Strange rumors had been filtering in about some queer beast that the Indians of the Beni region had seen. The scientists of the capital were trying to convince us that the description fitted a diplodocus, or some other prehistoric creature like it."

From the looks of interrogation, he knew that he was talking beyond most of them. "The diplodocus," he hastened to explain, "was a huge creature from ten to fifteen feet high and perhaps forty feet long that lived ages ago during the Pleistocene period before the tyrannosaurus came along and killed them off. You've probably seen reconstructions of them in museums, looking like a kangaroo with a long, tapering tail. At any rate, the jungle Indians were claiming to have seen a creature that has been extinct for at least 25,000 years.

"Frankly, I didn't believe a word of the story. I thought that some of those coca-crazed savages had gone on a spree; it was good newspaper stuff, however, like the creature that was reported in Argentina later. The upshot was that my committee at home read about it and cabled me to investigate. I didn't object. I love Bolivia. There's not a country I know of that is richer in interest for foreigners, and here was a chance to visit a part I'd never seen.

"I needed a few more pongos — those Indians that can carry anything up to a trunk on their shoulders — and while I was looking for them, I ran across Manion, or rather he ran across me. Nobody knew Manion. He was a silent chap who did nothing in the daytime but sun himself in front of the Congressional Building on the plaza, and when the cold evenings of the *alto plano* descended, he would disappear into the *pensíon* where he boarded. People said he was cracked. He had drifted into La Paz a few months before, no one knew from where. Where so many foreigners are fugitives, it doesn't do to make too many inquiries, but I half suspected he didn't know any too much about himself. He had a lot of uncomfortable habits. One was to tap incessantly at a silver plate embedded in his skull, when he was pondering. It reminded me of the old-fashioned wireless decoder where a hammer jars apart the filings. Perhaps he was trying to clarify his thoughts in the same way.

"But he would never tell us how he acquired the plate or the limp. Once, later when I had taken him with me, I saw scars on his body and he explained that he thought he had had an argument and after it they had given him some false ribs, which wasn't any explanation at all.

"Since he was a likable chap and could take the place of my secretary, who was down with dysentery, I gave him a job. He wrote a copperplate hand, could handle the porters, and was a big help.

"The day we left La Paz he appeared in a faded and worn flying suit with double wings on the breast. He apologized for it by saying he had no other roughing costume and had not wanted to bother me about an advance on his wages. Later he let drop that he had been in the Lafayette Escadrille, but that was a lie. I've looked over their records and no Manion or name like it appears in their roster.

"If I had been superstitious or gifted with prophecy we never should have left La Paz; but unfortunately, man can't see what lies ahead. I won't describe that trip, day after weary day. All the colors of an artist's palette could never reproduce its splendor, but all the tortures of the Inquisition are puny beside the sufferings it laid upon us. Sometimes we would toil for hours through knee-deep grasses with rain so heavy that it was like a curtain to push against. Then the torrid sun would transform the jungle in a twinkling into a vapor bath where we could scarcely breathe. But through all the hardships, Manion was always ready with a song. He seemed to know only one, but when we were dog-tired and needed to push on farther, his singing helped.

"He had evidently never been in the jungle before, and everything was wonderful. When all I could see was the next three feet of the trail, he would want to stop to be told about a new bird he had seen in one of the snakewood trees.

"But where he excelled was as a revolver shot. I never saw anyone so quick on the draw and so sure in aim. Once"—Winslow shuddered—"a boa constrictor, twined about a branch above the trail, swung down its head like a battering ram and with a single blow dislocated the neck of one of our Indian bearers. I was next in line, but before I could get out my revolver or that battering head could swing back, Manion put three shots into it. Then with hands absolutely steady, he stopped to reload his revolver. Out of curiosity, I felt his pulse—as slow as a child's. When not a single tremor betrayed his excitement, I thought he must be a man without nerves. That's what makes the rest of it so horrible."

Again the explorer stopped and took a sip of water. His own hand shook slightly as he set down the glass. After a moment he went on. "Manion had shot a twenty-eight-foot boa without disturbing his calm. You can see the skin in the museum, for I brought it back. He wanted to take the head, too, with the three bullet holes below the frontal bone so close together that a quarter would have covered them. We were rather short of carriers, however, so he had to give up the idea.

"It was a long journey to the place where the guides told us the animal had been seen, and far from any beaten path. No white people had penetrated that far before, so Manion, Jenkins (the botanist and geologist) and I—the only white people of the party—were a constant source of interest and fear to the few Indians we met. When we reached the tribe whose members had seen the animal, I found that neither my Aimara or Quechua, nor any of the Beni dialects Jenkins thought he knew were any use. Even the guide had difficulty making himself understood, but he did make out that they had recently seen that prehistoric animal. We were soon led to the place.

"If—mark I say 'if'—there's a place in this world where creatures of the Miocene and Pleistocene Ages might be expected to survive down to our own day, the valley we reached is the one. It was a sunken plain, about twenty or thirty miles square and full of that riot of vegetation which must have covered the earth when the diplodocus roamed it, for they ate only grass. You know how La Paz is situated—a sheer drop of one thousand feet below the surrounding plain. Well, this region was something like it, except that it had no exit, no river winding out of it, no path up the slope—only straight, sheer cliffs. Without elaborate tackle nothing down there could get out, and nothing outside, falling by accident over the edge, would live to want to get out. We went three-quarters of the way around before we found the place where the walls were lowest and least steep. There we made camp.

"We intended to make a permanent camp in the valley itself, but when we ordered the carriers to go down the three-hundred-foot vine ladder that they had constructed, there was a mutiny. Don't tell me sign language doesn't exist. Not one of our carriers had been told by us the reason for our coming, and yet all of them, without understanding a word of the jargon of that region, knew all about the beasts supposed to be hidden by the tangle of foliage below.

"They were afraid even of staying near the place, and I am sure that if we had carried out our plan and had us three white men make our camp below, they would have deserted, leaving us helpless in the jungle. It was Manion's idea to have two of us explore the lower valley by daylight, the other one staying with the carriers.

"Jenkins, who had been ill for a large part of the trip, suddenly took a turn for the worse. He was useless. He could do nothing but lie in the smaller of the lean-tos, leaving Manion and me to set in place the ladder the Indians had woven.

"It was almost dark before we completed the work, and we were so excited that we could not wait till morning. We descended to the lower level, not knowing what we should find, perhaps some footprints in the soft ground. But in our brief survey we found nothing, so, as it was growing dark, I suggested we had better return to camp.

"Manion wouldn't leave. He wanted to spend the night there in the valley, hoping to hear something. With Jenkins sick, I could not very well accompany him, especially as the Indians had been nervous and jumpy all day. Yet I hesitated to leave Manion. He laughed at my fears. He had two revolvers and was not at all afraid. Finally I gave in after he promised to sleep close to the ladder, to which he could retreat in case of danger.

"As I climbed the vine ladder, I looked back. I shall never forget the sight. Already the valley foliage was deepening in color where it lay closest to the western ledge. It would not have been difficult to imagine anything in that tangle of green. I called down a warning as I saw Manion brushing the ground where he was going to sleep. And as I went up the ladder, I heard him singing to himself that song that was so continually on his lips. It certainly had a haunting strain; I've never heard anybody else sing it. *Bonny Eloise* I think it is called. It goes—"

A cry like that of a stricken bird broke into his story. Grace Demming, her face suddenly dead white, leaned forward, clutching the table for support. Her glass of water overturned and the water spread slowly across the tablecloth, but no one moved. "Jimmy!" she moaned. "Then he didn't die in France."

Instant confusion reigned. Several of the company protested that she must be mistaken, that he could not possibly have reached South America. In the babble of sound, Miss Beardsley told Winslow that Miss Demming had been engaged to an aviator who had been reported killed in battle. Could that wound in the head have played pranks with his memory? The whole thing sounded preposterous, but Miss Demming was convinced.

"It was Jimmy," she insisted. "Something you said made me begin to suspect. Then you mentioned his writing, and now the only song he ever sang. Wait!" She burst out of the room, her mother following. In an instant she had returned with a photograph of a man in a flying suit. There was no doubt about it, then. Manion and the Jimmy Kent to whom Miss Demming had been engaged were the same. The explorer recognized him at once.

"Where is he?" she cried. "Tell me, where is he?"

Winslow looked at her sadly. "I am sorry, miss Demming," he said gently. "He's dead."

It seemed as though a whisper echoed his words. The girl clutched at her throat, pale as the lace that edged her collar. Her gray eyes appealed for more details.

"Yes, there's no doubt of it. Manion—I mean Kent—came back the next day, convinced that we had been hoaxed and that no animal existed except in some Indian's delirious imagination. We started back toward La Paz, but somewhere in the lowlands, perhaps the night he roamed the sunken valley, he had contracted jungle fever. We did all we could to make him comfortable, but in spite of all, he died, conscious to the end and entirely without pain. I wish you could see the paradise where we buried him, under a beautiful chonta palm, and we scattered orchids over the place before we left."

There was a scattered volley of questions. "Didn't you see the animal?"

The explorer shook his head. "How could one see a beast that has been extinct for centuries?"

Then the bald old man beside Miss Demming spoke up. "But I don't see what your story proves, Mr. Winslow. Where was the fear you spoke of?"

"Didn't I say? It was—it was in the faces of the Indians when they talked about the valley. The superstitious terror in their countenances when we told them we were going to camp in the valley was enough to make strong men shiver. But I don't blame them, exactly. It was the fear of the unknown that gripped them, so that I was glad enough to leave them and return to civilization. But I wonder whether there aren't almost as many superstitious terrors among the civilized."

The conversation switched, and soon the guests left the table and went to the porch, where coffee was served.

The explorer, wishing to escape from the others, had slipped into the house and was standing alone, watching the light of an automobile on the mountain road above him, when he sensed a presence. He had withdrawn from the group but Mr. Demming had found him. "Perhaps the others believed your story, perhaps not. But Kent was engaged to my daughter. He fell behind the German lines and we never had definite proof of his death. Grace has never been herself since, always hoping that he would someday return. Now I want the truth."

The explorer nodded wearily. "It's your right," he acknowledged dully. "I should never have begun the story in the first place. Again and again I have tried to efface its horror from my mind, but it leaps out, as it did tonight."

"Then part of it is true? I beg of you, be careful."

"I know, Mr. Demming. Unfortunately, it is true—true to the point where the boy and I parted. The rest of it I have never told a soul. Sometimes at night it fairly screams for utterance.

"I said he came up in the morning. He didn't. Shortly after I reached the camp, I threw down a blanket for him and some food. Then he made a fire and I went into the lean-to. Suddenly I heard a scream—his voice. It was too dark to see or do anything. Again and again I called his name. Only the echoes and the scream of the vampire bats answered me. All night I shuddered, waiting, waiting. When the first streak of light came, I took a gun and went down after him. At first I found nothing. Then I picked up his footprints, far apart, slipping and dodging as though he had been running. The reason for his haste was not apparent until I saw in the muck the mark of a gigantic foot. About ten feet farther on was another, and in between the trail of a heavy tail.

"Farther on was a trodden space about a thick, bushy growth. The tracks were mute evidence of the story. A mad chase and flight, dodging about the bush, with the huge creature finally breaking down the vegetation. Then I noticed other footprints, smaller, coming from another direction, from where the ladder hung.

"And finally, under the trampled bushes, I found Manion, dead. His face! Deadly terror had graven unforgettable lines on it, such horror and loathing as I never saw before. Please God I'll never have to see it again! And his body—not a sign of bruise or hurt upon it, the only mark, a messy green slime on one hand, as though an animal had slobbered over it.

"As I caught the significance, the world began making dizzying circles about me, and when next I knew anything, it was almost evening. Manion was lying in the same place, his sightless eyes staring as though seeing into hell. Hastily I buried him, as I said, at the foot of a palm and dropped orchids over his grave.

"Jenkins, when I found him, was in a fever of excitement. The carriers had deserted with most of our provisions. It was imperative to start back at once to save the lives of both of us. My nerves were in terrible shape, and Jenkins was about helpless, but we eventually reached La Paz."

"And you left Manion's body for that horrible animal to dig up and eat?"

The explorer shook his head. "No, that's the thing that makes me believe an unbelievable fact. Manion, who, as I knew, was a cool, accurate shot, had died of fright, paralyzed by the sight of some monster, and the beast had the chance to eat him any time during the night. His hand bore evidence that the creature had sniffed him, but there was no sign of a bite. Do you know any modern South American animal of any size that would not have eaten him? I don't. I know, however, that the diplodocus is herbivorous. Grass forms its diet. So I think he may have seen such a prehistoric animal as the Indians mentioned. I don't know. People would call me crazy if I told them I believed it. But some day I'm going back to Bolivia. The nights when I think about Manion, I can not sleep. I must go back to see what it was that shocked him lifeless with that horror that I saw painted indelibly on his features. Perhaps—who knows?"

THE BEETLE

GARNETT RADCLIFFE

Any moment the trap that had taken months to set might be expected to snap. Inspector Knowles had his watch on the blotting pad as he waited for news of the arrest of the sadistic strangler they called Captain 'Y.'

Instead of the expected ring Detective Scott walked into the office. The look on his face brought the Inspector to his feet. He spoke hoarsely.

"What happened?"

"He slipped us," Scott said. "Vanished like a puff of smoke. My fault, I'm afraid."

He seated himself wearily opposite the Inspector's desk. He was looking white, and haggard. After a pause he spoke.

51

"I've alerted all squads; they are certain to pick him up before long. I shouldn't worry too much."

"I do worry. Suppose another woman is found strangled tomorrow?"

"Captain 'Y' won't strangle another woman. He's dodged us for the moment, but he's still in the net. It's just a question of waiting."

"But how on earth did he give you the slip?"

"Put it down to a moment of mental aberration on my part which coincided with an unfortunate disturbance in the Roebuck Arms, of which he took advantage. He's cleverer than I gave him credit for. I was flattering myself he had not the faintest idea he was being shadowed."

The Inspector sighed.

"You've lost him, that's all I can think about. Anyway, tell me exactly what happened."

Scott smiled. He was thinking that that was just what he *couldn't* do. Captain 'Y's' disappearance from the Roebuck Arms had been as inexplicable as a clever conjuring trick.

One could make a fantastic surmise, but not aloud to a man like Inspector Knowles. Knowles was a practical man and was concerned only with plain facts.

He could have his plain facts. Scott proceeded to lay them before his superior as if he was dealing a hand of cards.

"We worked on Plan 'S,' sir. When Nesbitt phoned me that Captain 'Y' had gone into the saloon bar of the Roebuck Arms in Crewe Street I went there at once. Nesbitt, Brown, and Simmons met me outside. I told Simmons to keep an eye on Captain 'Y's' Mercedes, which he'd parked in Cotton Mews. Nesbitt and Brown I told to wait outside the entrance to the saloon bar in case he gave trouble when I arrested him. There's only the one door to that bar so I knew they couldn't miss him.

"I went inside alone. It was known he was meeting Mrs. Banbury and the idea was I should try to overhear what he said to her before arresting him. We thought if we could get a line on his methods it might help us to work out how he murdered Nina Mason and Mrs. Sorelli.

"It was seven thirty-five when I went into the Roebuck. Mrs. Banbury hadn't arrived and Captain 'Y' was at the bar talking to the barmaid. He was wearing a duffle coat over a blue blazer with gold buttons, gray flannels, and suede shoes. Very smart indeed, Inspector. No one would have suspected he was—well, what we know he was."

Had Knowles been a different type he would have liked to enlarge about how he had felt at that moment. The cosy bar with its glittering shelves and bright fire had seemed like a jungle glade; Captain 'Y' like the tiger he was stalking.

As he'd stood beside the tall, well-groomed man with the brushed-back hair and curiously cold eyes he'd felt like a hunter leveling his sights on an unsuspecting quarry.

"The question is," the Inspector snapped, "did he suspect who *you* were?"

Scott smiled.

"One for me, Inspector! No, I honestly don't think he had the least idea he was being shadowed. He was in a self-satisfied, boastful mood. As I stood beside him he was actually talking to the barmaid about the Sorelli murder. 'The police are a lot of numbskulls,' I heard him say. 'I'll lay a fiver they'll never catch the fellow who strangled her'."

"Bravado?" suggested the Inspector. "He knew who you were and he was pulling your leg."

Scott shook his head.

"I'll stake my experience he hadn't the least idea. If he had known anything he wouldn't have walked into the trap at the Roebuck Arms."

"He seems to have walked out again," the Inspector commented.

Scott ignored the remark and went on dealing out the plain facts.

"At ten to eight Mrs. Banbury arrived. She was dressed to kill—or be killed, perhaps, I should say. Mink coat, pearl necklace, and diamond rings. . . . I saw a glint in the eye of the tiger when he kissed her plump, white hand."

"What?"

"Sorry, Inspector, I was only repeating what crossed my mind at the time. You want just the bare facts. Well, after salutations Captain 'Y' ordered a pink gin for the lady and a double whiskey for himself—she paid, incidentally—and then they took their drinks to a small table on the left of the fireplace. And I took my humble glass of stout to a settee just behind where I could both see and hear.

"I was hoping to learn something of the methods by which our tiger decoyed his victims to their death. Well, I didn't. Circumstances decreed their conversation should take quite a different turn.

"What *did* they talk about? You'd never guess so I'll tell you. They talked of monkeys. It appeared that when Mrs. Banbury was getting out of her car outside the pub she had seen a monkey in the street outside. The poor little thing had looked so cold and lonely and lost crouching on the pavement! She hoped its owner would find it before some nasty dog came along. . . .

"That was her opening gambit, and Captain 'Y' followed it up. Apparently, he'd also seen a monkey when he was coming into the Roebuck. But he was used to seeing monkeys lost in London. He'd seen several during the last couple of months or so. His theory was that someone had forgotten to shut the doors of one of the cages at the Zoo, but the authorities were keeping it dark. That made Mrs. B. giggle and say, 'You are funny, Colonel Fitzgerald!' "

"Colonel Fitzgerald?" the Inspector repeated. "When he killed Nina Mason he was calling himself Major Robinson!"

"He'd promoted himself for Mrs. Banbury. A couple of customers were going out and as the chap was holding the door for his wife Mr. Monkey himself came hopping in. I suppose he'd got fed up sitting on the cold pavement. So we'd quite a menagerie in the Roebuck Arms that evening! A human tiger, a mink-coated lamb, and a real live monkey! Talk of the jungle!"

"What?"

"Nothing, Inspector. I'll get on with the facts. The monkey was quite tame. He hopped on the counter and when the barmaid, greatly daring, picked him up he put his arms round her neck like a baby. He was a jolly little chap, one of the ordinary brown *sangu* variety. I've seen thousands of them in Southern India."

Inspector Knowles made an impatient movement.

"Damn the monkey! What I want to hear is how Captain 'Y' gave you the slip."

Scott sighed.

"I don't know, Inspector, I can only give you the facts as they happened. The sight of the monkey started Captain 'Y' reminiscing. He went back to his days in India. Incidentally, he really was in India during the war, wasn't he?"

"He was until he was cashiered from the Poona Cavalry for pinching the mess funds."

"He didn't tell that to Mrs. B. What he told her was how he used to shoot monkeys when he was stationed at Ferozepore. I've been at Ferozepore myself, and I think he was telling the truth. The place is overrun with sacred monkeys, as tame as London sparrows. *Sacred* monkeys, Inspector. . . . Monkeys under the special protection of the great Monkey God Harathi Ram . . ."

"You mean it's forbidden to shoot them?"

"One doesn't shoot monkeys unless one happens to be a sadist like Captain 'Y.' He told Mrs. Banbury it was great fun potting the little beggars. She asked if he'd ever eaten one and he said he had and it had tasted like chicken."

"What about it?"

Inspector, your knowledge of Hindu mythology is nil, Scott thought. Have you never heard of the black magic of Harathi Ram, the terrible Monkey God? Have you never heard how Harathi Ram wreaks vengeance on those who harm his children?

When he'd been in India he had visited a temple of the Monkey God. There had been a monstrous statue of the most fearsome of all the Hindu deities. Half monkey, half human, with upraised arms and horrible snarling face, it had filled him with a sense of dread as he stood dwarfed by its shadow in the dim temple. A priest had whispered to him that if you offended Harathi Ram his magic would find you and punish you though you fled to the utmost parts of the earth.

Superstition? The Inspector would have thought him mad had he dared to voice his thoughts.

"Next thing happened," he went on, "was that the monkey sprang off the counter, hopped across the bar, and climbed into the fireplace. It wanted to get warm, I suppose. Everyone crowded round to watch. A monkey in a London bar is quite a novelty.

"Captain 'Y' knelt down to stroke it. I think he wanted to show off his familiarity with monkeys. I heard him speak to it in Urdu, 'Barra jao, chota souer ki butcha.' That means in English, 'Get out, you little son of a pig,' and is a most insulting thing to say."

Had the Inspector been a different sort of man he might have enlarged. Captain 'Y's' expression hadn't been the expression of a man who loved animals. His lurking smile, the slow caressing movements of his manicured hands, and the way the monkey seemed to shrink from his touch—somehow all those things had made him think of little Nina Mason, the girl who had been found strangled in a Mayfair flat.

He had noticed the monkey's eyes had suddenly gone red. They looked hypnotic and baleful as it lifted its little head to stare at the man. Then it put its paws on his beautiful white hand and made as if it were trying to draw him down toward the fire. . . .

A monkey pulling a man's hand playfully like a kitten! What had there been in that to give him such a sense of intangible horror? Other customers had laughed.

He continued speaking to the Inspector.

"Then the disturbance happened. A beetle of some sort fell with a flop into the fireplace. It began to run round and round inside the curb.

The monkey began playing with it, letting it get almost to safety and then scooping it back with its paw like a cat playing with a mouse."

While he spoke his mind was asking questions. *Had* it been a beetle, that frantic inch-high thing that ran upright on two legs, its wings flapping behind like a brown coat? *Had* it been a beetle that jumped over cinders, fell into hot ash, made wild leaps for the top of the curb and even tried to dash into the fire in its mad fear of the monkey?

Its terror had been most unpleasant to watch. The other customers had stopped laughing. Scott could remember their ejaculations of disgust: "It's a mouse. . . . No, it's a young bat. . . . I tell you it's a moth . . ." Then a woman had begun to scream. *"The monkey's torturing it. . . . Get it away from the monkey. . . . It's like a little man!"*

A barman had come running with a coal shovel. He tried to scoop up the—well, whatever the thing was. It had jumped on to the shovel and for a second the firelight glow had shown it to him like the tiny figure of a running man seen through the wrong end of a telescope. Its antennae had looked like arms raised above its head, its wings had been like a duffle coat flapping round its legs, and it had left drops of blood on the shovel.

It hadn't buzzed. It had uttered tiny sounds like the echoes of screams from Hell.

Scott wiped a face that had suddenly gone wet. The Inspector was staring at him.

"Are you ill?"

"I felt a bit faint, overwork I suppose. I was talking about the—the beetle. Someone tried to scoop it out of the fireplace with a shovel. But the monkey was too quick. It grabbed it off the shovel and stuffed it struggling into its mouth. Then before you could say 'Jack Robinson' it leapt on to the mantlepiece and then to a shelf and from there out through an upper window that was open."

Again he wiped his forehead. He had seen the monkey's shadow on the wall and ceiling as it leapt for the window. Some trick of lighting had made it look like a monstrous, crouching, simian nightmare, as if the shadow of the Monkey God himself had fallen on that London bar. He had seen the legs of the beetle, two twitching threads protruding from the great pouched-up mouth. . . .

Aware of the Inspector's curious stare he forced himself to go on.

"It was then I noticed that Captain 'Y' had disappeared. He must have taken advantage of the confusion to slip away."

"You never saw him go?"

"No. The men I'd posted outside didn't see him either."

"Is there any other exit?"

"None that I could discover. Mrs. Banbury was as mystified as we were. She said she shut her eyes because the monkey gave her the horrors, and when she opened them Captain 'Y' had disappeared."

The telephone on the desk rang. The Inspector snatched up the receiver. After a minute he turned to his subordinate. His face wore a grim smile as he spoke.

"They've found him! A burned and mangled body that has been identified as his has been found in the Crewe Street tube. I gather a couple of trains had gone over him. My idea is that he knew the game was up. While you were goggling at a beetle he made his get-away from the Roebuck, ran down to the tube, and jumped on the line. Any better explanation?"

Scott had one, but he preferred to keep it to himself. After all, it *might* have been only his own morbid imagination!

A Birthday Present for Tommy

CHARLES KING

I am a little girl. People say that I am small, even for my age. Sometimes when I walk in the park nearby my house, well-meaning strangers will ask me if I am not afraid to be alone. I always answer "No," and it is the truth.

Maybe it isn't the complete truth because I am sometimes afraid at night. That is, unless I have company. I live by myself and the house does get kind of scary without company. I like company very much. . . .

"Hello, little girl."

"How do you do, sir."

"Dear me. But you *are* a polite little girl. . . ."

"Thank you, sir."

"How old are you, my dear?"

"How old do I look, sir?"

"Ha! Ha! Bears out my contention that a woman's a coquette no matter what her age. To please you, child, I'd say you were about twelve. And very pretty."

I made believe that I saw a friend of mine and went away. It is always about this time that they start talking about my parents. That makes me very uneasy because I have no parents. And I just know that if I told that to a grown-up there would be trouble. There would be more questions. And if they ever found out that I live alone . . . well, I just know they would take me away from my house. I would not like that. It does scare me when I am alone, but sometimes I have company. And that is nice. I remember Tommy. He was *very* nice. I will tell you about him. . . .

It was about a month ago. I think it was a month. Time is funny. It is not always easy to remember.

I was walking along one of my favorite paths in the park. On a sunny day you can always find children there. It is fun to play with them. I can forget so many, many things when I play with them. But, even at my happiest, it is always saddening to know that I will see some of them for so very short a time. Even so, I must not depress myself. I promised to tell about Tommy, and I will. A ball came rolling along the walk. . . .

"Here is your ball, little boy. . . ."

"Huh. I'm not so little!"

"I'm sorry. I guess you're a pretty big boy."

"Sure, I am. And I'm strong, too."

"You must be. You threw that ball very far."

"I bet that girls can't throw like that."

"No . . . we can't. We learn different things. . . ."

"What kind of things?"

This would have been a very hard question to answer. There are many things you can tell little boys; there are so many things that one cannot. I have known many of them . . . very many . . . and yet each one thinks a little bit differently. That is where the danger lies. One cannot give the wrong answer because then they never trust you again. And yet one must have company. It is all quite tiring . . . and confusing. . . .

I was wondering just how to answer Tommy, when his governess ran up. She seemed most worried. And then she saw us together. She smiled, I suppose in relief, and then grew quite angry.

"Tommy! You are a bad, bad boy!"

"Why?"

"Because you ran away and I didn't see you."

"But I only was chasing my ball. . . ."

"Don't you know that there are bad people who steal little boys?"

"B-but I was only . . ."

"That will be enough, Tommy. On top of making me worry myself sick, you give me silly excuses. Little boys should always tell the truth."

"I am *not* little! I am almost seven years old, and . . ."

". . . and you are being very nasty to me. You . . . you are making me very unhappy. . . ."

You must agree that grown-ups are peculiar. Tommy's governess was worried about him. She said so. But when she found him she became angry. This has always been a grown-up sort of reaction that has been very hard to understand . . . for a long, long time. . . .

Do you see what I mean?

"Who is this little girl?"

"She gave me back my ball."

"That was very kind of you, my dear."

"Thank you. I like to do nice things for other people . . . like Tommy."

"Oh, you know his name?"

"Not till now. You just mentioned it."

"What is *your* name?"

It was a simple enough question. And yet, sometimes the simplest of questions are the hardest to answer. Haven't you found it so? Things that are hard you can somehow fight through, but, unless something warns you, it is the simple word that causes the most worry; makes you press your hands against your ears and pretend that you never heard the question. Bless little Tommy. He spoke up bravely as he could:

"She is my friend!"

"Of course, she is, Tommy. Let's all go back together and have her meet the rest of the children."

I was a bit worried. There were bound to be grown-ups as well as children, and grown-ups always get around to asking one's age. And though I have been answering that question for a long, long time, I am always thinking that some day I will be called a liar . . . and that somebody will start to investigate. The truth? Oh, no. I could never tell *that*.

There were little babies in carriages, and that also worried me. Babies are always frightened when they see me. Even those very new ones, that cannot see as yet, thrash their little limbs about when I am near. Sometimes they go into convulsions. Maybe it is because they have come only recently. Perhaps, in the world they left, they had much knowledge; and they haven't been in *this* world long enough to forget everything. They are dangerous. . . .

I left quickly, as soon as the first baby began to wail. But I promised Tommy I would play with him tomorrow.

As I walked up the steps to my house I began to feel afraid. It is hard for me to describe this fear. It isn't just what grown-ups call an emotion. It is . . . it is . . . like something solid. I can feel this fear. I always have. I kept hoping that, this time, *they* would let me alone.

It was no use. As I walked into the house *they* all started talking at once.

"Where is our food?"

"You know we are hungry!"

"We haven't eaten in *weeks!*"

I was frightened. I always am because *they* have so much power. I tried not to look at them as I answered:

"It is very dangerous to feed you so often. The last time I nearly got caught."

They began again—but not talking this time. It was much more horrible. I will call it "laughing," even though it didn't sound at all like any of the different kinds of laughter you have ever heard. *They* do not know what laughter means. In fact, *they* have no idea of most of your emotions. *They* once knew, of course, but that was a long time ago. Now *they* just regard others as being useful. Like myself.

"Behold! The Little One is frightened."

"She is always frightened."

"I am hungry!"

One of them uncoiled from the high chandelier and dropped to the floor. The floor was uncarpeted but the great body made no sound. I have seen this happen thousands of times but I never get used to it.

I closed my eyes; but had to open them at once. *They* can make me do anything. The scaly, three-cornered head was swaying close to mine. Some of the eyes on the ends of the wobly tentacles were closed; but enough of them remained open, blinking at me. Enough, I mean, to keep me from moving.

"What are you afraid of, Little One?"

"Of people finding out about . . . about *me*."

"Ah! You almost expressed fear that people would find out about *us!*"

❊   ❊   ❊

From behind a picture hanging crookedly on the wall, a lot of thick, grayish liquid dripped down to the floor. It shivered a little bit and then changed into a hairy, ropy, horrible thing. It scuttled soundlessly across the floor and joined us. I tried not to look at it. I kept silent while *they* talked.

"Is the Little One becoming dangerous?"

"No. She cannot. You know that."

"We built her so long ago that sometimes I forget."

"We built her well—for our purpose."

"But have we blocked ourselves by our own cleverness? The Little One is a weak vessel at times."

"That is because we made her so. If she is to mingle with humans then she must appear to them as such. She must share their weaknesses."

I tried not to listen. *They* had talked this way many, many times. My eyes kept sliding to a pile of dirt in the corner. I should be used to it by now, but my heart jumped with fright as a huge, red eye, dragging some disgusting threads of flesh, suddenly rolled out of the dirt. It joined the others. I could get used to the way they constantly change their shapes; it is just that *they* are so *quiet*.

Even with a whole roomful of them talking at once, their voices cannot be heard by anyone but me. That is the truth. And now the three of them were speaking in their soundless voices.

"It is too bad that we must depend upon the Little One for food. . . ."

"But we must. It is part of the agreement with *him*."

"Yes—I know. And sometimes I think *he* got the best of the bargain."

"How can you tell? After all, the agreement is but a few thousand years old."

"You are right."

"And you must remember—in justice to *him*—that our method of eating gives us wondrous enjoyment. *He* tacked that on to the agreement."

"True. The vivid ecstasy of tasting food, while somebody else eats, is a never-ending source of new pleasures. . . ."

"And do not forget that the Little One, who eats for us, not only transfers the delightful sensations to us . . . but enhances our gratification with *her* sensations!"

"Hm-m. Perhaps we did get the best of the bargain."

"All this talk has made me hungrier than ever. . . ."

I wanted so badly to run away. Wanted it more than anything. Because I knew what was coming.

"Listen well, Little One."

"I listen. . . ."

"And?"

". . . obey!"

"Good. You will feed us tomorrow night."

"Tomorrow night?"

"Yes. There must be no failure on your part."

"But. . . ."

"*Yes?*"

"N-nothing. I was just thinking. I met someone today. . . ."

"Excellent, Little One. That will make your task so much the easier."

I tried to go. But I couldn't. It meant *they* were not through talking to me. I always feel funny when I hear their voices. It is because their voices do not make any sound.

"Do not forget what we enjoy best, Little One."

"I . . . I will not forget."

"That is well. You once made a mistake. . . ."

"But that was long ago. So very long ago."

"We have not forgotten. Remember that!"

This time *they* let me go. As I turned, my eye caught a pretty shaft of moonlight coming through the window. *They* knew, immediately, that I enjoyed what I saw. So I was not surprised when the moonray was cut off. *They* simply blotted it out.

I suppose the reason is to save my emotions for the feasts. *All* my emotions are wanted then; for, at those times, *they* relish and savor my thoughts and feelings as much as the food I eat. You would find it very unpleasant to watch them the times that I eat. I think that you would go quite mad.

Next day I walked to the same spot in the park. Tommy was very happy to see me. And I was happy to see him.

"Hello, Tommy."

"Hello . . . gosh . . . gee!"

Tommy was so excited that he kept hopping from one foot to the other. He just couldn't keep his little body still. He tried to speak again, but spilled his words out so fast that it was impossible to understand him. So I spoke to him. I had to, anyway. There was so little time until tonight; and I had so much to do.

"What are you so excited about, Tommy?"

He couldn't help himself. He kept wiggling and wiggling. He hopped up and down. Then, finally he blurted:

"I'm seven years old!"

"No. Really?"

"Honest. It's my birthday today. I'm every bit seven years old."

I had to think very hard. This would make things much more difficult. But I knew I daren't fail. No. *They* wouldn't like it. Even thinking of it made me feel weak.

"Let's play catch, Tommy, I want to learn how to throw like you do."

"Sure, I'll show you. It's easy."

"Thank you, Tommy."

"Aw shucks. You're my friend, aren't you?"

"Yes, Tommy."

"Then why shouldn't I help you?"

I kept throwing the ball in such a way that we drifted apart from the other children and grown-ups. It was important. Dear little Tommy was very patient. He kept showing me what I was doing wrong. Over and over. When we were far enough away from the others I whispered to him:

"Do you know what's most fun to do on birthdays?"

"No. What?"

"Surprising people."

"What do you mean?"

"I mean playing tricks. Suppose we take a little walk and then come back to them from another direction."

"Oh boy! They wouldn't know *where* we came from. . . ."

"That's right. Wouldn't that be fun?"

His face fell. "My Mummy wouldn't like it. She always tells me never to go far away from my nurse. . . ."

"But, Tommy, you're not a little boy anymore. You're seven years old. And besides we won't go very far."

"You promise?"

"Of course. And then I've got my own surprise for you—"

"A present?"

I didn't answer him because it wasn't necessary. His mind was completely occupied with thinking about what I was going to give him.

And now time was getting short. I knew that in a few minutes Tommy would be missed; and they would begin looking for him. By this time we were on the lane that leads out of the park and onto the avenue. A light breeze carried along a frightening message. Someone was already calling for Tommy.

As we left the park Tommy started to hang back.

"We're going too far."

"No, Tommy. We're only going to get your present. My house is very near."

"And then we'll go right back?"

"Right back."

"Good. I wouldn't want nurse to worry about me." His face was all lit up with eagerness as he trotted along next to me.

"Why are you walking so fast?"

"So that we can get back quickly."

At the house Tommy stopped. He bent his neck to one side. Then to the other. He was peering so hard that his eyes squinted up.

"What's the matter, Tommy?"

"I don't like this house. It's funny."

"But I live here. It's a pretty house."

"I don't care. It's funny."

In another minute Tommy would go chasing pell-mell down the street, back to the park. I quickly looked up and down the quiet side street. It was absolutely deserted.

It came so fast that Tommy was only capable of an astonished squawk. I twisted one of his arms behind him and shot him up the steps and into the room.

And then he saw them.

His mouth opened. Shocked surprise left his eyes to be replaced by blank, unreasoning terror. A pulse in his temple began beating like a tiny hammer. Saliva started running out one corner of his mouth.

And then *they* were on him.

The room was filled with their shoutings and gigglings. But I knew that nobody outside could hear them. Only I can hear them.

Tommy was going fast. He was now in a corner, one hand held up before his eyes. His body was jerking faster and faster and a thin, steady whimpering fell from his wide-open mouth. Suddenly he fell. It was all over.

I knew what I had to do.

I hauled him to the center of the floor. Then *they* gathered around me in a circle. The room was filled with their noisy, hungry yelling. And yet the room was absolutely soundless. *They* were now ready to enjoy Tommy through me.

It was for me to begin the feast. . . .

The Cactus

MILDRED JOHNSON

The package came by first-class mail. It was from Edith's old friend in Los Angeles, Abby Burden. She opened it with interest, picked out some cotton wadding, a bulky letter, more cotton wadding. That was apparently all, but since nobody, not even Abby, would package a letter so tenderly, she reinspected the cotton and found a small prickly object. The explanation was undoubtedly in the letter.

It was written, as usual, on thin paper, typewritten with hand interlineations and annotations crawling about the pages and into the margins, and Edith had to turn it upside down and endways and trail sentences for sheets before capturing the sense. It dealt with the Burdens' trip to Mexico, but not until the end did it divulge the mystery of the enclosure.

"And now about the cutting," Abby wrote. "I may as well tell you Robert is against my sending it to you. He thinks I'm very silly. Let me tell you about it, though:

"I picked it up in an out-of-the-way, God-forsaken spot about a hundred miles from Chihuahua, where we had a flat tire. It was desert country, ninety in the shade—although there was no shade—and there was poor Robert faced with the prospect of changing a tire. I offered to help but he said the best way for me to help him would be to keep quiet for a while. You know how cranky a man can get under those conditions. The car was like an oven so I took a little walk around to look at the vegetation, such as it was, but there seemed to be nothing for hundreds of miles but sage and scrub and sand, and heat rising and shimmering all about. And then, a short distance away, I seemed to see a kind of fog, an overhanging mist. I thought it was an optical illusion— because whoever heard of a fog in the desert?—but, since it wasn't far away, I walked over to it. And as I approached it I smelled the sweetest, sourest, muskiest odor I've ever known. Suddenly the ground dipped and I was looking at a strange and lovely thing. Do you remember the meteor crater in Arizona? What I saw there was the same thing, much smaller, of course. It was a scoop in the earth, like a great dimple, and it was filled with cactus growths, marvelous, unearthly, beautiful—eight, nine, ten feet tall—gray-green giants stretching their twisted arms to the sky. There were hundreds of them, some of them already blooming with dark red flowers. It was the latter that gave off the strange, sweet smell.

"Edith—actually I felt as if I were on another planet, and what with the heavy perfume and the heat, my head swam. But finally I pulled myself together and rushed back to Robert to beg him to come and see what I had found, and ask him to cut me a slip of one of those weird plants. But his reaction was most peculiar. You know how sensible Robert usually is, but for some private reason he took a dislike to the whole area and became very difficult about getting a cutting for me. He said he wouldn't want a thing like that. He said they looked like goats and smelled like them too. He was positively silly. He said there was something about the little valley and the phalanxes of tortured shapes that gave him the creeps. But finally he gave in and cut me a tiny piece from the nearest plant. He scratched himself doing so and that didn't make him any happier. The spikes on the stem are rather tricky, you'll notice.

"As soon as I got it home I planted it. Edith, it's the finest specimen I've ever seen and grows like—I was going to say like a weed but it's faster than that. In a week I had to transplant it to a larger plant pot.

"Robert is still angry about it, though, and that's why he thinks I'm crazy to send you a cutting of it. But knowing your fondness for cacti, I had to share my discovery with you."

Edith folded up the letter and inspected the little cutting, holding it in her palm. It was no more than an inch in length, brown and shriveled, and so lifeless she doubted that it would grow at all. However, she would give it a chance. She found a small pot, pressed it in, watered it and set it on the shelf with her other cactus plants. "If you're going to be a giant cactus," she said, "you've a long way to go, little friend."

On examination the next morning, she was pleased to see that apparently its grip on life was secure. Watering it on the following Monday with the rest of her cactus collection she decided the infant was going to be a prodigy, for not only had it changed its wizened brown covering for one of healthy green but had straightened up and grown fully two inches. Its shape was somewhat comical: with the fat, spinous stem and the two little horns sprouting from the top, it resembled a rampant tomato caterpillar. Edith wrote to Abby that afternoon thanking her for the little plant.

Six weeks afterward, by the end of May, it was no longer little. In fact it had outstripped all the other cacti on the shelf. Now fifteen inches tall, it had been transplanted to a large urn and, in Edith's mind, was being groomed for a star appearance at the horticultural show in the autumn. Her friends admired it and, at club meetings, inquired about its health as they would about a child's.

When Mrs. Ferguson, her next door neighbor, viewed it, however, she asked the question: "When's it supposed to stop growing?"

"Well," laughed Edith, "my friend who sent it to me said they were eight, nine, and ten feet tall—the ones she saw growing in Mexico, but I don't imagine it will grow so much. I haven't a container large enough for it, for one thing."

"And your porch roof isn't high enough." Leaning over and tentatively feeling the two parallel spikes at the head of the plant, she added, "Not that it couldn't bore a hole right through if it wanted to with these things. They're like daggers."

Her remark prompted Edith to ask Abby how the parent was getting along, and she heard, with slight dismay, that it too was hyperexpansive, already two feet high and showing no signs of stopping. When it outgrew the house, wrote Abby, she had plans for it in the yard, but Edith thought grimly: when it outgrows my house it outgrows me. Goodbye, cactus, in that case.

It blossomed early in June with flowers of a peculiar liverish color. Though she never would have admitted it publicly, Edith thought them unattractive, almost repellent. They were almost like sores, she thought. And their odor was pungent enough to cause comment, the baker's delivery man asking if gas was escaping, the meter reader wanting to know if she had something burning in the oven. But her handy man, Mr. Krakaur, who came on Mondays to put out trash cans, mow the lawn, and so on, and who was the local philosopher on the side, stated frankly that it "stank." "Stinks like a goat," he said.

"Mr. Krakaur, how can you say that?" Laughing, she recalled what Robert Burden had said about it.

"And it looks like one too," Mr. Krakaur went on, shifting his cud reflectively. "Got horns and everything. Looks like a sick goat with boils."

But in two weeks the blooms were gone. Most of the smell went with them, although it lingered unaccountably in various portions of the house far away from the porch, in closets, in her bedroom, and seemed to be contained in air pockets for often, usually at night, she would smell it strong and musky, but in the next second lose it. It was as if the cactus itself had passed her open door. She smiled at her fancy, but was surprised to hear from Abby that Robert Burden had the same idea, although he was carrying it to ridiculous extremes, averring, for instance, that he had caught a glimpse of the cactus floating along in its own emanations like a jellyfish in an ocean current. Abby wrote that if he thought that frightening her would make her dispose of the cactus he was mistaken. He was being very stupid and unreasonable, she said. He was even threatening to warn Edith about the danger—"So if you hear a lot of nonsense from him you'll know what it's about."

She was not going to allow herself to be influenced by such palpable friction in the Burden household, Edith thought, but just the same, after reading Abby's letter, she went to the porch and took a good look at her cactus. It *was* a grotesque thing, she admitted, a frame on which mental aberrations could easily be hung. Cruciform in shape, its upraised "arms" were terminated in spiked nodules, like taloned fingers; the forward-sweeping horns were truly formidable; and the withered flowers at the "head" were arranged to suggest an evil face, a demonic, leering, loathsome face.

In sudden revulsion she decided she must destroy it but then, remembering her promise to exhibit it at the flower show and the admiration and interest of her friends, canceled the impulse by laughing herself out of it. "You're not going to pay any attention to Robert Burden's crazy notions, are you?" she asked herself, reminding herself in addition that she had always thought him neurotic. He sounded positively psychotic now.

But that night she dreamed about the cactus. It seemed that she was in bed and, awakened by a slipping, slithering sound from the hall, got up to investigate. In a shaft of moonlight there sat a tiny animal, like a chipmunk, all agleam with silver light, dainty and pretty, and she was about to approach it when suddenly Ted appeared. He looked young and slim, the way he had been when they were married, but his face was grave. Laying a hand on her shoulder, he shook his head as if to restrain her, but she paid no attention and walked towards the little animal clucking softly. But, as she reached it and was crouching to it, it began to swell and grow and in a second had become the cactus, writhing with vile delight, its malevolent face close to hers, its long arms pinioning hers to her sides in sickening embrace. She screamed for Ted but he had gone. He had left her.

Choking, heart beating wildly, she awoke and lay shaking in terror. Oriented at last, she looked towards the door, and it was as if a hand clutched her heart for the area in the hall was bathed, it seemed, in a deep, oily fog, like a swamp miasma, behind which something gray and green was stirring. She sat up, stared hard, cautiously reached for the bedlamp and quickly turned it on. There was nothing.

There was nothing but moonshine and sinister groupings of shadows and her own heavy breathing.

In the sensible light of day she marveled and was ashamed of the mantle of fear she was weaving for herself out of odds and ends of suggestions, fancied resemblances, and nightmares—she, Edith Porter, middle-aged, matter-of-fact, a professed scoffer at all superstition. Was she going to allow an odor, a shape, and a bad dream to push her into unreason? And as for Robert Burden's vaporings, for all she knew he might be joking.

She would take hold of herself firmly and, in the meantime, try to rid the house of the meandering gamy stench.

It was nine o'clock on the following Sunday evening. Having spent the day riding in the country with the Fergusons, Edith was finishing reading the newspaper and was beginning to yawn with delicious weariness and plan early retirement when the telephone rang.

It was a girl's voice, blurred with crying, sharpened by hysteria, and Edith could not recognize it.

"Mrs. Porter? This is Nancy, Nancy Winnick, the Burdens' daughter."

"Oh, yes, Nancy—how are you? Is anything the matter?" Edith's mind skipped about frantically for an explanation.

The girl was apparently trying to control herself. At last she said. "The most horrible thing happened this morning. Dad's dead!"

"Oh, no! How—how did it happen?" She felt herself turning cold with shock.

"I don't know the whole story because Mother is half out of her mind and she's given it to us in bits and pieces. She's resting now under a sedative, but all afternoon she's kept begging me to call you and let you know. It's about that cactus she gave you. She wants you to destroy it, because she says—" Here Nancy burst into sobs and was a few seconds recovering herself. "She says it killed him. She knows it killed him deliberately, and it's all her fault. She's afraid something will happen to you too and she'll have two deaths on her conscience."

"But how? How did it kill him?"

"This morning Mother finally agreed that he could get rid of it. You know what controversy there's been about it. Mother said she wrote you about it, how Dad hated it so and Mother was set on keeping it. Well, this morning they had it out, it seems, and she told him to go ahead and destroy it if he felt so strongly about it. He didn't wait a minute. He took it out to the rubbish can—it grew to an enormous size, you know—and threw it on top of the rubbish, pot and all and then—" Nancy started whimpering again. "I don't know what made him do it, except that he wanted to get rid of it quickly and couldn't wait for the trash collection, but he set it afire and stood there watching it burn. Mother said she shouted to him from the window, but he seemed fascinated by the sight of the flames traveling up it, and then all of a sudden it broke in the middle and the top half flew at him, all ablaze, and landed on him— and it clung to him—he couldn't tear it off—it was all over his face and head—"

"Oh—how horrible—how terrible!" Edith broke down then and wept with Nancy, who at length completed the story:

"When my husband and I arrived we found Mother in a faint, and when she came to she just screamed and screamed; and then my husband went out into the yard, but he wouldn't let us see Dad. He himself was sick because his face and head were all—they took him away to be cremated. We thought that was best."

Lenitive words, condolences—what good were they now? And Edith could not say them; she was too shocked.

After hanging up she sat frozen, staring ahead; then she rose quickly, strode to the porch, lifted down the cactus from the shelf, and, grasping the horns as one would the ears of a rabbit, tore it up by the roots. From the gaping hole there rose the fetid odor so concentrated and powerful that she choked and coughed, but her anger gave her courage and, without looking at the plant in her hand, holding it far off, she ran down cellar and threw it into the trash barrel. She returned for the pot and carried it down too, set it on top of the barrel, took a hammer and smashed it.

She was still panting when she sat at her desk in the living room to write to Abby all the sympathy she had been unable to express on the telephone and her hand shook so much she had to rest before beginning.

A hand touched her shoulder, gentle but firm—a warning hand; it rested there; she felt the pressure of the fingers. Slowly she unveiled her eyes. All about her was a mist pouring in ever-thickening clouds from the area behind her and obscuring the light, and a foul stink wafted to her nostrils, but she could not move: in that growing fetor, that dankness, that accrescence of vileness, she sat still. The hand pressed hard, and, coming to her senses, she half-turned her head. On the wall, just behind her head, was the shadow of horns.

She lurched to her feet, tore open the casement and flung herself into the darkness, landing on her hands and knees in the soft earth of a flower bed, scrambling to her feet and hurling herself forward across the field separating her house from the Fergusons'. She stumbled, fell, clambered up, ran on and at last reached the back door and pounded on it. When it was opened to her she fell in and pressed against the wall.

Mrs. Ferguson was staring at her, plump, red-faced, round-eyed. "What's wrong?" Edith could not answer.

"Harry!" Mrs. Ferguson called. "Come here!"

Ferguson appeared and together they led Edith to a chair. "Somebody trying to break into your house?" he asked.

"I don't know," she gasped. "I don't know. I've just had a terrible fright."

She sipped the glass of water they gave her, her teeth chattering against the rim.

"Call the police, Harry!" urged Mrs. Ferguson as Edith Porter sat frightened.

Edith raised a protesting hand. The police to rout something from another universe, another stratum of existence; the law to command the supernatural? "Don't call the police," she said, setting the glass on the table and sighing.

"But if there's a prowler around—"

"There's no prowler, I'm sure. I imagined it." She looked at these solid sane people and wondered if it were true. Perhaps she had dreamed it all. Nevertheless she could not return to the house. It was difficult to confess her fear of staying alone, but she had to do it. They said they understood, offered their guest room, but were puzzled. Ferguson went over and locked up and brought her keys back as directed.

When Mr. Krakaur put in an appearance on the street the next morning she joined him and walked with him.

"What you doing out so early, Mrs. Porter?" he asked.

"Last night I had a kind of brainstorm. I had a notion something— someone was breaking in, and so I ran over to the Fergusons and there I stayed. You know how we women get nervous at times."

"At times?" cackled Mr. Krakaur who fancied himself something of a misogynist. "I'd say all the time."

She was in no mood for badinage. Trying to be casual, she said, "I wonder if you'd be good enough to put out the trash barrel right away. I want to straighten up the cellar."

Standing fearfully in the kitchen, not daring to go down the cellar stairs but filled with curiosity, she heard him open the outer doors and come back for the barrel. She was not too surprised, though, when he called from the foot of the stairs: "Mrs. Porter, what happened to your cactus?"

"I broke it," she said from the door.

"Did it fall off the shelf?"

"Yes." If one waited others would always provide the answers.

Without realizing it she had moved to the head of the stairs and was peering over the rail just as he was picking up from the floor one of the pieces of the plant pot. Her heart leaped. It could not be coincidence this time, nor a dream. That every piece of the pot had remained in the barrel and none had fallen out she was positive. The sickness of terror rolled over her.

"It don't look too bad," he was saying. "All you got to do is put it in another pot. I think it'll grow just as good."

"No," she said.

"Okay. You're the boss."

She must go away and rest, cleanse her brain of this viscid horror that kept her trembling, made her afraid to go to bed, had her staring hard at shadows, sniffing the air, starting and glancing over her shoulder. She was sure now that the hand on her shoulder had been Ted's and that only her enormous danger had enabled him to get through to her. But it was over; the peril was gone; and perhaps a summer in Maine, at the little hotel in Winter Harbor where she and Ted had spent their honeymoon, would eradicate its immediate effects.

When she took one of her keys over to Mrs. Ferguson the latter expressed approval of her decision. "To tell you the truth Harry and I have been worried about you. It's so easy to go into a nervous breakdown, you know." She gave some instances of friends who had slipped into them. She would step in once a week and water the plants and see that everything was all right, she promised. "That was too bad about your big cactus," she said then. "Krakaur told me it fell off the shelf. And after you set such store by it too. But that's the way it is: it's always the things we like most that get smashed."

It was September when Edith returned. Riding in the taxi from the station, listening to the church clock bong eleven in the clear air, she felt calm, able to pick up her life where she had abandoned it on that Sunday evening in June. It seemed far away now. The peaceful summer, the new friends, the fresh stimuli, they had helped her forget. And she was not afraid. Never again would she be completely sure of herself and of the order of existence, for something strange and unearthly had touched her she knew, but she was not afraid. There was good to surmount evil, a tender hand to warn her of its approach.

The driver set her trunk in the hall, took his money, thanked her for the tip and left, closing the door behind him. And now she was alone; but everything was in its place, familiar and dear and homey: the grandmother's clock tick-tocking in the corner (Mrs. Ferguson hadn't forgotten to wind it, then), the Meissen figurines, a man and woman, in their perpetual saraband on the table, the Regency mirror reflecting a portion of the living room and beyond it the porch with its greenery of plants. She released the breath she had been holding, smiled, walked to the mirror and took off her hat. Then she felt it, the hand on her shoulder.

"This is ridiculous!" she said aloud. "Now I'm sure I dreamed the whole thing!" The pressure was renewed and she wheeled about and shouted, "It's gone, don't you know that?" In hysterical triumph she ran to the porch and turned on the light. "See?" she cried, standing in the middle and sweeping her arm around. "It's gone, I tell you. It's *gone!*"

But, on the wall, she saw the outline of its horns and, simultaneously, smelled its sickly odor. Her cry was guttural. With hands stretched out protectively, mouth squared in fear, she stepped backwards, crashed into a hard object, turned, and in the last second of consciousness saw the cactus teetering and falling. . . .

"But I feel responsible. I feel that it's my fault." Mrs. Ferguson had said it over and over. She would never be done saying it nor forget the sight which had met her eyes when, seeing the light, she had gone over to welcome Edith home. Again she explained. "I knew she was fond of that cactus and when I found it growing with the rubber plant I was so pleased. I didn't tell her. I wanted to surprise her. And so I planted it in a pot of its own and it grew even faster than the other one. I should have let her know, though—shouldn't I?"

"It was an accident," Harry Ferguson said patiently. "You're not to blame. Anybody would have done the same in the same circumstances. It was an accident, that's all."

"But it would never have happened if I hadn't done it. Oh, God, when I walked in and saw her lying there with those spikes in her throat—"

Call First

RAMSEY CAMPBELL

It was the other porters who made Ned determined to know who answered the phone in the old man's house.

Not that he hadn't wanted to know before. He'd felt it was his right almost as soon as the whole thing had begun, months ago. He'd been sitting behind his desk in the library entrance, waiting for someone to try to take a bag into the library so he could shout after them that they couldn't, when the reference librarian ushered the old man up to Ned's desk and said, "Let this gentleman use your phone." Maybe he hadn't meant every time the old man came to the library, but then he should have said so. The old man used to talk to the librarian and tell him things about books even he didn't know, which was why he let him phone. All Ned could do was feel resentful. People weren't supposed to use his phone, and even he wasn't allowed to phone outside the building. And it wasn't as if the old man's calls were interesting. Ned wouldn't have minded if they'd been worth hearing.

"I'm coming home now." That was all he ever said; then he'd put down the receiver and hurry away. It was the way he said it that made Ned wonder. There was no feeling behind the words, they sounded as if he were saying them only because he had to, perhaps wishing he needn't. Ned knew people talked like that: his parents did in church and most of the time at home. He wondered if the old man was calling his wife, because he wore a ring on his wedding finger, although in the claw where a stone should be was what looked like a piece of yellow fingernail. But Ned didn't think it could be his wife; each day the old man came he left the library at the same time, so why would he bother to phone?

Then there was the way the old man looked at Ned when he phoned: as if he didn't matter and couldn't understand, the way most of the porters looked at him. That was the look that swelled up inside Ned one day and made him persuade one of the other porters to take charge of his desk while Ned waited to listen in on the old man's call. The girl who

74

always smiled at Ned was on the switchboard, and they listened together. They heard the phone in the house ringing then lifted, and the old man's call and his receiver going down: nothing else, not even breathing apart from the old man's. "Who do you think it is?" the girl said, but Ned thought she'd laugh if he said he didn't know. He shrugged extravagantly and left.

Now he was determined. The next time the old man came to the library Ned phoned his house, having read what the old man dialed. When the ringing began its pulse sounded deliberately slow, and Ned felt the pumping of his blood rushing ahead. Seven trills and the phone in the house opened with a violent click. Ned held his breath, but all he could hear was his blood thumping in his ears. "Hello," he said and after a silence, clearing his throat, "Hello!" Perhaps it was one of those answering machines people in films used in the office. He felt foolish and uneasy greeting the wide silent metal ear, and put down the receiver. He was in bed and falling asleep before he wondered why the old man should tell an answering machine that he was coming home.

The following day, in the bar where all the porters went at lunchtime, Ned told them about the silently listening phone. "He's weird, that old man," he said, but now the others had finished joking with him they no longer seemed interested, and he had to make a grab for the conversation. "He reads weird books," he said. "All about witches and magic. Real ones, not stories."

"Now tell us something we didn't know," someone said, and the conversation turned its back on Ned. His attention began to wander, he lost his hold on what was being said, he had to smile and nod as usual when they looked at him, and he was thinking: they're looking at me like the old man does. I'll show them. I'll go in his house and see who's there. Maybe I'll take something that'll show I've been there. Then they'll have to listen.

But next day at lunchtime, when he arrived at the address he'd seen on the old man's library card, Ned felt more like knocking at the front door and running away. The house was menacingly big, the end house of a street whose other windows were brightly bricked up. Exposed foundations like broken teeth protruded from the mud that surrounded the street, while the mud was walled in by a five-story crescent of flats that looked as if it had been designed in sections to be fitted together by a two-year-old. Ned tried to keep the house between him and the flats, even though they were hundreds of yards away, as he peered in the windows.

All he could see through the grimy front window was bare floorboards; when he coaxed himself to look through the side window, the same. He dreaded being caught by the old man, even though he'd seen him sitting behind a pile of books ten minutes ago. It had taken Ned that long to walk here; the old man couldn't walk so fast, and there wasn't a bus he could catch. At last he dodged round the back and peered into the kitchen: a few plates in the sink, some tins of food, an old cooker. Nobody to be seen. He returned to the front, wondering what to do. Maybe he'd knock after all. He took hold of the bar of the knocker, trying to think what he'd say, and the door opened.

The hall leading back to the kitchen was long and dim. Ned stood shuffling indecisively on the step. He would have to decide soon, for his lunch hour was dwindling. It was like one of the empty houses he'd used to play in with the other children, daring each other to go up the tottering stairs. Even the things in the kitchen didn't make it seem lived in. He'd show them all. He went in. Acknowledging a vague idea that the old man's companion was out, he closed the door to hear if they returned.

On his right was the front room; on his left, past the stairs and the phone, another of the bare rooms he'd seen. He tiptoed upstairs. The stairs creaked and swayed a little, perhaps unused to anyone of Ned's weight. He reached the landing, breathing heavily, feeling dust chafe his throat. Stairs led up to a closed attic door, but he looked in the rooms off the landing.

Two of the doors which he opened stealthily showed him nothing but boards and flurries of floating dust. The landing in front of the third looked cleaner, as if the door were often opened. He pulled it toward him, holding it up all the way so it didn't scrape the floor, and went in.

Most of it didn't seem to make sense. There was a single bed with faded sheets. Against the walls were tables and piles of old books. Even some of the books looked disused. There were black candles and racks of small cardboard boxes. On one of the tables lay a single book. Ned padded across the fragments of carpet and opened the book in a thin path of sunlight that came through the shutters.

Inside the sagging covers was a page Ned slowly realized had been ripped from the Bible. It was the story of Lazarus. Scribbles that might be letters filled the margins, and at the bottom of the page: "p. 491." Suddenly inspired, Ned turned to that page in the book. It showed a drawing of a corpse sitting up in his coffin, but the book was all in the language they sometimes used in church: Latin. He thought of asking one of the librarians what it meant. Then he remembered that he needed proof he'd been in the house. He stuffed the page from the Bible into his pocket.

As he crept swiftly downstairs, something was troubling him. He reached the hall and thought he knew what it was. He still didn't know who lived in the house with the old man. If they lived in the back perhaps there would be signs in the kitchen. Though if it was his wife, Ned thought as he hurried down the hall, she couldn't be like Ned's mother, who would never have left torn strips of wallpaper hanging at shoulder height from both walls. He'd reached the kitchen door when he realized what had been bothering him. When he'd emerged from the bedroom, the attic door had been open.

He looked back involuntarily, and saw a woman walking away from him down the hall.

He was behind the closed kitchen door before he had time to feel fear. That came only when he saw that the back door was nailed rustily shut. Then he controlled himself. She was only a woman, she couldn't do much if she found him. He opened the door minutely. The hall was empty.

Halfway down the hall he had to slip into the side room, heart punching his chest, for she'd appeared again from between the stairs and the front door. He felt the beginnings of anger and recklessness, and they grew faster when he opened the door and had to flinch back as he saw her hand passing. The fingers looked famished, the color of old lard, with long yellow cracked nails. There was no nail on her wedding finger, which wore a plain ring. She was returning from the direction of the kitchen, which was why Ned hadn't expected her.

Through the opening of the door he heard her padding upstairs. She sounded barefoot. He waited until he couldn't hear her, then edged out into the hall. The door began to swing open behind him with a faint creak, and he drew it stealthily closed. He paced toward the front door. If he hadn't seen her shadow creeping down the stairs he would have come face to face with her.

He'd retreated to the kitchen, and was near to panic, when he realized she knew he was in the house. She was playing a game with him. At once he was furious. She was only an old woman, her body beneath the long white dress was sure to be as thin as her hands, she could only shout when she saw him, she couldn't stop him leaving. In a minute he'd be late for work. He threw open the kitchen door and swaggered down the hall.

The sight of her lifting the phone receiver broke his stride for a moment. Perhaps she was phoning the police. He hadn't done anything, she could have her Bible page back. But she laid the receiver beside the phone. Why? Was she making sure the old man couldn't ring?

As she unbent from stooping to the phone she grasped two uprights of the banisters to support herself. They gave a loud splintering creak and bent together. Ned halted, confused. He was still struggling to react when she turned towards him, and he saw her face. Part of it was still on the bone.

He didn't back away until she began to advance on him, her nails tearing new strips from both walls. All he could see was her protruding eyes, unsupported by flesh. His mind was backing away faster than he was, but it had come up against a terrible insight. He even knew why she'd made sure the old man couldn't interrupt until she'd finished. His calls weren't like speaking to an answering machine at all. They were exactly like switching off a burglar alarm.

CATERPILLARS

E. F. BENSON

I saw a month or two ago in an Italian paper that the Villa Cascana, in which I once stayed, had been pulled down, and that a manufactory of some sort was in process of erection on its site. There is therefore no longer any reason for refraining from writing of those things that I myself saw (or imagined I saw) in a certain room and on a certain landing of the villa in question, nor from mentioning the circumstances that followed, which may or may not (according to the opinion of the reader) throw some light on or be somehow connected with this experience.

The Villa Cascana was in all ways but one a perfectly delightful house, yet, if it were standing now, nothing in the world—I use the phrase in its literal sense—would induce me to set foot in it again, for I believe it to have been haunted in a very terrible and practical manner. Most ghosts, when all is said and done, do not do much harm; they may perhaps terrify, but the person whom they visit usually gets over their visitation. They may on the other hand be entirely friendly and beneficent. But the appearances in the Villa Cascana were not beneficent, and had they made their "visit" in a very slightly different manner, I do not suppose I should have got over it any more than Arthur Inglis did.

The house stood on an ilex-clad hill not far from Sestri di Levante on the Italian Riviera, looking out over the iridescent blues of that enchanted sea, while behind it rose the pale green chestnut woods that climb up the hillsides till they give place to the pines that, black in contrast with them, crown the slopes. All round it the garden in the luxuriance of mid-spring bloomed and was fragrant, and the scent of magnolia and rose, borne on the salt freshness of the winds from the sea, flowed like a stream through the cool vaulted rooms.

On the ground floor a broad pillared loggia ran round three sides of the house, the top of which formed a balcony for certain rooms of the first floor. The main staircase, broad and of gray marble steps, led up from the hall to the landing outside these rooms, which were three in number, namely two big sitting rooms and a bedroom arranged en suite. The latter was unoccupied, the sitting rooms were in use. From these the main staircase was continued to the second floor, where were situated certain bedrooms, one of which I occupied, while from the other side of the first-floor landing some half-dozen steps led to another suite of rooms, where, at the time I am speaking of, Arthur Inglis, the artist, had his bedroom and studio. Thus the landing outside my bedroom at the top of the house commanded both the landing of the first floor and also the steps that led to Inglis's rooms. Jim Stanley and his wife, finally (whose guest I was), occupied rooms in another wing of the house, where also were the servants' quarters.

I arrived just in time for lunch on a brilliant noon of mid-May. The garden was shouting with color and fragrance, and not less delightful after my broiling walk up from the marina, should have been the coming from the reverberating heat and blaze of the day into the marble coolness of the villa. Only (the reader has my bare word for this, and nothing more), the moment I set foot in the house I felt that something was wrong. This feeling, I may say, was quite vague, though very strong, and I remember that when I saw letters waiting for me on the table in the hall I felt certain that the explanation was here: I was convinced that there was bad news of some sort for me. Yet when I opened them I found no such explanation of my premonition: my correspondents all reeked of prosperity. Yet this clear miscarriage of a presentiment did not dissipate my uneasiness. In that cool fragrant house there was something wrong.

I am at pains to mention this because to the general view it may explain that though I am as a rule so excellent a sleeper that the extinction of my light on getting into bed is apparently contemporaneous with being called on the following morning, I slept very badly on my first night in the Villa Cascana. It may also explain the fact that when I did sleep (if it was indeed in sleep that I saw what I thought I saw) I dreamed in a very vivid and original manner, original, that is to say, in the sense that something that, as far as I knew, had never previously entered into my consciousness, usurped it then. But since, in addition to this evil premonition, certain words and events occurring during the rest of the day, might have suggested something of what I thought happened that night, it will be well to relate them.

After lunch, then, I went round the house with Mrs. Stanley, and during our tour she referred, it is true, to the unoccupied bedroom on the first floor, which opened out of the room where we had lunched.

"We left that unoccupied," she said, "because Jim and I have a charming bedroom and dressing room, as you saw, in the wing, and if we used it ourselves we should have to turn the dining room into a dressing room and have our meals downstairs. As it is, however, we have our little flat there, Arthur Inglis has his little flat in the other passage; and I remembered (aren't I extraordinary?) that you once said that the higher up you were in a house the better you were pleased. So I put you at the top of the house, instead of giving you that room."

It is true, that a doubt, vague as my uneasy premonition, crossed my mind at this. I did not see why Mrs. Stanley should have explained all this, if there had not been more to explain. I allow, therefore, that the thought that there was something to explain about the unoccupied bedroom was momentarily present to my mind.

The second thing that may have borne on my dream was this.

At dinner the conversation turned for a moment on ghosts. Inglis, with the certainty of conviction, expressed his belief that anybody who could possibly believe in the existence of supernatural phenomena was unworthy of the name of an ass. The subject instantly dropped. As far as I can recollect, nothing else occurred or was said that could bear on what follows.

We all went to bed rather early, and personally I yawned my way upstairs, feeling hideously sleepy. My room was rather hot, and I threw all the windows wide, and from without poured in the white light of the moon, and the love song of many nightingales. I undressed quickly, and got into bed, but though I had felt so sleepy before, I now felt extremely wide awake. But I was quite content to be awake; I did not toss or turn,

I felt perfectly happy listening to the song and seeing the light. Then, it is possible, I may have gone to sleep, and what follows may have been a dream. I thought anyhow that after a time the nightingales ceased singing and the moon sank. I thought also that if, for some unexplained reason, I was going to lie awake all night, I might as well read, and I remembered that I had left a book in which I was interested in the dining room on the first floor. So I got out of bed, lit a candle, and went downstairs. I went into the room, saw on a side table the book I had come to look for, and then, simultaneously, saw that the door into the unoccupied bedroom was open. A curious gray light, not of dawn nor of moonshine, came out of it, and I looked in. The bed stood just opposite the door, a big four-poster, hung with tapestry at the head. Then I saw that the grayish light of the bedroom came from the bed, or rather from what was on the bed. For it was covered with great caterpillars, a foot or more in length, which crawled over it. They were faintly luminous, and it was the light from them that showed me the room. Instead of the sucker-feet of ordinary caterpillars they had rows of pincers like crabs, and they moved by grasping what they lay on with their pincers, and then sliding their bodies forward. In color these dreadful insects were yellowish gray, and they were covered with irregular lumps and swellings. There must have been hundreds of them, for they formed a sort of writhing, crawling pyramid on the bed. Occasionally one fell off on to the floor, with a soft fleshy thud, and though the floor was of hard concrete, it yielded to the pincer-feet as if it had been putty, and, crawling back, the caterpillar would mount on to the bed again, to rejoin its fearful companions. They appeared to have no faces, so to speak, but at one end of them there was a mouth that opened sideways in respiration.

Then, as I looked, it seemed to me as if they all suddenly became conscious of my presence. All the mouths at any rate were turned in my direction, and next moment they began dropping off the bed with those soft fleshy thuds on to the floor, and wriggling toward me. For one second a paralysis as of a dream was on me, but the next I was running upstairs again to my room, and I remember feeling the cold of the marble steps on my bare feet. I rushed into my bedroom, and slammed the door behind me, and then—I was certainly wide awake now—I found myself standing by my bed with the sweat of terror pouring from me. The noise of the banged door still rang in my ears. But, as would have been more usual, if this had been mere nightmare, the terror that had been mine when I saw those foul beasts crawling about the bed or dropping softly on to the floor did not cease then. Awake now, if dreaming before, I did not at all recover from the horror of dream: it did not seem to me that I had dreamed. And until dawn, I sat or stood, not daring to lie down, thinking that every rustle or movement that I heard was the approach of the caterpillars. To them and the claws that bit into the cement the wood of the door was child's play: steel would not keep them out.

But with the sweet and noble return of day the horror vanished; the whisper of wind became benignant again; the nameless fear, whatever it was, was smoothed out and terrified me no longer. Dawn broke, hueless at first; then it grew dove-colored, then the flaming pageant of light spread over the sky.

The admirable rule of the house was that everybody had breakfast where and when he pleased, and in consequence it was not till lunch time that I met any of the other members of our party, since I had breakfast on my balcony, and wrote letters and other things till lunch. In fact, I got down to that meal rather late, after the other three had begun. Between my knife and fork was a small pillbox of cardboard, and as I sat down Inglis spoke.

"Do look at that," he said, "since you are interested in natural history. I found it crawling on my counterpane last night, and I don't know what it is."

I think that before I opened the pillbox I expected something of the sort that I found in it. Inside it, anyhow, was a small caterpillar, grayish yellow in color, with curious bumps and excrescences on its rings. It was extremely active, and hurried round the box, this way and that. Its feet were unlike the feet of any caterpillar I ever saw: they were like the pincers of a crab. I looked, and shut the lid down again.

"No, I don't know it," I said, "but it looks rather unwholesome. What are you going to do with it?"

"Oh, I shall keep it," said Inglis. "It has begun to spin: I want to see what sort of a moth it turns into."

I opened the box again, and saw that these hurrying movements were indeed the beginning of the spinning of the web of its cocoon. Then Inglis spoke again.

"It has got funny feet, too," he said. "They are like crabs' pincers. What's the Latin for crab? Oh, yes, Cancer. So in case it is unique, let's christen it: 'Cancer Inglisensis.' "

Then something happened in my brain, some momentary piecing together of all that I had seen or dreamed. Something in his words seemed to me to throw light on it all, and my own intense horror at the experience of the night before linked itself on to what he had just said. In effect, I took the box and threw it, caterpillar and all, out of the window. There was a gravel path just outside, and beyond it, a fountain playing into a basin. The box fell on to the middle of this.

Inglis laughed.

"So the students of the occult don't like solid facts," he said. "My poor caterpillar!"

The talk went off again at once on to other subjects, and I have only given in detail, as they happened, these trivialities in order to be sure myself that I have recorded everything that could have borne on occult subjects or on the subject of caterpillars. But at the moment when I threw the pillbox into the fountain, I lost my head; my only excuse is that, as is probably plain, the tenant of it was, in miniature, exactly what I had seen crowded on to the bed in the unoccupied room. And though this translation of those phantoms into flesh and blood—or whatever it is that caterpillars are made of—ought perhaps to have relieved the horror of the night, as a matter of fact it did nothing of the kind. It only made the crawling pyramid that covered the bed in the unoccupied room more hideously real.

After lunch we spent a lazy hour or two strolling about the garden or sitting in the loggia, and it must have been about four o'clock when Stanley and I started off to bathe, down the path that led by the fountain into which I had thrown the pillbox. The water was shallow and clear, and at the bottom of it I saw its white remains. The water had disintegrated the cardboard, and it had become no more than a few strips and shreds of sodden paper. The center of the fountain was a marble Italian cupid that squirted the water out of a wineskin held under its arm. And crawling up its leg was the caterpillar. Strange and scarcely credible as it seemed, it must have survived the falling-to-bits of its prison, and made its way to shore, and there it was, out of arm's reach, weaving and waving this way and that as it evolved its cocoon.

Then, as I looked at it, it seemed to me again that, like the caterpillars I had seen last night, it saw me, and breaking out of the threads that surrounded it, it crawled down the marble leg of the cupid and began swimming like a snake across the water of the fountain toward me. It came with extraordinary speed (the fact of a caterpillar being able to swim was new to me), and in another moment was crawling up the marble lip of the basin. Just then Inglis joined us.

"Why, if it isn't old 'Cancer Inglisensis' again," he said, catching sight of the beast. "What a tearing hurry it is in."

We were standing side by side on the path, and when the caterpillar had advanced to within about a yard of us, it stopped, and began waving again, as if in doubt as to the direction in which it should go. Then it appeared to make up its mind, and crawled on to Inglis' shoe.

"It likes me best," he said, "but I don't really know that I like it. And as it won't drown I think perhaps—"

He shook it off his shoe on to the gravel path and trod on it.

All afternoon the air got heavier and heavier with the sirocco that was without doubt coming up from the south, and that night again I went up to bed feeling very sleepy; but below my drowsiness, so to speak, there was the consciousness, stronger than before, that there was something wrong in the house, that something dangerous was close at hand. But I fell asleep at once, and—how long after I do not know—either woke or dreamed I awoke, feeling that I must get up at once, *or I should be too late*. Then (dreaming or awake) I lay and fought this fear, telling myself that I was but the prey of my own nerves disordered by sirocco or what not, and at the same time quite clearly knowing in another part of my mind, so to speak, that every moment's delay added to the danger. At last this second feeling became irresistible, and I put on coat and trousers and went out of my room on to the landing. And then I saw that I had already delayed too long, and that I was now too late.

The whole of the landing of the first floor below was invisible under the swarm of caterpillars that crawled there. The folding doors into the sitting room, from which opened the bedroom where I had seen them last night, were shut, but they were squeezing through the cracks of it, and dropping one by one through the keyhole, elongating themselves into mere string as they passed, and growing fat and lumpy again on emerging. Some, as if exploring, were nosing about the steps into the passage at the end of which were Inglis's rooms, others were crawling on the lowest steps of the staircase that led up to where I stood. The landing, however, was completely covered with them: I was cut off. And of the frozen horror that seized me when I saw that, I can give no idea in words.

Then at last a general movement began to take place, and they grew thicker on the steps that led to Inglis's room. Gradually, like some hideous tide of flesh, they advanced along the passage, and I saw the foremost, visible by the pale gray luminousness that came from them, reach his door. Again and again I tried to shout and warn him, in terror all the time that they would turn at the sound of my voice and mount my stair instead, but for all my efforts I felt that no sound came from my throat. They crawled along the hinge-crack of his door, passing through as they had done before, and still I stood there making impotent efforts to shout to him, to bid him escape while there was time.

At last the passage was completely empty: they had all gone, and at that moment I was conscious for the first time of the cold of the marble landing on which I stood barefooted. The dawn was just beginning to break in the eastern sky.

Six months later I met Mrs. Stanley in a country house in England. We talked on many subjects and at last she said:

"I don't think I have seen you since I got that dreadful news about Arthur Inglis a month ago."

"I haven't heard," said I.

"No? He has got cancer. They don't even advise an operation, for there is no hope of a cure: he is riddled with it, the doctors say."

Now during all these six months I do not think a day had passed on which I had not had in my mind the dreams (or whatever you like to call them) that I had seen in the Villa Cascana.

"It is awful, is it not?" she continued, "and I feel, I can't help feeling, that he may have—"

"Caught it at the villa?" I asked.

She looked at me in blank surprise.

"Why did you say that?" she asked. "How did you know?"

Then she told me. In the unoccupied bedroom a year before there had been a fatal case of cancer. She had, of course, taken the best advice and had been told that the utmost dictates of prudence would be obeyed so long as she did not put anybody to sleep in the room, which had also been thoroughly disinfected and newly whitewashed and painted. But—

Dagon

H. P. LOVECRAFT

I am writing this under an appreciable mental strain, since by tonight I shall be no more. Penniless, and at the end of my supply of the drug which alone makes life endurable, I can bear the torture no longer; and shall cast myself from this garret window into the squalid street below. Do not think from my slavery to morphine that I am a weakling or a degenerate. When you have read these hastily scrawled pages you may guess, though never fully realize, why it is that I must have forgetfulness or death.

It was in one of the most open and least frequented parts of the broad Pacific that the packet of which I was supercargo fell a victim to the German sea-raider. The great war was then at its very beginning, and the ocean forces of the Hun had not completely sunk to their later degradation; so that our vessel was made a legitimate prize, whilst we of her crew were treated with all the fairness and consideration due us as naval prisoners. So liberal, indeed, was the discipline of our captors, that five days after we were taken I managed to escape alone in a small boat with water and provisions for a good length of time.

When I finally found myself adrift and free, I had but little idea of my surroundings. Never a competent navigator, I could only guess vaguely by the sun and stars that I was somewhat south of the equator. Of the longitude I knew nothing, and no island or coastline was in sight. The weather kept fair, and for uncounted days I drifted aimlessly beneath the scorching sun; waiting either for some passing ship, or to be cast on the shores of some habitable land. But neither ship nor land appeared, and I began to despair in my solitude upon the heaving vastnesses of unbroken blue.

The change happened whilst I slept. Its details I shall never know; for my slumber, though troubled and dream-infested, was continuous. When at last I awaked, it was to discover myself half sucked into a slimy expanse of hellish black mire which extended about me in monotonous undulations as far as I could see, and in which my boat lay grounded some distance away.

Though one might well imagine that my first sensation would be of wonder at so prodigious and unexpected a transformation of scenery, I was in reality more horrified than astonished; for there was in the air and in the rotting soil a sinister quality which chilled me to the very core. The region was putrid with the carcasses of decaying fish, and of other less describable things which I saw protruding from the nasty mud of the unending plain. Perhaps I should not hope to convey in mere words the unutterable hideousness that can dwell in absolute silence and barren immensity. There was nothing within hearing, and nothing in sight save a vast reach of black slime; yet the very completeness of the stillness and the homogeneity of the landscape oppressed me with a nauseating fear.

The sun was blazing down from a sky which seemed to me almost black in its cloudless cruelty; as though reflecting the inky marsh beneath my feet. As I crawled into the stranded boat I realized that only one theory could explain my position. Through some unprecedented volcanic upheaval, a portion of the ocean floor must have been thrown to the surface, exposing regions which for innumerable millions of years had lain hidden under unfathomable watery depths. So great was the extent of the new land which had risen beneath me, that I could not detect the faintest noise of the surging ocean, strain my ears as I might. Nor were there any seafowl to prey upon the dead things.

For several hours I sat thinking or brooding in the boat, which lay upon its side and afforded a slight shade as the sun moved across the heavens. As the day progressed, the ground lost some of its stickiness, and seemed likely to dry sufficiently for traveling purposes in a short time. That night I slept but little, and the next day I made for myself a pack containing food and water, preparatory to an overland journey in search of the vanished sea and possible rescue.

On the third morning I found the soil dry enough to walk upon with ease. The odor of the fish was maddening; but I was too much concerned with graver things to mind so slight an evil, and set out boldly for an unknown goal. All day I forged steadily westward, guided by a far-away hummock which rose higher than any other elevation on the rolling desert. That night I encamped, and on the following day still traveled toward the hummock, though that object seemed scarcely nearer than when I had first espied it. By the fourth evening I attained the base of the mound, which turned out to be much higher than it had appeared from a distance; an intervening valley setting it out in sharper relief from the general surface. Too weary to ascend, I slept in the shadow of the hill.

I know not why my dreams were so wild that night; but ere the waning and fantastically gibbous moon had risen far above the eastern plain, I was awake in a cold perspiration, determined to sleep no more. Such visions as I had experienced were too much for me to endure again. And in the glow of the moon I saw how unwise I had been to travel by day. Without the glare of the parching sun, my journey would have cost me less energy; indeed, I now felt quite able to perform the ascent which had deterred me at sunset. Picking up my pack, I started for the crest of the eminence.

I have said that the unbroken monotony of the rolling plain was a source of vague horror to me; but I think my horror was greater when I gained the summit of the mound and looked down the other side into an immeasurable pit or canyon, whose black recesses the moon had not yet soared high enough to illumine. I felt myself on the edge of the world; peering over the rim into a fathomless chaos of eternal night. Through my terror ran curious reminiscences of *Paradise Lost*, and of Satan's hideous climb through the unfashioned realms of darkness.

As the moon climbed higher in the sky, I began to see that the slopes of the valley were not quite so perpendicular as I had imagined. Ledges and outcroppings of rock afforded fairly easy footholds for a descent, whilst after a drop of a few hundred feet, the declivity became very gradual. Urged on by an impulse which I cannot definitely analyse, I scrambled with difficulty down the rocks and stood on the gentler slope beneath, gazing into the Stygian deeps where no light had yet penetrated.

All at once my attention was captured by a vast and singular object on the opposite slope, which rose steeply about a hundred yards ahead of me; an object that gleamed whitely in the newly bestowed rays of the ascending moon. That it was merely a gigantic piece of stone, I soon assured myself; but I was conscious of a distinct impression that its contour and position were not altogether the work of Nature. A closer scrutiny filled me with sensations I cannot express; for despite its enormous magnitude, and its position in an abyss which had yawned at the bottom of the sea since the world was young, I perceived beyond a doubt that the strange object was a well-shaped monolith whose massive bulk had known the workmanship and perhaps the worship of living and thinking creatures.

Dazed and frightened, yet not without a certain thrill of the scientist's or archaeologist's delight, I examined my surroundings more closely.

The moon, now near the zenith, shone weirdly and vividly above the towering steeps that hemmed in the chasm, and revealed the fact that a far-flung body of water flowed at the bottom, winding out of sight in both directions, and almost lapping my feet as I stood on the slope. Across the chasm, the wavelets washed the base of the Cyclopean monolith; on whose surface I could now trace both inscriptions and crude sculptures. The writing was in a system of hieroglyphics unknown to me, and unlike anything I had ever seen in books; consisting for the most part of conventionalized aquatic symbols such as fishes, eels, octopi, crustaceans, molluscs, whales, and the like. Several characters obviously represented marine things which are unknown to the modern world, but whose decomposing forms I had observed on the ocean-risen plain.

It was the pictorial carving, however, that did most to hold me spell-bound. Plainly visible across the intervening water on account of their enormous size, were an array of bas-reliefs whose subjects would have excited the envy of a Doré. I think that these things were supposed to depict men — at least, a certain sort of men; though the creatures were shewn disporting like fishes in the waters of some marine grotto, or paying homage at some monolithic shrine which appeared to be under the waves as well. Of their faces and forms I dare not speak in detail; for the mere remembrance makes me grow faint. Grotesque beyond the imagination of a Poe or a Bulwer, they were damnably human in general outline despite webbed hands and feet, shockingly wide and flabby lips, glassy, bulging eyes, and other features less pleasant to recall. Curiously enough, they seemed to have been chiseled badly out of proportion with their scenic background; for one of the creatures was shewn in the act of killing a whale represented as but little larger than himself. I remarked, as I say, their grotesqueness and strange size; but in a moment decided that they were merely the imaginary gods of some primitive fishing or seafaring tribe; some tribe whose last descendant had perished eras before the first ancestor of the Piltdown or Neanderthal Man was born. Awestruck at this unexpected glimpse into a past beyond the conception of the most daring anthropologist, I stood musing whilst the moon cast queer reflections on the silent channel before me.

Then suddenly I saw it. With only a slight churning to mark its rise to the surface, the thing slid into view above the dark waters. Vast, Polyphemus-like, and loathsome, it darted like a stupendous monster of nightmares to the monolith, about which it flung its gigantic scaly arms, the while it bowed its hideous head and gave vent to certain measured sounds. I think I went mad then.

Of my frantic ascent of the slope and cliff, and of my delirious journey back to the stranded boat, I remember little. I believe I sang a great deal, and laughed oddly when I was unable to sing. I have indistinct recollections of a great storm some time after I reached the boat; at any rate, I know that I heard peals of thunder and other tones which Nature utters only in her wildest moods.

When I came out of the shadows I was in a San Francisco hospital; brought thither by the captain of the American ship which had picked up my boat in mid-ocean. In my delirium I had said much, but found that my words had been given scant attention. Of any land upheaval in the Pacific, my rescuers knew nothing; nor did I deem it necessary to insist upon a thing which I knew they could not believe. Once I sought out a celebrated ethnologist, and amused him with peculiar questions regarding the ancient Philistine legend of Dagon, the Fish-God; but soon perceiving that he was hopelessly conventional, I did not press my inquiries.

It is at night, especially when the moon is gibbous and waning, that I see the thing. I tried morphine; but the drug has given only transient surcease, and has drawn me into its clutches as a hopeless slave. So now I am to end it all, having written a full account for the information or the contemptuous amusement of my fellow-men. Often I ask myself if it could not all have been a pure phantasm—a mere freak of fever as I lay sun-stricken and raving in the open boat after my escape from the German man-of-war. This I ask myself, but ever does there come before me a hideously vivid vision in reply. I cannot think of the deep sea without shuddering at the nameless things that may at this very moment be crawling and floundering on its slimy bed, worshipping their ancient stone idols and carving their own detestable likenesses on submarine obelisks of water-soaked granite. I dream of a day when they may rise above the billows to drag down in their reeking talons the remnants of puny, war-exhausted mankind—of a day when the land shall sink, and the dark ocean floor shall ascend amidst universal pandemonium.

The end is near. I hear a noise at the door, as of some immense slippery body lumbering against it. It shall not find me. God, *that hand!* The window! The window!

The Damned Thing

AMBROSE BIERCE

I

ONE DOES NOT ALWAYS EAT WHAT IS ON THE TABLE

By the light of a tallow candle which had been placed on one end of a rough table a man was reading something written in a book. It was an old account book, greatly worn; and the writing was not, apparently, very legible, for the man sometimes held the page close to the flame of the candle to get a stronger light on it. The shadow of the book would then throw into obscurity a half of the room, darkening a number of faces and figures; for besides the reader, eight other men were present. Seven of them sat against the rough log walls, silent, motionless, and the room being small, not very far from the table. By extending an arm any one of them could have touched the eighth man, who lay on the table, face upward, partly covered by a sheet, his arms at his sides. He was dead.

The man with the book was not reading aloud, and no one spoke; all seemed to be waiting for something to occur; the dead man only was without expectation. From the blank darkness outside came in, through the aperture that served for a window, all the ever unfamiliar noises of night in the wilderness—the long nameless note of a distant coyote; the stilly pulsing thrill of tireless insects in trees; strange cries of night birds, so different from those of the birds of day; the drone of great blundering beetles, and all that mysterious chorus of small sounds that seem always to have been but half heard when they have suddenly ceased, as if conscious of an indiscretion. But nothing of all this was noted in that company; its members were not overmuch addicted to idle interest in matters of no practical importance; that was obvious in every line of their rugged faces—obvious even in the dim light of the single candle. They were evidently men of the vicinity—farmers and woodsmen.

The person reading was a trifle different; one would have said of him that he was of the world, worldly, albeit there was that in his attire which attested a certain fellowship with the organisms of his environment. His coat would hardly have passed muster in San Francisco; his footgear was not of urban origin, and the hat that lay by him on the floor (he was the only one uncovered) was such that if one had considered it as an article of mere personal adornment he would have missed its meaning. In countenance the man was rather prepossessing, with just a hint of sternness; though that he may have assumed or cultivated, as appropriate to one in authority. For he was a coroner. It was by virtue of his office that he had possession of the book in which he was reading; it had been found among the dead man's effects—in his cabin, where the inquest was now taking place.

When the coroner had finished reading he put the book into his breast pocket. At that moment the door was pushed open and a young man entered. He, clearly, was not of mountain birth and breeding: he was clad as those who dwell in cities. His clothing was dusty, however, as from travel. He had, in fact, been riding hard to attend the inquest.

The coroner nodded; no one else greeted him.

"We have waited for you," said the coroner. "It is necessary to have done with this business tonight."

The young man smiled. "I am sorry to have kept you," he said. "I went away, not to evade your summons, but to post to my newspaper an account of what I suppose I am called back to relate."

The coroner smiled.

"The account that you posted to your newspaper," he said, "differs, probably, from that which you will give here under oath."

"That," replied the other, rather hotly and with a visible flush, "is you please. I used manifold paper and have a copy of what I sent. It was not written as news, for it is incredible, but as fiction. It may go as a part of my testimony under oath."

"But you say it is incredible."

"That is nothing to you, sir, if I also swear that it is true."

The coroner was silent for a time, his eyes upon the floor. The men about the sides of the cabin talked in whispers, but seldom withdrew their gaze from the face of the corpse. Presently the coroner lifted his eyes and said: "We will resume the inquest."

The men removed their hats. The witness was sworn.

"What is your name?" the coroner asked.

"William Harker."

"Age?"

"Twenty-seven."

"You knew the deceased, Hugh Morgan?"

"Yes."

"You were with him when he died?"

"Near him."

"How did that happen—your presence, I mean?"

"I was visiting him at this place to shoot and fish. A part of my purpose, however, was to study him and his odd, solitary way of life. He seemed a good model for a character in fiction. I sometimes write stories."

"I sometimes read them."

"Thank you."

"Stories in general—not yours."

Some of the jurors laughed. Against a sombre background humor shows highlights. Soldiers in the intervals of battle laugh easily, and a jest in the death chamber conquers by surprise.

"Relate the circumstances of this man's death," said the coroner. "You may use any notes or memoranda that you please."

The witness understood. Pulling a manuscript from his breast pocket he held it near the candle, and turning the leaves until he found the passage that he wanted, began to read.

II

WHAT MAY HAPPEN IN A FIELD OF WILD OATS

The sun had hardly risen when we left the house. We were looking for quail, each with a shotgun, but we had only one dog. Morgan said that our best ground was beyond a certain ridge that he pointed out, and we crossed it by a trail through the *chaparral*. On the other side was comparatively level ground, thickly covered with wild oats. As we emerged from the *chaparral* Morgan was but a few yards in advance. Suddenly we heard, at a little distance to our right and partly in front, a noise as of some animal thrashing about in the bushes, which we could see were violently agitated.

" 'We've started a deer,' I said. 'I wish we had brought a rifle.'

"Morgan, who had stopped and was intently watching the agitated *chaparral*, said nothing, but had cocked both barrels of his gun and was holding it in readiness to aim. I thought him a trifle excited, which surprised me, for he had a reputation for exceptional coolness, even in moments of sudden and imminent peril.

" 'O, come,' I said. 'You are not going to fill up a deer with quail-shot, are you?'

"Still he did not reply; but catching a sight of his face as he turned it

93

slightly toward me I was struck by the intensity of his look. Then I understood that we had serious business in hand and my first conjecture was that we had 'jumped' a grizzly. I advanced to Morgan's side, cocking my piece as I moved.

"The bushes were now quiet and the sounds had ceased, but Morgan was as attentive to the place as before.

" 'What is it? What the devil is it?' I asked.

" 'That Damned Thing!' he replied, without turning his head. His voice was husky and unnatural. He trembled visibly.

"I was about to speak further, when I observed the wild oats near the place of the disturbance moving in the most inexplicable way. I can hardly describe it. It seemed as if stirred by a streak of wind, which not only bent it, but pressed it down—crushed it so that it did not rise; and this movement was slowly prolonging itself directly toward us.

"Nothing that I had ever seen had affected me so strangely as this unfamiliar and unaccountable phenomenon, yet I am unable to recall any sense of fear. I remember—and tell it here because, singularly enough, I recollected it then—that once in looking carelessly out of an open window I momentarily mistook a small tree close at hand for one of a group of larger trees at a little distance away. It looked the same size as the others, but being more distinctly and sharply defined in mass and detail seemed out of harmony with them. It was a mere falsification of the law of aerial perspective, but it startled, almost terrified me. We so rely upon the orderly operation of familiar natural laws that any seeming suspension of them is noted as a menace to our safety, a warning of unthinkable calamity. So now the apparently causeless movement of the herbage and the slow, undeviating approach of the line of disturbance were distinctly disquieting. My companion appeared actually frightened, and I could hardly credit my senses when I saw him suddenly throw his gun to his shoulder and fire both barrels at the agitated grain! Before the smoke of the discharge had cleared away I heard a loud savage cry—a scream like that of a wild animal—and flinging his gun upon the ground Morgan sprang away and ran swiftly from the spot. At the same instant I was thrown violently to the ground by the impact of something unseen in the smoke—some soft, heavy substance that seemed thrown against me with great force.

"Before I could get upon my feet and recover my gun, which seemed to have been struck from my hands, I heard Morgan crying out as if in mortal agony, and mingling with his cries were such hoarse, savage sounds as one hears from fighting dogs. Inexpressibly terrified, I struggled to my feet and looked in the direction of Morgan's retreat; and may

Heaven in mercy spare me from another sight like that! At a distance of less than thirty yards was my friend, down upon one knee, his head thrown back at a frightful angle, hatless, his long hair in disorder and his whole body in violent movement from side to side, backward and forward. His right arm was lifted and seemed to lack the hand—at least, I could see none. The other arm was invisible. At times, as my memory now reports this extraordinary scene, I could discern but a part of his body; it was as if he had been partly blotted out—I cannot otherwise express it—then a shifting of his position would bring it all into view again.

"All this must have occurred within a few seconds, yet in that time Morgan assumed all the postures of a determined wrestler vanquished by superior weight and strength. I saw nothing but him, and him not always distinctly. During the entire incident his shouts and curses were heard, as if through an enveloping uproar of such sounds of rage and fury as I had never heard from the throat of man or brute!

"For a moment only I stood irresolute, then throwing down my gun I ran forward to my friend's assistance. I had a vague belief that he was suffering from a fit, or some form of convulsion. Before I could reach his side he was down and quiet. All sounds had ceased, but with a feeling of such terror as even these awful events had not inspired I now saw again the mysterious movement of the wild oats, prolonging itself from the trampled area about the prostrate man toward the edge of a wood. It was only when it had reached the wood that I was able to withdraw my eyes and look at my companion. He was dead."

III

A MAN THOUGH NAKED MAY BE IN RAGS

The coroner rose from his seat and stood beside the dead man. Lifting an edge of the sheet he pulled it away, exposing the entire body, altogether naked and showing in the candle-light a claylike yellow. It had, however, broad maculations of bluish black, obviously caused by extravasated blood from contusions. The chest and sides looked as if they had been beaten with a bludgeon. There were dreadful lacerations; the skin was torn in strips and shreds.

The coroner moved round to the end of the table and undid a silk handkerchief which had been passed under the chin and knotted on the top of the head. When the handkerchief was drawn away it exposed what had been the throat. Some of the jurors who had risen to get a better view repented their curiosity and turned away their faces. Witness Harker went to the open window and leaned out across the sill, faint and sick. Dropping the handkerchief upon the dead man's neck the coroner stepped to an angle of the room and from a pile of clothing produced one garment after another, each of which he held up a moment for inspection. All were torn, and stiff with blood. The jurors did not make a closer inspection. They seemed rather uninterested. They had, in truth, seen all this before; the only thing that was new to them being Harker's testimony.

"Gentlemen," the coroner said, "we have no more evidence, I think. Your duty has been already explained to you; if there is nothing you wish to ask you may go outside and consider your verdict."

The foreman rose—a tall, bearded man of sixty, coarsely clad.

"I should like to ask one question, Mr. Coroner," he said. "What asylum did this yer last witness escape from?"

"Mr. Harker," said the coroner, gravely and tranquilly, "from what asylum did you last escape?"

Harker flushed crimson again, but said nothing, and the seven jurors rose and solemnly filed out of the cabin.

"If you have done insulting me, sir," said Harker, as soon as he and the officer were left alone with the dead man, "I suppose I am at liberty to go?"

"Yes."

Harker started to leave, but paused, with his hand on the door latch. The habit of his profession was strong in him—stronger than his sense of personal dignity. He turned about and said:

"The book that you have there—I recognize it as Morgan's diary. You seemed greatly interested in it; you read in it while I was testifying. May I see it? The public would like—"

"The book will cut no figure in this matter," replied the official, slipping it into his coat pocket; "all the entries in it were made before the writer's death."

As Harker passed out of the house the jury reentered and stood about the table, on which the now covered corpse showed under the sheet with sharp definition. The foreman seated himself near the candle, produced from his breast pocket a pencil and scrap of paper and wrote rather laboriously the following verdict, which with various degrees of effort all signed:

"We, the jury, do find that the remains come to their death at the hands of a mountain lion, but some of us thinks, all the same, they had fits."

IV

AN EXPLANATION FROM THE TOMB

In the diary of the late Hugh Morgan are certain interesting entries having, possibly, a scientific value as suggestions. At the inquest upon his body the book was not put in evidence; possibly the coroner thought it not worth while to confuse the jury. The date of the first of the entries mentioned cannot be ascertained; the upper part of the leaf is torn away; the part of the entry remaining follows:

". . . would run in a half-circle, keeping his head turned always toward the center, and again he would stand still, barking furiously. At last he ran away into the brush as fast as he could go. I thought at first that he had gone mad, but on returning to the house found no other alteration in his manner than what was obviously due to fear of punishment.

"Can a dog see with his nose? Do odors impress some cerebral center with images of the thing that emitted them? . . .

"Sept. 2.—Looking at the stars last night as they rose above the crest of the ridge east of the house, I observed them successively disappear—from left to right. Each was eclipsed but an instant, and only a few at the same time, but along the entire length of the ridge all that were within a degree or two of the crest were blotted out. It was as if something had passed along between me and them; but I could not see it, and the stars were not thick enough to define its outline. Ugh! I don't like this." . . .

Several weeks' entries are missing, three leaves being torn from the book.

"Sept. 27.—It has been about here again—I find evidences of its presence every day. I watched again all last night in the same cover, gun in hand, double-charged with buckshot. In the morning the fresh footprints were there, as before. Yet I would have sworn that I did not sleep —indeed, I hardly sleep at all. It is terrible, insupportable! If these amazing experiences are real I shall go mad; if they are fanciful I am mad already.

"Oct. 3.—I shall not go—it shall not drive me away. No, this is *my* house, *my* land. God hates a coward. . . .

"Oct. 5.—I can stand it no longer; I have invited Harker to pass a few weeks with me—he has a level head. I can judge from his manner if he thinks me mad.

"Oct. 7.—I have the solution of the mystery; it came to me last night—suddenly, as by revelation. How simple—how terribly simple!

"There are sounds that we cannot hear. At either end of the scale are notes that stir no chord of that imperfect instrument, the human ear. They are too high or too grave. I have observed a flock of blackbirds occupying an entire treetop—the tops of several trees—and all in full song. Suddenly—in a moment—at absolutely the same instant—all spring into the air and fly away. How? They could not all see one another—whole treetops intervened. At no point could a leader have been visible to all. There must have been a signal of warning or command, high and shrill above the din, but by me unheard. I have observed, too, the same simultaneous flight when all were silent, among not only blackbirds, but other birds—quail, for example, widely separated by bushes—even on opposite sides of a hill.

"It is known to seamen that a school of whales basking or sporting on the surface of the ocean, miles apart, with the convexity of the earth between, will sometimes dive at the same instant—all gone out of sight in a moment. The signal has been sounded—too grave for the ear of the sailor at the masthead and his comrades on the deck—who nevertheless feel its vibrations in the ship as the stones of a cathedral are stirred by the bass of the organ.

"As with sounds, so with colors. At each end of the solar spectrum the chemist can detect the presence of what are known as 'actinic' rays. They represent colors—integral colors in the composition of light—which we are unable to discern. The human eye is an imperfect instrument; its range is but a few octaves of the real 'chromatic scale.' I am not mad; there are colors that we cannot see.

"And, God help me! the Damned Thing is of such a color!"

Dark Brother

Donald R. Burleson

They can't see him. It's hard to believe, but they really can't see him.

The woman with her eternal magazines, the man with his eternal can of beer, the television blaring unendingly, an evening like any other. What unimaginative creatures they are.

I suppose they think *I'm* the unimaginative one. They don't give me credit for having a whole lot of sense, it would seem. It's a pity; I could teach them a great deal.

But look at them, how satisfied they are with their comically circumscribed little world, their narrow sensibilities. How complacent they seem. I wonder what they would think of Dark Brother if they could see him. Now the man belches and rubs his belly and smacks his lips, the television swells to a higher din, the woman widens her eyes at it and giggles, Dark Brother undulates in pale gossamer swirls at their feet.

Waiting.

Another night, like any other. They come home, from wherever it is they go all day. While they were out of the house, he was quiet as usual; I scarcely saw him out at all. He takes my presence for granted, and I understand that. Mostly he likes to come out and sniff around when they come home. He's curious about them, sizing them up. Tonight as always he'll wait till they settle down in the living room. For now, they cook their dinner, and the woman sets down a bowl of milk and some of that food that they imagine I like. Here, kitty, kitty, indeed. Nice kitty, pretty-pretty little puss, isn't she sweet, come have 'ums din-din. God, what simpletons.

They plunk themselves down for the evening, television puling away, the beer can solid in the hand as if it grew there, the woman's magazines rustling. The woman chatters from time to time, the man grunts and looks at the screen and wipes his mouth on his sleeve. And out comes Dark Brother.

I always love seeing him come out, so silent, so graceful. From the baseboards he slides slowly out like a long, translucent ribbon of pallid smoke; up from the tiny spaces between the floorboards he emerges, many parallel sheets of gray wisp, all nodding and swirling together, joining into a single mist hanging in the air near the floor. He flows around me, stroking my fur, and it feels so good I can't help purring. The way he eddies and slides around the coffee table, the edges of the sofa, the woman's feet, the man's feet, flowing, so smooth and silky and silent. This musty old house has bred him, nurtured him, grown him. They probably fancy that *they* own the house, and what a delectable piece of irony that is. Dark Brother was here long, long before they came, before I came; he told me so. How odd it is, that their senses can be so narrow—they really don't see him, and it would probably never occur to them that they live in an old, old house, and that old houses can breed things, can spawn higher forms of life, as every cat knows. What crude organisms they are, these sofa-sitters.

Dark Brother shapes part of himself into a long, probing finger of gray-blue haze and insinuates himself snakelike between them on the sofa, bobbing about the man's face for a closer look, touching the woman's hair tentatively. They watch the babbling bright screen, unaware.

Another evening. They've noticed that I see something that they don't. Dark Brother has been spectacular coming out tonight, shimmering and waving with a vigor and a sheer beauty that has made me sit up and admire. The woman points at me and says something to the man, and they watch me with that atrophied sense that I suppose passes for curiosity with them, then go back to watching television. I have to remember not to be so obvious about it.

Dark Brother oozes about them where they sit, probing, looking, sensing. They still don't see him.

But I do. And he's growing stronger.

Now when the people are gone during the day, he comes out and plays with me. He slithers through the hall, the kitchen, the bedroom, under the bed, pursuing me with smoky tendrils of gray substance, flipping me over on my back on the living room floor where I kick and meow while he tickles my tummy. He's darker now, bigger, stronger; he's drawing strength from the house, from the man and the woman, and, in a special way, from me. Rearing up in an undulating hood of haze, he pounces upon me anew, and we dart off down the hall, tumbling, frolicking. What a time we have!

Tonight they're beginning to notice Dark Brother.

The man and the woman—actually beginning to sense that there's something in the house watching them.

They look tired, drawn, sitting there on the sofa. Dark Brother runs a spidery play of gray fog fingers up to the man, brushing him, feeling at his face, and the man frowns and rubs the back of his hand across his cheek, looking puzzled. The woman eyes him, and says something. He shakes his head, looking around him and shrugging. Dark Brother, still formed into a wriggling cluster of fingers on a sinewy arm pinched up out of the general haze at the floor, withdraws a little and watches. Watches with many, many eyes. I can feel his malign humor, see him gently throbbing with it. They still can't see him, but they're sensing something, finally. He retracts the smoky arm and swirls thickly about their feet. The man is wearing shoes and doesn't seem to feel anything. But with a sharp little yell the woman draws her bare feet up under her on the couch and says something rapid and petulant-sounding to the man, waving her arms. He gets up and looks under the couch, shaking his head; all the while, Dark Brother flows gently around him, leaving him a little clearance. They go back to watching the gabbling bright screen, but look preoccupied; every now and then the man puts his hand to his face.

Today, with the man and the woman out, Dark Brother has waxed bolder. Racing in misty out-thrown tentacles through the house, he scatters papers off the coffee table, overturns a candle holder on a shelf, and whirls a little mess of tissue paper up out of the wastebasket onto the kitchen floor. We cavort together from room to room, delighting in our rapport, our timeless affinity. The things we understand together, the things he makes me remember!

The man and the woman have come home and noticed the mess Dark Brother has made. Bad kitty. Frowns, finger-shakings; bad, bad kitty. I don't mind.

Later now, they have settled down on the sofa with the television babbling away, and they look even more tired, and a little apprehensive. Dark Brother slithers back out, darker, more insolent-looking now, and swirls about the floor, caressing me, covering the whole room, but not touching the feet at the base of the sofa. Suddenly he forms an append-age up out of the ground haze and rushes at the woman, fidgeting at her face and hair with misty fingers. She yelps, drops her magazine, and brushes at her face with her hands. The man sets his beer down with a clack and jumps up, looking comically helpless, irresolute, searching. Incredibly, they still can't see him, even as much darker as he has grown. While the woman stands and the man disarranges the sofa cushions, and looks behind the sofa itself, Dark Brother withdraws, quivering with something that is now more eager than mere humor. But, he decides, enough for tonight.

The next evening. I think the woman can see him now.

Dark Brother slides up from behind the sofa and drags an arm of mist quickly across the man's face, and he jumps up, yelling and spilling his beer. The woman screams, startled wide-eyed. Dark Brother withdraws behind the couch and flows along the wall back into the hallway, seeping back in at the baseboards. Just as he is almost back in, the woman points there, shouting. The man bounds into the hall, dropping to his knees and examining the area of the baseboards. Naturally, he finds nothing, but he and the woman talk late into the night with troubled faces.

Dark Brother is avid now; I can tell, I can feel it.

Tonight there will be no mere toying with them.

They sit on the sofa, talking quietly, the television off for once. A good deal of time passes, and nothing happens, but the man and the woman seem more nervous as the evening wears on.

Dark Brother suddenly appears, gushing up out of the ancient woodwork with a hungry determination, a multitude of throbbing sheets of purposeful, sentient mist running together in the air. They see him now, by God. The woman shrieks, pressing herself back into the sofa. The man leaps to his feet, his eyes wide and rolling. At once Dark Brother fastens upon him, dragging him to the floor kicking and yelling. The woman, drooling with fear, powerful fear that I can smell, is up and sprinting for the hall, but Dark Brother, without leaving the man, shoots out a tendril to thicken upon her and take her down, moaning, in the hallway, where, pulsating, he worries at her face until the screaming stops.

Now Dark Brother tells me he will take me into himself, let me become part of him, teach me to flow into the woodwork and nurture myself there and really live *in* the house. Our house. We'll be quiet if anyone comes in to see about the man and the woman. They won't find anything, and they'll go away.

Then, sooner or later, of course, new people will come to the house to live. And that's when the fun will really begin.

Deep Wood

STEPHEN M. RAINEY

When Starmont Corporation announced its plans to construct a new housing development practically in my very backyard, I was—to put it mildly—enraged, infuriated, and a little pissed off. I had not moved out of Gainesville's city limits a few years previously, at the cost of my entire life's savings, with the desire to be thrust back into another sterile subdivision of matchbox houses cranked out by an assembly line. Gainesville realtors couldn't even sell half the property they already had developed; why on earth should they want to build more?

Because all of their lots lay inside the city limits. People wanted country living! *That* was the secret: cut down the nearest forest and plant some homes!

I owned a meager three-quarters of an acre ten miles north of town, well off of US 129. Mine was a modest two-story brick house that had been built in the late 1930s, when the nearest neighbor lived two miles away and the forest that began at the back door didn't stop until it crossed the Appalachians, some thirty miles distant. Certainly there is much greater human infestation today, but the land is still predominantly woodland, broken only by a few paved roads and populated mostly by families who have lived in the same place for generations.

It isn't the sort of place that decent people would raze to build a subdivision.

Legal petitions had been filed and failed. My wife and I had joined our neighbors in praying that Starmont would go bankrupt before the land could be cleared. We prayed for inclement weather—a tornado, even; anything to delay the beginning of the project.

It didn't happen.

On that morning, I watched the bulldozers, the scrapers, the earth movers rumbling down the road, heading toward their target like armored combat vehicles. The sight sickened me. Sixty acres of woods were about to be clobbered by giant eating machines in a famous Starmont blitzkrieg. And in a matter of days, innumerable rows of giant shoeboxes would miraculously appear, their windows overlooking my backyard—a yard where children had once faced the deep wood, marveling at its secrets. Wood that fed the air, provided homes for deer, raccoons, even bear and bobcat. I told myself that sixty acres out of countless thousands amounted to a mere drop in the bucket. But sixty here, eighty there, a hundred somewhere else. . . .

Five days after the first tree was felled, I awoke to an early morning sun, and an April breeze that hummed through the pine towers that guarded my home in blissful ignorance of what soon lay in store. Far in the distance, I could hear the engines of the mechanized assassins grinding to life, and closer at hand, the sharp buzzing of a chainsaw sinking its teeth into yielding timber.

"Jeff," my wife, Martha, called from the bathroom. "The toilet is full of ick."

"I flushed," I replied groggily, dragging myself from the bed.

She stood next to the toilet, pointing a belligerent finger toward the bowl. "Will you look at this?"

I peered into it, finding a thick mass of brown and gray scum in place of our Sani-Flush blue water. I reached for the handle to flush it, but Martha slapped my hand away.

"Don't do that! What if it overflows? You'll have more than a mess to clean up."

"Guess we'd better call the plumber, then," I muttered, my sleep-swollen eyes trying to convince me I was not yet awake.

"I guess you may as well."

I heaved a sigh, annoyed to be annoyed so early in the morning. Unfortunately, I couldn't very well blame this on the developers chopping, digging, and clearing less than a mile away—though I very much wanted to—because our septic tank was buried just out back. The pipes were old. Probably some tree roots had grown into them.

The people in those new houses would certainly never have *that* problem.

No plumbers would be open yet, so I assured Martha I would make the necessary calls from the office. I owned a graphic arts studio just this side of Gainesville's city limits, from which I managed to earn a fairly decent living, though all my clients were small, local businesses of less-than-extravagant means. All the bigger ones had their work done in Atlanta, an hour away. Gainesville isn't and never will be a Big Town, but with the exceptional growth of Atlanta in recent years, it was inevitable that the sprawl should encompass such a nearby town. Nowadays, there's a real rush hour here that lasts about forty-five minutes, and lots of traffic chokes the main roads all day long. Still, it's a pleasant enough community, and would likely remain so if they'd boot all the developers.

Later that morning I made arrangements for the plumber to call at my house. My office affairs kept me moving at a fairly frantic pace all day, so our backed-up toilet didn't again enter my head until just about quitting time. Apparently, though, it had been foremost in Martha's mind, for when I came in, she was waiting in the kitchen holding a bill from Millard Wiegman, our local waterworks expert.

"Eighty dollars!" Martha snapped. "And all he did was snake the pipe."

"Did he fix it?"

"Sure he fixed it."

"Then be happy," I said, nevertheless finding my spirits dampened by the unexpected expense.

"He said the trouble wasn't roots. The pipes weren't even clogged up. He didn't know what it was."

I hoped this wasn't leading up to further expense, but for the time being, I had no desire to dwell upon it. Instead, I sat down to enjoy Martha's excellent cooking, tonight's special being honey-roasted ham and corn on the cob. Afterward, we watched some television together on one of the four channels our set picked up (there's no cable out here, which I reckoned might devastate some potential town house buyers), drank two beers each, and occasionally grumbled about the development moving closer to our door. Despite the occasional squabble, Martha and I have had a good twenty years together. You can't beat that with a stick.

Martha went to bed at eleven, but I stayed up to watch the news and read the paper until about midnight. That quiet hour was always a favorite time for me—a period to enjoy the rustic atmosphere of our house, and the sheltered solitude provided by the forest. With the windows open, I could hear the crickets and other night creatures making their melodic racket, and occasionally a whippoorwill mourned in the distance. They'd be gone soon, seeking the deeper recesses of the forest where no one would cut their trees. Listening to them, I felt a deep pang of melancholy, as though sensing the passing of an era.

For a time, I sat in my recliner next to the window, trying to focus on the paper. My attention kept wandering, however, and after about ten minutes, I realized it was because a sound—an unfamiliar sound—was pouring almost subliminally from the woods. I could barely distinguish it above the chirping of the crickets, yet I knew that *something* unusual was singing out there. A low drone, or a whine, softly rising and falling, growing briefly louder, then receding almost into silence. I leaned forward with my ear to the open window, listening . . . waiting. The noise didn't seem to vary much; certainly it was neither approaching nor retreating. But it was nothing I had ever heard in the past.

For a period of perhaps ten minutes it went on, then slowly faded and fell silent. The sound reminded me of the whirring mating song of cicadas, but this was somehow deeper, *bigger*. I realized it made me uneasy. And once it had stopped, I noticed that all the other sounds—the crickets, the night birds—had also ceased.

After a time, I rose and prepared myself for bed. Martha was already sound asleep, breathing softly in our dark room. A few crickets eventually began to chatter again, and all seemed normal about the night. But as I lay down and nestled beneath the blanket, I felt, for the first time ever in this house, a strange unease, as if something malevolent might be peering in from the wooded blackness outside.

The next day was Saturday, and after a breakfast of bacon, eggs, grits, and toast, I set out walking down the old path that led from our backyard to a small pond about a half mile to the north, at the edge of the land the developers had already claimed. In the daylight, the pines and cedars wore their friendliest faces, their leaves having just opened for the spring. I often walked on this path, and knew every curve, every root, every stump along the way. It would all be gone soon, and I felt as if someone were about to erase a part of my soul. Yet after last night, something about the wood seemed different—less welcoming than it ever had in the past.

Shortly, I came to a tall maple, just to the right of the path, that had probably stood for most of a century. In its bark was ingrained a most remarkable pattern, one shaped by nature's hand as if by more than happenstance: a grotesque, cyclopean face, its staring eye a gaping knothole, blackened over the course of countless years. This image had always struck me as somewhat repulsive, yet it seemed as natural a part of the tree as its limbs and leaves. A personality existed here, one that predated even the tree itself, and one that cared not a whit for the economic well-being of developers.

Now, looking at this countenance, I could see dark streaks of thick fluid running down the trunk—pouring from the eye of the ancient wooden face. For all the world, it appeared that the tree was weeping tears of blood. I touched the liquid, and found it sticky, but thinner than typical maple sap. Something about its color—a rich brown, tinted with gray—reminded me of the scum we had seen in our toilet bowl.

A bit puzzled, I continued on, soon able to see an open patch of sky that had never been there before. The pond lay just ahead, and from it, I could hear a soft gurgling, like someone blowing bubbles from under the water. I hurried forward, curious about the source of this noise.

At the path's end, I came to a short crescent of thick weeds and fronds, beyond which the pond lapped gently at its muddy banks. A few frogs croaked from their hiding places, and a cloud of flying insects swarmed just above the murky water. I could still hear the gurgling sound, and scanning the area, I saw a disturbance near the opposite bank that sent ripples spiraling toward me. Something seemed to be moving just beneath the aqua surface. A moment later, a dark shape appeared in the center of the pond, something small and oblong, which I at first thought might be a beaver. But as it drew nearer, I realized that a beaver would not move with such a thrashing motion, nor did beavers possess the kind of prehensile limb that rose and fell quickly, to splash me with cool spray. I froze, finding myself suddenly awed and shocked. A large, dark stain then began to spread across the surface of the pond: more of the brownish slime that my wife had so aptly termed "ick."

Ignoring my every impulse to flee, I stood stock still and waited while the scum flowed to the near bank and began to seep into the weeds at my feet. The organism from which it flowed remained near the center of the pond, just far enough under the water to prevent me seeing it clearly. Just before the viscous mass reached me, I took one step back, and it halted its advance. Swallowing my cold dread, I leaned forward and peered at the submerged shape, trying to study the new life I seemed to have found.

Then, I heard an eruption of water, and a small fountain burst up from the center of the pond. A second later, a low, droning sound—like that which I'd heard the night before, only at a lower volume—rose from the thing, gradually rising in pitch. Almost musical, the sound held me enraptured. I halfway wondered if I were about to be dragged into the water as a feast for some unknown carnivorous horror.

Instead, I felt as if some sort of message were being conveyed to me, something to which I remained deaf, as if my own senses were primitive compared to those of the thing in the pond. All I could do was stare and listen dumbly while the creature sang to me with its almost lulling, woodwind voice. After a few minutes of this, the sound subsided and the surface of the water stilled. At my feet, the dull ick suddenly seemed to be absorbed by the soft mud, for within seconds, all traces of it were gone. And the organism in the pond slowly sank completely out of sight.

But then I heard another splash, and in the corner of my eye, saw something dark quickly shoot from the water and disappear into the tall reeds along the far bank. The fronds suddenly began to wave, as the thing moved purposefully through them. All around me, I perceived a vague sensation of movement, spreading through the trees like a ripple, with the pond at its center. Branches creaked softly and leaves rustled together like rough fingers, though not so much as a whisper of wind stirred them.

This thing—whatever it might be—must not be the only one of its kind.

And then I heard voices: men talking in normal tones, but from too great a distance to understand what they were saying. I knew they were at the development site—probably some inspectors come to see the result of the week's labor. I stood and listened for a few minutes, seized by a strong feeling of anticipation and cold fear. Nothing out of the ordinary happened while I stood there, and finally, gathering my wits as much as possible, I began to make my way toward the cleared area of the forest, compelled to relate to someone—anyone—the things I had just seen and heard, regardless that I might be taken for a lunatic.

And then I stopped, finding my path blocked by a barrier of vines and thorns, an impenetrable wall of vegetation that separated me from the clearing ahead. I started to call out, but as I did, I heard the musical drone behind me, and my tongue froze. Ahead, I could hear the voices of the men much more clearly now, and it seemed they were searching for one of their companions. I counted three of them.

"He was over here a minute ago," said one, a gruff, gravelly voice.

"Hey, Bill!" called a young-sounding tenor.

"Are you hurt?" Another youthful, tremulous voice.

"Answer us!"

A rustling came from my left.

"Hey, Alex, look over here."

"What is it?"

"I don't know. Some kind of ick."

"Hey . . . what's that?"

"Jesus, God. . . ."

And then came the screams. Rising higher and higher, animalistic screeches that would not stop. My heart leaped to my throat, and I found myself on my knees, my muscles turned to jelly. Grating howls that couldn't come from human throats—though I knew that they must—pierced my eardrums, and a deep squelching sound, followed by a sharp *rip*, silenced one voice. Immediately after, the same sounds were repeated, and finally, the forest again fell silent except for the fading echoes of screams and the faintest of dronings coming from somewhere behind me.

It grew louder again, rising all around me. The trees seemed to vibrate with the sound, and as its volume mounted, I began to sense in it a note of triumph, a victorious howl from the soul of the forest. From the lowest of bass tones to the highest soprano, the wail covered an entire tonal range, both smooth and grating in texture. I fell to my knees as the woods exulted, covered my ears with my palms, but to no avail. I had to escape, I knew, for death lay close at hand. Yet all I could do now was crawl, for I felt the burn of something horrible gazing at me from places unseen.

I had only just begun to move when I was frozen by the sight of something small and dark emerging from the wall of vines that encircled me. I could barely discern its shape, for its coloring matched the grays and greens of the surrounding foliage. But the pair of glistening, blood-colored eyes that stared at me separated themselves from the tangled backdrop like dim, hovering suns, withering my will with their intensity. I saw several segmented appendages beneath a domed carapace that might have been legs, and something—a tail, perhaps?—waved slowly behind it, almost hypnotic in its smoothness.

The woodwind song rose from some unseen organ, again submitting something to me that I sensed held a meaning, but which eluded me in my shock and fear. It was when a pool of the brownish scum began to flow from beneath the body of this creature, slowly spreading toward me along the ground, that I realized the fluid must be a sort of appendage in itself—perhaps something with sensory purpose. But when it touched flora, the grasses and weeds began to sway slowly of their own accord, as if the excretion were some sort of life-giving elixir.

My god. Whatever this tissue was, it had been in my house. I had *touched* it . . . on the tree, where it leaked from the face in the bark.

I knew then that through this contact, the creature had somehow come to perceive *me*, physically, and perhaps in other ways. Spiritually, even.

Then, suddenly, the thing simply vanished into the darkness of the brush. And I managed to get back to my feet and hurry toward my home. As I came upon the tree with the sentient face, I stopped and regarded it with a new curiosity. The dark streaks remained, but now a clear fluid oozed slowly from the knothole. I reached out to touch the bark; it was warm, like living flesh, rather than wood. And I understood the meaning in the sounds as I could not have only a short time before. There had been no triumph in the killing of the developers; only anger and regret. The forest was crying. Some primal life had been driven forth by the land-clearers, something that lived within the earth itself, older than even the trees.

When I returned home, there were tears in my own eyes.

Many nights thereafter, I heard the droning sounds in the woods, and though I still felt a certain fear, my understanding of their true nature prevented me from packing up and leaving for the artificial surroundings of Atlanta—as Martha was for a time determined to do following the deaths of the company men. Her first reaction to the sounds was like mine: a terror born of the unknown, augmented by the continued ill fortune of the developing crews that attempted to complete the Starmont project. Finally, however, the bulldozers, the earth movers, the chainsaws, and the axemen retreated, and since then the woods have remained quiet. Martha's fear eventually passed as well, though she still refuses to join me on my frequent walks to the pond. I continue to try persuading her, as it is my sincerest wish that she might come to share the rapport that I have developed with the woods—a bond that has only made my life more compassionate, more *feeling*. Perhaps in time, it will happen.

While the urban advance into the wilds goes on, I know at some point it must stop; if not for the forest's sake, then for our own. You see, the message came down that day in these north Georgia woods, in terms clear and precise and with absolute authority:

Should any man enter here intending to cut the living wood, he will never walk out alive.

Demons of the Sea

William Hope Hodgson

"**C**ome out on deck and have a look, 'Darky!'" Jepson cried, rushing into the half deck. "The Old Man says there's been a submarine earthquake, and the sea's all bubbling and muddy!"

Obeying the summons of Jepson's excited tone, I followed him out. It was as he had said; the everlasting blue of the ocean was mottled with splotches of a muddy hue, and at times a large bubble would appear, to burst with a loud "pop." Aft, the skipper and the three mates could be seen on the poop, peering at the sea through their glasses. As I gazed out over the gently heaving water, far off to windward something was hove up into the evening air. It appeared to be a mass of seaweed, but fell back into the water with a sullen plunge as though it were something more substantial. Immediately after this strange occurrence, the sun set with tropical swiftness, and in the brief afterglow things assumed a strange unreality.

The crew were all below, no one but the mate and the helmsman remaining on the poop. Away forward, on the topgallant forecastle head the dim figure of the man on lookout could be seen, leaning against the forestay. No sound was heard save the occasional jingle of a chain sheet, of the flog of the steering gear as a small swell passed under our counter. Presently the mate's voice broke the silence, and, looking up, I saw that the Old Man had come on deck, and was talking with him. From the few stray words that could be overheard, I knew they were talking of the strange happenings of the day.

Shortly after sunset, the wind, which had been fresh during the day, died down, and with its passing the air grew oppressively hot. Not long after two bells, the mate sung out for me, and ordered me to fill a bucket from overside and bring it to him. When I had carried out his instructions, he placed a thermometer in the bucket.

"Just as I thought," he muttered, removing the instrument and showing it to the skipper; "ninety-nine degrees. Why, the sea's hot enough to make tea with!"

"Hope it doesn't get any hotter," growled the latter; "if it does, we shall all be boiled alive."

At a sign from the mate, I emptied the bucket and replaced it in the rack, after which I resumed my former position by the rail. The Old Man and the mate walked the poop side by side. The air grew hotter as the hours passed and after a long period of silence broken only by the occasional "pop" of a bursting gas bubble, the moon arose. It shed but a feeble light, however, as a heavy mist had arisen from the sea, and through this, the moonbeams struggled weakly. The mist, we decided, was due to the excessive heat of the sea water; it was a very wet mist, and we were soon soaked to the skin. Slowly the interminable night wore on, and the sun arose, looking dim and ghostly through the mist that rolled and billowed about the ship. From time to time we took the temperature of the sea, although we found but a slight increase therein. No work was done, and a feeling as of something impending pervaded the ship.

The fog horn was kept going constantly, as the lookout peered through the wreathing mists. The captain walked the poop in company with the mates, and once the third mate spoke and pointed out into the clouds of fog. All eyes followed his gesture; we saw what was apparently a black line, which seemed to cut the whiteness of the billows. It reminded us of nothing so much as an enormous cobra standing on its tail. As we looked it vanished. The grouped mates were evidently puzzled; there seemed to be a difference of opinion among them. Presently as they argued, I heard the second mate's voice:

"That's all rot," he said. "I've seen things in fog before, but they've always turned out to be imaginary."

The third shook his head and made some reply I could not overhear, but no further comment was made. Going below that afternoon, I got a short sleep, and on coming on deck at eight bells, I found that the steam still held us; if anything, it seemed to be thicker than ever. Hansard, who had been taking the temperatures during my watch below, informed me that the sea was three degrees hotter, and that the Old Man was getting into a rare old state. At three bells I went forward to have a look over the bows, and a chin with Stevenson, whose lookout it was. On gaining the forecastle head, I went to the side and looked down into the water. Stevenson came over and stood beside me.

"Rum go, this," he grumbled.

He stood by my side for a time in silence; we seemed to be hypnotized by the gleaming surface of the sea. Suddenly out of the depths, right before us, there arose a monstrous black face. It was like a frightful caricature of a human countenance. For a moment we gazed petrified; my blood seemed to suddenly turn to ice water; I was unable to move. With a mighty effort of will, I regained my self-control and, grasping Stevenson's arm, I found I could do no more than croak, my powers of speech seemed gone. "Look!" I gasped. "Look!"

Stevenson continued to stare into the sea, like a man turned to stone. He seemed to stoop further over, as if to examine the thing more closely. "Lord," he exclaimed, "it must be the devil himself!"

As though the sound of his voice had broken a spell, the thing disappeared. My companion looked at me, while I rubbed my eyes, thinking that I had been asleep, and that the awful vision had been a frightful nightmare. One look at my friend, however, disabused me of any such thought. His face wore a puzzled expression.

"Better go aft and tell the Old Man," he faltered.

I nodded and left the forecastle head, making my way aft like one in a trance. The skipper and the mate were standing at the break of the poop, and running up the ladder I told them what we had seen.

"Bosh!" sneered the Old Man. "You've been looking at your own ugly reflection in the water."

Nevertheless, in spite of his ridicule, he questioned me closely. Finally he ordered the mate forward to see if he could see anything. The latter, however, returned in a few moments, to report that nothing unusual could be seen. Four bells were struck, and we were relieved for tea. Coming on deck afterward, I found the men clustered together forward. The sole topic of conversation with them was the thing that Stevenson and I had seen.

"I suppose, Darky, it couldn't have been a reflection by any chance, could it?" one of the older men asked.

"Ask Stevenson," I replied as I made my way aft.

At eight bells, my watch came on deck again, to find that nothing further had developed. But, about an hour before midnight, the mate, thinking to have a smoke, sent me to his room for a box of matches with which to light his pipe. It took me no time to clatter down the brass-treaded ladder, and back to the poop, where I handed him the desired article. Taking the box, he removed a match and struck it on the heel of his boot. As he did so, far out in the night a muffled screaming arose. Then came a clamor as of hoarse braying, like an ass but considerably deeper, and with a horribly suggestive human note running through it.

"Good God! Did you hear that, Darky?" asked the mate in awed tones.

"Yes, sir," I replied, listening—and scarcely noticing his question—

113

for a repetition of the strange sounds. Suddenly the frightful bellowing broke out afresh. The mate's pipe fell to the deck with a clatter.

"Run for'ard!" he cried. "Quick, now, and see if you can see anything."

With my heart in my mouth, and pulses pounding madly I raced forward. The watch were all up on the forecastle head, clustered around the lookout. Each man was talking and gesticulating wildly. They became silent, and turned questioning glances toward me as I shouldered my way among them.

"Have you seen anything?" I cried.

Before I could receive an answer, a repetition of the horrid sounds broke out again, profaning the night with their horror. They seemed to have definite direction now, in spite of the fog that enveloped us. Undoubtedly, too, they were nearer. Pausing a moment to make sure of their bearing, I hastened aft and reported to the mate. I told him that nothing could be seen, but that the sounds apparently came from right ahead of us. On hearing this he ordered the man at the wheel to let the ship's head come off a couple of points. A moment later a shrill screaming tore its way through the night, followed by the hoarse braying sounds once more.

"It's close on the starboard bow!" exclaimed the mate, as he beckoned the helmsman to let her head come off a little more. Then, singing out for the watch, he ran forward, slacking the lee braces on the way. When he had the yards trimmed to his satisfaction on the new course, he returned to the poop and hung far out over the rail listening intently. Moments passed that seemed like hours, yet the silence remained unbroken. Suddenly the sounds began again, and so close that it seemed as though they must be right aboard of us. At this time I noticed a strange booming note mingled with the brays. And once or twice there came a sound that can only be described as a sort of "gug, gug." Then would come a wheezy whistling, for all the world like an asthmatic person breathing.

All this while the moon shone wanly through the steam, which seemed to me to be somewhat thinner. Once the mate gripped me by the shoulder as the noises rose and fell again. They now seemed to be coming from a point broad on our beam. Every eye on the ship was straining into the mist, but with no result. Suddenly one of the men cried out, as something long and black slid past us into the fog astern. From it there rose four indistinct and ghostly towers, which resolved themselves into spars and ropes, and sails.

"A ship! It's a ship!" we cried excitedly. I turned to Mr. Gray; he, too, had seen something, and was staring aft into the wake. So ghostlike, unreal, and fleeting had been our glimpse of the stranger, that we were not sure that we had seen an honest, material ship, but thought that we had been vouchsafed a vision of some phantom vessel like the *Flying Dutchman*. Our sails gave a sudden flap, the clew irons flogging the bulwarks with hollow thumps. The mate glanced aloft.

"Wind's dropping," he growled savagely. "We shall never get out of this infernal place at this gait!"

Gradually the wind fell until it was a flat calm. No sound broke the deathlike silence save the rapid patter of the reef points, as she gently rose and fell on the light swell. Hours passed, and the watch was relieved and I then went below. At seven bells we were called again, and as I went along the deck to the galley, I noticed that the fog seemed thinner, and the air cooler. When eight bells were struck I relieved Hansard at coiling down the ropes. From him I learned that the steam had begun to clear about four bells, and that the temperature of the sea had fallen ten degrees.

In spite of the thinning mist, it was not until about a half an hour later that we were able to get a glimpse of the surrounding sea. It was still mottled with dark patches, but the bubbling and popping had ceased. As much of the surface of the ocean as could be seen had a peculiarly desolate aspect. Occasionally a wisp of steam would float up from the nearer sea, and roll undulatingly across its silent surface, until lost in the vagueness that still held the hidden horizon. Here and there columns of steam rose up in pillars, which gave me the impression that the sea was hot in patches. Crossing to the starboard side and looking over, I found that conditions there were similar to those to port. The desolate aspect of the sea filled me with an idea of chilliness, although the air was quite warm and muggy. From the break of the poop the mate called to me to get his glasses.

When I had done this, he took them from me and walked to the taffrail. Here he stood for some moments polishing them with his handkerchief. After a moment he raised them to his eyes, and peered long and intently into the mist astern. I stood for some time staring at the point on which the mate had focused his glasses. Presently something shadowy grew upon my vision. Steadily watching it, I distinctly saw the outlines of a ship take form in the fog.

"See!" I cried, but even as I spoke, a lifting wraith of mist disclosed to view a great four-masted bark lying becalmed with all sails set, within a few hundred yards of our stern. As though a curtain had been raised, and then allowed to fall, the fog once more settled down, hiding the strange bark from our sight. The mate was all excitement, striding with quick, jerky steps, up and down the poop, stopping every few moments to peer through his glasses at the point where the four-master had disappeared in the fog. Gradually, as the mists dispersed again, the vessel could be seen more plainly, and it was then that we got an inkling of the cause of the dreadful noises during the night.

For some time the mate watched her silently, and as he watched the conviction grew upon me that in spite of the mist, I could detect some sort of movement on board of her. After some time had passed, the doubt became a certainty, and I could also see a sort of splashing in the water alongside of her. Suddenly the mate put his glasses on top of the wheel box and told me to bring him the speaking trumpet. Running to the companionway, I secured the trumpet and was back at his side.

The mate raised it to his lips, and taking a deep breath, sent a hail across the water that should have awakened the dead. We waited tensely for a reply. A moment later a deep, hollow mutter came from the bark; higher and louder it swelled, until we realized that we were listening to the same sounds we had heard the night before. The mate stood aghast at this answer to his hail; in a voice barely more than a hushed whisper, he bade me call the Old Man. Attracted by the mate's hail and its unearthly reply, the watch had all come aft and were clustered in the mizzen rigging in order to see better.

After calling the captain, I returned to the poop, where I found the second and third mates talking with the chief. All were engaged in trying to pierce the clouds of mist that half hid our strange consort and to arrive at some explanation of the strange phenomena of the past few hours. A moment later the captain appeared carrying his telescope. The mate gave him a brief account of the state of affairs and handed him the trumpet. Giving me the telescope to hold, the captain hailed the shadowy bark. Breathlessly we all listened, when again, in answer to the Old Man's hail, the frightful sounds rose on the still morning air. The skipper lowered the trumpet and stood with an expression of astonished horror on his face.

"Lord!" he exclaimed. "What an ungodly row!"

At this, the third, who had been gazing through his binoculars, broke the silence.

"Look," he ejaculated. "There's a breeze coming up astern." At his words the captain looked up quickly, and we all watched the ruffling water.

"That packet yonder is bringing the breeze with her," said the skipper. "She'll be alongside in half an hour!"

116

Some moments passed, and the bank of fog had come to within a hundred yards of our taffrail. The strange vessel could be distinctly seen just inside the fringe of the driving mist wreaths. After a short puff, the wind died completely, but as we stared with hypnotic fascination, the water astern of the stranger ruffled again with a fresh catspaw. Seemingly with the flapping of her sails, she drew slowly up to us. As the leaden seconds passed, the big four-master approached us steadily. The light air had now reached us, and with a lazy lift of our sails, we, too, began to forge slowly through that weird sea. The bark was now within fifty yards of our stern, and she was steadily drawing nearer, seeming to be able to outfoot us with ease. As she came on she luffed sharply, and came up into the wind with her weather leeches shaking.

I looked toward her poop, thinking to discern the figure of the man at the wheel, but the mist coiled around her quarter, and objects on the after end of her became indistinguishable. With a rattle of chain sheets on her iron yards, she filled away again. We meanwhile had gone ahead, but it was soon evident that she was the better sailor, for she came up to us hand over fist. The wind rapidly freshened and the mist began to drift away before it, so that each moment her spars and cordage became more plainly visible. The skipper and the mates were watching her intently when an almost simultaneous exclamation of fear broke from them.

"My God!"

And well they might show signs of fear, for crawling about the bark's deck were the most horrible creatures I had ever seen. In spite of their unearthly strangeness there was something vaguely familiar about them. Then it came to me that the face that Stevenson and I had seen during the night belonged to one of them. Their bodies had something of the shape of a seal's, but of a dead, unhealthy white. The lower part of the body ended in a sort of double-curved tail on which they appeared to be able to shuffle about. In place of arms, they had two long, snaky feelers, at the ends of which were two very humanlike hands, which were equipped with talons instead of nails. Fearsome indeed were these parodies of human beings!

Their faces, which, like their tentacles, were black, were the most grotesquely human things about them, and the upper jaw closed into the lower, after the manner of the jaws of an octopus. I have seen men among certain tribes of natives who had faces uncommonly like theirs, but yet no native I had ever seen could have given me the extraordinary feeling of horror and revulsion I experienced toward these brutal-looking creatures.

"What devilish beasts!" burst out the captain in disgust.

117

With this remark he turned to the mates, and as he did so, the expressions on their faces told me that they had all realized what the presence of these bestial-looking brutes meant. If, as was doubtless the case, these creatures had boarded the bark and destroyed her crew, what would prevent them from doing the same with us? We were a smaller ship and had a smaller crew, and the more I thought of it the less I liked it.

We could now see the name on the bark's bow with the naked eye. It read *Scottish Heath*, while on her boats we could see the name bracketed with Glasgow, showing that she hailed from that port. It was a remarkable coincidence that she should have a slant from just the quarter in which yards were trimmed, as before we saw her she must have been drifting around with everything "aback." But now in this light air she was able to run along beside us with no one at her helm. But steering herself she was, and although at times she yawed wildly, she never got herself aback. As we gazed at her we noticed a sudden movement on board of her, and several of the creatures slid into the water.

"See! See! They've spotted us. They're coming for us!" cried the mate wildly.

It was only too true, scores of them were sliding into the sea, letting themselves down by means of their long tentacles. On they came, slipping by scores and hundreds into the water, and swimming toward us in droves. The ship was making about three knots, otherwise they would have caught us in a very few minutes. But they persevered, gaining slowly but surely, and drawing nearer and nearer. The long, tentacle-like arms rose out of the sea in hundreds, and the foremost ones were already within a score of yards of the ship before the Old Man bethought himself to shout to the mates to fetch up the half dozen cutlasses that comprised the ship's armory. Then, turning to me, he ordered me to go down to his cabin and bring up the two revolvers out of the top drawer of the chart table, also a box of cartridges that was there.

When I returned with the weapons he loaded them and handed one to the mate. Meanwhile the pursuing creatures were coming steadily nearer, and soon half a dozen of the leaders were directly under our counter. Immediately the captain leaned over the rail and emptied his pistol into them, but without any apparent effect. He must have realized how puny and ineffectual his efforts were, for he did not reload his weapon.

Some dozens of the brutes had reached us, and as they did so, their tentacles rose into the air and caught our rail. I heard the third mate scream suddenly, and turning, I saw him dragged quickly to the rail, with a tentacle wrapped completely around him. Snatching a cutlass, the second mate hacked off the tentacle where it joined the body. A gout of blood splashed into the third mate's face, and he fell to the deck. A dozen more of those arms rose and wavered in the air, but they now seemed some yards astern of us. A rapidly widening patch of clear water appeared between us and the foremost of our pursuers, and we raised a wild shout of joy. The cause was soon apparent; for a fine fair wind had sprung up, and with the increase in its force, the *Scottish Heath* had got herself aback, while we were rapidly leaving the monsters behind us. The third mate rose to his feet with a dazed look, and as he did so something fell to the deck. I picked it up and found that it was the severed portion of the tentacle of the third's late adversary. With a grimace of disgust I tossed it into the sea, as I needed no reminder of that awful experience.

Three weeks later we anchored in San Francisco. There the captain made a full report of the affair to the authorities, with the result that a gunboat was despatched to investigate. Six weeks later she returned to report that she had been unable to find any signs, either of the ship herself or of the fearful creatures that had attacked her. And since then nothing, as far as I know, has ever been heard of the four-masted bark *Scottish Heath*, last seen by us in the possession of creatures that may rightly be called demons of the sea.

Whether she still floats, occupied by her hellish crew, or whether some storm has sent her to her last resting place beneath the waves is purely a matter of conjecture. Perchance on some dark, fog-bound night, a ship in that wilderness of waters may hear cries and sounds beyond those of the wailing of the winds. Then let them look to it, for it may be that the demons of the sea are near them.

The Deserted Garden

August Derleth

Mr. Jerym Waring's archeological researches had brought him at last to the Gower coast of Wales. He stood now in the center of the highway that ran through the unnamed hamlet that he had reached with the aid of kind tourists. In one hand he held a suitcase; in the other the clipping that had brought him there. He looked askance at the headline—"Dead Man in Mysterious Deserted Garden"—and hoped fervently that any prying investigators would have completed their work. The article went on to say that a tourist had been found dead in a strange, out-of-the-way garden overlooking the sea, and that his death was supposed to have been by murder, though it was rather late to ascertain definitely, the body having gone long undiscovered. There were curious marks about the throat, it seemed, and the intrepid detective in charge of the case insisted on murder. This, instead of contributing to the clarity of the matter, tangled it still more. Mr. Jerym Waring had a penchant for anything that suggested the ancient; consequently, when he read the last paragraph of the article, telling about the antiquity of the garden, he lost no time in making for the place. Unfortunately he lost himself, and arrived seven days later than he had scheduled.

Mr. Jerym Waring looked up from the article to find himself the cynosure of several pairs of eyes. Two of them were directed at him from behind a curtain to his left; another came from a large frame dwelling on the other side of the road. Mr. Waring fixed his eyes on this building, reflecting to himself that it suspiciously resembled a hostelry. The eyes abruptly vanished, and a moment later a large, rotund man ambled casually out of the building and planted himself against the doorjamb. The archeologist took hold of his suitcase and went over to him.

"I say, brother," he began, "can you tell me where I can find some place to put up for a week or a fortnight?" He shifted his weight from one foot to the other.

The rotund man slowly removed a pipe from his mouth, made a little bow, and answered him, with a faraway look in his eyes, as if he were watching for sailboats along the distant sea horizon, "You can make yourself right at home here, sir. This has always been as good a hotel as you can find hereabouts." He bowed again, and imperturbably turned to lead the way into the building. Mr. Jerym Waring saw nothing to do but to follow his host.

At table that night Mr. Jerym Waring casually mentioned the mysterious garden. Was it far from there? And could one get to it easily? And how?

"It's a good many steps," said his host, "but it's not what I'd call far." He turned to his wife for corroboration; she nodded hastily. "The path's pretty clear, now that all those detectives and doctors have worn it down so. You follow it right down to the sea, and there you turn northward and start going up on the cliffs. You'd best be pretty careful there, sir, for the path's narrow as can be, and the sea's below, and there's sharp rock under the water." His wife nodded again, and Mr. Waring nodded, too. The host was using his fork to punctuate his remarks.

The following morning Mr. Jerym Waring rose especially early and made his way out of his hotel to the sea coast. It was as yet somewhat misty, and he stood for some moments debating on the advisability of ascending the cliffs in the half light. The path upward seemed fairly clear, but it was also dangerously close to the edge of a sheer wall to the sea. He resolved at last to continue his jaunt, and he made his way carefully up along the cliff wall. At times gulls flew screaming past him, so close that he might have reached out and touched them, had it not been for the danger of upsetting himself. He emerged from the rocky path finally in a sort of ravine, equally as rocky. This he followed to its end, where he came upon the deserted garden.

At first glance it looked like a forlorn cemetery; there were a great many vine-grown rocks and slabs of stone to be seen among the trampled weeds. Here and there were sickly-looking flowers—not at all what Mr. Waring had expected. He walked about among the stones, examining them under his glass, and leaving one after the other with a disappointed air. About half-way through the garden he discovered himself to be in the middle of the ruins of what had once been a stone building. He stood for some minutes looking around him, trying to trace the outlines of this old ruin, when his eye lighted on a peculiar flat slab, close to the wall line of the ruin. It struck him at once as being infinitely older than any of the other stones, and he hurried over to it eagerly.

It was certainly a marker for a grave, reflected Mr. Waring, and he bent closer in a vain effort to decipher the cryptic scrawls on the stone.

But the writing was totally strange to Mr. Waring, well versed as he was in ancient lore. Mr. Jerym Waring was chagrined, and he stood up and glanced shamefacedly about, as if on the lookout for anyone who might have seen him. He rambled through the remainder of the garden, but his fancy drew him at last back to the slab. He tried, halfheartedly to move it, but the effort was futile; the stone was too large, and besides, it was half imbedded in the earth.

It was somewhat after 12 when Mr. Jerym Waring reached his hostelry. The archeologist noticed at once that his host's manner was rather strained, and he wondered vaguely whether this had to do with his presence. At table he mentioned casually his intention to return to the garden for the afternoon. A quick glance passed between his host and hostess, and for a moment after his announcement there was complete silence. Mr. Jerym Waring's host coughed nervously and put his teacup in his saucer.

"You'll be back before nightfall, I suppose, sir?"

"That depends," said Mr. Waring reflectively, "on what I find. I have a flashlight with me, so don't worry if I fail to come back for lunch."

"We'd like to have you with us for lunch, Mr. Waring. All afternoon, in fact. You needn't go up there today—you've all week to visit, sir."

"There's never a time like the present. Besides, there may be nothing there after all; so that I may leave you tonight. If I waited and found nothing, I should lose that much time."

"I don't like to mention it, sir, but that garden is a bad spot—an unhealthful spot at night."

"There's a queer slab up there. It has a lot of curious carvings on it," Mr. Waring went on, as if he had not heard his host.

His hostess suddenly set her cup of tea on the table, and moved her chair slightly away.

"It was beside that stone," said his host slowly, "that the body was found."

"Is that so? Well, that's most interesting. I wonder, now. . . . How old do you take the garden to be?"

"I don't know, sir. That garden was there before this town was founded. Some say it's Roman."

"Do you know what night this is?" asked his hostess suddenly. Mr. Waring stared blankly at her. "May Eve, sir. And for years past there've been queer doings up in that garden on May Eve, to say nothing of All Souls and All Hallows."

"What do you mean—'queer doings?' "

"Lights, greenish-blue lights," his host broke in. "And often weird, uncanny music that scares you."

"And no one ever investigated?" asked Mr. Waring incredulously.

"Yes. One of us went up." There was a significant silence. "He never came back; we never found his body." His host coughed again. "But we heard him in the night, screaming."

"What do you suppose—?" begain Mr. Waring.

"There is," said his host stolidly, "it is said, an old god named Pan—a Greek god—of good and of evil, of nature. On May Eve, on All Hallows, on All Souls, the evil predominates, and it is better for man to avoid the spot Pan and his satyrs frequent."

Mr. Waring made an effort to speak, but he said nothing. The eyes of his hostess were staring blankly into the past; her face had gone a pasty white.

Mr. Jerym Waring was somewhat perplexed. But in the afternoon he went up, and by evening he had quite forgotten about the matter.

He learned nothing from the slab, save that it might have been moved. Had it not been for this discovery, Mr. Waring would have returned to his hostelry in time for lunch. As the matter stood, his lingering was pardonable. His first reaction on sight of the disturbed ground about the base of the slab was one of intense surprise. It was clear to him that it would take more than one man to move the slab, and it was fairly certain that not more than one man at a time had been up here, save perhaps the detectives who had investigated the death some weeks before. Yes, that was most probably it. But it did not seem to him that the stone had been disturbed at all that morning.

Mr. Jerym Waring stood up, relieved. The discovery had been made at sundown, and when the archeologist rose from his crouching position there was only a deep red fringe on the horizon to show where the sun had been. A gull wheeled about high up in the sky, and another followed it, screaming raucously. Mr. Waring stood for a tentative moment. All was strangely silent, with that curious silence that falls in still places when the birds have ceased their crying. It was getting rapidly darker, and all that was left of the day was a faint, darkening line of red on the sea, as if someone were dying there, and bleeding from a hundred wounds. A dim moon was making its way slowly through great clouds of fog rolling up from the lowlands.

Mr. Waring stood there until the fog had entirely surrounded the peak he surmounted; it was as if he had suddenly been thrust out into the far reaches of the sky; as if the earth were thousands and thousands of miles below him.

He turned to go at last, even while the wisps of vapor were curling around him. He sought out the slab once more, and directed his flashlight at it. He had not anticipated what he saw: the slab had been raised fully an inch from the ground, and it stood on one edge at a distinct angle. Mr. Waring had a sudden, unaccountable vision of his hostess's drawn face. Then his flashlight went out. He stood quite still for a moment; then he ran forward—and fell over a stone. He picked himself up, bewildered, and ran again, only to fall a second time. Again he stood still, and looked in vague fright toward the place where the slab should be.

The fog was too thick to see anything, but the archeologist was not unaware of the faint greenish luminosity that hovered in the vapor near him. He had yet to assure himself of its reality, and he knew of no way to go about it. He was frightened, though he could not himself tell why. Within him stirred indistinct fears, and he felt in the air about him a power, as of a strong charge of electrical current released close by. He anticipated something, though he could not say what.

For some minutes nothing whatever happened, and he was just about to make a tentative step forward, when suddenly, in his immediate propinquity, sounded a succession of weird notes, as if from a group of flutes or willow pipes—sounds as of some diabolic *Danse Macabre.* At almost the same instant a brilliant flash of green light came into being before his eyes, and in its midst he saw a curious, swirling outline, suggestive of a face framed in curling black hair, crowned by a pair of odd upright structures, as of horns. From pipes that the weird creature held at its lips came awful music. Mr. Waring was chilled. He felt in some unaccountable manner that this thing before him was not destined for human eyes, and he wondered if he, too, were seen. The greenish light spread and undulated as he watched, and beyond it he could see hundreds of little black figures dancing.

But suddenly Mr. Waring became acutely conscious of the music that the creature was playing on the pipes. From pianissimo it rose sharply to crescendo after crescendo in a succession of piercing notes that came to Mr. Waring as sharp stabs inflicted. For a moment he had no knowledge of what was passing; even while he strove to reassert himself, he felt the music drawing him, and looking around him in his terror, he saw the vague outlines of the trees writhe and twist to the notes. The last thing he saw was a hawthorn bush, whose great white flowers were limned on his consciousness like dead things. Then he felt within him a searching and prodding, as if the strains of that melancholy, weird music had gained entrance to his body, and were now seeking for something to which to ally themselves. And then, finally, a terrific withdrawal. He collapsed, striking his head against the slab as he fell.

Mr. Waring's host found his body at about noon on the following day. He came at the head of an exploring party, organized for the express purpose of discovering Mr. Waring's whereabouts. The archeologist was lying close to the slab, and it was assumed by many that he had slipped and fallen, striking his head on the slab, thus mortally injuring himself. Mr. Waring's host said nothing. He interested himself mainly in the disposal of the body, but he did not fail to note the hundreds of minute hoofprints in evidence on the grass.

Then, too, quite close to the dead man's hand, almost hidden by a clump of grass and an overhanging hawthorn bush, lay a brown, discolored group of willow pipes.

The Devil of the Marsh

H. B. MARRIOTT-WATSON

It was nigh upon dusk when I drew close to the Great Marsh, and already the white vapors were about, riding across the sunken levels like ghosts in a churchyard. Though I had set forth in a mood of wild delight, I had sobered in the lonely ride across the moor and was now uneasily alert. As my horse jerked down the grassy slopes that fell away to the jaws of the swamp I could see thin streams of mist rise slowly, hover like wraiths above the long rushes, and then, turning gradually more material, go blowing heavily away across the flat. The appearance of the place at this desolate hour, so remote from human society and so darkly significant of evil presences, struck me with a certain wonder that she should have chosen this spot for our meeting. She was a familiar of the moors, where I had invariably encountered her; but it was like her arrogant caprice to test my devotion by some such dreary assignation. The wide and horrid prospect depressed me beyond reason, but the fact of her neighborhood drew me on, and my spirits mounted at the thought that at last she was to put me in possession of herself. Tethering my horse upon the verge of the swamp, I soon discovered the path that crossed it, and entering struck out boldly for the heart. The track could have been little used, for the reeds, which stood high above the level of my eyes upon either side, straggled everywhere across in low arches, through which I dodged, and broke my way with some inconvenience and much impatience. A full half-hour I was solitary in that wilderness, and when at last a sound other than my own footsteps broke the silence the dusk had fallen.

I was moving very slowly at the time, with a mind half disposed to turn from the melancholy expedition, which it seemed to me now must surely be a cruel jest she had played upon me. While some such reluctance held me, I was suddenly arrested by a hoarse croaking that broke out upon my left, sounding somewhere from the reeds in the black mire. A little further it came again from close at hand, and when I had passed on a few more steps in wonder and perplexity, I heard it for the third time. I stopped and listened, but the marsh was as a grave, and so taking the noise for the signal of some raucous frog, I resumed my way. But in a little the croaking was repeated, and coming quickly to a stand I pushed the reeds aside and peered into the darkness. I could see nothing, but at the immediate moment of my pause I thought I detected the sound of somebody trailing through the rushes. My distaste for the adventure grew with this suspicion, and had it not been for my delirious infatuation I had assuredly turned back and ridden home. The ghastly sound pursued me at intervals along the track, until at last, irritated beyond endurance by the sense of this persistent and invisible company, I broke into a sort of run. This, it seemed, the creature (whatever it was) could not achieve, for I heard no more of it, and continued my way in peace. My path at length ran out from among the reeds upon the smooth flat of which she had spoken, and here my heart quickened, and the gloom of the dreadful place lifted. The flat lay in the very center of the marsh, and here and there in it a gaunt bush or withered tree rose like a specter against the white mists. At the further end I fancied some kind of building loomed up; but the fog that had been gathering ever since my entrance upon the passage sailed down upon me at that moment and the prospect went out with suddenness. As I stood waiting for the clouds to pass, a voice cried to me out of its center, and I saw her next second with bands of mist swirling about her body, come rushing to me from the darkness. She put her long arms about me, and, drawing her close, I looked into her deep eyes. Far down in them, it seemed to me, I could discern a mystic laughter dancing in the wells of light, and I had that ecstatic sense of nearness to some spirit of fire that was wont to possess me at her contact.

"At last," she said, "at last, my beloved!" I caressed her.

"Why," said I, tingling at the nerves, "why have you put this dolorous journey between us? And what mad freak is your presence in this swamp?" She uttered her silver laugh, and nestled to me again.

"I am the creature of this place," she answered. "This is my home. I have sworn you should behold me in my native sin ere you ravished me away."

"Come, then," said I; "I have seen; let there be an end of this. I know you, what you are. This marsh chokes up my heart. God forbid you should spend more of your days here. Come."

"You are in haste," she cried. "There is yet much to learn. Look, my friend," she said, "you who know me, what I am. This is my prison, and I have inherited its properties. Have you no fear?"

For answer I pulled her to me, and her warm lips drove out the horrid humors of the night; but the swift passage of a flickering mockery over her eyes struck me as a flash of lightning, and I grew chill again.

"I have the marsh in my blood," she whispered: "the marsh and the fog of it. Think ere you vow to me, for I am the cloud in a starry night."

A lithe and lovely creature, palpable of warm flesh, she lifted her magic face to mine and besought me plaintively with these words. The dews of the nightfall hung on her lashes, and seemed to plead with me for her forlorn and solitary plight.

"Behold!" I cried, "witch or devil of the marsh, you shall come with me! I have known you on the moors, a roving apparition of beauty; nothing more I know, nothing more I ask. I care not what this dismal haunt means; not what these strange and mystic eyes. You have powers and senses above me; your sphere and habits are as mysterious and incomprehensible as your beauty. But that," I said, "is mine, and the world that is mine shall be yours also."

She moved her head nearer to me with an antic gesture, and her gleaming eyes glanced up at me with a sudden flash, the similitude (great heavens!) of a hooded snake. Starting, I fell away, but at that moment she turned her face and set it fast toward the fog that came rolling in thick volumes over the flat. Noiselessly the great cloud crept down upon us, and all dazed and troubled I watched her watching it in silence. It was as if she awaited some omen of horror, and I too trembled in the fear of its coming.

Then suddenly out of the night issued the hoarse and hideous croaking I had heard upon my passage. I reached out my arm to take her hand, but in an instant the mists broke over us, and I was groping in the vacancy. Something like panic took hold of me, and, beating through the blind obscurity, I rushed over the flat, calling upon her. In a little the swirl went by, and I perceived her upon the margin of the swamp, her arm raised as in imperious command. I ran to her, but stopped, amazed and shaken by a fearful sight. Low by the dripping reeds crouched a small squat thing, in the likeness of a monstrous frog, coughing and choking in its throat. As I stared, the creature rose upon its legs and disclosed a horrid human resemblance. Its face was white and thin, with long black hair; its body gnarled and twisted as with the ague of a thousand years. Shaking, it whined in a breathless voice, pointing a skeleton finger at the woman by my side.

"Your eyes were my guide," it quavered. "Do you think that after all these years I have no knowledge of your eyes? Lo, is there aught of evil in you I am not instructed in? This is the Hell you designed for me, and now you would leave me to a greater."

The wretch paused, and panting leaned upon a bush, while she stood silent, mocking him with her eyes, and soothing my terror with her soft touch.

"Hear!" he cried, turning to me, hear the tale of this woman that you may know her as she is. She is the Presence of the marshes. Woman or Devil I know not, but only that the accursed marsh has crept into her soul and she herself is become its Evil Spirit; she herself, that lives and grows young and beautiful by it, has its full power to blight and chill and slay. I, who was once as you are, have this knowledge. What bones lie deep in this black swamp who can say but she? She has drained of health, she has drained of mind and of soul; what is between her and her desire that she should not drain also of life? She has made me a devil in her Hell, and now she would leave me to my solitary pain, and go search for another victim. But she shall not!" he screamed through his chattering teeth; "she shall not! My Hell is also hers! She shall not!"

Her smiling untroubled eyes left his face and turned to me; she put out her arms, swaying toward me, and so fervid and so great a light glowed in her face that, as one distraught of superhuman means, I took her into my embrace. And then the madness seized me.

"Woman or devil," I said, "I will go with you! Of what account this pitiful past? Blight me even as that wretch, so be only you are with me."

She laughed, and, disengaging herself, leaned, half-clinging to me, toward the coughing creature by the mire.

"Come," I cried, catching her by the waist. "Come!" She laughed again a silver-ringing laugh. She moved with me slowly across the flat to where the track started for the portals of the marsh. She laughed and clung to me.

But at the edge of the track I was startled by a shrill, hoarse screaming, and behold, from my very feet, that loathsome creature rose up and wound his long black arms about her, shrieking and crying in his pain. Stooping, I pushed him from her skirts, and with one sweep of my arm drew her across the pathway; as her face passed mine her eyes were wide and smiling. Then of a sudden the still mist enveloped us once more; but ere it descended I had a glimpse of that contorted figure trembling on the margin, the white face drawn and full of desolate pain. At the sight an icy shiver ran through me. And then through the yellow gloom the shadow of her darted past me, to the further side. I heard the hoarse cough, the dim noise of a struggle, a swishing sound, a thin cry, and then the sucking of the slime over something in the rushes. I leapt forward; once again the fog thinned, and I beheld her, woman or devil, standing upon the verge, and peering with smiling eyes into the foul and sickly bog. With a sharp cry wrung from my nerveless soul, I turned and fled down the narrow way from that accursed spot; and as I ran the thickening fog closed round me, and I heard far off and lessening still the silver sound of her mocking laughter.

THE DEVILISH RAT

ALBERT PAGE MITCHELL

You know that when a man lives in a deserted castle on the top of a great mountain by the side of the river Rhine, he is liable to misrepresentation. Half the good people of the village of Schwinkenschwank, including the burgomaster and the burgomaster's nephew, believed that I was a fugitive from American justice.

The other half were just as firmly convinced that I was crazy, and this theory had the support of the notary's profound knowledge of human character and acute logic.

The two halves to the interesting controversy were so equally matched that they spent all their time in confronting each other's arguments, and I was left, happily, pretty much to myself.

As everybody with the slightest pretension to cosmopolitan knowledge is already aware, the old Schloss Schwinkenschwank is haunted by the ghosts of twenty-nine medieval barons and baronesses. The behavior of these ancient specters was very considerate. They annoyed me, on the whole, far less than the rats, which swarmed in great numbers in every part of the castle.

When I first took possession of my quarters, I was obliged to keep a lantern burning all night, and continually to beat about me with a wooden club in order to escape the fate of Bishop Hatto. Afterward I sent to Frankfurt and had made for me a wire cage in which I was able to sleep with comfort and safety as soon as I became accustomed to the sharp gritting of the rats' teeth as they gnawed the iron in their impotent attempts to get in and eat me.

Barring the specters and the rats, and now and then a transient bat or owl, I was the first tenant of the Schloss Schwinkenschwank for three or four centuries.

After leaving Bonn, where I had greatly profited by the learned and ingenious lectures of the famous Calcarius, Herr Professor of Metaphysical Science in that admirable university, I had selected this ruin as the best possible place for the trial of a certain experiment in psychology.

The Hereditary Landgraf, von Toplitz, who owned Schloss Schwinkenschwank, showed no signs of surprise when I went to him and offered six thalers a month for the privilege of lodging in his ramshackle castle. The clerk of a hotel could not have taken my application more coolly or my money in a more businesslike spirit.

"It will be necessary to pay the first month's rent in advance," said he.

"That I am fortunately prepared to do, my well-born Hereditary Landgraf," I replied, counting out six thalers. He pocketed them, and gave me a receipt for the same. I wondered whether he ever tried to collect rent from his ghosts.

The most inhabitable room in the castle was that in the northwest tower, but it was already occupied by the Lady Adelaide Maria, eldest daughter of the Baron von Schotten, who was starved to death in the thirteenth century by her affectionate papa for refusing to wed a one-legged freebooter from over the river.

As I could not think of intruding upon a lady, I took up my quarters at the head of the south turret stairway, where there was nobody in possession except a sentimental monk, who was out a good deal nights and gave me no trouble at any time.

In such calm seclusion as I enjoyed in the Schloss it is possible to reduce physical and mental activity to the lowest degree consistent with life. Saint Pedro of Alcantara, who passed forty years in a convent cell, schooled himself to sleep only an hour and a half a day, and to take food but once in three days.

While diminishing the functions of his body to such an extent, he must also, I firmly believe, have reduced his soul almost to the negative character of an unconscious infant's. It is exercise, thought, friction, activity, that brings out the individuality of a man's nature. Prof. Calcarius's pregnant words remained burned into my memory:

"What is the mysterious link that binds soul to the living body? Why am I Calcarius, or rather why does the soul called Calcarius inhabit this particular organism? (Here the learned professor slapped his enormous thigh with his pudgy hand.) Might not I as easily be another, and might not another be I? Loosen the individualized Ego from the fleshy surroundings to which it coheres by force of habit and by reason of long contact, and who shall say that it may not be expelled by an act of volition, leaving the living body receptive, to be occupied by some nonindividualized Ego, worthier and better than the old?"

This profound suggestion made a lasting impression upon my mind. While perfectly satisfied with my body, which is sound, healthy, and reasonably beautiful, I had long been discontented with my soul, and constant contemplation of its weakness, its grossness, its inadequacy, had intensified discontentment to disgust.

Could I but escape myself, could I but tear this paste diamond from its fine casket and replace it with a genuine jewel, what sacrifices would I not consent to, and how fervently would I bless Calcarius and the hour that took me to Bonn!

It was to try this untried experiment that I shut myself up in the Schloss Schwinkenschwank.

Excepting little Hans, the innkeeper's son, who climbed the mountain three times a week from the village to bring me bread and cheese and white wine, and afterward Hans's sister, my only visitor during the period of my retirement was Professor Calcarius. He came over from Bonn twice to cheer and encourage me.

On the occasion of his first visit night fell while we were still talking of Pythagoras and metempsychosis. The profound metaphysicist was a corpulent man and very short-sighted.

"I can never get down the hill alive," he cried, wringing his hands anxiously. "I should stumble, and, Gott im Himmel, precipitate myself peradventure upon some jagged rock."

"You must stay all night, Professor," said I, "and sleep with me in my wire cage. I should like you to meet my roommate, the monk."

"Subjective entirely, my dear young friend," he said. "Your apparition is a creature of the optic nerve and I shall contemplate it without alarm, as becomes a philosopher."

I put my Herr Professor to bed in the wire cage and with extreme difficulty crowded myself in by his side. At his especial request I left the lantern burning. "Not that I have any apprehension of your subjective specters," he explained. "Mere figments of the brain they are. But in the dark I might roll over and crush you."

"How progresses the self-suppression?" he asked at length—"the subordination of the individual soul? Eh! What was that?"

"A rat, trying to get in at us," I replied. "Be calm: you are in no peril. My experiment proceeds satisfactorily. I have quite eliminated all interest in the outside world. Love, gratitude, friendship, care for my own welfare and the welfare of my friends have nearly disappeared. Soon, I hope, memory will also fade away, and with my memory my individual past."

"You are doing splendidly!" he exclaimed with enthusiasm, "and rendering to psychologic science an inestimable service. Soon your psychic nature will be a blank, a vacuum, ready to receive—God preserve me! What was that?"

"Only the screech of an owl," said I, reassuringly, as the great gray bird with which I had become familiar fluttered noisily down through an aperture in the roof and lit upon the top of our wire cage.

Calcarius regarded the owl with interest, and the owl blinked gravely at Calcarius.

"Who knows," said the Herr Professor, "but what that owl is animated by the soul of some great dead philosopher? Perhaps Pythagoras, perhaps Plotinus, perhaps the spirit of Socrates himself, abides temporarily beneath those feathers."

I confessed that some such idea had already occurred to me.

"And in that case," continued the Professor, "you have only to negate your own nature, to nullify your own individuality, in order to receive into your body this great soul, which, as my intuitions tell me, is that of Socrates, and is hovering around your physical organization, hoping to effect an entrance. Persist, my worthy young student, in your most laudable experiment, and metaphysical science—Merciful Heaven! Is that the devil?"

It was the huge gray rat, my nightly visitor. This hideous creature had grown in his life, perhaps of a century, to the size of a small terrier. His whiskers were perfectly white and very thick. His immense tushes had become so long that they curved over till the points almost impaled his skull. His eyes were big and blood red. The corners of his upper lip were so shrivelled and drawn up that his countenance wore an expression of diabolical malignity, rarely seen except in some human faces.

He was too old and knowing to gnaw at the wires; but he sat outside on his haunches, and gazed in at us with an indescribable look of hatred. My companion shivered. After a while the rat turned away, rattled his callous tail across the wire netting, and disappeared in the darkness. Professor Calcarius breathed a deep sigh of relief, and soon was snoring so profoundly that neither owls, rats, nor specters ventured near us till morning.

I had so far succeeded in merging my intellectual and moral qualities in the routine of mere animal existence that when it was time for Calcarius to come again, as he had promised, I felt little interest in his approaching visit. Hansel, who constituted my commissariat, had been taken sick of the measels, and I was dependent for my food and wine upon the coming of his pretty sister Emma, a flaxen-haired maiden of eighteen, who climbed the steep path with the grace and agility of a gazelle.

She was an artless little thing, and told me of her own accord the story of her simple love. Fritz was a soldier in the Emperor Wilhelm's army. He was now in garrison at Cologne. They hoped that he would soon get a lieutenancy, for he was brave and faithful, and then he would come home and marry her.

She had saved up her dairy money till it amounted to quite a little purse, which she had sent him that it might help purchase his commission. Had I ever seen Fritz? No? He was handsome and good, and she loved him more than she could tell.

I listened to this prattle with the same amount of romantic interest that a proposition in Euclid would excite, and congratulated myself that my old soul had so nearly disappeared.

Every night the gray owl perched above me. I knew that Socrates was waiting to take possession of my body, and I yearned to open my bosom and receive that grand soul.

Every night the detestable rat came and peered through the wires. His cool, contemptuous malice exasperated me strangely. I longed to reach out from beneath my cage and seize and throttle him, but I was afraid of the venom of his bite.

My own soul had by this time nearly wasted away through disciplined disuse. The owl looked down lovingly at me with his great placid eyes. A noble spirit seemed to shine through them and to say, "I will come when you are ready." And I would look back into their lustrous depths and exclaim with infinite yearning, "Come soon O Socrates, for I am almost ready!"

Then I would turn and meet the devilish gaze of the monstrous rat, whose sneering malevolence dragged me back to earth and to earth's concerns.

My detestation of the abominable beast was the sole lingering trace of the old nature. When he was not by, my soul seemed to hover around and above my body, ready to take wing and leave it free forever. At his appearance, an unconquerable disgust and loathing undid in a second all that had been accomplished, and I was still myself. To succeed in my experiment I felt that the hateful creature whose presence barred out the grand old philosopher's soul must be dispatched at any cost of sacrifice or danger.

"I will kill you, you loathsome animal!" I shouted to the rat, "and then to my emancipated body will come the soul of Socrates which awaits me yonder."

The rat turned on me his leering eyes and grinned more sardonically than ever. His scorn was more than I could bear. I threw up the side of the wire cage and clutched desperately at my enemy.

I caught him by the tail. I drew him close to me. I crunched the bones of his slimy legs, felt blindly for his head, and when I got both hands to his neck, fastened upon his life with a terrible grip.

With all the strength at my command, and with all the recklessness of a desperate purpose, I tore and twisted the flesh of my loathsome victim. He gasped, uttered a horrible cry of wild pain, and at last lay limp and quiet in my clutch. Hate was satisfied, my last passion was at an end, and I was free to welcome Socrates.

When I awoke from a long and dreamless sleep, the events of the night before and, indeed, of my whole previous life were as the dimly remembered incidents in a story read years ago.

The owl was gone but the mangled corpse of the rat lay by my side. Even in death his face wore its horrible grin. It now looked like a Satanic smile of triumph.

I arose and shook off my drowsiness. A new life seemed to tingle in my veins. I was no longer indifferent and negative. I took a lively interest in my surroundings and wanted to be out in the world among men, to plunge into affairs and exult in action.

Pretty Emma came up the hill bringing her basket. "I am going to leave you," said I. "I shall seek better quarters than the Schloss Schwinkenschwank."

"And shall you go to Cologne," she eagerly asked; "to the garrison where the emperor's soldiers are?"

"Perhaps so—on my way to the world."

"And will you go for me to Fritz?" she continued, blushing. "I have good news to send him. His uncle, the mean old notary, died last night. Fritz now has a small fortune and he must come home to me at once."

"The notary," said I slowly, "died last night?"

"Yes sir; and they say he is black in the face this morning. But it is good news for Fritz and me."

"Perhaps," continued I, still more slowly—"perhaps Fritz would not believe me. I am a stranger, and men who know the world, like your young soldier, are given to suspicion."

"Carry this ring," she quickly replied, taking from her finger a worthless trinket. "Fritz gave it to me and he will know by it that I trust you."

My next visitor was the learned Calcarius. He was quite out of breath when he reached the apartment I was preparing to leave.

"How goes our metempsychosis, my worthy pupil?" he asked. "I arrived last evening from Bonn, but rather than spend another night with your horrible rodents, I submitted my purse to the extortion of the village innkeeper. The rogue swindled me," he continued taking out his purse and counting over a small treasure of silver. "He charged me forty groschen for a bed and breakfast."

The sight of the silver, and the sweet clink of the pieces as they came in contact in Professor Calcarius's palm, thrilled my new soul with an emotion it had not yet experienced.

Silver seemed the brightest thing in the world to me at that moment, and the acquisition of silver, by whatever means, the noblest exercise of human energy. With a sudden impulse that I was unable to resist, I sprang upon my friend and instructor and wrenched the purse from his hands. He uttered a cry of surprise and dismay.

"Cry away!" I shouted; "it will do no good. Your miserly screams will be heard only by rats and owls and ghosts. The money is mine."

"What's this?" he exclaimed. "You rob your guest, your friend, your guide and mentor in the sublime walks of metaphysical science? What perfidy has taken possession of your soul?"

I seized the Herr Professor by the legs and threw him violently to the floor. He struggled as the gray rat had struggled. I tore pieces of wire from my cage, and bound him hand and foot so tightly that the wire cut deep into his fat flesh.

"Ho! Ho!" said I, standing over him; "what a feast for the rats your corpulent carcass will make," and I turned to go.

"Good Gott!" he cried. "You do not intend to leave me. No one ever comes here."

"All the better," I replied, gritting my teeth and shaking my fist in his face; "the rats will have uninterrupted opportunity to relieve you of your superfluous flesh. Oh, they are very hungry, I assure you, Herr Metaphysician, and they will speedily help you to sever the mysterious link that binds soul to living body. They will know how to loosen the individualized Ego from the fleshly surroundings. I congratulate you on the prospect of a rare experiment."

The cries of Professor Calcarius grew fainter and fainter as I made my way down the hill. Once out of hearing I stopped to count my gains. Over and over again, with extraordinary joy, I counted the thalers in his purse, and always with the same result. There were just thirty pieces of silver.

My way into the world of barter and profit led me through Cologne. At the barracks I sought out Fritz Schneider of Schwinkenschwank.

"My friend," said I, putting my hand upon his shoulder, "I am going to do you the greatest service which one man may do another. You love little Emma the innkeeper's daughter?"

"I do indeed," he said. "You bring news of her?"

"I have just now torn myself away from her too ardent embrace."

"It is a lie!" he shouted. "The little girl is as true as gold."

"She is as false as the metal in this trinket," said I with composure, tossing him Emma's ring. "She gave it to me yesterday when we parted."

He looked at the ring, and then put both hands to his forehead. "It is true," he groaned. "Our bethrothal ring!" I watched his anguish with philosophical interest.

"See here," he continued, taking a neatly knitted purse from his bosom. "Here is the money she sent to help me buy promotion. Perhaps that belongs to you?"

"Quite likely," I replied, very cooly. "The pieces have a strangely familiar look."

Without another word the soldier flung the purse at my feet and turned away. I heard him sobbing, and the sound was music. Then I picked up the purse and hastened to the nearest cafe to count the silver.

There were just thirty pieces again.

To acquire silver, that is the chief joy possible to my new nature. It is a glorious pleasure, is it not? How fortunate that the soul, which took possession of my body in the Schloss, was not Socrates's, which would have made me, at best, a dismal ruminator like Calcarius; but the soul that had dwelt in the gray rat till I strangled him.

At one time I thought that my new soul came to me from the dead notary in the village. I know, now, that I inherited it from the rat, and I believe it to be the soul that once animated Judas Iscariot, that prince of men of action.

Dog, Cat, and Baby

JOE R. LANSDALE

When my son, Keith, was born, we had a dog and a cat. Both fine critters, but there was a certain jealousy in the air when we brought Keith home. Up until that time, the pets had ruled the roost. This made me nervous. I had heard horrible stories and read horrible newspaper accounts of babies being killed by jealous pets.

The pets and the baby were never left alone, no matter how innocent they seemed. Fear of what might happen if they were left alone fostered this story.

For John Maclay

Dog did not like Baby. For that matter, Dog did not like Cat. But Cat had claws—sharp claws.

Dog had always gotten attention. Pat on head. "Here, boy, here's a treat. Nice dog. Good dog. Shake hands. Speak! Sit. Nice dog."

Now there was Baby.

Cat had not been problem, really.

Cat was liked, not loved by family. They petted Cat sometimes. Fed her. Did not mistreat her. But they not love her. Not way they loved Dog—before Baby.

Damn little pink thing that cried.

Baby got "Oooohs and Ahhhs." When Dog tried to get close to Masters, they say, "Get back, boy. Not *now*."

When would be *now?*

Dog never see now. Always Baby get now. Dog get nothing. Sometimes they so busy with Baby it be all day before Dog get fed. Dog never get treats anymore. Could not remember last pat on head or "Good Dog!"

Bad business. Dog not like it.

Dog decide to do something about it.

Kill Baby. Then there be Dog, Cat again. They not love Cat, so things be okay.

Dog thought that over. Wouldn't take much to rip little Baby apart. Baby soft, pink. Would bleed easy.

Baby often put in Jumper that hung between doorway when Master Lady hung wash. Baby be easy to get then.

So Dog waited.

One day Baby put in Jumper and Master Lady go outside to hang wash. Dog looks at pink thing jumping, thinks about ripping to pieces. Thinks on it long and hard. Thought makes him so happy his mouth drips water. Dog starts toward Baby, making fine moment last.

Baby looks up, sees Dog coming toward it slowly, almost creeping. Baby starts to cry.

But before Dog can reach Baby, Cat jumps.

Cat been hiding behind couch.

Cat goes after Dog, tears Dog's face with teeth, with claws. Dog bleeds, tries to run. Cat goes after him.

Dog turns to bite.

Cat hangs claw in Dog's eye.

Dog yelps, runs.

Cat jumps on Dog's back, biting Dog on top of head.

Dog tries to turn corner into bedroom. Cat, tearing at him with claws, biting with teeth, makes Dog lose balance. Dog running very fast, fast as he can go, hits the edge of doorway, stumbles back, falls over.

Cat gets off Dog.

Dog lies still.

Dog not breathing.

Cat knows Dog is dead. Cat licks blood from claws, from teeth with rough tongue.

Cat has gotten rid of Dog.

Cat turns to look down hall where Baby is screaming.

Now for *other* one.

Cat begins to creep down hall.

Dummy

SIMON MacCULLOCH

"Hi, I'm Fred, this is Ed. Say 'hi,' Ed."

"Fuck off."

(Christ, that *still* gets them. Every time. Talk about a cheap laugh.)

"Ed, that won't do. I'm telling you, you mind your manners or I'm trading you in for Sooty and Sweep."

(Actually, old son, I do believe it's time for a trade-in anyway. This routine's as lame as a double amputee.)

"All right, sulk then. I'll just go ahead and do the show without you."

(Now *there's* an idea . . .)

"Actually, ladies and gentlemen, I'd been hoping for a chance to tell you about what happened to me the other day when I . . . Ed, what are you *doing* with that?"

Etcetera. You get the picture. The set had all the sparkling originality of beans on toast. The Foul-Mouthed Schoolboy bit—I was well sick of it by the start of last season and I'll bet my dumb partner would've been too if he'd had a brain. Three years of flogging the same dead jokes round the same dead-end circuit's enough to tell anyone it's time for a change.

So why haven't I done something about it? Inertia, I suppose. It's hard to break the mold your life's been poured into even when you hate it. And to be honest, I don't hate performing, however stale the act gets—it's all I really know. As long as there are engagements to fill, I'll grit my teeth and go on with whatever I've got. Yeah, a regular bloody trouper, me.

The thing is, I know I can do better than Mr. Fuck Off. Last night I plucked up the courage to tell him. The final crappy show of the season had just ended, and he was propped up in front of the "dressing room" (hah!) mirror with his reflection staring smugly back at him—"I'm okay." "You're okay," that all's-well-in-my-little-world look of cretinous complacency that he always has. "Don't know what you've got to look pleased about. You and me, we're through, get it? No, not through for tonight, not through for the year—through for good. No more 'mind your manners.' You. Are. Redundant. Follow me?"

Of course he ignored me. He just sat there, his round shiny face glowing with self-satisfaction in the light of the bare overhead bulb. If the cleaner hadn't come by right then to toss us both out, I swear I'd've belted the little bastard one.

But it was different later. We share a mobile home, just him and me since the missus packed her bags, right bloody cosy. It's set a bit back from the main site, and that's a fair step off the road, about five minutes drive out of town. It gets quiet and lonely here at night, and the gigs never finish before eleven. I'd cooled off by the time I stood looking down at him in the after-midnight darkness—electric light not being a feature chez nous. And suddenly getting rid of him seemed to be a bigger deal than I'd thought. His eyes were closed—he's fitted with moveable eyelids that shut automatically when he's on his back—and just then I didn't want them to snap open in case there'd be something in them I hadn't seen before.

Of course, that sounds as goddamn stupid to me now, in daylight, as it does to you. So, first thing this morning, I got up and slung my ex-partner out with the garbage, right?

Wrong, as you probably guessed. I wouldn't be bothering to tell you this if it had been that simple, would I? For a start, after mellowing out a bit on the subject I'm beginning to wonder how vital it really is to dispose of my good friend just so I can make a fresh start next season. I could always go out, find a replacement, and forget about him.

Yeah, but would he let me? I mean, when you've relied on the same prop in front of an audience for years, it's hard to let go. The laughs *are* still there for Fuck Off Etcetera—and a mindless knee-jerk laugh is better than nothing. Something tells me that as long as I let him hang around like a jealous ex, there'll be the danger that I'll end up back with him. If I don't make a clean break of it. . . .

Who am I kidding? The truth is, leaving out the practicalities, dumping him like a worn-out shoe isn't enough—I want to *destroy* him. Those smooth chubby cheeks already look like they're bulging to hold in the spew of rancid jokes he's expecting to regurgitate at my audiences again next summer. His too-wet-looking lips make me nauseous—they're like plump worms, and when we're on stage I'd swear they wriggle. He's just

140

somehow horribly—*soft*, softer than he ought to be, like his wood's gone spongy. And he's the soft spot in my career where I let myself wallow in the easy laughs and the applause of morons, until I'm too flabby-minded to try for anything better. I look at him and see myself rotting, and feebly enjoying it.

That's it. He's a rotten limb, and it's time to lop him off. What then? Obvious. Whatever stopped me going through with it last night was a bloody godsend—it's made sure that I'll do the job right. And I'll do it next month—on Bonfire Night.

Two weeks to go. Am I impatient? Three years of creative constipation almost over—what do you think? Sure, I could go ahead with it now, and to hell with ceremony. There's the neighbors, of course—they're not near enough to pay any attention normally, but an early bonfire might draw a few of them—and this is one event I know will be best savored alone. Anyway, the night's right—Mr. Fawkes was a pathetic failure too.

So how is the lucky Guy? Nice of you to ask. You probably know how it is when you've put up with someone's little faults and foibles at close quarters for a good old while, then finally realized you won't have to put up with them for much longer. It seems a shame to spoil your good behavior record when you're about to be paroled, so you strain to keep the sick grin on your face for them just a few days more. Meanwhile, every little wart and pimple of their personality swells up like gangrene until you can't get the stink out of your nostrils.

There's the feeling he's always listening for my slightest move. I tell myself it's only a kink in his neck that makes his head tilt slightly to one side all the time, like he's cocking an ear for me. But when I move around the shadowy clutter of the caravan in the night, skirting the corner he lies in, I see the head twitch a tiny fraction further. I stop. I wait for the eyes to open.

When they don't, I go on with whatever I'm doing, more quietly. Thinking that maybe the self-congratulatory little smile that I hate when I see it and hate more when I can't might be putting a tiny dimple in a rosy baby cheek, in the knowledge of another point scored in a petty game.

Silly me. But then there's his hands. They don't match his face. They're not to scale—too big; the color's wrong—too white. They were obviously made for a different model altogether, and they hang low out of his sleeves like they're trying to detach themselves. Then what do they think they'll do—flop off into the night to look for their true owner?

I can't wait to watch those stupid big hands burn.

One week left. I'm at the stage now where I can almost enjoy the agony of waiting. I've gotten so used to the pleasure of roasting my old friend in my imagination that I'll almost regret giving up the fantasies for the reality. Almost.

Ah, but there are questions that only the real thing can answer. How long will it take? Which parts of him will go quickest? Will he smell as bad as my opinion of him says he should?

Unlikely—nothing could reek like that. My loathing's hung pretty thick around our little home this past week, I can tell you. He pretends to ignore it. *I* pretend he can see every detail of the movie playing in my head, hear every delicious snap, crackle, and pop of its soundtrack.

That's only my little daydream, though. I couldn't really wish for the creep to know what's in store for him. I want surprise on my side when it comes to the crunch. Well, I don't know what he's capable of when the chips are really down. You can't guess what anyone or anything will do when it becomes a matter of survival, can you? All bets are off in that situation—you shouldn't rely on the normal rules applying.

Actually, I'm not sure if they still apply now. All right, I'm getting flaky. In the circumstances, you won't convince me I shouldn't worry about noises I can't account for in the small hours. You don't have to tell me how idiotic it is to stand looking at his hands as dawn breaks, waiting for them to let slip what he's up to, until my staring makes them jitter if nothing else does. I know I sound totally paranoid, and yet . . .

Maybe he's planning a surprise for me too. In that case, may the best man win.

I can taste that smoke already. Yum!

Red. That's what I'll remember from that November 5. That was the color of the last firework of the night, the one rocket some jerk had found buried under the wrappings when everything else had been blown to glory and it was time to clear up.

It must have been about midnight. I was in the caravan, gazing happily at my victim-to-be, relishing the last few moments of his ignorance before I made my move. I'd been at work since dark in the empty field out back, building the bonfire quietly and quickly. Thinking all the time that perhaps he'd notice I was gone and come creeping out like a shadow I'd somehow managed to leave behind for a while, eager to attach itself to me again.

Well, he didn't, of course, and if he'd been planning to turn the tables on me I reckoned he'd left it too late by the time I was standing over him with the paraffin can.

Then the rocket whooshed and banged, rattling the windows, lighting the place up like a goddamn ghost train ride and pasting a great thick smear of bloody light right across his eyelids.

Which snapped open. I froze, and for a moment we could only stare blankly at each other. I almost lost my nerve, but I forced myself to stand my ground, and I'd swear I saw something come into his eyes, something that wasn't the hatred and menace I'd been expecting. It was fear, I realized triumphantly, and disbelief—the feeble-minded jerk couldn't believe I was really doing this, actually going through with what I'd threatened.

That's probably why he didn't struggle. Maybe he was still telling himself he was dreaming as I tied him up into a neat, easily combustible bundle with garden twine. All he did was gawk, those dumb baby-blues of his bugging out at me like painted ping-pong balls.

Goggle all you like now, me old mate, I thought. The cards are on the table, and I've got the winning hand.

His mouth fell open. Oh no you don't. I grabbed a sock to stuff in it and a T-shirt to complete the gag. Couldn't have him squawking away in that oh-so-familiar grating little-boy voice as I took him outside. The neighbors might wonder.

That was when the bastard bit me. His jaws weren't strong enough to injure me, but I lost my temper. As soon as I'd knotted the T-shirt behind his head, I gave him a few good bashes with the paraffin can. His eyes fell shut again.

He stayed limp as I got him outside and, looking over my shoulder for snooping neighbors this time, planted him on the bonfire. I'd stuck a long garden rake firmly in the ground in the middle of the pyre, to tie him to. It added a nice touch of history to the procedure, and made sure he stayed upright where I could see him. I certainly didn't fancy having to drag him back on to the blaze again if he rolled off half-done.

Now came the bit I'd been looking forward to for weeks. His last show. The audience was smaller than usual, but I was willing to bet it'd be the most appreciative he'd ever had.

His eyes opened again as I splashed the paraffin over him. So much the better. It was far too late now for him to do anything, as I fumbled the match out of its box, struck it, flicked it at him, and danced back into the dark to watch the fun.

He burned well. Better than I'd imagined, thinking of rotten wood, though the smell was worse. I think he twitched and wriggled quite a while. The smoke and shadows, I suppose. If he made any sounds they didn't get past the gag, and by the time that had disintegrated I reckon whatever he could've used to make sounds with had too.

It's still dark now, but the fire has finally died. I've been poking carefully through the ashes—they're still hot—to see what's left. At dawn I'll dig a hole for the bits and pieces the flames didn't gobble. I'll skip the prayers by the graveside.

Among the cinders I found a glowing red eye. It's cooled enough now for me to work out what it is. It's a sign for me. A little beacon in the night, telling me what I should do now that I'm free at last. No, I won't be going back to the stage after all. I've realized there are better things than that—things that make a difference in the world. Things I never knew I had the power to do before.

So tonight's not really the end—it's the beginning. I'll be taking the only part of Our Dear Departed that survived his incineration in one piece with me on my new adventure, to remind me that his elimination must be the first of many. Because the job won't be finished until I've dealt with those others, and one other in particular, whose kinship with him makes them my enemies, threats to my newly won independence that I can't afford to ignore.

Yeah, it'll be the perfect celebration of my victory over poor old useless Fred, and a symbol of the long revenge to come on all his loud-mouthed meat-soft "master" race for the slavery they keep my kind in from the moment they carve us out of the quiet wood in their own hateful image—to wear his wedding ring as I bury him, and as I hunt down his wife.

THE DUMP

JOE R. LANSDALE

I have a soft spot in my heart—or maybe it's my head—for this one, though I hated it when I wrote it. It's a simple little Fred Brown/Robert Bloch sort of story, and it was the result of a popcorn dream, as well as the fact that I was listening to a lot of old radio shows my friend Jeff Banks had lent to me.

About the popcorn dreams. The nuttiness in many of my stories, especially stories of this period, was the result of popcorn. I avoid the stuff most of the time, but when the urge hits, or when the bank account looks low, my wife makes up a huge batch. Her popcorn is the only popcorn that does it to me. She has her own special method of popping it up, and I tend to overeat. I go to bed. I have weird dreams. I get up and write the dreams and sell them. So far, every popcorn dream I've written down—a few were just too nonsensical—has sold. I guess it could be said I owe my career to my wife and her popcorn.

Radio shows. Bloch. Brown. Popcorn dreams. It all came together. I woke up in the middle of the night and wrote this story down. (I seldom do any writing in the middle of the night by the way, but then I was working full time and wrote when I could manage it.) When I finished, I thought it was, to put it mildly, dumb. I didn't even make a copy. I folded it immediately, put it in an envelope so I wouldn't change my mind, went back to bed, and next day mailed it off to the then new ROD SERLING'S TWILIGHT ZONE MAGAZINE, a magazine I badly wanted to appear in.

More I thought about the story, dumber I felt. Boy was I an idiot, and I didn't even have a copy of the story to look over and see how big an idiot I was.

Couple of days later, one night actually, Ted Klein, then editor of TWILIGHT ZONE MAGAZINE, phoned to say he loved it and wanted to buy it for the magazine. Later it appeared in BEST OF THE TWILIGHT ZONE, a magazine anthology. I suddenly began to like it better.

For Ted Klein

Me, I like it here just fine. Don't see no call for me to move on. Dump's been my home nigh on twenty years, and I don't think no high-falutin' city sanitation law should make me have to pack up and move on. If I'm gonna work here, I ought to be able to live here.

Me and Otto . . . where is that sucker anyway? I let him wander about some on Sundays. Rest of the time I keep him chained inside the hut there, out of sight. Wouldn't want him bitin' folks.

Well, as I was sayin', the dump's my home. Best damn home I ever had. I'm not a college man, but I got some education. I read a lot. Ought to look inside that shack and see my bookshelves. I may be a dump-yard supervisor, but I'm no fool.

Besides, there's more to this dump than meets the eye.

'Scuse me. Otto! Otto. Here, boy. Dadbum his hide, he's gotten bad about not comin' when I call.

Now, I was sayin' about the dump. There's more here than meets the eye. You ever thought about all that garbage, boy? They bring anything and everything here, and I doze her under. There's animal bodies— that's one of the things that interests old Otto—paint cans, all manner of chemical containers, lumber, straw, brush, you name it. I doze all that stuff under and it heats up. Why, if you could put a thermometer under that earth, check the heat that stuff puts out while it's breakin' down and turnin' to compost, it would be up *there*, boy, way up *there*. Sometimes over a hundred degrees. I've plowed that stuff open and seen the steam flow out of there like a cloud. Could feel the heat of it. It was like bein' in one of them fancy baths. Saunas, they call 'em. Hot, boy, real hot.

Now you think about it. All that heat. All those chemicals and dead bodies and such. Makes an awful mess, a weird blend of nature's refuse. Real weird. And with all that incubatin' heat. Well, you consider it.

I'll tell you somethin' I ain't told nobody else. Somethin' that happened to me a couple years ago.

One night me and Pearly, that was a friend of mine, and we called him that on account of he had the whitest teeth you ever seen. Darn things looked *painted* they were so white. . . . Let's see, now where was I? Oh, yeah, yeah, me and Pearly. Well, we were sittin' around out here one night shootin' the breeze, you know, sharin' a pint. Pearly, he used to come around from time to time and we'd always split a bottle. He used to be a legit, old-time hobo. Rode the rails all over this country. Why, I reckon he was goin' on seventy years if not better, but he acted twenty years younger.

He'd come around and we'd talk and sit and snort and roll us some of that Prince Albert, which we'd smoke. We had some good laughs, we did, and I miss old Pearly sometimes.

So that night we let the bottle leak out pretty good, and Pearly, he's tellin' me about this time down in Texas in a boxcar with a river trash whore, and he stops in midsentence, right at the good part, and says: "You hear that?"

I said, "I don't hear nothin'. Go on with your story."

He nodded and told the tale, and I laughed, and he laughed. He could laugh better at his own stories and jokes than anyone I'd ever seen.

After a bit Pearly gets up and walks out beyond the firelight to relieve himself, you know. And he comes back right quick, zippin' his fly, and walkin' as fast as them old stiff legs of his will take him.

"There's somethin' out there," he says.

"Sure," I say. "Armadillos, coons, possums, maybe a stray dog."

"No," he says. "Something else."

"Awww."

"I been a lot of places, boy," he says—he always called me boy on account of I was twenty years younger than he was—"and I'm used to hearin' critters walk about. That don't sound like no damn possum or stray dog to me. Somethin' bigger."

I start to tell him that he's full of it, you know—and then I hear it too. And a stench like you wouldn't believe floats into camp here. A stench like a grave opened on a decomposin' body, one full of maggots and the smell of earth and death. It was so strong I got a little sick, what with all the rotgut in me.

Pearly says, "You hear it?"

And I did. It was the sound of somethin' heavy, crunchin' down that garbage out there, movin' closer and closer to the camp, like it was afeared of the fire, you know.

I got the heebie-jeebies, and I went into the hut there and got my double-barrel. When I came out Pearly had pulled a little old thirty-two Colt out of his waistband and a brand from the fire, and he was headin' out there in the dark.

"Wait a minute," I called.

"You just stay put, boy. I'll see to this, and I'll see that whatever it is gets a hole in it. Maybe six."

So I waited. The wind picked up and that horrible stench drifted in again, very strong this time. Strong enough so I puked up that hooch I'd drunk. And then suddenly from the dark, while I'm leanin' over throwin' my guts out on the ground, I hear a shot. Another one. Another.

I got up and started callin' for Pearly.

"Stay the hell where you are," he called. "I'm comin' back." Another shot, and then Pearly seemed to fold out of the darkness and come into the light of the fire.

"What is it, Pearly?" I said. "What is it?"

Pearly's face was as white as his teeth. He shook his head. "Ain't never seen nothin' like it. . . . Listen, boy, we got to get the hell out of Dodge. That sucker, it's—" He let his voice trail off, and he looked toward the darkness beyond the firelight.

"Come on, Pearly, what is it?"

"I tell you, I don't know. I couldn't see real good with that there firebrand, and it went out before too long. I heard it down there crunchin' around, over there by that big hill of garbage."

I nodded. That was a pile I'd had heaped up with dirt for a long time. I intended to break it open next time I dozed, push some new stuff in with it.

"It—it was comin' out of that pile," Pearly said. "It was wrigglin' like a great gray worm, but . . . there were legs all over it. Fuzzy legs. And the body—it was jellylike. Lumber, fence wire, and all manner of crap was stickin' out of it, stickin' out of it like it belonged there, just as natural as a shell on a turtle's back or the whiskers on a cougar's face. It had a mouth, a big mouth, like a railway tunnel, and what looked like teeth. But the brand went out then. I fired some shots. It was still wrigglin' out of that garbage heap. It was too dark to stay there—"

He cut in midsentence. The smell was strong now, solid as a wall of bricks.

"It's movin' into camp," I said.

"Must've come from all that garbage," Pearly said. "Must've been born in all that heat and slime."

"Or come up from the center of the earth," I said, though I figured Pearly was a mite near closer to right.

Pearly put some fresh loads in his revolver. "This is all I got," he said.

"I want to see it eat buckshot," I said.

Then we heard it. Very loud, crunchin' down those mounds of garbage like they was peanut hulls. And then there was silence.

Pearly, he moved back a few steps from the double-barrel toward the shack. I aimed the double-barrel toward the dark.

Silence went on for a while. Why, you could've heard yourself blink. But I wasn't blinkin'. I was a watchin' out for that critter.

Then I heard it—but it was behind me! I turned just in time to see a fuzzy tentacle slither out from behind the shack and grab old Pearly. He screamed, and the gun fell out of his hand. And from the shadows a head showed. A huge, wormlike head with slitted eyes and a mouth large enough to swallow a man. Which is what it did. Pearly didn't make that thing two gulps. Wasn't nothin' left of him but a scrap of flesh hangin' on the thing's teeth.

I emptied a load of buckshot in it, slammed the gun open and loaded her again. By that time it was gone. I could hear it crashin' off in the dark.

I got the keys to the dozer and walked around back of the shack on tiptoe. It didn't come out of the dark after me. I cranked the dozer, turned on the spotlights, and went out there after it.

It didn't take long to find it. It was movin' across the dump like a snake, slitherin' and a-loopin' as fast as it could go—which wasn't too fast right then. It had a lump in its belly, an undigested lump. Poor old Pearly!

I ran it down, pinned it to the chain-link fence on the far side of the dump, and used my dozer blade to mash it up against it. I was just fixin' to gun the motor and cut that sucker's head off when I changed my mind.

Its head was stickin' up over the blade, those slitted eyes lookin' at me . . . and there, buried in that wormlike face, was the face of a puppy. You get a lot of them here. Well, it was alive now. Head was still mashed in like it was the first time I saw it, but it was movin'. The head was wrigglin' right there in the center of that worm's head.

I took a chance and backed off from that thing. It dropped to the ground and didn't move. I flashed the lights over it.

Pearly was seepin' out of that thing. I don't know how else to describe it, but he seemed to be driftin' out of that jellylike hide; and when his face and body were halfway out of it, he stopped movin' and just hung there. I realized somethin' then. It was not only created by the garbage and the heat—it lived off of it, and whatever became its food became a part of it. That puppy and old Pearly were now a part of it.

Now don't misunderstand me. Pearly, he didn't know nothin' about it. He was alive, in a fashion, he moved and squirmed, but like that puppy, he no longer thought. He was just a hair on that thing's body. Same as the lumber and wire and such that stuck out of it.

And the beast—well, it wasn't too hard to tame. I named it Otto. It ain't no trouble at all. Gettin' so it don't come when I call, but that's on account of I ain't had nothin' to reward it with, until you showed up. Before that, I had to kind of help it root dead critters out of the heaps. . . . Sit down! I've got Pearly's thirty-two here, and if you move I'll plug you.

Oh, here comes Otto now.

THE EDGE OF THE SHADOW

R. ERNEST DUPUY

That you should believe this would be remarkable. I have no explanation. Limited knowledge I have, and hearsay for the rest. The hearsay at first I did not believe. But when the man who lifted the curtain had gone West—and he was a hard-headed soldier man—I wondered. For his going, when one takes everything into consideration, fitted in. And to that, at least, I can bear witness.

We were lying in our dugout at Romagne, waiting for zero hour. Outside, Fritz's counter preparation was messing things up considerably. Through an instant's lull came the long-drawn howl of a dog—if it was a dog. And something scratched and slithered against the sturdy logs of our shelter. A spray of shrapnel, perhaps.

"It's calling me," was all that he said.

I can still see his face and the quizzical lift of his eyebrows in the glare of our gasoline lantern—we were motorized artillery and did things in style. And as I returned his stare, his yarn, forgotten for two years, came back.

He had to go out a few minutes later to check up data at the guns, and when we found him in the dawning a splinter—or something—had ripped away his throat. Nothing else. But even now, when a dog gives dismal tongue in the quiet of the night, I feel my hackles rise and the ice creep up my backbone, and I wonder.

It was a book that had made him open up to me in the first place—a book called *Dracula*. Ever read it? No? Well, sometime when you want a good crawly chill, look it over. He noticed it on the shelf one night when he had dropped in at my quarters for a chat, some time before we went into the war. And he asked me what I thought of it. He didn't pay much attention to my opinion, I guess, but sat there sucking his pipe and nodding while I talked. And then he said:

"I've scraped against the edge of that stuff. Just the edge. It's not so good."

Now, he wasn't at all the type of man that one would link up with that sort of yarn. And for that reason it made all the more impression on me. He didn't attempt any explanation either; just told it as it struck him. And do not get the idea that he was boasting of his conquest. I didn't know the girl, never would know her. And we had been friends too long for him to fear that I might blab. His thoughts had just come to a boil, I imagine, looking at the book and bringing back the thing, so he had to get it out of his system.

It seems that he had met her in a casual way, but first glance had been like fire to tow. Headlong they went into it, with open eyes, a well-matched pair. She must have been a wonder. A Russian, with all the Slavic grasp of the *ars amandi*, one moment all fire and passion, the next an iceberg. A thoroughbred, too. "Gone wrong," if you will, but always a thoroughbred. And he—was my friend. Not that he elaborated on their adventure. I simply filled in, in my mind's eye, the brief, bold outline he blocked out.

The climax came one night when they were riding. They had had several nocturnal prowls on horseback, I gathered; brief intervals of dalliance. This night they took a trail that was new to both. Imagine them jogging side by side, the August moon rising over the treetops, throwing the masses of foliage into deep relief; great blocks of velvet blackness against the cloudless sky. About them fields shining silver in the moonlight.

The shadows swallowed them up as the trail twisted into the woods, the man leading, his white-shirted back gleaming vaguely to the woman following close, the horses picking their way up hill and down. Through brush and trees the trail ran, now sloping upward on hillsides whose inky depths defied the faint moonlight; now plunged in woodland pockets. I could feel the gloom that closed them in, as he talked; a tangible thing seemingly, ever surrounding, yet ever giving way before their advance until at last they broke through to a moonlit plateau and cantered together over the swelling ridges to draw rein on the very crest of the cliff.

Below them the lowlands spread in tawny languor till they touched the silver-flashing edge of the moon-swept sea on the horizon; behind them the swale of plateau ran clear to the curtain of the woods.

And then, he said, they decided to explore farther. Again they entered the woods—this time a clump of trees guarded by a fringe of stunted, desolate-looking deadwood. And somehow the air felt different. There was a chill and dankness about it he had not noticed in the other woods. The girl shivered. Up a slight incline and then into the open again and on their right a dark mass—the gloomy pile of a deserted house, its empty windows black leering dead eyes, the moonlight heaping fantastic shadows about its front and through the ruins of what had once been a noble porte cochère. A bit of broken pane in one of the lower windows flickered eerily in the moon rays. The girl brought her animal close to his, her eyes shielded with one hand as she passed the house with averted head.

"What's the matter, dear?" he joked. "Afraid that you will see the goblins holding carnival inside?"

But she only cowered closer in the saddle. And that was so odd, so different from her usual bold demeanor that it chilled him. And then something, vague, unformed, brushed between them. He felt it touch his boot, he said.

The girl screamed, the horses plunged, and she wheeled her beast, crowding the man into the brush as she spurred past him. He followed, only to see her throw her horse once more upon its haunches as she turned again, squarely in front of the house. And the thought passed through his mind of the house as a finite being, an unclean object squatting there inside its circle of blasted trees.

He rode up beside her as she sat, with staring eyes and heaving breasts. And to his question she answered simply.

"It is the end," she said.

And then her mood changed and her lips sought his and covered them with voluptuous kisses.

"Dismount," she whispered. I could see the perspiration gather on his forehead as he told this part, although his voice never changed.

"Dismount," she coaxed again, and her lips caressed his throat. Her arms were about him now as they pressed closely, the horses jammed against one another.

"We are going in there together, dear boy," and the white teeth touched his flesh. And through him passed a wave of pure terror.

"I'm damned if we are!" he snapped, and tearing himself loose, snatched at her bridle and urged the horses into a gallop. He didn't remember how they got out, he said. The horses must have found the way. All he remembered was a rush through the restraining underbrush, the girl sobbing as they went, until at last they broke through to the high road and sanity.

That night she told him her story. Told him, with his arms about her; and he quivered now and then at the telling, and once, as a dog howled somewhere in the distance, he pushed her from him for a moment. She understood and laughed, though the tears were close beneath.

She was twelve, she said, when the Terror first came to her. In her home on the Dniester, almost in the shadow of the Carpathians—a feudal hold whose foundations went back to time immemorial, one wing was forbidden territory. Blocked off from the rest of the old castle it was, with its own tiny court, the only entrance a door giving from the east tower to the courtyard. The gatekeeper, old Portal, was the only human she had ever seen go through its entrance.

Playing with her jacks one afternoon she found the courtyard door open, and with the curiosity of a child overcoming the strict injunction, had slipped in.

It was late and the rays of the setting sun were striking the massive tower door. Sitting on the lintel she idly threw the jackstones against the oak. Deeper the shadows grew except for one bright spot, at the height of a man's head, where the sunlight struck. Once again she carelessly tossed the jacks against the door. There was a rattle and stir inside, and with a creaking groan the door swung inward and the child found herself staring at something that lurked and mewed in the opaque shadow. Startled, she rose to her feet, and It rose too, and stood with head and shoulders framed in the light of the dying sun, gazing down on her.

Terror froze the girl, for through the dusk she could see the body— the body of the Thing That Should Not Have Been. And she cowered there. It bent toward her and she felt herself picked up in arms that were not human, crushed against a form not human, while the face that was human but should not have been blew its fetid breath upon her. In a voice rasping and metallic, like no human voice, it spoke, in a horrid, unforgettable monotone that thrilled and bit deep into her brain.

"You have come to me of your own free will; you have called me. Again will I come to you and yet again. And you shall belong to me, body and soul, to do my bidding, for the ages and ages to come."

One arm forced the girl's head back, passing over her neck in a dreadful caress. The Face bent over her throat, the slavering lips touched her skin, the pointed teeth pressed against her flesh. Came one shriek of terror from her and then oblivion.

She was sixteen when she met the Terror again. Riding through the woods near Garenstein with her cousin Ivan, the pair of them madly in love, she had felt the icy blast of a wave of horror and sensed the shadowy Thing that loped on all fours by her stirrup, its hot breath on her boot and the touch of fearsome lips on its leather. All that evening she had cowered in her room, gazing at the boot that lay where she had flung it, a broad white mark blasted on its shining surface. For she was certain then, she told him, that what they had said was a terrible dream, four years ago, had been no dream at all.

Ivan, called to the colors the next day by the mobilization, lay, a few months later, a sprawling corpse in the blood-soaked morasses of the Mazurian lakes, she told him.

Whether or not my friend ever saw the girl after that I don't know. At any rate he never mentioned the thing to me from that day until the night he died. So there the matter lies. I can not give any explanation. Perhaps you can. But the howl of a dog at night annoys me.

Exhibit A

Anne Harris Hadley

The wreckage of the plane has all been cleared away and disposed of according to orders, sir," continued Lieutenant Gorham. "It was undoubtedly Captain Rowell's plane, although this is a thousand miles from where the flight started; and it is very evident that he broke the altitude record as he had been trying so hard to do. Now, sir, if you will read this—" Lieutenant Gorham extended a small black notebook. "I found it in the breast pocket of his leather outside jacket. I can not imagine why the plane did not take fire in falling from such a terrific height. And you will perhaps be interested to know, sir—" he hesitated —"that that same queer odor you can still detect on the book was quite noticeable as we were clearing up."

The Major sniffed the book.

"Um—odd," he said. "All right, I'll look it over."

Lieutenant Gorham saluted and went out. The Major opened the little book and read, at first casually, then intently:

"I am writing this" [ran the words written in Captain Rowell's familiar, irregular handwriting] "in the hope that it may fall into the hands of human beings and reveal the things I have found up here. It now seems improbable I will be able to return and report personally my amazing experiences.

"It is impossible to measure accurately the lapse of time, as my watch has stopped, but I broke the altitude record more easily than I had hoped for the continued mounting. The cold was intense, breathing became increasingly difficult. I must have become dizzy, for the next recollection I have is of a sensation of lightness, as if my body were about to rise out of the still mounting plane and soar ahead of it. I assume I had then reached a point so distant from the earth that the attraction of some other heavenly body about counterbalanced the earth's pull. My life belt, however, held me securely, and I lapsed again into unconsciousness.

"The next conscious moment found me lying prone on the softest, most restful substance I can conceive of. I had a sensation as of gentle zephyrs puffing into my face and I opened my eyes. There was an indefinite, shapeless mass above me. As I watched it, I became convinced that it was endowed with intelligence and that its actions were the source of the pleasant, revivifying puffs of air I felt.

"Observing more closely, the mass above me looked somewhat like a huge oyster about the size of a man and of a cloudy, semitransparent substance. Its outline was not clearly defined. Imagine my sensations when I realized that it appeared able at will to put forth from any portion of itself streams of its substance that remained connected with the main body and performed the functions of arms! Think of it! An extra arm or two or three—any number of them projected at will from any part of the body! The unnaturalness of it, the slimy horror that the formless gray mass induced made me shiver. Though its actions appeared friendly, though it made no effort to harm me, yet an icy sweat broke out all over my body as I gazed fascinated at the unearthly being.

"I found afterward that it transported itself from place to place without apparent bodily movement and by means of some interior energy instead of by the use of legs, of which in fact the creature had none. It was just as if an airplane could glide along without movement of the propeller, driven by sheer inner impetus of its engine.

"As my mind became clearer I realized that the strange creature was projecting a portion of itself into an apparently stationary object, and then gently waving the part so transported over me, thus puffing the currents of air that were reviving me. The eerie, creepy sensation this gave me is indescribable. I felt it must be part of some fantastic dream, and yet I knew all too well that I was awake, that no sudden, grateful earth noise would jar me back to the realm of familiar things.

"Somehow, by what strange trick of Fate or machinations of this pallid, semitransparent creature I know not, but while I sat unconscious, my swiftly mounting plane had passed from the realms of the known to this ghostlike region, the borderland between the earth and the moon, that thin portion of space where the gravity of the earth is almost exactly counterbalanced by that of the moon. And I, a human being, a dweller on old Mother Earth, was here in this unutterably strange place —and one of the beings who dwell in it was reviving me. Doubtless he recognized me as earthborn and knew my inability to live comfortably in the thin atmosphere of the place, hence he was pouring air in my face as a man on earth might pour water in the face of one who had fainted.

"As my senses revived my amazement knew no bounds. I sat up, very awkwardly to be sure, for the least effort moved me much farther than I anticipated.

" 'How do you do?' I said, by way of showing I was ready for whatever might be in store.

"The creature emitted a queer, whistling noise, which I found afterward is the manner of speech of these creatures who inhabit the zone at the point and near where the gravity of the earth and that of the moon neutralize each other. On account of the small density of their bodies and the great power of their interior means of locomotion, which for lack of a better name I will call engines, these creatures can go a considerable distance on either side of the plane of neutrality and return, but are careful not to go far enough so that the gravity of either earth or moon can exercise on them a pulling power greater than their engines can resist. Later on I made an effort to find out if any had ever done so, but on account of the difficulty I had in making myself understood, I could get no satisfactory information.

"They have great intelligence and have perfected antigravity screens, though I do not understand fully for what purpose they are used. I do know, however, that they are used as resting places for such as are disabled in any way, especially when trouble is experienced in their locomotive apparatus.

"It was on one of these screens that I was lying when I regained consciousness. This screen was a huge affair, in appearance like a thin layer of rose-tinted cloud, yet it bore the weight of myself and my machine, which I rejoiced to see close by.

"I stood up, feeling quite light-headed and dizzy, but the creature, who had revived me and whose captive I apparently was, indicated to me that I should keep still, then he placed near me the object into which he had been dipping. This object was oval in shape and reminded me of a semisolidified cloud.

"The creature made queer noises and wavings of those surprisingly outthrust portions of his body. At last I understood that I was to make use of the cloud-bowl. I discovered that it was filled with air, breathable by a human being—containing real, life-sustaining oxygen.

"Whenever the thin atmosphere around became too devoid of oxygen and breathing became difficult, I would dip my hands into the bowl and dash oxygen in my face. The effect was quite lasting. The oxygen (or whatever the oxygen-containing substance was, for of its exact nature I am uncertain) permeated surrounding space as perfume does the air, and for many minutes I could breathe comfortably.

"Seeing that I understood what was expected of me, my captor began making mysterious motions near the edge of the cloud mass, which was in reality a gravity screen, and I watched, wondering what would happen next. After a minute or so I moved over to my plane, carrying the oxygen-bowl along.

"The sensation of moving about was extremely odd, and that of carrying the bowl was no less so. Nothing seemed to have any appreciable weight. This was due at least partly to the gravity screen, which was adjustable to counterbalance part of the pull of either earth or moon as need might be and thus make the attraction of the two bodies practically equal at a given spot. The result of the use of such screens is that the neutral zone, instead of a plane a hair's thickness, becomes for their purposes portion of space perhaps some miles in depth.

"I examined my machine, which seemed to be in good condition, although the gasoline was quite low. The being watched me curiously, then suddenly attached itself to the gravity screen by a tentacle put out, and started hurtling through space drawing the screen that bore me and my plane behind him. This dissipated the oxygen around me and I found the only way I could breath was by dipping my head into the bowl. Then I managed with fair comfort. After some time I felt the speed decrease and raised my head to look around.

"All about me were numbers of beings of all colors and sizes, but fundamentally similar to my strange captor. Among these strange creatures color apparently denotes rank or occupation. Their voices, or whistles, which more accurately describes what they have in place of voices, are all in a very high key and vary from the sweetest fairy notes of dreamland to the siren note of a factory whistle. I noticed that those of dark, indistinct color had the siren-whistle voices, while some of the orange and pink and blue bodies gave forth extremely sweet sounds.

"My appearance caused great excitement among them; and I cannot begin to describe my own sensations as I stood on that soft, cloudlike screen and leaned for companionship against the only familiar thing in sight—my plane. All about me was a confusion of these extraordinarily high-pitched whistle voices, and everywhere these indistinct, variously colored bodies put forth most surprisingly the tentacles that served for arms and as surprisingly drew them back. And I was the subject of the hubbub. Evidently there was a difference of opinion as to what to do with me and my plane.

"And while the discussion went on, they observed due regard for my person. Not one of them touched me, but their long tentacles came darting out here and there touching, investigating the plane and its mechanism. They recognized and respected me as a sentient being. The plane was a created object, as were their gravity screens. As I realized their consideration, I could not but wonder, even in the midst of this strange scene, if a crowd of human beings coming suddenly upon one of these unearthly creatures would show equal courtesy.

"At last the hubbub suddenly quieted and I witnessed another surprising occurrence. The strange forms stood still, expectant, moved by the approach of something unseen by me. Then while I, too, waited breathless for the next development, I saw coming from the direction toward which attention seemed turned a glowing, orange-colored being, bearing a blue-white sphere that quivered and sparkled. The bearer of the sphere came forward and paused in the midst, then suddenly put forth two tentacles in addition to the ones with which it bore the glowing sphere. With these second two tentacles it separated the sphere into halves, and a strange gas—a cloud of perfume, the most exquisite I could imagine—came forth. I could think of nothing but the almost divine sweetness of the odor. I drank in all my lungs could hold, and breathed deeply again and again.

"I found afterward that the odor is to them what food is to us, and is distributed at intervals by orange-colored beings. I also noted that the gray and brown ones always shifted the gravity screens and seemed to be most interested in the intricacies of my ship, hence I infer they are the mechanics of this strange community.

"After breathing in that wondrous odor, I remembered nothing more until I found myself alone. Where my strange captors had gone I could not guess. Impenetrable screen masses were above and below me. My plane was nearby and undisturbed. The space between the cloud masses had been flooded with oxygen, the source of which is still unknown to me.

"Whether these creatures have homes and gardens and laboratories, I do not know, but certain it is that somewhere beyond what I have seen, there must be abodes, apparatus with which to work, to prepare the oxygen, the heavenly food-odors, to make the intricate gravity screens. I am consumed with a burning desire to penetrate beyond the cloud-screen barriers and learn more of the life and wisdom of these eerie but highly intelligent beings.

"Finding myself alone, I wandered about between the cloud masses, but dared not attempt to force my way through them lest I should impair their ability to counteract the force of gravity and should find myself falling headlong toward earth or moon. No, it is better to wait and wonder. And after a while, worn out by the wonder of it all, I lay down and slept.

"When I awoke, three of the gray creatures had returned and were curiously investigating my plane. I rose from the cloud-screen on which I had been sleeping and joined them. They were eager to learn about the machine, and I was quite willing to explain, but since we had no common language, no common gestures, not even similar limbs in common with which to gesticulate, we made rather poor headway. . . .

"These things have gone on for some time. How long I cannot accurately tell, as my watch has long since stopped, and the periods of twelve hours light and twelve of darkness of course do not obtain here. I imagine from the growth of beard on my face that about three days have passed. And now a new and ominous disturbance has arisen—ominous for me.

"More of these beings than I have seen before have gathered and are hurrying about, first in one direction, then in another. Some are quite angry. They swish back and forth like specters in a dream, moving with incredible rapidity and always most unexpectedly putting forth those surprising tentacles. As they mull about, first one and then another, and sometimes several at once, emit those odd, unearthly, whistlelike screeches, my blood runs cold. I am the cause of the disturbance; just how and why I do not understand, but I am the issue at stake.

"Now they are tearing at the gravity screens. Some pull in one direction, some in another. I do not know the strength of the beings or of the screens, but if a screen should break—

"Well, I have my plane ready—as ready as I can make it. Possibly the engine will pick up and start when the fall begins. But suppose the fall should be away from the earth and toward the moon—what then?

"I have taken my seat in the plane and adjusted the safety belt. There is nothing more I can do. My action seems to have added to the excitement, but there is still dissension among them.

"They are tugging in good earnest at the screens. They surely cannot stand the strain. The one beneath me is parting. Instead of cloudiness, I see merely space beneath me.

"My engine—"

There the account ended.

The Major sat staring a long time at the little black book and sniffing the odor, faint, elusive, but still delightful beyond anything he had ever encountered. Then he shook his head, sighed, and, picking up a pencil, marked in red letters prominently on the cover "Exhibit A" before he laid the little book carefully in the top drawer of his desk ready to accompany his report to Washington.

Fairy Gossamer

HARRY HARRISON KROLL

If you find spider gossamer in the autumn of the year when the spider balls hatch and the young go forth into the world, it's a sign that the fairies are leading you on to good fortune.

—OLD FOLKS' SAYING.

William Thompson sat at the opening of the sinkhole absorbedly watching tiny strands of spider gossamer issue from the orifice. He had come to this spot in the cavernous limestone region of Kentucky in search of a specimen of the genus *Arimnes*, the most brilliantly colored of temperate zone spiders, his college work in biology at Vanderbilt necessitating his discovering such a specimen. Hearing of a legend current in this neighborhood about spiders, he had come here in the hope of satisfying his requirement.

The story related that years ago one Israel Hicks, suddenly gone crazy and believing himself pursued by an evil spirit, had come out here and begun the breeding of spiders that he might devise a web to entangle the demon that vexed him. It was averred that, previous to his going insane, he had been a wealthy bluegrass farmer; and many believed that

160

he possessed considerable riches. At any rate, the last of his name and kind, he had come here and lived alone, spending his time and energies in catching spiders and shutting them up in a mysterious insectary, which he never permitted any one to visit. And now the old man had been dead these many long years, and likely was well rid of his evil spirit, and none would probably ever know much more about him and his peculiar hallucination.

"There are spiders somewhere in this locality," William told himself, as he continued to observe the strands of silk wafted up out of the hole. "And if I could investigate down in that sink-hole, I believe I might find just what I am looking for."

He tried getting down into the hole, but apparently it would not readily admit passage of his body.

"Strange about that draft," he continued to meditate. "I never knew one of these glacial blowouts to have a draft before."

He tested the strength of the air current by casting some leaves into the opening. These fragments rose several feet above the surrounding ground level before the force of the air was sufficiently modified to permit them to drop.

"Well, well," he said thoughtfully; "if I could find the other end of this passage, the chances are that I would find my spider."

He began an examination of sink-holes nearby, of which there were many; for in a past geological age a great explosion of natural gas had honeycombed the entire undersurface region, these pits being outlets of the force of the detonation. But none of the others appeared to have a draft. An ignited match (a certain test of air movement) burnt over them as undisturbed as a candle flame in a closed room. It was apparent to William that there was no direct connection between the pit with a draft and its kindred near by.

"The air has to get in some way, though," he reasoned. "If it comes out, it surely has to go in. One of the holes hereabouts has to have a downward draft."

But no amount of search revealed it. Presently, after an extended exploration, he returned to the chimney hole.

"Israel Hicks," he recalled meditatively out of the traditions of this authority as they had been recounted to him, "used to say that you never see gossamer except in the fall of the year, it being the spinning of the new spider brood. Now, any idiot knows that where there is gossamer there are spiders. I've got to locate the other end of this hole. Likely as not when I do I will have located old man Hicks's spider incubator. I'll wager that it is one gloriously interesting place for the biologist."

The idea fascinated him, for the old lunatic was reputed to have had a fancy collection of spiders. William obtained a long, slender stick, and prodded down into the hole. He found by the experiment that the passageway went deep into the earth, and bent in the direction of the old house, several hundred yards away on a hill, where the old man had made his home. William scratched his head in perplexity. Did the hole come out somewhere near, or under, the house?

He dashed up the hill and into the yard. An eager search of the abandoned enclosure, however, disclosed no such hole as he looked for. He continued his search into the ruinous old house. The floor was gone, and he found an open cellar glaring vacantly back at the patches of sky that showed through the holes in the clapboards. He stood baffled, for nothing of interest met his eyes. Then suddenly he became aware, across the spot where he stood on the stone cellar bottom, of a draft that chilled his feet. Bending down for a test with his hand, he discerned a steady air movement fanning his feet and entering a crack in the cobbles. By listening he could even hear the sound of it whistling into the hole.

"Aha!" he ejaculated. "The old lunatic had a secret passageway down to his spider hatchery. Let's raise this rock and take a peek inside."

This he did, and there was disclosed, leading deep into the cavernous maw of the earth, a natural tunnel. He had his flashlight with him; and slipping down through the opening, he began the descent. Presently daylight behind him had disappeared. Another turn of the passageway thrust him into Stygian darkness. Down, down he went. Had he not been somewhat familiar with caves, he probably would have lost his nerve and refused to penetrate any farther. Cobwebs hung everywhere —millions of them, lodged here over the long years since old Israel Hicks had first introduced the spinners. There was no question in William's mind that he had found the previously unknown spider hatchery of the crazy old loon. The chances were that he would find the specimen he sought, since Hicks had been a connoisseur in his line of business and likely had overlooked none of the types in the region.

Presently, as he had surmised, he arrived at a widening of the passageway, which in turn opened into a large, cavernous chamber. As he stepped down into the larger room, quite unexpectedly a pivoted rock, not unlike some vast door to a sepulcher, swung to behind him. He paused fearfully, believing that his egress was cut off. But far ahead of him a speck of daylight reassured him—evidently the sinkhole came out into the cavern there, and he could make his escape at the same outlet as the fairy gossamer. He went on, flashing his light on every hand.

❊   ❊   ❊

162

What a dreary, haunted den it was! The endless walls of slimy, irregular ceiling were gray with the ashen webs of innumerable spiders. Beads of moisture clung to many of the festoons, which besprinkled him with chill showers. Literally thousands of the curious, agile creatures, leaping out into view for possible prey at his entrance, as suddenly and uncannily withdrew to their silken refuges when he turned his light upon them. Their myriad cunning eyes, in that momentary scrutiny, almost frightened him, and caused a cold shudder to run up his spine.

Then with a sudden and involuntary exclamation he stopped. He had found the prize, a beautiful *Arimnes*, possessing perhaps the loveliest geometric markings he had ever observed in the type: almost as large as a silver dollar, with long, graceful legs, and a brilliant figure on its head and another on its back, and intensely black eyes.

His problem, now that he had found it, was to snare it. And no easy problem would it be, as he well knew, for the *Arimnes* is as cunning as it is beautiful, and as fearless and savage as it is cunning. Moreover, William had no desire to risk being bitten by this gentleman. Although the type is regarded as nonpoisonous, or but mildly so, nevertheless there were authentic cases where individuals were deadly venomous. He had with him a device manufactured from a fishing reel, section of hat wire, and gauze, intended to capture insects. With this contrivance he began craftily stalking the prey.

The spider retreated, William following. Then, with cunning suddenness, the creature darted down into a crevice of the rock wall. Out of this retreat William could not budge him. No amount of mild persuasion appeared in the least to affect this crafty gentleman. Finally, at his wits' end, William as a last desperate expedient punched down into the crack with his reel. He desired the specimen alive, but a dead one would be better than none.

It was, as he was to perceive when too late, an ill-advised move. Seemingly the hordes of spiders were waiting for just such a signal, for suddenly they were upon him in one great, hungry mob. Great, hairy demons dropped upon his head from above; they crawled across his unprotected face; he felt them creeping up his trouser legs! Although he frantically brushed them off, slapping them out of his eyes and trying in the darkness to stamp upon them, his efforts seemed only to attract other packs of them.

His mind worked rapidly. Knowing the habits of spiders, and the fact that they may go without food for as long as a year and a half, and in such a state are ravenous, he realized that it would be only a question of time before they would overpower him by their very numbers and devour his body. There in the darkness with no protection and only his flashlight to show the way, it might seem a hopeless task to cope with them. Neither could he beat his way back as he had come, for the pivoted rock cut off his retreat. He could only strive forward, knocking the spiders from his face as he went, and trust to providence to effect his escape by way of the chimneylike suckhole. He therefore began moving forward as best he might, his hat pulled low over his eyes, his coat collar turned up, and his free hand acting as a relentless brush against the stinging, voracious arachnids.

He sensed dimly that the nebula of light increased on the opposite side of the chamber as he approached that quarter. In fact, it shortly began to take definite shape. If he could hold out for another span of moments, he would make it. But already he was feeling sensations of pain in all parts of his body, and he was becoming giddy, whether from fear or poison he could not be sure, but his hands and face were swelling from bites. And then he stopped in frozen horror!

Immediately in the opening that would give him egress from this terrible place to the good open sunshine above, he saw the form of the most gigantic spider he had ever beheld! From where he stood, even after making allowance for his unreliable perception, it seemed to measure two feet across! It belonged to a genus about which he had read, but which had never been seen before by the eyes of a white man—the monster golden spider, native of the tropics. Where the light fell upon it from above, it gave back an untarnished reflection of the precious metal from which it derived its name.

Curiously enough, as he beat his way closer in spite of the hazard, he found the smaller pests to be dropping off and falling back. He was in the circle of light, too, and that aided him in brushing them off. Many he succeeded in crushing under his heels.

And well might this smaller fry retire, William vaguely reasoned. For this fat old demon had sufficient capacity to devour them as they came.

He took a fresh, firm grip upon his reel, and approached nearer for the inevitable conflict. He would have to fight here, and to the deadly finish. Either he or the giant spider must fall. Nor did the creature move as he crept nearer and nearer. Its golden eyes never flinched. It still maintained its masterful composure as William, staking his fate upon one accurate cut of the steel fishing rod, prepared to cleave its body in twain with the tubing.

His aim proved true, he saw even before the blow fell. It descended clean and sharp across the middle of the spider's body. And then William, almost collapsing from the letdown of his nerves, saw something he could not bring himself for a moment to believe. Instead of the creature writhing about in the death agony, it scattered, not unlike an apparition, with a sudden metallic clanking and jingling! Until his senses returned to him, and the weakness of his legs gave way to some degree of composure, William was unable to examine the results of this singular metamorphosis. When he did, he found the spider to have been made of golden coins, in an artful similitude of the insect.

When able to think constructively, he conjectured the why of it all. Old man Hicks had had two gods: his money, about which but few knew, and spiders, which he bred and loved. He had placed his money here under the protection of the spiders. The arranging of the coins in form of one of them was a curious slant of the old man's fad. And true to their trust all of these long years, the spiders had all but succeeded in their task.

William got out of the cave as quickly as he could, but not before he had collected the coins in his pockets and the overplus in his hat. Out in the glorious open sunshine he breathed free, finding that none of the bites inflicted upon him would result in more than temporary discomfort.

The adventure recalled to his mind two curious superstitions about spiders: one, that the creatures will not attach their webs to, or come near, gold; and the other that if you find the gossamer in the autumn of the year when the spider balls hatch and the young go forth into the world, it's a sign that the fairies are leading you on to good fortune!

Familiar Face

ROBERT M. PRICE

Why white rats? Oh, Randy wasn't one of those animal rights nuts on campus who questioned using animals for scientific testing. He didn't even wonder why rats in particular were used for the tests. The more of the little buggers offed the better, he figured. But why specifically *white* rats? Was it possibly to overcome the fear and disgust you just couldn't help feeling when you were around them? Maybe long ago scientists had decided that they could get along better with rats in their labs if they were snow-white albinos that looked almost like rabbits with bobbed ears. Yes, that might be it. Snow-white. Washed clean of any rattish taint. Almost as if they were wearing little lab coats of their own.

Such were Randy's random ramblings as he sought to delay getting down to work in the lab section of his biology course at Aylesbury State College. He told himself he just didn't want to start without Claudia, his lab partner. Of course, he could have gone ahead and gotten things ready, but it was more than half true: Claudia was the life form he was really interested in. And there were tests he was downright eager to perform upon her animal body. He imagined she, too, was pure white.

But no Claudia yet. He'd better start seeming to be busy before the grad student proctor came a-snooping. He made the rats his business again, pretending to study them more intently. The bemused little vermin were, without knowing it, on death row, like lobsters in the fish tank in a supermarket. One of them, in fact, looked for all the world like a convict gripping the bars of the cell, and . . . Randy's beady eyes widened—did that rat actually have *a human hand?*

No need to pretend interest now. Randy was up and slipping open the door to the cage, doing fast and furtively what he'd never been able to do without a good shudder of disgust before—putting his hand and arm into the rat cage. Oddly, the little beast made no motion to avoid him. They usually did, as if they'd managed to evolve enough intelligence to realize what was happening once it was too late to do anything about it.

He moved along to the coat tree, his new pet secreted as best he could in his pocket. On the way out the room and down the hall, he brushed against Claudia. She gave him a look that might have been more appropriate for a rat with a human hand. "Where the hell are *you* off to?"

"My dorm room, babe. Forgot my, uh, notes for today's experiment."

"*Exper*iment? What the fuck are you *talk*ing about?"

"Back in a minute! Feel free to start without me!" Claudia shook her head in disdain as she continued on into the lab. Randy, looking backward at her, stumbled into another latecomer, but he didn't hear the cursing his reckless elbow had evoked; he was absorbed in how beautiful she was when she was being contemptuous. Was contempt enough of a basis for a relationship?, he wondered. Probably not, but her body was.

And speaking of bodies, what was he to make of the strange specimen he held, surprisingly quiet and still, in his capacious coat pocket? And what would he do with it?

Randy unlocked the door, looking around for the best place to hide the little monster. He felt sure that opportunity had come squeaking, if only he could figure how to take advantage of it. His eye fell upon an empty bird cage, the one vacated last month when a stray cat had assassinated his roommate Walt's parakeet. Randy popped the rodent inside, crumbled a bit of bread and sprinkled it through the tiny prison bars. "Sorry, pal. I'll try to get you the deluxe menu this afternoon. Consider yourself lucky! You got a reprieve from the governor!"

Randy didn't want Walt to see his prize, so he draped a towel over the cage, moving it flush against the window to allow some daylight in the one exposed side. If he were lucky, Walt wouldn't notice anything till he was ready to explain what he intended to do with the little freak. Now back to the lab.

His brief absence was hardly noticed, but Claudia heralded his return with one of her usual icy remarks. Randy countered this with a typically crude proposal, and they finally got to work dissecting a rat that had four ordinary paws.

When the festivities were over she left abruptly, leaving the cleanup to her partner. Claudia was apparently as glad to be rid of him as she was to take her leave of the verminous carcass they had shared. This time Randy's gaze did not linger on her smart-marching hindquarters. He was occupied with the thought of his new pet, his new opportunity.

Maybe it would be possible to unveil the little beast to one of the senior professors on the condition that Randy be promised a share of the credit for whatever might be discovered. Lackluster scientist that he was, even Randy could recognize what might be at stake with a find like this: it might reveal volumes about unsuspected genetic similarities or crossovers between far-removed species. Mutations usually involved only the misfiring of a single chromosome. And if his man-handed rodent were possible, what sort of latent genetic fund might the species share? The implications for genetic medicine were dizzying. And that couldn't hurt a guy's career.

These thoughts occupied him on the way back to his room, the excitement quickening his pace. He jiggled the door knob. Not locked. And there was roommate Walt staring eye to eye with the rat.

"Notice anything odd, Walt?"

"Yeah, he has a long love line."

"So you've discovered my secret. I'm going to try to solve *his*." The two scrawny college juniors sat on beds across from one another.

Randy's bunk had witnessed some recent attempt to tidy it up; Walt's looked like the primordial ooze from which its occupant might have emerged as a new life form only this morning.

"I figure it's a mutant, though I guess that's obvious even to a layman like you."

"Listen, Mr. Science, you can't impress me. What is he, one of the X-Men? Mutant, schmutant! That thing's a *familiar*."

"What? What are you talking about? It doesn't look familiar to *me!*"

"This is too good to be true! I was *hop*ing you'd say that!" Walt burst into hilarity, then into a coughing fit. He was none too healthy-looking. Finally he stopped for a breath and said, *"Now* who's the layman? Being a Medieval Studies major comes in handy sometimes."

Randy's slow boil began to subside, even though Walt's pathetic attempts at humor only added insult to injury. "Okay, it's obvious you know something I don't—for once. Just what the hell *is* a familiar, then?"

Walt took off his horn-rims to wipe the tears from his eyes. "It's a familiar *spirit*. You know—a demon, kind of a mascot sent by the devil to help a witch or a wizard. A familiar would give you special knowledge and powers. It might even grant wishes. They always looked like small animals, though with a difference of some sort—not usually this obvious, though."

By now Randy found himself looking steadily at the rat, or rather, he found himself the object of the rat's scrutiny. For a split second he found himself half-thinking what Walt said might have some truth in it. But then when did anything Walt said have any truth to it? No way.

Walt had pulled a book from his chaotic shelves, letting loose a cascade of old *Playboy*s and occult paperbacks. He held a copy of *Man, Myth, and Magic*. "See, it's right here. Here's one that looks like a two-headed rooster."

Randy saw geekhood beckoning if he took this seriously; he didn't even look at the page. "You're crazy! It's just a mutant. It's scientific, not magic."

"Yeah? Suit yourself, Einstein," Walt mumbled as he cast the book aside and reached for the swimsuit issue. "But why not check it out? Try a little experiment. That's the scientific way, isn't it?"

"What," asked a wary Randy, "have you got in mind?"

"Go pick him up and make a wish. What's the harm?"

For some reason Randy went along with it. "Okay, but this is just between us, all right? Anybody hears about this, and you'll be as dead as the Middle Ages!" But Walt seemed oblivious, stretched out on his bunk, apparently now thoroughly absorbed in an informal study of human anatomy.

Randy flipped the cage door open, and the rat walked out onto his palm, exactly like a trained pet. It was eerie, even though Randy felt about as foolish as he did the first time Claudia turned down one of his juiciest propositions. Claudia! Now *there* was wish fodder!

The lab didn't meet again for half a week, and when Claudia showed up as aloof as ever, Randy had to admit he was more than a little disappointed. Yet even this paled beside the embarrassment he felt at having taken the damn thing as seriously as he had; he'd tried telling himself he knew nothing would happen, but deep down he must have believed it would. His usual smart-ass manner was more subdued for the rest of the lab. He left with hardly a suggestive innuendo.

The rest of the day held little to cheer him, except the prospect of telling Walt that he was in fact full of crap. That he looked forward to. He made his usual Tuesday rounds to the Rathskeller and the library, returning on schedule to the dorm. He knew Walt had some kind of seminar in medieval metaphysics and wouldn't be back till late. That's why it alarmed him to see his door was not locked. Oh no! Not another CD player ripped off!

He flung the door open and took in the scene in one glance. The room was not as he had left it, that was for sure. The rat's cage was draped again and turned back to the window, but that wasn't the first thing Randy noticed. The first thing was the naked form of Claudia astride his bed. There was a look on her face he had never seen before. He was speechless but she was not: "What are you waiting for? Let's try an experiment." Wordlessly, Randy fumbled with his zipper.

When he awoke she was gone. The incredible thought occurred to him—did he, could he possibly, have the rat to thank? It seemed absurd, but then, to be honest, was it any less absurd than the idea of Claudia putting herself at his disposal as she had? He turned the cage away from the window. The rat now held two bars of its miniature prison with opposable thumbs.

Randy might have appreciated the strangeness of his situation more had his emotions not been otherwise preoccupied. How should he approach Claudia now? How would they relate? He hadn't really gotten to know her; she was just there and willing to do it, no explanation offered. And he'd relished the opportunity, no questions asked. But what would things be like now? How to approach her? He hated this sort of uncertainty.

Up and out of the shower, he decided to skip paleontology and go straight to the library, dressed only in jeans and shirt, heedless of the late-autumn chill. He had to find out more on this "familiar" business. The librarian, luckily, knew what he was talking about. She had studied library science not far away at Miskatonic, and she knew just where to look.

"There's not much, I'm afraid; you'd have better luck over at the University. But I'll show you what we've got."

Randy paged impatiently through a short stack of books that mentioned witch's familiars, but mostly as pieces of amusing local folklore. Goody Watkins, Abbie Prinn—several of the old women had been burned because they had these little pets, probably just tame squirrels, Randy thought as he tossed aside the last book. On a hunch he went to the card catalog and rounded up a few of the older science tomes, stuff innocent of modern genetics, but sometimes more open to the reality of what was nowadays dismissed as superstition.

Here, too, he was largely disappointed. The only thing he was able to turn up was a brief discussion of familiars in a discreditable volume called *Marvels of Science* by someone named V. Morryster. It was pretty wild stuff, and it contented itself with cataloging oddball items, pretty much like Charles Fort. Besides a couple of silly-looking artist's renderings of familiar spirits in vermin form, there was only the vague caution that the familiar would not work its wonders without exacting a price. Yeah, well, he'd just have to wait and see. A look at his watch showed he'd missed supper at the Refectory; the Rat Factory they called it.

Back to the dorm. Walt should be in, but the door was locked. Cupping his ear to the door, Randy thought he could hear something, couldn't imagine what. Hoping he wouldn't be disturbing anything, he clicked in his key and eased the door open.

"Hey, Walt, I owe you an apology. Looks like it does. . . . *What the fuck?*"

So Walt kept his horn-rims on even when he was screwing—screwing Claudia! She was bending over him, but Randy recognized her ass.

Then she hopped off the bed, faced him with a blank slate of a face, grabbed the sheet and made for the bathroom. Realizing he had no business standing there, Randy nonetheless found himself rooted to the spot. The hastily draped Claudia brushed past him as impersonally as if both were navigating a crowded hall.

Walt tried with palsied motions to pull his pants and shirt on and began to cough. "I . . . uh, came in last night and found you both asleep. I figured it must have worked pretty good. I guess I used one of your wishes, old pal. Hope you don't mind."

Randy had uncovered the cage and was now holding the rat up to the desk lamp, just to be sure. Yeah, now it had a human foot, too. And before he put the rodent down he paused and made another wish. He didn't look at or speak a word to Walt as he shucked his clothes and climbed into bed, face to the wall.

Next morning he skipped the lab, not a good idea this late in the semester, but he didn't know how to face Claudia. He flipped a coin and headed across campus to the library again. He was in such a funk that he hardly noticed the ambulance siren till the vehicle almost knocked him over in its rush past him. It seemed headed in his direction. Overdue book, Randy thought with an inane chuckle. He followed it, elbowed his way through the gathering crowd. Suddenly a familiar-looking form drifted into him, almost into his arms as he recognized the young librarian he had queried the previous afternoon. She seemed choked with nausea.

". . . anything like it! The poor guy . . . it just fell off and dropped like a bomb. His head . . . like a smashed pumpkin . . ." She rushed off, maybe to puke at the edge of the crowd. Randy shoved forward, shook off the hindering arms of the rescue squad, who really had no rescuing left to do. There was the shattered form of Walt, recognizable to Randy from his thrift shop clothes—and his glasses. But there was no longer any face to wear them. Witnesses swore, so said the article in the *Aylesbury Record* the next week, that a chunk of apparently sound masonry had detached itself from the library arch and *swerved* to drop directly onto the poor fellow's skull.

After this it was easy for the rat to stand squarely on two human feet. In fact, by now it almost looked like some kind of monkey.

Somewhere Randy felt a little remorse. But he could hardly believe it had been his irate ill will that had caused his roomie's death. That just couldn't be true. How *could* it be his fault?

Well, he'd have to go back to class sooner or later. He'd have to face Claudia one way or another. Next day he did. It was as he'd feared: the old contempt. But why? Had Walt, may he rest in peace, really been able to woo her away from him? No, remember, it was the wishes. But no, that would mean he had wished Walt to his grave.

From somewhere he heard the grad assistant droning on about repeatability as the criterion of the scientific method. Repeatability, yes, there might be something in that, after all. After class, Randy rushed out, sparing Claudia not a glance, not a crudity. He had plans for her, though. She was not far from his thoughts.

Back at the dorm the rat seemed to be waiting for him. The cage was facing the door, not the outside window, though Randy had not moved it. As before, the little creature paced cooperatively into his outstretched hand. Randy's flesh crawled, though, at the unmistakably human feel of the hands and feet. He was just thankful that the thing hadn't walked out erect. It could have.

He had scarcely finished his wishing. There wouldn't have been time even to blow out a birthday candle. And there was Claudia's lithe form filling the doorway, entering it, locking the door behind her. "We shouldn't be this way with each other, Randy. Let's . . ." Her lips smothered him and he thought of eating a peach. And then he was falling back onto the bed.

He came gradually out of the pleasant daze of sexual satiety. He savored the sight of Claudia tucking her voluptuous form into her clothes, but an uneasy suspicion drew his eye to the cage. Oh God! Had Claudia seen the thing? Did it matter? Was she hypnotized or something? Maybe she wouldn't remember what she had seen in such a state. Just to be safe, he quickly rose and reached for the cage, turned it to the wall. It wouldn't do for her to see a rat or a monkey with human hands and feet, and a human penis dangling there.

He felt chilled, turned back to her, but she was already mostly out the door without a word. Maybe she *was* hypnotized. Randy guessed that meant he was sort of raping her. Well, too late to worry about that.

Over the next weeks, Randy concluded, to his displeasure, that Claudia's amours had to be renewed each time. She was her old self whenever he saw her on campus, even worse, as if somehow she subconsciously knew what he was doing to her and hated him for it. He wanted to have her again, but somehow he was scared. He stopped going to biology.

Suddenly finals week was upon him. Randy's adventures — his extracurricular experiments, as he liked to think of them — had taken his mind altogether off his studies. He was going to go down in flames, and then he would catch it from his folks, lose his financial aid, you name it. But, come to think of it, maybe there was some recourse. Maybe the rat could help him. It couldn't hurt to try.

Aced. Every single one. Maybe he'd graduate summa, magna anyway. The future looked bright. Christmas music was piping into the Rathskeller. He felt like celebrating. He went back to the room. He was, truth to tell, kind of afraid of looking at his little pal.

Yes, yes, it did have a human face this time, as he knew it would. He didn't want to look too carefully as he took it into his hands; he didn't want to find out that it was his own face, like in the dreams. As he held it

172

he wished again for Claudia. For an instant he toyed with the notion of closing his hands, crushing the life out of the rodent. But then he felt a sharp pain, and wetness. He dropped the rat and it scurried away. He felt suddenly dizzy. He knew he was going to fall and tried to aim himself at the bed. He didn't stay awake long enough to know whether he was successful.

Claudia took a bit longer this time. She had a suitcase with her. Maybe she had sensed Randy's summons from the train platform, on her way home for the holidays. She was from the Berkshires. But she didn't complain at the change of plans. She never did.

Randy awakened just in time to see her welcome face, but something was wrong. Something had happened to his sense of perspective. How sick had that damned rat made him? He felt a rush of nervous energy, began to pace back and forth on bare feet, tried to speak and couldn't. His eyes widened as a second figure entered his field of vision, closing the door behind Claudia, slipping her coat off, kissing her.

What? Another betrayal? Who this time? Had someone discovered his secret like Walt had? The *bastard!* This time Randy wouldn't let things go so far. If only he could get up and grab that guy and plant one on him. But he seemed big, like a giant. But then so did Claudia.

In paralyzed outrage, he had no choice but to silently watch them make love, urgently, sweatily, shamelessly, right in front of him! Her face was vacant with the transport of orgasm; the interloper's face he could not see, damn him!

Claudia must have heard his impotent whisperings; her eyes turned toward him, focused, but no recognition registered. Her nose wrinkled in disgust. She sat up and spoke, her voice oozing disdain, "Oh, Randy, why did you bring *that* thing here? Don't you know I hate the little bastards? Can't you get rid of it?"

He tried to answer, but he was mute. But he heard his voice answer anyway. It came from the other figure, turning now, and approaching him. It was his own vast face, his own form, still scrawny, yet big as a colossus.

"You're right. This lab rat's outlived its usefulness. I'll take care of it. You may not want to look at this."

He tried to struggle. He got a bite in, but it was nothing against the gigantic pair of squeezing hands.

Father's Vampire

ALVIN TAYLOR AND LEN J. MOFFATT

Father is a little mad, of course, and someday I suppose I will have to have *him* put away too. He is quite harmless right now, however, and as long as I'm around to keep an eye on him he shouldn't cause anyone any real trouble.

Father collects things. Even when we were poor as church mice and Father was earning a meager living for Mother and me by digging wells, cesspools and graves around the town . . . yes, even when we were on relief during the depression years Father collected things.

One thing about Father, though. He wasn't in a rut like many collectors are. He didn't specialize in any one thing. He would bring home odds and ends, old books, torn halves of magazines, bits of string and rope, used ice cream sticks, pieces of metal from worn-out machines and so on.

And, of course, after we became fabulously wealthy there seemed to be no end to Father's collecting. We became wealthy when Uncle Henry died. Uncle Henry was Father's brother who struck it rich in Texas or some such Godforsaken place and for some reason or other (we were never on very friendly terms with Uncle Henry) he willed us his vast fortune. It was a little disconcerting because we weren't used to having all that money and we didn't quite know what to do with it. It was then that Father went a little mad.

Oh, he was practical enough at first. We had the old house done over and he bought Mother a pretty new cotton dress and gave me a ten-dollar bill to do with just whatever I pleased. I gave some of it to Mother to buy groceries with and am afraid I spent the rest of it rather foolishly on a girl.

Then Aunt Mabel came to live with us. She was Uncle Henry's widow. The lawyer who came with her (he didn't stay very long, although Mother was polite enough when she invited him to stay for supper) said we had inherited the money all right but there was a provision in the will that said we must look after Aunt Mabel until she died if we wanted to *keep* the money.

Mother said, "I knew there was a catch to it, but of course, Mabel is welcome here anytime."

Father said, "I always did dislike you less than I did Henry, Mabel." He gave me a look that meant I was supposed to say something nice to Aunt Mabel so I told her she could have one of my pet rats. Not the pregnant one, however, as I wanted the little rats from it to use in my home laboratory experiments.

Aunt Mabel didn't seem too happy with us at first but I think she got used to our dull, normal way of living after a while. I suppose she was used to a more adventurous life in Texas and just didn't feel at home with us right away. Anyway she didn't have to live with us very long because we found her dead in bed one morning.

Father sent for a doctor right away. As I said, he can be practical when he wants to be and he knew a doctor would have to pronounce her dead, make out a certificate, and so on. The doctor called in the constable and some other authorities because he said Aunt Mabel had been murdered.

This made Mother hysterical. She began to scream that she didn't do it and no one could prove she did it. But the constable claimed that the tiny pricks in Aunt Mabel's throat were caused by Mother's hatpin and the doctor said there was hardly a drop of blood in Aunt Mabel's body.

They were a little put out though because there was no blood on the bedclothes or anywhere in the room. They searched the entire house and grounds, but they couldn't find Aunt Mabel's blood anywhere.

So Father signed the papers and had Mother put away in the asylum just up the road from here. We buried Aunt Mabel in the old churchyard. We asked Reverend Worthy in to say a few words over her as Aunt Mabel had been a religious woman, always quoting the Bible or a bit now and then from the Decameron of Boccaccio.

It was several days after the funeral when Father called me into his study and gave me his best chair to sit in. He perched his lank frame on the edge of a table and smiled knowingly. I smiled knowingly back at him. I know how to humor Father.

"Being a bright and intelligent young man you no doubt have some idea concerning what I am about to reveal," said Father.

I kept on smiling.

"Of course," he said. "Your own father's son. Well, you realize then that it wasn't your mother who killed poor dear Mabel."

"Oh?" I said quietly.

"Of course not," said Father. "It was the vampire I am keeping in the cellar. I couldn't very well tell the authorities I had collected a vampire, coffin and all, now could I? Your mother knew about it, naturally. It was always hard to keep secrets from her. But then that is the way it is with people who are a little—er—demented? I'm afraid the strain of Mabel's demise was just too much for your poor mother, so it is just as well that she is where she is and that things have turned out so nicely without me having to give up my vampire. . . ."

I was fascinated. Vampires have always fascinated me. I couldn't control my eagerness as I questioned Father.

"What does it look like? Is it in the form of a man or woman or what? Is it thin or fat? Does . . ."

Father raised a thin hand to ward off my questions.

"Please, son," he smiled. "One thing at a time. I really couldn't tell you about the nature of the vampire as I haven't seen it yet."

"You haven't? Then how do you know it killed Aunt Mabel?"

"The markings on her throat and the fact that we could not find the blood she obviously lost," said Father, impatiently. "Why it was so obvious that I was sorely afraid the authorities would suspect the presence of a vampire. They did not, however, or perhaps they assumed that your mother had gotten rid of the blood in some other way or drunk it herself. Authorities being what they are—politicians—are generally a stupid lot. Clever at times, but always stupid."

"If you really have a vampire, Father, I want to see it. I must see it!"

"Whatever for? They are dangerous, you know. I just collected this one for the curiosity of having one about. Besides it doesn't seem to get out of its coffin, lazy fellow that it is. Except for its escapade with Mabel. It is probably a very old vampire who prefers to sleep most of the time and needs little nourishment. Just as well though, as I considered inviting tramps and other such riffraff in to supper now and then so it would not starve and thus not give *us* any trouble. One must be practical, you know."

"Of course," I agreed. "But I really do want to see it and talk with it. I have always wanted to interview a vampire. I could write it up for the local paper and then maybe Editor Stanley would put me on his staff."

"Why on earth do you want to write for that two-bit rag?" frowned Father. "And if you did write such an interview you would have to present it as fiction and use a pseudonym. I don't want notoriety, you know. I want to be alone with my collection."

Father was beginning to weep. I handed him my handkerchief and tried to change the subject. One of Father's pet peeves is the town's weekly paper, which stirred up such a fuss when we inherited the money. Such inaccurate reporting! If Stanley had let me write it up as I wanted to and offered to but . . .

"Look, Father," I said. "Please let me visit the vampire. I'll be very polite and I'll write the interview for some other publication. One of the 'little magazines,' perhaps. They don't pay much but they are awfully literary. Lord knows we don't need the money."

"Well," said Father, managing a weak smile. "I guess it will be all right. I doubt if you will get to see it, though. I admit I was a little curious when the coffin arrived. I even tapped on the box and asked it to come out but nothing happened at all. I tried to lift the lid but it is evidently locked or bolted from the inside. Very clever vampire. The coffin is made of wood that must be six inches thick. I thought once of prying it open, forcing the lock or bolt or whatever it is but I was afraid of ruining the coffin itself. It's a wonderful piece of woodcarving. I know there is a vampire in there all right because I have the papers that go with the box—a kind of written guarantee. And then, of course, there was Mabel. . . ."

I waited impatiently for Father to dismiss me. He had given his permission and there was nothing on earth I wanted more to see than a real undead vampire. I thought of all the questions I could ask and of other things, too, for I must admit I have peeked into some of Father's old books when he wasn't around. . . .

Finally Father let me go with a parting warning to be very careful, and above all, to be polite. I thanked him heartily and left him playing with his collection of handpainted cockroaches. He painted them himself—all the colors of the rainbow. Father really has the soul of an artist.

As I descended the cellar steps I thought I heard a bumping noise but wasn't sure where it was coming from. I was carrying a flashlight, my notebook and ballpoint pen, and two cans of cold beer. I had thought of wearing some garlic or a crucifix but decided that wouldn't be very polite, though it struck me as humorous at the time. I knew the vampire wouldn't hurt me any. I have made a study of vampires and although I hate to appear immodest I believe I probably know more about them than any other being in the world. Even more than Father because I know he hasn't read all of his books.

The coffin was indeed beautiful, obviously hand carved. It was covered with engravings depicting all sorts of fascinating rites as well as scenes from the private lives of famous beauties of history. There were also some very patriotic scenes showing the battle of Bunker Hill, the Spanish-American War, and so on, with a likeness of George Washington in bas-relief smiling down upon it all.

I knocked quietly on the coffin lid. There was a noise inside.

"Maybe just an echo," I thought, but I knocked again—harder.

"Oh, go away and let me sleep!" said a voice from inside the coffin.

"You're there!" I shouted with joy. "You're really there! A real true vampire at last! Please come out and talk to me."

"Why should I?" muttered the voice, definitely masculine.

I decided to fib a bit. It seemed the only way to get it out of its coffin.

"I've heard a lot about you, Mr. Vampire. I understand you have lived a fascinating life and that when you died your life after death—if I may call it that—was even more fabulous. But I would like to hear the details from your own lips. I'm sure you are a genius at storytelling and can thrill me with tales of the places you have been, the women you have known, the people you have dined with and dined on. . . ."

I could hear it moving about inside its coffin."

"Naturally," came the voice. "But why do you want to know?"

"I have always been fond of vampires and vampire stories," I replied promptly. "But most of the stories were silly fiction and I want to hear the truth from a real vampire. I want my facts from an authority. In short, I want to interview you. I can promise you a very nice write-up in all of the Sunday papers. If you wish, I'll use a pseudonym and will not reveal your location so no one will come around and bother you. . . ."

I heard a clicking sound inside the coffin and then the lid raised up. The vampire, in the form of a fat, healthy-looking man, climbed out, stretched, and yawned.

"So you want the story of my life and undeath," it grinned, showing white, pointed teeth. "Aren't you afraid I'll attack you?"

"Why should I be afraid?" I smiled, ever so innocently. "You belong to my father and besides you have recently dined on Aunt Mabel, who must have had enough blood to satisfy you for weeks to come."

"Perhaps," said the vampire, sitting down on the coffin's edge beside me. "You look like an interesting morsel though. . . ."

"Oh, skip that nonsense," I said. "Let's get to your history. Now, first give me the basic facts, statistics, you know. Birthdate. Where born? And so on up to time of death, cause of same, and the like. You just talk away and I'll take it down in shorthand. . . ."

"Very well," it said, trying to keep its eyes away from my neck. They were rather nice blue eyes, though. "I was born on April 9, 1652. . . ."

It began to give a very boring account of its life in a small Hungarian village, going into some detail regarding its various conquests of girls and the amount of wine it could consume in one evening. But I patiently took it all down. While it talked it kept gazing at me as though hypnotized and when it began to drool I moved away a little.

It must have noticed my moving for it immediately stopped talking and edged closer to me.

"Do not sit so far away," it whispered, placing a cold hand on my shoulder.

"Please continue your story," I said as quietly as possible.

"Another time," murmured the vampire. "You can best enjoy it when you become one of us. Your poor aunt is having the devil's own time trying to get out of that churchyard, but perhaps you will be more fortunate. In fact, I will take the trouble to instruct your father to let your coffin rest here with mine. We can be death-long companions. But first you must let me . . ."

His face was close to mine now and I could feel his cold breath on my throat. This wouldn't have been so bad but he had a bad case of halitosis. I stood up and stepped away from him, fingering the flashlight and letting the notebook and pen drop to the floor. It arose and moved towards me.

"The light will not help you," it smiled. "It won't hurt much, really. Just a little nip, a little pressure and you will be dead and I will be fed. Then you will evolve into undeadness and join me forever. . . ."

"Not interested, really," I said, insistently enough.

"But why not? You said you have always been fascinated by vampires. Why not become one? It is so easy and so much fun after all. . . ."

"I am not going to be a vampire," I told it firmly. "I have a definite interest in them but I would never think of being one, believe me. I'm happy the way I am."

"Please do not be difficult," said the vampire. It was close to me now and I could feel the wall behind me. Somehow it had got between me and the stairs. "If I want to I can force you into submission. I am stronger than a mere mortal man, you know."

I smiled right into its leering face.

"You may as well know," I said. "It is impossible for me to become a vampire. The most powerful vampire in existence cannot harm me. I know."

The vampire began to look a little unsure of itself. But it managed a grin combined with a sneer.

"And why can't you become a vampire? All I have to do is attack you, drink your blood. . . ."

"You just can't do it," I said. "Perhaps you're not as bright as I thought. But surely all vampires know about *druds* and have learned to fear them."

The vampire shuddered.

"*Druds!* There are no *druds* here. *Druds* are rare; perhaps one is born every few centuries, but . . ."

"I'm a *drud*," I said. "I found out by reading one of Father's old books. Even Father doesn't know about me, or about *druds*, for that matter, as he doesn't read half the stuff he collects. I might never have known if I hadn't read that book. Or perhaps I would have learned about myself naturally once I met you or some other vampire. I know I have often felt the hunger, the thirst, but I always tried to satisfy it with a sandwich or a glass of beer. I assumed it was an unusual hunger but I hate to bother with doctors and as I appeared to be quite healthy otherwise. . . ."

The vampire was leering again.

"You are not a *drud*," it said. "You may have read about the accursed creatures in some old book but you couldn't be a *drud*. A *drud* is a vampire's vampire. It drinks the blood of vampires after the vampire has dined on some mortal being. *Druds* have the disgusting taste for distilled blood . . . the blood of my kind after we have taken it from some human. But you are not a *drud* and now I shall have your life!"

I ducked just in time to avoid its grabbing arms and clicking teeth.

"I am too a *drud!*" I shouted. "What makes you think I'm not? You better look out or *I'll* have *your* blood. I'm awfully thirsty, you know. I didn't come down here just to get a story from you. That was just to get you out of your coffin so I could get at you!"

"You cannot be a *drud*," grinned the vampire, closing in again. "You have eyebrows. *Druds* do not have eyebrows!"

"Of course, they haven't," I said, reaching up and pulling off the fake eyebrows I had been wearing. I advanced on the vampire.

It screamed horribly, I'm sure, and ran from me to its coffin. I raced madly after it but stumbled over an empty beer can. By the time I got to my feet the vampire was in its coffin and I could hear the lock clicking on the inside.

"You can't reach me now!" It cried. "You'll never get me! I'll stay here forever! You can't reach me now!"

I hammered heavily on the coffin lid and could hear it weeping hysterically inside. Finally, I picked up my notes and pen and found my way to the stairs. As I climbed up into the house I smiled and thought that I really hadn't gotten much of a story for all my trouble. Shaving off my eyebrows had been a nuisance but, oh well, they will grow back in a little while.

Father is peeved at me for frightening the vampire so that it won't come out of its coffin, but he'll get over it eventually. Of course, we'll have to find some other use for the hobo Father invited in to supper tonight.

The Feather Pillow

Horacio Quiroga

Alicia's entire honeymoon gave her hot and cold shivers. A blonde, angelic, and timid young girl, the childish fancies she had dreamed about being a bride had been chilled by her husband's rough character. She loved him very much, nonetheless, although sometimes she gave a light shudder when, as they returned home through the streets together at night, she cast a furtive glance at the impressive stature of her Jordan, who had been silent for an hour. He, for his part, loved her profoundly but never let it be seen.

For three months—they had been married in April—they lived in a special kind of bliss. Doubtless she would have wished less severity in the rigorous sky of love, more expansive and less cautious tenderness, but her husband's impassive manner always restrained her.

The house in which they lived influenced her chills and shuddering to no small degree. The whiteness of the silent patio—friezes, columns, and marble statues—produced the wintry impression of an enchanted palace. Inside the glacial brilliance of stucco, the completely bare walls, affirmed the sensation of unpleasant coldness. As one crossed from one room to another, the echo of one's steps reverberated throughout the house, as if long abandonment had sensitized its resonance.

Alicia passed the autumn in this strange love nest. She had determined, however, to cast a veil over her former dreams and live like a sleeping beauty in the hostile house, trying not to think about anything until her husband arrived each evening.

It is not strange that she grew thin. She had a light attack of influenza that dragged on insidiously for days and days; after that Alicia's health never returned. Finally one afternoon she was able to go into the garden, supported on her husband's arm. She looked around listlessly. Suddenly Jordan, with deep tenderness, ran his hand very slowly over her head, and Alicia instantly burst into sobs, throwing her arms around his neck. For a long time she cried out all the fears she had kept silent, redoubling her weeping at Jordan's slightest caress. Then her sobs subsided, and she stood a long while, her face hidden in the hollow of his neck, not moving or speaking a word.

This was the last day Alicia was well enough to be up. On the following day she awakened feeling faint. Jordan's doctor examined her with minute attention, prescribing calm and absolute rest.

"I don't know," he said to Jordan at the street door. "She has a great weakness that I am unable to explain. And with no vomiting, nothing. . . . If she wakes tomorrow as she did today, call me at once."

When she awakened the following day, Alicia was worse. There was a consultation. It was agreed there was an anaemia of incredible progression, completely inexplicable. Alicia had no more fainting spells, but she was visibly moving toward death. The lights were lighted all day long in her bedroom, and there was complete silence. Hours went by without the slightest sound. Alicia dozed. Jordan virtually lived in the drawing room, which was also always lighted. With tireless persistence he paced ceaselessly from one end of the room to the other. The carpet swallowed his steps. At times he entered the bedroom and continued his silent pacing back and forth alongside the bed, stopping for an instant at each end to regard his wife.

Suddenly Alicia began to have hallucinations, vague images, at first seeming to float in the air, then descending to floor level. Her eyes excessively wide, she stared continuously at the carpet on either side of the head of her bed. One night she suddenly focused on one spot. Then she opened her mouth to scream, and pearls of sweat suddenly beaded her nose and lips.

"Jordan! Jordan!" she clamored, rigid with fright, still staring at the carpet.

Jordan ran to the bedroom, and, when she saw him appear, Alicia screamed with terror.

"It's I, Alicia, it's I!"

Alicia looked at him confusedly; she looked at the carpet; she looked at him once again; and after a long moment of stupefied confrontation, she regained her senses. She smiled and took her husband's hand in hers, caressing it, trembling, for half an hour.

Among her most persistent hallucinations was that of an anthropoid poised on his fingertips on the carpet, staring at her.

The doctors returned, but to no avail. They saw before them a diminishing life, a life bleeding away day by day, hour by hour, absolutely without their knowing why. During their last consultation Alicia lay in a stupor while they took her pulse, passing her inert wrist from one to another. They observed her a long time in silence and then moved into the dining room.

"Phew. . . ." The discouraged chief physician shrugged his shoulders. "It is an inexplicable case. There is little we can do."

"That's my last hope!" Jordan groaned. And he staggered blindly against the table.

Alicia's life was fading away in the subdelirium of anaemia, a delirium that grew worse through the evening hours but that let up somewhat after dawn. The illness never worsened during the daytime, but each morning she awakened pale as death, almost in a swoon. It seemed only at night that her life drained out of her in new waves of blood. Always when she awakened she had the sensation of lying collapsed in the bed with a million-pound weight on top of her. Following the third day of this relapse she never left her bed again. She could scarcely move her head. She did not want her bed to be touched, not even to have her bedcovers arranged. Her crepuscular terrors advanced now in the form of monsters that dragged themselves toward the bed and laboriously climbed upon the bedspread.

Then she lost consciousness. The final two days she raved ceaselessly in a weak voice. The lights funereally illuminated the bedroom and drawing room. In the deathly silence of the house the only sound was the monotonous delirium from the bedroom and the dull echoes of Jordan's eternal pacing.

Finally, Alicia died. The servant, when she came in afterward to strip the now empty bed, stared wonderingly for a moment at the pillow.

"Sir!" she called Jordan in a low voice. "There are stains on the pillow that look like blood."

Jordan approached rapidly and bent over the pillow. Truly, on the case, on both sides of the hollow left by Alicia's head, were two small dark spots.

"They look like punctures," the servant murmured after a moment of motionless observation.

"Hold it up to the light," Jordan told her.

The servant raised the pillow but immediately dropped it and stood staring at it, livid and trembling. Without knowing why, Jordan felt the hair rise on the back of his neck.

"What is it?" he murmured in a hoarse voice.

"It's very heavy," the servant whispered, still trembling.

Jordan picked it up; it was extraordinarily heavy. He carried it out of the room, and on the dining room table he ripped open the case and the ticking with a slash. The top feathers floated away, and the servant, her mouth opened wide, gave a scream of horror and covered her face with her clenched fists. In the bottom of the pillowcase, among the feathers, slowly moving its hairy legs, was a monstrous animal, a living, viscous ball. It was so swollen one could scarcely make out its mouth.

Night after night, since Alicia had taken to her bed, this abomination had stealthily applied its mouth—its proboscis one might better say—to the girl's temples, sucking her blood. The puncture was scarcely perceptible. The daily plumping of the pillow had doubtlessly at first impeded its progress, but as soon as the girl could no longer move, the suction became vertiginous. In five days, in five nights, the monster had drained Alicia's life away.

These parasites of feathered creatures, diminutive in their habitual environment, reach enormous proportions under certain conditions. Human blood seems particularly favorable to them, and it is not rare to encounter them in feather pillows.

The Fisherman's Special

H. L. THOMSON

And so," said my lean-jawed share-of-a-seat on the Fisherman's Special from New York to Montauk, "there's more—much more, to it than backwoods superstition. Man—" he leaned over and pounded my knee with his hard, brown fist. "I tell you, I know."

I laughed. I had to. This big, hulking chap, who had seated himself beside me when the Special pulled out of Pennsylvania Station, had me jittery with his talk about the supernatural powers of man. He'd been at it for over an hour. I shivered, Patchogue and the Hamptons were behind us and the wind blasting through the opened windows of the coach was cold. Besides, this talk of werewolves and other things I had relegated to my adolescence caused goosebumps to shoot along my spine.

"I'll tell you a queer story," commenced my seatmate. "Back in my country—"

I looked at him quickly. He didn't look like a foreigner to me.

He grinned. "I've been here a long time," he said.

"You certainly have no trace of an accent," I said. "English?"

"No. Swedish. A man who has to travel a lot—first in one country, then another—soon loses his accent."

"I suppose so," I told him.

"I come from a small town in the extreme northern part of Sweden," he said. "Many queer and unnatural things happen there. There are werewolves—men who, at will, turn themselves into wolfmen and roam the countryside, bringing death, misery, and stark, wild-eyed horror." He shuddered and continued. "It's nothing new. It's old—old. It's been going on since the beginning of time. It's written of in musty books and talked of furtively as darkness falls. Every year at the beginning of the Christmas season, that's when it happens. It's when the snow burns blue with the coming dark, and squeals beneath your boots. The conversion of men into beasts! It has always been so. They descend upon the helpless inhabitants of ancient villages and destroy them."

"A lot of good yarns have been spun around that sort of thing," I said. "Interesting reading. Good stuff!"

His steady eyes stared straight ahead and he didn't answer me for a minute or two. Then he jerked his head impatiently. "Up there—just before night—when the snow is so white it turns blue and squeals beneath your boots like a living thing—" His voice died away as if he were living a million miles away.

He continued in the same singsong voice, "There, in the town where I grew up, lived two brothers. Both were tall, straight, and strong. They loved the same girl, but she preferred the older brother. He was good and steady, and the young one"—his voice became harsh—"was a fool. Selma—that was her name. She married the older brother early one spring, and the three of them lived together in their old, whitewashed house near the end of the village. But, the happiness of his brother and Selma kept misery gnawing at the innards of the younger brother. He grew morose and ugly. He spent his nights in the town tavern. He'd stay there until all the lights in the little house were out. Then he'd go in and throw himself into bed and fall into drunken slumber."

I commenced to fidget. I wished soundly that I was at Montauk or back in New York. This fellow got on my nerves, dreamily. I made up my mind to check him fast during the rush from the train. I must have missed part of the conversation. I caught myself up short when I hear him say "werewolves."

"What's that?" I asked.

"I said that the stranger he met in the tavern one winter's night told him he could change himself into a wolfman and join the other werewolves on the eve of Christmas."

I shoved my tongue in my cheek. "He told the younger brother that?"

He nodded. "Yes. He told him how it might be done."

"Did he do it?" I asked.

My somber friend nodded again.

"How?" I asked, smirking. "I might try it myself if the fish aren't biting out here."

He gripped my arm. "My friend, if you value your sanity, if you would not rove the world with the screams of the innocents in your ears, if you value your hope of immortality—never try it. The poor misguided younger brother was a victim of jealousy—fancied wrongs."

"We all have 'em," I said. "How's it done?"

"It is done," he said, glancing over his shoulder, quickly, "by muttering certain words—"

"What words?" I interrupted.

"Those I shall not tell you. By muttering certain words and drinking a cup of ale to a man-wolf. If he accepts, it renders the man-natural worthy of acceptance of the werewolf state."

"I'll have to remember that," I said. "I've had many a cup of ale with strangers. All of which reminds me—how about a drink?" I reached for my gunny sack.

"I never drink."

"Well, here's to you," I said, peeling off the top of my "jug." Whether the road bed was rougher than usual, or whether the train went around a curve, I don't know. But, suddenly, my friend fell, almost in my lap, and my bottle of rye went out of the window.

Old gloom-face smiled. "I'm sorry," he said. "Possibly, I can make it up to you by finishing my story."

I grinned with only one side of my mouth. "Forget it. Shoot. Did the younger brother turn himself into a werewolf?"

"He did. On the eve of Christmas, when they strung the tree with popcorn and red cranberries, his hatred and jealousy boiled over. He tore out of the house and went to the tavern. There he filled himself with spirits and brooded over his loss of Selma. After a time, he got to his feet and went into the forest. There, in his drunkenness, he pronounced the words and assumed the wolf form."

"What'd he do? Go back and gnaw up his brother?"

"He came back, but first he traveled to the spot that had been made known to him by the stranger in the tavern. It was many miles north, beneath the wall of a ruined castle of some feudal lord. There he joined hundreds of others, who, in natural form, were weak, frustrated men such as he.

"Then the pack set out en masse. Strong doors were paper before them, white, unprotected throats their aim. Shrill gurgling screams of their victims on the still, cold air whetted their appetites."

"What about the younger brother—our hero?" I asked.

"I haven't forgotten the younger brother. He ran with great, leaping bounds straight to his home. His red tongue lolled from his gaping mouth. His eyes were green—green in their madness."

I frowned. This fellow certainly threw himself into his story like a professional. He had goose-flesh on my neck.

"This werewolf—this beast—attacked his brother and the lovely Selma as they lay in their bed. He felt his own brother's hot blood in his dry throat. He shook him as a terrier does a rag.

"The lovely Selma screamed and tore at him with her little hands."

"And no one came to help them?" I asked.

"You forget. The town was in an uproar. The whole pack attacked."

"And—Selma?" I said.

"Yes—Selma. Selma grabbed the other brother's hunting-knife from his belt on the back of the chair and stabbed at the werewolf, screaming curses."

"My God, how ghastly! Did she kill him?"

He shook his head. "No, she didn't kill him—she only tore off his right ear with the sharp knife, and, in the manner of all things who attack in the night his own pain defeated him. He ran out of the house and from the village. He disappeared into the dark forest. His red blood stained the white snow for miles."

"They could have trailed him that way."

He shook his head. "No. He assumed the human form once he was in the forest and staunched the flow of blood."

"But the wound," I protested. "How could he explain that to the townspeople—to Selma?"

"He never went back. He ran away. The people of the town must have thought he too was a victim of the werewolves that bloody, gory night."

The conductor pulled the door of the coach open. "Montauk! Montauk!" he called.

All around us men started whooping and grabbing up their equipment. I sat quietly for a minute.

"What a story!" I finally managed to say. "What a story to tell a man when he's out at the end of nowhere! I've got the creeps."

He shrugged. "It was merely to pass the time. Any sort of conversation to pass the time. Good luck—good fishing." He got up to get his stuff.

"Same to you," I said, sticking out my hand.

As my eyes met his, I started, and my hand dropped nervelessly to my side.

He grinned crookedly, but that lopsided twitching of his face only accentuated the horror of the livid hole where his right ear should have been.

THE FROG

GRANVILLE S. HOSS

November 4th.—It has long been my contention that the great difference in the intelligence and advancement of man, in comparison with the lower animals, has not been due to any innate superiority or peculiar advantage arbitrarily bestowed by the creator. I have held the theory that man's leadership of all created life has been due to the more rapid absorption by his brain of certain chemical properties that have tended to promote growth of the brain cells with corresponding expansion of his intellect.

I have believed that if it were possible to reduce to concrete form the chemical elements that have given growth and development to the mind of man, it would be possible to inject the resulting substance into the brain of one of the lower forms of life and raise the subject of the experiment to the intellectual level of man.

This thought first came to me in my college days. It has been with me throughout all the years since that time. Never but once have I shared these views with another. Fifteen years ago I admitted my closest friend, Dr. Mark Potter, to my thoughts. I talked enthusiastically and at length, giving in detail what I considered substantial reasons for my conclusions, ending by suggesting that he join me in the effort to verify the deductions at which I had arrived.

His laughter was like a basin of ice water dashed in my face. "Illingham," he cried, "you are crazy, or soon will be if you continue to dwell on such thoughts. Forget that idle twaddle and give your time to advancing in your profession. One way leads to fortune and renown; the other, to the madhouse."

I made no reply to this tirade, but changed the conversation and for the remainder of the time we were together discussed the latest issue of the *Medical and Surgical Review*.

But my efforts were continued. My leisure hours and for the past ten years my whole time has been given to what has become the one absorbing interest of my life, and now I am ready for the final grand test. I shall soon know if the years have been wasted or if I have found one of the great secrets of life.

I am too nervous to write any more tonight. I must go out for a walk.

November 5th. — While this diary is not meant to be seen by other eyes than my own, I shall nevertheless not go into details of the composition of my brain serum, as life is uncertain and the record might fall into the hands of others. It has been a weary task to gain the small phial of the precious substance now reposing in my safe. In order to get it, I have been many times guilty of what the law pronounces to be serious crimes. I have not hesitated to violate the grave and betray the most sacred trusts. If failure is my portion, then my life will have been worse than wasted. In that event I shall not face the light of another day, but seek rest in Nirvana. On the other hand, success will wipe clean the slate and I will have added inestimably to the world's knowledge. The veil that hides many of the phenomena of earthly life will have been pierced.

November 8th. — For three days I have been attempting to decide on a subject for the final great test. Shall it be bird, beast, or reptile? In my opinion, any specimen will answer. As my supply of brain serum is very limited, I think I shall select a small creature, so if the results are not immediately what I expect, I can discontinue the injections and select some other species. I must give this matter the thought it deserves.

November 11th. — My decision is made. I have chosen a bullfrog, a fine, healthy fellow I obtained from the lake adjacent to the city. I have constructed him a home in my laboratory, a small pool of cement with a bottom of mud and water plants. My greatest difficulty will be suitable food, but I think it can be managed. Tonight I shall administer the first injection of brain serum. I am nervous and laboring under great excitement. This will not do. I must be calm.

November 12th. — Mr. Frog withstood the operation beautifully. I was quite alarmed at first, as he lay in a comatose state for an hour and was quite dazed for a much longer period. He is active now. I am unable to observe any change in him, unless it is that he moves about more than formerly. I feel much encouraged. The results are all I have hoped for from the first tiny injection of serum.

November 17th. — Eureka! Success has attended me. After three more injections of serum, my frog shows unmistakable signs of an awakening intelligence. He starts at sudden noises, and, instead of at once plunging into the basin, he immediately faces in the direction from whence they come, seeming to ponder the cause. He apparently watches me as I move about the room and seems to have no fear. He spends less time in the water and moves about the room in a restless manner. I wish now my selection had been different. A creature higher in the scale of life — a monkey, for instance — might in time have been taught to communicate with me. However, it is too late now for regrets and I shall keep on with the frog.

November 25th. — Undoubtedly, my theory has been proven correct. Each day my frog grows in intelligence. He watches my every movement and observes me at my meals, which I have formed the habit of preparing in my laboratory, where I also sleep. At first he would eat nothing but insects, but the other day I tried him with a small piece of vegetable on the end of my knife. His tongue at once seized the morsel, which he promptly swallowed. Since then, he always partakes with me when I eat. He seems to be losing his appetite for insects, for when offered a fly alongside a tiny bit from my plate, he rejected the fly for the other. He spends less and less time in the water.

I have been under a nervous strain since commencing the experiment and seem unable to throw it off. This positively will not do. I must relax.

November 30th. — My frog has developed a memory. He has seemed to recognize me for several days, and when I enter the room from an excursion to the outside he hops toward me with every appearance of delight, uttering queer little croaking noises. Last night I offered him a small portion of food sprinkled with quinine powder; he accepted it, but immediately emitted a raucous cry and attempted to eject the bitter dose. He acted completely disgusted, moved from my vicinity and would have nothing more to do with me the whole evening. This episode is full of interest.

December 4th. — Mr. Bullfrog has become quite an imitator. He not only follows me about, seemingly interested in my every movement, but tonight attempted to stand upright. He was only partly successful, maintaining his balance for but a few seconds, then falling to the floor. He also tries to use his hands, keeping one continually moving, while resting on the other. He picks up small articles, such as match sticks and any other tiny objects he finds in his way. I now call him and he responds. He quails at a note of anger in my voice, much in the manner of a puppy. In the light of my present success, I now wish more than ever I had selected some creature higher in the scale of life for the experiment. However, it is too late. My malady increases. My nights are broken.

December 10th. — I am disappointed. While my frog develops in mind each day, I can now see that he has not a human mind and never will have. His brain might expand to the utmost in cunning, but it would still be reptilian. I experienced an example of this a few nights ago. I crossed the room hurriedly in answer to the ringing of the telephone and stepped on one of the frog's feet, with the result that he is now a cripple. He uttered a loud cry, sprang upon my foot and attempted to bite me. Of course this was impossible, considering that he has no teeth, but his actions quite shocked me. He now will have nothing to do with me, backing away at my approach and uttering ribald, raucous cries. I know of no other words to describe his noise. He has formed a bitter hatred for me, watching me unceasingly with what appears to be a baleful glare in his eyes, ready at my first movement in his direction to back away with his awful cries.

December 15th. — My old nervous disorder has returned upon me with full vigor. I have been unable to sleep for three nights and suppose I shall have to go back to drugs in order to get necessary sleep. The frog still refuses all my friendly advances and exhibits an unholy cunning.

December 20th. — Last night I enjoyed the first sound sleep I have had for a week, but was awakened in the most extraordinary manner, which would be ridiculous were it not for the shattered condition of my nerves. I was aroused by a cold sensation on my chest, to find the frog seated there, his little hands gripping my throat and apparently attempting to the utmost of his puny strength to strangle me. At my first awakening, he leaped to the floor and retreated to his pool, uttering his unearthly cries, which to my half-aroused senses seemed to be charged with threats. I wish I could kill the monster, but cannot. He seems like a creature of my own creation, being, as he is, the culminating result of years of preparation.

December 22nd.—I was reawakened last night in the same ghoulish manner, with the addition that this time he was attempting to bite. Had he been gifted with fangs, they would certainly have been buried in my throat. I shall be compelled to confine the beast if this continues. I wonder if my snores annoy him. I am aware that I snore dreadfully and know it must be worse than ever when sleep is induced by artificial means, as is now necessary with me. Anyway, the hatred of the frog is mounting, as shown by attacks on two successive nights.

December 23rd.—Again! This time the rascal was clawing and tearing at my mouth. As I sat up, he leaped to the floor and hurried to his pool, where I heard him plunge in. His cries were fearful, baleful, and to my drug-clouded senses, laden with warning. This positively will not do. Today I shall build a fine wire fence about his pool. Let him use the brain I have given him and climb out if he can.

Extract from the Evening Star,
December 24th

Dr. John Illingham, a well-known retired physician of this city, was discovered dead in his bed today. Death was due to strangulation. Lodged firmly in his throat, as though he had made an effort to swallow it, was a full-grown bullfrog.

Medical examination disclosed the fact that Dr. Illingham had been in the habit of using large quantities of drugs, and it has been suggested that he had become temporarily insane and attempted to swallow the frog. Only a crazed man would attempt such a feat. The frog was quite dead when removed from the throat of the deceased.

In the combined laboratory and bedroom, where the body was discovered, a small concrete pool had been built and around it erected a fine wire fence about five feet in height.

A strange diary was found among Dr. Illingham's effects, which seems to bear out the insanity theory. In this diary is mentioned the name of Dr. Mark Potter, a well-known physician of this city. In the absence of any known relatives of Dr. Illingham, the diary has been turned over to Dr. Potter.

I have read the diary of my old friend Dr. Illingham and have been asked to make a statement thereon. There is little I can say. It is true that years ago he mentioned some such theory as that described in the diary. Whether it contained any truth or not, who can now say? If the diary is a strict record of fact, then it is apparent that the frog took the only method at his command to make an end of one whom he had come to hate and fear. If the coroner's theory is correct and the diary contains the ravings of a madman, then the conclusion arrived at by that official is probably true.

Frogfather

MANLY WADE WELLMAN

No, I never liked frogs' legs very much, not even before what happened. And I wouldn't eat them now if I was starving. This is why.

Though I'd known and worked for Ranson Cuff for two years, all of each day and part of most nights, I remember him clearly only in the dark of that particular night we went frog hunting. Ranson Cuff was the sort of man who shoved himself into your mind, like a snake crawling into a gopher hole. I defy anyone to find anyone else who liked Ranson Cuff—maybe his wife liked him, but she didn't live with him for more than three weeks. Nobody around the Swamps liked him, though he was the best off in money. He ran a string of hunting camps for strangers from up north, who came to hunt deer or fish for bass, once in a while to chase bear with dogs. He did his end of that job well, and if he was rude the strangers figured him for a picturesque character. I've heard them call him that. The Swamps people called him other things, to his face if he didn't have mortgages on their houseboats, cabins, and trapping outfits.

This night we were paddling, he and I and an old, old Indian whose name I never knew, in a really beautiful boat he'd taken for a bad debt. Cuff was going to get a mess of frogs' legs, which he loved, and which he'd love three times as much because he'd killed the frogs for them. Cuff would have killed people if he'd dared, just for fun. I know he would. I'd gone to work for him when I was fifteen—my old maid aunt, who raised me, owed him money she could never pay. When he told her to, she gave me to him, and I suppose what I earned went into settling the debt. Slavery—and he was the quickest and oftenest to remind me of it.

That night was clear and dark, not a speck of moon and all the stars anyone ever saw at once. They sheened the swamp water, up to where the great fat clumps of trees cuddled it in at the edges. I paddled, the old Indian paddled, and Cuff sat like a fat toad—not a frog—in the bow with his lantern and his gig. The lantern light gave his face the kind of shadows that showed us what he was. His face was as round as a lemon, and as yellow and as sour. His mouth was small, and his eyes couldn't have been closer together without mixing into each other, and his little nose was the only bony thing about him.

"Head for that neck of water northeast," he said. "I haven't ever been in there, but I hear frogs singing. And none of them are out along these banks."

He cursed the frogs for not being there to kill. I began to scoop with my paddle to turn the boat the way he said, but the old Indian pulled his paddle out with a little dripping slop.

"We don't go there," said the old Indian. He spoke wonderful English, better than Cuff or myself.

"Don't go where?" snarled Cuff. He always snarled, at people who had to take it. The old Indian had come to work for him, hungry and ragged, and wasn't exactly fat or well dressed now.

"I'm speaking for your good, Mr. Cuff," said the old Indian. "That's no place to stick frogs."

"I can hear them singing!" Cuff said. "Listen, there must be a whole nation of them."

"They're there because they're safe," said the old Indian.

"Khaa!" Cuff spit into the water. "Safe! That's what they think. We're going in there to stick a double mess."

"I'm of the first people here, and I can tell you the truth of it, Mr. Cuff," went on the old Indian, with Indian quiet and Indian stubbornness. "I'm surprised you don't know about that neck of water and what's beyond. It's the home of Khongabassi."

"Don't know him," growled Cuff.

"Khongabassi," repeated the old Indian. "The Frogfather. He's lived there since the world was made. The oldest ones say he dug the waterways and planted the trees along them. And the frogs are his children."

"Oh, heaven deliver me!" Cuff screwed his fat face into the sourest frown I had ever seen, even on him. "Indian talk I came out to hear. You make me sick. Get going northwest."

"No," and the old Indian laid his paddle inside the boat.

"You're fired, you old—" and Cuff cursed the Indian every way he knew. He knew a great many ways, including the Indian's ancestry back to Adam and his children down to the last generation. "You're fired," he said again. "Get out of this boat."

"Yes, Mr. Cuff," said the old Indian gently. "Put it to the shore—"

"Get out right here," blustered Cuff, "I'm not taking you to the shore."

"Yes," said the old Indian again, and slipped overboard sidewise, like a muskrat. He barely rippled the water as he swam away. Cuff spit after him, and cocked his head.

"Hark at those frogs singing!" he said. "Frogfather—I'll frogfather them! Right in their pappy's dooryard. Johnny," he said to me, "get us going there."

I did all the paddling, and we came to the neck of water. Trees were close on both sides, shutting out the little, little gleam of starlight, but there seemed to be a sort of green brightness beyond. Cuff swore at me to make me ship my paddle.

"Look at the glow from under the surface," said Cuff. He reached right down into his half-knowledge for a cozy explanation. "Must be full of those little shiny bugs like the ones in the sea. Makes it easy for us to find the frogs."

I remembered how my grandfather had once said you're better off knowing a few things than to know so many things that aren't so. My hunch was that maybe there was rotten wood somewhere around, what old-timers call foxfire. Cuff, at the bow, knelt with his lantern in one hand and his gig in the other. The gig had a hand-forged fork for its head, three sharp barbed spikes. The shaft was a piece of hickory, about four feet long and as thick as your hand could hold comfortably.

"Snake us along the bank, Johnny," he said. "Now hold her. I see one."

I saw it too, in the light of his lantern, a nice fat green frog on a rock set in some roots. It squatted with its knees high and its hands together in front of it, like a boy waiting his turn at a marble game. Its head was lifted, its eyes fixed by the dazzling glare of the lantern, and those eyes were like precious jewels. Cuff stabbed down, and brought it up, squirming and kicking, its mouth gaped open, all three tines of his gig in it. He smacked it on the inside of the boat to quiet it, and shoved it off at my feet.

"Got your knife?" he growled. "Then slice off its legs—no, snake me along again, I see a bigger one yonder.

"You're tipping me away," he said. "Balance me back, or I'll put a knot on your head with this gig-handle."

"It's not me, Mr. Cuff," I argued, but not with any heart in it, because he always frightened me. "You must be tipping us—"

"My weight's here next the frog, you fool," he said. "And you're tipping us toward the water. You'll have us over in a minute!"

The boat was tipping, and I shifted to bring her back on an even keel, but she tipped more, and I looked around to see what snag might have hooked us.

Over the thwart lay something like a long, smooth piece of wood, darkish and dampish in the dim light. Yes, a snag, I thought. But Cuff turned and lifted the lantern, and I saw it was no snag.

It was a long green arm!

From elbow to fingertip it was visible above the thwart, weighting down that side of the boat and tipping us in the direction of the open water. The ordinary human arm is eighteen inches long, I hear, the length of the old-fashioned Bible cubit. This was longer than that. Two feet at least, and probably more. It was muscled smoothly and trimly from the neat point of the elbow to the slender, supple wrist, and beyond this stretched slim, pointed fingers, but not enough. The hand spread, and it had three fingers and a thumb, with no gap where the other finger had been lost. Between them was a shiny wet web, and it was dead gray, while the arm was covered with sleek green skin blotched twice or three times with brown-black spots as big as saucers.

What Cuff said I wouldn't want written down as my own last words. He said it loudly, and at the noise another arm came up across the other, and hooked there. Then a head came into view and looked at us.

The lantern light caught the eyes first, great popped-out eyes of every jewel-flashing color known to the vainest woman that lives. They looked at Cuff. They were set in a heavy, blunt head the size of a fish basket, and in some ways the head was like Cuff's. But it had no bony nose, no nose at all, and the mouth was a long curved slit like a tight-closed Gladstone bag. Under the mouth, where the chin ought to be, the white throat dipped in and out, in and out, breathing calmly.

196

The creature lifted a hand, quicker than Cuff could stab. It took hold of the gig just below the head. That hickory was as strong as a hoe-handle, but the big green webbed hand snapped off the iron fork just like picking a daisy, and tossed it away with a splash. At that splash every frog stopped singing. And the big elbows heaved a little, shoulders came into view, and I saw what there was to see of the creature, down to where its waist came out of the water.

All blotchy green and brown, with a white belly and a wet smoothness, it was a frog. But it was bigger than a man by twice, I suppose. Our boat went over, and I flew through the air and splashed in. That moment in the air was enough to see Cuff caught by neck and shoulder in those two green hands. And he went down under water, lantern and all. He hadn't time for another curse.

As I sank, I got my arms and legs working. I was more anxious to swim away than swim up. My eyes were open, and I saw under the water by the green light that was there. That part of the Swamps must have been the deepest, and many times my length below I could make out old drowned tree-trunks, a lost forest from some ancient time of storm and washaway. They were mixed up together as if something had tried to make a hut or nest of them, and I suppose something had. There was a hole among them like a door, with the green light coming from it, and down toward that hole swam a long green shape, nine feet at least from its blunt head to the heels of its flipping webbed feet. Under one arm it carried Cuff, tucked like a stolen baby, and the other hand helped swim it along.

Then I broke surface and churned away, sick and faint and ready to burst with my pounding heart, but making for the little channel by which we had come into the place.

I made it, and when I swam out, I heard a long, soft whistle. It made me almost jump out of the water. Another whistle, and something dark and swift and silent came toward me. I tried to turn away, but my strength was gone. The dark shape bore close, and it was a canoe. The old Indian put down his hand and helped me get in. Then I lay there and came to life, while he paddled the canoe idly around and around, here and there, on the peaceful starlit water.

He did not seem surprised or even curious. He asked me nothing. When I was able, I told him what had happened.

"It was Khongabassi," he said quietly when I had finished. "Khongabassi, the Frogfather. When a stranger comes to kill children in their very home, will not their father help them?"

That was something new to think about. I got strength to sit up.

"We'll have to get help," I said, "and go back and—"

"And challenge Khongabassi?" he finished for me. "Why? He saved his children. He took only Mr. Cuff and let you go. Khongabassi never takes any more prey than he needs. But if many men go there, with grappling hooks and weapons—then Khongabassi will have a way to deal with them, and I do not want to see it."

I didn't want to see it, either. I asked a question. "You knew all about Khongabassi, didn't you? You knew what he would do?"

I saw the old Indian's head nod against the stars. "Of course. He has done that to others who came to his home without permission. We first people learned many lives ago to keep to our ways and leave him to his. Khongabassi is not terrible, he is only Khongabassi. You think of him as what we call a *djibaw*, an evil spirit. We think of him as a part of nature, that defends nature's weak things. Men should be a part of nature, too, and perhaps they would escape what Mr. Cuff has not escaped."

"What shall we do, though?" I persisted.

"Oh," said the old Indian, "we shall think of a story, you and I, that explains Mr. Cuff's death. A story that white men will believe."

The Gargoyle Sacrifice

Tina L. Jens

The gargoyle's red eyes flashed. Its distended belly seemed to pulsate as its tongue flicked the air.

Marissa would have sworn the gargoyle was watching her through the doubled-paned glass cage. Its body was made of sterling silver, its belly a ruby-colored stone the size of the lenses in her Lennon glasses. Smaller rubies were embedded in the demon's eye sockets. Finely engraved taloned claws stretched to form the sides of the collar necklace. Marissa imagined what it would feel like to clamp the talons down over her shoulder bones.

She wanted the monster—wanted it badly.

But it was trapped in the display case, just as surely as she was

198

trapped in the Sun King's Occult Book Store. She'd come at her boy-friend's urging. After hours Pharaoh, the store manager and the Sun King's servant, did body piercings, tattooing, and pagan earth ceremonies in the back room.

Marissa's excursion into the front room was a brief reprieve. Any moment Rudy would come looking for her to drag her back for her turn in the chair. Rudy wanted her to get her nipples pierced, promised to buy her a gold chain to suspend between them. Probably wanted to yank on it while he was doing it to her.

She wouldn't mind having a gold chain. But she didn't see how he could afford it when he'd begged ten dollars off her that afternoon to help pay last month's rent. She'd taken it out of her old man's wallet. With any luck he'd be drunk before he noticed it was missing. He didn't hit as hard when he was drunk.

She rubbed her hand over her breast, the flannel softly comforting her. It would hurt. Last week Mindy had cried for half an hour. It had taken forever to stop the bleeding. When she finally left, the whole front of her shirt was red with blood.

The ruby eyes flashed again. The gargoyle was laughing at her for being such a chicken-shit. Marissa turned away from the display case. Maybe she'd have *one* done, see how it felt.

She pulled her worn leather jacket tighter around her and drifted down the aisle. She scanned the ancient Egyptology book section, then turned away in boredom. The next counter held incense and candles. She wrinkled her nose, disgusted at the smell. Still, she liked the little brass burners; they were dainty, delicate.

She heard the beads in the doorway clacking. Probably Rudy looking for her.

"Come on, Marissa. You're going to lose your turn," Rudy whined.

Marissa studied her boyfriend. He wasn't much to look at. Tall and too thin, with dirty brown hair that fell past his shoulders. But he was one of the oldest guys in the group and he could French inhale his Camel cigarettes. Marissa had to be careful. A lot of the girls would be happy to steal him.

"I'm comin'," she said shrugging. Her leather jacket squeaked loud in the silence. "Wanna show you something first."

She led him to the counter and crouched down in front of the display case. He hunched down to see what she was pointing at.

"Isn't he beautiful!" Marissa whispered.

" 's okay."

He pointed to the card sitting beside it. FOR DISPLAY ONLY. "Means it's expensive."

He sounded more interested now.

"I heard about this necklace," Rudy told her. "The guys were talkin' about it last week. It's supposed to be magic. The last piece the Sun King made. The night before he went to jail, they had this big midnight ceremony, took a blood sacrifice from all three of his kids."

"That's why his belly glows," Marissa murmured.

Rudy laughed. "They're full of shit!"

"What'd the Sun King go to jail for?" Marissa asked.

She'd just turned fourteen and started coming to the store. She was too young to have met the store owner. Rudy was eighteen. He'd been coming here a long time.

"Bunch of stuff," Rudy said casually. "Statutory rape, animal mutilation, possession of controlled substances. That kind of thing. Got twenty years. But the Sun King's got connections. He won't be in long."

He stared at the necklace thoughtfully.

"Those are supposed to be real rubies and silver," he said slowly. "I bet it's worth some money."

"Would it cost more than a gold chain?" Marissa hinted.

"Doesn't have to," Rudy said, daring her.

"I already checked," Marissa said, the disappointment heavy in her voice. "The case is locked."

She felt Rudy's arm snake around her waist. He leaned close and whispered in her ear.

"Look baby, I'm short on cash tonight. I was going to have you pay for the pierc—"

Marissa jerked away and glared at him.

"Hey! I was gonna pay you back," Rudy said, defensively.

He pulled her body back to him.

"I got a better idea, now. You can get both your nips pierced *and* get the necklace—free of charge."

With a flip of his head he tossed the hair out of his eyes.

"How?" Marissa demanded.

"Tell the Pharaoh you want to make Alternate Arrangements for payment," Rudy said, smoothly.

Marissa shook her head. "Pharaoh's not gonna trade the necklace for Alternate Arrangements. Besides, the card says it's not for sale."

She stroked the glass, wishing desperately she could pet the gargoyle. She would have sworn its belly was glowing, beckoning to her.

Rudy's breath tickled her ear again.

"He'll make Arrangements for the piercings. If you keep him busy long enough, I'll do some arranging of my own." He smiled at her encouragingly.

"I don't know, Rudy," Marissa said, slowly.

"You want the gargoyle don't you?"

She nodded.

He shoved her toward the beaded door.

"Remember, get the hoops. They'll work better with the chain."

Marissa whispered "Alternate Arrangements" in the Pharaoh's ear. He grinned a fat, greasy smile at her and led her to the reclining chair. She stared at the dozen faces that had gathered around the chair to watch.

Around the room teenagers were flopped down on ratty furniture, drinking cheap beer and smoking rolled cigarettes. A New Age music tape was blaring from a portable tape player, the sound heavy with flutes and wind chimes. Clouds of incense hung in the air.

Marissa's head was swimming.

"Want a shot?" one of the older boys asked her.

She nodded and he poured her some whiskey in the community shot glass. She choked it down, coughing.

"You'll be all right," the boy told her.

Pharaoh sat down beside her. "Rudy tells me you want hoops."

Marissa nodded, dumbly.

"I am just the Sun King's servant," Pharaoh said, as he fumbled with the buttons of her gray flannel shirt. "But I think he would approve."

He pulled the material away and caressed her. "Very nice," he hissed, rolling her nipples between the thumb and finger of each hand.

A sea of faces nodded in agreement.

Marissa swallowed hard, forcing back the bile that was welling up in her throat. The incense and whiskey were making her sick. She stared at the Pharaoh's blood-splattered shirt.

It was bad enough to be pawed in front of everybody. She tried not to think about what would happen when the piercing was done. Pharaoh would take her to the bathroom for that part.

A crack rang out, loud as a gun shot, in her ears. It was just Pharaoh at the ice tray. She moaned and tried to concentrate on the gargoyle, as he advanced toward her wielding an ice cube and a carpet needle.

❀ ❀ ❀

201

Marissa huddled against the wall under the El tracks, and stroked the gargoyle's red belly. The necklace seemed to emit its own heat lying against her skin. It comforted her in the chilly night.

She let her fingers stray down to her breasts. They still ached from the piercing. It hadn't helped that Rudy had kept trying to pinch them.

She'd rushed straight out of the shop after she'd paid off the Pharaoh. Ran the whole five blocks to the alley where she and Rudy always met. He wouldn't tell her if he got the gargoyle. Demanded that she show him first. She opened her jacket and unbuttoned her blouse, displaying herself for his approval. The cold had turned her nipples hard, making them ache even more.

He'd wanted to pull on them, play with them. He started pouting when she told him to knock it off. But he stopped her when she tried to button her shirt. Marissa saw the gargoyle's eyes flash as Rudy pulled it out of his pocket.

The metal should have felt cold in the night air, but it was warm, almost hot, as Rudy slipped it on her.

Marissa stroked the gargoyle's belly again. She almost thought she could feel its heart beating.

Rudy had wanted to screw her. But one fat, humping pig a night was enough. Of course, she hadn't said that to Rudy. After twenty minutes of trying to force her, he'd stalked off in a huff.

Marissa was glad he left. Except that she'd been counting on sleeping over at his place. She wanted to avoid the old man for a few days.

She'd be all right under the tracks for the night. It was too cold for the drug pushers to hang out. They'd stay in their cars. And the street people would be fighting over the heating grates.

She was getting hungry. Marissa unwrapped and ate the other half of the candy bar she'd stolen out of a vending machine. She arranged some old newspapers she pulled out of the dumpster into a seat against the wall, then leaned her head back and closed her eyes.

Marissa slept fitfully. The cold bit at her. The El rumbled overhead. Awful images filled her dreams. Fat old men pawing at her naked body. Rudy, forcing her down on all fours, whipping her, dragging her around by a long gold chain. Her old man backhanding her across the room, pulling her across the kitchen by the hair, grabbing her by the throat and bending her backwards over the kitchen table, then choking her, harder and harder.

Marissa jerked awake, gasping. She choked and tried to catch her breath. The nightmares were gone but the viselike grip on her neck remained. Tears leaked from her eyes as she fought to unzip her jacket. She tried to wedge her fingers under the metal collar. It was sticky. Her hands kept slipping. A sharp pain shot across her neck, as the collar cut through her skin. Rivulets of blood seeped down her chest.

She felt the body of the gargoyle move. Its claws dug deep into her shoulders as it slowly pulled itself up her chest. She felt its hot breath against her skin. A dark chuckle rumbled in her ear, its grip ever tighter cutting through her neck. Then more pain, as its teeth ripped her ear-lobe.

"You've done well," the Sun King said to his fat, ingratiating servant through the plexiglass pane in the prison's visiting hall.

"Decapitated body discovered at Lawrence Street El," the newspaper clipping said. "The as yet unidentified girl is just another suspected casualty of the mounting gang war over the Uptown territory," the Sun King read aloud.

"Is the necklace back in your possession?" he said suddenly.

"No, but soon," his servant assured him. "I'll stop at the police station on the way home."

The Sun King nodded his pleasure and dismissed the man. He signalled to the guard to escort him back to his cell. He had a much more important visitor to greet there.

When the guard had left him, the Sun King turned to the shadowy figure lurking in the corner. The Sun King suppressed a shiver. It would not do to show his true feelings toward the creature who reeked of sulphur and spoke with the voice of a hundred hissing reptiles.

"That's thirteen," the creature said.

"No, sixteen," the Sun King said firmly. "You persist in forgetting my children. Surely this one meets—exceeds—our agreement. I'd be paroled after twelve years—fourteen at the very outside."

The form of the dark shadow shifted. The Sun King was glad he could see no more than a vague outline of the figure.

"The deal was one soul for each year of your *sentence*," the shadowy figure hissed. "Deliver just seven more, Sun King, and you'll be a free man."

Ghouls of the Sea

J.B.S. Fullilove

Most readers of the daily papers, and especially those persons who follow with interest those accounts relating to the men of the sea, will recall the strange disappearance of the freighter *Kay Marie* some seven months ago. They will recall the brief flurry of excitement attending her reported foundering with all hands aboard. Desperately storm-ridden and swept far off her course, she sent forlorn appeals for aid, reporting that her rudder had been swept away and her engines seriously damaged. Nearby ships immediately put out to her aid, but her wireless signals suddenly ceased. Apparently she had drifted far, for no trace of her was ever found.

In common with most others, I accepted as the most plausible explanation the theory that, in her crippled condition, she had either been swamped by the mountainous waves or driven to her doom upon some uncharted reef in unknown waters.

But today, with the *Kay Marie* farthest from my mind and all but forgotten, I chanced upon something else. As is often my habit, I had risen before the sun and gone down to a favorite stretch of beach to cast in the surf for bass. As I walked along the shore I stumbled upon a large glass jug lying amid a pile of driftwood and debris. Even before I smashed it with my heavy sand-pike I knew that it contained some message from the sea, for through its salt-caked sides I had seen a flash of white.

And message indeed it was! Part of the manuscript was missing, but the remainder comprises a bizarre and incredible tale that I set down here precisely as I found it. The true account of the *Kay Marie* disaster? That is for the reader to decide.

Here is the account:

". . . calm, and immediate danger is past. But we are completely cut off from the rest of the world and there is nothing to do but wait and hope that some ship picked up our S.O.S. and will find us before our food and water become exhausted.

"There are many sharks about, and to relieve the monotony of waiting, the crew for a time engaged in fishing for them. Two were caught, and then the fishing suddenly stopped. Here is something very strange, something that arouses superstitious fears in the men. Until now I have been unable to ascertain exactly what it is, because the men are all strangely reticent concerning the whole affair. All I have been able to get out of them is that the sharks they caught were dead.

"Svensen, the big Swedish mate, however, tells me that there were curious gobs of pinkish jelly covering their heads. He says that Doctor Curey took samples of the stuff to his cabin for examination.

"It is indeed surprizing that men like Svensen, who can laugh in the teeth of a storm, should exhibit fear at sight of a few dead fish.

"I have just left Doctor Curey in his makeshift laboratory busily engaged in working on the specimen he took from the head of the shark. It somewhat resembles a huge, pink jellyfish. It has the same disgusting feel, and is without definite form. Still, there are differences. This thing is continually in motion; shimmering at all times as though someone were shaking the table upon which it is placed. A mephitic odor hovers about it, and an indefinable something about it fills me with a kind of loathing and a queer feeling almost of fear. At times I felt as if it were alive and possessed some uncanny power of sight and were watching me.

"Doctor Curey is very much excited. He says that it is an entirely new form of parasitic growth secreting a powerful, bone-dissolving acid that enables it to get at the flesh and blood of its victims. But he, too, is at a loss to explain their immediate and deadly effect when the sharks were taken from the water.

"Captain Wilkes picked up a trail of smoke on the horizon this morning; but they passed us by. We are far from shipping lanes, and it is good to know that some one is looking for us.

"God is indeed merciful! Had the ship we sighted picked us up, what a ghastly horror might have been loosed upon the world! My fear of the strange specimen of Doctor Curey was well founded. It is a spawn of the nethermost depths of some hell of the sea.

"I was engaged in working on my hopelessly damaged apparatus when suddenly a scream echoed through the ship. It was a scream of paralyzing horror and fraught with agony, but through its terror I recognized it as the voice of Doctor Curey.

"Perhaps no one else knew wherefrom the scream had come, for I was the first to reach the cabin of the stricken man. As I rushed in, I saw the doctor seated in a darkened corner, where, I judged, he must have fallen asleep. Only the pale rays of the moon lighted the room, and I could not see plainly, but there was something peculiar about the way he sat. He seemed strangely stiff and as straight as a statue. Apoplexy! instantly flashed through my mind. I shouted to him and stepped closer.

"At the sound of my voice, he half turned and rose slowly from his chair. Something about his movements abruptly checked my rush toward him. The peculiar, frightful *stiffness* of his actions is impossible to describe. They were the movements of a reawakened corpse who tries to force worm-eaten muscles into the forgotten movements of life.

"With my heart still, I stood motionless and watched him as he painfully arose. Once again I called to him in a voice hoarsened by strange fear. As if in answer, he turned. At the same time my hand darted swiftly to my pocket, and with trembling fingers I lighted a match against the wall. As it flared up, I looked into his face and sank to my knees with a low gasping cry. The flickering light of the match was dim, but, even so, that first view of the horror was so indelibly stamped upon my brain that even now—days later—as I write, I can still see it vividly, frightfully.

"The face staring sightlessly into mine was a white, drawn mask of insupportable agony. The blackened tongue, grown sickeningly to astounding length, protruded from half-open lips. He seemed to be trying to scream. His eyes were leaping from their sockets, and already there was forming over them a cold and ghastly glaze. . . . *The man walking stiffly toward me was plainly dead!*

"And then as the last flickering rays of the match burned out between my fingers, I saw . . .

"Until now, I had not thought of any connection between the doctor's experiments and *this.* I had unconsciously supposed him to have fallen victim to some new and horrible disease. But with the last dimming ray of the match, a glimmering of the incredible truth burst upon me with terrible clearness. Even then my dazed and weakened mind refused to grasp the full significance of what I saw in all its ghastliness.

"The top of his head was a shimmering mask of dark red jelly, and from it I could see a long tongue of the same unspeakable stuff slithering down the back of his neck. The whole loathsome mass seemed to swell and grow from his skull with unbelievable rapidity. Despite the awful dazedness of my mind, I still noted the significant change in the color of the mass . . . and that mingled with its grisly red, there were flecks of white and gray.

"As in a dream I heard excited voices and knew that the room had filled with men. I saw the captain, with a curious glance at me, dart forward and catch the swaying doctor in his arms. Frozen with horror, I could only stare—and wait.

"As swiftly as the movement of a striking snake—too swiftly for the eye to follow—a tongue of the dribbling mass hanging nearly to the doctor's shoulders licked out and spattered upon the captain's head. He clawed madly at his hair for a moment, gave vent to a single agonized scream, then slumped forward. He stiffened almost before he struck the floor; then with the same frightful rigidity that the doctor had shown, he slowly sat up, then rose to his feet.

"The horror upon his head had sunk in, disappearing beneath his matted hair. Now it reappeared, growing, swelling like a toy balloon—a shuddersome mass of quivering, sensate jelly, whose soul-chilling scarlet was thickly dotted with white and gray. . . .

"Miraculously then my power of movement returned. Gasping weakly, I stumbled toward the door. I saw the thing that had been the doctor move also, and a ghastly hint of its intention thrust itself into my stunned consciousness, lending speed to my laggard limbs. Close behind me, it circled the milling, craning crowd, who still could not understand; or having seen, stood rooted, held powerless to move by sheer ecstasy of horror. I staggered through the door and sank exhausted to the deck. Behind me the door slammed shut, and there came the sound of a heavy body falling against it.

"For some moments, then, there was silence; then from behind the door there came the ghastly sound of scream after scream of mortal agony and horror, the sound of thudding bodies and of madly stamping feet; but now and then above this hellish din I could hear with terrible distinctness a faint *splat, splat,* like the sound of wet rags falling upon the floor.

"Only a short time I lay thus. Then I remember somewhat vaguely running madly and mingling my screams with the screams of the imprisoned men. For the madness of terror that had descended upon me was now complete. *Just in time I had risen, warned by reflected moonbeams shining into my eyes, and seen the faintly luminous, slithering rill of the jelly that was flowing out toward me from under the door. . . .*

"When I regained consciousness later—whether days or weeks I do not know—I found that I had bolted myself within my own cabin. In the fever of madness I had stuffed up every crack and hole in the walls and door. Still there is everywhere the indescribable stench of the things. I am now certain that I must have been insane much longer than I at first believed, for now I can detect another odor. But upon that I dare not dwell. The picture it brings is too unutterably horrible for contemplation in my weakened state . . . rotting corpses, animated by hellish creatures who supplant their brains, walking in ghastly parades across the decks! . . .

"Am I alone? Outside I can hear the slow tramping of feet. Whether they are the feet of living men or of the horror I dare not look to see. I shout, but never is there an answer. The things I hear outside number many.

"But there is a way out if I am swift. There is powder in the hold. If I can reach it, a match will save me through quick death from the other end I face. Besides, the *Kay Marie* must never be found or allowed to drift too near to land.

"If the things are waiting when I step outside the door, at least I shall have tried to send them back to where they belong — at the bottom of the sea."

THE GRAY WOLF

GEORGE MACDONALD

One evening twilight in spring, a young English student, who had wandered northward as far as the outlying fragments of Scotland called the Orkney and Shetland islands, found himself on a small island of the latter group, caught in a storm of wind and hail, which had come on suddenly. It was in vain to look about for any shelter; for not only did the storm entirely obscure the landscape, but there was nothing around him save a desert moss.

At length, however, as he walked on for mere walking's sake, he found himself on the verge of a cliff, and saw, over the brow of it, a few feet below him, a ledge of rock, where he might find some shelter from the blast, which blew from behind. Letting himself down by his hands, he alighted upon something that crunched beneath his tread, and found the bones of many small animals scattered about in front of a little cave in the rock, offering the refuge he sought. He went in, and sat upon a stone. The storm increased in violence, and as the darkness grew he became uneasy, for he did not relish the thought of spending the night in the cave. He had parted from his companions on the opposite side of the island, and it added to his uneasiness that they must be full of apprehension about him. At last there came a lull in the storm, and the same instant he heard a footfall, stealthy and light as that of a wild beast, upon the bones at the mouth of the cave. He started up in some fear, though the least thought might have satisfied him that there could be no very dangerous animals upon the island. Before he had time to think, however, the face of a woman appeared in the opening. Eagerly the wanderer spoke. She started at the sound of his voice. He could not see her well, because she was turned toward the darkness of the cave.

"Will you tell me how to find my way across the moor to Shielness?" he asked.

"You cannot find it tonight," she answered, in a sweet tone, and with a smile that bewitched him, revealing the whitest of teeth.

"What am I to do, then?" he asked.

"My mother will give you shelter, but that is all she has to offer."

"And that is far more than I expected a minute ago," he replied. "I shall be most grateful."

She turned in silence and left the cave. The youth followed.

She was barefooted, and her pretty brown feet went catlike over the sharp stones, as she led the way down a rocky path to the shore. Her garments were scanty and torn, and her hair blew tangled in the wind. She seemed about five and twenty, lithe and small. Her long fingers kept clutching and pulling nervously at her skirts as she went. Her face was very gray in complexion, and very worn, but delicately formed, and smooth-skinned. Her thin nostrils were tremulous as eyelids, and her lips, whose curves were faultless, had no color to give sign of indwelling blood. What her eyes were like he could not see, for she had never lifted the delicate films of her eyelids.

At the foot of the cliff they came upon a little hut leaning against it, and having for its inner apartment a natural hollow within it. Smoke was spreading over the face of the rock, and the grateful odor of food gave hope to the hungry student. His guide opened the door of the cottage; he followed her in, and saw a woman bending over a fire in the middle of the floor. On the fire lay a large fish broiling. The daughter spoke a few words, and the mother turned and welcomed the stranger. She had an old and very wrinkled but honest face, and looked troubled. She dusted the only chair in the cottage, and placed it for him by the side of the fire, opposite the one window, whence he saw a little patch of yellow sand over which the spent waves spread themselves out listlessly. Under this window there was a bench, upon which the daughter threw herself in an unusual posture, resting her chin upon her hand. A moment after the youth caught the first glimpse of her blue eyes. They were fixed upon him with a strange look of greed, amounting to craving, but as if aware that they belied or betrayed her, she dropped them instantly. The moment she veiled them, her face, notwithstanding its colorless complexion, was almost beautiful.

When the fish was ready, the old woman wiped the deal table, steadied it upon the uneven floor, and covered it with a piece of fine table linen. She then laid the fish on a wooden platter, and invited the guest to help himself. Seeing no other provision, he pulled from his pocket a hunting knife, and divided a portion from the fish, offering it to the mother first.

"Come, my lamb," said the old woman; and the daughter approached the table. But her nostrils and mouth quivered with disgust.

The next moment she turned and hurried from the hut.

"She doesn't like fish," said the old woman, "and I haven't anything else to give her."

"She does not seem in good health," he rejoined.

The woman answered only with a sigh, and they ate their fish with the help of a little rye bread. As they finished their supper, the youth heard the sound as of the pattering of a dog's feet upon the sand close to the door; but ere he had time to look out of the window, the door opened and the young woman entered. She looked better, perhaps from having just washed her face. She drew a stool to the corner of the fire opposite him. But as she sat down, to his bewilderment, and even horror, the student spied a single drop of blood on her white skin within her torn dress. The woman brought out a jar of whisky, put a rusty old kettle on the fire, and took her place in front of it. As soon as the water boiled, she proceeded to make some toddy in a wooden bowl.

Meantime the youth could not take his eyes off the young woman, so that at length he found himself fascinated, or rather bewitched. She kept her eyes for the most part veiled with the loveliest eyelids fringed with darkest lashes, and he gazed entranced; for the red glow of the little oil lamp covered all the strangeness of her complexion. But as soon as he met a stolen glance out of those eyes unveiled, his soul shuddered within him. Lovely face and craving eyes alternated fascination and repulsion.

The mother placed the bowl in his hands. He drank sparingly, and passed it to the girl. She lifted it to her lips, and as she tasted—only tasted it—looked at him. He thought the drink must have been drugged and have affected his brain. Her hair smoothed itself back, and drew her forehead backward with it; while the lower part of her face projected towards the bowl, revealing, ere she sipped, her dazzling teeth in strange prominence. But the same moment the vision vanished; she returned the vessel to her mother, and rising, hurried out of the cottage.

Then the old woman pointed to a bed of heather in one corner with a murmured apology; and the student, wearied both with the fatigues of the day and the strangeness of the night, threw himself upon it, wrapped in his cloak. The moment he lay down, the storm began afresh, and the wind blew so keenly through the crannies of the hut, that it was only by drawing his cloak over his head that he could protect himself from its currents. Unable to sleep, he lay listening to the uproar that grew in violence, till the spray was dashing against the window. At length the door opened and the young woman came in, made up the fire, drew the bench before it, and lay down in the same strange posture, with her chin propped on her hand and elbow, and her face turned towards the youth. He moved a little; she dropped her head, and lay on her face, with her arms crossed beneath her forehead. The mother had disappeared.

Drowsiness crept over him. A movement of the bench roused him, and he fancied he saw some four-footed creature as tall as a large dog trot quietly out of the door. He was sure he felt a rush of cold wind. Gazing fixedly through the darkness, he thought he saw the eyes of the damsel encountering his, but a glow from the falling together of the remnants of the fire revealed clearly enough that the bench was vacant. Wondering what could have made her go out in such a storm, he fell fast asleep.

In the middle of the night he felt a pain in his shoulder, came broad awake, and saw the gleaming eyes and grinning teeth of some animal close to his face. Its claws were in his shoulder, and its mouth in the act of seeking his throat. Before it had fixed its fangs, however, he had its throat in one hand, and sought his knife with the other. A terrible struggle followed; but regardless of the tearing claws, he found and opened his knife. He had made one futile stab, and was drawing it for a surer, when, with a spring of the whole body, and one wildly contorted effort, the creature twisted its neck from his hold, and with something betwixt a scream and a howl, darted from him. Again he heard the door open; again the wind blew in upon him, and it continued blowing; a sheet of spray dashed across the floor and over his face. He sprung from his couch and bounded to the door.

It was a wild night—dark, but for the flash of whiteness from the waves as they broke within a few yards of the cottage; the wind was raving, and the rain pouring down the air. A gruesome sound as of mingled weeping and howling came from somewhere in the dark. He turned again into the hut and closed the door, but could find no way of securing it.

The lamp was nearly out, and he could not be certain whether the form of the young woman was upon the bench or not. Overcoming a strong repugnance, he approached it, and put out his hands—there was nothing there. He sat down and waited for the daylight: he dared not sleep any more.

When the day dawned at length, he went out yet again and looked around. The morning was dim and gusty and gray. The wind had fallen, but the waves were tossing wildly. He wandered up and down the little strand, longing for more light.

At length he heard a movement in the cottage. By and by the voice of the old woman called to him from the door.

"You're up early, sir. I doubt you didn't sleep well."

"Not very well," he answered. "But where is your daughter?"

"She's not awake yet," said the mother. "I'm afraid I have but a poor breakfast for you. But you'll take a dram and a bit of fish. It's all I've got."

Unwilling to hurt her, though hardly in good appetite, he sat down at the table. While they were eating, the daughter came in, but turned her face away and went to the further end of the hut. When she came forward after a minute or two, the youth saw that her hair was drenched, and her face whiter than before. She looked ill and faint, and when she raised her eyes, all their fierceness had vanished, and sadness had taken its place. Her neck was now covered with a cotton handkerchief. She was modestly attentive to him, and no longer shunned his gaze. He was gradually yielding to the temptation of braving another night in the hut, and seeing what would follow, when the old woman spoke.

"The weather will be broken all day, sir," she said. "You had better be going, or your friends will leave without you."

Ere he could answer, he saw such a beseeching glance on the face of the girl that he hesitated, confused. Glancing at the mother, he saw the flash of wrath in her face. She rose and approached her daughter, with her land lifted to strike her. The young woman stooped her head with a cry. He darted round the table to interpose between them. But the mother had caught hold of her; the handkerchief had fallen from her neck; and the youth saw five blue bruises on her lovely throat—the marks of the four fingers and the thumb of a left hand. With a cry of horror he darted from the house, but as he reached the door he turned. His hostess was lying motionless on the floor, and a huge gray wolf came bounding after him.

There was no weapon at hand; and if there had been, his inborn chivalry would never have allowed him to harm a woman even under the guise of a wolf. Instinctively, he set himself firm, leaning a little forward, with half outstretched arms, and hands curved ready to clutch again at the throat upon which he had left those pitiful marks. But the creature as she sprung eluded his grasp, and just as he expected to feel her fangs, he found a woman weeping on his bosom, with her arms around his neck. The next instant, the gray wolf broke from him, and bounded howling up the cliff. Recovering himself as he best might, the youth followed, for it was the only way to the moor above, across which he must now make his way to find his companions.

All at once he heard the sound of a crunching of bones—not as if a creature was eating them, but as if they were ground by the teeth of rage and disappointment; looking up, he saw close above him the mouth of the little cavern in which he had taken refuge the day before. Summoning all his resolution, he passed it slowly and softly. From within came the sounds of a mingled moaning and growling.

Having reached the top, he ran at full-speed for some distance across the moor before venturing to look behind him. When at length he did so, he saw, against the sky, the girl standing on the edge of the cliff, wringing her hands. One solitary wail crossed the space between. She made no attempt to follow him, and he reached the opposite shore in safety.

The Green-and-Gold Bug

J. M. ALVEY

The inquest was over. The coroner had gone, and so had the twelve men who formed his jury. The police officials and reporters for the press had ceased to ring our doorbell. The undertaker, polite and low-spoken, had got his work well in hand and the two coffins lay side by side in the dimly lighted parlor. An awed silence was in the house where but a few hours ago grim tragedy stalked its hideous way.

But I am starting my story at the wrong end. Let us turn back forty-eight hours to the beginning.

It was early on Wednesday night, and my uncle and I, dressed for dinner, sat, each at a window in the living room watching every passing taxi in the street. At last one stopped outside; two figures stepped out into the cold night, and while one paid the taxi driver, the other rushed up the front steps and came into the front hall and flung her arms round my uncle's neck. It was my kid sister Joe, back from a five-month honeymoon in the far-distant and mysterious countries of the orient.

"Well, well," said my uncle, "is the little rosebud glad to be home again and rest once more in her uncle's arms?"

And Joe said, "Yes—oh, yes!" and burst out crying and hid her face on my uncle's oversize vest and held his coat lapels, each with a tiny, girlish hand.

I went out to greet her husband but fell back before him as he advanced, so shocked was I at the change in his appearance. From a handsome youth, well built and smiling, he had become a pale, shriveled figure who staggered under the weight of the light hand baggage he was dragging into the house.

My uncle and I had planned to give the travelers a royal welcome. Our plans, however, were rudely swept aside, and the bridegroom was rushed upstairs to bed and the doctor summoned.

Just what the sick man's ailment was the physician was unable to determine. There were times when his heart raced like fury and his breath came in gasps and his neck swelled and his eyes bulged. At such times he clutched the bed clothes with an iron claw and tried to raise himself. Then the spell would pass like a snap of the fingers, and the patient would relax and fall back as if exhausted from a violent struggle.

About midnight he rested easier, and Joe, my uncle, and I sat down to the untasted dinner.

"A month ago, in China," said Joe, "we went up into the mountains one day, to a temple where a horrible old creature sat on the floor with incense burning all around him. He was a magician, or priest, or soothsayer or something, and had power with the Chinese gods. But Dick laughed at him and said the poor Chinamen were suckers to fall for his line.

"And the magician was angry and rose up in all his ugliness and put a curse on Dick and on his family. Dick was going to fight him right there, and we would have been murdered, I'm sure, only I pulled him away and made him take me quickly back into the city.

"And that night," said Joe, "Dick had the first attack."

"Josephine!" cried my uncle. "Do you know what you are saying? I'm—Confound it, my dear, what nonsense! 'Put a curse on him?' You know better than to believe such trash. 'Curse,' the devil, my dear! Dick has got some low-down foreign plague. It don't matter whether the Democrats or the Republicans are in power, there's no place like the U.S.A. Confound these outlandish, God-forsaken, evil-smelling places, where all the pests and misery of the world are bred. Dick's got bubonic plague, or the beri-beri or some such fool thing."

Joe told us that Dick got over the first attack in a few hours, but two weeks later on the first night out at sea on the way home he had the second, and it was worse than the first. After that they became more frequent and more violent, and Dick was wasting away and poor Joe's heart was breaking.

"Fiddlesticks!" said my uncle. "Bosh and tommyrot! 'Curse,' my eye! I'm no doctor, but the lad's got some heathen disorder. But cheer up, little woman. We'll have your lover overhauled and in A-1 shape in a jiffy. It may take a month to get real sick in China, but that's China. You're home now, my dear, and it don't take all day to get a pain in the tummy here, nor all night to get over it. Just smile, little girl, and get ready to go to housekeeping. That's what."

It was two o'clock before the house settled down. It was three when I heard a noise outside my door. I went out to see what it was.

The light at the top of the stairs had been left burning, and as I opened my door there was enough light to show me the deformed creature that was creeping along the wall of the hallway, a hideous man, a weird beast, some terrible imp from hell, what I could not say, so awful was it, so unlike anything I have ever seen, or heard of, or fancied.

And this thing opened the door of the honeymooners' room and passed in.

I had no revolver, so I took up a dumbbell that I used of a morning for exercise and went to the door of the room where the thing had entered. I opened it, and reached in and snapped on the lights. In the bed lay the travelers sound asleep. I went over and touched them to make sure they were only sleeping. I looked under the bed, in the closet and out on the porch roof under the windows. There was nothing there.

Joe, open-mouthed and wide-eyed, caused me to pull my head in from the window.

"What's the matter? What's the matter?"

"Nothing," said I. "Don't be frightened. I thought I heard the fire engines going downtown and came over to look."

I went downstairs to look around a bit. The hall, the parlors, the dining room were all empty, but in the little passage that runs from the dining room to the kitchen I thought I heard a footstep. I was sure I did. I stood and listened. And then somebody sneezed.

I pulled the swinging door open. There stood my uncle in his night-shirt.

"God bless my soul!" he said. "I was about to shoot you."

"You're catching cold," I told him. "Go to bed. What are you tramping around here for this hour of the night?"

"And why are you, sir?"

"I heard a noise," I explained.

"So did I."

"And I thought I saw something."

" 'Thought!' " he cried. " 'Thought,' hell. I *did*."

"You did. Where?"

"You saw it, too?"

"Yes, in the corridor outside my room."

"You're lucky," said my uncle. "I saw it in my room."

He smiled a grim smile.

"I was so shocked that I could not move. After it left I got up and came down here. I thought it might have come this way."

"No," I said. "It came past my room and went into their room."

The next day the sick man was much improved. Joe was brighter. My uncle smiled in spite of his troubled mind. I said nothing.

That night we went to bed early. I was tired out and soon fell asleep. It was three o'clock again when I heard a noise. This time I rushed out and came face to face with the unearthly visitor. It gave me one mighty crack on the chin that sent me back into my room. I lay on the floor in a semidazed condition for full five minutes as well as I can estimate. Then I grabbed my dumbbell and went out again.

As on the previous night, I went to the door of Joe's room and opened it and switched on the lights.

On the floor lay Joe, blood at her mouth and nose. Across the foot of the bed lay her husband, looking more like his old self than I had seen him since the day of his wedding.

I told my story at the inquest. The police officials laughed at it. The reporters seized upon it as great stuff for the papers. The coroner's jury considered it gravely, and then gave it as their verdict "that Josephine

Blackton was murdered by her husband Richard Blackton, who afterward died by his own hand."

They are right and yet they are wrong. I have found new evidence. I shall make it known.

In the trunks of the honeymooners, which arrived tonight, was a collection of curios. Among them was a small bottle containing a strange insect, a green-and-gold-colored bug, and the bottle was labeled: "Shangtang Jan. 15. The strange bug that stung Dick last night. We believe that someone threw it in the window."

I don't like the idea of a murder and a suicide in our family. I don't want that coroner's verdict to stand. I'm going to prove that an enraged old magician in the mountains near Shangtang caused the green-and-gold bug to be thrown in the window where the Americans were staying and it poisoned Dick and slowly drove him mad; destroyed his human qualities, mind and body; and that the two who lay side by side in their coffins were both murdered and that the murderer sits among his incense burners seven thousand miles away. I'm going to prove it if I have to go to China!

The House on the Rynek

DERMOT CHESSON SPENCE

I

Camborne twisted his hands and looked into the fire.

"The most dreadful affair that ever came my way," he said, "happened in Poland. You boys have been artlessly trying to cap each other's horrors all evening, so perhaps you'll give an older man an innings."

We said that we would, and he began.

I have always been interested in ghosts and spirit manifestations of all kinds—being an Irishman—and Count Paul Lewandowski proved to be a mine of information on the folklore of his country. Werewolves are no half-forgotten monstrosities of fabulous ancestry when you are on the edge of the Tatras. You can believe a lot of things in the shadow of those mountains that you would smile at in London.

Paul's own and very noble family had a curse, and he told me about it over the nuts and the wine, and his little countess helped and checked him on many points. They had evidently been rather proud of that curse until, in due course, it had swung around and pointed at him. But even now it didn't seem sensible to be frightened by the last few words of an old and dirty Jewish furrier who had died in a three-century-old pogrom. Even Paul did not know what the curse precisely was, but since that snowy night, few heads of that vastly interconnected family had died in their beds. Certainly the title had never gone by direct descent from father to son. There was at least a suspicion that Paul's two immediate predecessors had committed suicide. One on a hunting trip round Morskie Okoe had had an accident with a loaded rifle, and the other had taken his yacht out into a capful of wind on the Baltic and never been seen again. This was but ten short months ago, and so Paul became a power in the land. Identifiable timbers had come ashore between Gdynia and Zoppot, and his death was beyond a doubt. Those, said Paul, were strange if not impossible fortuities for the great sportsmen these men had been.

The old story ran—and not very creditably either—that Mattheus Levine the furrier had lent much money to the Count Lewandowski of his day, and had been indiscreet enough to press for repayment. It was suggested, though never proved, that the massacre in which Levine had died had been promoted for his particular benefit. Be that as it may, it was certain history that the Jew had dragged his dying body into the court of their house in Cracow to curse their name forever.

There is a well in the forecourt, said Paul, with a walled coping, and on this Levine had leant to tell them what this night's work would cost them; it would cost them death and division, no one of their strain should become master of those vastly mortgaged estates and live to enjoy them or to pass them to his sons. It was snowing as the old furrier sprawled there, and the undermaid took a great traveling rug of fine fur and flung it over him, though Lewandowski, erect and sneering in the gallery, cursed her for a nameless and interfering fool. Mattheus had roused himself at that and had smiled a little, caressing the rich texture of his covering with his broken hands. Then he had looked up at the young count and said something in Yiddish, spat at him, and died. The young count threw the body out into the Rynek with his own hands.

Paul paused for a moment.

"You've married into a sweet family," I said to Sonia, "Paul is very proud of that ancestor of his, really."

"I've not married into it," said Sonia, "I'm of it," and she smiled and showed her splendid teeth. "I was born as much and more of a Lewandowski than Paul—only I'm a girl."

I shall never forget how lovely she looked sitting there at the foot of a priceless refectory table, gazing down it at her young husband, her heart-shaped face white and calm under her crown of black hair. There was a beauty of spirit as well. . . .

"And the curse is still working?" I asked hurriedly of them both.

"It was until I took the matter in hand," said Paul, with a gravity that I had never before seen in him. "We are going to break this curse together, Sonia, you—Nicholas—and I. We have always run from before this old furrier in the past—we, Lewandowskis, who do not run. But we are going to meet him face to face. You know that tonight is the night on which he crawled in out of the square."

This was hurrying with a vengeance, I said to myself, and smiled at my own unintentional jest, a pitiful thing.

"Each year," said Paul, "he comes in from the Rynek to die again by the well head and maybe to claim his due. He has let ten, twenty, or more years go by without claiming a life sometimes. But the longer a Lewandowski lives the darker across his days falls the shadow of Mattheus Levine. Uncle Andrew had the estates twelve years before he went deliberately to his death in the Baltic."

"*Deliberately* is a hard word," I said judicially.

"We are Lewandowskis and we know our breed," put in Sonia sharply. "Something so terrible had come on daddy that he couldn't bear his body to be found, even for Christian burial."

"We are first cousins," said Paul, "she was in Paris at the time. But can you wonder that we take the thing seriously?"

There was a little silence.

"Anyway," said Paul, "this will be the first time since the Austrians vacated the Wahvel that our house has been open on this night. My superstitious Irish friend, are you with us? Are you game?"

And Paul went on, almost with his usual gaiety, to tell us of the Holy Water and the crucifixes. In his excitement he limped the length of his great dining room to prove to me from some old book or other that his cure was infallible, and that his and Sonia's days would be long in the land. So and so would he break the grim sequence—if sequence indeed there was and not a self-induced panic exaggerating the ordinary misfortunes of life into major disasters. Even with Sonia here to defend her father's memory, belief wavered. . . .

II

We drove back to Cracow in his open Austro-Daimler. It was clear and frosty, and the roads had fully recovered from the recent floods of the Vistula. Sonia sat next to Paul as he drove and I huddled behind under a bearskin, thinking what a fool's errand it all must prove. My Irish mind could not help but feel that this spirit of aristocratic intolerance was not the best in which to approach a family curse. Even so, such foolhardiness was better than craven retreat or helpless waiting like a rabbit before a weasel. . . .

In a bare two hours we swung along the river bank for the last time, and so into Cracow. Our objective stood on the corner of the central square, the Rynek, and looked much as it did when first built. I had never been to the Lewandowskis' town house before. The titular owner of the mansion was Paul's aunt and Sonia's mother, who gave them the run of the dust-sheeted rooms any time they wanted to spend the night in Cracow—any night but this night, said a voice in my inner consciousness.

Paul had handed Sonia out of the car and was waiting for me.

"You might bring the rug in," he said, "it might get stolen, and in any case it'll make a show of comfort inside. The old lady never leaves any servants here. There might be a little of their old vodka left."

As he spoke, he unlocked a small door set in the surface of the great gate, and he led the way in.

"And this is the famous well head," said Paul, pointing with his electric torch at the low coping in the center of the cobbled yard. "And there," and he turned around and flashed his lamp on the inner side of the gate, "is our insurance against jokers. No strangers can gate-crash those bars!"

"As if anyone in Cracow would want to, this night of all nights," said Sonia. "Let's get under cover. I'm cold. It shouldn't take long to get a fire going. We've got an hour or more to kill before anything starts—if anything starts!"

While Sonia was coaxing a blaze out of the logs in the open hearth, and Paul, draped in the fur rug, was busying himself with the silver flask of Holy Water and his textbook on ghost baiting, I made a brief inspection of the drawing room floor with a candlestick in my hand. It seemed wiser to save the torch for any work that might need to be done out of doors. I had Paul's word for it that all but this floor was locked up and uninhabited, but I felt that it was more prudent to make sure. He was quite right—we were so far as it was humanly possible to tell, alone in the house.

Despite what I have told you of its history, this old mansion on the Rynek was not exactly the perfect setting for a ghost story. When I looked out of the drawing room window I could see Paul's open touring car by the curb, and, upstairs or down, I could hear through the closed shutters the cheerful clanking of the electric trams. The house, too, had all modern conveniences, excepting electric light—the old countess apparently would not stand for that innovation. Candles and lamps had been good enough for the centuries before her, and they would last for her time too! The family portraits that covered the walls were themselves shrouded in sheeting, and the great pieces of furniture suddenly would loom out before me like snow-whitened boulders of strange and frightening shapes.

When I came back to the fire, Paul was showing signs of nervous impatience.

"It is getting late," he said, and again, "Tonight is the night." Then he pointed back through the open door of the salon to the balcony overlooking the courtyard. "Mattheus is due any time now."

"It's a business appointment," said Sonia brightly. "I hope he won't commit the solecism of being late."

She spoke casually enough, but I could feel a growing nervous tension behind her words, and again I was glad of the gross mechanical comfort of a particularly strident tram. It passed under our window in a crescendo of noise and then stopped abruptly.

"Loiterers' harvest," said Paul, and the horn from the tower in the square blew the hour of midnight.

"Dear faithful Hainault," said Sonia. Then, with a pretty little shiver, she added, "I'm still cold. Pass me some more wood, Paul, there's a dear."

"I'll shut the window," I said, and went off to do it. "It's snowing, you know?" And as I went across the parquet flooring great soft flakes were flocking silently into the room. Then I too was cold, but my cold was something more than physical.

At first I thought of calling Paul—it was his concern rather than mine, since it was his car that had gone—but then I looked a little more closely, and little though I knew the Rynek, I could see that more than the Daimler had vanished. The tram standards, the gleaming lines had

221

gone too. The great square had changed from its daylight self, from what it had been forty minutes ago. Then the market hall had been flood-lit, and there had been pigeons on the tower protesting volubly at this travesty of night. The travel agency across a hundred yards of neat paving had flaunted a red neon sign. But now the very roof lines had changed about us, and the paving was nothing but rutted and beaten earth, desolate under the sky. The silence was absolute. Despite myself, I clutched at the window jamb and stared and stared for minutes on end. The flurry of snow had passed, and the moon rode high among frost-bright stars.

"What is happening?" I asked—and the effort to find my voice was enormous. But only the firelight flickered derisively in answer. Then I was, frankly, terrified, and ran out on to the landing, recklessly. Anything, I felt, was better than that empty and silent room fronting on to an altered world.

III

To my relief I found Paul and Sonia standing side by side in the gallery gazing down into the darkness of the courtyard. They were still chattering idly together of what Paul was to do with his flask of water and his crucifix against the old enemy of his family. But I guessed somehow that even now he was too late. Someone had already turned time against all of us. And I hated that worse than death at that moment.

"You were a long time at the window," said Sonia. "See a pretty market-girl?"

I said nothing. How could I explain? And how could I tell that they would see what I had seen? We were all in dire danger now, and I could not bring myself to break their spirit too. There was more—but Paul cut into my somber thoughts.

"There's a grand old hullabaloo going on over this side," he said. "Some of the University lads making a night of it. . . ."

From the streets behind the house came a shouting and general uproar, such as I have never heard before, and the night sky was lined with the glow of flame.

"There's a fire," said Sonia eagerly. "Let's go and see it!"

"And leave our posts," said Paul. "Never."

The memory of that old story of greed and murder stirred in me the thought that this noise was that of a frantic mob urged on by one of Paul's kin for his own private and detestable purposes. By door and

222

window the Lewandowski house was opening on to another world than ours, and I was going to tell them both of the many things I'd rather do than go out again through that little wicket gate, when it swung for a moment lazily open, and then swung as idly to.

Paul looked at me, moistened his lips with his tongue, and spoke: "I must have left it unlatched when we came in. Very careless of me. Eh, Sonia?"

Sonia did not answer, but continued to stare down into the court. I strained my eyes to their utmost, but could see nothing whatsoever. Paul, I imagine, did the same. Then she did speak—but not to us.

"You poor, poor man," she said to the darkness, and opened her arms wide. "We are the same blood, Paul and I, take your due—but take me."

Then bizarre nightmare moved so swiftly about us that I forgot my fears of the silent square and the Jew-baiting hooligans loose in the streets outside. They had each served their turn as opening chords to that night's fugue of horror.

"What nonsense is this?" cried Paul, and then more sharply, "Sonia! Are you mad?" and he clutched wildly at her, but she dodged him easily, and, scrambling like a cat, was away over the rail of the gallery with the speed of a trained acrobat.

Paul with his game leg could never hope to follow.

"I'll go," I said, and made after her.

"She's all right," said Paul, and pointed across the court. Sonia had made the round, hand over hand, and was standing on the gallery facing us. "That's the old servants' quarters, and it'd take us a month of Sundays to break in. The keys are with the old lady down at Myslience. You let her be. Sonia, I mean. She does these queer things sometimes— besides, these rails would never stand your weight."

(And indeed I was a very heavy man.)

Sonia's clear voice carried right across the intervening space to us.

"You must be very cold," she said, "take these. It's all I've got for you."

And before our eyes, despite the curses and pleas of Paul, she slowly stripped herself, until she stood there mother-naked, a glimmering Dresden figurine, as beautiful as—snow. The storm had come back again over us and already a stray flake or so was settling gently on the balcony rail.

"The little idiot," said Paul. "She'll catch her death of cold. What is it? A joke?"

And Sonia answered him by stepping forward to the edge of her own gallery and tipping her rumpled finery down into the yard.

223

Then and not till then—and I must ask you to believe this—did we think of the original purpose of our night's adventure.

"So *he* opened the door," said Paul in a grim whisper. "I'll fix *him!*" And he drew the stopper from his silver flask and leant over the balcony as far as he could, scattering the Holy Water as much into the middle of the dark quadrangle as he could contrive, all the while mumbling rapidly to himself in what seemed to be Latin. He thought he was winning all along the line, and I thought that we were already worse than lost. I cannot tell you what was in Sonia's mind, and it cannot greatly matter now. But something was to happen in a very few moments to reorientate my whole conception of the night's happenings, to make me see myself as the silly self-hypnotising savage finding fear where no fear was, an Irishman and a superstitious fool . . . if those can be two separate things!

IV

Paul had finished the last drop in his flask, and turned again to me. "That's the lot," he said. "That should do. And if I catch Sonia before she gets hold of her things, I'll treat her to a good old-fashioned smacking in the old-fashioned way across my knee."

Neither then nor later did it strike either of us as funny that we had tacitly never even considered the idea of going down into the courtyard. One thinks of these things afterward.

While Paul was engaged in his exorcism I had been watching the shadowy gallery forty feet away. Now I spoke.

"Paul," I said, "I'm your old friend, and I'm going over. There's something I don't quite like. Of course she's only fainted or something, but I don't see her any more. Those shutters are all bolted up, so she can't have climbed in, and I'm positive she hasn't climbed out."

Paul laughed his usual fat and jovial laugh. "I'd trust you with Sonia anywhere, even under the present unusual conditions! I'll even lend you my torch. Good luck and good hunting. Remember she's uncommon quick to box a man's ears if he gets fresh." And he laughed again. He was satisfied and at ease, was Paul Lewandowski.

Gingerly I entrusted my fourteen stone to the moist and creaking balustrading, and eventually but with none of the agility of my quarry I climbed on to Sonia's balcony. My sense of decency foolishly made me leave my torch unused in my pocket. Besides, I thought that this marble nymph would be easy enough to find.

Everything was silent and the darkness was Stygian. And then I heard a little noise—a suppressed whimper or a giggle, and I made for it. In the furthest corner I found somebody who twisted and wriggled in my arms like a monkey, and the skin was smooth and furry to the touch like a monkey or a seal.

It was at that moment that this evening of terror collapsed for me in a gust of laughter. Heaven knows how many weeks ago the little demon had put one of her fur coats up here in the balcony, and then when she wanted to frighten her ghost-hunting husband and his fat friend into fits, all she had to do was to go through that clever farce of stripping and slip out of sight into the enveloping darkness of the coat. The audacity of it all. And I was just going to snatch a kiss, for which I would not have been responsible to Paul, when the creature gave another sudden twist and was out of my arms and away.

A joke's a joke—but I wanted no more climbing that night, so I called out to Paul to watch her and turned my flashlight after the fleeting figure. It shone on a smooth surface of glistening fur—a fine coat, uncommonly high in the neck since I couldn't see where Sonia's own hair began. Then in a curious, blinded sort of way she fetched up against the rail with a bump, and swung out as though to climb. As she did so, her face was toward me, full in the light of the torch. Only there was no face, only the same dark, hairy flat surface unbroken by mouth or eyes. That closed me up for good.

By one of God's greater mercies she fell to her death on the snowy cobbles in that very instant, and Paul, who saw and remained sane, was able to do what he could about the body. He knew how to call a doctor who was a confidential friend of the family, and the funeral went off without a hitch. He was also able to conceal the fact that we had spent the night—where we had spent it. As far as the world knew, young Countess Lewandowski had died on a frenzied motor run up through the night from the South. We were well content that they should think so.

Paul of course was broken-hearted, and kept asking me again and again, when once I was well enough to see him, if I thought she realized what she invited when she offered herself for him. What more than a life for a life? I queried. You prove yourself unworthy of her love by that very question. Did she cry out to us when the nature of her fate was made known to her?

Camborne was silent for a moment. Then he ruminated again, talking to himself as it seemed.

225

"Paul, you know, saw nothing of what I or she saw—except—excepting for Sonia herself. Was she mad? Perhaps so great a love is madness, and in such madness is triumph. I should like to think that enough has now been paid. As Sonia was brave, so was the doom quick, and so by comparison merciful. But can you put yourself in the place of those old lords of creation on the day when the first patch of strange hair appeared on bull neck, maybe, or scarred forearm?"

One of us answered with a further question.

"Yes, I did find out what the last words of the old Jew were, but they seem so monstrous now that we know what happened. Six quite simple words that I'd give a lot to forget. 'You shall have your furs back,' said Mattheus Levine, usurer and furrier, fingering the sealskin that the servant girl had tossed him."

I'll Be Glad When I'm Dead

CHARLES KING

Get up, you lazy bum!"

Julius didn't need an alarm clock.

"Get your skinny feet out've that bed before I clout that bald skull of yours!"

He had a wife.

"You wanna be late to work?" Then, as usual, she answered herself: "Sure! There's prob'ly nothin' better you'd like than to take the roof offa my head and the food outa my mouth."

Julius agreed. But, being a hundred and seventeen pounds against his wife's one hundred and ninety, he kept his generous assent a deep secret.

"Get up!"

Squirming unhappily out of bed, Julius perched on the edge a moment. Gradually, his small, vaguely colored eyes focused downward. No getting away from it, he brooded unhappily, his feet were skinny.

Slewing sideways, his eyes took in the bony arms that poked out of his undershirt. Though, at certain times, he fondly imagined that he was

226

starting to put on some weight, this was an off day. He saw himself for exactly what he was . . . a skinny little runt.

And he hated it.

And he hated *them*.

Them? They were the well-padded people who unconcernedly waddled through life.

They were the ones whose several chins quivered as they laughed.

They were the ones whose plump bellies shook as they walked.

They were the ones who flaunted their flesh proudly . . . the flesh that Julius didn't possess.

So he hated.

"Awright, awright, slow poke. I don't wanna stay over the sink all day. Feed your face and scram."

"Yes, m'dear," mumbled Julius as he hastily swallowed a scratchy piece of burnt toast. Then, squashing his hat atop his head, he fled to the outside world.

Nobody gave the forlorn, shabby little man a second glance as he mooched down the street. They would have done much more than that, however, if they could have read his morbid thoughts. For Julius was engrossed in his favorite occupation: reducing all fleshy hulks to dried up, wizened specimens such as himself. His methods were quite grisly.

He was three minutes late for work that morning. His boss—a two-hundred-pounder, of course—didn't let Julius forget it all day. The daily kicking around, which he had grown to accept as a part of his miserable job, was, this day, excruciatingly enhanced by the blobby behemoth who paid his salary. By the day's end Julius was almost witless with helpless rage. As he slammed from the office into the street he hardly knew where he was heading.

What made it that much worse was that his bony hands were completely tied. There was nothing he could do—absolutely nothing. If he spoke up to his boss that bulbous bully would flatten him on the spot with painful promptness . . . and then fire him. And his wife. Oh, his ever-loving wife. When she got her beefy paws on him that would be the end. He'd be a dead pigeon, for certain.

Now, there is a definite group of men who revert to childlike actions when they are under severe strain of temper. Some of them wave their arms wildly as they rant and bellow; others, frenetic with fury, clench their fists and hop up and down in paroxysms of vocally silenced rage.

Julius belonged to both groups . . . and to neither. Internally he churned with a violence that was unbelievable in its sheer fury; externally he presented the front of a pallid, little character with curiously strained features.

But there is always a breaking point—and today was it. He was going to revenge himself upon a world loaded with fat enemies. He entered a small stationery store, made a quick, unobtrusive purchase, and then darted around the corner to where there was an empty lot. Then he took the machinery for his vengeance out of his pocket.

A box of chalk.

Then, squatting on his heels, he drew, upon a slab of concrete walk, the two symbols designating both sexes of the lumpish, corpulent people that he envied and loathed . . . his Wife and his Boss. They represented, to him, all *the others*.

If he had been a good artist—if he had been *any* sort of an artist—it wouldn't have happened. The egregious part of it was that he couldn't draw at all. What he fondly hoped was the faces of his enemy symbols were merely childish distortions.

Angles and curves overlapped without any harmonic lines or perspective, presenting a veritable distortion of ungoverned traceries. Still, nothing would have happened if he hadn't completed his job so thoroughly.

Underneath what would have been unrecognizable to any one but himself, he scrawled every nasty obscenity he could pluck from the stilled vocabulary of years. From the chalk in his hand rolled all the pent-up viciousness that had been contained so long; viciousness that had grown by feeding and festering upon itself.

The completion of his destiny was simplicity itself. He lit a cigarette and tossed the flaming match into the center of his drawn and written depravities.

"Well?"

Shocked surprise rode across Julius's face as he spun around. Where *had* that squeaking voice come from?

"Damn it, I haven't got all day! Well?"

He looked around again. Nothing there. Sweat coursed freely down his face. Had he become subject to squeaking hallucinations? He looked down. *He looked down*. There it was . . . in his vest pocket.

"Well?" queried the single-eyed crimson little horror poking its head out of his pocket. "D'you think I have all day? Ask me what you want—and hurry up!"

Somehow Julius found what was left of his voice: "Who . . . what . . . are you?"

"Oh, oh," moaned the red mite, "did I get called away from a bit of the most gratifying torturing it has been my lot to administer in centuries . . . called away just to answer the stupid questions of a moron human?"

"B-but . . . b-but . . ."

"Stop repeating yourself. Don't you realize that the precise curves and angles of the figures you drew—coupled with the obscenities and the burning match—called me up to you?"

"Then—"

"Of course! Your combined acts geared together to form a spell. You're entitled to one wish, stupid, and I wish you'd get the lead out of your baggy pants."

Slowly . . . torturously . . . the enormity of what had happened enveloped the bulging-eyed Julius. His voice came in whistling gasps: "You . . . you are . . ."

"*A Demon*. And now will you *please* hurry."

Whirling worlds, with Julius as their core, came to a sudden, jarring, rending stop. The still, small voice of caution forced itself through his accustomed cloak of timorousness. "But I always thought . . . read . . . that demons were large—with horns and forked tails—and . . ."

"Shut *up*, you misbegotten human," squalled the raging horror. "Did you ever *see* a demon?"

"I only meant . . ."

"Quiet, damn your human soul! You used a vest-pocket-sized spell and got a vest-pocket-sized demon. Anything wrong with that?"

"No . . . *wait!* Did you say I get a wish? *Any* wish?"

The other shuddered. "Questions, questions. I'll go mad. Yes, dope, you get any wish. Only hurry—I've got *work* to do."

Julius seemed to gain sudden height. "All right, I've got a wish."

"Yes?"

"*I want to be a vampire!*"

"Mm-mm. Interesting. If you'll pardon my demonic curiosity, I'd appreciate knowing just why."

For perhaps the first time in his life Julius spoke surely. The words came steadily: "All my life I've hated fat people. They pick on me—remind me of what I am—"

"You are a rather sad specimen," observed the other.

"I want to get back at them . . . cut them down to my size. . . ."

The other nodded. "I quite see your point. By returning as a vampire and sucking their blood you'll cut their weight down."

"Exactly," Julius agreed happily.

"Of course, though, you will have to die first. Only way it can be done, you know."

"But—but—you'll definitely bring me back?"

"As a vampire? Oh yes. The spell guarantees you one wish . . . and you'll get it."

"Then," smiled Julius, "I'll be glad when I'm dead."

"Wait, human, are you sure?"

"You—you're not backing out on me, are you?"

"Dope! Certainly not! It's just that . . . well . . . in all my centuries I've never seen such a miserable specimen as yourself. What I'm trying to say, human, is that I'm *sorry* for you."

Julius' voice rose shrilly: "You're tricking me . . . trying to cheat me. . . ."

"No, human, it's merely the first authenticated case of a demon trying to help anybody."

"Lies—broken promise—" the skinny man's voice died away to a despairing gurgle.

"Very well, then, and stop that lousy snivelling. Only don't forget that I warned you. I'm a vest-pocket-sized demon, and my spells . . ."

Julius broke in eagerly, as if afraid the other would change its mind. "Let's go to my house and get it over with."

Muttering something about "Vest pocket size" and "spells having to balance," the demon grumpily subsided.

Julius lay down, in his house, but asked one last question before he died.

"Don't worry," spat the demon in answer, "you'll come back and drink blood . . . damned, dopey, human fool!"

The awakening was sudden. Julius knew he was alive. Things were slightly blurred . . . there seemed a limitless expanse of space about him . . . but he was alive. And he was *flying*. Good old demon. He'd more than kept his promise. This was great.

Flying . . . *look!* An enormous blob of flesh beneath him. What a lovely beginning. What a wonderful subject to practice upon. Careful now . . . land softly. Ah. His first victim was a veritable giant, extending away in amazing manner. But no time to puzzle over that now. *Drink.*

Funny . . . very funny. Not the taste of the blood. No, that was good. But he had found out something. Vampires do *not* sink needle-sharp teeth into their victims' necks. All wrong. False. What they do is insert an incredibly sharp nose and . . .

Look. Run!

Grotesquely shaped like a mammoth starfish, a fleshy appendage was swinging down with horrifying speed. Run . . . fly . . . *splat!*

Punctuating the night with her steady snoring, Julius' wife turned over, her hand dropping off the side of the bed.

And, on the floor, a mashed mosquito quivered once . . . twice . . . and lay still.

Indigestion

BARRY N. MALZBERG

Ah well. Then again I sometimes wonder how it might have been if instead of the anonymous and forlorn I had ingested instead the bodies of the famous. The cells of Spinoza swimming to mingle with my own bright and burbling blood, the obsessions of Beethoven, the clear and cunning visions of W.J. Bryan taken unto me and merged with my glutinous bloodstream . . . why, I might have been anything. Anything at all! I would have been a congregation, a celebration unto myself, not Henry of this common nature (which for all the ecstasy of my activities is what I am; I know my limitations) but Henry Transmogrified, carrying within himself the seeds and decomposition of hundreds of the best.

If the ingestion of a corpse enables one (as I humbly do believe, your honor) to take on many of the intellectual qualities of the deceased, then it is clear that I am limited only by the limitations of those within me. Still, that is absolute.

Still. I frequent bleak graveyards located far from the fashionable suburbs; I content myself with fresh grave sites unattended—which can only mean that the deceased left as little of a mark in the departure from life as in the partaking—I observe the amenities of my cruel and inexplicable trade by working as much as I can on the periphery of feeling. Not for me the leap into the still-open grave surrounded by mourning relatives and creditors, not for me either an attempt to insinuate myself nearer the deceased by obtaining a job in the trade: mortician, laboratory attendant, morgue custodian, and so on. For me there is an appreciation of the amenities of feeling. I observe them. I do what I must, not without a bright thread of shame. I admit that I am a fiend.

Spinoza and Beethoven, the Kennedys or the cellular decomposition of Nobel Prize winners revolve with me not; I suit myself with simpler game, not a little of it (I will admit this, too) gathered from the potter's fields. I own a shortwave radio and keep up with the latest police reports; if a derelict is delivered anonymously DOA to a hospital I want to be prepared to call upon him tomorrow. But it is not me, it is Henry no longer, it is (as I have said) a congregation that now takes itself upon these tours; the dead feed upon the dead and all two hundred and fifty-five of us, the original Henry and parts of the two hundred and fifty-four he has consumed, prowl about their obsessive errands. I am more than a congregation, I am a civilization, an urban culture (or at least a medium-sized village) to myself. At the end of all of this, I am sure, lies a knowledge so absolute that only the amorphous outlines of the goal, rosy in their radiance, are there to tantalize me. I do not know what I (what we) am (are), I only know that I must go forward. Besides, the dead are very tasty. Eating parts of decomposed corpses is exciting, not only a bizarre gourmet treat but, as a meal taken on the run, heightened by a sense of mortality, of imminent capture. One can enjoy the task for its own sake. I enjoy eating the dead. (I already warned you that I was a fiend.)

So much for exposition and all of this in the persona of the original Henry, the corpse-eating Henry who began his journey just three and a half years ago. But Henry, now thirty-seven, can hardly be said to exist anymore, his fragile, mean soul has been overtaken by the souls of the two hundred and fifty-four ingested so that the congregation clangs and bangs against itself nervously within the confines of the tenement that is Henry's persona. Each of the two hundred and fifty-four would have its tale to tell; each of them could make its own case. They have found their immortality within Henry; this is firmly believed and each of them (as are all the living, too) is an individual, but the stories would remit to a common banality, a reiteration of the germinal act of *having been eaten;* this would be rather repetitious and thus Henry, the true and final narrator of these adventures, Henry will suppress the other two hundred and fifty-four in the interests of economy and fictional imperative, dealing only with the present instances as they refract into the past, as they summon up the future. It is he, after all, who has devised for the two hundred and fifty-four their immortality.

Into his rooms at some careful hour of the dawn Henry comes, his congregation chanting within him. Fluids roil murkily; Henry has spent the hours of the night at a cemetery in Forest Hills (Forest Hills!) where he has eaten richly of parts of an old woman buried not sixteen hours before. From his careful reading of the obituaries, from his tennis shoes and alert stalk, from his gloved hands, strong shoulders, and wood-cutting devices, from his energy and ambition Henry has derived rich proceeds; not only has he gorged himself with a hand, a foot, and an eyeball but (in a festival of gluttony) Henry has also eaten part of the chin and a weary, crushed-in nose, these last two superfluities sickening him, but Henry could not stop. Sometimes he is unable to control himself. Tossing over the dirt with shaking hands, replacing the marker guiltily, Henry stumbled away from the graveyard and onto a Queens Boulevard bus at the end of the line, his appearance bringing only desultory attention from the three inhabitants of the bus: a workman, a driver, a drug addict who sat nodding secretly in the back. Looking at Henry, it is impossible to know what they might have made of his appearance, the dirt on his shoes, the dirt on his nostrils, his flushed and yet pallid demeanor, but Henry knew what to make of them: looking at them, it was as if he regarded not people but metaphors, metaphors for the corpses that they would be. Shyly and tentatively, yet with increasing boldness, Henry and his congregation regarded these three, wondering what it might be like at some date in the indefinite future to eat them, what their personalities might be like added to the two hundred and fifty-four already in his bloodstream, and the two hundred and fifty-fifth making sliding entrance through gullet and bowels, and they in turn looked back. Did they judge his thoughts? Regarding his shovel, the valise in which he held his cutter, did these three have any inkling of that secret buzzing greedily in Henry's brain and throat like a demented insect? Or did they simply think nothing at all; were their minds as clean and darkly paneled as the minds of the dead? Henry looked between his feet and thought nothing at all, afflicted with an indigestion so severe that it drove metaphysical speculation clear from the pulpit of his consciousness, from the church of his interior, from the congregation of his choice. He returned to his rooms.

Not unaware that he was a fiend, Henry took the usual precautions when he had emerged from the 102 Queens Boulevard bus at the intersection of two numbered avenues. At one wastebasket he disposed of his gloves, at another the woolen hat which he had worn for customary disguise and which had become smeared in a somewhat implicatory fashion; at a third (Henry, staggering from his indigestion, reeling down the length of Queens Boulevard, pausing at wastebaskets to hurl objects, might have had a riotous aspect to anyone who was watching; Henry is not unaware of his appearance or how his activities might strike an appalled and unreasoning world; for this reason he takes more than the usual precautions over his activities and tries to write about himself in the third person as much as possible so that anyone stumbling across these well-secreted notes posthumously might well think that I was talking about someone *else*, which is more than a few senses is the case) Henry paused to retch, his insides convulsing as certain displacements took effect (he should not have had that eyeball), and then, somewhat eased in the flesh if not in the murmurings of the spirit, he returned to his rooms where he found the Other waiting for him as the Other so often does after these expeditions.

It might be necessary, by laws of fictional imperative already referred to, to discuss the Other, to talk about the background of the beast, to explain what it was doing in the rooms and why it and Henry have such undue familiarity, but if it is all the same to everyone, Henry will refuse this task. Henry will not discuss this anymore, being quite familiar with the appearance of the Other and the Other's reasons for being there and having discussed this at length in previous narratives. Besides, there are certain things that lie, perhaps, outside of any decent opinion of mankind, outside of any normal range of human behavior, and which, when written about, when even *hinted* about, can cause only the most unusual disgust and revulsion, open up emotions and responses that are archaic and long since buried. Let them stay buried. There will be no discussion of the Other here other than to state that it was there again and that Henry felt the old twisting fear in his vitals. He had never gotten over his terror of the Other. Try as he had to supersede that terror, to realize that much of it was imaginary, that all of it could be overcome, he could not stop that feeling but indeed found himself in its thrall. Very much as did his congregation, which squirmed, trembled in place, murmured warnings and imprecations. Half a congregation, three-quarters Henry, four-fifths what he had most recently consumed, Henry faced the Other as bravely as he could and said, "I thought I told you that I didn't want you here anymore. I thought that we settled that last time. Come on. Get out of here."

The Other took a slightly different posture and said, "Come now, Henry, enough of this." It eyed him, saw the look on his face that must have told him everything, not that a ringing, foaming belch from Henry did not tell him more; small specks of blood that were not his then pouring from Henry's mouth to the corners of his lips. Henry wiped them slowly, trying not to call attention to this disaster, but it was already too late. The face of the Other congealed. It licked its horrid lips.

"You've been doing it again," it said.

"That's none of your business. That's none of your affair."

"But I'm afraid that it is my affair, Henry. It's very much my responsibility; I'm implicated in this up to the hilt. Haven't I warned you?"

"Warn away," Henry said rather sullenly. He was terrified but still sullen; sullen but yet terrified; part of this having to do with the reactions of his congregation. Some of them were sullen but then again others of them were terrified. His reactions were never consistent because his congregation was inconsistent. It involved a cross section. If Henry had partaken of a better class of person, if Henry had determined unto himself that he would seek only the best and the most consistent of personality traits, then things might have been quite different, but then again Henry could not control himself. Gluttony predominated, and the urge to multiply. If one cannot multiply in one way then one must do it in another, but this is a line of speculation that Henry finds very arcane and *he will not pursue it under any circumstances.* "Get out of here," he said again sullenly and with terror. "Get out now."

"You've been eating people," the Other said flatly. "You've been going to graves and tearing them open and you've been taking out corpses and eating them. A finger here, an eyeball there, sometimes a whole hand, occasionally even an arm. I know what you're doing, Henry. Do you think I'm a fool? You've been warned again and again."

"It's none of your business," Henry said. He put down the valise with a clatter, walked then into the second of the two rooms of his two-room furnished apartment, in which second room he walked to the window, looked down the clear pipe of the air shaft to the sheer drop, three stories below, the implacable stones of the courtyard assuming to him, in the first intimations of the dawn, the aspect of a kind of destiny. "None of your business," he repeated, hearing the footsteps of the Other as it came through the doorway and closed distance between them. There was no way to keep the horrid creature out.

"You've been warned and warned, Henry," the Other said, somewhat repetitiously. "You've been warned nicely and you've been warned harshly. You've been begged and you've been threatened. You've been reasoned with and once we even looked at pictures together while I tried to explain to you nicely why you can't go around eating corpses. Every time I thought you got the point but you're hopeless, Henry. You just keep on doing it. It's got to stop."

Henry shook his head, standing against the window. "What I do is my business," he said. "Besides," he added, "I've got not only myself to consider now. I'm eating for two hundred and fifty-six."

"That is lunacy, Henry. There are no two hundred and fifty-six. There is only you. Your personality does not increase through the personalities of those you ingest. The soul is ephemeral; it flies away at the moment of death. There is nothing but flesh. You lust to eat flesh, Henry. There is no congregation. It is only yourself and the rest is rationalization."

"Get out of here," Henry said severely. His stomach roiled at the thought that he might not be two hundred and fifty-six but only himself. Alone, alone: always alone; the suggestion was obscene. It could not be. He knew if nothing else that ingestion had given him *companionship*. He put the thought away. "Get out or I'll strike you."

The Other giggled in a rather feminine way. It has a rather high voice when under stress, very much as Henry does, although Henry can control himself better. "Don't be ridiculous," it said, "I can't get out. I won't get out. You can't get rid of me. This has got to stop."

"I mean it," Henry said, turning from the window, raising his hand in a threatening way. "I've had quite enough of this now. Be gone with you."

The Other paused, looming, hanging just beyond Henry's reach. Its horrid little eyes turned meditative, its green scales prickled. It shook its beaked head. "I'm sorry," it said, "I'm sorry, Henry. This has gone too far. You're quite dangerous and you won't be held back. I've tried reasoning and threatening, begging and explanations. Still you go on looting graves, desecrating the friendless dead. This is hopeless. It has got to stop." It nodded solemnly, in a sudden and decisive way. "Yes," it said, "this has got to stop."

It closed upon Henry and a claw came out; suddenly Henry felt himself held within a tremendous and beckoning claw, yanked up against the scales of the creature. They exuded a foul odor; Henry felt the strength and conviction of the Other pouring into him and regrets suddenly spun the tumblers of his mind. Why hadn't he listened? Why hadn't he heeded the warnings? Why had he not understood that the Other was merely, as it had oft repeated, doing this for his own good in lieu of more horrid actions? But it was too late for any of this, of course. Henry knew how late it was. The Other had indeed threatened him and Henry had not thought that the threats would come to pass but now they had, and as he clung to the horrid green of the creature, a slimy ooze coming from little pores like abcesses in the scales of the Other,

Henry's whole life seemed to flick before his eyes, right up to his thirty-fifth year when these activities (and the Other) had entered his life. Why had he done it? Why had he found it necessary to look to the dead for sustenance when there were so many of the living? Insight like a belch exploded and expanded his consciousness, but of course it was too late for any of this. With little peeps and cries his congregation fled the temple of his insides, plunged gabbling into the vestry of his unconscious, and Henry realized that he was indeed alone, always to be alone.

"I'm afraid that I'm going to have to kill you now," the Other said. It inclined its tentacled head in a gesture gracious and somehow touching, something humanoid in the aspect. "It's for your own good, Henry," it pointed out, "this would just go on and on and eventually you'd wind up doing something really dangerous and stupid like frequenting funeral homes, looking around open coffins. This has got to be brought to an end."

And Henry said, "Yes, yes, I see what you mean," his breath cut off by that suffocating embrace, his body arched in a spasm of agreement, for he did see, he truly saw what the Other was saying; he saw too that the Other, all along, had merely been trying to help him, to educate him into a better way of life, and like all of the other opportunities offered him Henry had mocked and lost this last of them but too late, too late for any of this. "I'm sorry," the Other said, "Henry, I'm truly sorry but there must come an end to this," and guided him toward the windows, centered Henry against it and then with one terrific thrust sent Henry arching and vaulting through the glass; for one instant hanging high in the air, his skin severed by a thousand cuts, his body at dreadful stillness, looking at the Other, Henry thought that he understood everything up to the Other's identity . . . but in the next instant as he began that long, expiring fall to the courtyard beneath he realized that he understood nothing at all and that all of it must be, as it had always been, a mystery.

His last thought before his body explodes is not for himself but his congregation as truly befits the minister he has tried to be . . . but his congregation is out of touch, no time for benediction, and all two hundred and fifty-six of them slant to the stones before rebounding, the organs of his dismembered body spokes. The impact fire.

The impact fire.

The Inn

Rex Ernest

Barlow cursed as his foot plunged into a pocket of slimy mud and ice-cold water slithered in over the top of his shoe. He strained his eyes into the darkness, but could distinguish nothing more than heavier blackness of the trees that crowded down upon him. The rain poured down, making a monotonous dirge in the leaves. The weather was bad enough without getting himself lost. Taking a fresh grip on his case he pushed on through the murk and muck of the lonely country lane.

This was one thing he had not bargained for when he had applied for poor old Gough's territory—he had been thinking too much of the fat commissions that would be his. Still, travelers in strange parts must expect this sort of thing. It was queer about Gough. They had never been satisfied about his death—there was something funny about the whole business! Anyway, he wasn't married, left no wife and kids behind.—Thank God! A light!

Casting aside his ruminations, Barlow gazed ahead at the pallid yellow light that showed through the gloom. It was the window of some sort of building, and he steered his course toward it. When he was close enough to make out its looming bulk, he guessed it was an inn, and the thought cheered him greatly. Here was warmth and shelter, anyway. The rusty creaking of a signboard, hidden in the darkness, confirmed his guess, and soon he felt cobblestones beneath his feet. He tried to make out what the sign said, but found the darkness too thick; so he stooped and got the swinging board limned against the faint luminance of the night sky. It could be just made out: the crude figure of a bird. A name shuffled forward from the recesses of his memory: *The Blind Crow*. The recollection dragged behind it a grim fact; this was the inn where Gough had died!

Disquieted, Barlow stood a moment lost in strange sensations; then, as the cold discomfort of the rain again asserted itself, he shrugged his shoulders and scurried into the porch. Setting down his bag, he swept his sodden hat from his head, and slashed it through the air to rid it of its heavy wetness. He opened his coat and shook off some of the rain, and then looked around for bell or knocker that would bring someone to open the heavy door.

He was reaching for the heavy iron knocker when the door swung open, silently. Its silence jarred on his already jumpy nerves: it was the sort of door that is expected to groan and protest. He blinked his eyes in the sickly radiance that crept out, seeking to distinguish the man who stood there. Tall, gaunt, and bald, the man regarded him without interest. Here was no rubicund, cheery host; more, it seemed to Barlow, of a keeper, a guardian of grimmer places. The traveler was conscious that his voice was curiously subdued, as he said:

"Good evening! I'd like a room for the night!"

The other made no answer; just stood to one side and opened the door wider. Barlow stepped into the wide passage, waited for the taciturn innkeeper to close the door, then followed him into a large stone-flagged room. He was greeted by a warm atmosphere. A log fire hissed and crackled on the open hearth, filling the room with cheerful red light and dancing shadows, and a big table bore indications of toothsome fare. His spirits rose, and flinging his wet clothes across a chair, he rubbed his hands briskly together.

"I'll be grateful if you'll put me out something to eat. Some cold meat and pickles if you have it, and, of course, some beer."

The host nodded and uttered a grunt, and set about producing the food. When everything was on the table, he threw down a heavy key attached to a small billet of wood. When he spoke, his voice was dry and rustling:

"Here's the key to your room. It's the second door on the landing. Good night!"

And without further conversation, the strange host shuffled away to the remote regions back of the kitchen.

Barlow stared after him. He had intended getting him to talk about Gough, but somehow he feared to intrude upon the man's morose aloofness. He fingered the big key, and then turned to the goodly viands before him.

He took time over the meal. The cold meat was good and the beer was the best he had yet encountered. Mentally, he praised the host's foresight in serving an ample supply of the drink. Under the cheering influence of a satisfied stomach and the cozy warmth, a mellow contentment settled over him. Leisurely, he filled his pipe, and glanced around the big room. The log fire was still crackling redly, and, filling up his glass

239

anew, Barlow turned down the lamp and walked across to the big settle, stretching his legs toward the blaze. He lit his pipe, and with that drawing well, relaxed luxuriously. Ah! This was good!

With half-closed eyes gazing into the friendly heart of the fire, he sank into dreamy rumination. When he retired, he'd have a place like this. Nothing to beat it. Then his mind came back to Gough. Poor old Gough! Quite a decent fellow, in his way. Funny he should happen on the very place where he had died; still, in a way it was not so funny,—wasn't he traveling over the same ground? Still . . . wonder what really happened! He hadn't read the account; he only knew that some sort of mystery surrounded the case. Half aloud, he murmured: "Poor old Gough!" and prepared to dismiss the matter from his mind.

"Yes, it was unfortunate!" answered a deep voice.

Barlow sat bolt upright, stared about the room. Then, just as he was beginning to think the voice had been a figment of his imagination, he discerned a figure hunched up in the shadows on the opposite side of the fire. Gradually, his fright subsided. He peered at the other, trying to see more than the indistinct outlines that merged into the surrounding shadows, changing shape with each vagary of the flickering flames. His sense of companionship came to the fore.

"Good evening!" he said. "I thought I was alone. I didn't notice you there."

He paused a moment, then, as the other made no reply, he continued: "Beastly weather! Are you 'on the road'?"

"No!"

"Oh, you live here, then?"

"No, I don't live here." The deep voice seemed to come from the very depths of the deepest shadow. "But I am here very frequently."

Barlow drew on his pipe, and sought for some new lead to fresh fields of conversation. Then he remembered the stranger's entry into his consciousness.

"Didn't you make some remark about Gough—the fellow that died here?"

"I said that it was unfortunate."

"Yes, it was a sad affair. He worked for the same firm as I do. I knew him well. Not a bad chap. Funny nobody seems to know exactly what happened. All I seem to be able to get is that he was found in bed here dead, with an expression of great fear on his face! The doctors said heart failure, but if you had known Gough—why, the man was like a horse!"

"The symptoms stated were indicative of death from fear—extreme terror."

"Fear? Why, man, Gough feared nothing on earth. It would take something to frighten him at all, let alone scare him to death."

"Scared of nothing on earth? Maybe, but he died from terror."

The traveler pondered this. Outside, the wind moaned and sent the rain scrabbling at the windowpanes. He plucked up courage, and blurted out the question that had been burning on his lips since the conversation started.

"You seem to know a lot about it. Perhaps you would tell me?"

"I know all about it."

Following the abrupt admission, the other fell silent for so long that Barlow feared he had offended him in some way. Just as he was about to make some effort at making amends for any offense he might have caused, the other began to speak.

"Gough arrived here in much the same manner as you—he had lost the last train, and it was raining hard. He was given the second room off the landing, and after a good supper, he retired.

"He settled down to read for an hour or so, but the old four-poster was so comfortable, he soon extinguished the light, cuddled down under the warm blankets, and dropped off to sleep. Just after midnight he awoke. He did not know what had caused him to awake, and he gave a sleepy glance around and then tried to get to sleep again. In a few minutes, he was awake again. This time, he tried to define the cause. It was not long before he realized that there was something in the room—another Presence.

"He sat up in the bed, and peered into the shadows. He could see nothing, and hear nothing beyond the dismal drip-drip of the rain from the eaves. Still, he knew that something was there. Suddenly, he stiffened, stared intently into the darkest corner. Something moved, deep in the shadows—more like the swirl of thick smoke than actual movement. Faintly, but distinctly, a peculiar musty smell reached his nostrils. There was an evil tension in the air that caused the short hairs on his neck to tingle, and a moisture to break out on his brow.

"Fascinated, he watched the vague movements gather strength; saw them become a virile, sinister writhing. Soon, something bulked large and menacing within the depths of the shadow, something that began to move toward the foot of the bed. By now, Gough was clutching the sheets tightly, unable to do more than watch with terrified eyes. His vocal cords were frozen, and his muscles refused to obey his spellbound mind. He had to sit there and wait, wait.

"The thing moved out from the shadows, itself only a black shadowy bulk. It reached the foot of the bed, where it seemed to grow yet more, rearing up, looming hungrily toward the terrified man. Then, the cold, white moonlight came from a rift in the storm-rack, poured through the window, full upon the thing.

"Gough's eyes widened, bulged. He tried to scream, but no sound issued from his dry throat. He thrust out shaking hands to ward off the thing from the shadows—a futile gesture. Then, with a tortured sob, he fell back onto the pillows, dead!

"Thus they found him the next morning!"

For some minutes after the other ceased speaking Barlow sat as if in a trance. His pipe had gone cold, and the fire had died away to red embers, where an occasional flame flickered its brief life. Outside, the rain still poured, beating against the sides of the house. With a sigh, Barlow came back to earth, and leaned back, mopping his forehead. His heart was still racing with the horror of what he had heard. Then a thought struck through his daze, a thought that sent his fears scurrying back to their hiding places. The more he thought of it, the more he wanted to laugh. He was careful to speak with nonchalance:

"How terrible! What a horrible death!"

The figure in the shadows made no reply. Barlow went on, allowed a little triumph to creep into his tone:

"Your story was very vivid, my friend. Too vivid! Gough was *alone*— and only he could have known what happened!"

He leaned forward, waiting for an answer to his challenge. Somewhere, a clock chimed twelve times. From the shadows, the reply came.

"Yes! Only Gough *and the thing from the shadows!*"

And the figure moved forward into the dying light of the fire.

Itching for Action

Charles Garofalo

or crying out loud!" grumbled Arlene. "Will you quit tossin' around like that! I wanna sleep!"

"Yeah," Joe Borden growled. "You try t' sleep when you're being et alive! See how far you get!"

"No thanks, it's hard enough tryin' to sleep with somebody break dancing next to you! Hey, I know you don't got to go to work till ten, but I gotta be up an' about by six. So give me a break and settle down, will ya'? What's eatin' you anyhow?"

"Mosquitos," her husband growled. "And I ain't jokin'. I got a dozen bites so far at least. How come they ain't botherin' you?"

"Just lucky I guess," sighed Arlene wearily, getting up and flicking on the light. "Come on, let's find that damn bug so I can get some sleep."

As she turned on the light she realized her husband wasn't exaggerating about being bitten up. There was a bright red bump on his forehead, just above the eyebrow; another five running down his left arm; and a cluster on his bare chest. She felt itchy just looking at him.

"Boy, oh boy, he's really zeroed in on you," she remarked. "Must be a swarm of 'em in here."

"Yeah, they like me," said Joe sourly as he scanned the walls, hoping to spot one hovering or crawling around.

Neither he nor his wife were able to find any mosquitos in the room. Joe was about to pull the mattress up looking for bedbugs when Arlene saw the black speck on his neck . . . a black speck that hopped out of sight even as she glanced at it.

"Joe, ya got fleas," she said quietly.

She flinched back when she saw her husband's reaction to her words. For a second she thought Joe was going to hit her . . . if he didn't hit the ceiling first.

"Fleas!" roared Joe. "You know damn well I can't have fleas! I never go near dogs! Or cats either, for that matter!"

"Yeah, but they're all over this time a' year. Musta jumped on ya

243

when ya went into the woods this afternoon, remember? You were in and out about a dozen times."

Joe tended to use the patch of woods by his house to dump dead leaves, fallen branches, and this afternoon a dead tree he'd cut down. He didn't consider it littering; after all, it wasn't tin cans or household garbage he dumped in there.

"Fleas! Jesus Christ!" he cursed. "If ya can't dodge 'em by staying away from animals, how the hell do you dodge 'em?!"

At this point he flinched, and his scowl became even more pronounced.

"Brother, you can feel it when they bite ya!" he muttered, looking like he didn't believe it.

Arlene looked as his pillow and pointed. Joe squinted his eyes and spotted the two specklike insects hopping off his pillow.

"See?" she said. "You must've got a whole swarm of 'em on ya. Go take a bath before they give ya anemia!"

She expected an argument from her husband, but instead he immediately got up and went charging down the stairs to the bathroom. As he left she saw a several bites on his back as well. In less than a second, she heard the tap running.

"Boy, they must really be doin' a number on him," she said to herself.

Monday morning was always the most hectic morning of the week, as the Bordens forgot the weekend and got back into the work routine. This morning was a little more hectic than most for Arlene, as her husband chose this one to get up about the same time she did. Unable to just stay put at the breakfast table, he moped around the kitchen as she tried to get ready, getting in the way just enough to make her wonder if he was doing it on purpose.

"What's the matter?" she asked, biting back her natural inclination to complain.

"Ahh, couldn't sleep last night," he grunted. "I was itching like crazy."

"Even after the bath? You musta' soaked yourself a good half hour."

"Yeah, and then I smeared myself with that calamine and I still felt like I was going to itch myself to death!" her husband groaned. "Never thought fleas could drive ya crazy!"

"Well don't forget, ya had a good head start in that department," said Arlene, less miffed about last night than some things her husband had said over the weekend.

"Very funny. You should be on television."

"Squattin' on top and holdin' up the antenna. Ha, ha," said Arlene. "Anyhow, Joe, you got to stop scratchin'."

"Be glad to," grumbled her husband, not pausing a second at his vigorous rubbing. "Just tell me f—in' how!"

"Well, it ain't gonna look good if you do that at work. Besides, your irritatin' the bites and makin' 'em worse!"

"They irritated me first!"

"Take another bath and put some more stuff on 'em. You know, that cream that's supposed t' kill itches. There's a couple tubes of it in the bathroom cabinet."

"Believe me, Arlene, I'm gonna," grumbled Joe.

As her grumbling husband turned to grab himself the last of the coffee, Arlene spotted the flea on his neck. The bug quickly hopped down the collar of his bathrobe. She decided not to tell Joe about it. He was cranky enough this morning without any bad news of that sort.

Mrs. Borden quietly breathed a prayer of thanks that she hadn't picked the fleas up from her husband. The way he had them it was downright amazing she hadn't gotten them on her so far.

"He musta walked through a whole nest of 'em yesterday," she muttered after she'd wished her husband good day and headed out to the car.

Or did you call it a nest with fleas? A swarm? Whatever.

"Stay outta my way tonight," Joe warned his wife as he came home that evening. "I'm in a shitty mood."

"The itching?" she asked.

"Yeah, I nearly itched myself to death at work today. Couldn't scratch, couldn't do nothin'! Just had t' put up with it," he growled.

"That soothing cream didn't work?" she dared to ask.

"Oh it worked . . . for the first three hours or so. Then it wore off. And I swear I still got those goddamned fleas," Joe continued. "Felt 'em crawling over me and bitin' me all day."

"Great stuff to talk about just before dinner."

"Talk about it, hell! Try feeling it all day. We got any bug repellant?"

"I don't think so," said Arlene, thoughtfully. "Used up that can we had at the picnic."

"Then I'm goin' to the store and buying six cans right after dinner! You shouldn't let us run outta stuff like that!"

Without bothering to ask what was for dinner, Joe turned on his heel and went back out again.

"I'm gonna be outside till dinner's ready," he said.

245

Arlene appreciated the action more than it deserved. At least when Joe knew he was in a bad mood he tried to keep away from her.

Outside Joe tried to stop from scratching, which he found hard, and then checked his arms and legs for any loose fleas. He found one, and had the satisfaction of catching the bug and squashing it between his thumb and forefinger. Not that it really helped much. He could feel the others crawling all over him. He knew part of it was imagination, but he also knew for a fact he really did have more fleas than a mangy mutt in a junkyard.

"Oh. Hi there, Joe," came a voice behind him.

Joe turned to see his neighbor Stan Barbour. Stan lived down the block and was on pretty good terms with Joe and his wife.

"Hi, Stan," said Joe as his neighbor came out of the woods. "What are you up to?"

"Ahh, lookin' for my damn cat," sighed Stan. "Been missin' the past couple days."

"Mmph," said Joe, noncommittally.

"My kid's hysterical," Stan continued. "Phillis's worried, too. She's afraid that poisoner we had a few months back might be up to his old tricks."

Although Stan didn't say it, it was clear he was upset about the cat's disappearance as well.

"Well, I haven't seen your cat around here," said Stan, truthfully. "Or in the woods."

"Didn't think so, this isn't the usual place she wanders. Say, isn't your wife allergic to cats?" asked Stan.

"Very. Dogs as well. If one of either comes near her, it's like she's got a king-sized cold," said Joe. "Sneezes her head off. Though when I hear about missin' pets, and poisoners, I'm kinda glad we can't keep one."

"You might be right at that," said Stan, sadly. "You might be right at that."

Joe's neighbor suddenly gave him an odd look. Joe, after the initial apprehension, realized Stan was staring at his face. Joe instinctively slapped at his cheek, catching the flea crawling across it more by luck than skill.

"Damn, a flea," he said, as if it were the first time he realized he had 'em. "Musta picked it up in the woods. Better watch yourself if you're fooling around in there, Stan."

"I know I ought to stay outta there, but I gotta look for Bootsie."

Stan went back to combing the woods. Joe forced himself not to smile. If anything had happened to the Barbour's cat, he knew for a fact it hadn't happened on his property—or anywhere near it, for that matter.

He'd made sure none of his neighbors knew the way his guts churned whenever he saw any sort of animal at all, or the fact when a dog or cat wandered across his property, it was he, not Arlene (who really was allergic) who got upset.

In spite of the rain coming into the house, Arlene didn't want to close the windows. Joe had set off a bug bomb in the house a couple days earlier and she was afraid all the fumes hadn't dissipated yet. She could still smell it.

She wondered where her husband was right now. He was late home from work, but not so late that it couldn't be traffic.

Ahh, there he was now.

Joe was grimly carrying a large paper bag. As Arlene watched, he dumped the contents out on the kitchen table.

"Flea dip? Flea powder?" she read aloud. "Joe, have you gone crazy? Those are for dogs!"

"I know!" said her husband through clenched teeth. "I checked the drugstore first. They didn't have anything for humans with fleas."

"But you can't use that on yourself! It's not for people—you'll make yourself sick!"

"I'll have to risk it. The boss took me aside today and talked to me about my hygiene. They've been noticing the fleas at work. And the scratchin'. I can't afford to lose this job, Arlene!"

"But you're takin' two baths a day now," his wife protested.

"When a guy's covered with fleas, who can believe that?" demanded Joe. "Anyhow, I got to do something about those goddamned bugs! This is no way to live!"

Arlene had to agree. It had been going on eight days now. No matter what Joe did, he couldn't get rid of the fleas. In spite of twice-daily baths, they showed no signs of abating. He'd bug-bombed the house, but the fleas seemed to have been all outside with him while the bomb was fumigating their home. He'd even, in the privacy of their bedroom, stripped naked and gone over himself with that little hand vacuum-cleaner they used on the cars. If he had gotten rid of a lot of the fleas, a whole batch must have survived his various onslaughts on them. Either that, or else a whole new brigade of them jumped on him every time he stepped outside in the yard.

And she could see the results of Joe's flea trouble. All the little bites, all over his body. The sudden appearance of a flea on his hand or face, hopping about like it owned Joe. The scabs on his arms where Joe had scratched too hard and make himself bleed, so he had to wear long-sleeved shirts in midsummer to hide them like a junkie concealing his needle marks. The repulsive black specks of "flea dirt" he had to brush off whenever he washed. And the big pouches under his eyes.

Not that Arlene didn't have bags under her eyes at this point, what with her husband keeping her up half the night with his tossing, turning, and cursing. Between that and the bugs, she was tempted to go downstairs and sleep on the couch these nights, only she dreaded the fight that would cause with Joe.

Besides, against all probability, she hadn't been bit once; hadn't found one flea crawling on her. For that matter, she didn't believe that any of the neighbors Joe had talked to had gotten any fleas off him, or any of his coworkers, despite the fact they'd noticed his problem.

Arlene suspected her husband had some sort of odor or flavor that made the bugs favor him over everybody else, though she wouldn't dare tell Joe that. State he was in, he'd probably throw a fit.

"She kep' a dozhen cats in her house," Joe slurred. "An jus' as many dogs. Hated the smell. Hated the dirt. Alwaysh came home with scratches. Got bit once so bad doctor had to sew it up. And you know what she shaid? She tol' the doctor I'd pulled the dog'sh tail. I didn't pull hish tail. I ben't down to pet him and he bit me!"

"Don't take it so hard," soothed the barkeep. "Old ladys are like that."

"Yeah, but to blame her own . . . her own gran'son when it was the dog what acted up . . . was that right? Was it right when she whipped me bloody with a strap because one of her cats got run over?" Joe continued. "I wasn't even there when it happened. She was already cryin' over the cat when my folks dropped me off. Then, the minute . . . the second they left she accused me of lettin' the cat out so it got onto th' road."

The barkeep, who'd discovered he'd led a very happy childhood by comparing it to his customer's, could only nod his head in a commiserating fashion.

Joe's complaints lowered into a dull, monotonous grumble.

"It wasn't fair! My Dad couldn't shtand her. My Mom couldn't take her! But they kep' sendin' me over there to visit her because she nagged about it! Her and those animals. An the smell. And those damn fleas . . . I came home with fleas ev'ry time I was there. Hated that. Itchin', crawlin' on me . . ."

"Cab's here," the assistant barkeep announced.

"Here," said the bartender. "Let me help you."

Joe got up by himself and waved him away.

"Thanksh," he muttered. "Don't need help. Not gettin' to a cab. I jush need t' get rid of thoshe goddamned fleas."

Scratching and mumbling, he lurched his way out of the saloon to his cab.

"What was that all about?" asked a regular who'd come in at the end of the performance, after the cab had taken Joe safely out of earshot.

"That big guy comes in," explained the barkeep. "Orders a couple whiskeys, then starts cryin' his eyes out. Kept sayin' he had fleas. Can you imagine somebody goin' on a crying jag over fleas? Anyhow, I'm glad he didn't put up a fight when I called a cab for him. Was afraid he was gonna start a fight."

"I just hope he didn't leave any of those fleas here," said the other bartender. "See how he was scratchin'? Those weren't D.T. bugs—he had bites all over his hands."

The dog had died before they found him. All they could've done would've been to put him out of his misery, anyhow.

For a while they were silent (it hadn't been their dog). Then the father announced harshly:

"Well, he's back."

"Think it was the same bastard as last time?" his near-grown son asked.

"Had to be!" growled the father. "It's all happening in the same patch of woods! Christ Almighty, first poison meat and fish, now leghold traps! What next?"

"Stan Barbour found his cat caught in one of these traps last week," sighed the son. "Vet saved the cat's leg, but it'll limp for the rest of its life. Cost Stan a lot to save the animal, too."

"Boy, if ever someone should go to jail for cruelty to animals, it's this character. And they won't catch him, either, that's the worst part," the father complained.

"I wouldn't say that. We can hope they make a mistake sooner or later," said the son.

"You still think it's those Yodice kids, don't you?" demanded the old man. "It ain't them. Throwing rocks at a dog is more their speed. This is some cunning, sneaky guy who nobody suspects. This shows real thought behind it. Wouldn't even be surprised if it's a guy who lives in a different neighborhood, who comes over here at night to take it out on the animals. If the cops find him, it'll be by luck. This guy doesn't even return to see what he's done, just leaves his traps and poison and forgets about it. He probably wouldn't care if he injured a kid with those lousy traps."

"Four dogs, seven cats, a raccoon, two rabbits, and a muskrat so far," the son counted off. "If I thought curses worked, I'd wish that dirty shit would never have a good day."

"Don't worry about cursin' him," said the father. "This guy's pissed off so many people that if *anybody's* curses work, he got to have one workin' on him already."

JIKININKI

Lafcadio Hearn

Once, when Musō Kokushi, a priest of the Zen sect, was journeying alone through the province of Mino, he lost his way in a mountain district where there was nobody to direct him. For a long time he wandered about helplessly, and he was beginning to despair of finding shelter for the night when he perceived, on the top of a hill lighted by the last rays of the sun, one of those little hermitages, called *anjitsu*, that are built for solitary priests. It seemed to be in a ruinous condition, but he hastened to it eagerly and found that it was inhabited by an aged priest, from whom he begged the favor of a night's lodging. This the old man harshly refused; but he directed Musō to a certain hamlet in the valley adjoining where lodging and food could be obtained.

Musō found his way to the hamlet, which consisted of less than a dozen farm cottages, and was kindly received at the dwelling of the headman. Forty or fifty persons were assembled in the principal apartment at the moment of Musō's arrival, but he was shown into a small separate room, where he was promptly supplied with food and bedding. Being very tired, he lay down to rest at an early hour, but a little before midnight he was roused from sleep by a sound of loud weeping in the next apartment. Presently the sliding screens were gently pushed apart and a young man, carrying a lighted lantern, entered the room, respectfully saluted him, and said:

"Reverend sir, it is my painful duty to tell you that I am now the responsible head of this house. Yesterday I was only the eldest son. But when you came here, tired as you were, we did not wish that you should feel embarrassed in any way, therefore we did not tell you that father had died only a few hours before. The people whom you saw in the next room are the inhabitants of this village: they all assembled here to pay their last respects to the dead; and now they are going to another village, about three miles off—for, by our custom, no one of us may remain in this village during the night after a death has taken place. We make the proper offerings and prayers, then we go away, leaving the corpse alone. Strange things always happen in the house where a corpse has thus been left, so we think that it will be better for you to come away with us. We can find you good lodging in the other village. But perhaps, as you are a priest, you have no fear of demons or evil spirits, and, if you are not afraid of being left alone with the body, you will be very welcome to the use of this poor house. However, I must tell you that nobody, except a priest, would dare to remain here tonight."

Musō made answer:

"For your kind intention and your generous hospitality, I am deeply grateful. But I am sorry that you did not tell me of your father's death when I came, for, though I was a little tired, I certainly was not so tired that I should have found any difficulty in doing my duty as a priest. Had you told me, I could have performed the service before your departure. As it is, I shall perform the service after you have gone away; and I shall stay by the body until morning. I do not know what you mean by your words about the danger of staying here alone, but I am not afraid of ghosts or demons; therefore, please to feel no anxiety on my account."

The young man appeared to be rejoiced by these assurances, and expressed his gratitude in fitting words. Then the other members of the family, and the folk assembled in the adjoining room, having been told of the priest's kind promises, came to thank him—after which the master of the house said:

"Now, reverend sir, much as we regret to leave you alone, we must bid you farewell. By the rule of our village, none of us can stay here after midnight. We beg, kind sir, that you will take every care of your honorable body while we are unable to attend upon you. And if you happen to hear or see anything strange during our absence, please tell us of the matter when we return in the morning."

✿ ✿ ✿

All then left the house, except the priest, who went to the room where the dead body was lying. The usual offerings had been set before the corpse, and a small Buddhist lamp—*tōmyō*—was burning. The priest recited the service and performed the funeral ceremonies, after which he entered into meditation. So meditating, he remained through several silent hours, and there was no sound in the deserted village. But, when the hush of the night was at its deepest, there noiselessly entered a Shape, vague and vast; and in the same moment Musō found himself without power to move or speak. He saw that Shape lift the corpse, as with hands, and devour it, more quickly than a cat devours a rat—beginning at the head, and eating everything: the hair and the bones and even the shroud. And the monstrous Thing, having thus consumed the body, turned to the offerings, and ate them also. Then it went away, as mysteriously as it had come.

When the villagers returned next morning, they found the priest awaiting them at the door of the headman's dwelling. All in turn saluted him, and when they had entered and looked about the room, no one expressed any surprise at the disappearance of the dead body and the offerings. But the master of the house said to Musō:

"Reverend sir, you have probably seen unpleasant things during the night: all of us were anxious about you. But now we are very happy to find you alive and unharmed. Gladly we would have stayed with you, if it had been possible. But the law of our village, as I told you last evening, obliges us to quit our houses after a death has taken place, and to leave the corpse alone. Whenever this law has been broken, heretofore, some great misfortune has followed. Whenever it is obeyed, we find that the corpse and the offerings disappear during our absence. Perhaps you have seen the cause."

Then Musō told of the dim and awful Shape that had entered the death chamber to devour the body and the offerings. No person seemed to be surprised by his narration, and the master of the house observed:

"What you have told us, reverend sir, agrees with what has been said about this matter from ancient time."

Musō then inquired:

"Does not the priest on the hill sometimes perform the funeral service for your dead?"

"What priest?" the young man asked.

"The priest who yesterday evening directed me to this village," answered Musō. "I called at his *anjitsu* on the hill yonder. He refused me lodging, but told me the way here."

The listeners looked at each other, as in astonishment; and, after a moment of silence, the master of the house said:

"Reverend sir, there is no priest and there is no *anjitsu* on the hill. For the time of many generations there has not been any resident priest in this neighborhood."

Musō said nothing more on the subject, for it was evident that his kind hosts supposed him to have been deluded by some goblin. But after having bidden them farewell and obtained all necessary information as to his road, he determined to look again for the hermitage on the hill, and so to ascertain whether he had really been deceived. He found the *anjitsu* without any difficulty; and, this time, its aged occupant invited him to enter. When he had done so, the hermit humbly bowed down before him, exclaiming: "Ah! I am ashamed!—I am very much ashamed!—I am exceedingly ashamed!"

"You need not be ashamed for having refused me shelter," said Musō. "You directed me to the village yonder, where I was very kindly treated; and I thank you for that favor."

"I can give no man shelter," the recluse made answer, "and it is not for the refusal that I am ashamed. I am ashamed only that you should have seen me in my real shape—for it was I who devoured the corpse and the offerings last night before your eyes. . . . Know, reverend sir, that I am a *jikininki*—an eater of human flesh. Have pity upon me, and suffer me to confess the secret fault by which I became reduced to this condition.

"A long, long time ago, I was a priest in this desolate region. There was no other priest for many leagues around. So, in that time, the bodies of the mountain folk who died used to be brought here—sometimes from great distances—in order that I might repeat over them the holy service. But I repeated the service and performed the rites only as a matter of business; I thought only of the food and the clothes that my sacred profession enabled me to gain. And because of this selfish impiety I was reborn, immediately after my death, into the state of a *jikininki*. Since then I have been obliged to feed upon the corpses of the people who die in this district: every one of them I must devour in the way that you saw last night. . . . Now, reverend sir, let me beseech you to perform a *Ségaki* service for me: help me by your prayers, I entreat you, so that I may be soon able to escape from this horrible state of existence."

No sooner had the hermit uttered this petition than he disappeared, and the hermitage also disappeared at the same instant. And Musō

Kokushi found himself kneeling alone in the high grass, beside an ancient and moss-grown tomb, of the form called *go-rin-ishi,* which seemed to be the tomb of a priest.

John Mortonson's Funeral

AMBROSE BIERCE

Rough notes of this tale were found among the papers of the late Leigh Bierce. It is printed here with such revision only as the author might himself have made in transcription. (Note by Bierce.)

John Mortonson was dead; his lines in "the tragedy 'Man'" had all been spoken and he had left the stage.

The body rested in a fine mahogany coffin fitted with a plate of glass. All arrangements for the funeral had been so well attended to that had the deceased known he would doubtless have approved. The face, as it showed under the glass, was not disagreeable to look upon; it bore a faint smile, and as the death had been painless, had not been distorted beyond the repairing power of the undertaker. At two o'clock of the afternoon the friends were to assemble to pay their last tribute of respect to one who had no further need of friends and respect. The surviving members of the family came severally every few minutes to the casket and wept above the placid features beneath the glass. This did them no good; it did no good to John Mortonson; but in the presence of death reason and philosophy are silent.

As the hour of two approached the friends began to arrive and after offering such consolation to the stricken relatives as the proprieties of the occasion required, solemnly seated themselves about the room with an augmented consciousness of their importance in the scheme funereal. Then the minister came, and in that overshadowing presence the lesser lights went into eclipse. His entrance was followed by that of the widow, whose lamentations filled the room. She approached the casket and, after leaning her face against the cold glass for a moment, was gently led to a seat near her daughter. Mournfully and low the man of God began his eulogy of the dead, and his doleful voice, mingled with the sobbing that it was its purpose to stimulate and sustain, rose and fell, seemed to come and go, like the sound of a sullen sea. The gloomy day grew darker as he spoke; a curtain of cloud underspread the sky and a few drops of rain fell audibly. It seemed as if all nature were weeping for John Mortonson.

When the minister had finished his eulogy with prayer a hymn was sung and the pallbearers took their places beside the bier. As the last notes of the hymn died away the widow ran to the coffin, cast herself upon it, and sobbed hysterically. Gradually, however, she yielded to dissuasion, becoming more composed; and as the minister was in the act of leading her away her eyes sought the face of the dead beneath the glass. She threw up her arms and with a shriek fell backward insensible.

The mourners sprang forward to the coffin, the friends followed, and as the clock on the mantel solemnly struck three all were staring down upon the face of John Mortonson, deceased.

They turned away, sick and faint. One man, trying in his terror to escape the awful sight, stumbled against the coffin so heavily as to knock away one of its frail supports. The coffin fell to the floor, the glass was shattered to bits by the concussion.

From the opening crawled John Mortonson's cat, which lazily leapt to the floor, sat up, tranquilly wiped its crimson muzzle with a forepaw, then walked with dignity from the room.

THE KEEN EYES AND EARS OF KARA KEDI

CLAUDE FARRÈRE

January 13, 1937

I have been writing all the evening, alone in my room, alone in my little house in the uncomprehending city of Toulon, the lonely refuge I have crept into to get away from the world. When a man tires himself out, when he takes too strenuous a part in the various painful agitations of active life, he grows old rapidly. I have not yet lived fifty years on this earth, but my hair is white and my thoughts are as gray as ashes. . . .

I am writing in my room, all alone. Alone in a sense, that is. My black cat is with me. He is asleep, curled up in his armchair, which is an exact duplicate of mine. He and I spend a great deal of time together in these great, heavy twin chairs, upholstered in tan velvet. My black cat's name is Kara Kedi, which is Turkish for just that—I mean, for "black cat." I didn't waste a great deal of imagination in naming him. Kara Kedi was born in Turkey, at Stamboul, in the holy suburb of Eyoub. That was back in the days when I was deep in love with the Circassian girl. Ah, how blond her hair was, and how brown her skin was! And how sweet her kisses were!

But there is no burning passion in my cottage tonight. Kara Kedi's chair is comfortable, and he sleeps very soundly, so that I am really alone in my room, alone in my dreary little house.

My little house is a gimcrack of a place, with a little garden that runs all around it. To the right and left are little gardens very much like mine, about tiny little houses very much like mine. My neighbor on the right is a very dirty, very polite, and very deaf old sailor. My neighbor on the left is a pretty little young woman, very charming and very candid, who is constantly laughing and rattling her bracelets, as she gambols about in her sunny little garden. She has a great many friends, all of them gentlemen, and I am afraid they do not all come merely for the sake of a look at her pretty face and the pleasure of hearing her silvery voice. But of course it isn't any affair of mine what they come for. And they are reasonably quiet about it, so that I scarcely know when they come and go.

At night, our part of the city is absolutely quiet. It is so still at night that even when the sea is calm I can hear it lapping lazily against the rocks. For the sea is not many feet away from me. I could see it from my windows, if my windows were not so low. But as it is, the cabins of the fishermen's families hide the sea away from me.

But tonight, for some reason or other, I can't hear a sound of any sort, not even the caressing whispers of the waves. It is too calm even for that. There is not a hint of a breeze in the air, not a ripple on the surface of the sea. The winds and the waves are asleep, quite as soundly asleep as Kara Kedi, my black cat.

Kara Kedi, in his velvet-upholstered armchair, is as completely motionless as if he were cast in bronze. I can't see his paws or his tail, or the exact shape of his head. He is rolled up into a tightish ball, with a

256

soft outline of ink-colored fur. Kara Kedi is an enormous cat. I think he is probably the biggest cat I ever saw. You could scarcely call him fat. He is not one of those round, formless cats you see sometimes, who doze day and night because they have more fat flesh than they have energy. He is longer, larger-boned, taller on his feet, than the ordinary housecat. When he crosses my garden, gravely, gracefully, but with unmistakable evidence of personality and power, to meditate in the branches of the great fig tree at the end of my garden, my little neighbor on the left says he makes her nervous. She tells me that she is almost afraid of him, and since her zoological attainments are not extensive enough to include black panthers, she reproachfully calls him a big awful bear.

I am writing at this journal of mine . . . there is a great feeling of calmness and peace about me in the room and in the house . . . in the garden, and in all the quiet night that reaches out beyond. . . .

I discover that my pen is empty. I raise my head and reach out my hand for the inkwell. . . . Ah! Kara Kedi is not asleep any longer. His head has suddenly emerged from the placid ball of dark fur. His head moves upward and forward, and his glaring eyes fix themselves on the dim rectangle of the window. And I can see that his pointed ears have turned straight upward. He is listening with all his might.

"Kara Kedi, old fellow, is there something wrong out beyond that window?"

Kara Kedi is still motionless and silent. But I can see his ears twitch, in a gesture that tells me he has heard me, but implores me to be quiet. He is right. There is no reason why I should distract his attention from the faint and distant noises, which may mean much, by the noisy futilities of human speech. . . .

They *do* mean much, I am sure of that. Something is wrong, mysteriously wrong. Kara Kedi rises upright on his four long, strong legs, his head held straight forward and his long tail standing straight out behind him. He has disdained the thousand-year tradition of cats awakened from a nap. He has not stopped to arch his back, to yawn, to stretch himself magnificently. There must be something ominous in the air, or at least it must seem ominous to Kara Kedi . . . perhaps it might seem less so to me. . . .

It *is* a serious matter in Kara Kedi's opinion; there is no longer any doubt about that! Kara Kedi descends from the armchair and walks toward the window. He walks resolutely, determinedly, like a strong nature meeting a crisis. When he left his chair, he did not leap down from the chair to the floor. He lengthened himself out, muscle after

257

muscle, until he touched the floor with one paw, then with a second, then with a third, and a fourth. . . . I realize perfectly by this time that I must maintain an absolute silence. Kara Kedi's head moves forward till his nose touches the strangely disquieting windowpane. Then, very slowly, the great body swings around till it faces toward the wall that lay to the animal's left before. My windows are so low that I can see the great panther profile now, standing out rather distinctly against the faint light of the window. I should not be able to see him so distinctly if the animal's hair had not suddenly risen to a perpendicular all over his body and begun, as I had seen it do once or twice before on very stormy days, to emit a myriad of tiny crackling electric sparks.

"Kara Kedi! Kitty! What's the matter with you?"

"Meow!"

It was not Kara Kedi's usual "meow" of inquiry, petition, or complaint; it was merely an expression of impatience. Kara Kedi, so courteous on most occasions, is nervously irritated at my foolish prattle. I accept his rebuke, in all meekness. I shall not breathe another sound.

Kara Kedi's eyes are fixed on that left wall with glaring insistence. The eyes are two green flames of dazzling glory. All at once the great feline turns his head and gazes at me, and—it sounds supremely foolish —and I am unable to ward off a feeling of superstitious, dazed terror. I am as sure as Kara Kedi is that something ghastly is happening out beyond that wall. It is a feeling, nothing more. There is no trace of rational knowledge. . . .

Kara Kedi, phosphorescent from his tail to his mustache, moves entirely away from the window. Then he begins to creep straight along that left wall, as if he were following, step by step, some unknown being that moved or was moved slowly along on the other side of the wall. Kara Kedi is making no apparent use of his sense of smell. He is listening with all the intense keenness of his ears, and he is looking, looking with all his eyes. . . . The wall is covered with a plain gray paper, and I can't remember ever to have seen anything on that wall or that paper that had anything unusual about it. . . .

Oh—oh!

Kara Kedi draws himself together, and with all the power of his marvelous muscles he flings himself backward into the room, away from the wall. He runs around in a bewildered circle, his tail thrust out perfectly stiff. He looks this way and that for a place to flee to. I can see that he is driven by blind and agonizing terror. He is so troubled that his mind and his memory are not functioning; he has forgotten that I am there to guard and protect him as I have done so many times before. It is

258

only after a long period of anguish and dashing madly hither and thither that his dazed eyes chance to meet mine. The message of my presence reaches his poor fuddled brain at last. And suddenly, like an animal hunted for prey, he flings himself toward me, he leaps to my knees, but he does not stop there. He crawls deep into my arms, up against my breast. He buries his head between my neck and my shoulder, but he is unable to resist the wretched fascination that keeps drawing his eyes toward that miserable wall, that wall of pain and horror.

And his trouble has taken possession of me. The frightened cat has driven his fear into the very marrow of my bones. I am paralyzed with craven foreboding. Like the cat, I am unable to move my eyes from the mysterious gray wall, the wall that is hiding from me some blood-curdling happening that I have not the courage to try to imagine. Kara Kedi trembles and shivers in the protecting grasp of my two cold hands. Then suddenly an even more terrible thing happens.

Kara Kedi tears himself free from my embrace, drops from my knees, leaps into the air three or four times and falls to the floor in violent convulsions. His throat is torn by raucous cries, cries that are no more like the familiar meowing of his normal life than the sinister gurglings of an epileptic in the midst of a seizure are like the healthy human voice. . . .

I think I suffered a temporary period of derangement. I have a feverish recollection that I seized my revolver and stood a long time with the weapon pointed at the ominous wall, waiting for the wall to open and admit some shape of terror. . . .

Jan. 14.

My poor, pretty young neighbor, the giddy little person of accommodating virtue whose bracelets rattled so gayly in her sunny garden, is dead. They found her body this morning.

Nobody has the slightest inkling of what the motive of the crime may have been. The assassin does not appear to have taken anything. The poor little corpse still wears all its gaudy jewelry. Nor was there any sign of a struggle or of violence. An extraordinarily long gold pin, an ornament but a deadly weapon at need, was found driven into her body below the fifth rib. And the eyes of the dead woman, wide open and staring, are dilated with a horror that is one of the most dreadful things I have ever seen.

Everybody is mystified. Nobody saw anything, nobody heard anything. It is likely that the mystery will never be solved. Till the body was found, nobody had any suspicion that anything was wrong.

Nobody, that is, but Kara Kedi—Kara Kedi and I.

Kara Kedi followed me over when I went into the little cottage to look at the body. He glanced carelessly at the pathetic little corpse; then he looked away. It appears that dead people have no particular interest for Kara Kedi. But he did look at me again, with a strange earnest expression in his eyes.

Then he walked out of the open door, crossed the garden pensively, and moved out on a branch of the great fig tree to meditate. To meditate—perhaps to ruminate on his memories.

The Kelpie

MANLY WADE WELLMAN

No sooner had Cannon closed and latched the door than Lu was in his arms, and they were kissing with the hungry fierceness of lovers who doubt their own good fortune. Thus for a delirious, heart-battering moment; then Lu pulled nervously away.

"We're being watched," she whispered breathlessly.

The big, dark man laughed down at her worried blue eyes, her shining wealth of ale-brown hair, her face like an ivory heart, the apprehensive tautness of her slender figure. "That's guilty conscience, Lu," he teased. "You know I wouldn't have invited you to my apartment without giving my man the night off. And even if someone did see us, why be afraid? Don't we love each other?"

She allowed him to bring her into the parlor and draw her down beside him on a divan, but she still mused apprehensively.

"I could swear there were eyes upon us," she insisted, half apologetically. "Hostile eyes."

"Maybe they're spirits," Cannon cried gayly, his own twinkling gaze sweeping around to view in turn the paintings on the walls, the hooded lamps, the bookshelves, the rich, comfortable furniture, the big box-shaped aquarium in the darkest corner. Again he chuckled. "Spirits—that's a pun, you know. The lowest form of wit."

From a taboret at his elbow he lifted a decanter of brandy and poured two drinks with a humorous flourish. Lu, forgetting her uneasiness of a moment before, lifted her glass. "To us," she toasted.

But Cannon set his own drink down untasted and peered around a second time, this time without gaiety. "You've got me thinking it now," he muttered.

"Thinking what?"

"That something is watching—and not liking what it sees." He glanced quickly over his shoulder, then continued, as if seeking to reassure them both. "Nothing in that corner, of course, except the aquarium."

"What's the latest tenantry there?" Lu asked, glad to change the disquieting subject.

"Some Scotch water plants—new laboratory project." Cannon was at ease the moment his hobby came into the conversation. "They arrived this afternoon in a sealed tin box. Doctor MacKenzie's letter says they were gathered from the Pool Kelp, wherever that is in his highland wildernesses. I'm letting them soak and wash overnight. In the morning I'll begin experimenting."

Lu sipped more brandy, her eyes interested. "Pool Kelp," she repeated. "It sounds seaweedy."

"But these are fresh-water growths. As I say, I never heard of the pool before." Cannon broke off. "Here, though, why talk botany when we can—"

His lips abruptly smothered hers, his arms gathered her so close as to bruise her. But even as she yielded happily to his embrace the telephone rang loudly in the front entry. Cannon released her with a muttered curse of impatience, rose, and hurried out to answer. He closed the door behind him, and his voice, muffled and indistinct, sounded aggrieved as he spoke into the transmitter.

Lu, finishing her brandy alone, picked up the drink Cannon had set down. As she lifted it to her lips she glanced idly over the rim of the glass at the moist tangle in the aquarium. In the dim light it seemed to fall into all manner of rich greens—darkest emerald, beryl, malachite, olive, grass, lettuce. Something moved, too, filliped and swerved in the heart of the little submerged grove.

Cannon was still talking. Lu rose, drink in hand, to stroll curiously toward the big glass box. As she did so the moving trifle seemed to glide upward toward the surface. Coming closer yet, Lu paused to peer in the half-light.

A fish? If so, a very green fish and a very small one—perhaps a tadpole. A bubble broke audibly on top of the water. Lu, genuinely interested, bent closer, just as something rose through the little ripples and hooked its tip on the rim of the aquarium.

It was a tiny, spinach-colored hand.

Half a second later another fringe of tiny fingers appeared, clutching the rim in turn. Lu, woodenly motionless, stared in her effort to rationalize. She could see the tiny digits, each tapering and flexible, each armed with a jet-colored claw. Through the glass, under and behind the fingers, she made out thumbs—deft, opposable thumbs—and smooth, wet palms of a dead, oystery gray. Her breath caught in mute, helpless astonishment. A blunt head rose slowly into view behind and between the fists, something with flat brow, broad lump of nose and wide mouth, like a grotesque Mayan mask—and it was *growing*.

Lu told herself, a little stupidly, that she must not have seen clearly at first. She had thought the creature a little green minnow, but it was as big as a squirrel. No, as big as a baby! Its bright eyes, white-ringed, fixed hers, projecting a wave of malignant challenge that staggered her like a blow. The full, lead-hued lips parted loosely and the forked tip of a purple tongue quivered out for a moment. A snaky odor steamed up to Lu's nostrils, making her dizzy and weak. Wet, scabby-green shoulders had heaved into view by now, and after them the twin mounds of a grotesquely feminine bosom. The thing was climbing out at her, and as it did so it swelled and grew, grew. . . .

The brandy glass fell from her hand and loudly exploded into splinters upon the floor. The sound of the breaking gave Lu back her voice, and she screamed tremulously, then managed to move back and away, half stumbling and half staggering. The monster, all damp and green and stinking, was writhing a leg into view. Lu noted that, and then everything went into a whirling white blur and she began to collapse.

Faintly she heard the rush of Cannon's feet, felt the clutch of his strong arms as though many thicknesses of fabric separated them from her. He almost shouted her name in panic. After a moment her sight and mind cleared, and she looked up into his concerned face. With all her shaken strength she clung to him.

"That thing," she chattered, "that horrid female thing in the aquarium—"

262

Cannon managed a comforting tone. "But there's nothing, dearest, nothing at all. Those two brandies—you took mine, too, you shameless glutton—went to your head."

"Look at it!" She pointed an unsteady finger. "Deep down there in the weeds."

He looked. "Oh, that?" he laughed. "I noticed it, too, just before you came. It's a little frog or toad—must have been gathered with the weeds and shipped all the way from Scotland."

Lu caressed her throbbing forehead with her slender white hand and mumbled something about "seeing things." Already she believed that she had somehow dreamed of the green water-monster. Still, it was a distinct effort to walk with Cannon to the aquarium and look in.

Through the thick tangle of stems and fronds that made a dank stew in the water she could make out a tiny something that wriggled and glided. It was only minnow-size after all, and seemed smooth and innocuous. Funny what notions two quick drinks will give you. . . . She lowered a cupped palm toward the surface, as if to scoop down and seize the little creature, but the chilly touch of the topmost weed tips repelled her, and she drew back her arm.

"You'd never catch it," Cannon told her. "It won't wait for you to grab. I had a try when I first saw it, and got a wet sleeve—and this."

He held out his left hand. For the first time that evening Lu saw the gold band that he wore on his third finger.

"A ring," her lover explained. "It was lying on the bottom. Apparently it came with the weeds, too."

"You put it on your wedding finger!" Lu wailed.

"That was the only one it would fit," Cannon defended as she caught his hand and tugged with all her might at the ring. It did not budge.

"Please," she begged, "get rid of it."

"Why, Lu, what's the trouble? Are you being jealous because a present was given me by that mess of weed—or maybe by the little lady frog?"

The tiny swimmer in the tank splashed water, as if in punctuation of his joke, and Cannon, falling abruptly silent, suddenly began wrenching at the gold circlet. But not even his strength, twice that of Lu, could bring it over the joint.

"Here, I don't like this," he announced, his voice steady but a little tight. "I'm going to put soap on my finger. That will make the thing slip off."

Lu made no reply, but her eyes encouraged him. Cannon kissed her pale forehead, strode across the room and into a little corridor beyond.

After a moment Lu could hear the spurt of a water jet in a bowl, then the sound of industrious scrubbing with lather.

In command of herself once again but still a trifle faint and shaky, Lu leaned her hand lightly upon the thick, smooth edge of the aquarium glass. A fond little smile came to her lips as she pondered on Cannon's eagerness to please her whim. Not even in a silly little matter like this one did he cross her will or offer argument that might embarrass or hurt her. The shedding of that ring would be a symbol between them, of understanding and faith.

Her eyes dropped to the table that stood against the aquarium, with its litter of papers and notebooks. At the edge nearest Lu lay a thick volume bound in gray—a dictionary. What was the term she had puzzled over? Oh, yes. . . . Still lounging with one hand on the glass, she flipped the book open with the other and turned the pages to the Ks:

> Kelp: Any one of various large brown seaweeds of the families *Laminariaceae* and *Fucaceae*.

Her hazy memory had been right, then, about the word. But why should a body of fresh water be called Pool Kelp? Glancing back at the page, her eyes caught the next definition.

It answered her question.

> Kelpie: (*Gael. Myth.*) A malicious water spirit or demon believed to haunt streams or marshes. Sometimes it falls in love with human beings, striving jealously against mortal rivals. . . .

The words swam before her vision, for the snake smell had risen sickeningly around her. And something was gripping the hand that rested on the rim of the tank.

Lu's mouth opened, but, as before, terror throttled her. Like a sleeper in the throes of nightmare, she struggled half-heartedly. She dared not look, yet some power forced her head around.

The grip had shifted to her wrist. Long, claw-tipped fingers were clamped there—fingers as large as her own, scrofulous green and of a swampy chill. Lu's eyes slid in fascinated horror along the scale-ridged, corded arm to the moldy-looking body, stuck and festooned over with weed fronds, that was rising from the water. Another foul hand stole swiftly out, fastened on Lu's shoulder, and jerked her close. The flat, grotesque face, grown to human size, was level with hers, its eyes triumphant within their dead white rings, its dark tongue quivering between gaping lips.

Yet again Lu tried to find her voice. All she could achieve was a wordless moan, no louder than a sigh.

"Did you call, sweetheart?" came Cannon's cheery response from his washing. "I'll be with you in a minute now; this thing is still hanging on like a poor relation!"

The reptilian jaw dropped suddenly, like the lid of a box turned upside down. Lu stared into the slate-gray cave that was the yawning mouth. Teeth, sharp teeth, gleamed there—not one row, but many.

Lu's hands lifted feebly in an effort at defense, then dropped wearily to her sides. The monster crinkled its humid features in something like a triumphant grin. Then its blunt head shot forward with incredible swiftness, nuzzling Lu at the juncture of neck and shoulder.

For a moment she felt exquisite pain, as of many piercing needles. After that she neither felt, heard, nor saw anything.

The medical examiner was drawing a sheet over the still, agony-distorted body of the dead girl. The police sergeant, scribbling his final notes, addressed Cannon with official sternness.

"Sorry," he said, "but you haven't explained this business at all satisfactorily. You come down to headquarters with me."

Cannon glanced wanly up from his senseless wrestling with the ring that would not quit his wedding finger. "I didn't do it," he reiterated dully.

The medical examiner was also speaking, more to himself than anyone: "An autopsy might clear up some points. Those inflamed, suppurated wounds on the neck might have been made by a big water snake. Or," he added, with a canny glance at the sergeant, "by a poisoned weapon constructed to simulate such a creature's bite."

Cannon's last vestige of control went. "I tell you," he snarled desperately, "that she and I were the only living things here tonight—the only living things." He broke off, becoming aware of movement in the aquarium. "Except, of course, that little frog in there."

The creature among the weeds, a tiny sliver of agile greenness, cavorted for a moment on the surface of the water as if in exultation, then, before any of the three watchers could get a fair look at it, dived deep into the heart of the floating mess.

Ladies in Waiting

Hugh B. Cave

Halper, the village real-estate man, said with a squint, "You're the same people looked at that place back in April, aren't you? Sure you are. The ones got caught in that freak snowstorm and spent the night there. Mr. and Mrs. Wilkes, is it?"

"Wilkins," Norman corrected, frowning at a photograph on the wall of the old man's dingy office: a yellowed, fly-spotted picture of the house itself, in all its decay and drabness.

"And you want to look at it again?"

"Yes!" Linda exclaimed.

Both men looked at her sharply because of her vehemence. Norman, her husband, was alarmed anew by the eagerness that suddenly flamed in her lovely brown eyes and as suddenly was replaced by a look of guilt. Yes—unmistakably a look of guilt.

"I mean," she stammered, "we still want a big old house that we can do over, Mr. Halper. We've never stopped looking. And we keep thinking the Creighton place just might do."

You keep thinking it might do, Norman silently corrected. He himself had intensely disliked the place when Halper showed it to them four months ago. The sharp edge of his abhorrence was not even blunted, and time would never dull his remembrance of that shocking expression on Linda's face. When he stepped through that hundred-seventy-year-old doorway again, he would hate and fear the house as much as before, he was certain.

Would he again see that look on his wife's face? God forbid!

"Well," Halper said, "there's no need for me to go along with you this time, I guess. I'll just ask you to return the key when you're through, same as you did before."

Norman accepted the tagged key from him and walked unhappily out to the car.

It was four miles from the village to the house. One mile of narrow blacktop, three of a dirt road that seemed forlorn and forgotten even in

266

this neglected part of New England. At three in the afternoon of an awesomely hot August day the car made the only sound in a deep green silence. The sun's heat had robbed even birds and insects of their voices.

Norman was silent too—with apprehension. Beside him his adored wife of less than two years leaned forward to peer through the windshield for the first glimpse of their destination, seeming to have forgotten he existed. Only the house now mattered.

And there it was.

Nothing had changed. It was big and ugly, with a sagging front piazza and too few windows. It was old. It was gray because almost all its white paint had weathered away. According to old Halper the Creightons had lived here for generations, having come here from Salem, where one of their women in the days of witchcraft madness had been hanged for practicing demonolatry. A likely story.

As he stopped the car by the piazza steps, Norman glanced at the girl beside him. His beloved. His childhood sweetheart. Why in God's name was she eager to come here again? She had not been so in the beginning. For days after that harrowing ordeal she had been depressed, unwilling even to talk about it.

But then, weeks later, the change, Ah, yes, the change! So subtle at first, or at least as subtle as her unsophisticated nature could contrive. "Norm . . . do you remember that old house we were snowbound in? Do you suppose we might have liked it if things had been different? . . ."

Then not so subtle. "Norm, can we look at the Creighton place again? Please? Norm?"

As he fumbled the key into the lock, he reached for her hand. "Are you all right, hon?"

"Of course!" The same tone of voice she had used in Halper's shabby office. Impatient. Critical. *Don't ask silly questions!*

With a premonition of disaster he pushed the old door open.

It was the same.

Furnished, Halper had called it, trying to be facetious. There were dusty ruins of furniture and carpets and—yes—someone or something was using them; that the house had *not* been empty for eight years, as Halper claimed. Now the feeling returned as Norman trailed his wife through the downstairs rooms and up the staircase to the bed chambers above. But the feeling was strong! He wanted desperately to seize her hand again and shout, "No, no, darling! Come out of here!"

Upstairs, when she halted in the big front bedroom, turning slowly to look about her, he said helplessly, "Hon, please—what is it? What do you *want?*"

No answer. He had ceased to exist. She even bumped into him as she went past to sit on the old four-poster with its mildewed mattress. And, seated there, she stared emptily into space as she had done before.

He went to her and took her hands. "Linda, for God's sake! What *is* it with this place?"

She looked up and smiled at him. "I'm all right. Don't worry, darling."

There had been an old blanket on the bed when they entered this room before. He had thought of wrapping her in it because she was shivering, the house was frigid, and with the car trapped in deepening snow they would have to spend the night here. But the blanket reeked with age and she had cringed from the touch of it.

Then—"Wait," he had said with a flash of inspiration. "Maybe if I could jam this under a tire! . . . Come on. It's at least worth a try."

"I'm cold, Norm. Let me stay here."

"You'll be all right? Not scared?"

"Better scared than frozen."

"Well . . . I won't be long."

How long was he gone? Ten minutes? Twenty? Twice the car had seemed about to pull free from the snow's mushy grip. Twice the wheel had spun the sodden blanket out from under and sent it flying through space like a huge yellow bird, and he'd been forced to go groping after it with the frigid wind lashing his half-frozen face. Say twenty minutes; certainly no longer. Then, giving it up as a bad job, he had trudged despondently back to the house and climbed the stairs again to that front bedroom.

And there she sat on the bed, as she was sitting now. White as the snow itself. Wide-eyed. Staring at or into something that only she could see.

"Linda! What's wrong?"

"Nothing. Nothing . . ."

He grasped her shoulders. "Look at me! Stop staring like that! What's happened?"

"I thought I heard something. Saw something."

"Saw *what?*"

"I don't know. I don't . . . remember."

Lifting her from the bed, he put his arms about her and glowered defiantly at the empty doorway. Strange. A paper-thin layer of mist or smoke moved along the floor there, drifting out into the hall. And there were floating shapes of the same darkish stuff trapped in the room's corners, as though left behind when the chamber emptied itself of a larger mass. Or was he imagining these things? One moment they seemed to be there; a moment later they were gone.

And was he also imagining the odor? It had not been present in the musty air of this room before; it certainly seemed to be now, unless his senses were playing tricks on him. A peculiarly robust smell, unquestionably male. But now it was fading.

Never mind. There *was* someone in this house, by God! He had felt an alien presence when Halper was here; even more so after the agent's departure. Someone, something, following them about, watching them.

The back of Linda's dress was unzipped, he realized then. His hands, pressing her to him, suddenly found themselves inside the garment, on her body. And her body was cold. Colder than the snow he had struggled with outside. Cold and clammy.

The zipper. He fumbled for it, found it drawn all the way down. What in God's name had she tried to do? This was his wife, who loved him. This was the girl who only a few weeks ago, at the club, had savagely slapped the face of the town's richest, handsomest playboy for daring to hint at a mate-swapping arrangement. Slowly he drew the zipper up again, then held her at arm's length and looked again at her face.

She seemed unaware he had touched her. Or that he even existed. She was entirely alone, still gazing into that secret world in which he had no place.

The rest of that night had seemed endless, Linda lying on the bed, he sitting beside her waiting for daylight. She seemed to sleep some of the time; at other times, though she said nothing even when spoken to, he sensed she was as wide awake as he. About four o'clock the wind died and the snow stopped its wet slapping of the windowpanes. No dawn had ever been more welcome, even though he was still unable to free the car and they both had to walk to the village to send a tow truck for it.

And now he had let her persuade him to come back here. He must be insane.

"Norman?"

She sat there on the bed, the same bed, but at least she was looking *at* him now, not through him into that secret world of hers. "Norman, you do like this house a little, don't you?"

"If you mean could I ever seriously think of living here—" Emphatically he shook his head. "My God, no! It gives me the horrors!"

"It's really a lovely old house, Norman. We could work on it little by little. Do you think I'm crazy?"

"If you can even imagine living in this mausoleum, I *know* you're crazy. My God, woman, you were nearly frightened out of your wits here. In this very room, too."

"Was I, Norman? Really?"

"Yes, you were! If I live to be a hundred, I'll never stop seeing that look on your face."

"What kind of look was it, Norman?"

"I don't know. That's just it—I don't know! What in heaven's name *were* you seeing when I walked back in here after my session with the car? What was that mist? That smell?"

Smiling, she reached for his hands. "I don't remember any mist or smell, Norman. I was just a little frightened. I told you—I thought I heard something."

"You *saw* something too, you said."

"Did I say that? I've forgotten." Still smiling, she looked around the room—at the garden of faded roses on shreds of time-stained wallpaper; at the shabby bureau with its solitary broken cut-glass vase. "Old Mr. Halper was to blame for what happened, Norman. His talk of demons."

"Halper didn't do that much talking, Linda."

"Well, he told us about the woman who was hanged in Salem. I can see now, of course, that he threw that out as bait, because I had told him you write mystery novels. He probably pictured you sitting in some sort of Dracula cape, scratching out your books with a quill, by lamplight, and thought this would be a marvelous setting for it." Her soft laugh was a welcome sound, reminding Norman he loved this girl and she loved him—that their life together, except for her inexplicable interest in this house, was full of gentleness and caring.

But he could not let her win this debate. "Linda, listen. If this is such a fine old house, why has it been empty for eight years?"

"Well, Mr. Halper explained that, Norman."

"Did he? I don't seem to recall any explanation."

"He said that last person to live here was a woman who died eight years ago at ninety-three. Her married name was Stanhope, I think he said, but she was a Creighton—she even had the same given name, Prudence, as the woman hanged in Salem for worshipping demons. And when she passed away there was some legal question about the property because her husband had died some years before in an asylum, leaving no will."

Norman reluctantly nodded. The truth was, he hadn't paid much attention to the real-estate man's talk, but he did recall the remark that the last man of the house had been committed to an asylum for the insane. Probably from having lived in such a gloomy old house for so long, he had thought at the time.

Annoyed with himself for having lost the debate—at least, for not having won it—he turned from the bed and walked to a window, where he stood gazing down at the yard. Right down there, four months ago, was where he had struggled to free the car. Frowning at the spot now, he suddenly said aloud, "Wait. That's damn queer."

"What is, dear?" Linda said from the bed.

"I've always thought we left the car in a low spot that night. A spot where the snow must have drifted extra deep, I mean. But we didn't. We were in the highest part of the yard."

"Perhaps the ground is soft there."

"Uh-uh. It's rocky."

"Then it might have been slippery?"

"Well, I suppose—" Suddenly he pressed closer to the window glass. "Oh, damn! We've got a flat."

"What, Norman?"

"A flat! Those are new tires, too. We must have picked up a nail on our way into this stupid place." Striding back to the bed, he caught her hand. "Come on. I'm not leaving you here this time!"

She did not protest. Obediently she followed him downstairs and along the lower hall to the front door. On the piazza she hesitated briefly, glancing back in what seemed to be a moment of panic, but when he again grasped her hand, she meekly went with him down the steps and out to the car.

The left front tire was the flat one. Hunkering down beside it, he searched for the culprit nail but failed to find any. It was underneath, no doubt. Things like flat tires always annoyed him; in a properly organized world they wouldn't happen. Of course, in such a world there would not be the kind of road one had to travel to reach this place, nor would there be such an impossible house to begin with.

Muttering to himself, he opened the trunk, extracted jack, tools, and spare, and went to work.

Strange. There was no nail in the offending tire. No cut or bruise, either. The tire must have been badly made. The thought did not improve his mood as, on his knees, he wrestled the spare into place.

Then when he lowered the jack, the spare gently flattened under the car's weight and he knelt there staring at it in disbelief. "What the hell . . ." Nothing like this had *ever* happened to him before.

He jacked the car up again, took the spare off and examined it. No nail, no break, no bruise. It was a new tire, like the others. Newer, because never yet used. He had a repair kit for tubeless tires in the trunk, he recalled—bought one day on an impulse. "Repair a puncture in minutes without even taking the tire off the car." But how could you repair a puncture that wasn't there?

"Linda, this is crazy. We'll have to walk back to town as we did before." He turned his head. "Linda?"

She was not there.

He lurched to his feet. "Linda! Where are you?" How long had she been gone? He must have been working on the car for fifteen or twenty minutes. She hadn't spoken in that time, he suddenly realized. Had she slipped back into the house the moment he became absorbed in his task? She knew well enough how intensely he concentrated on such things. How when he was writing, for instance, she could walk through the room without his even knowing it.

"Linda, for God's sake—no!" Hoarsely shouting her name, he stumbled toward the house. The door clattered open when he flung himself against it, and the sound filled his ears as he staggered down the hall. But now the hall was not just an ancient, dusty corridor; it was a dim tunnel filled with premature darkness and strange whisperings.

He knew where she must be. In that cursed room at the top of the stairs where he had seen the look on her face four months ago, and where she had tried so cunningly to conceal the truth from him this time. But the room was hard to reach now. A swirling mist choked the staircase, repeatedly causing him to stumble. Things resembling hands darted out of it to clutch at him and hold him back.

He stopped in confusion, and the hands nudged him forward again. Their owner was playing a game with him, he realized, mocking his frantic efforts to reach the bedroom yet at the same time seductively urging him to try even harder. And the whisperings made words, or seemed to. "Come Norman . . . sweet Norman . . . come come come. . . ."

In the upstairs hall, too, the swirling mist challenged him, deepening into a moving mass that hid the door of the room. But he needed no compass to find that door. Gasping and cursing—"Damn you, leave me alone! Get out of my way!" He struggled to it and found it open as Linda and he had left it. Hands outthrust, he groped his way over the threshold.

The alien presence here was stronger. The sense of being confronted by some unseen creature was all but overwhelming. Yet the assault upon him was less violent now that he had reached the room. The hands groping for him in the eerie darkness were even gentle, caressing. They clung with a velvet softness that was strangely pleasurable, and there was something voluptuously female about them, even to a faint but pervasive female odor.

An *odor*, not a perfume. A body scent, druglike in its effect upon his senses. Bewildered, he ceased his struggle for a moment to see what would happen. The whispering became an invitation, a promise of incredible delights. But he allowed himself only a moment of listening and then, shouting Linda's name, hurled himself at the bed again. This time he was able to reach it.

But she was not now sitting there staring into that secret world of hers, as he had expected. The bed was empty and the seductive voice in the darkness softly laughed at his dismay. "Come Norman . . . sweet Norman . . . come come come. . . ."

He felt himself taken from behind by the shoulders, turned and ever so gently pushed. He fell floating onto the old mattress, half-heartedly thrusting up his arms to keep the advancing shadow-form from possessing him. But it flowed down over him, onto him, into him, despite his feeble resistance, and the female smell tantalized his senses again, destroying his will to resist.

As he ceased struggling he heard a sound of rusty hinges creaking in that part of the room's dimness where the door was, and then a soft thud. The door had been closed. But he did not cry out. He felt no alarm. It was good to be here on the bed, luxuriating in this sensuous, caressing softness. As he became quiescent it flowed over him with unrestrained indulgence, touching and stroking him to heights of ecstacy.

Now the unseen hands, having opened his shirt, slowly and seductively glided down his body to his belt. . . .

He heard a new sound then. For a moment it bewildered him because, though coming through the ancient wall behind him, from the adjoining bedroom, it placed him at once in his own bedroom at home. Linda and he had joked about it often, as true lovers could—the explosive little syllables to which she always gave voice when making love.

So she was content, too. Good. Everything was straightforward and aboveboard, then. After all, as that fellow at the club had suggested, mate-swapping was an in thing in this year of our Lord 1975 . . . wasn't it? All kinds of people did it.

He must buy this house, as Linda had insisted. Of course. She was absolutely right. With a sigh of happiness he closed his eyes and relaxed, no longer made reluctant by a feeling of guilt.

·But—something was wrong. Distinctly, now, he felt not two hands caressing him, but more. And were they hands? They suddenly seemed cold, clammy, frighteningly eager.

Opening his eyes, he was startled to find that the misty darkness had dissolved and he could see. Perhaps the seeing came with total surrender, or with the final abandonment of his guilt feeling. He lay on his back, naked, with his nameless partner half beside him, half on him. He saw her scaly, misshapen breasts overflowing his chest and her monstrous, demonic face swaying in space above his own. And as he screamed, he saw that she did have more than two hands: she had a whole writhing mass of them at the ends of long, searching tentacles.

The last thing he saw before his scream became that of a madman was a row of three others like her squatting by the wall, their tentacles restlessly reaching toward him as they impatiently awaited their turn.

LAURA

SAKI

You are not really dying, are you?" asked Amanda.

"I have the doctor's permission to live till Tuesday," said Laura.

"But today is Saturday; this is serious!" gasped Amanda.

"I don't know about it being serious; it is certainly Saturday," said Laura.

"Death is always serious," said Amanda.

"I never said I was going to die. I am presumably going to leave off being Laura, but I shall go on being something. An animal of some kind, I suppose. You see, when one hasn't been very good in the life one has just lived, one reincarnates in some lower organism. And I haven't been very good, when one comes to think of it. I've been petty and mean and vindictive and all that sort of thing when circumstances have seemed to warrant it."

"Circumstances never warrant that sort of thing," said Amanda hastily.

"If you don't mind my saying so," observed Laura, "Egbert is a circumstance that would warrant any amount of that sort of thing. You're married to him—that's different; you've sworn to love, honor, and endure him: I haven't."

"I don't see what's wrong with Egbert," protested Amanda.

"Oh, I dare say the wrongness has been on my part," admitted Laura dispassionately; "he has merely been the extenuating circumstance. He made a thin, peevish kind of fuss, for instance, when I took the collie puppies from the farm out for a run the other day."

"They chased his young broods of speckled Sussex and drove two sitting hens off their nests, besides running all over the flower beds. You know how devoted he is to his poultry and garden."

"Anyhow, he needn't have gone on about it for the entire evening and then have said, 'Let's say no more about it' just when I was beginning to enjoy the discussion. That's where one of my petty vindictive revenges came in," added Laura with an unrepentant chuckle; "I turned the entire family of speckled Sussex into his seedling shed the day after the puppy episode."

"How could you?" exclaimed Amanda.

"It came quite easy," said Laura; "two of the hens pretended to be laying at the time, but I was firm."

"And we thought it was an accident!"

"You see," resumed Laura, "I really *have* some grounds for supposing that my next incarnation will be in a lower organism. I shall be an animal of some kind. On the other hand, I haven't been a bad sort in my way, so I think I may count on being a nice animal, some thing elegant and lively, with a love of fun. An otter, perhaps."

"I can't imagine you as an otter," said Amanda.

"Well, I don't suppose you can imagine me as an angel, if it comes to that," said Laura.

Amanda was silent. She couldn't.

"Personally I think an otter life would be rather enjoyable," continued Laura; "salmon to eat all the year around, and the satisfaction of being able to fetch the trout in their own homes without having to wait for hours till they condescend to rise to the fly you've been dangling before them; and an elegant svelte figure—"

"Think of the other hounds," interposed Amanda; "how dreadful to be hunted and harried and finally worried to death!"

"Rather fun with half the neighbourhood looking on, and anyhow not worse than this Saturday-to-Tuesday business of dying by inches; and then I should go on into something else. If I had been a moderately good otter I suppose I should get back into human shape of some sort; probably something rather primitive—a little brown, unclothed Nubian boy, I should think."

"I wish you would be serious," sighed Amanda; "you really ought to be if you're only going to live till Tuesday."

As a matter of fact Laura died on Monday.

"So dreadfully upsetting," Amanda complained to her uncle-in-law, Sir Lulworth Quayne. "I've asked quite a lot of people down for golf and fishing, and the rhododendrons are just looking their best."

"Laura always was inconsiderate," said Sir Lulworth; "she was born during Goodwood week, with an Ambassador staying in the house who hated babies."

"She had the maddest kind of ideas," said Amanda; "do you know if there was any insanity in her family?"

"Insanity? No, I never heard of any. Her father lives in West Kensington, but I believe he's sane on all other subjects."

"She had an idea that she was going to be reincarnated as an otter," said Amanda.

"One meets with those ideas of reincarnation so frequently, even in the West," said Sir Lulworth, "that one can hardly set them down as being mad. And Laura was such an unaccountable person in this life that I should not like to lay down definite rules as to what she might be doing in an after state."

"You think she really might have passed into some animal form?" asked Amanda. She was one of those who shape their opinions rather readily from the standpoint of those around them.

Just then Egbert entered the breakfast room, wearing an air of bereavement that Laura's demise would have been insufficient, in itself, to account for.

"Four of my speckled Sussex have been killed," he exclaimed; "the very four that were to go to the show on Friday. One of them was dragged away and eaten right in the middle of that new carnation bed that I've been to such trouble and expense over. My best flower bed and my best fowls singled out for destruction; it almost seems as if the brute that did the deed had special knowledge how to be as devastating as possible in a short space of time."

"Was it a fox, do you think?" asked Amanda.

"Sounds more like a polecat," said Sir Lulworth.

"No," said Egbert, "there were marks of webbed feet all over the place, and we followed the tracks down to the stream at the bottom of the garden; evidently an otter."

Amanda looked quickly and furtively across at Sir Lulworth.

Egbert was too agitated to eat any breakfast, and went out to superintend the strengthening of the poultry yard defenses.

"I think she might at least have waited till the funeral was over," said Amanda in a scandalized voice.

"It's her own funeral, you know," said Sir Lulworth; "it's a nice point in etiquette how far one ought to show respect to one's own mortal remains."

Disregard for mortuary convention was carried to further lengths next day; during the absence of the family at the funeral ceremony the remaining survivors of the speckled Sussex were massacred. The marauder's line of retreat seemed to have embraced most of the flower beds on the lawn, but the strawberry beds in the lower garden had also suffered.

"I shall get the otter hounds to come here at the earliest possible moment," said Egbert savagely.

"On no account! You can't dream of such a thing!" exclaimed Amanda. "I mean, it wouldn't do, so soon after a funeral in the house."

"It's a case of necessity," said Egbert; "once an otter takes to that sort of thing it won't stop."

"Perhaps it will go elsewhere now that there are no more fowls left," suggested Amanda.

"One would think you wanted to shield the beast," said Egbert.

"There's been so little water in the stream lately," objected Amanda; "it seems hardly sporting to hunt an animal when it has so little chance of taking refuge anywhere."

"Good gracious!" fumed Egbert, "I'm not thinking about sport. I want to have the animal killed as soon as possible."

Even Amanda's opposition weakened when, during church time on the following Sunday, the otter made its way into the house, raided half a salmon from the larder, and worried it into scaly fragments on the Persian rug in Egbert's studio.

"We shall have it hiding under our beds and biting pieces out of our feet before long," said Egbert, and from what Amanda knew of this particular otter she felt that the possibility was not a remote one.

On the evening preceding the day fixed for the hunt Amanda spent a solitary hour walking by the banks of the stream, making what she imagined to be hound noises. It was charitably supposed by those who overheard her performance, that she was practicing for farmyard imitations at the forthcoming village entertainment.

It was her friend and neighbor, Aurora Burret, who brought her news of the day's sport.

"Pity you weren't out; we had quite a good day. We found it at once, in the pool just below your garden."

"Did you—kill?" asked Amanda.

"Rather. A fine she-otter. Your husband got rather badly bitten in trying to 'tail it.' Poor beast, I felt quite sorry for it, it had such a human look in its eyes when it was killed. You'll call me silly, but do you know who the look reminded me of? My dear woman, what is the matter?"

When Amanda had recovered to a certain extent from her attack of nervous prostration Egbert took her to the Nile Valley to recuperate. Change of scene speedily brought about the desired recovery of health and mental balance. The escapades of an adventurous otter in search of a variation of diet were viewed in their proper light. Amanda's normally placid temperament reasserted itself. Even a hurricane of shouted curses, coming from her husband's dressing-room, in her husband's voice, but hardly in his usual vocabulary, failed to disturb her serenity as she made a leisurely toilet one evening in a Cairo hotel.

"What is the matter? What has happened?" she asked in amused curiosity.

"The little beast has thrown all my clean shirts into the bath! Wait till I catch you, you little—"

"What little beast?" asked Amanda, suppressing a desire to laugh; Egbert's language was so hopelessly inadequate to express his outraged feelings.

"A little beast of a naked brown Nubian boy," spluttered Egbert.

And now Amanda is seriously ill.

Left by the Tide

Edward E. Schiff

Were it not for that four-inch scar upon my forehead, I would have thought it a nightmare—some ghastly hallucination, even though it happened in broad daylight. But there is that scar, which mars my features for life, tangible and terrible evidence to prove that I did not dream it.

I had gone down to the beach with the rising sun, but I was the only one there. None of the other guests from the hotel had yet come down to take their early morning plunge. A charity affair that did not break up till 3 o'clock that morning kept them abed. So I was alone upon that sun-drenched stretch of sand.

The tide was low and I had to walk some hundred yards before I was waist-deep and breasting the invigorating waters of old ocean. I swam out at once to a pile of rocks, a good quarter of a mile from the shore, and climbed out upon them. Now, at low tide, they formed a nearly circular, barnacle- and weed-covered island, about fifty feet in diameter and rising only a few feet above the waters. After resting a few minutes I clambered over the jagged stones toward the center, where there was a depression about six or seven feet deep and about the same width, and where the retreating waters sometimes left strange denizens of the deep, which could be observed under ideal conditions.

Just before I reached the little pool, I thrilled to the sound of a splash of a heavy body. The tide had left something there with a vengeance, I thought gleefully, and I hastened forward to see what it was.

I stared, sickened by what I saw—a dead man, with shriveled, shrunken skin, hollow cheeks, and hideous in apparently the last stages of putrefaction. There he was floating on his back a bare few inches below the surface. His hands were under him, and at first I thought he was naked. Then, as I overcame my first horror, I noted that he had a sort of apron about his loins—an apron made of what appeared to be the scales of a large fish. It was a curious garment and covered with green algae or sea moss. The man must have been dead a long time to

279

have allowed for the formation of that slime. I puzzled over this, wondering how it was he remained whole and not half devoured by the scavengers of the sea. Then suddenly I remembered the splash I had heard. Who had made it? Not the dead man. Closely I searched the pool for some other sign of life, but except for a sea crab or two there was none.

Turning my attention to the body again, I scrutinized it closely and felt my scalp twitch when I thought I detected a barely perceptible rising and falling of the chest. The more I stared the more certain I was that I was not mistaken. But drowned men do not breathe, I told myself; I must be laboring under a hallucination. I turned my eyes away and gazed out over the sea and sky to rest them, and when I turned them back again I was shocked into an exclamation. The body had moved toward me. I could still see the faint traces of the eddy it had made to reach me. But dead men cannot move and there was no wave or tide or any breath of wind that could propel it within that enclosed space.

Now I was certain it was breathing. The slight but definitely regular expansion and contraction of the chest were caused by respiration. I could not be mistaken.

Then suddenly the lids flashed open and I was staring into its eyes. And they were the eyes of a living creature, sea-green and evil, that probed through mine into the very recesses of my brain with satanic curiosity. Then, still holding me with its baleful gaze, the thing reached for the brink with huge hands that were webbed like the feet of some aquatic bird, and started to pull itself up.

Somehow I broke the spell by which the thing held me, and, half mad with loathing and horror, I kicked him with my bare foot back into the pool.

I think I stumbled half back to the open water before I recovered my courage and paused to look back. It had come out of the pool and was dragging its slimy length over the rocks toward me. I realized at once it could not walk upright and that I would have no difficulty in evading it. With unmitigated loathing I watched it crawl until it approached to within a few feet of me. Then I backed away from it, taking care to avoid being crowded into the sea where it could easily outmaneuver me with its finlike appendages.

Again it tried to hold me with its hypnotic stare, but I avoided its eyes, and, stooping down, picked up a fragment of rock and tried to threaten it back. Suddenly it, too, reached out and picked up a stone, and we both threw at the same moment. But I was completely beside myself with horror and missed him by inches, while he caught me fairly on the chest—a blow that knocked the breath out of me and dropped me to my knees. The next moment he was upon me, his powerful hands closing about my throat, his cold, slimy body against my cringing, warm flesh, his fetid breath in my nostrils.

But I fought, fought in a stark, frenzied madness that promised to rid me of his clinging, hateful weight, when suddenly he released one of his hands from my throat, and I could feel him fumble around his waist. The next moment I would have been free of him, but his hand came up again wielding a stone or coral knife.

I screamed and tried to evade the blow, but while I spoiled his aim for my throat he managed to inflict that awful gash on my forehead.

When I came back to consciousness it was with a cry of terror, in the arms of two men who were lifting me into a skiff; and for some minutes I struggled with them, before I realized they were my rescuers.

Their story is briefly told. They had observed me from the beach apparently trying to avoid some creature which they thought was a seal. They quickly got into a skiff and rowed to the rocks, shouting to frighten off the creature when they saw me struggling with it. Then for a minute or two I was out of their sight, hidden by a projecting rock, and when they again saw me I was alone and lying flat on my back, though a moment before they had heard the thing splash into the sea.

That is their story. Mine they would not believe. In fact, they tried to stop me in the telling of it, and attempted to soothe me as if I were a terror-stricken child, or crazy. They said I had injured my forehead by falling on a jagged stone.

But that day two bathers were pulled down to their death by some creature of the sea. Sharks, they all said. But I know better.

The Lesser Brethren Mourn

SEABURY QUINN

This happened back in the days when the other Roosevelt was in the White House and everybody was whistling tunes from "King Dodo" and the "Burgomaster," but I don't often speak about it, for no one but my mother-in-law believes me, and she comes from County Mayo.

I was serving my apprenticeship with Ambrose McGonigle over at Centerville. Mac had a good practice for a country town, fifty or sixty cases a year, enough to make him a good living and pay me fair wages, but not enough to keep him from his semiweekly poker session back of McGhee's grocery, or to interfere too seriously with my courting Monica Duffy. Mac was playing poker the night Bert Emmons barged into the office.

It's always seemed to me there are three sorts of drinkers—those who drink for sociability, those who drink to drown their troubles, and those who do it out of sheer perversity and meanness. Bert fitted into the third category. He was mean and quarrelsome cold sober, and got meaner with each drink.

This evening he was three-drinks mean as he stopped in front of my desk and pushed his hat back till its rim rested on his neck. I'd seen him do that before starting a fight in the Biggs House bar, and slid my chair back from the desk so I could be up and out of reach if he made a pass at me.

We eyed each other for a moment, then he grinned. One of those mean grins that twist the corners of the mouth but leave the eyes cold and bleak.

"Where's Mac?" he wanted to know.

"He's out," I told him. "Anything I can do for you?"

"Not me," he answered, with a hiccup. "You can for Uncle Wash, though. He died this evenin'."

"I'm sorry," I replied, and I was. I used to pass the time of day with Washington Kearney on my way to and from Monica's, and a pleasant-spoken gentleman he was.

His hard grin widened. "You'll be sorrier when you hear this. I want him buried as cheap as you can do it. I'm his only livin' kin, so I got the say, an' I say plant him cheap as possible. I been waitin' long enough for him to croak."

"But his estate will pay the funeral expenses," I began.

That was as far as I got, for he banged a fist down on the desk and glared at me.

"His estate? Who the hell says it's his? It's all mine now, every red-headed penny, an' I'm goin' to give you buzzards just as little of it as I can. What's your cheapest coffin cost?"

I hadn't worked a year for Ambrose McGonigle for nothing.

"We haven't a coffin in stock," I answered, taking refuge in a technicality, for as I suppose you know a coffin is kite-shaped while a casket is oblong. "I can let you have a casket with everything complete for a nice funeral for a hundred dollars, though."

You'd have thought I'd tried to pick his pocket, but I held out, and finally he tossed a key down on the desk.

"There you are," he grunted. "Doc Abernathy'll sign the death certificate an' you can bury Uncle Wash in the family plot out on the farm. Don't let me see or hear of you till it's finished. I'll be at the Biggs House."

"Who's going to officiate?" I asked, as I picked up the key.

"If those old Grand Army cripples want to put a show on, let 'em. Don't bother me with it. You just run the funeral and bring me that key when you're done. . . ."

I was off at six next evening, and was just getting into my other suit when old Ambrose came back to the little room they'd set aside for me back of the office.

"You'll be droppin' in on Monica tonight, belike?" he asked.

"If Prince doesn't cast a shoe on the way out," I answered.

Prince was the little black horse, too light for hearse or brougham duty that we kept to pull the sidebar buggy we used on first calls. He was a good little fellow, gentle as a kitten and almost as playful, but he had a habit of shuffling his forefeet when he trotted, and it was seldom a week went by without his dropping a shoe.

"Arrah"—Mac grinned at me—"shoe or no shoe, ye'll be sparkin' Monica widin th' hour, or ye're not th' lad I take ye for. But would ye be after doin' me a favor on th' way out?"

"Of course," I promised, as I finished tightening the knot of my red four-in-hand. Morticians' assistants generally wore black string bows those days, and getting into a colored necktie was to me what slipping into civvies is to a soldier. "What is it, Mr. McGonigle?"

"Look in on old Wash Kearney. I'd take it kindly if ye'd stop by on yer way to Monica's just to see if everything's all right. It don't seem decent for 'im to be layin' there alone this way, wid his nearest kin down at th' Biggs House bar, a-drinkin' himself pie-eyed. Nobody's there a-mourning Wash."

"Certainly," I told him. I agreed with McGonigle.

The Kearney farm was on the way to Monica's, and she wouldn't be the girl to quarrel if business made me just a little late.

Fall had set in early, and the shadows had already started forming round the trees and bushes by the roadside as I set off for Monica Duffy's. The farmers had been breaking ground for winter wheat and the fields smelled pleasantly of fresh-turned earth. Somehow the quiet restfulness of the evening made me think of old Wash Kearney.

He was a character, old Washington. Except on Decoration Day when he came in to march with the G.A.R., and every other Thursday when he drove in to McGhee's for his two-weeks' supply of groceries, we never saw him in town by daylight, and the only times he came in after dark were when the Zebulon B. Lipschutz Post was meeting in the Odd Fellows Temple. The rest of his time was spent puttering around the little garden patch that was all he tried to cultivate of the hundred and twenty acres his father left him.

There was considerable mystery about old Wash. Except for the farm, which was pretty well worked out when it came to him, his father left him nothing, yet he was the richest man in the county and could have been a lot richer if it hadn't been for his habit of never foreclosing a mortgage. Nearly everyone for miles around had owed him money at one time or other, and though most of them had paid, he had enough outstanding notes to make a sizeable fortune.

Where his money came from set the gossips nearly wild. According to one story—and from some things he'd let drop in our casual conversations I believed it—he'd been one of that host of reckless youngsters who just couldn't settle down when they were mustered out in '65. Some of them went West to build the railroads, some went to Mexico to help Juarez drive Maximilian from the throne, some went filibustering in Cuba and South America, a few just knocked around anywhere there was excitement and money to be had.

Washington Kearney was one of these. Egyptology was just then on the threshold of its present importance, and desperate characters were organizing expeditions to loot the old tombs systematically. Besides the gold and jewels, they found they had a ready market for the mummies, which were worth anywhere from ten to fifty pounds, according to condition and importance, in London, Paris, or Berlin.

Native Egyptians didn't take too kindly to the foreign grave-robbers, but the men who had fought with Grant and Farragut and Sherman made small account of Arabs armed with smooth-bore muzzle-loaders. The expeditions marched and countermarched across the sands at will, taking what they found and shooting down all opposition.

By the time the newly organized *gendarmerie du désert* became effective, the tomb looters were ready to retire on their profits. When Washington Kearney came back to Centerville he had two buckskin bags of British sovereigns to deposit in the First National.

Those were the days of greenbacks and "shin-plasters." There was hardly any silver in circulation, and Washington's English gold brought a huge premium. When specie payment was resumed in '79 and his paper money redeemed he was worth almost a hundred thousand dollars. Which was about fifty thousand more than anybody else in the county could count.

You'd never have suspected he was a wealthy man. He wore blue denim in summer and the same old suit of frayed cheviot year after year in winter. One hobby was his flowers, but a bigger one was giving shelter to stray animals. Once he had twenty cats, five dogs, a spavined, spring-halted old mare he'd bought when its owner was about to shoot it, and a blind mule, all boarding with him at the same time.

I'd seen him take a cat that had lost eight of its nine lives and nurse it back to health as if it had been a sick child. He wouldn't have a rat trap on his place. The chipmunks nested in the gables of his house, squirrels came and went at will through a broken window in his attic.

"Someone has to help the lesser brethren in distress," he told me once, when I joked about the size of his menagerie.

"The lesser brethren?" I repeated. I was pretty literal those days, the way most youngsters are.

"That's right. I picked that up from a *mollah* in Egypt. The old boy tried to make a Moslem out of me. Most of what he said went in one ear and out the other, but a little lodged between 'em, especially a verse from the sixth book of the Koran, the one they call 'the Flocks.' "

He rattled off something that sounded like Spanish to me, then translated:

" 'There is no kind of beast on earth, no fowl that flieth with its wings, but the same is a people like unto you; then unto their Lord shall they return.' Pretty good philosophy, eh, son?"

"Sure," I agreed, not knowing any more what he was driving at than if he hadn't bothered to translate.

But I kept thinking about it, and the more I thought the clearer it seemed. Here was an old man, rich and lonely and with nothing but his memories for company, putting in his time being good to dumb beasts, just as some folks feel a call to work with people in prison or almshouses or insane asylums. There used to be a picture of Saint Francis of Assisi preaching to the birds on the wall of the third-grade room at Saint Dominic's School. Maybe the blessed Francis and Wash Kearney had the same idea.

Anyway, the old man lived the last years of his long life peacefully. Now he'd slipped away in the calm of early fall, when they gather in the harvest. It seemed appropriate. All but that hellion nephew of his, drinking himself blind at the Biggs House and waiting for the estate to be settled.

I was mulling all this over when something by the roadside caught my eye. At first I thought it was a rabbit, but when I looked again I saw it was a cat. It was walking along leisurely as if it had no place to go and no special time to get there when all of a sudden it seemed to think of something and started running, head down and tail trailed out behind it like a plume.

Half a mile, perhaps three-quarters down the road, I passed five more. First, an old tom, marching like a regimental sergeant-major on parade, and right behind him a little jennie stepping daintily as if walking on thin ice, with three half-grown kittens stringing out behind her.

"Somebody must have called a cat convention," I muttered, and fell to laughing over the fool notion the way a person sometimes will at something utterly silly.

Then I stopped laughing, for from somewhere in a copse of pine trees by the road I heard a cat's *meaul*—you know the sound, a sort of low, deep, growling moan that rises to a shrieking wail and swells into a tortured howl, then sinks into a moan again—and from off across the hills an answer came, the long-drawn, quavering howling of a dog.

It was warm that evening, so warm I'd left my topcoat home, but as I heard those cries I felt as if a breath of January wind had blown on me. Everything inside me seemed to knot together. I've read since that we're instinctively affected by a cat's cry or a dog's howl in the night, because our prehistoric ancestors' worst enemies were wolves and leopards.

I wouldn't know about that, but I remember there was a chilling feeling right between my shoulder blades and my scalp began to itch as if a thousand small red ants were crawling over it. Prince seemed afraid, too, for he hooked his tail across the lines and threw his head up with a snort and started down the road as if I'd laid the whip to him.

A light breeze sighed among the bare-boughed 'lanthus trees that shaded Kearney's front yard and played with the black crêpe as a kitten might play with a string. It knocked it against the door as if it rapped for admission, fluttered it like a pennant, let it drop till it dangled straight again, then caught it up once more to shake it as a woman shakes a dust rag.

I let the check-rein down and hitched Prince to the picket fence, pushed the front gate open with my foot, and felt in one pocket for the key and in another for my matches. We didn't have flashlights those days.

Perhaps I'd gone five yards, maybe a little more, when I heard Prince give a frightened nicker. I swung round and saw him straining at the hitching-strap until nails that held the picket to the string-piece of the fence began to give with a sharp, rasping squeal. That wouldn't do. I went back, patted him and stroked his neck until he quieted, then hitched him to a tree, snubbing the line around the trunk so that he'd have some play if he took fright again, but couldn't possibly pull loose.

I was halfway back to the house when I heard it. At first I thought it was the breeze among the crisp, curled brown leaves that lay all over the lawn, but in a moment I knew better. It was the scampering patter of small feet, feet that moved when I moved, drawing closer every step I took, and stopped when I stopped—waiting.

We didn't know the phrase then, but only it can describe how I felt. My goat was gone. I was running in a panic by the time I reached the porch and began fumbling with the key. Somehow, I couldn't seem to make it fit, but at last the bolt clicked back. I jumped across the threshold and slammed the door behind me, bracing my heel against it as I slipped the key into the lock. Whatever waited outside was going to have to break that door in before it came to me.

Everything seemed normal in the house. Old Washington lay in his casket, his head as comfortably pillowed on the silk cushion as it had ever been in bed. His thin gray hair was parted as he always wore it, and the buttons on his Grand Army blouse made small pools of brightness in the candlelight.

I wanted to stay with him. He represented something I understood, my usual daily work. Outside was something terrifying, vague and formless as a child's fear of the dark, and all the more frightening because I couldn't name it. Maybe I'd better take another look at him, I told myself, but before I could put the candle down I heard a noise at the back door.

It wasn't quite a knock nor yet a scratching, but a sort of combination of the two, as if something clawed the panels with a kind of dreadful eagerness. My breath stopped absolutely still for a full second, then I got a grip upon myself.

Bert Emmons! He'd been fuller than a fiddler's tyke all afternoon, boasting how he would splurge with old Washington's money. Maybe he'd drunk his credit up at the Biggs House and come out here to search the place for money.

He would get nothing but a bloody nose if I caught him, I promised myself, as I hurried toward the rear of the house. There was rag carpet on the kitchen floor. My feet made no sound as I crossed it and ripped the back door open.

The moon was shining through the bare trees, making alternate lines of shadow and brightness on the roofless porch. And that was all. If there'd been anything bigger than a mouse on the stoop I couldn't have missed seeing it.

Then I jumped as if a wasp had stung me. This time there was no mistake. A window had been smashed in the front of the house. I heard the shatter of the glass followed by the tinkle of the fragments on the bare floor. Instinctively I reached out for a weapon, and the first thing that my hand touched was a potato masher, one of those old-fashioned things with a turned handle ending in a heavy knob. It must have weighed three pounds and made a first class shillalah.

I swung it back and forth a time or two, getting the heft of it in my hand, then started up the hall. Curiously, I was more angry than frightened. Whatever had smashed that window, man or devil, ghost or burglar, was going to know it had been in a battle before I finished with it. Old Wash Kearney might be helpless to defend his house, but I wasn't, not by a . . .

My mind was wiped as clear of thought as a child's slate is sponged clean with an eraser as I reached the parlor door.

A big splash of moonlight, white as spilled milk, lay in the center of the room, but the corners were as black as soot. The light shone full on Washington, and his face looked peaked and ghostly in it, colorless and gaunt, with shadows in his eye sockets and the angles where his nose and cheeks joined, even in the wrinkles that traced little networks on his smooth-shaved upper lip.

Beyond the casket was the sheen of broken glass where the lower light of the French window had been smashed. That didn't make sense. The break was too low for a man to come through unless he went on his hands and knees. Anyway, a burglar should have smashed the glass beside the latch, so he could reach his hand in.

I realized what it was, then. Something was moving in the shadow, and the movement seemed to spread and widen like a ripple spreading from a stone dropped in a quiet pool.

Then, just where the light and darkness joined, a rat came creeping out, an old, gray, whiskered corncrib-robber, and right beside him, and paying him no more attention than if he weren't there, a cat stepped daintily as if the floor were paved with eggs. Just beyond the cat a squirrel came into sight, moving as squirrels do in a series of short runs, stopping a moment to twitch its nose and flirt its tail, then running forward again with a nervous jerk.

Everywhere I looked I saw the movement of small bodies and the shine of little eyes. They were almost so close-packed you couldn't lay a hand between them—cats, mice, squirrels, rats, chipmunks, and more cats. I heard a scratching at the window, and a mongrel hound with one ear and no more than half a tail crouched down, crept through the broken window and joined the company that formed about the casket.

A big old tomcat left the front rank, stopped a moment by the pedestal that held the casket's lower end, then jumped up to the table where we'd put the old man's G.A.R. hat, ready to go on his casket with the flag next morning. He was a monster, that cat. A big gray tiger with a ruff of white fur at his throat and eyes that were all bright black pupils.

I drew my club back, ready to let fly. The memory of one of Ambrose Bierce's stories flashed across my mind—the one about the pet cat that jumped into its master's casket. If the beast made one more move toward old Wash I was going to smash him to a pulp.

But he didn't. For what seemed like five minutes he just stood there, looking down into the old man's face. Then, dignified as a retired brigadier, he turned and jumped down from the table, stalked across the room, and went out through the broken window.

And every creature in the room followed suit. Mice, squirrels, rats, chipmunks—even the mother cat who made three extra trips to lift her kittens in her mouth so they could look down in the casket—mounted that table, took a long farewell of old Washington, and went out through the hole smashed in the window. None of them made a sound. They were as quiet, dignified, and ritualistic about it as a delegation of lodge members passing round the casket of a deceased brother.

It must have taken an hour, but finally the last one left and I stepped into the death chamber, found a sheet of newspaper, and stuffed the broken window with it. I wasn't afraid any more. I knew that there was nothing outside in the darkness now. And Monica was waiting for me.

The Marmot

ALLISON V. HARDING

I have never admired my brother. Edward Allis was a vain, selfish blusterer. He had no use for hard work, for ethics, and not much use for me. After a small family inheritance was divided between us, I didn't see much of him. I invested my share in a small business while Edward preferred to jog off for some exotic alien soil. Good riddance!

Still he was my brother, and when I got that agonized telegram, "Jim come quick. Need you. Desperate," I reacted the way any man would, I guess.

I hadn't seen Edward for quite some time, and the tone of the wire from my usually confident, self-sufficient kin puzzled and upset me. The address was in a city not more than a few hours distant and I was able to get there by the evening of that same day.

I remember the shock of surprise that hit me when I saw Edward. True, it had been two and a half years since I'd laid eyes on him, but a normal man shouldn't change as much as Edward had. He greeted me almost hysterically.

"My God, I'm glad you're here, Jim." His palm was moist with sweat as we shook hands.

"Well, Edward, what's this all about? You look done in!"

I noted that his rooms were comfortable, in an apartment of good taste. Without speaking, he motioned me absently to a chair. I sat down and looked up at my brother pacing in front of me. His small pig eyes that I had disliked in the old days, their furtiveness always a signal of

290

some devilment, were dilated with fear now. I kept quiet, waiting for him to break the silence. His quick, nervous little movements stopped all of a sudden and he stood in front of me.

"Jim, the doctors tell me I'm, well, mad. They tell me I'm insane. They want me to go away somewhere to be treated."

I controlled my surprise and he made no comment. Edward went on. "But it's outrageous!"

"It's not as simple as all that. I wish I could make you believe me."

"Start at the beginning," I suggested. "You and your affairs are strange to me after all this time."

Edward forced himself into a chair at my side. He had lost weight, I noted, and his once round, pouting face had thinned unbelievably.

"Look, Jim. I want you to go to see Dr. Jeffries. He's the man who's taking care of me. Oh, I've been to a lot of others, but he's supposed to be tops. You and I haven't always gotten along but you know I'm not crazy. You know that's absurd!"

"I don't understand. . . ." I started.

Edward hurried on, "You see I do have kind of an affliction, but it's a physical thing. It isn't mental. I know it isn't. I *know* it isn't!"

I cleared my throat. "What this boils down to, Ed, is that you want me to go to Dr. Jeffries and vouch for your sanity. Isn't that a little silly? I mean, what weight would my opinions have? I haven't laid eyes on you for, well, what's it been? Thirty months?"

Edward got up and came over to me. He gripped my arm in a nervous spasm. "Jim, at least go with me. Go with me to Dr. Jeffries tomorrow morning. We've never asked much of each other. This you've got to do for me."

I nodded wearily. "All right, Ed. Can you put me up here for the night?"

He smiled and patted me. "Sure, sure. I'm so glad you're staying."

I bedded down in the spare room next, to Edward's room. I had brought some order blanks along and decided to study them after I got into bed. My business was still young, and I had a consuming interest in it.

I guess my concentration on these personal matters was so great that the noises from the next room grew into full-throated cries before I heard them. Without waiting to slipper my feet, I padded across the cold floor to the door leading into the adjoining room. It was unlocked and I burst into my brother's room. He was on top of his bed doubled over in agony. A strange, horrible whistling cry came from him. I reached him in a split second.

"For God's sake, Ed, what's wrong?"

I thought fleetingly of an acute appendicitis attack but then I saw he was gripping the upper part of his right leg. As I laid my hands on him, the paroxysms of pain seemed to pass. He shuddered beneath my grip and straightened from his jackknife posture, though still clutching his thigh. I stood helplessly alongside.

"You see! This is what they've been telling me is mental," he said in a voice weakened by his ordeal. "Mental! Get that, Jim? They tell me I'm imagining this thing."

"What thing?"

"This pain. This hideous something in my leg."

"In heaven's name, man, tell me what you mean."

Edward turned a look of horror and hopelessness toward me. He prodded his thigh.

"There's something in there, Jim. Something alive. Something that means to kill me!"

We saw Dr. Jeffries at 10 o'clock the next morning. The psychiatrist, for that is what he turned out to be, was an elderly man whose forceful personality could be felt the minute one stepped into his consultation room.

Edward immediately launched into a minute description concerning his attack of the previous night. He turned to me for corroboration. I nodded slowly. "Yes, I saw it, Doctor. Obviously my brother was in great pain."

Dr. Jeffries smiled kindly. "Of course, of course. He *is* in great pain, Mr. Allis, but the cause of that pain," he tapped his forehead significantly, "is *here.*"

Edward's reaction to this announcement was immediate.

"It's impossible, impossible I tell you. I know what I feel. It *is* there! There's something there in my leg. I'll go elsewhere. I'll try another doctor."

Dr. Jeffries shook his head. "Do as you wish."

He looked directly at Edward. "Now I wonder if you'd mind if I had a few words with your brother."

Edward went ungracefully out of the room. After the door was shut again the physician turned to me.

"It's good that you're here to take care of him, Mr. Allis. Your brother is a very sick man."

"Won't you tell me the situation, Doctor? I know so little. I saw him last night for the first time in two and a half years. He's been away. Out of the country for a great deal of that time, I believe. I knew he traveled, but we never kept in touch."

"Then I probably know more about him, Mr. Allis, than you do. It's an interesting case. He doesn't make things easy for us. He should be under constant treatment."

I leaned forward. "I don't question your judgment on the case, Dr. Jeffries. However, as I said before, I saw this attack last night. I will swear that my brother was suffering hellish torture. Actual physical pain. He clutched his leg in agony and told me that there was something —that's what he said—something there that would destroy him."

"Precisely. That has been his story all along, Mr. Allis. Originally he went to general practitioners and made a fool of himself demanding X-rays and undergoing other clinical procedures. You know, the mind does many strange things. It can deceive us into believing that one part or another of our anatomy is the site of excruciating pain."

"You mean then that he really is insane?"

Dr. Jeffries tut-tutted. "Insane? What does that word mean? That is a loose, ineffectual term at best. Perhaps all of us are a bit what the layman calls 'insane.' Let's say simply that your brother is in desperate need of care. He is distinctly a mental case."

"Well, what do we do, Doctor?"

Jeffries fiddled with the blotter on his desk. "Simple. He must be sent away somewhere where he can be under supervision. I recommend that you get Edward's consent so that we can send him to Harwood Home. He'll get excellent care there. If there is any hope of bringing him out of this condition, it lies in following such a course."

I considered a few moments. "What you say seems to make good sense. Of course, I feel in fairness to my brother that I should get another opinion."

Jeffries smiled. "By all means, Mr. Allis. Edward has been to several other psychiatrists here in town. I am sure you will find they concur in my diagnosis. I have discussed his problem with them."

"Well, I guess that's good enough," I said after a moment's thought. "Tell me something else. Edward's phraseology was so strange last night. I was tired and the shock of being startled by his cries was terrific, but I found myself morbidly fascinated by his insistence that there was something in his leg. Doctor, he used the term 'something alive.'"

"Oh, that's very simple, Mr. Allis. As a matter of fact, I found the key to that when I psychoanalyzed your brother some time ago. Under a sedative, hypnosis revealed a rather grisly little episode that took place during his travels abroad. I say 'grisly' advisedly, for frankly it is not complimentary to Edward's character. He's never even hinted at this story except, as I say, when under hypnotic influence."

"Go on," I urged eagerly.

"Well," started Dr. Jeffries. "You know that your brother liked to move around a lot. He was an adventurous, greedy man, fond of collecting valuable curios and women's hearts, if he could. This is nothing new to you?"

I shook my head. "Edward has done many things I have disapproved of, Doctor. I know his shortcomings."

"You knew he went to Serbia?"

"Well, I knew vaguely he was going to that part of Europe."

"Well, in Serbia, Edward, pursuing his usual selfish objectives, had a most unfortunate experience with a Eurasian household of some standing and power in the community. Moreover, the episode must have made an abnormally powerful impression on his mind, for the details he revealed to me were minute.

"It seems that he became enamoured with the woman of a Eurasian. He courted her and apparently quite won her. One time, though, despite her cautions, he followed her home."

Dr. Jeffries shuffled some papers on his desk. "I took a very complete record of this impression. I have it here with Edward's case history."

He looked down. "Yes. Aside from beauty, this woman represented wealth. Edward, a little the worse for wear I believe, trailed her home one evening and broke into the Eurasian's house. Once inside, he stated to the ancient Eurasian master of the house that the woman must be his. Further, he began to help himself to any objects around the house that struck his fancy. The aged man, although a cripple, defied him and Edward struck him brutally. At this, the Eurasian began to pronounce certain unintelligible syllables that infuriated Edward even more.

"But Edward refused to retreat and instead laughed and poked fun at the old Eurasian calling him crazy and finally striking him again. At this point Edward became aware of a small animal. From his description I would say a tiny marmot. This creature was crouched at the ancient Eurasian's side. The Eurasian called to Edward that he would never have his woman or his valuables and that he, Edward, would be the one to go crazy. And of all he had, he was giving only his marmot to stay with Edward until he should lose his reason.

"At this, according to Edward's story, the marmot sprang at him and bit him severely in the thigh and then magically disappeared before Edward could kill the little creature. The pain of this knifed through Edward's drunkenness and he lurched out of the house with the Eurasian cackling in glee behind.

"He never returned to this place again. Apparently the whole episode filled him with a morbid superstitious dread so that he immediately left the country."

Jeffries raised his eyes from the case-history papers.

"Sounds like a good fiction story," I offered.

"A man of your brother's caliber could easily get into a scrape like that. He has fastened on that experience. He has a sense of guilt and superstitious fear about it."

"Well," I pushed, "what about this thing in his leg?"

"Don't you see?" said Dr. Jeffries. "He thinks the marmot's in his leg!"

I gasped. "It's strange," I mused after a minute. "The Eurasian's curse or whatever you want to call it seems to have come true. Edward *has* gone crazy."

Jeffries pursed his lips. "All that's nonsense. Your brother, because of the sort of life he's lived, and probably because of certain inherent qualities, is susceptible to the sort of nagging ill-suggestion that this constituted. You know, it's often been said and proved that the power of the voodoo curse lies in the morbid beliefs of the victims."

I saw his point. Jeffries went on.

"That's why he keeps insisting on physical examinations and X-rays. He even has suggested to me that we do an exploratory operation on his leg. Although he hasn't admitted it consciously, he's looking for the marmot."

"All right, Doctor. I guess I must agree with you. We've got to put him somewhere he'll be cared for, wherever you think."

Three of the hardest days of my life I spent trying to convince Edward of the necessity of going to Harwood Home. Finally, I succeeded, but only because Dr. Jeffries and I conceived the brilliant idea of suggesting that it might very well be advisable to open up the leg for an investigation, and this of course would require hospitalization.

Edward signed the necessary papers then without much difficulty. I saw him to the Home and satisfied myself that he would receive every care. Dr. Jeffries was still in charge and was to visit him several times a week. I intended to come over once in a while from my home.

It was three weeks later that I received Dr. Jeffries's summons. It was cryptic, bidding me come to Harwood Home as soon as possible.

When I arrived, Jeffries sent for me and explained at once the reason for his wire.

"It's not for a moment that I doubt our original diagnosis, Mr. Allis, but I thought you ought to know. Your brother is a very sick man physically now as well as mentally. These paroxysms of pain occur more often. He hardly ever eats. We keep him under sedatives as much as is possible. I thought I ought to explain to you before you see him. His appearance may be something of a shock to you."

I was glad he warned me, for I was braced lest I reveal to my brother any inkling of my surprise at his appearance. For he had wasted away to almost nothingness. His face had a pointed, hunted look, his nose seemed to have lengthened and sharpened, his ears and lips had a pinched bluish tinge. His eyes were bright with fever or eagerness to see me, I did not know which.

"Well, old man," I said with an attempt at heartiness. "Dr. Jeffries tells me you're not being such a good patient."

"Jim," he said. "It's been hell. Every day it's been worse." He frowned at the nurse fixing his water decanter until she left the room. "Look. Look at this," and with a convulsive movement he pulled the blankets and sheet from his legs. I looked at his right thigh beneath the rolled-up pajama leg. This time with all my control, I could not contain myself from starting. For his leg was swollen. It was purplish in color and swollen at the top.

"Don't you see?" he cried. "They're neglecting me. There's something horrible, I tell you. It's crawling right up my leg and they won't do anything about it. It's eating me from within!"

His voice rose in hysteria and a nurse bustled in from outside. I patted his shoulder and went out into the hall. Indignantly I demanded to see Dr. Jeffries and finally cornered him on a downstairs floor.

"What's the meaning of his leg?" I demanded. "Doctor, it's swollen. It looks wrong to me."

Jeffries frowned. "So you saw it. We're all aware of that, Mr. Allis. You know the mind does strange . . ."

"Mind be damned!" I said. "That's not imagination. He has a swelling there and that leg looks like there's poison in it."

"Hear me out, Mr. Allis. I must stick to my original diagnosis. Do you know, sir, that your brother spends almost the entire day prodding and kneading and poking that leg? He's obsessed with the idea that his leg is being eaten away. We have even allowed him the concession of another series of X-ray pictures here at the Home. They show no pathology, yet he insists there's something in his thigh. It's the marmot he's looking for, of course."

I was silent. Jeffries spoke again:

"Can you arrange to stay for a few days? It might be beneficial for Edward."

I agreed.

But it wasn't to be for a few days, for that night my brother died. I was at his bedside, as was Dr. Jeffries, when he passed away. So frenzied had been his convulsions, so fanatic his obsession, that with his own hands he had torn cruelly at his already swollen leg, drawing blood. In his weakened, near-starved state, the anguish and agony of those last few moments were too much for him. I remember my disgust as I sat at his bedside. The loosely hanging bed clothes were wet with blood from his final throes. My brother had been a stark madman the last few minutes of his life. I got up finally with Dr. Jeffries to leave the room.

We were alone then for a minute, and we walked toward the door, his hand on my shoulder.

"Maybe it's better this way, Mr. Allis."

I opened my mouth to speak when my eye caught a slight movement in the dark far corner of the room. I moved closer, Jeffries still at my side. I looked, and a feeling of chill liquid horror stole through me until my scalp crawled with an unearthly dampness. For there, crouched in the corner, was a tiny yet stout-bodied, short-legged little creature, its coarse fur matted with blood from small ears to short bushy tail. It just sat there silently observing us.

I gasped then and reeled into the hall. I felt rather than saw Jeffries still beside me. Outside I turned and looked at him. His face was green gray with pallor. But neither of us spoke. Thinking it over afterward, that fact doesn't seem strange, for God knows I value my sanity above everything else in the world!

METZENGERSTEIN

EDGAR ALLAN POE

Pestis eram vivus—moriens tua mors ero.

—*Martin Luther*

Horror and fatality have been stalking abroad in all ages. Why then give a date to the story I have to tell? Let it suffice to say that at the period of which I speak, there existed, in the interior of Hungary, a settled although hidden belief in the doctrines of the Metempsychosis. Of the doctrines themselves—that is, of their falsity, or of their probability—I say nothing. I assert, however, that much of our incredulity—(as La Bruyère says of all our unhappiness) *"vient de ne pouvoir être seuls."*[1]

But there were some points in the Hungarian superstition that were fast verging to absurdity. They—the Hungarians—differed very essentially from their Eastern authorities. For example, *"The soul,"* said the former—I give the words of an acute and intelligent Parisian—*"ne demeure qu'une seule fois dans un corps sensible: au reste—un cheval, un chien, un homme même, n'est que la ressemblance peu tangible de ces animaux."*

The families at Berlifitzing and Metzengerstein had been at variance for centuries. Never before were two houses, so illustrious, mutually embittered by hostility so deadly. The origin of this enmity seems to be found in the words of an ancient prophecy—"A lofty name shall have a fearful fall when as the rider over his horse, the mortality of Metzengerstein shall triumph over the immortality of Berlifitzing."

To be sure, the words themselves had little or no meaning. But more trivial causes have given rise—and that no long while ago—to consequences equally eventful. Besides, the estates, which were contiguous, had long exercised a rival influence in the affairs of a busy government. Moreover, near neighbors are seldom friends; and the inhabitants of the Castle Berlifitzing might look from their lofty buttresses into the very windows of the Palace Metzengerstein. Least of all had the more than

---

[1] Mercier, in *"L'An deux mille quatre cents quarante,"* seriously maintains the doctrines of the Metempsychosis, and J. D'Israeli says that "no system is so simple and so little repugnant to the understanding." Colonel Ethan Allen, the "Green Mountain Boy," is also said to have been a serious metempsychosist.

feudal magnificence, thus discovered, a tendency to allay the irritable feelings of the less ancient and less wealthy Berlifitzing. What wonder, then, that the words, however silly, of that prediction, should have succeeded in setting and keeping at variance two families already predisposed to quarrel by every instigation of hereditary jealousy? The prophecy seemed to imply—if it implied anything—a final triumph on the part of the already more powerful house; and was of course remembered with the more bitter animosity by the weaker and less influential.

Wilhelm, Count Berlifitzing, although loftily descended, was, at the epoch of this narrative, an infirm and doting old man, remarkable for nothing but an inordinate and inveterate personal antipathy to the family of his rival, and so passionate a love of horses, and of hunting, that neither bodily infirmity, great age, nor mental incapacity prevented his daily participation in the dangers of the chase.

Frederick, Baron Metzengerstein, was, on the other hand, not yet of age. His father, the Minister G——, died young. His mother, the Lady Mary, followed him quickly. Frederick was, at that time, in his eighteenth year. In a city, eighteen years are no long period; but in a wilderness—in so magnificent a wilderness as that old principality, the pendulum vibrates with a deeper meaning.

From some peculiar circumstances attending the administration of his father, the young baron, at the decease of the former, entered immediately upon his vast possessions. Such estates were seldom held before by a nobleman of Hungary. His castles were without number. The chief in point of splendor and extent was the "Palace Metzengerstein." The boundary line of his dominions was never clearly defined; but his principal park embraced a circuit of fifty miles.

Upon the succession of a proprietor so young, with a character so well known, to a fortune so unparalleled, little speculation was afloat in regard to his probable course of conduct. And, indeed, for the space of three days, the behavior of the heir out-Heroded Herod, and fairly surpassed the expectations of his most enthusiastic admirers. Shameful debaucheries, flagrant treacheries, unheard-of atrocities gave his trembling vassals quickly to understand that no servile submission on their part—no punctilios of conscience on his own—were thenceforward to prove any security against the remorseless fangs of a petty Caligula. On the night of the fourth day, the stables of the Castle Berlifitzing were discovered to be on fire; and the unanimous opinion of the neighborhood added the crime of the incendiary to the already hideous list of the Baron's misdemeanours and enormities.

But during the tumult occasioned by this occurrence, the young nobleman himself sat apparently buried in meditation, in a vast and desolate upper apartment of the family palace of Metzengerstein. The rich although faded tapestry hangings that swung gloomily upon the walls represented the shadowy and majestic forms of a thousand illustrious ancestors. *Here*, rich-ermined priests and pontifical dignitaries, familiarly seated with the autocrat and the sovereign, put a veto on the wishes of a temporal king, or restrained with the fiat of papal supremacy the rebellious sceptre of the Archenemy. *There*, the dark, tall statures of the Princes of Metzengerstein—their muscular war-coursers plunging over the carcasses of fallen foes—startled the steadiest nerves with their vigorous expression; and *here*, again, the voluptuous and swanlike figures of the dames of days gone by floated away in the mazes of an unreal dance to the strains of imaginary melody.

But as the Baron listened, or affected to listen, to the gradually increasing uproar in the stables of Berlifitzing—or perhaps pondered upon some more novel, some more decided act of audacity—his eyes were turned unwittingly to the figure of an enormous and unnaturally colored horse, represented in the tapestry as belonging to a Saracen ancestor of the family of his rival. The horse itself, in the foreground of the design, stood motionless and statuelike—while, farther back, its discomfited rider perished by the dagger of a Metzengerstein.

On Frederick's lip arose a fiendish expression, as he became aware of the direction which his glance had, without his consciousness, assumed. Yet he did not remove it. On the contrary, he could by no means account for the overwhelming anxiety that appeared falling like a pall upon his senses. It was with difficulty that he reconciled his dreamy and incoherent feelings with the certainty of being awake. The longer he gazed the more absorbing became the spell—the more impossible did it appear that he could ever withdraw his glance from the fascination of that tapestry. But the tumult without becoming suddenly more violent, with a compulsory exertion he diverted his attention to the glare of ruddy light thrown full by the flaming stables upon the windows of the apartment.

The action, however, was but momentary; his gaze returned mechanically to the wall. To his extreme horror and astonishment, the head of the gigantic steed, had, in the meantime, altered its position. The neck of the animal, before arched, as if in compassion, over the prostrate body of its lord, was now extended at full length, in the direction of the Baron. The eyes, before invisible, now wore an energetic and human expression, while they gleamed with a fiery and unusual red; and the distended lips of the apparently enraged horse left in full view his sepulchral and disgusting teeth.

Stupefied with terror, the young nobleman tottered to the door. As he threw it open, a flash of red light, streaming far into the chamber, flung his shadow with a clear outline against the quivering tapestry; and he shuddered to perceive that shadow—as he staggered awhile upon the threshold—assuming the exact position, and precisely filling up the contour, of the relentless and triumphant murderer of the Saracen Berlifitzing.

To lighten the depression of his spirits, the Baron hurried into the open air. At the principal gate of the palace he encountered three equerries. With much difficulty, and at the imminent peril of their lives, they were restraining the convulsive plunges of a gigantic and fiery-colored horse.

"Whose horse? Where did you get him?" demanded the youth, in a querulous and husky tone, as he became instantly aware that the mysterious steed in the tapestried chamber was the very counterpart of the furious animal before his eyes.

"He is your own property, sire," replied one of the equerries, "at least he is claimed by no other owner. We caught him flying, all smoking and foaming with rage, from the burning stables of the Castle Berlifitzing. Supposing him to have belonged to the old Count's stud of foreign horses, we led him back as an estray. But the grooms there disclaim any title to the creature; which is strange, since he bears evident marks of having made a narrow escape from the flames."

"The letters W.V.B. are also branded very distinctly on his forehead," interrupted a second equerry; "I supposed them, of course, to be the initials of William Von Berlifitzing—but all at the castle are positive in denying any knowledge of the horse."

"Extremely singular!" said the young Baron, with a musing air, and apparently unconscious of the meaning of his words. "He is, as you say, a remarkable horse—a prodigious horse! although, as you very justly observe, of a suspicious and untractable character; let him be mine, however," he added, after a pause, "perhaps a rider like Frederick of Metzengerstein may tame even the devil from the stables of Berlifitzing."

"You are mistaken, my lord; the horse, as I think we mentioned, is *not* from the stables of the Count. If such had been the case, we know our duty better than to bring him into the presence of a noble of your family."

"True!" observed the Baron, drily; and at that instant a page of the bedchamber came from the palace with a heightened color and a precipitate step. He whispered into his master's ear an account of the sudden disappearance of a small portion of the tapestry, in an apartment he designated; entering, at the same time, into particulars of a minute and circumstantial character; but from the low tone of voice in which these latter were communicated, nothing escaped to gratify the excited curiosity of the equerries.

The young Frederick, during the conference, seemed agitated by a variety of emotions. He soon, however, recovered his composure, and an expression of determined malignancy settled upon his countenance, as he gave peremptory orders that the apartment in question should be immediately locked up, and the key placed in his own possession.

"Have you heard of the unhappy death of the old hunter, Berlifitzing?" said one of his vassals to the Baron, as, after the departure of the page, the huge steed that that nobleman had adopted as his own, plunged and curveted, with redoubled fury, down the long avenue that extended from the palace to the stables of Metzengerstein.

"No!" said the Baron, turning abruptly towards the speaker, "dead! say you?"

"It is indeed true, my lord; and, to the noble of your name, will be, I imagine, no unwelcome intelligence."

A rapid smile shot over the countenance of the listener. "How died he?"

"In his rash exertions to rescue a favorite portion of the hunting stud, he has himself perished miserably in the flames."

"I-n-d-e-e-d!" ejaculated the Baron, as if slowly and deliberately impressed with the truth of some exciting idea.

"Indeed!" repeated the vassal.

"Shocking!" said the youth, calmly, and turned quietly into the palace.

From this date a marked alteration took place in the outward demeanour of the dissolute young Baron Frederick Von Metzengerstein. Indeed, his behavior disappointed every expectation, and proved little in accordance with the views of many a maneuvering mamma; while his habits and manner, still less than formerly, offered anything congenial with those of the neighboring aristocracy. He was never to be seen beyond the limits of his own domain, and in his wide and social world, was utterly companionless—unless, indeed, that unnatural, impetuous, and fiery-colored horse, which he henceforward continually bestrode, had any mysterious right to the title of his friend.

Numerous invitations on the part of the neighborhood for a long time, however, periodically came in. "Will the Baron honor our festivals with his presence?" "Will the Baron join us in a hunting of the boar?"— "Metzengerstein does not hunt"; "Metzengerstein will not attend" were the haughty and laconic answers.

These repeated insults were not to be endured by an imperious nobility. Such invitations became less cordial, less frequent; in time they ceased altogether. The widow of the unfortunate Count Berlifitzing was even heard to express a hope "that the Baron might be at home when he did not wish to be at home, since he disdained the company of his equals; and ride when he did not wish to ride, since he preferred the society of a horse." This, to be sure, was a very silly explosion of hereditary pique; and merely proved how singularly unmeaning our sayings are apt to become, when we desire to be unusually energetic.

The charitable, nevertheless, attributed the alteration in the conduct of the young nobleman to the natural sorrow of a son for the untimely loss of his parents; forgetting, however, his atrocious and reckless behavior during the short period immediately succeeding that bereavement. Some there were, indeed, who suggested a too-haughty idea of self-consequence and dignity. Others again (among whom may be mentioned the family physician) did not hesitate in speaking of morbid melancholy, and hereditary ill-health; while dark hints, of a more equivocal nature, were current among the multitude.

Indeed, the Baron's perverse attachment to his lately acquired charger—an attachment that seemed to attain new strength from every fresh example of the animal's ferocious and demonlike propensities—at length became, in the eyes of all reasonable men, a hideous and unnatural fervor. In the glare of noon—at the dead hour of night—in sickness or in health—in calm or in tempest—the young Metzengerstein seemed riveted to the saddle of that colossal horse, whose intractable audacities so well accorded with his own spirit.

There were circumstances, moreover, which, coupled with late events, gave an unearthly and portentous character to the mania of the rider, and to the capabilities of the steed. The space passed over in a single leap had been accurately measured, and was found to exceed, by an astounding difference, the wildest expectations of the most imaginative. The Baron, besides, had no particular *name* for the animal, although all the rest in his collection were distinguished by characteristic appellations. His stable, too, was appointed at a distance from the rest; and, with regard to grooming and other necessary offices, none but the owner in person had ventured to officiate, or even to enter the enclosure of that horse's particular stall. It was also to be observed, that although the three grooms, who had caught the steed as he fled from the conflagration at Berlifitzing, had succeeded in arresting his course by means of a chain-bridle and noose—yet not one of the three could with any certainty affirm that he had, during that dangerous struggle, or at any period thereafter, actually placed his hand upon the body of the beast. Instances of peculiar intelligence in the demeanor of a noble and high-spirited horse are not to be supposed capable of exciting unreasonable attention, but there were certain circumstances that intruded themselves perforce upon the most skeptical and phlegmatic; and it is said there were times when the animal caused the gaping crowd who stood around to recoil in horror from the deep and impressive meaning of his terrible stamp—times when the young Metzengerstein turned pale and shrunk away from the rapid and searching expression of his human-looking eye.

Among all the retinue of the Baron, however, none were found to doubt the ardor of that extraordinary affection that existed on the part of the young nobleman for the fiery qualities of his horse; at least, none but an insignificant and misshapen little page, whose deformities were in everybody's way, and whose opinions were of the least possible importance. He (if his ideas are worth mentioning at all) had the effrontery to assert that his master never vaulted into the saddle without an unaccountable and almost imperceptible shudder; and that, upon his return from every long-continued and habitual ride, an expression of triumphant malignity distorted every muscle in his countenance.

One tempestuous night, Metzengerstein, awaking from a heavy slumber, descended like a maniac from his chamber, and, mounting in hot haste, bounded away into the mazes of the forest. An occurrence so common attracted no particular attention, but his return was looked for with intense anxiety on the part of his domestics, when, after some hours' absence, the stupendous and magnificent battlements of the Palace Metzengerstein were discovered crackling and rocking to their very foundation, under the influence of a dense and livid mass of ungovernable fire.

As the flames, when first seen, had already made so terrible a progress that all efforts to save any portion of the building were evidently futile, the astonished neighborhood stood idly around in silent if not pathetic wonder. But a new and fearful object soon riveted the attention of the multitude, and proved how much more intense is the excitement wrought in the feelings of a crowd by the contemplation of human agony, than that brought about by the most appalling spectacles of inanimate matter.

Up the long avenue of aged oaks that led from the forest to the main entrance of the Palace Metzengerstein, a steed, bearing an unbonneted and disordered rider, was seen leaping with an impetuosity that outstripped the very Demon of the Tempest.

The career of the horseman was indisputably, on his own part, uncontrollable. The agony of his countenance, the convulsive struggle of his frame, gave evidence of superhuman exertion; but no sound, save a solitary shriek, escaped from his lacerated lips, which were bitten through and through in the intensity of terror. One instant, and the clattering of hoofs resounded sharply and shrilly above the roaring of the flames and the shrieking of the winds; another, and, clearing at a single plunge the gateway and the moat, the steed bounded far up the tottering staircases of the palace, and, with its rider, disappeared amid the whirlwind of chaotic fire.

The fury of the tempest immediately died away, and a dead calm sullenly succeeded. A white flame still enveloped the building like a shroud, and, streaming far away into the quiet atmosphere, shot forth a glare of preternatural light; while a cloud of smoke settled heavily over the battlements in the distinct colossal figure of—*a horse.*

MIMIC

DONALD A. WOLLHEIM

It is less than five hundred years since an entire half of the world was discovered. It is less than two hundred years since the discovery of the last continent. The sciences of chemistry and physics go back scarce one century. The science of aviation goes back forty years. The science of atomics is being born.

And yet we think we know a lot.

We know little or nothing. Some of the most startling things are unknown to us. When they are discovered they may shock us to the bone.

We search for secrets in the far islands of the Pacific and among the ice fields of the frozen North while under our very noses, rubbing shoulders with us every day, there may walk the undiscovered. It is a curious fact of nature that that which is in plain view is oft best hidden.

I have always known of the man in the black cloak. Since I was a child he has always lived on my street, and his eccentricities are so familiar that they go unmentioned except among casual visitors. Here, in the heart of the largest city in the world, in swarming New York, the eccentric and the odd may flourish unhindered.

As children we had hilarious fun jeering at the man in black when he displayed his fear of women. We watched, in our evil, childish way, for those moments; we tried to get him to show anger. But he ignored us completely, and soon we paid him no further heed, even as our parents did.

We saw him only twice a day. Once in the early morning, when we would see his six-foot figure come out of the grimy dark hallway of the tenement at the end of the street and stride down toward the elevated to work—again when he came back at night. He was always dressed in a long black cloak that came to his ankles, and he wore a wide-brimmed black hat down far over his face. He was a sight from some weird story out of the old lands. But he harmed nobody, and paid attention to nobody.

Nobody—except perhaps women.

When a woman crossed his path, he would stop in his stride and come to a dead halt. We could see that he closed his eyes until she had passed. Then he would snap those wide watery blue eyes open and march on as if nothing had happened.

He was never known to speak to a woman. He would buy some groceries maybe once a week, at Antonio's—but only when there were no other patrons there. Antonio said once that he never talked, he just pointed at things he wanted and paid for them in bills that he pulled out of a pocket somewhere under his cloak. Antonio did not like him, but he never had any trouble with him either.

Now that I think of it, nobody ever did have any trouble with him.

We got used to him. We grew up on the street; we saw him occasionally when he came home and went back into the dark hallway of the house he lived in.

One of the kids on the block lived in that house too. A lot of families did. Antonio said they knew nothing much about him either, though there were one or two funny stories.

He never had visitors, he never spoke to anyone. And he had once built something in his room out of metal.

He had then, years ago, hauled up some long flat metal sheets, sheets of tin or iron, and they had heard a lot of hammering and banging in his room for several days. But that had stopped and that was all there was to that story.

Where he worked I don't know and never found out. He had money, for he was reputed to pay his rent regularly when the janitor asked for it.

Well, people like that inhabit big cities and nobody knows the story of their lives until they're all over. Or until something strange happens.

I grew up, I went to college, I studied. Finally I got a job assisting a museum curator. I spent my days mounting beetles and classifying exhibits of stuffed animals and preserved plants, and hundreds and hundreds of insects from all over.

Nature is a strange thing, I learned. You learn that very clearly when you work in a museum. You realize how nature uses the art of camouflage. There are twig insects that look exactly like a leaf or a branch of a tree. Exactly. Even to having phony vein markings that look just like the real leaf's. You can't tell them apart, unless you look very carefully.

Nature is strange and perfect that way. There is a moth in Central America that looks like a wasp. It even has a fake stinger made of hair, which it twists and curls just like a wasp's stinger. It has the same colorings and, even though its body is soft and not armored like a wasp's, it is colored to appear shiny and armored. It even flies in the daytime when wasps do, and not at night like all the other moths. It moves like a wasp. It knows somehow that it is helpless and that it can survive only by pretending to be as deadly to other insects as wasps are.

I learned about army ants, and their strange imitators.

Army ants travel in huge colums of thousands and hundreds of thousands. They move along in a flowing stream several yards across and they eat everything in their path. Everything in the jungle is afraid of them. Wasps, bees, snakes, other ants, birds, lizards, beetles—even men run away, or get eaten.

But in the midst of the army ants there also travel many other creatures—creatures that aren't ants at all, and that the army ants would kill if they knew of them. But they don't know of them because these other creatures are disguised. Some of them are beetles that look like ants. They have false markings like ant-thoraxes and they run along in imitation of ant speed. There is even one that is so long it is marked like three ants in single file. It moves so fast that the real ants never give it a second glance.

There are weak caterpillars that look like big armored beetles. There are all sorts of things that look like dangerous animals. Animals that are the killers and superior fighters of their groups have no enemies. The army ants and the wasps, the sharks, the hawk and the felines. So there are a host of weak things that try to hide among them—to mimic them.

And man is the greatest killer, the greatest hunter of them all. The whole world of nature knows man for the irresistible master. The roar of his gun, the cunning of his trap, the strength and agility of his arm place all else beneath him.

It was, as often happens to be the case, sheer luck that I happened to be on the street at that dawning hour when the janitor came running out of the tenement on my street shouting for help. I had been working all night mounting new exhibits.

The policeman on the beat and I were the only people besides the janitor to see the things that we found in the two dingy rooms occupied by the stranger of the black cloak.

The janitor explained—as the officer and I dashed up the narrow rickety stairs—that he had been awakened by the sound of heavy thuds and shrill screams in the stranger's rooms. He had gone out in the hallway to listen.

Severe groaning as of someone in terrible pain—the noise of someone thrashing around in agony—was coming from behind the closed door of the stranger's apartment. The janitor had listened, then run for help.

When we got there the place was silent. A faint light shone from under the doorway. The policeman knocked; there was no answer. He put his ear to the door and so did I.

We heard a faint rustling—a continuous slow rustling as of a breeze blowing paper. The cop knocked again but there was still no response.

Then, together, we threw our weight at the door. Two hard blows and the rotten old lock gave way. We burst in.

The room was filthy, the floor covered with scraps of torn paper, bits of detritus and garbage. The room was unfurnished, which I thought was odd.

In one corner there stood a metal box, about four feet square. A tight box, held together with screws and ropes. It had a lid, opening at the top, which was down and fastened with a sort of wax seal.

The stranger of the black cloak lay in the middle of the floor—dead.

He was still wearing the cloak. The big slouch hat was lying on the floor some distance away. From the inside of the box the faint rustling was coming.

We turned over the stranger, took the cloak off. For several instants we saw nothing amiss—

At first we saw a man, dressed in a somber, featureless black suit. He had a coat and skin-tight pants.

His hair was short and curly brown. It stood straight up in its inch-long length. His eyes were open and staring. I noticed first that he had no eyebrows, only a curious dark line in the flesh over each eye.

It was then that I realized that he had no nose. But no one had ever noticed that before. His skin was oddly mottled. Where the nose should have been there were dark shadowings that made the appearance of a nose, if you only just glanced at him. Like the work of a skillful artist in a painting.

His mouth was as it should be, and slightly open—but he had no teeth. His head perched upon a thin neck.

The suit was—not a suit. It was part of him. It was his body.

What we thought was a coat was a huge black wing sheath, like a beetle has. He had a thorax like an insect, only the wing sheath covered it and you couldn't notice it when he wore the cloak. The body bulged out below, tapering off into the two long, thin hind legs. His arms came out from under the top of the "coat." He had a tiny secondary pair of arms folded tightly across his chest. There was a sharp round hole newly pierced in his chest just above these arms still oozing a watery liquid.

The janitor fled gibbering. The officer was pale but standing by his duty. I heard him muttering under his breath an endless stream of *Hail Marys*.

The lower thorax—the "abdomen"—was very long and insectlike. It was crumpled up now like the wreck of an airplane fuselage.

I recalled the appearance of a female wasp that had just laid eggs—her thorax had had that empty appearance.

The sight was a shock such as leaves one in full control. The mind rejects it, and it is only in afterthought that one can feel the dim shudder of horror.

The rustling was still coming from the box. I motioned the white-faced cop and we went over and stood before it. He took his nightstick and knocked away the waxen seal.

Then we heaved and pulled the lid open.

A wave of noxious vapor assailed us. We staggered back as suddenly a stream of flying things shot out of the huge iron container. The window was open, and straight out into the first glow of dawn they flew.

There must have been dozens of them. They were about two or three inches long and they flew on wide gauzy beetle wings. They looked like

309

little men, strangely terrifying as they flew—clad in their black suits, with expressionless faces and their dots of watery blue eyes. And they flew out on transparent wings that came from under their black beetle coats.

I ran to the window, fascinated, almost hypnotized. The horror of it had not reached my mind at once. Afterward I have had spasms of numbing terror as my mind tries to put the things together. The whole business was so utterly unexpected.

We knew of army ants and their imitators, yet it never occurred to us that we too were army ants of a sort. We knew of stick insects and it never occurred to us that there might be others that disguise themselves to fool, not other animals, but the supreme animal himself—man.

We found some bones in the bottom of that iron case afterward. But we couldn't identify them.

Perhaps we did not try hard. They might have been human—

I suppose the stranger of the black cloak did not fear women so much as it distrusted them. Women notice men, perhaps, more closely then other men do. Women might become suspicious sooner of the inhumanity, the deception. And then there might perhaps have been some touch of instinctive feminine jealousy. The stranger was disguised as a man, but its sex was surely female. The things in the iron box were its young.

But it is the other thing I saw when I ran to the window that has shaken me most. The policeman did not see it. Nobody else saw it but me, and I only for an instant.

Nature practises deceptions in every angle. Evolution will create a being for any niche, no matter how unlikely.

When I went to the window, I saw the small cloud of flying things rising up into the sky and sailing away into the purple distance. The dawn was breaking and the first rays of the sun were just striking over the housetops.

Shaken, I looked away from that fourth-floor tenement room over the roofs of the lower buildings. Chimneys and walls and empty clotheslines made the scenery over which the tiny mass of horror passed.

And then I saw a chimney, not thirty feet away on the next roof. It was squat and red brick and had two black pipe ends flush with its top. I saw it suddenly vibrate, oddly. And its red brick surface seem to peel away, and the black pipe openings turn suddenly white.

I saw two big eyes staring up into the sky.

A great, flat-winged thing detached itself silently from the surface of the real chimney and darted hungrily after the cloud of flying things.

I watched until all had lost themselves in the sky.

MIVE

CARL JACOBI

Carling's Marsh, some called it, but more often it was known by the name of Mive. Strange name that — Mive. And it was a strange place. Five wild, desolate miles of thick water, green masses of some kind of kelp, and violent vegetable growth. To the east the cypress trees swelled more into prominence, and this district was vaguely designated by the villagers as the Flan. Again a strange name, and again I offer no explanation. A sense of depression, of isolation perhaps, which threatened to crush any buoyancy of feeling possessed by the most hardened traveler, seemed to emanate from this lonely wasteland. Was it any wonder that its observers always told of seeing it at night, before a storm, or in the spent afternoon of a dark and frowning day? And even if they had wandered upon it, say on a bright morning in June, the impression probably would have been the same, for the sun glittering upon the surface of the olive water would have lost its exuberant brilliance and become absorbed in the roily depths below. However, the presence of this huge marsh would have interested no one, had not the east road skirted for a dismal quarter-mile its melancholy shore.

The east road, avoided, being frequently impassable because of high water, was a roundabout connection between the little towns of Twellen and Lamarr. The road seemed to have been irresistibly drawn toward the Mive, for it cut a huge half-moon across the country for seemingly no reason at all. But this arc led through a wilderness of an entirely different aspect from the land surrounding the other trails. Like the rest it started among the hills, climbed the hills, and rambled down the hills, but after passing Echo Lake, that lowering tarn locked in a deep ravine, it straggled up a last hillock and swept down upon a large flat. And as

311

one proceeded, the flat steadily sank lower; it forgot the hills, and the ground, already damp, became sodden and quivering under the feet.

And then looming up almost suddenly — Mive! . . . a morass at first, a mere bog, then a jungle of growth repulsive in its overluxuriance, and finally a sea of kelp, an inland Sargasso.

Just why I had chosen the east road for a long walk into the country I don't really know. In fact, my reason for taking such a hike at all was rather vague. The day was certainly anything but ideal; a raw wind whipping in from the south, and a leaden sky typical of early September lent anything but an inviting aspect to those rolling Rentharpian hills. But walk I did, starting out briskly as the inexperienced all do, and gradually slowing down until four o'clock found me plodding almost mechanically along the flat. I dare say every passerby, no matter how many times he frequented the road, always stopped at exactly the same spot I did and suffered the same feeling of awe and depression that came upon me as my eyes fell upon that wild marsh. But instead of hurrying on, instead of quickening my steps in search of the hills again, I for some unaccountable reason that I have always laid to curiosity, left the trail and plunged through oozing fungi to the water's very edge.

A wave of warm humid air, heavy with the odor of growth, swept over me as though I had suddenly opened the door of some monstrous hothouse. Great masses of vines with fat creeping tendrils hung from the cypress trees. Razor-edged reeds, marsh grass, long waving cattails, swamp vegetation of a thousand kinds flourished here with luxuriant abundance. I went on along the shore; the water lapped steadily the sodden earth at my feet, oily-looking water, grim-looking, reflecting a sullen and overcast sky.

There was something fascinating in it all, and while I am not one of those adventurous souls who revel in the unusual, I gave no thought of turning back to the road, but plodded through the soggy, clinging soil, and over rotting logs as though hurrying toward some destination. The very contrast, the voluptuousness of all the growth seemed some mighty lure, and I came to a halt only when gasping for breath from exertion.

For perhaps half an hour I stumbled forward at intervals, and then from the increasing number of cypress trees I saw that I was approaching that district known as the Flan. A large lagoon lay here, stagnant, dark, and entangled among the rip grass and reeds, reeds that rasped against each other in a dry, unpleasant manner like some sleeper constantly clearing his throat.

All the while I had been wondering over the absolute absence of all animate life. With its dank air, its dark appeal, and its wildness, the

Eden recesses of the Mive presented a glorious place for all forms of swamp life. And yet not a snake, not a toad, not an insect had I seen. It was rather strange, and I looked curiously about me as I walked.

And then . . . and then as if in contradiction to my thoughts it fluttered before me.

With a gasp of amazement I found myself staring at an enormous, a gigantic ebony-black butterfly. Its jet coloring was magnificent, its proportions startling, for from wing tip to wing tip it measured fully fifteen inches. It approached me slowly, and as it did I saw that I was wrong in my classification. It was not a butterfly; neither was it a moth; nor did it seem to belong to the order of the *Lepidoptera* at all. As large as a bird, its great body came into prominence over the wings, disclosing a huge proboscis, ugly and repulsive.

I suppose it was instinctively that I stretched out my hand to catch the thing as it suddenly drew nearer. My fingers closed over it, but with a frightened whir it tore away, darted high in the air, and fluttered proudly into the undergrowth. An exclamation of disappointment burst from me, and I glanced ruefully at my hand where the prize should have been.

It was then that I became aware that the first two fingers and a part of my palm were lightly coated with a powdery substance that had rubbed off the delicate membrane of the insect's wings. The perspiration of my hand was fast changing this powder into a sticky bluish substance, and I noticed that this gave off a delightfully sweet odor. The odor grew heavier; it changed to a perfume, an incense, luring, exotic, fascinating. It seemed to fill the air, to crowd my lungs, to create an irresistible desire to taste it. I sat down on a log; I tried to fight it off, but like a blanket it enveloped me, tearing down my resistance in a great attraction as magnet to steel. Like a sword it seared its way into my nostrils, and the desire became maddening, irresistible.

At length I could stand it no longer, and I slowly brought my fingers to my lips. A horribly bitter taste that momentarily paralyzed my entire mouth and throat was the result. It ended in a long coughing spell.

Disgusted at my lack of willpower and at this rather foolish episode, I turned and began to retrace my steps toward the road. A feeling of nausea and of sluggishness began to seep into me, and I quickened my pace to get away from the stifling air. But at the same time I kept watch for a reappearance of that strange butterfly. No sound now save the washing of the heavy water against the reeds and the sucking noise of my steps.

313

I had gone farther than I realized, and I cursed the foolish whim that had sent me here. As for the butterfly—whom could I make believe the truth of its size or even of its existence? I had nothing for proof, and . . . I stopped suddenly!

A peculiar formation of vines had attracted my attention—and yet not vines either. The thing was oval, about five feet in length, and appeared to be many weavings or coils of some kind of hemp. It lay fastened securely in a lower crotch of a cypress. One end was open, and the whole thing was a grayish color like a cocoon . . . a cocoon! An instinctive shudder of horror swept over me as the meaning of my thoughts struck me with full force.

With a cocoon as large as this, the size of the butterfly would be enormous. In a flash I saw the reason for the absence of all other life in the Mive. These butterflies, developed as they were to such proportions, had evolved into some strange order and become carnivorous. The fifteen-inch butterfly which had so startled me before faded into insignificance in the presence of this cocoon.

I seized a huge stick for defense and hurried on toward the road. A low muttering of thunder from somewhere off to the west added to my discomfort. Black threatening clouds, harbingers of an oncoming storm, were racing in from the horizon, and my spirits fell even lower with the deepening gloom. The gloom blurred into a darkness, and I picked my way forward along the shore with more and more difficulty. Suddenly the mutterings stopped, and there came that expectant, sultry silence that precedes the breaking of a storm.

But no storm came. The clouds all moved slowly, lavalike, toward a central formation directly above me, and there they stopped, became utterly motionless, engraved upon the sky. There was something ominous about that monstrous cloud bank, and in spite of the growing feeling of nausea, I watched it pass through a series of strange color metamorphoses, from a black to a greenish black, and from a decided green to a yellow, and from a yellow to a blinding, glaring red.

And then as I looked those clouds gradually opened; a ray of peculiar colorless light pierced through as the aperture enlarged disclosing an enormous vault-shaped cavern cut through the stratus. The whole vision seemed to move nearer, to change from an indistinguishable blur as though magnified a thousand times. And then towers, domes, streets, and walls took form, and these coagulated into a city painted stereoscopically in the sky. I forgot everything and lost myself in a weird panorama of impossible happenings above me.

Crowds, mobs, millions of men clothed in medieval armor of chain mail with high helmets were hurrying on, racing past in an endless procession of confusion. Regiment upon regiment, men and more men, a turbulent sea of marching humanity were fleeing, retreating as if from some horrible enemy!

And then it came, a swarm, a horde of butterflies . . . enormous, ebony-black, carnivorous butterflies, approaching a doomed city. They met—the men and that strange form of life. But the defensive army and the gilded city seemed to be swallowed up, to be dissolved under this terrible force of incalculable power. The entire scene began to disintegrate into a mass, a river of molten gray, swirling and revolving like a wheel—a wheel with a hub, a flaming, fantastic, colossal ball of effulgence.

I was mad! My eyes were mad! I screamed in horror, but like Cyprola turned to stone, stood staring at this blasphemy in the heavens.

Again it began to coalesce; again a picture took form, but this time a design, gigantic, magnificent. And there under tremendous proportions with its black wings outspread was the butterfly I had sought to catch. The whole sky was covered by its massive form, a mighty repulsive tapestry.

It disappeared! The thunder mutterings, which had become silenced before, now burst forth without warning in unrestrained simultaneous fury. The clouds suddenly raced back again, erasing outline and detail, devouring the sight, and there was only the blackness, the gloom of a brooding, overcast sky.

With a wild cry, I turned and ran, plunged through the underbrush, my sole thought being to escape from this insane marsh. Vines and creepers lashed at my face as I tore on; knife reeds and swamp grass penetrated my clothing, leaving stinging burns of pain. Streak lightning of blinding brilliance, thunderations like some volcanic upheaval belched forth from the sky. A wind sprang up, and the reeds and long grasses undulated before it like a thousand writhing serpents. The sullen water of the Mive was black now and racing in toward the shore in huge waves, and the thunder above swelled into one stupendous crescendo.

Suddenly I threw myself flat upon the oozing ground and with wild fear wormed my way deep into the undergrowth. It was coming!

A moment later with a loud flapping the giant butterfly raced out of the storm toward me. Scarcely ten feet away I could see its enormous, swordlike proboscis, its repulsive, disgusting body, and I could hear its sucking inhalations of breath. A wave of horror seared its way through my very brain; the pulsations of my heart throbbed at my temples and at

315

my throat, and I continued to stare helplessly at it. *A thing of evil it was, transnormal, bred in a leprous, feverish swamp, a hybrid growth from a paludinous place of rot and overluxuriant vegetation.*

But I was well hidden in the reeds. The monstrosity passed on unseeing. In a flash I was up and lunging on again. The crashing reverberations of the storm seemed to pound against me as if trying to hold me back. A hundred times I thought I heard that terrible flapping of wings behind me, only to discover with a prayer of thanks that I was mistaken. But at last the road! Without stopping, without slackening speed, I tore on, away from the Mive, across the quivering flat, and on and on to the hills. I climbed; I stumbled; I ran; my sole thought was to go as far as possible. At length exhaustion swept over me, and I fell gasping to the ground.

It seemed hours that I lay there, motionless, unheeding the driving rain on my back, and yet fully conscious. My brain was wild now. It pawed over the terrible events that had crowded themselves into the past few hours, repictured them, and strove for an answer.

What had happened to me? What had happened to me? And then suddenly I gave an exclamation. I remembered now, fool that I was. The fifteen-inch butterfly that had so startled me near the district of the Flan . . . I had tried to catch the thing, and it had escaped, leaving in my hand only a powderish substance that I had vainly fought off and at last brought to my lips. That was it. What had happened after that? A feeling of nausea had set in, a great inward sickness like the immediate effects of a powerful drug. A strange insect of an unknown order, a thing resembling and yet differing from all forms of the *Lepidoptera*, a butterfly and yet not a butterfly. . . . Who knows what internal effect that powder would have on one? Had I been wandering in a delirium, a delirium caused by the tasting of that powder from the insect's wings? And if so, where did the delirium fade into reality? The vision in the sky . . . a vagary of a poisoned brain perhaps, but the monstrosity that had pursued me and the telltale cocoon . . . again the delirium? No, and again no! That was too real, too horrible, and yet everything was all so strange and fantastic.

But what master insect was this that could play with a man's brain at will? What drug, what unknown opiate existed in the membrane of its ebony-black wings?

And I looked back, confused, bewildered, expecting perhaps an answer. There it lay, far below me, vague and indistinct in the deepening gloom, the black outlines of the cypress trees writhing in the night wind, silent, brooding, mysterious—the Mive.

THE MOON-SLAVE

BARRY PAIN

The Princess Viola had, even in her childhood, an inevitable submission to the dance; a rhythmical madness in her blood answered hotly to the dance music, swaying her, as the wind sways trees, to movements of perfect sympathy and grace.

For the rest, she had her beauty and her long hair, which reached to her knees, and was thought lovable; but she was never very fervent and vivid unless she was dancing; at other times there almost seemed to be a touch of lethargy upon her. Now, when she was sixteen years old, she was betrothed to Prince Hugo. With others the betrothal was merely a question of state. With her it was merely a question of obedience to the wishes of authority; it had been arranged; Hugo was *comme ci, comme ça* —no good in her eyes; it did not matter. But with Hugo it was quite different—he loved her.

The betrothal was celebrated by a banquet, and afterward by a dance in the great hall of the palace. From this dance the Princess soon made her escape, quite discontented, and went to the furthest part of the palace gardens, where she could no longer hear the music calling her.

"They are all right," she said to herself as she thought of the men she had left, "but they cannot dance. Mechanically they are all right; they have learned it and don't make childish mistakes; but they are only one-two-three machines. They haven't the inspiration of dancing. It is so different when I dance alone."

She wandered on until she reached an old forsaken maze. It had been planned by a former king. All round it was a high crumbling wall with foxgloves growing on it. The maze itself had all its paths bordered with high opaque hedges; in the very center was a circular open space with tall pine trees growing round it. Many years ago the clue to the maze had been lost; it was but rarely now that anyone entered it. Its gravel paths were green with weeds, and in some places the hedges, spreading beyond their borders, had made the way almost impassable.

For a moment or two Viola stood peering in at the gate—a narrow

317

gate with curiously twisted bars of wrought iron surmounted by a heraldic device. Then the whim seized her to enter the maze and try to find the space in the center. She opened the gate and went in.

Outside everything was uncannily visible in the light of the full moon, but here in the dark shaded alleys the night was conscious of itself. She soon forgot her purpose, and wandered about quite aimlessly, sometimes forcing her way where the brambles had flung a laced barrier across her path, and a dragging mass of convolvulus struck wet and cool upon her cheek. As chance would have it she suddenly found herself standing under the tall pines, and looking at the open space that formed the goal of the maze. She was pleased that she had got there. Here the ground was carpeted with sand, fine and, as it seemed, beaten hard. From the summer night sky immediately above, the moonlight, unobstructed here, streamed straight down upon the scene.

Viola began to think about dancing. Over the dry, smooth sand her little satin shoes moved easily, stepping and gliding, circling and stepping, as she hummed the tune to which they moved. In the center of the space she paused, looked at the wall of dark trees all round, at the shining stretches of silvery sand and at the moon above.

"My beautiful, moonlit, lonely, old dancing room, why did I never find you before?" she cried; "but," she added, "you need music—there must be music here."

In her fantastic mood she stretched her soft, clasped hands upward toward the moon.

"Sweet moon," she said in a kind of mock prayer, "make your white light come down in music into my dancing room here, and I will dance most deliciously for you to see." She flung her head backward and let her hands fall; her eyes were half closed, and her mouth was a kissing mouth. "Ah! sweet moon," she whispered, "do this for me, and I will be your slave; I will be what you will."

Quite suddenly the air was filled with the sound of a grand invisible orchestra. Viola did not stop to wonder. To the music of a slow saraband she swayed and postured. In the music there was the regular beat of small drums and a perpetual drone. The air seemed to be filled with the perfume of some bitter spice. Viola could fancy almost that she saw a smouldering camp fire and heard far off the roar of some desolate wild beast. She let her long hair fall, raising the heavy strands of it in either hand as she moved slowly to the laden music. Slowly her body swayed with drowsy grace, slowly her satin shoes slid over the silver sand.

The music ceased with a clash of cymbals. Viola rubbed her eyes. She fastened her hair up carefully again. Suddenly she looked up, almost imperiously.

"Music! more music!" she cried.

Once more the music came. This time it was a dance of caprice, pelting along the violin strings, leaping, laughing, wanton. Again an illusion seemed to cross her eyes. An old king was watching her, a king with the sordid history of the exhaustion of pleasure written on his flaccid face. A hook-nosed courtier by his side settled the ruffles at his wrists and mumbled *"Ravaissant! Quel malheur que la vieillesse!"* It was a strange illusion. Faster and faster she sped to the music, stepping, spinning, pirouetting; the dance was light as thistle down, fierce as fire, smooth as a rapid stream.

The moment that the music ceased Viola became horribly afraid. She turned and fled away from the moonlit space, through the trees, down the dark alleys of the maze, not heeding in the least which turn she took, and yet she found herself soon at the outside iron gate. From thence she ran through the palace garden, hardly ever pausing to take breath, until she reached the palace itself. In the eastern sky the first signs of dawn were showing; in the palace the festivities were drawing to an end. As she stood alone in the outer hall Prince Hugo came toward her.

"Where have you been, Viola?" he said sternly. "What have you been doing?"

She stamped her little foot.

"I will not be questioned," she replied angrily.

"I have some right to question," he said.

She laughed a little.

"For the first time in my life," she said, "I have been dancing."

He turned away in hopeless silence.

The months passed away. Slowly a great fear came over Viola, a fear that would hardly ever leave her. For every month at the full moon, whether she would or no, she found herself driven to the maze, through its mysterious walks into that strange dancing room. And when she was there the music began once more, and once more she danced most deliciously for the moon to see. The second time that this happened she had merely thought that it was a recurrence of her own whim, and that the music was but a trick that the imagination had chosen to repeat. The third time frightened her, and she knew that the force that sways the tides had strange power over her. The fear grew as the year fell, for each month the music went on for a longer time—each month some of the pleasure had gone from the dance. On bitter nights in winter the moon

319

called her and she came, when the breath was vapor, and the trees that circled her dancing room were black bare skeletons, and the frost was cruel. She dared not tell anyone, and yet it was with difficulty that she kept her secret. Somehow chance seemed to favor her, and she always found a way to return from her midnight dance to her own room without being observed. Each month the summons seemed to be more imperious and urgent. Once when she was alone on her knees before the lighted altar in the private chapel of the palace she suddenly felt that the words of the familiar Latin prayer had gone from her memory. She rose to her feet, she sobbed bitterly, but the call had come and she could not resist it. She passed out of the chapel and down the palace gardens. How madly she danced that night!

She was to be married in the spring. She began to be more gentle with Hugo now. She had a blind hope that when they were married she might be able to tell him about it, and he might be able to protect her, for she had always known him to be fearless. She could not love him, but she tried to be good to him. One day he mentioned to her that he had tried to find his way to the center of the maze, and had failed. She smiled faintly. If only she could fail! But she never did.

On the night before the wedding day she had gone to bed and slept peacefully, thinking with her last waking moments of Hugo. Overhead the full moon came up the sky. Quite suddenly Viola was wakened with the impulse to fly to the dancing room. It seemed to bid her hasten with breathless speed. She flung a cloak around her, slipped her naked feet into her dancing shoes and hurried forth. No one saw her or heard her —on the marble staircase of the palace, on down the terraces of the garden, she ran as fast as she could. A thorn plant caught in her cloak, but she sped on, tearing it free; a sharp stone cut through the satin of one shoe, and her foot was wounded and bleeding, but she sped on. As the pebble that is flung from a cliff must fall until it reaches the sea, as the white ghost-moth must come in from cool hedges and scented darkness to a burning death in the lamp by which you sit so late—so Viola had no choice. The moon called her. The moon drew her to that circle of hard, bright sand and the pitiless music.

It was brilliant, rapid music tonight. Viola threw off her cloak and danced. As she did so, she saw that a shadow lay over a fragment of the moon's edge. It was the night of a total eclipse. She heeded it not. The intoxication of the dance was on her. She was all in white; even her face was pale in the moonlight. Every movement was full of poetry and grace.

The music would not stop. She had grown deathly weary. It seemed to her that she had been dancing for hours, and the shadow had nearly covered the moon's face, so that it was almost dark. She could barely see the trees around her. She went on dancing, stepping, spinning, pirouetting, held by the merciless music.

It stopped at last, just when the shadow had quite covered the moon's face, and all was dark. But it stopped only for a moment, and then began again. This time it was a slow, passionate waltz. It was useless to resist; she began to dance once more. As she did so she uttered a sudden shrill scream of horror, for in the dead darkness a hot hand had caught her own and whirled her round, *and she was no longer dancing alone.*

The search for the missing Princess lasted during the whole of the following day. In the evening Prince Hugo, his face anxious and firmly set, passed in his search the iron gate of the maze, and noticed on the stones beside it the stain of a drop of blood. Within the gate was another stain. He followed this clue, which had been left by Viola's wounded foot, until he reached that open space in the center that had served Viola for her dancing room. It was quite empty. He noticed that the sand round the edges was all worn down, as though someone had danced there, round and round, for a long time. But no separate footprint was distinguishable there. Just outside this track, however, he saw two footprints clearly defined close together: one was the print of a tiny satin shoe; the other was the print of a large naked foot—a cloven foot.

Monsters in the Night

CLARK ASHTON SMITH

The change occurred before he could divest himself of more than his coat and scarf. He had only to step out of the shoes, to shed the socks with two backward kicks, and shuffle off the trousers from his lean hind legs and belly. But he was still deep-chested after the change, and his shirt was harder to loosen. His hackles rose with rage as he slewed his head around and tore it away with hasty fangs in a flurry of falling buttons and rags. Tossing off the last irksome ribbons, he regretted his haste. Always heretofore he had been careful in regard to small details. The shirt was monogrammed. He must remember to collect all the tatters later. He could stuff them in his pockets, and wear the coat buttoned closely on his way home, when he had changed back.

Hunger snarled within him, mounting from belly to throat, from throat to mouth. It seemed that he had not eaten for a month—for a month of months. Raw butcher's meat was never fresh enough: it had known the coldness of death and refrigeration, and had lost all vital essence. Long ago there had been other meals, warm, and sauced with still-spurting blood. But now the thin memory merely served to exasperate his ravening.

Chaos raced within his brain. Inconsequently, for an instant, he recalled the first warning of his malady, preceding even the distaste for cooked meat: the aversion, the allergy, to silver forks and spoons. It had soon extended to other objects of the same metal. He had cringed even from the touch of coinage, had been forced to use paper and to refuse change. Steel, too, was a substance unfriendly to beings like him; and the time came when he could abide it little more than silver.

What made him think of such matters now, setting his teeth on edge with repugnance, choking him with something worse than nausea?

The hunger returned, demanding swift appeasement. With clumsy pads he pushed his discarded raiment under the shrubbery, hiding it from the heavy-jowled moon. It was the moon that drew the tides of madness in his blood, and compelled the metamorphosis. But it must not betray to any chance passerby the garments he would need later, when he returned to human semblance after the night's hunting.

The night was warm and windless, and the woodland seemed to hold its breath. There were, he knew, other monsters abroad in that year of the twenty-first century. The vampire still survived, subtler and deadlier, protected by man's incredulity. And he himself was not the only lycanthrope: his brothers and sisters ranged unchallenged, preferring the darker urban jungles, while he, being country-bred, still kept the ancient ways. Moreover, there were monsters unknown as yet to myth and superstition. But these too were mostly haunters of cities. He had no wish to meet any of them. And of such meeting, surely, there was small likelihood.

He followed a crooked lane, reconnoitered previously. It was too narrow for cars and it soon became a mere path. At the path's forking he ensconced himself in the shadow of a broad, mistletoe-blotted oak. The path was used by certain late pedestrians who lived even farther out from town. One of them might come along at any moment.

Whimpering a little, with the hunger of a starved hound, he waited. He was a monster that nature had made, ready to obey nature's first commandment: *Thou shalt kill and eat.* He was a thing of terror . . . a fable whispered around prehistoric cavern fires . . . a miscegenation allied by later myth to the powers of hell and sorcery. But in no sense was he akin to those monsters beyond nature, the spawn of a new and blacker magic, who killed without hunger and without malevolence.

He had only minutes to wait, before his tensing ears caught the faroff vibration of footsteps. The steps came rapidly nearer, seeming to tell him much as they came. They were firm and resilient, tireless and rhythmic, telling of youth or of full maturity untouched by age. They told, surely, of a worthwhile prey; or prime lean meat and vital, abundant blood.

There was a slight froth on the lips of the one who waited. He had ceased to whimper. He crouched closer to the ground for the anticipated leap.

The path ahead was heavily shadowed. Dimly, moving fast, the walker appeared in the shadows. He seemed to be all that the watcher had surmised from the sound of his footsteps. He was tall and well-shouldered, swinging with a lithe sureness, a precision of powerful tendon and muscle. His head was a faceless blur in the gloom. He was hatless, clad in dark coat and trousers such as anyone might wear. His steps rang with the assurance of one who has nothing to fear, and has never dreamt of the crouching creatures of darkness.

Now he was almost abreast of the watcher's covert. The watcher could wait no longer but sprang from his ambush of shadow, towering high upon the stranger as his hind paws left the ground. His rush was irresistible, as always. The stranger toppled backward, sprawling and helpless, as others had done, and the assailant bent to the bare throat that gleamed more enticingly than that of a siren.

It was a strategy that had never failed . . . until now. . . .

The shock, the consternation, had hurled him away from that prostrate figure and had forced him back upon teetering haunches. It was the shock, perhaps, that caused him to change again, swiftly, resuming human shape before his hour. As the change began, he spat out several broken lupine fangs; and then he was spitting human teeth.

The stranger rose to his feet, seemingly unshaken and undismayed. He came forward in a rift of revealing moonlight, stooping to a half-crouch, and flexing his beryllium-steel fingers enameled with flesh-pink.

"Who—what—are you?" quavered the werewolf.

The stranger did not bother to answer as he advanced, every synapse of the computing brain transmitting the conditioned message, translated into simplest binary terms, "Dangerous. Not human. *Kill!*"

THE MOTHER OF MONSTERS

GUY DE MAUPASSANT

I was reminded of this horrible story and this horrible woman on the sea-front the other day, as I stood watching—at a watering place much frequented by the wealthy—a lady well known in Paris, a young, elegant, and charming girl, universally loved and respected.

My story is now many years old, but such things are not forgotten.

I had been invited by a friend to stay with him in a small country town. In order to do the honors of the district, he took me about all over the place; made me see the most celebrated views, the manor houses and castles, the local industries, the ruins; he showed me the monuments, the churches, the old carved doors, the trees of specially large size or uncommon shape, the oak of St. Andrew and the Roqueboise yew.

When, with exclamations of gratified enthusiasm, I had inspected all the curiosities in the district, my friend confessed, with every sign of acute distress, that there was nothing more to visit. I breathed again. I should be able, at last, to enjoy a little rest under the shade of the trees. But suddenly he exclaimed:

"Why, no, there *is* one more. There's the Mother of Monsters."

"And who," I asked, "is the Mother of Monsters?"

He answered: "She is a horrible woman, a perfect demon, a creature who every year deliberately produces deformed, hideous, frightful children, monsters, in a word, and sells them to peep-show men.

"The men who follow this ghastly trade come from time to time to discover whether she has brought forth any fresh abortion, and if they like the look of the object, they pay the mother and take it away with them.

"She has dropped eleven of these creatures. She is rich.

"You think I'm joking, making it up, exaggerating. No, my friend, I'm only telling you the truth, the literal truth.

"Come and see this woman. I'll tell you afterwards how she became a monster-factory."

He took me off to the outskirts of the town.

She lived in a nice little house by the side of the road. It was pretty and well kept. The garden was full of flowers, and smelled delicious. Anyone would have taken it for the home of a retired lawyer.

A servant showed us into a little parlor, and the wretched creature appeared.

She was about forty, tall, hard-featured, but well built, vigorous, and wealthy, the true type of robust peasantry, half animal and half woman.

She was aware of the disapproval in which she was held, and seemed to receive us with malignant humility.

"What do the gentlemen want?" she inquired.

My friend replied: "We have been told that your last child is just like any other child, and not in the least like his brothers. I wanted to verify this. Is it true?"

She gave us a sly glance of anger and answered:

"Oh, no, sir, oh dear no! He's even uglier, mebbe, than the others. I've no luck, no luck at all, they're all that way, sir, all like that, it's something cruel; how can the good Lord be so hard on a poor woman left all alone in the world!"

She spoke rapidly, keeping her eyes lowered, with a hypocritical air, like a scared wild beast. She softened the harsh tone of her voice, and it was amazing to hear these tearful high-pitched words issuing from that great bony body, with its coarse, angular strength, made for violent gesture and wolfish howling.

"We should like to see your child," my friend said.

She appeared to blush. Had I perhaps been mistaken? After some moments of silence she said, in a louder voice: "What would be the use of that to you?"

She had raised her head, and gave us a swift, burning glance.

"Why don't you wish to show him to us?" answered my friend. "There are many people to whom you show him. You know whom I mean."

She started up, letting loose the full fury of her voice.

"So that's what you've come for, is it? Just to insult me? Because my bairns are like animals, eh? Well, you'll not see them, no, no, no, you shan't. Get out of here. I know you all, the whole pack of you, bullying me about like this!"

She advanced toward us, her hands on her hips. At the brutal sound of her voice, a sort of moan, or rather a mew, a wretched lunatic screech, issued from the next room. I shivered to the marrow. We drew back before her.

In a severe tone my friend warned her:

"Have a care, She-devil"—the people all called her She-devil—"have a care, one of these days this will bring you bad luck."

She trembled with rage, waving her arms, mad with fury, and yelling:

"Get out of here, you! What'll bring me bad luck? Get out of here, you pack of beasts, you!"

She almost flew at our throats; we fled, our hearts contracted with horror.

When we were outside the door, my friend asked:

"Well, you've seen her; what do you say to her?"

I answered: "Tell me the brute's history."

And this is what he told me, as we walked slowly back along the white high road, bordered on either side by the ripe corn that rippled like a quiet sea under the caress of a small, gentle wind.

The girl had once been a servant on a farm, a splendid worker, well-behaved and careful. She was not known to have a lover, and was not suspected of any weakness.

She fell, as they all do, one harvest night among the heaps of corn, under a stormy sky, when the still, heavy air is hot like a furnace, and the brown bodies of the lads and girls are drenched with sweat.

Feeling soon after that she was pregnant, she was tormented with shame and fear. Desirous at all costs of hiding her misfortune, she forcibly compressed her belly by a method she invented, a horrible corset made of wood and ropes. The more the growing child swelled her body, the more she tightened the instrument of torture, suffering agony, but bearing her pain with courage, always smiling and active, letting no one see or suspect anything.

She crippled the little creature inside her, held tightly in that terrible machine; she crushed him, deformed him, made a monster of him. The skull was squeezed almost flat and ran to a point, with the two great eyes jutting right out from the forehead. The limbs, crushed against the body, were twisted like the stem of a vine, and grew to an inordinate length, with the fingers and toes like spiders' legs.

The trunk remained quite small and round like a nut.

She gave birth to it in the open fields one spring morning.

When the women weeders, who had run to her help, saw the beast that was appearing, they fled shrieking. And the story ran round the neighborhood that she had brought a demon into the world. It was then that she got the name "She-devil."

She lost her place. She lived on charity, and perhaps on secret love, for she was a fine-looking girl, and not all men are afraid of hell.

She brought up her monster, which, by the way, she hated with a savage hatred, and which she would perhaps have strangled had not the *curé*, foreseeing the likelihood of such a crime, terrified her with threats of the law.

At last one day some passing showmen heard tell of the frightful abortion, and asked to see it, intending to take it away if they liked it. They did like it, and paid the mother five hundred francs down for it. Ashamed at first, she did not want to let them see a beast of this sort; but when she discovered that it was worth money, that these people wanted it, she began to bargain, to dispute it penny by penny, inflaming them with the tale of her child's deformities, raising her prices with peasant tenacity.

In order not to be cheated, she made a contract with them. And they agreed to pay her four hundred francs a year as well, as though they had taken this beast into their service.

The unhoped-for good fortune crazed the mother, and after that she never lost the desire to give birth to another phenomenon, so that she would have a fixed income like the upper classes.

As she was very fertile, she succeeded in her ambition, and apparently became expert at varying the shapes of her monsters according to the pressure they were made to undergo during the period of her pregnancy.

She had them long and short, some like crabs and others like lizards. Several died, whereat she was deeply distressed.

The law attempted to intervene, but nothing could be proved. So she was left to manufacture her marvels in peace.

She now has eleven of them alive, which bring her in from five to six thousand francs, year in and year out. One only is not yet placed, the one she would not show us. But she will not keep it long, for she is known now to all the circus proprietors in the world, and they come from time to time to see whether she has anything new.

She even arranges auctions between them, when the creature in question is worth it.

My friend was silent. A profound disgust surged in my heart, a furious anger, and regret that I had not strangled the brute when I had her in my hands.

327

"Then who is the father?" I asked.

"Nobody knows," he replied. "He or they have a certain modesty. He, or they, remain concealed. Perhaps they share in the spoils."

I had thought no more of that far-off adventure until the other day, at a fashionable watering place, when I saw a charming and elegant lady, the most skillful of coquettes, surrounded by several men who have the highest regard for her.

I walked along the front, arm-in-arm with my friend, the local doctor. Ten minutes later I noticed a nurse looking after three children who were rolling about on the sand.

A pathetic little pair of crutches lay on the ground. Then I saw that the three children were deformed, hunch-backed, and lame; hideous little creatures.

The doctor said to me: "Those are the offspring of the charming lady you met just now."

I felt a profound pity for her and for them.

"The poor mother!" I cried. "How does she still manage to laugh?"

"Don't pity her, my dear fellow," replied my friend. "It's the poor children who are to be pitied. That's the result of keeping the figure graceful right up to the last day. Those monsters are manufactured by corsets. She knows perfectly well that she's risking her life at that game. What does she care, so long as she remains pretty and seductive?"

And I remembered the other, the peasant woman, the She-devil, who sold hers.

MOTHER OF TOADS

CLARK ASHTON SMITH

Why must you always hurry away, my little one?"

The voice of Mere Antoinette, the witch, was an amorous croaking. She ogled Pierre, the apothecary's young apprentice, with eyes full-orbed and unblinking as those of a toad. The folds beneath her chin swelled like the throat of some great batrachian. Her short, flat fingers, outspread on her soiled apron, revealed an appearance as of narrow webs between their first flanges.

Pierre Baudin, as usual, gave no answer but turned his eyes from Mere Antoinette with an air of impatience. Her voice, raucously coaxing, persisted:

"Stay awhile tonight, my pretty orphan. No one will miss you in the village. And your master will not mind."

Pierre tossed his head with the disdain of a young Adonis. The witch was more than twice his age, and her charms were too uncouth and unsavory to tempt him for an instant. She was repellently fat and lumpish, and her skin possessed an unwholesome pallor. Also, her repute was such as to have nullified the attractions of a younger and fairer sorceress. Her witchcraft had made her feared among the peasantry of that remote province, where belief in spells and philters was still common. The people of Averoigne called her La Mere des Crapauds, Mother of Toads, a name given for more than one reason. Toads swarmed innumerably about her hut; they were said to be her familiars; and dark tales were told concerning their relationship to the sorceress, and the duties they performed at her bidding. Such tales were all the more readily believed because of those batrachian features that had always been remarked in her aspect.

The youth disliked her, even as he disliked the sluggish, abnormally large toads on which he had sometimes trodden in the dusk, upon the path between her hut and the village of Les Hiboux. He could hear some of these creatures croaking now; and it seemed, weirdly, that they uttered half-articulate echoes of the witch's words.

It would be dark soon, he reflected. The path along the marshes was not pleasant by night, and he felt doubly anxious to depart. Still without replying to Mere Antoinette's invitation, he reached for the black triangular vial she had set before him on her greasy table. The vial contained a philter of curious potency that his master, Alain le Dindon, had sent him to procure. Le Dindon, the village apothecary, was wont to deal surreptitiously in certain dubious medicaments supplied by the witch, and Pierre had often been on such errands to her osier-hidden hut.

The old apothecary, whose humor was rough and ribald, had sometimes rallied Pierre concerning Mere Antoinette's preference for him. Remembering certain admonitory gibes, more witty than decent, the boy flushed as he turned to go.

"Stay," insisted Mere Antoinette. "The fog is cold on the marshes, and it thickens apace. I knew that you were coming, and I have mulled for you a goodly measure of the red wine of Ximes."

She removed the lid from an earthen pitcher and poured its steaming contents into a large cup. The purplish-red wine creamed delectably, and an odor of hot, delicious spices filled the hut, overpowering the less agreeable odors from the simmering cauldron; the half-dried newts, vipers, bat wings, and evil, nauseous herbs hanging on the walls; and the reek of the black candles of pitch and corpse-tallow that burned always, by noon or night, in that murky interior.

"I'll drink it," said Pierre, a little grudgingly. "That is, if it contains nothing of your own concoctions."

"Tis naught but sound wine, four seasons old, with spices of Arabia," the sorceress croaked ingratiatingly. " 'Twill warm your stomach . . . and . . ." She added something inaudible as Pierre accepted the cup.

Before drinking, he inhaled the fumes of the beverage with some caution but was reassured by its pleasant smell. Surely it was innocent of any drug, any philter brewed by the witch, for, to his knowledge, her preparations were all evil-smelling.

Still, as if warned by some premonition, he hesitated. Then he remembered that the sunset air was indeed chill; that mists had gathered furtively behind him as he came to Mere Antoinette's dwelling. The wine would fortify him for the dismal return walk to Les Hiboux. He quaffed it quickly and set down the cup.

"Truly, it is good wine," he declared. "But I must go now."

Even as he spoke, he felt in his stomach and veins the spreading warmth of the alcohol, of the spices . . . of something more ardent than these. It seemed that his voice was unreal and strange, falling as if from a height above him. The warmth grew, mounting within him like a golden flame fed by magic oils. His blood, a seething torrent, poured tumultuously and more tumultuously through his members.

There was a deep, soft thundering in his ears, a rosy dazzlement in his eyes. Somehow the hut appeared to expand, to change luminously about him. He hardly recognized its squalid furnishings, its litter of baleful oddments, on which a torrid splendor was shed by the black candles.

It came to him, for an instant, that all this was a questionable enchantment, a glamour wrought by the witch's wine. Fear was upon him and he wished to flee. Then, close beside him, he saw Mere Antoinette.

Briefly he wondered why he had thought her old and gross and repulsive, for it seemed that he looked upon Lilith, the first witch. The lumpish limbs and body had grown voluptuous; the pale, thick-lipped mouth enticed him with a promise of ampler kisses than other mouths could yield. He knew why the magic warmth mounted ever higher and hotter within him. . . .

"Do you like me now, my little one?" she questioned. . . .

Pierre awoke in the ashy dawn, when the tall black tapers had dwindled down and had melted limply in their sockets. Sick and confused, he sought vainly to remember where he was or what he had done. Then, turning a little, he saw beside him on the couch a thing that was like some impossible monster of ill dreams: a toadlike form, as large as a fat woman. Its limbs were somehow like a woman's arms and legs. Its pale, warty body pressed and bulged against him, and he felt the rounded softness of something that resembled a breast.

Nausea rose within him as memory of that delirious night returned. Most foully he had been beguiled by the witch, and had succumbed to her evil enchantments.

It seemed that an incubus smothered him, weighing upon all his limbs and body. He shut his eyes, that he might no longer behold the loathsome thing that was Mere Antoinette in her true semblance. Slowly, with prodigious effort, he drew himself away from the crushing nightmare shape. It did not stir or appear to waken; and he slid quickly from the couch.

Again, compelled by a noisome fascination, he peered at the thing on the couch—and saw only the gross form of Mere Antoinette. Perhaps his impression of a great toad beside him had been but an illusion, a half-dream that lingered after slumber. He lost something of his nightmarish horror; but his gorge still rose in a sick disgust, remembering the lewdness to which he had yielded.

Fearing that the witch might awaken at any moment and seek to detain him, he stole noiselessly from the hut. It was broad daylight, but a cold, hueless mist lay everywhere, shrouding the reedy marshes, and hanging like a ghostly curtain on the path he must follow to Les Hiboux. Moving and seething always, the mist seemed to reach toward him with intercepting fingers as he started homeward. He shivered at its touch, he bowed his head and drew his cloak closer about him.

Thicker and thicker the mist swirled, coiling, writhing endlessly, as if to bar Pierre's progress. He could discern the twisting, narrow path for only a few paces in advance. It was hard to find the familiar landmarks, hard to recognize the osiers and willows that loomed suddenly before him like gray phantoms and faded again into the white nothingness as he went onward. Never had he seen such fog; it was like the blinding, stifling fumes of a thousand witch-stirred cauldrons.

Though he was not altogether sure of his surroundings, Pierre thought that he had covered half the distance to the village. Then, all at once, he began to meet the toads. They were hidden by the mist till he came close upon them. Misshapen, unnaturally big and bloated, they squatted in his way on the little footpath or hopped sluggishly before him from the pallid gloom on either hand.

Several struck against his feet with a horrible and heavy flopping. He stepped unaware upon one of them, and slipped in the squashy noisomeness it had made, barely saving himself from a headlong fall on the bog's rim. Black, miry water gloomed close beside him as he staggered there.

Turning to regain his path, he crushed others of the toads to an abhorrent pulp under his feet. The marshy soil was alive with them. They flopped against him from the mist, striking his legs, his bosom, his very face with their clammy bodies. They rose up by scores like a devil-driven legion. It seemed that there was a malignance, an evil purpose in their movements, in the buffeting of their violent impact. He could make no progress on the swarming path, but lurched to and fro, slipping blindly, and shielding his face with lifted hands. He felt an eery consternation, an eldritch horror. It was as if the nightmare of his awakening in the witch's hut had somehow returned upon him.

The toads came always from the direction of Les Hiboux, as if to drive him back toward Mere Antoinette's dwelling. They bounded against him like a monstrous hail, like missiles flung by unseen demons. The ground was covered by them, the air was filled with their hurtling bodies. Once, he nearly went down beneath them.

Their number seemed to increase, they pelted him in a noxious storm. He gave way before them, his courage broke, and he started to run at random, without knowing that he had left the safe path. Losing all thought of direction, in his frantic desire to escape from those impossible myriads, he plunged on amid the dim reeds and sedges, over ground that quivered gelatinously beneath him. Always at his heels he heard the soft, heavy flopping of the toads; sometimes they rose up like a sudden wall to bar his way and turn him aside. More than once they drove him back from the verge of hidden quagmires into which he would otherwise have fallen. It was as if they were herding him deliberately and concertedly to a destined goal.

Now, like the lifting of a dense curtain, the mist rolled away, and Pierre saw before him in a golden dazzle of morning sunshine the green, thick-growing osiers that surrounded Mere Antoinette's hut. The toads had all disappeared, though he could have sworn that hundreds of them were hopping close about him an instant previously. With a feeling of helpless fright and panic, he knew that he was still within the witch's toils; that the toads were indeed her familiars, as so many people believed them to be. They had prevented his escape, and had brought him

332

back to the foul creature—whether woman, batrachian, or both—who was known as the Mother of Toads.

Pierre's sensations were those of one who sinks momently deeper into some black and bottomless quicksand. He saw the witch emerge from the hut and come toward him. Her thick fingers, with pale folds of skin between them like the beginnings of a web, were stretched and flattened on the steaming cup that she carried. A sudden gust of wind arose as if from nowhere, and bore to Pierre's nostrils the hot, familiar spices of the drugged wine.

"Why did you leave so hastily, my little one?" There was an amorous wheedling in the very tone of the witch's question. "I should not have let you go without another cup of the good red wine, mulled and spiced for the warming of your stomach. . . . See, I have prepared it for you . . . knowing that you would return."

She came very close to him as she spoke, leering and sidling, and held the cup toward his lips. Pierre grew dizzy with the strange fumes and turned his head away. It seemed that a paralyzing spell had seized his muscles, for the simple movement required an immense effort.

His mind, however, was still clear, and the sick revulsion of that nightmare dawn returned upon him. He saw again the great toad that had lain at his side when he awakened.

"I will not drink your wine," he said firmly. "You are a foul witch, and I loathe you. Let me go."

"Why do you loathe me?" croaked Mere Antoinette. "I can give you all that other women give . . . and more."

"You are not a woman," said Pierre. "You are a big toad. I saw you in your true shape this morning. I'd rather drown in the marsh waters than stay with you again."

An indescribable change came upon the sorceress before Pierre had finished speaking. The leer slid from her thick and pallid features, leaving them blankly inhuman for an instant. Then her eyes bulged and goggled horribly, and her whole body appeared to swell as if inflated with venom.

"Go, then!" She spat with a gutteral virulence. "But you will soon wish that you had stayed."

The queer paralysis had lifted from Pierre's muscles. It was as if the injunction of the angry witch had served to revoke an insidious, half-woven spell. With no parting glance or word, Pierre turned from her and fled with long, hasty steps, almost running, on the path to Les Hiboux.

He had gone little more than a hundred paces when the fog began to return. It coiled shoreward in vast volumes from the marshes; it poured like smoke from the very ground at his feet. Almost instantly, the sun dimmed to a wan silver disk and disappeared. The blue heavens were lost in the pale seething voidness overhead. The path before Pierre was blotted out till he seemed to walk on the sheer rim of a white abyss that moved with him as he went.

Like the clammy arms of specters, with death-chill fingers that clutched and caressed, the weird mists drew closer still about Pierre. They thickened in his nostrils and throat, they dripped in a heavy dew from his garments. They choked him with the fetor of rank waters and putrescent ooze, and a stench as of liquefying corpses that had risen somewhere to the surface amid the fen.

Then, from the blank quietness, the toads assailed Pierre in a surging, solid wave that towered above his head and swept him from the dim path with the force of falling seas as it descended. He went down, splashing and floundering, into water that swarmed with the numberless batrachians. Foul slime was in his mouth and nose as he struggled to regain his footing. The water, however, was only knee-deep, and the bottom, though slippery and oozy, supported him with little yielding when he stood erect.

He discerned indistinctly through the mist the nearby margin from which he had fallen. But his steps were weirdly and horribly hampered by the toad-seething waters when he strove to reach it. Inch by inch, with a hopeless panic deepening upon him, he fought toward the solid shore. The toads leaped and tumbled about him with a dizzying eddying motion. They swirled like a viscid undertow around his feet and shins. They swept and swirled in great loathsome undulations against his retarded knees.

However, he made slow and painful progress, till his outstretched fingers could almost grasp the wiry sedges that trailed from the low bank. Then, from that mist-bound shore, there fell and broke upon him a second deluge of those demoniac toads; and Pierre was borne helplessly backward into the filthy waters.

Held down by the piling and crawling masses, and drowning in nauseous darkness at the thick-oozed bottom, he clawed feebly at his assailants. For a moment, ere oblivion came, his fingers found among them the outlines of a monstrous form that was somehow toadlike . . . but large and heavy as a fat woman.

Mummy

Kelsey Percival Kitchel

I have always prided myself on being a practical man; prosaic, if you will. In the old days the boys used to call me the man from Missouri.

Well, so I was. I had to be shown — and I was shown. Let me tell you. . . .

It was in South America that the thing happened. I had been engaged by the Babylonia Copper Company to go to their mine and smelter two miles high in the Andes. Being a metallurgical engineer and having had blast-furnace experience in the New Jersey plant, I was put in charge of the furnaces there in the desert.

At that time Babylonia was in process of growth and organization; it was not the finished affair that it is nowadays with its hospital, married quarters, white women, and a club. When I went down from New York there wasn't a wife in camp. We men — a handful of us — lived at the mess house and worked eighteen hours a day for seven days a week. Oh, yes, the pay was good; we would not have stayed if it had not been for the high salaries. You see, there was not a thing to amuse a chap. We were fifteen miles from railhead, living in a tiny village clinging to a mountainside that is a desert in the absolute meaning of that much-abused word. You yourself have seen so-called deserts, haven't you? And they were usually graced with sage-brush, lizards, mosses, and lichens, weren't they? Well, the Atacama has nothing on it that may be called "life." Not a thing. Rolling reaches and ridges of black, volcanic rocks and red gray sands; great salt-caked basins; leagues and leagues of alkaline dust blown westward at night by the winds pouring down from the Andes, then blown eastward during the day with the winds coming from the coast.

Yes, you have to be pretty hard-boiled to keep your sanity in such a place. We worked on eight-hour shifts there at the furnaces, of course. My buddy was Preston, a good scout who roomed with me and had the next shift to mine, knew his business and all that. Kellogg looked after the third shift in the twenty-four hours.

After I'd been there a year, more or less, I had naturally absorbed plenty of information about the surrounding country. I'd heard stories of the Indian burying grounds over at Chiu-Chiu; some of the boys had managed to get leave and ride over there—twenty miles of vile going through the desert. They had brought back a few turquoise beads, some pots, and so forth. I had never been particularly interested in archeology, but since I couldn't pry a vacation loose from the G. M.—and by "vacation" I mean a trip to port where there is a decent hotel; there's a movie palace, too, and you can sit on a plaza bench and look at white women—as I could not be spared for that, I asked for, and got, a couple of days. Having nothing better to do I decided on Chiu-Chiu and the burying ground. I believe that one should try everything once, and it seemed a pity to go back home to New York, at the end of my contract, without being able to show some honest-to-goodness relics. And I had a notion to get a skull and have it made into a tobacco jar. You can tell by that how young I was.

This place was situated on the River Loa, but don't run away with a fancy picture of a meadow-fringed stream, clumps of woodland, and fields of waving grain. Nature does not work that way in northern Chile. The Loa struggles down from the snows across a region as desolate and terrible as any inferno. For untold centuries the river has been eating its way through variegated strata laid down eons ago—like the Colorado, you know. In most places the canyon is so steep and deep that no human being could tap enough water for a window box; but in a very few places the escarpment has broken away, leaving an approach to the narrow, turbid stream. In these rare spots the aborigines have, from time immemorial, irrigated and cultivated the ground. Yes, oases, with skimpy fig and pepper trees, some highland corn and alfalfa and small, stony patches of puny vegetables. Life is unbelievably difficult for the desert farmer there in the Andes. The huts, made of stone and mud, cluster around a squat, gray church.

Chiu-Chiu, being the seat of a posthouse on the Inca highway long before Pizarro dreamed of coming to the New World, had buried its dead for centuries in the sandy wastes outside the little sun-baked oasis.

I rode over there alone. I had always preferred doing things by myself because it seemed to me a mark of weakness to want somebody tagging along for company. I do not think so now, but—well, let me go on.

One does not suffer on such a ride. You and your tough pampa horse have a good drink before starting and you take along a brace of water bottles—the horse gets a sip from your hat, you understand—and the sun blisters your parched skin, and your eyes squint in the merciless

336

glare, and you sneer at the deceitful mirages that mock you with their glimpses of blue lake water. . . .

Chiu-Chiu has a hotel—at least a hovel goes by that name; but you can get a meal there and a shakedown. Being so high in the air you are not troubled with insect life, with the exception of flies.

The horse was fed and watered while I got a snack myself; then I started for the burying ground; the hotel keeper was a trifle reluctant to direct me but he did not hold off long. You see, the farmers depended on selling their green stuff to the Babylonia Mine, and consequently nobody wanted to offend a gringo. We foreigners could arrange to secure our pumpkins and green corn from the port, you see, and the people at the oasis knew it.

Well, I found the place and, with a trench shovel that I'd fastened to the saddle, I began to dig after having done a little preliminary stamping, which, I had been told at Babylonia, was the way to locate a grave. If there is a hollow sound underfoot, why, you have come to a likely place to dig, see?

It was interesting, that delving there in the limitless desert under the towering, snowy peaks of the Andes.

I uncovered a brown, dried figure, mummied by the arid climate. It sat with its arms wrapped around its bony knees and with its head bent; clinging to it were fragments of ancient cloth, and from the fine sand close to it I lifted out darts, lances, arrows, pots, and a few rough necklaces of shell and low-grade turquoise. No, he was not a prince; or if he was from a royal house he must have been desperately poor. God knows how long he had been squatting there, looking east and waiting for Judgment Day.

The face was a splendid aquiline one with deep eye sockets; the brown skin was drawn incredibly snug over the skull. Every bit of flesh was gone—dried away; there was nothing left but what is popularly termed "skin and bone."

He was quite freed of sand by the time I had laid my discoveries on the crusted surface of the desert. I sat down to roll a cigarette and have a swig at the canteen, and I fell to thinking that what I was doing would be called grave robbery if it were carried on in a modern cemetery; but if a burying ground is ancient, why, we illogical little microbes called men name our digging "archeological excavation."

I had a feeling of discomfort that I could not understand; I wondered whether the long ride in the blistering heat had anything to do with it. An intuition came to me that I'd better leave that mummy alone with his worthless trumpery; but being a practical man and taking no stock in intuitions, I pulled myself together and rather halfheartedly selected the best of the trash from the sandy grave and packed it in the saddlebag. That one hole in the ground was enough for me; I did not search for any more; somehow the whole affair seemed a dubious sort of pleasure. I was sick of it and decided suddenly that I would change my plans and return to Babylonia that night instead of sleeping in the *tambo*. I knew that by going slow the horse would be able to make the trip.

I went to work at the head, which I intended using for a tobacco jar. There was little difficulty in cracking it loose. Brittle, friable, dusty, musty, it came off in my two hands and I stuffed it in the bag along with the other things. . . .

Something seemed to impel me to cover up that stark, headless thing; something seemed to tell me that I should leave him as I had found him. But I obstinately ignored these intuitions.

Back at the *tambo* I bought the horse a good feed and rested him, but could not eat the disgusting supper of beans and tough steak offered me. As the moon rose I started for Babylonia, going slowly for the sake of the tired animal under me. There was no danger of my getting lost, as there is a fairly clear trail from the oasis to railhead; and from there I had the mine lights to guide me.

There was a curious tingling sensation all over me; I thought that perhaps I had a touch of sun; or maybe I was getting scurvy, for in those days that disease was not infrequent in the more remote mining camps in the Andes; we could not depend with any certainty on the oasis vegetables and it was pretty hard to get fresh food up from port. I felt sick, and had delusions. I was sure I was being followed. . . . Now, the natives are as gentle as sheep; they never bother gringos. In spite of that I kept looking behind me; I saw nothing but the long shadows of the rocks. It was cold. You know that at an altitude of ten thousand feet the nights are bitter even in the tropics. The sudden changes of temperature crack the rocks, night and day, and in the pampa silence you can hear the soft whispering "ping" of flaking granite as it comes away and rolls down to the skirt of sand at the base of every boulder.

Once I was sure that the saddlebag quivered and wriggled. The horse was aware of something extraordinary, to judge by his behavior, because tired as he was he acted the terrified child that night, jumping, shying, shaking.

The lights grew brighter and larger as I neared camp, and I heard the roar of the ore crushers; for the first time I liked the sound. It seemed almost homelike. It meant that there were human beings round about—

lots of 'em! Mostly Bolivian and Chilean laborers, to be sure, but humans at any rate. I was ashamed of myself for wanting to be with my own kind; I was unreasonable, foolish, I told myself.

The corral was below the plant and I stopped there to leave the horse, which was pretty well tuckered out. I left the saddlebags, too; common sense warned me that I should go up to the mess house and turn in, for night was nearly gone and I needed sleep. But I did not do that. Preston was on shift at the furnaces and I wanted to get near my buddy. I wanted to tell him what a fizzle my *paseo* had been. He would laugh at my disappointment, perhaps, but I didn't care. He had told me before I started that burying grounds are not what they are cracked up to be. He had tried that sort of dissipation himself and had found it dull.

So I plowed through the heavy dust and sand, over loose stones, up to the furnaces.

Preston was on the feed floor; he had one man working under his eye, a burly fellow who pulled the loaded barrow of mixed charge off the elevator and dumped the contents into the furnace mouths. As I drew near I saw Preston on the platform above me and climbed up to him. Again I felt that there was something behind me; it was close, too; I seemed to feel two hands on my shoulders—bony, clawlike hands—and yet when I reached back quickly there was nothing there—nothing.

Preston watched me mounting the iron steps but instead of his cheery grin I saw, in the bright glare of the sputtering arclight, an odd, startled expression on his face.

"What in hell?" he shouted as he looked over my shoulder and down toward the lower floor. I turned, too, but there was nothing unusual to be seen.

"There was somebody behind you—with the thinnest face that ever came down the pike!" Preston laughed sheepishly. "Guess I must have been half asleep. I didn't expect you back for another twelve hours—what's the matter?"

I was thinking of that bony face in the saddlebag at the corral; the head that was to be cleaned up and fashioned into a jar—bah! I shuddered while I was angry with myself for giving in to nerves. Before I could formulate an answer Preston glanced down from the feed floor, then ran past me down the stairs, two steps at a time. Below, a laborer, tapping the copper, could not stop the flow when the ladle was full. The sparkling, iridescent stream ran wild, and Preston was needed, pronto. The Bolivian on the platform had no business to leave his job, but he caught the excitement and ran down the stairs, too, leaving me alone.

A full barrow was standing on the elevator facing the furnace mouth. It came up just as the Bolivian ran below. There was no reason why I should stay there and do his work, but I saw that the furnace needed another charge, so I stepped across and took hold of the handles of the car, thinking to dump it and close the furnace.

Then two hands seized mine—and, man, *I saw them!* . . . Disembodied hands, clawlike, brown, and shriveled, with each bone showing through the papery, dark skin. They clutched my wrists, holding me fast while they forced the barrow and me along with it toward the open door where the white-hot hellfire raged. . . .

I struggled while the car trundled slowly, jerkily, straight toward the fury of the fire. The gripping hands dug dark nails into my wrists. . . . I have the scars yet. Look! You see them? Ten white crescents that I shall always carry. . . .

The barrow moved faster and I felt a cold breath on my cheek in spite of the searing heat from the open furnace. For a second I looked over my shoulder into the eye sockets of a mummied head with skin drawn thin and tight over the bones; coarse, harsh hair brushed me. . . . I saw it, felt it—yes. . . . The barrow tipped.

I slid with it—down. . . .

You have guessed, of course, that Preston returned to the platform just in time to grab me as I fell.

A wave of unconsciousness swept over me. When I opened my eyes I was flat on my back panting like a branded steer and Preston was examining my bleeding wrists. The workmen from various parts of the building had gathered near, and one of them said, in his slurred, rapid Spanish: "Those wounds never came from the car. The *patrón* has had dealings with a spirit!" He spoke with the surety, the finality of an Indian who sees and knows, perhaps, more than we foreigners do.

Just then Kellogg, the lad in charge of the 7-to-3-o'clock shift, came along fresh from his bed and breakfast; so Preston was free to get me back to the mess house.

But after we were away from the furnaces I refused to go to my room. I told him everything—"and I've got to get that thing back to its body— now!" I finished.

He was a good sport; he did not laugh as many a man might have done, although I think that I could have killed him if he had sneered. No, he looked at me, nodded, and remarked quietly: "I saw something behind you as you came up the steps." He put his arm through mine and without another word we went to the corral; he had his own horse

340

saddled and chose a fresh mount for me. The bags he took care of himself, remarking as he picked them up: "You cannot have those relics, old man."

Together we rode back to Chiu-Chiu. I no longer felt that there was something behind me; the thing, whatever it was, moved at my side, waiting.

It did not have to wait long. The horses were fresh and we arrived at Chiu-Chiu before noon, making a wide circuit around the oasis to avoid curious villagers.

Back on the shoulders I put the head of that seated Thing and I replaced each piece of trash I had pilfered. Then we covered the mummy from the light of day. The sand was smooth when we had finished. . . .

That's all. I've never had a haunted feeling since; being a practical man I won't either, for I shall never again disturb a dead man. No, never again.

My Father, the Cat

HENRY SLESAR

My mother was a lovely, delicate woman from the coast of Brittany, who was miserable sleeping on less than three mattresses, and who, it is said, was once injured by a falling leaf in her garden. My grandfather, a descendant of the French nobility whose family had ridden the tumbrils of the Revolution, tended her fragile body and spirit with the same loving care given rare, brief-blooming flowers. You may imagine from this his attitude concerning marriage. He lived in terror of the vulgar, heavy-handed man who would one day win my mother's heart, and at last this persistent dread killed him. His concern was unnecessary, however, for my mother chose a suitor who was as free of mundane brutality as a husband could be. Her choice was Dauphin, a remarkable white cat that strayed onto the estate shortly after his death.

Dauphin was an unusually large Angora, and his ability to speak in cultured French, English, and Italian was sufficient to cause my mother to adopt him as a household pet. It did not take long for her to realize that Dauphin deserved a higher status, and he became her friend, protector, and confidante. He never spoke of his origin, nor where he had acquired the classical education that made him such an entertaining companion. After two years, it was easy for my mother, an unworldly woman at best, to forget the dissimilarity in their species. In fact, she was convinced that Dauphin was an enchanted prince, and Dauphin, in consideration of her illusions, never dissuaded her. At last, they were married by an understanding clergyman of the locale, who solemnly filled in the marriage application with the name of M. Edwarde Dauphin.

I, Etienne Dauphin, am their son.

To be candid, I am a handsome youth, not unlike my mother in the delicacy of my features. My father's heritage is evident in my large, feline eyes, and in my slight body and quick movements. My mother's death, when I was four, left me in the charge of my father and his coterie of loyal servants, and I could not have wished for a finer upbringing. It is to my father's patient tutoring that I owe whatever graces I now possess. It was my father, the cat, whose gentle paws guided me to the treasure houses of literature, art, and music, whose whiskers bristled with pleasure at a goose well cooked, at a meal well served, at a wine well chosen. How many happy hours we shared! He knew more of life and the humanities, my father, the cat, than any human I have met in all my twenty-three years.

Until the age of eighteen, my education was his personal challenge. Then, it was his desire to send me into the world outside the gates. He chose for me a university in America, for he was deeply fond of what he called "that great raw country," where he believed my feline qualities might be tempered by the aggressiveness of the rough-coated barking dogs I would be sure to meet.

I must confess to a certain amount of unhappiness in my early American years, torn as I was from the comforts of the estate and the wisdom of my father, the cat. But I became adapted, and even upon my graduation from the university, sought and held employment in a metropolitan art museum. It was there I met Joanna, the young woman I intended to make my bride.

Joanna was a product of the great American southwest, the daughter of a cattle raiser. There was a blooming vitality in her face and her body, a lustiness born of open skies and desert. Her hair was not the gold of antiquity; it was new gold, freshly mined from the black rock. Her eyes were not like old-world diamonds; their sparkle was that of sunlight on a cascading river. Her figure was bold, an open declaration of her sex.

She was, perhaps, an unusual choice for the son of a fairylike mother and an Angora cat. But from the first meeting of our eyes, I knew that I would someday bring Joanna to my father's estate to present her as my fiancée.

I approached that occasion with understandable trepidation. My father had been explicit in his advice before I departed for America, but on no point had he been more emphatic than secrecy concerning himself. He assured me that revelation of my paternity would bring ridicule and unhappiness upon me. The advice was sound, of course, and not even Joanna knew that our journey's end would bring us to the estate of a large, cultured, and conversing cat. I had deliberately fostered the impression that I was orphaned, believing that the proper place for revealing the truth was the atmosphere of my father's home in France. I was certain that Joanna would accept her father-in-law without distress. Indeed, hadn't nearly a score of human servants remained devoted to their feline master for almost a generation?

We had agreed to be wed on the first of June, and on May the fourth, emplaned in New York for Paris. We were met at Orly Field by François, my father's solemn manservant, who had been delegated not so much as escort as he was chaperone, my father having retained much of the old-world proprieties. It was a long trip by automobile to our estate in Brittany, and I must admit to a brooding silence throughout the drive that frankly puzzled Joanna.

However, when the great stone fortress that was our home came within view, my fears and doubts were quickly dispelled. Joanna, like so many Americans, was thrilled at the aura of venerability and royal custom surrounding the estate. François placed her in the charge of Madame Jolinet, who clapped her plump old hands with delight at the sight of her fresh blonde beauty, and chattered and clucked like a mother hen as she led Joanna to her room on the second floor. As for myself, I had one immediate wish: to see my father, the cat.

He greeted me in the library, where he had been anxiously awaiting our arrival, curled up in his favorite chair by the fireside, a wide-mouthed goblet of cognac by his side. As I entered the room, he lifted a paw formally, but then his reserve was dissolved by the emotion of our reunion, and he licked my face in unashamed joy.

François refreshed his glass, and poured another for me, and we toasted each other's well-being.

"To you, *mon purr*," I said, using the affectionate name of my child-hood memory.

"To Joanna," my father said. He smacked his lips over the cognac, and wiped his whiskers gravely. "And where is this paragon?"

"With Madame Jolinet. She will be down shortly."

"And you have told her everything?"

I blushed. "No, *mon purr*, I have not. I thought it best to wait until we were home. She is a wonderful woman," I added impulsively. "She will not be—"

"Horrified?" my father said. "What makes you so certain, my son?"

"Because she is a woman of great heart," I said stoutly. "She was educated at a fine college for women in eastern America. Her ancestors were rugged people, given to legend and folklore. She is a warm, human person—"

"Human," my father sighed, and his tail swished. "You are expecting too much of your beloved, Etienne. Even a woman of the finest character may be dismayed in this situation."

"But my mother—"

"Your mother was an exception, a changeling of the fairies. You must not look for your mother's soul in Joanna's eyes." He jumped from his chair, and came toward me, resting his paw upon my knee. "I am glad you have not spoken of me, Etienne. Now you must keep your silence forever."

I was shocked. I reached down and touched my father's silky fur, saddened by the look of his age in his gray, gold-flecked eyes, and by the tinge of yellow in his white coat.

"No, *mon purr*," I said. "Joanna must know the truth. Joanna must know how proud I am to be the son of Edwarde Dauphin."

"Then you will lose her."

"Never! That cannot happen!"

My father walked stiffly to the fireplace, staring into the gray ashes. "Ring for François," he said. "Let him build the fire. I am cold, Etienne."

I walked to the cord and pulled it. My father turned to me and said: "You must wait, my son. At dinner this evening, perhaps. Do not speak of me until then."

"Very well, father."

When I left the library, I encountered Joanna at the head of the stairway, and she spoke to me excitedly.

"Oh, Etienne! What a *beautiful* old house. I know I will love it! May we see the rest?"

344

"Of course," I said.

"You look troubled. Is something wrong?"

"No, no. I was thinking how lovely you are."

We embraced, and her warm full body against mine confirmed my conviction that we should never be parted. She put her arm in mine, and we strolled through the great rooms of the house. She was ecstatic at their size and elegance, exclaiming over the carpeting, the gnarled furniture, the ancient silver and pewter, the gallery of family paintings. When she came upon an early portrait of my mother, her eyes misted.

"She was lovely," Joanna said. "Like a princess! And what of your father? Is there no portrait of him?"

"No," I said hurriedly. "No portrait." I had spoken my first lie to Joanna, for there was a painting, half-completed, which my mother had begun in the last year of her life. It was a whispering little watercolor, and Joanna discovered it, to my consternation.

"What a magnificent cat!" she said. "Was it a pet?"

"It is Dauphin," I said nervously.

She laughed. "He has your eyes, Etienne."

"Joanna, I must tell you something—"

"And this ferocious gentleman with the moustaches? Who is he?"

"My grandfather. Joanna, you must listen—"

François, who had been following our inspection tour at shadow's length, interrupted. I suspected that his timing was no mere coincidence.

"We will be serving dinner at seven-thirty," he said. "If the lady would care to dress—"

"Of course," Joanna said. "Will you excuse me, Etienne?"

I bowed to her, and she was gone.

At fifteen minutes to the appointed dining time, I was ready, and hastened below to talk once more with my father. He was in the dining room, instructing the servants as to the placement of the silver and accessories. My father was proud of the excellence of his table, and took all his meals in the splendid manner. His appreciation of food and wine was unsurpassed in my experience, and it had always been the greatest of pleasures for me to watch him at table, stalking across the damask and dipping delicately into the silver dishes prepared for him. He pretended to be too busy with his dinner preparations to engage me in conversation, but I insisted.

"I must talk to you," I said. "We must decide together how to do this."

"It will not be easy," he answered with a twinkle. "Consider Joanna's view. A cat as large and as old as myself is cause enough for comment. A cat that speaks is alarming. A cat that dines at table with the household is shocking. And a cat whom you must introduce as your—"

"Stop it!" I cried. "Joanna must know the truth. You must help me reveal it to her."

"Then you will not heed my advice?"

"In all things but this. Our marriage can never be happy unless she accepts you for what you are."

"And if there is no marriage?"

I would not admit to this possibility. Joanna was mine; nothing could alter that. The look of pain and bewilderment in my eyes must have been evident to my father, for he touched my arm gently with his paw and said:

"I will help you, Etienne. You must give me your trust."

"Always!"

"Then come to dinner with Joanna and explain nothing. Wait for me to appear."

I grasped his paw and raised it to my lips. "Thank you, father!"

He turned to François, and snapped: "You have my instructions?"

"Yes, sir," the servant replied.

"Then all is ready. I shall return to my room now, Etienne. You may bring your fiancée to dine."

I hastened up the stairway, and found Joanna ready, strikingly beautiful in shimmering white satin. Together, we descended the grand staircase and entered the room.

Her eyes shone at the magnificence of the service set upon the table, at the soldierly array of fine wines, some of them already poured into their proper glasses for my father's enjoyment: Haut Medoc, from St. Estephe, authentic Chablis, Epernay Champagne, and an American import from the Napa Valley of which he was fond. I waited expectantly for his appearance as we sipped our aperitif, while Joanna chatted about innocuous matters, with no idea of the tormented state I was in.

At eight o'clock, my father had not yet made his appearance, and I grew ever more distraught as François signaled for the serving of the *bouillon au madere*. Had he changed his mind? Would I be left to explain my status without his help? I hadn't realized until this moment how difficult a task I had allotted for myself, and the fear of losing Joanna was terrible within me. The soup was flat and tasteless on my tongue, and the misery in my manner was too apparent for Joanna to miss.

"What is it, Etienne?" she said. "You've been so morose all day. Can't you tell me what's wrong?"

346

"No, it's nothing. It's just—" I let the impulse take possession of my speech. "Joanna, there's something I should tell you. About my mother, and my father—"

"Ahem," François said.

He turned to the doorway, and our glances followed his.

"Oh, Etienne!" Joanna cried, in a voice ringing with delight.

It was my father, the cat, watching us with his gray, gold-flecked eyes. He approached the dining table, regarding Joanna with timidity and caution.

"It's the cat in the painting!" Joanna said. "You didn't tell me he was here, Etienne. He's beautiful!"

"Joanna, this is—"

"Dauphin! I would have known him anywhere. Here, Dauphin! Here, kitty, kitty, kitty!"

Slowly, my father approached her outstretched hand, and allowed her to scratch the thick fur on the back of his neck.

"Aren't you the pretty little pussy! Aren't you the sweetest little thing!"

"Joanna!"

She lifted my father by the haunches, and held him in her lap, stroking his fur and cooing the silly little words that women address to their pets. The sight pained and confused me, and I sought to find an opening word that would allow me to explain, yet hoping all the time that my father would himself provide the answer.

Then my father spoke.

"Meow," he said.

"Are you hungry?" Joanna asked solicitously. "Is the little pussy hungry?"

"Meow," my father said, and I believed my heart broke then and there. He leaped from her lap and padded across the room. I watched him through blurred eyes as he followed François to the corner, where the servant had placed a shallow bowl of milk. He lapped at it eagerly, until the last white drop was gone. Then he yawned and stretched, and trotted back to the doorway, with one fleeting glance in my direction that spoke articulately of what I must do next.

"What a wonderful animal," Joanna said.

"Yes," I answered. "He was my mother's favorite."

THE NECROMANCER

ARTHUR GRAY

This is a story of Jesus College, and it relates to the year 1643. In that year Cambridge town was garrisoned for the Parliament by Colonel Cromwell and the troops of the Eastern Counties' Association. Soldiers were billeted in all the colleges, and contemporary records testify to their violent behavior and the damage they committed in the chambers that they occupied. In the previous year the Master of Jesus College, Doctor Sterne, was arrested by Cromwell when he was leaving the chapel, conveyed to London, and there imprisoned in the Tower. Before the summer of 1643 fourteen of the sixteen Fellows were expelled, and during the whole of that year there were, besides the soldiers, only some ten or twelve occupants of the college. The names of the two Fellows who were not ejected were John Boyleston and Thomas Allen.

With Mr. Boyleston this history is only concerned for the part that he took on the occasion of the visit to the college of the notorious fanatic William Dowsing. Dowsing came to Cambridge in December 1642, armed with powers to put in execution the ordinance of Parliament for the reformation of churches and chapels. Among the devastations committed by this ignorant clown, and faithfully recorded by him in his diary, it stands on record that on December 28, in the presence and perhaps with the approval of John Boyleston, he "digg'd up the steps (i.e., of the altar) and brake down Superstitions and Angels, 120 at the least." Dowsing's account of his proceedings is supplemented by the Latin History of the college, written in the reign of Charles II by one of the Fellows, a certain Doctor John Sherman. Sherman records, but Dowsing does not, that there was a second witness of the desecration — Thomas Allen. Of the two he somewhat enigmatically remarks: "The one (i.e., Boyleston) stood behind a curtain to witness the evil work; the other, afflicted to behold the exequies of his Alma Mater, made his life a filial offering at her grave, and, to escape the hands of wicked rebels, laid violent hands on himself."

That Thomas Allen committed suicide seems a fairly certain fact, and that remorse for the part he had unwillingly taken in the sacrilege of December 28 prompted his act we may accept on the testimony of Sherman. But there is something more to tell that Sherman either did not know or did not think fit to record. His book deals only with the college and its society. He had no occasion to remember Adoniram Byfield.

Byfield was a chaplain attached to the Parliamentary forces in Cambridge, and quarters were assigned to him in Jesus College, in the first-floor room above the gate of entrance. Below his chamber was the porter's lodge, which at that time served as the armory of the troopers who occupied the college. Above it, on the highest floor of the gate tower "kept" Thomas Allen. These were the only rooms on the staircase. At the beginning of the Long Vacation of 1643 Allen was the only member of the college who continued to reside.

Some light is thrown on the character of Byfield and his connection with this story by a pudgy volume of old sermons of the Commonwealth period that is contained in the library of the college. Among the sermons bound up in it is one that bears the date 1643 and is designated on the title page:

> A FAITHFUL ADMONICION of the Baalite sin of *Enchanters & Stargazers*, preacht to the Colonel Cromwell's Souldiers in Saint Pulcher's (i.e., Saint Sepulchre's) church, in Cambridge, by the fruitfull Minister, *Adoniram Byfield*, late departed unto God, in the yeare 1643, touching that of *Acts* the seventh, verse 43, *Ye took up the Tabernacle of Moloch, the Star of your god Remphan, figures which ye made to worship them; & I will carrie you away beyond Babylon.*

The discourse, in its title as in its contents, reveals its author as one of the fanatics who wrought on the ignorance and prejudice against "carnal" learning that actuated the Cromwellian soldiers in their brutal usage of the University "scholars" in 1643. All Byfield's learning was contained in one book—*the* Book. For him the revelation that gave it sufficed for its interpretation. What needed Greek to the man who spoke mysteries in unknown tongues, or the light of comment to him who was carried in the spirit into the radiance of the third heaven?

Now Allen, too, was an enthusiast, lost in mystic speculation. His speculation was in the then-novel science of mathematics and astronomy. Even to minds not darkened by the religious mania that possessed Byfield that science was clouded with suspicion in the middle of the seventeenth century. Anglican, Puritan, and Catholic were agreed in regarding its great exponent, Descartes, as an atheist. Mathematicians were looked upon as necromancers, and Thomas Hobbes says that in his days at Oxford the study was considered to be "smutched with the black art," and fathers, from an apprehension of its malign influence, refrained from sending their sons to that university. How deep the prejudice had sunk into the soul of Adoniram his sermon shows. The occasion that suggested it was this. A pious cornet, leaving a prayer meeting at night, fell down one of the steep, unlighted staircases of the college and broke his neck. Two or three of the troopers were taken with a dangerous attack of dysentery. There was talk of these misadventures among the soldiers, who somehow connected them with Allen and his studies. The floating gossip gathered into a settled conviction in the mind of Adoniram.

For Allen was a mysterious person. Whether it was because he was engrossed in his studies, or that he shrank from exposing himself to the insults of the soldiers, he seldom showed himself outside his chamber. Perhaps he was tied to it by the melancholy to which Sherman ascribed his violent end. In his three months' sojourn on Allen's staircase Byfield had not seen him a dozen times, and the mystery of his closed door awakened the most fantastic speculations in the chaplain's mind. For hours together, in the room above, he could hear the mumbled tones of Allen's voice, rising and falling in ceaseless flow. No answer came, and no word that the listener could catch conveyed to his mind any intelligible sense. Once the voice was raised in a high key and Byfield distinctly heard the ominous ejaculation "Avaunt, Sathanas, avaunt!" Once through his partly open door he had caught sight of him standing before a board chalked with figures and symbols that the imagination of Byfield interpreted as magical. At night, from the court below, he would watch the astrologer's lighted window, and when Allen turned his perspective glass upon the stars the conviction became rooted in his watcher's mind that he was living in perilous neighborhood to one of the peeping and muttering wizards of whom the Holy Book spoke.

An unusual occurrence strengthened the suspicions of Byfield. One night he heard Allen creep softly down the staircase past his room; opening his door, he saw him disappear round the staircase foot, candle in hand. Silently, in the dark, Byfield followed him and saw him pass into the porter's lodge. The soldiers were in bed and the armory was unguarded. Through the lighted pane he saw Allen take down a horse pistol from a rack on the wall. He examined it closely, tried the lock, poised it as if to take aim, then replaced it and, leaving the lodge, disappeared up the staircase with his candle. A world of suspicions rushed on Byfield's mind, and they were not allayed when the soldiers

350

reported in the morning that the pistols were intact. But one of the sick soldiers died that week.

Brooding on this incident Adoniram became more than ever convinced of the Satanic purposes and powers of his neighbor, and his suspicions were confirmed by another mysterious circumstance. As the weeks passed he became aware that at a late hour of night Allen's door was quietly opened. There followed a patter of scampering feet down the staircase, succeeded by silence. In an hour or two the sound came back. The patter went up the stairs to Allen's chamber, and then the door was closed. To lie awake waiting for this ghostly sound became a horror to Byfield's diseased imagination. In his bed he prayed and sang psalms to be relieved of it. Then he abandoned thoughts of sleep and would sit up waiting if he might surprise and detect this walking terror of the night. At first in the darkness of the stairs it eluded him. One night, light in hand, he managed to get a glimpse of it as it disappeared at the foot of the stairs. It was shaped like a large black cat.

Far from allaying his terrors, the discovery awakened new questionings in the heart of Byfield. Quietly he made his way up to Allen's door. It stood open and a candle burned within. From where he stood he could see each corner of the room. There was the board scribbled with hieroglyphs; there were the magical books open on the table; there were the necromancer's instruments of unknown purpose. But there was no live thing in the room, and no sound save the rustling of papers disturbed by the night air from the open window.

A horrible certitude seized on the chaplain's mind. This Thing that he had caught sight of was no cat. It was the Evil One himself, or it was the wizard translated into animal shape. On what foul errand was he bent? Who was to be his new victim? With a flash there came upon his mind the story how Phinehas had executed judgment on the men that were joined to Baal-peor, and had stayed the plague from the congregation of Israel. He would be the minister of the Lord's vengeance on the wicked one, and it should be counted unto him for righteousness unto all generations for evermore.

He went down to the armory in the porter's lodge. Six pistols, he knew, were in the rack on the wall. Strange that tonight there were only five—a fresh proof of the justice of his fears. One of the five he selected, primed, loaded, and cocked it in readiness for the wizard's return. He took his stand in the shadow of the wall, at the entrance of the staircase. That his aim might be surer he left his candle burning at the stair foot.

In solemn stillness the minutes drew themselves out into hours while Adoniram waited and prayed to himself. Then in the poring darkness he became sensible of a moving presence, noiseless and unseen. For a moment it appeared in the light of the candle, not two paces distant. It was the returning cat. A triumphant exclamation sprang to Byfield's lips, "God shall shoot at them, suddenly shall they be wounded"—and he fired.

With the report of the pistol there rang through the court a dismal outcry, not human nor animal, but resembling, as it seemed to the excited imagination of the chaplain, that of a lost soul in torment. With a scurry the creature disappeared in the darkness of the court, and Byfield did not pursue it. The deed was done—that he felt sure of—and as he replaced the pistol in the rack a gush of religious exaltation filled his heart. That night there was no return of the pattering steps outside his door, and he slept well.

Next day the body of Thomas Allen was discovered in the grove that girds the college—his breast pierced by a bullet. It was surmised that he had dragged himself thither from the court. There were tracks of blood from the staircase foot, where it was conjectured that he had shot himself, and a pistol was missing from the armory. Some of the inmates of the court had been aroused by the discharge of the weapon. The general conclusion was that recorded by Sherman—that the fatal act was prompted by brooding melancholy.

Of his part in the night's transactions Byfield said nothing. The grim intelligence, succeeding the religious excitation of the night, brought to him questioning, dread, horror. Whatever others might surmise, he was fatally convinced that it was by his hand that Allen had died. Pity for the dead man had no place in the dark cabin of his soul. But how was it with himself? How should his action be weighed before the awful Throne? His lurid thought pictured the Great Judgment as already begun, the Book opened, the Accuser of the Brethren standing to resist him, and the dreadful sentence of Cain pronounced upon him, "Now art thou cursed from the earth."

In the evening he heard them bring the dead man to the chamber above his own. They laid him on his bed, and, closing the door, left him and descended the stairs. The sound of their footsteps died away and left a dreadful silence. As the darkness grew the horror of the stillness became insupportable. How he yearned that he might hear again the familiar muffled voice in the room above! And in an access of fervor he prayed aloud that the terrible present might pass from him, that the hours might go back, as on the dial of Ahaz, and all might be as yesterday.

Suddenly, as the prayer died on his lips, the silence was broken. He could not be mistaken. Very quietly he heard Allen's door open, and the old, pattering steps crept softly down the stairs. They passed his door. They were gone before he could rise from his knees to open it. A momentary flash lighted the gloom in Byfield's soul. What if his prayer was heard, if Allen was not dead, if the events of the past twenty-four hours were only a dream and a delusion of the Wicked One? Then the horror returned intensified. Allen was assuredly dead. This creeping Thing— what might it be?

For an hour in his room Byfield sat in agonized dread. The thought of the open door possessed him like a nightmare. Somehow it must be closed before the foul Thing returned. Somehow the mangled shape within must be barred up from the wicked powers that might possess it. The fancy gripped and stuck to his delirious mind. It was horrible, but it must be done. In a cold terror he opened his door and looked out.

A flickering light played on the landing above. Byfield hesitated. But the thought that the cat might return at any moment gave him a desperate courage. He mounted the stairs to Allen's door. Precisely as yesternight it stood wide open. Inside the room the books, the instruments, the magical figures were unchanged, and a candle, exposed to the night wind from the casement, threw wavering shadows on the walls and floor. At a glance he saw it all, and he saw the bed where, a few hours ago, the poor remains of Allen had been laid. The coverlet lay smooth upon it. The dead necromancer was not there.

Then as he stood footbound, at the door a wandering breath from the window caught the taper, and with a gasp the flame went out. In the black silence he became conscious of a moving sound. Nearer, up the stairs, they drew—the soft creeping steps—and in panic he shrank backward into Allen's room before their advance. Already they were on the last flight of the stairs; then in the doorway the darkness parted and Byfield saw. In a ring of pallid light that seemed to emanate from its body he beheld the cat—horrible, gory, its foreparts hanging in ragged collops from its neck. Slowly it crept into the room, and its eyes, smoking with dull malevolence, were fastened on Byfield. Further he backed into the room, to the corner where the bed was laid. The creature followed. It crouched to spring upon him. He dropped in a sitting posture on the bed and as he saw it launch itself upon him, he closed his eyes and found speech in a gush of prayer, "O my God, make haste for my help." In an agony he collapsed upon the couch and clutched its covering with both hands. Beneath it he gripped the stiffened limbs of the dead necromancer, and, when he opened his eyes, the darkness had returned and the spectral cat was gone.

Night Shapes

Robert Weinberg

The whole thing occurred because Raymond's bed was next to the window. Not that it was an unusual window. On the contrary, it was a quite pleasant window, or so his mother said, and it fit in nicely with the decorum of the rest of the room, if there is such a thing as decorum in the room of a very imaginative twelve-year-old boy. However, judged by most standards, the window was just an ordinary second-floor window.

It was a hot night in the middle of the summer. Raymond's parents, both physical-fitness fanatics, didn't believe in air conditioning. Ceiling fans that futilely circulated hot air from floor to ceiling were their only concession to comfort. Needless to say, as was the way in an unfair world, Raymond's parents slept soundly in their bedroom, while their son remained wide awake in his. Fortunately, Raymond didn't mind. He liked staying up late, and he liked the heat. It gave him a chance to peer out the open window and invent shapes in the night.

All twelve-year-old boys did the same. Lying with their heads propped up on pillows next to the window, they made sinister shapes out of the neighborhood scenery that appeared so ordinary during the daylight. For a few hours each night, imagination ruled and reason ceased to exist. The darkness gave everything and anything a mysterious, exciting new life.

The house on the corner became an ogre's monstrous face, with eyes closed in slumber. The mailbox turned into an alien death machine sliding down the street. And the clouds high in the sky usually turned into giant gray elephantlike beasts floating through the atmosphere. At night, the only boundaries were those you imposed on yourself. It was a wonderful time to be awake.

Raymond wasn't sure if there would be any clouds tonight. All day, the sky had been a bright blue without a hint of overcast. The weather report right before bed promised more of the same tomorrow. The sky was a huge velvet sheet, with white dots of light shining through. The moon, immense and round, coated everything in sight with a bright silver glow. Raymond searched and searched, but there were no clouds to be found. Until he looked directly overhead, his face pressed right against the screen covering the window.

There was one cloud. A solitary, small white fluffy one, floating directly over his house. Which was why he hadn't spotted it earlier.

Pursing his lips together, he tried to decide what it resembled. A cat, a dog, or a white elephant? None of those descriptions fit, so he turned to his secondary list. A mouse? A house? Maybe even a baseball cap? He couldn't make up his mind.

Finally, Raymond resorted to his one sure answer. He settled on a face. The two indentations near the top worked as eyes. The cloud creature had no nose. The curve of night showing through became the mouth, turned up in a grin. While not perfect, it was good enough. Nodding his satisfaction, Raymond turned to other, easier-to-identify shapes.

The bungalow across the street, where his friend Marvin lived, became a massive tank, ready for battle against invaders. The old dead tree on the corner changed into a troll, gigantic arms outstretched to snatch some unsuspecting child from the curb. The street lamp turned into the giant glowing eye of a cyclops.

The gnarled oak tree in front of his house, not far from the window, became a dragon. Odd how he had never noticed the resemblance before. Concentrating, he envisioned a great big, mean, and very, very hungry dragon!

Swiftly, the creature took shape. The twisted branches covered with green leaves became its huge mouth, opened wide with terrible appetite. The thick, bent trunk became its massive body, hidden by the undergrowth. Branches that stretched out almost to his window transformed into long claws reaching out for prey. The night sky shining through two holes in the creature's head were its eyes.

Raymond paused suddenly, his own eyes widening. He shook his head, trying to make sense out of nonsense. It couldn't be—but it was. His imaginary vision was moving!

He gulped, swallowing hard. Making shapes in trees was fine, but it was another thing altogether when those shapes turned out to be real.

He felt a sudden twinge of panic. Maybe he should have slept with his feet by the window.

With a clatter, the dragon's claws twitched close by the window, scraping against the side of the house. They just missed the screen next to his head.

The breath froze in Raymond's throat. He hadn't noticed before that the monster's mouth was filled with long white teeth. Teeth that had no possible relation to any shadow shape. Teeth that gnashed and ground together. But now, Raymond knew exactly what the dragon wanted for his midnight snack. But he couldn't move an inch.

A weird, supernatural force emitting from the eyes of the beast held Raymond glued to the spot. He was trapped, the unsuspecting victim of a shadow dragon—a monster that devoured unsuspecting children just like him.

The dragon's mouth gaped open wide, wider, widest. It was at the window, ready to chomp through the screen, through the casement, and right through Raymond.

Tears of anger and frustration glistened in Raymond's eyes. Night shapes were supposed to be fun. They weren't allowed to come to life!

The dragon's claws reached again for the screen, hooking onto the metal. Raymond cringed, knowing it was all over.

A long white arm, thick as a barrel but insubstantial as mist, reached down from above. Immense, marshmallowlike fingers wrapped around the dragon, pulling it off its perch in the tree like some pesky insect. With a "whoosh!" the monster disappeared upward.

High above the house, there was a crunch, then another, as if someone had just munched down on a giant pretzel.

A cheerful voice, out of the night, whispered softly in Raymond's mind.

"Thanks for the assist. I knew the shape-dragon wouldn't dare venture out of the shadows unless he saw an innocent victim to devour. He was getting pretty desperate lately, knowing I was on his trail. Guess we put an end to his schemes."

Looking up out of his window, Raymond was not overly surprised to see the face in the cloud wink.

The Owl on the Moor

Marc Schorer and August Derleth

[*The following letter, crumpled and yellow with age, was found among the personal effects of the late M. R. Bentley, Barrister.*]

Brandon,
Egdon Heath,
17th May, 1908.

My Dear Morris:

I am all excited! Do you remember the controversy we had about witchcraft a summer ago? I'm sure you can recall it. It is about an unusual development that hinges directly upon this controversy that I am excited.

On May first I arrived here in this small hamlet bordering the famous Egdon heath, the setting of Thomas Hardy's noted *Return of the Native*, for my annual month's vacation. Of course, the furze and bracken attracted me the very first day, and I began to wander about alone on the heath. I often walked far out; sometimes, even, I was perplexed as to my direction. One day I chanced to wander farther than usual and I came upon the lowlands of the heath—a dank, miry moor far in the heart of it.

I was startled that I had wandered so far, and, as twilight was not far distant, I hastily began to return when my eyes caught sight of a solitary cottage, or possibly I should call it a shack, for, indeed, it resembled the latter much more than the former. I stared in bewilderment, thinking that perhaps my eyes had deceived me, and that I had conjured up a hallucination. But no; the shack didn't vanish as I half expected it to when I closed my eyes. Not that the appearance of a shack in this lone place surprised me to that extent, but there was smoke curling up from the crumbling chimney. I hesitated for some little time, and then turned and proceeded moodily homeward, determined to question the villagers about the dweller in the shack.

And question them I did. A woman lives there. Don't laugh, for that's all they told me. Who is she, where does she come from, what is her business, how does she subsist—of that they know nothing; they do not even hint at the answers to these questions. The people here are peace-loving folk, and it takes much to stir them, but it was clear to see that they hated that woman with all their hearts. This fact perplexed me sorely, but after incessant prying I found the reason.

She had been out there on the moor living her life of solitude for two years. She never came to the village, or if she did come she was never seen. Shortly after her coming a mysterious death came to one of the villagers: he was found out on the moor, his face a marble carving of fear and fascination. An examination revealed several minute scratches on the head and face of the dead man, which the doctor failed to diagnose. This, in itself, was extraordinary. And several months later another man was found dead on the heath, a good distance from the moor, with the same peculiar scratches about the head, and with that same expression of awful horror. The next death bore the same distinctive marks, but this time it was a woman who suffered. And other deaths occurred, and because the dead were always found out upon the lonely heath where only the woman walked, the villagers came to regard her with loathing and suspicion. Even the furze-cutters ceased their work, and people seldom rambled on the heath, for they did not know in what form this malignant death might approach and overcome them.

You can well imagine my astonishment at learning these things. However, this tale of sudden deaths did not deter me from my daily rambles on the heath. But I will admit that I was constantly on the alert for any hidden danger that might descend upon me.

For the first few days I gave the shack a wide berth, and wended my way within sight of the village. But I soon reflected what childish folly this was, and I became bolder and bolder.

One day I ventured within sight of the shack. I crouched half-hidden in the gorse for an appreciable length of time, but I observed no signs of life. This surprised me, perhaps unduly, and I moved cautiously nearer. Again I halted, breathless. I wondered what would happen should the woman discern me, and I kept my eyes fastened upon the door of the shack, which swung loosely open on one hinge that creaked loudly in the silence as a fanciful breeze came against the door. But nothing happened. There was no indication of life; all was an oppressive, death-like stillness, broken only at intervals by the eerie call of a bird, which came to me across the bracken, and, sweeping past me, died lingeringly away in the distance.

I halted there for some time, half expecting some fearful apparition to emerge from the darkness of the doorway and pounce upon me and devour me before I could so much as move. But finally, annoyed at this apparently overcautious attitude, I rose and strode boldly forward, fully determined to enter the evidently forsaken shack. Then suddenly I stopped short, for to my ears came the low, almost imperceptible sound of moaning.

That the moaning proceeded from the shack I could not doubt. Indubitably the mysterious inhabitant was ill. With this conviction in mind I proceeded forward, hesitating only at the threshold. The moaning was very distinct now, and I entered almost at once.

Picture, if you can, my astonishment at finding the one-room structure totally devoid of all human inhabitation. My eyes swept the room in a vain endeavor to pierce the shadows and discover the source of the sound that dinned in my ears. But I could perceive nothing. I then gave my attention to the squalid interior. The furniture in the room consisted of a table, upon which some broken dishes were standing, and three chairs, one broken and sadly in need of repair. The odd feature of this assembly of furniture was the fact that there was no bed. Surely this woman did not sleep upon the floor! I ridiculed the idea, but the fact remained that there was no bed.

It was soon impressed upon me that the room lacked the essentialities of a living room. There was no evidence of a container of food of any sort, nor were there signs of the remains of any recently eaten meal. My eyes swept in these things at a glance, and meanwhile the low moaning continued in the same monotonous tone.

This hidden moaning irritated me, and I began to peer intently on all sides. I glanced under the table and moved the chairs about. Quite suddenly I saw the source of the mysterious moaning sound. Looking up in the rafters I saw two great, round eyes turned upon me in an unblinking stare. It was a huge owl!

This incident seemed very odd to me at first. I had not seen an owl in the vicinity during my stay, and the sudden appearance of this bird startled me. It showed no inclination to leave its perch, nor did I endeavor to excite it. To be sure, I lost no time in beating a retreat, whether or not I was justified in doing so. I ran swiftly through the gorse toward the village. On a little knoll some distance from the shack I turned about and looked back. The woman, who had been nowhere about, was standing in the open door staring after me!

I was astounded; I readily confess it. A thousand questions perplexed me. How could she have gotten there? Where could she have been hiding, if indeed she was hiding? Could she have been in the gorse watching my every move? When she saw me gazing at her, she turned and went into the shack.

For some time I stood looking at the doorway where she had been. Then I went swiftly home, wondering about her untimely appearance.

Two nights later, while I was reading a treatise on witchcraft, I was seized with a horrible suspicion. I was, so to speak, as if a spell or charm had been cast over me. The suspicion rapidly became a conviction, and, acting upon it, I procured my pistol and without delay I ventured out upon the moor.

It was a beautiful night. The moon was out, and it lighted the moor as far as the eye could reach. But the waving of the bracken and gorse beneath the moon was not beautiful to me, for I thought of nothing but the terrible suspicion that had lodged in my mind.

Just as I reached the knoll upon which I had stood two days before, I saw a scene that I shall never forget. A man, who had evidently come from some point on the other side of the moor, was struggling with a huge owl! He was fending off the clutching talons as best he could, and the moonlight clearly showed the agony on his features.

The sight almost paralyzed me. But luckily for both of us, I retained my presence of mind, and, with the conviction of my suspicion in mind, I drew my pistol and fired pointblank at the monstrous bird, murmuring a prayer for the safety of the stranger. Both the man and the bird fell to the ground. I made the best of time to the spot to reckon what injuries the man had received.

The man was not severely injured; he was, however, unconscious. But the worst detail of the incident was the final confirmation of my awful suspicions.

Upon the ground near the man lay the body of a woman, a bullet hole through her breast!

Yours,
HARCOURT.

THE PHANTOM DRUG

A. W. KAPFER

This document, written in a clear, bold hand, was found in the burned ruins of an old insane asylum. The records of this institution had been saved, and upon investigation it was found that an eminent drug analyst was confined within its walls for one of the most horrible crimes ever recorded. He was judged and found insane after telling, as his defense, a fantastic story that was interpreted as a maniac's delusion. After reading his story, which coincides so well with the known facts, one cannot help but wonder. . . .

It's night again—one of those threatening, misty nights that you see in dreams. I'm afraid of it—it returns like a mockery to goad my memory to greater torture. It was on a night much like this that it happened; that horrible experience that gives my mind no rest—that fear that gives shadows ghostly forms and lends an added terror to the scream of an insane inmate. They put me in a madhouse because they judged me insane—me, whose mentality is so inexpressibly superior to those that judged me mentally unbalanced.

They wouldn't believe the facts I told them—said my story was the fabrication of an unsound mind, as an alibi for the horrible crime I had committed. I swore on my honor that I had told the truth, but even my friends refused to believe me; so it is with little hope of winning your credence that I leave this written document. But here are the facts.

I was at work in my laboratory analyzing some drugs that I had received in a new consignment from India. A tube containing a phosphorescent liquid attracted my attention, and I read the note my collector had sent with it.

He stated that it was supposed to have the power of transforming the mind of a human into the body of an animal; a superstition that the natives of the inner jungle firmly believe. They claim it is compounded from the brains of freshly slain animals, each brain containing an amount of this substance relative to its size.

I naturally scoffed at the claims for this drug, but decided to test it on

361

one of my laboratory animals so that I could place it in its proper category. I injected a small amount into the system of a rabbit and watched closely the reaction. For a minute it was motionless except for the natural movements of breathing. Then its eyelids closed slowly until they were completely shut and it appeared to be in a deep lethargy. For half a minute more there appeared no change; then its eyes flicked open and I looked, not into the timid eyes of a rabbit, but those of a scared animal.

With a sudden spring it leaped for the laboratory light, which was suspended by a chain from the ceiling. Its paws, however, were unfitted to grip the chain or the sloping reflector, and it fell to the floor, only to spring frantically at the curtain in a vain attempt to climb it. Another leap sent it to the top of a cabinet, where it upset several bottles, which fell to the tiled floor and smashed.

This aroused me from my stupor and I endeavored to catch it. I might as well have tried to catch its shadow. From cabinet to mantel, from mantel to curtain, curtain to shelf, leaving a trail of spilled and broken bottles in its wake. As it sprang about, strange squeaky barks came from its throat.

Perspiring and out of wind I gave up the chase, picked up an overturned chair and sat down to ponder the matter out. I observed the rabbit's actions closely. Now it was on a shelf looking at its short stump of a tail and chattering excitedly. Then it rubbed its ears and seemed startled at their length.

I wondered what was the explanation of this. It flew around like a monkey. A monkey—that was it. The drug made animals act like monkeys. Then the claim of the natives was true and the drug did have the power of performing a transition! I wondered if the drug always had the same result and decided to test it again on a white mouse that I took from another cage.

I carefully injected a small amount into its bloodstream. After a minute had expired, during which it made no move, it began to twitch about. The blood was pounding in my temples and my eyes were glued to its quivering form. Slowly it roused from its stupor and then stood on its hind legs while it flapped the front ones by its side.

"What the deuce—" I began. Then I understood. The drug affected each animal differently, dependent on the amount of the dose. As I arrived at this conclusion I noticed the rabbit was hopping about in its natural way, all trace of its former erratic movements gone. Never before in my experience had any drug such a startling effect on the brain as to give it the complete characteristics of a different animal.

* * *

My old and dearest friend, Rodney Caleb, was living with me and I went to his room to tell him what had occurred. He was lying on the bed covered by a heavy blanket that did not entirely conceal the hulking form, once the proud possessor of enormous strength, now robbed by sickness and old age. He was twenty years older than I. He liked to talk of the days when his prowess was commented upon where strength and courage counted. His voice still held some of its old timbre as he greeted me and noticed my excitement.

"Hello," he said. "Something interesting happen?"

With eager enthusiasm I detailed the effects the drug had had on the rabbit and the mouse. I could tell, from the expression on his face, that he was intensely interested, but when I had finished he lay back on his pillow as if in deep thought.

"Doc," he said quietly, "I think that at last I am going to have my wish fulfilled."

I looked at him uncomprehendingly.

"You know," he said, growing excited, "you know how I've longed to have my old strength back again, or, at least to be active for a time; well, there you have the substance that can perform that miracle."

"What do you mean?" I gasped.

"Why can't I take some of that drug," he reasoned, "and control the body of some animal for a while?"

"Rodney, you are crazy," I cried aghast. "I will not consent to your doing such an insensate thing. It would mean your death within a few minutes. Can you imagine yourself as a monkey, hopping and swinging about, with that old body of yours? It could never stand the strain."

"You forget something," he smiled.

"What?" I asked.

"My mind would no longer control this body, but that of some active and healthy animal."

"I should say not—" I began, then stopped and reasoned the matter out. The rabbit had been controlled by a monkey's mind; what happened to the rabbit's mind? It was only logical to suppose that they had been exchanged and that some monkey in far-off India had been hopping about like a rabbit during the transition.

"It is probable," I admitted, "that you would be controlling another body, but you forget that your body would be controlled by an animal's mind. That would be far more risky, as was proved by the rabbit's antics in the laboratory."

"You can take care of that," he argued, "by giving me a potion to

363

numb the motor area of my brain, and by giving me a sleeping powder. Then, no matter what impulse is aroused, it cannot be carried into an action."

I pondered his words carefully, and had to admit to myself that his reasoning was plausible. Rodney pleaded his cause with desperate earnestness.

"Here am I, an old man, chained to a bed for the rest of my life—a year or so at the most. Life holds little attraction for me, handicapped as I am. My body is weak, but the spirit of adventure is still strong within me. Surely you cannot deny me this favor; if not to gratify the wish of an old man, then on the claim of our friendship."

"I have but one thing left to say," I replied, "and that is—if you take some of this drug, then so will I."

Rodney hesitated at involving me in his rash wish.

"It is not necessary for you to do so," he said. "You are healthy, and in the name of your profession you owe the world a service. Nothing claims me."

"Nevertheless, that arrangement stands," I said. "Do you think I could ever bear to have anything happen to you through this enterprise, without my sharing it? Never. We have stood together in all things in the past and will continue to do so until the end."

Rodney placed his hand on mine. Neither of us spoke for a few minutes, but we felt the bond of friendship more closely than ever before.

"I can't ask you to risk it," he said huskily, and tried to hide the disappointment that his voice betrayed.

"And I cannot refuse your wish," I replied. "Besides, it is in a way my duty to undergo an experience that may prove of value in research. I must admit that I feel thrilled at the prospects of this adventure too. When shall we try it?"

"I am ready now," he replied. "What preparations are necessary?"

"Hardly any," I said. "I'll go down to the laboratory to get the sedatives and a hypodermic needle for this drug. I may as well bring my safety kit along."

Before I locked the back door I glanced out into the night. The air was surcharged and oppressive, and the uncanny stillness that precedes a storm sent a chilling premonition over me.

I locked the door, gathered the articles I needed and returned to the bedroom.

"An electrical storm is coming up," I said.

Rodney did not answer. His eyes were on the tube containing the phosphorescent drug. He was breathing faster and becoming excited and impatient.

"Better quiet down a bit, Rod," I admonished. My own heart was pumping strangely and the air seemed exceedingly warm. I thought it best to hide my perturbation from him, however. An unexpected crash of thunder made our nerves jump.

"We're as nervous as a couple of kids on their first pirate expedition," laughed Rod. His voice was high-pitched and taut.

I mixed a sedative and a sleeping potion for him and a stronger mixture for myself. These we drank. Then I took off my coat, bared my left arm and bade Rod roll up his pajama sleeve.

"We shall not feel the effects for a minute or two," I told him, "and by that time the potion we drank will start its work. Just lie quiet."

I forced my hand to be steady as I injected the drug into his arm, then hastily refilled the needle chamber from the tube and emptied it into my own arm. Rodney had put his hand by mine as I lay down beside him and I clasped it fervently. A drowziness crept over me as the seconds slipped by; then—something snapped, and I knew no more.

An unfamiliar atmosphere surrounded me when my mind began to function again. Slowly the haze wore away and I stirred restlessly as strange impressions flooded my brain. I was among a heavy growth of trees, rank grass, and bush. My nose felt peculiar to me; then I cried out in wonder. It was not a faint ejaculation that came from my throat, however, but a roar—a volume of sound that made the very earth tremble, and with good cause; for I, or rather my mind, was embodied in an elephant. My nose!—it was now a trunk!

I became intoxicated with the thought of the strength I now possessed, seized a tree with my trunk, and with a mighty tug, pulled its roots from the ground and hurled it aside. My cry of satisfaction was a boom that rolled like a peel of thunder.

A low growl sounded behind me and I swung my huge bulk quickly around. A tiger lay crouched in the undergrowth. I raised my trunk threateningly and stamped angrily, but the beast did not move. Then I looked into its eyes and understood. It was Rodney! He had possession of a tiger's body!

He was overjoyed at my recognizing him, and although we could not talk to each other, we showed our pleasure plainly enough. He gloried in the agility and strength that were now his, and took prodigious leaps and flips in a small clearing.

Finally, tired and winded from his play, he came to me and rubbed his back against my leg, purring like an immense cat. With a flip of my trunk I swung him on my back and raced through the jungle for miles. A river cut its way through this wilderness and we drank our fill—a gallon of water seemed but a cupful to my stupendous thirst. I was amusing myself by squirting water on Rodney when a roar came from a distance, accompanied by heavy crashings.

We faced the direction of the disturbance and waited breathlessly. Over the top of the waving jungle grass there appeared the head of an angry elephant. That its temper was up was all too plain. Its ears stuck out from its head like huge fans and its upraised trunk blasted forth a challenge as it charged along.

I looked anxiously at Rodney. The light of battle was in his eyes and I knew that he would be a formidable ally. It was too late to flee. My opponent was too close and the river was a barrier that, if I tried to cross, would give my adversary the advantage of firmer footing. My temper was aroused also, and as it was not my own body that was at stake, I did not fear the coming conflict.

The huge elephant facing me charged, and I met him halfway. Two locomotives crashing together would not have made that glade tremble more than it did when we met.

My enemy gave a scream of fear and pain when we parted and I soon saw the reason why. Rodney had waited until we were locked, then had launched himself at the throat of my rival. He had sunk his teeth deep into its tough hide and was tearing the flesh from its shoulder and chest with his bared claws.

All this I had seen in an instant, and as the monster turned on Rodney, I charged it from the side, driving both tusks deep in. Almost at the same instant Rodney severed its jugular vein. The elephant trembled, swayed, and toppled to the ground.

I was unhurt except for an aching head, the result of the first onslaught, but Rodney had not fared so well. As we turned from our fallen adversary I noticed that one of his legs had been crushed. The light of victory was in his eyes, however, and he seemed happy despite the pain he must have been suffering.

It was then that I noticed a change coming over me; a sort of drowsiness. At first I thought it was due to the exertion I had just gone through, but as its effect became more marked and insistent, I realized with a tremor of terror what it really was. The elephant's mind was trying to throw my own out of possession of its body!

I glanced at Rodney apprehensively to see if he was undergoing the same change. He was still in complete control. Then the truth dawned on me. The immense bulk I had been dominating had absorbed the power of the drug faster than the body Rodney controlled!

I hurried to his side and tried to make him understand that he should crawl into the jungle and hide until the effect of the drug had worn off. It was of no use. The more I stamped and raged, the more his eyes smiled at me as though he thought I was trying to show him how pleased I was at our victory.

More and more insistent and powerful did the elephant's mind become. It began to get control of its body and fixed its eyes with a baneful glare on Rodney's recumbent form. I struggled desperately to wrest control from that conquering mind, but in vain. The drug's force was ebbing fast.

One last warning I managed to blast out, and Rodney faced me. Horror of horrors! He thought I was calling him! Slowly and painfully he crept toward me. My thoughts became dim, and I struggled, as if in a dream, to conquer again the huge bulk he was approaching, but it was too late.

The monster I had once controlled was in almost complete possession now, and I was but an unwilling spectator viewing things through a veil that grew steadily heavier.

When Rodney was but a few feet away the body under me reared in the air—a flash of fear showed in Rodney's eyes as he realized the awful truth—and as his shrill scream rent the air, I was swallowed into blackness.

I don't know how long I lay in a daze, in Rodney's bedroom. Consciousness came back slowly. As events crowded themselves into my mind, I felt for Rodney's hand. It was not by my side. I sat up in bed, weak, and trembling all over.

At first I did not see him; then—I screamed in terror!

Rodney lay beside the bed, *every bone in his body broken as though something weighing several tons had crushed him!*

The Place of Hairy Death

Anthony M. Rud

At least not alone, Señor! If I were like you, young, handsome, and with the strength of two men in my arms, I would not venture at all down into those ancient workings. I foresee trouble; and in those horrible, dripping tunnels below Croszchen Pahna, where death may lurk in every slime-lined crevice, a comrade who will not flinch is even more necessary than your own great courage.

Ah, it is not a nice place down there! I have been part way, many years ago. I suppose every young *mozo* in all this district of Quintana Roo once could say as much. For there was a tale of treasure, of a room of gold and skeletons. Not this cheap ore that remains, and that costs more to mine than the ore will yield. A storeroom of the heavy nuggets found in rotten rock. And sealed up with that gold, the bodies of all the Indians who worked down in the bowels of the earth for their masters, the *Conquistadores*.

Not the first time I ventured there, but the second, death reached out with many hairy fingers and caught its prey. The first time I descended alone, and in terror. I returned to the blessed daylight very quickly—but not alone. A multitude of hairy horrors came with me! Even now after nearly thirty years, when I eat to a fullness of *carne* at nightfall, I know what will happen. Ever since then, in all my dreams I see—

But the señor shrugs. He is a hothead, like all *Americanos*. He wishes knowledge, not the fancies of an old man. It shall be so. Even today, the offer of fifty pesos is enough to tempt; for after all, one must eat. If the señor will get a good comrade, and both wish it, I shall guide them halfway. That is as far as my knowledge extends. I will build a fire, then, in the Room of Many Craters, and wait. But I will not go unless I judge the señor has a man of bravery for a comrade.

How do I know the Room of Many Craters is halfway? Well, it is a guess, Señor, but a good guess, I believe. The Indians who slaved in the mine for their Spanish masters never saw daylight. They dwelt in this huge room, which is a great bubble in the rock.

368

Also, a hundred or more of them worked here in this room. The round craters were worn in the floor by many men pushing against tree trunks, and walking endlessly in circles. This ground the rotten ore, and in time scoured out the craters in the floor.

According to old story, which has much sign of truth, the gold secured from the ore had to be stored many months. Ships came seldom, not every few weeks like today when steam drives ships as legs drive water beetles, wherever they wish to go. There were no strongholds above ground; so the gold was taken a long way through a secret passage, and stored in a barren room where guards watched night and day.

And that room once was found, though its unimaginable store of yellow gold still remains untouched. Unless more slides have come, it is probable that the señor will know the right passage or crevice, for before he may force a way it will be necessary to move a moldered skeleton.

That is not the short and rather frail bone frame of one of my people. That youth was strong, blue of eye like the señor himself. Yellow of hair. Easy to make smile or laugh. But he did not laugh once, from the time he, his companion, and I reached the Room of Craters, where I was to wait. There is a hot, wet atmosphere down there. And among the many things that hang in that heavy air is a queer, fetid stench that sends the heart of man down into his boots.

That time, when I saw the two men leave me by my fire in the Room of Craters, I crossed myself and prayed for their safe return. I did not even think of the gold, then, though they had promised me all I could carry, as my share. The one with blue eyes, the laughing one, was such as my mother's people worshiped in the old days, you understand. I was loyal to his companion, naturally; but to *him* I would render any service but one! I would not go farther into that place of hairy death! No, not even loyalty could take me there. That is why I caution the señor to choose his comrade with care.

Those two young men left me, and vanished into the wet dark. And only the wrong one returned. I must tell a little of those men and their story, so the señor can know how that could be. Usually it is the other way. In most struggles with darkness and evil, the strongest and most right it is who comes back to tell the tale. But not this time.

The tale, the señor must understand, is pieced together from fragments. It may not all be true exactly as I tell it. But the main facts are as I say. There is no need even to imagine a hatred or jealousy between the two men. There was none. One man was strong and poor. The other was weak—and the heir to millions of *Americano* gold. He, at least, should never have risked health and mind and life for more wealth. But thus it is in this world. No one is satisfied.

The blue-eyed, laughing man had been the superintendent of the great *jeniquen* rope factory in Valladolid, up north forty miles from here, in Yucatan. The señor doubtless knows the factory, for he came by narrow-gage railway, and Valladolid is the terminus.

The factory, and perhaps two hundred square miles of the great *jeniquen* plantations, were owned by the *Americano* father of the second man, the dark-skinned young fellow who was known as Señor Lester Ainslee.

It seems that the great father of Señor Lester did not approve of his boy. It was wished that Señor Lester get out into the jungle and what is called "rough it," drinking less wine, smoking fewer cigarettes, and learning to work hard with his hands. That was strange to me; for a sharp glance told me that one single day in the broiling sun, cutting *jeniquen*, would kill the delicate boy. But fathers are strange. They love and marry women who are delicate and nervous, and who die young. Then they demand their own strength in their offspring—when it is well known that Nature orders it otherwise. No breeder of fine horses would be such a fool. He would look for the characteristics of the dam to appear in the male colt; and those of the sturdy sire to show themselves in the female get.

Señor Jim Coulter—he was the blond, laughing one—was perhaps twenty-eight, though he looked not so much older than his companion. The boy, a fortnight or so before, had got drunk to celebrate his twenty-first birthday, and there were purple saucers under his eyes remaining from that bad time.

Then it was that the rich father could endure no more. He sent the boy down from the United States to work in the rope factory, or in the fields. Alongside the most ignorant peons, you understand—mere beasts who have slaved for generations under the lash of the overseers of the *haciendados!*

It was asking the impossible. The factory superintendent, Señor Jim Coulter, sent many telegraph messages; for the unreasonable father would hold him responsible, and he knew that nothing save quick death could happen to the frail young man in his charge.

In the end it was agreed that Señor Jim would take one month of holiday from the rope factory, and accompany the boy from the north on a trip into the jungle. The Señor Jim somewhere had got hold of a story that told of the treasure vault still remaining deep in this Madre d'Oro

Mine, two thousand feet below the ancient temple at Croszchen Pahna. The story was an old one to me, of course, and probably true.

When they came to me, hearing that I had ventured down into these old workings at much risk to my life, and I assured them that no one ever had dared go far enough to find the treasure room, they nearly burst with excitement. What to them were walls that fell at a touch? What were a few deadly vipers, a thousand ten-inch scorpions waving their armored tails, or the horrible hosts of *conechos*—those great, leaping spiders that *Americanos* call tarantulas?

True, Señor, you frown impatiently. You will say to me, ah, but everyone knows a tarantula is not deadly poison. Well, perhaps that is true. I once knew a man who was bitten in the lobe of the ear, and lived. But he had a sharp knife. And after all, part of an ear is not so much to sacrifice, when life itself is in hazard.

The *conechos*, Señor, that dwell in the slimy crevices of this old Madre d'Oro Mine below the wettest cellars of Croszchen Pahna, are of a larger variety than those one finds feeding on bananas. Also they are whitish-pink in color, and sightless. They do not need the eyes. They leap surely through the dark at what they wish to bite. . . .

The way down as far as the Room of Craters is not far, as miles are measured up here in the blessed sunshine. Perhaps there was a day when the bearded Spaniards walked safely enough from the broken shaft mouth, down the steep-slanted manways, helped here and there by rough ladders, in no more than one hour.

I know not if the way remains passable now. But if it is no worse than it was the day those two young *Americanos* and I descended to the Room of Craters, it will take three active, daring men more than ten times that space of time.

Roped to each other, we crawled and slid down the terrible passages. I led, and carried in my left hand a long and heavy broom of twigs bound with wire. With this I struck ahead before I placed my foot—or cleared a way of vipers and scorpions before lying down and wriggling feet foremost through narrow, low apertures where time and again my coming was the signal for a fall of wet, rotten rock.

I call to your attention, Señor, that the way to enter such unknown passages always is feet first. Then if there are creatures waiting unseen to strike or leap at one from the side, they are apt to waste their venom on the heavy boots, or on the thighs that are wrapped in many thicknesses of paper, under the heavy trousers.

Also it is easier to withdraw, if a serious slide occurs.

Señor Jim, who followed me, carried a strong lantern. Another, smaller one for my use in the Room of Craters was attached to his belt, near the taut rope. Señor Lester, who came last, bore a miner's pick, for use in breaking through walled-up passages.

Once I was knocked flat and pinned down by a flake of rock like a sheet of slate, which fell before I even touched it; jarred free, no doubt, by the vibrations of our footsteps.

With the pick, however, Señor Jim quickly released me. And while he was working there I heard him strike swiftly once, twice, thrice with the pick, though not on the rock which held me.

Then he cursed, and his voice held a note of wonderment.

"Fastest thing I ever saw!" he muttered; while behind him Señor Lester whimpered aloud. I knew he had viewed some frightful thing, and had failed to kill it with the pick.

That was the first of the sickly-white spiders, the *conechos*. I had warned the two young men, of course; but until one sees those horrible, sightless, hairy monsters, and learns how they can leap and dodge — even a swift bullet, some maintain! — there can be no understanding of the terror they inspire in men.

From then on the *conechos*, which never appear near the surface, became more numerous. It was necessary for us to shout, and to hurl small rocks ahead of us, to drive them into their crevices. Otherwise they might leap at us. And such is the weird soundless telegraphy of such creatures, that if any living thing is bitten by a spider, all the other spiders know it instantly, and come. Whatever the living thing may be, it is buried under an avalanche of horrid albino hunger.

Long before we reached the Room of Craters, Señor Lester — the weak one — was exhausted. He was a shivering wreck from terror, the foul air, and the heat, and was pleading with Señor Jim to go back.

The other one would not have it. He kept mocking the dangers, laughing shortly — and how soon that brave laugh was to be stilled! But Señor Lester got to stumbling; weeping as he staggered or crawled after us. He dropped the pick, and neither of us knew, until we reached a place where the enlargement of an opening had to be done. Then we had to retrace many weary steps to secure the tool.

At last we reached the Room of Craters, where a fire may be built from the old logs that were used by the Indian slaves in pushing the ore mill. There was comparative safety, and we rested, while Señor Jim did all he could to revive the courage of his companion.

I could have told him it was of no use; but in those days I too was young, and did not feel it my place to advise. Señor Lester quieted; but every minute or two his whole thin frame would be racked by a fit of shuddering. I was glad I had made it very plain I would go no farther, but would wait for them here. Señor Jim tried every inducement, but I held firm. The few pesos I had earned outright were enough. I did not care much whether or not they found gold. The one time before I had come this far, I had penetrated a few dozen yards farther, into a narrow passage I deemed might be the one leading to the treasure room. And I knew what that passage contained—white, hairy death!

So I huddled over my fire of punk logs, ate food from the small pack I carried, slept, and waited through the weary hours. I thought hideous things, though none was worse than reality. My knowledge of what happened, you understand, Señor, comes in great part from the ravings of a man to which I was forced to listen.

In the narrow, slide-obstructed passage that led on, those two young ones fought their way. How Señor Jim ever made the other follow as far as he did, is not for me to guess. But struggle on they did; and at length they reached a blank ending of the passage—a place where centuries before, the Spaniards had walled in their treasure, and with it the human slaves who had dug, ground, and carried the ore and gold.

There was one small hole pierced in this wall. *Quien sabe?* Perhaps the prisoners broke through that much. It is likely that the dons would have a swordsman waiting outside as a guard, ready to chop off the groping arms of those dying desperate ones.

But while Señor Lester sank on the rock floor, too spent now to help, Señor Jim set at the wall with the pick. In time, by dint of much sweat, and many pauses in which he used the broom to brush aside the spiders, which were numerous at this low level, he had broken in a hole large enough so that a man could crawl through feet first.

He flashed the lantern into the chamber which opened beyond the wall. *It was the treasure house!*

His yell at sight of the piles of gold, long since burst from their hide sacks and spilled together, aroused Señor Lester, who was able to stagger to his feet and look. They saw, besides the great mountain of gold, white traceries on the floor that might once have been the moldered human bones of the imprisoned slaves. Yes, it was the storehouse of treasure!

Frantically then, forgetting his caution that had brought him and his companion farther than any other white man, Señor Jim wriggled into the hole he had made. He would have got through, too—only there was a slight movement of the rock, just a subsidence of perhaps six inches.

It squeezed him at the waist! It held him horizontal and helpless, two feet from the rock floor!

Señor Lester cried out in weak terror, but Señor Jim did not lose his head.

"You'll have to break me out—quick!" he commanded. "It's slowly squeezing the insides out of me! Quick, the pick! Hit it right up above me—there!" He nodded with his head, both arms being pinioned so that he could not point.

Whimpering, whining, almost unable to lift the pick, the other tried to obey. But that was when the first hairy thing fell or leaped from above. It landed squarely on Señor Jim's upturned face. He screeched with horror—then with pain and realization that this was the end.

Almost before the sound had left his whitening lips, the *others* came, leaping, bounding, from the roof, along the walls, from the floor. The albino horde!

And from Señor Lester fled the last vestige of manhood. Jerking back on the rope that held him to his doomed companion, he sawed at it with his knife.

When it broke he fled, screaming himself to drown the awful, smothering sounds from the end of the passage. . . .

That is not quite all, Señor. I heard the ghastly tale, though not until I had slept safely many hours, there in the Room of Many Craters. The young *Americano* had taken at least seven or eight hours to fight his way back to me. There was no hope for the other.

I brought Señor Lester up into the blessed daylight, though because of his complete collapse we were a whole day and night on the way.

Until his father could come from the United States, I cared for the young man, who could not leave his bed. A part of his mind had gone, it seemed, and he raved about the death of his friend, saying the same things over and over. I was very glad to surrender Señor Lester to his saddened father, who took his boy home where good doctors could care for him.

It was almost a year later when a scarecrow came to my hut. It was Señor Lester, dressed now in rags, but with a sheaf of money with which he tried to bribe me to descend with him again into the old mine!

Valgame Dios! I would not have gone then for a million million dollars, *Americano* gold! The fear was too lately on me. So then he threw back his head, his voice shaking, and said:

"Then I must go alone! I can never rest till I bring up Jim's body! I —I was a coward! I *am* a coward!"

"Well, that is the truth," I admitted, "but there are many cowards. What difference can it make now?"

But he was resolute—in words. In actions, not so resolute. He had made up his mind to go again, this time alone; but days dragged by. He lived in my hut. He jumped each time a gamecock crowed, every time a door was closed. He was a nervous shadow, not even as strong as he had been when I saw him first. He had escaped from a sanatorium up north, and come back here secretly, I discovered. I decided to send a message to his father. When that message did go it was somewhat different from what I intended.

I was a bachelor then, Señor. The little spiders, the *malichos*, spun their webs where they would on the rafters of my hut. I did not care. The mice played around freely at night; for my striped cat was old and fat, sleeping much and doing little.

To keep the young *Americano* from those sudden screeching fits, though, I had to climb up with a broom and wipe away the spider webs. They would build new ones. It did not matter.

"I can't *stand* them!" he would wail, shuddering all over. I thought to myself then there was little danger he ever would go again into the Madre d'Oro Mine. And that was true. He never went again.

That very night as I slept in my blankets on the floor, I was awakened suddenly. Señor Lester had leapt up, screaming as I hope I never hear another man or woman scream! He jumped around. I could not quiet him. I made a light hurriedly, hearing him fall to the floor.

He was stiffening then, head arched back.

"It *bit* me! I killed it!" he shrieked. Then came a final shudder, and he went limp—dead!

Now that was too fast even for the bite of a great pit-viper. I tried to find what had killed him. His two hands had been clenched together, but now in death they relaxed. I drew them apart. I knew the truth, and my heart went faint within me. He had been dreaming of the hairy spiders, when—

Crushed between the palms of his thin, nervous hands, was the dead body of a small mouse!

The Plant-Thing

R. G. Macready

This morning, Dick, I have something special for you," said Norris, city editor of the *Clarion*, as I approached his desk. "Interview with Professor Carter. You've heard of him, of course?"

"Certainly," I replied. "There are some rather weird stories concerning him."

"Exactly. And the latest of these stories is that Carter is conducting wanton vivisection on a prodigious scale. Holder, of the local Society for the Prevention of Cruelty to Animals, went over yesterday to investigate but was turned away at the gate. He laid the matter before me and I promised to try for an interview."

"Who started the vivisection story?"

"Several farmers, according to Holder. During the past four months they've sold Carter more than a hundred and fifty pigs, sheep, and calves. It is well known that the professor is a scientist and not a stock raiser; ergo he dissects the animals. . . . Can you start now?"

En route to the Carter home I stopped at a hardware store and bought a thirty-foot length of rope. I foresaw difficulty in securing admittance to the professor's domain.

While driving, I brought to mind everything I knew about him. Four years ago he had bought the old Wells place, ten miles west of town. No sooner had it passed into his hands than he commenced the construction of a high board wall about the five acres, in the center of which the house was situated. The wall completed, he had moved in with a young lady, apparently his daughter, and eight Malay retainers. From that time on he and his household might have been dead for all the town saw of them. Our tradesmen made frequent trips to the place, but all their business was transacted with a Malay at the gate.

I drove rapidly and soon came in sight of my destination, which stood on a hill a half mile back from the road. Five minutes later I drew up before the gate, and in response to my hail the Malay appeared. He was a nice-looking young chap, dressed irreproachably, and spoke excellent English. I gave him my card and after a perfunctory glance at it he shook his head.

"I am sorry, sir, but it is the master's order that no one be admitted; and if you will pardon my saying so, least of all, representatives of the press."

"But my business is urgent. Serious charges have been laid against him, and it is possible that I may be the medium by which these charges are refuted."

The Malay's ivory teeth flashed in a smile.

"Thank you, sir, but I do not doubt that the master is able to take care of himself. Good day." This last was spoken in a tone of polite finality as he turned on his heel and walked away.

I entered my car and drove back to the highway. However, I was determined to get that interview by crook if not by hook; if I may say it, this policy of mine had made me star reporter of the *Clarion's* staff. So I continued on down the road a few hundred yards and parked the car in the grove, where it was hidden well. I then took the coil of rope and made my way through the grove, which swung in a huge, narrowing semicircle up the hillside to the northwest corner of the Carter grounds. Arrived there under the fifteen-foot wall, I looked cautiously about me. So far as I could see, I was unobserved.

Just within the wall grew a great oak, one of whose major branches extended well outside. Quietly I flung one end of my rope over this limb, fashioned a running noose, and drew the rope tight. Then slowly I wormed up the barrier.

From the top I gazed down upon a glory of wonderful, luxuriant flora. Stately ferns waved gently in the stirring air, beautiful flowering shrubs were interspersed here and there, while everywhere in the emerald grass, still wet with dew, nodded strange, exotic plants. Ever a lover of flowers, I forgot my mission as I looked. There came to my nostrils odors more fragrant and elusive than any I had heretofore known.

Suddenly I crouched low. On noiseless feet there passed beneath me a Malay, who had emerged without warning from a clump of ferns. He paused for a moment to brush an insect from a shrub, then disappeared from view in a thicket of high, green bushes.

Stealthily I slid to the ground and started toward the house, guiding myself by the observations I had made while on the wall. It was very likely, indeed, that the professor would kick me forth the instant he discovered my presence, but at any odds I should have something to tell the readers of the *Clarion*. Too, my audacity might count in my favor.

I had not gone far before I became conscious of an odor utterly different from the others. It was vague, but none the less disquieting. A feeling of loathing and dread pervaded me, a desire to clamber back over the wall and return to the city. The scent came again, much stronger, and I stood irresolute for several minutes, fighting down a sense of faintness as well as the longing to take flight. Then I advanced. In thirty seconds I came to the edge of a small, open space. At what I beheld, I put out a hand to a large fern to steady myself.

In the middle of that tiny clearing grew a thing that, even now, I shudder to describe. In form it was a gigantic tree, unspeakably stunted, fully twelve feet in diameter at the base and twenty-five feet high, tapering to a thickness of two feet at the top, from which depended *things* — I cannot call them leaves — for all the world resembling human ears. The whole was of a dead, drab color.

Dreadful as was the appearance of the thing, it was not that which made me reel as I looked. It was writhing and contorting, twisting itself into all manner of grotesque shapes. And *eyes* were boring into me, freezing the current of my blood.

Something rustled in the grass. I looked down and saw an immense creeper snaking toward me. For the first time I observed that it was joined to the trunk of that frightful thing, and so near the ground that I had not seen it for the tall grass. With a cry of horror I turned to run.

The creeper leapt at me and fastened around my middle with horrible force. I felt something in me give way. Frantically, I struck and tore at the ghastly, sinuous girdle that encircled me, undulating like the tentacle of an octopus. Fruitless, fruitless! I was drawn relentlessly forward.

I screamed. In the trunk of the thing there had appeared a mighty, red-lipped orifice. The tentacle tightened and I was lifted off my feet toward that orifice.

A beautiful girl was bending over me when I opened my eyes. She spoke, in a musical voice: "Please do not move. One of your ribs is broken."

A tall, gray-haired man who had been standing in the background now came to my bedside.

"I am glad that I came in time, my boy. Otherwise . . ."

He was Professor Carter. He presented the girl as his daughter Isobel.

Here one of the dark-skinned servants entered with some articles, which he deposited upon the center table.

"I am going to set your rib," announced the professor. And forthwith he took off his coat and rolled up his sleeves. When the job was finished to his satisfaction, I besought him to telephone to town for a taxicab.

"I shall certainly do no such thing," he said. "I insist that you remain our guest until you are recovered."

Isobel Carter proved a wonderful nurse during the three days that followed. Indeed, the moment I had first looked into her deep black eyes, I knew that I loved her. I should have liked to remain in bed indefinitely with her to care for me, but was ashamed to do so. On the third morning I was moving cautiously about the house, she supporting my steps, although there was no need of it. The professor joined us.

No mention had been made of my weird adventure in the grounds, but at my request he now told me how I had been saved from the hideous creature.

"Your first cry reached my ears as I was walking toward the house and I immediately dashed in its direction. You were about to be swallowed when I arrived. I gave a sharp command, and my travesty released you."

"It obeyed your command?" I exclaimed incredulously.

"Precisely. It acknowledges me as its master. For six months, its period of life so far, I have superintended its growth and ministered to its needs.

"But *what* is it?"

A dreamy look came into Carter's eyes.

"For many years my brother scientists have sought for the so-called 'missing link' between man and ape. For my part, I dare to believe that I have discovered the 'link' between the vegetable and animal kingdoms. The creature out there, however, has, to my mind, not as yet passed the initial stage of its development. Whether it will attain the power of locomotion remains to be seen."

He paused, gazing out of the window, then continued.

"Twenty years ago, in Rhodesia, I chanced upon a carnivorous plant that gave me my clue. Since then I have labored unremittingly, crossing and recrossing my specimens, and you have seen the result. It has cost me three-fourths of my fortune, and countless trips to Asia and Africa."

He indicated a vast pile of manuscript on the table.

"The life history, precedents included, of my travesty. It will form the basis of a work that, I do not doubt, will revolutionize science."

Glancing at the clock, he rose to his feet.

"It is feeding time. Do you care to accompany me?"

I assented, and we went out.

The thing remembered me, for the huge tentacle swept out in my direction, curling impotently in the empty air. I shuddered, and kept my distance.

A Malay appeared leading a calf. It was lowing piteously, for it had sensed danger.

The tentacle thrashed about, endeavoring to clutch the animal, which lunged back, wild with terror. The man wrapped his arms about it and hurled it forward. It was seized. A loud cracking of bones broke the momentary silence, and was followed by an agonized cry. Six feet from the ground the great orifice gaped wide. The calf disappeared. A fleeting second and the mouth closed. There was no sign of its location; the trunk was smooth and unbroken.

A nausea had gripped me during the scene. The professor and the Malay were apparently indifferent. They conversed briefly. Then, linking his arm in mine, Carter led the way back to the house. As we walked thither, I broached the subject of departure. He would not hear of it, insisting that I stay until Saturday.

While in his study I had noticed an elephant gun in a corner. I asked him whether he had done any big-game hunting.

"That gun? Tala had me get it. He asserted that he could foretell tragedy in connection with the creature; that a day would come when I should lose control of it. I scouted the idea, but to humor him purchased the weapon, which stands there loaded in the event need of it arises. Still, it would assuredly break my heart if anything necessitated the slaying of my travesty."

At the door of his study he excused himself and went in. Isobel carried me off to the veranda hammock. As we talked, it was inevitable that the subject of the plant-thing should come up, and a shadow crossed her face as we discussed it.

"Tala says that Father does not know how dangerous it is. He is right. But Father will not listen."

The next morning I again went with Professor Carter to the little clearing.

It was a sheep this time. The poor beast was paralyzed with fright, and stood passive, waiting for death.

The tentacle shot forth, wavered a second, then encircled, not the sheep, but Professor Carter, who seemed stricken by surprise.

He ripped out an order: "Off!"

The tentacle only tightened. Agony settled upon Carter's face. I sprang forward to drag him back. The tentacle released its hold for one lightning flash, then seized us both. We strove in vain against the vise-like cable. The Malay, with a wild cry, turned and rushed down the path, shouting as he ran.

The thing was playing with us as a cat plays with mice it has caught. It could have crushed us effortlessly, but the tentacle tightened by degrees. In spite of all we could do, we felt that we were being dragged forward to where the frightful red mouth yawned. Our eyes bulged, and I could see that Carter's face was taking on a greenish tinge. I extended my free arm and our hands clasped. Then there was the roar of a gun at close quarters and the tentacle gave a spasmodic jerk that flung us twenty feet. We rose, staggering.

Tala stood by, the smoking elephant gun in his hands, staring at the thing. Following his eyes we discerned a large, ragged hole in its trunk, from which a stream of *blood* was flowing and forming a great pool on the ground.

Even as we looked, the travesty went into the death agonies. And as it writhed it emitted a sound that forever haunts me. Presently its struggles ceased. The professor buried his face in his hands.

I had not noticed Isobel's presence. Now I turned and saw her beside me, gazing with horror-filled eyes at the terrible drooping form. I took her away from that tragic spot, for I knew that Professor Carter wished to be alone.

The Power of the Dog

G. G. PENDARVES

Greeting, effendi! I salute you in the name of Allah the Compassionate!"

Benson reined in his horse, as the Arab on the dusty brown camel approached. "You have no news?" he replied.

"None," said Abou Koi. "It is true that an Englishman was at the oasis of Wad Eles; we found him there with many servants—digging foolishly in the sand! But it was not *thy* Englishman."

The manager of the El Adrar mine frowned thoughtfully, staring out across the broad yellow plain. Up to the present, he had ruled his little community of natives and white men with marked success. He was straightforward in his methods, and although he had little sympathy with the subtle, devious ways of the Arabs, he was never unjust. He listened to them, often laughed at them, and gave them more rein than a weaker man would have thought wise.

Now, for the first time in his seven years of experience at El Adrar, he was faced with a problem that he could not solve. It was a month now since his head clerk, Stephen Adams, had vanished so unaccountably. It was a mystery—and above all things, Benson loathed a mystery!

"You are sure you have made no mistake?—you would recognize Adams effendi if you saw him?" Benson's gaze returned to the dark, sun-ravaged face of the old Arab.

"Hath Allah afflicted me with blindness, that I should not know him? What man could mistake his face—with one eye as blue as the lake of Kef-el-dour itself, and the other black as Eblis!"

"No—you could hardly fail to recognize him," admitted Benson. "Let us return to El Adrar now—I must see if the Bougie police have sent in their report yet."

As they approached El Adrar—with its handful of flat-roofed houses, and its native huts clinging like birds' nests to the rocky coast—Benson saw that an unusual crowd was gathered in the tiny market-square, and he rode up to ascertain the cause.

"It is Daouad!" Abou Koi informed him in an awed whisper.

Benson checked an angry exclamation. At every turn he came up against this name! Daouad the Wearer of the Veil, the worker of spells, the man whom Adams had named "dog" in a moment of provocation, and who had now avenged that insult in secret and terrible fashion, so the villagers said.

Always this everlasting Daouad! Benson was sick of the very sound of his name. There was not a shred of evidence to prove that Daouad had anything to do with Adams's disappearance; on the contrary there was indisputable proof that he had *not;* and yet the whispered rumors grew, and grew.

On horseback, Benson could see over the heads of the jostling, excited crowd. In their midst stood the veiled figure of Daouad, from whom the people shrank in awe, leaving a wide ring about him. He held a long whip in his hand, and its wicked lash flicked out continually, like a snake's tongue, to urge on a wretched yellow dog rolling in the dust before him.

The animal was being unmercifully punished by a vicious black-and-white mongrel, and its tawny coat was red with blood. The end was a matter of minutes now, for the black-and-white had a firm grip on the other's throat, and the yellow dog's struggles had almost ceased.

Benson slipped down from his horse, and was about to push his way through the crowd, when he felt a hand on his sleeve. He turned to find Abou Koi at his elbow, speaking low and urgently. "It is an evil thing to come between Daouad and his pleasure! He will do thee some ill!"

Benson was accustomed to the unthinking cruelty of the Arabs, and, up to a point, found it politic not to interfere; but an impulse stronger than himself now urged him to rescue the yellow dog from its fate. He shook off the restraining hand and elbowed the natives aside, and in another minute stood with a revolver smoking in his hand, while the black-and-white mongrel rolled over with a bullet in its brain.

Daouad and the Englishman faced each other over its dead body, while the yellow dog panted for breath.

The Arab laughed scornfully: "The effendi is merciful! May he obtain mercy when his hour comes!" There was a threat in his insolent words, and a murmur of fear ran round the ring of spectators.

Benson was stung to most unwonted fury. "You're making a nuisance of yourself, Daouad! I won't have you here in El Adrar frightening the women and children with your tales of devils and witchcraft! If I were a superstitious man, you would be in prison now for putting your spells on Adams effendi—but I won't flatter you by taking you so seriously. Let me hear no more of this foolishness!"

Without waiting for more, Benson turned on his heel, and beckoned to Abou Koi, who stood back with eyes full of fear.

"Bring the yellow dog to my stables," Benson ordered, and mounting his horse again, he rode through the village to his big white house by the sea.

Half an hour later Abou Koi presented himself before the veranda where Benson lounged with a long drink at his elbow.

"Is the dog in my stables?" asked the latter.

"No, effendi! Daouad the Chief hath taken the animal to his own dwelling."

"What!" ejaculated Benson, his recent anger returning in a hot wave.

"Master, I was afraid," replied the other simply. "Thou, with the magic of a white man, canst withstand Daouad and the devil that dwelleth in him, but with me it is not so."

"Then I must go myself and get the dog," replied Benson, after a long pause.

Abou Koi shrank back, holding his hand before his face, and wailed. "Thou too—thou too wilt vanish as did Adams effendi! Daouad will—"

"I tell you Daouad had nothing whatever to do with Adams effendi!" interrupted Benson impatiently. "That, I have proved. Daouad was up in the hills at Beni Gaza that day. And it was here, in this village, that Adams effendi vanished. He was seen approaching the village by the bridge, and walking along the road where it lies in the shadow of the eucalyptus trees!"

"Yea!" answered Abou Koi. "And beyond those trees doth Daouad dwell!"

"But Daouad was not there that day—and I had the house and gardens searched before he returned from Beni Gaza."

"Daouad *was* there that day," returned Abou Koi solemnly. "What if he was seen at Beni Gaza in that hour! Hath he not power to clothe a devil like to himself—and appear thus where he will?"

"Then I suppose you believe that both Daouad and Adams effendi were in the house when I searched it?"

"Master, I do believe it. They were there, but Daouad caused your eyes to be blind, that you might not see!"

"That is damned nonsense!" said Benson, striding across the veranda.

It was more than a question of rescuing a miserable yellow cur, reflected Benson, as he walked up the village street—where swift blue dusk fell softly, lit by braziers of glowing charcoal and the firefly gleam of the smokers' pipes. Yes—it was a challenge to Daouad! The man had defied him by keeping the dog, and Benson intended to humble this insolent chief in the eyes of the credulous villagers.

As he neared Daouad's dwelling, and was about to enter the belt of dense shadow thrown by the trees across the dusty road, a long-drawn howling rose and fell, with an indescribably mournful cadence. Benson was surprised at the stab of fear he felt, and squared his shoulders impatiently.

"It's infectious—this talk of ghosts and devils," he murmured. "I'll be as foolish as any ignorant beggar in El Adrar soon!"

Again that wailing inhuman sound—and the eucalyptus trees rustled trembling leaves in warning, as it died away.

Then as Benson looked ahead, he tasted fear again, so sharp and poignant that his joints seemed turned to water. A few yards away, on the little bridge beyond the trees, stood the tall veiled figure of Daouad —apparently risen from the ground!

The Englishman rallied all his common sense to his aid. "He's been expecting me, of course," he thought, "and he's going to try a few of his conjuring tricks."

Deliberately he took out a cigarette, and lit it with steady hands.

"Well, Daouad!" he said to the motionless figure. "I've come for that dog."

"The dog is my dog," came the deep answering voice.

"You can dispute that, if you like, before the magistrate next week. You don't know how to treat an animal, and I claim it. If you don't hand it over at once, I'll have you arrested!"

"Thou, too, art afraid then!"

"Not of an Arab dog!"

"Dog! That word again to me!"

The veiled figure approached, and Benson caught the glitter of the dark eyes, between hood and *littrem.*

"Look, white man! Look and see the power of the dog!"

Benson felt a swift wind fan his face, and his eyes smarted as though staring at the midday sun. The aromatic gloom of the eucalyptus trees vanished, and in its place he saw a vast stretch of gray desert, from whose sandy floor heat rose in visible waves, to meet the white glare of the sky above. Across the desert a dark moving mass of horsemen passed with tossing spears. A great army—and at their head, the proudest and most kingly of all that splendid tribe—rode Daouad the Chief!

"The servants of the dog!" A voice sounded faintly in Benson's ear.

The desert darkened swiftly, and under a red moon Benson saw a world of tents and the gleam of campfires—stretching over the sands to far-distant boundaries.

But his horror-stricken gaze was focused on something in the foreground of the picture. Something hardly human, that crawled blind and writhing in the shifting sands, while Daouad spurned it with sandaled foot and urged his slaves to further torture.

As Benson stared spellbound, the chief snatched a flaming brand from a brazier at his side, and beckoned with imperious hand. Powerless to resist, Benson stumbled forward until he was face to face with Daouad's victim. From its twisted, blackened features, two eyes met his

—the eyes of one in hell—but unmistakable to Benson! For one was blue as the Lake of Kef-el-dour and the other black as Eblis!

Daouad laughed insolently as he saw that Benson understood—then, with a fierce gesture, thrust the blazing brand into his victim's face.

Again that fiery wind fanned Benson's face; he saw the desert no longer—but only the little bridge, and the silver trunks of the eucalyptus trees, and the tall veiled figure of Daouad blotting out the moonlight before him.

He drew a deep breath, shaken to the very soul by that sudden opening of the gates of hell, yet he stood his ground stubbornly.

"Try again, Daouad!" he said, steadying his voice by an immense effort of will. "A very neat trick, I admit, but—"

"Yet you feared greatly, white man!" said the chief, pointing to the other's hands. Benson involuntarily glanced down, and saw the palms of them marked deep with the indents of his own fingernails. He bit his lip at the betrayal—but his eyes were steady as he confronted Daouad.

"I admit that you took me by surprise," he answered lightly. "However, as it is only a conjuring trick—"

Daouad smiled evilly. "It was a true vision you beheld. Did he not call me dog?"

"If I believed that," replied Benson, his words stumbling and indistinct, because of a sudden dryness of his mouth, "you should be hanged before dawn breaks, for the dog you are!"

The Arab's eyes blazed, and he lifted one hand in a threatening gesture. Benson drew his revolver and covered him instantly.

"Enough of this fooling!" he snapped. "I want that yellow dog—and at once!"

Daouad came a few paces nearer. "Shoot, white man! Try your magic against mine!" was the insolent reply.

In a white heat of rage, Benson drew the trigger, and—nothing happened.

"By Eblis!" mocked the Arab. "Said I not thou wert afraid? So lost in fear and wonder of my magic, that I have drawn thy sting without thy knowledge."

Benson could not repress a gasp. It was true—the devil had indeed removed his cartridges, while he himself had stood, fuddled and afraid, like any ignorant native.

"Your trick!" he said quietly, his strong face set in its grimmest lines, "You are a clever rogue—too clever altogether for El Adrar! And now that you have done your little turn, and satisfied yourself that you can impose on a white man—we may consider the show is ended."

"For you—yes! The show is ended!"

Benson controlled a shiver. There was a sinister ring he did not like in Daouad's slow words.

"You shall learn the power of the dog," went on the Arab. "You shall learn—as did that other one!"

With a sudden movement Benson flung himself forward on that tall veiled figure—but he clutched the empty air and fell, choking and gasping, his eyes and mouth full of hot sand. Utterly bewildered, he got to his knees, to find himself once more under that low-hung moon in the wilderness, among the tents and campfires of Daouad the Chief.

And then naked terror seized him. For again Daouad stood before the great brazier—his torturers in a ring about him—and within that circle of evil grinning faces he himself was hemmed.

"Deliver my soul from the power of the dog!" The words beat like a tattoo in Benson's brain. He knew now, too late to save himself, that such power was real—a blasting, devastating power that could destroy him, body and soul.

The chief pointed to him, and Benson strove desperately that he might not grovel before his enemy.

A pock-marked Arab tore the Englishman's coat from his back with slavering eagerness, and cruel fingers were at the collar of his shirt, when a swift, lean shape darted across the ring, and sprang at Daouad's throat.

"The yellow dog!" burst from Benson's dry lips, as he heard a choking, terrible cry, and the vast floor of the desert seemed to rise up around him. . . . Then he saw clearly again he was under the eucalyptus trees once more, his coat flung on the ground beside him, his shirt torn open at the throat; and before him, on the bridge, in the white moonlight, Daouad strove to fling off that savage, tawny shape hanging at his throat!

Inch by inch the Arab staggered back until he reeled against the light handrail of the bridge. It bent and broke with a report that rang out like a pistol shot, and man and dog fell into the deep water below.

Benson dragged himself forward and peered down. He saw the two locked together, sink and rise, and sink again. Then, after a long interval, both rose once more to the surface, and began to float slowly down the stream.

He watched and saw how they drifted apart at last—Daouad was carried on in midstream, while the dog was drawn into the shallows and lay washing gently to and fro among the long reeds by the bank.

A quick impulse stirred Benson. He must at least give the animal a decent burial—not leave it like a drowned rat there in the water! Had it not been for the yellow dog—! He shivered, and ran quickly down to the river's brink and drew the dog to land. The dead body was wet and heavy, and Benson staggered as he carried it up to the road.

He put out a hand to shut its eyes—those staring glassy eyes! But he did not shut them—his hand fell to his side, and violent, nauseating horror, too great for brain and body to bear, overwhelmed him; and he pitched forward on his face in the road.

One eye of the yellow dog was blue as the lake of Kef-el-dour, the other black as Eblis.

A Problem of the Dark

FRANCES ARTHUR

The Dennison home is a quiet, roomy place, neither new nor old. It has wide, kindly spaces; the walls smile at you.

The house has many closets, but not a skeleton in any of them—and as for ghosts, no one has ever died there.

There is no luxury, and equally, no mystery—not at all the place to tempt a night-marauding visitor, from this or any other world; and Mollie Dennison, its gentle mistress, finds it strange that her husband should be so insistent, of late, about having every door and window on the first floor tightly locked every night. Only last summer, many of them were commonly left open, and even when he forgot to hook the screens, he laughed at her for remonstrating.

What caused this change in him, she is never to know; so John Dennison has vowed to himself, to his son Robert, and to his friend Dr. Hedges.

"A woman couldn't know a thing like that!" he has told them.

At breakfast, on that day, late in the previous summer, which he is never to forget, he had asked Mollie casually, "Robert up yet?"

"Yes—or he was; he's lying on the couch in the library and he wants to see you before you go; he said wouldn't you please come in?"

"Nonsense! Why doesn't he come to the table?"

"John, dear, the boy's sick, and you're so hard with him! You wouldn't listen yesterday—"

"Dreams again, eh?"

"Yes, but he's very hoarse, too. I'm worried."

Dennison left the breakfast table impatiently.

The summer was passing, and the boy, who had come home from college in June with shadowed eyes and a puzzled frown between them, seemed more preoccupied, more listless, every day.

He was thinner, too; not in any way like the big, rollicking chap who had left them last September. He had visited a friend over the Christmas holidays, and both parents had anxiously noted the change in him, after nine months of absence.

"Keep having nightmares—guess I'm bilious!" was the only explanation they had been able to win from him; it had not seemed a sufficient one. Dennison resented the boy's lack of interest in the business (an automobile agency), and gave him hard work to do, tersely remarking that he'd sleep better for it. The tasks were well but wearily performed, and nothing gained besides.

"Morning, sir," he said as Dennison entered. He swung his slippered feet to the floor and sat up dizzily, supporting himself with a hand at each side upon the couch.

He was "his mother's boy," tall and fair; for Dennison was shorter, darker, more muscular.

"If you won't help me, Dad, I'll have to get somebody else."

"What's the matter, anyway?"

"I tried to tell you yesterday. Listen, Dad! This thing's killing me! Look here!" He showed a swollen and discolored throat; his eyes were bloodshot, and he was hoarse, as his mother had said.

"Hurt yourself?"

"It's that thing I dream about, I tell you—if it *is* dreaming. He—or It—"

"You do it yourself, in your sleep—but that's bad enough; need more exercise."

"I exercise until I can hardly crawl to bed. No trouble about going to sleep; it's all I can do—but afterward—"

"Well, what can I do about it?"

"Dad"—the boy's pale face flushed—"you'll say it's babyish, because you don't know—you don't know! I—want you to stay with me to-night!"

"Babyish enough! Ever leave the light on?"

"Yes. He came just the same! I couldn't see him, but—"

"Aha! And yet you're still afraid of him?"

"It was worse than ever. I can't move, you see, or fight, or even breathe; but I get wide awake, and then he goes away, but I don't sleep any more."

"Just a regular nightmare, Rob."

"Maybe. But oh, God! How I'd like to have one night of peace—one night when Bull Bayman—"

"Bull Bayman! So that's who it is, you think?"

"I don't know; it seems like him, somehow; only of course Bull didn't have—scales all over him."

"Scales!" There was an underlying note of panic in the man's exasperation. Was it more than dreams, then? Was it insanity?

"Honest, Dad. And claws."

His father observed in a tolerably controlled tone, "Bull Bayman was the quarterback who choked you because he thought you gave away the signals to the other team?"

"Did he choke me?" the lad returned vaguely.

"Don't you remember it? He knocked you down first. Kent Taylor told me about it; said they threw water on you to bring you out of it."

"I know we had a mix-up; I didn't play any more, of course, but in the very next scrimmage Bull got that welt on the head that sent him— where he is now."

"And you think he comes back every night to choke you?"

"I'd forgotten he choked me," mused the boy.

"But he comes back in a dream, Rob! Don't you see now that it's all a dream?"

"And don't you see that I'll lose my mind if this thing doesn't let up? And will you stay with me tonight, anyway until midnight, or—say—1 o'clock?"

John Dennison rose sharply.

"I will—to keep you from calling on somebody else. Nice thing to get around—ghosts!"

"Dad! You promise?"

"I said I would, didn't I?"

"Oh, God!" sobbed the boy hoarsely, as a flood of relief rolled over his parched nerves. "Oh, God!"

He flung himself face down on the leather couch, and his slender body shook in hysteria. His father looked down at him sadly.

"I didn't know it was so bad, Robby," he gruffly admitted.

"Don't tell him, but I'm going to see Hedges about him," he told his wife in the front hall, as he was leaving the house. "It's nerves. Let him sleep it off, if he can."

She had tried to believe, as John did, that the dreams would "wear off," but she was glad and relieved to know that their good friend Dr. Hedges, whose studies of late had taken a psychopathic turn, was to be asked to help her boy.

"It isn't as if Rob ever drank a drop, or smoked too much," John told this friend, at the latter's office, "and he was never afraid of the fellow; had forgotten, even, that he choked him!"

"Bull hadn't forgotten, though," muttered Hedges.

"Bull's dead."

"His body is. But what was he living for, just as he got that blow on the head that finished him? To be revenged on Rob, because he thought he had queered the game. Now, if the mass of molecules, or atoms, or even electrons, that must be released at death (for something is released, John), could retain an impression, a purpose—can't you find it possible to suppose that it could animate another body—even an elemental one?"

"But—even supposing that, Rob had the light on one night, and—he says he felt him, but couldn't see him!"

"It is by no means probable that all the elemental forms are visible to us. You've seen those beautiful little sea creatures, John, that are exactly like glass, yet have life and motion; and even that familiar thing, the eel, is transparent at one stage. You could imagine a being so perfectly transparent as to be invisible, yet alive. Now, supposing that the freed human particles enter into and animate an elemental, transparent body—"

"Where would they find such a thing? Why don't we ever hear of them?"

"Perhaps, being invisible, it is easy for them to keep out of our way. There are hundreds of religious beliefs—but we won't go into that. John, something living made those marks on that boy's neck. It's up to us to find out what it is."

"If—if there is anything, why hasn't it—or he—killed him?"

"That's the Bull Bayman part of it! He repeats the choking incident; possibly he has memory without intelligence.

"I think, John," he added after a pause, "that I'll show you something."

He unlocked a small safe, and paused again before he beckoned Dennison to his side. He had taken from the safe an envelope, the seal of which he now broke.

"These are photographs—of 'dreams,' " he said in a low tone; "I made them myself." He exposed them slowly, placing one behind another.

John staggered to a seat, nauseated, horror-stricken.

"I don't believe it!" he cried out suddenly.

"You wouldn't. But, John, if you want me to help Rob, you will have to do as I say. Your belief has nothing whatever to do with the case, you see. Now, first, I want the house quiet by 11; you're to sleep with Rob; Mollie's to sneak me into a room near him, without his knowing I'm there; then I want her to go and stay with her sister; I'd rather not have her in the house at all."

"No!" shuddered John, with an involuntary glance at the safe—a sarcophagus of nightmares.

"No lights, remember, and the doors unlocked. Now, I'll stop at your office and arrange about the films. Yes, as you say, if there's anything to make a film of. A corner of your basement will do for that; and I'll give you all the final instructions. Good-bye, John."

The daily routine calmed Dennison, though he felt rather old, rather lacking in the cocksureness of his own judgment. Had it made him cruel to the boy?

"You don't know—you don't know!" Robert had said.

"You wouldn't," Frank Hedges had told him, when he had given his friend the lie. Well, tonight—if he must—

At 11 o'clock, all had been arranged according to Dr. Hedges's instructions, and he himself waited in the room across the hall. Robert, who had worked that day with something like his old boyish enthusiasm, now lay sound asleep beside his father. The lights were out, but there was a switch near Dennison's left hand.

The streets grew more quiet; fewer vehicles passed.

Midnight tolled.

An even deeper quiet settled upon the house.

The quarter struck. Robert was still breathing deeply, softly, like a child. His father tried to believe that he was not listening for any other sound.

Two strokes announced the half-hour. His attention was gradually relaxing. There would be nothing tonight. Rob had felt so safe, to have him near; just as he himself had felt, to have Frank near.

Nonsense! He had always felt safe enough.

Those films—someone had fooled Frank, that was all.

And yet—he remembered the doctor's habit of accuracy; his extreme nicety of perception. Tomorrow he would ask him—but now he became aware that Robert was gradually drawing away from him. He still lay relaxed, not a muscle tense, and breathing easily, yet he was moving, or being moved, slowly away. Then, with a deep sigh, he rolled over on his back.

Nothing, after all, but an involuntary change of position.

But his breathing was getting shorter, thicker—he began to strangle, to moan—his whole body labored.

"Nightmare!" thought Dennison, and had almost reached out his hand to rouse the boy, when he remembered Hedges' command, "If he chokes I shall hear him. Don't move! Don't call!"

But suppose Frank had fallen asleep?

It was growing more terrible every second!

Dennison's head and hands were wet with the effort of holding still, when the sounds ceased—Robert lay as if dead.

His father could bear no more; he threw out his hands—they encountered the thick, rough, scaly neck of something bending over the bed. This he clutched desperately, shouting, "Frank! Help! Help!" For horrible claws snatched at his face, yet he dared not loose his hold.

"I'm—right here!" grated the doctor's voice, through set teeth, and Dennison knew that he, too, was struggling with the intruder; that they had attacked it simultaneously.

Was it to elude them both after all? It was a fearful antagonist, because of its strength, its sinuous, twisting motions, the repeated attacks on their hands and faces from its hideous claws—it was like some struggle of brute forces in the primordial darkness.

"There!" panted the doctor at last, "I've—got him—handcuffed! The light, John!

"Lie still, Bull Bayman, or I'll break your elbows!" he thundered; and then John turned the switch.

Staring half-dazed in the sudden light, he beheld his friend with one knee apparently poised in the air above the bed; his face swollen and set with the effort of holding something down; something that neither of them could see!

Rob's words raced through his mind, even while he again hurled himself forward to the doctor's assistance: "He came just the same—I couldn't see him—"

And he had jeered!

"Hold his shoulders down, while I hold his legs," directed Dr. Hedges.

"Listen, you! Are you Bull Bayman?"

There was not an instant's cessation in the thing's efforts to free itself.

"Listen, Bull Bayman! You're wrong about Robert Dennison—he never gave the other team your signals!"

There was no sign of understanding; only the continued struggle. They could feel and hear the harsh rattle of its breath, the heavily beating heart. As they held him, or it, firmly, but without too great a pressure, they felt the heartbeat becoming slower, the breath fluttering strangely.

The paroxysms grew weaker, then ceased. The shape lay inert.

"I don't believe he understands you," murmured Dennison.

"Yet he may be able to both hear and see us! As for his understanding—he is trying to leave this hulk even now! . . . In other words, he's dying!"

"I gave him a shot of cyanide solution before you ever called," he added, "as soon as I felt those damned scales. I knew then he wasn't human."

"Cyanide!"

"Enough to kill a horse; or an alligator. Well—he's dead."

"Frank, for God's sake, look after Rob, won't you?"

"Rob's all right; didn't even wake up, though we had this fellow right across his knees all the time. Let him sleep it off."

Only a few hours ago Dennison had used those words himself; it seemed to him that he had forged through strange worlds since then. Dr. Hedges' nonchalance as he rolled "the fellow" to the floor and reached to the table for his first-aid kit roused a sort of dull resentment in Dennison's mind.

"We'll bind up our wounds," said Dr. Hedges, "and then—say, John, this long scratch came mighty near the jugular!"

"It felt like it," muttered John.

"I've got one that just missed my left eye. We'll have a beautiful photo of our unseen friend in a few days, though."

"Good heavens, Frank!" exploded Dennison, "what do you want of a photo?"

"Want to see how it looks, of course!"

"Well, I don't! Feeling it was bad enough; let's chop it up and burn it in the furnace—it's a cool night."

"See here, John! These things belong to the hidden side of nature—but they exist, as I've told you, and they're very dangerous!"

"Well, you've killed it."

"Yes, and I'm going to study it. There must be some clue to its identity. They're rare, I grant you, but suppose they should increase on the earth?"

"Horrible!"

"Is the paint ready to smear on? And the stuff for the flashlight?"

"It's all in the back basement."

"Let's snake him down, then."

The doctor's safe holds another dream-photo now; Dennison refuses to look at it, and Robert does not know of its existence, though the rest of the story has been told him in detail. He was informed that the body was burned in the furnace, which was true. The photo shows a man's body, with the legs and scales of some great reptile or lizard, and with the face protected by ridges of bone. It is a truly horrific object, yet Dr. Hedges declares that it shows a decided resemblance to Bull Bayman.

Professor Jonkin's Cannibal Plant

HOWARD R. GARIS

After Professor Jeptha Jonkin had, by skillful grafting and care, succeeded in raising a single tree that produced, at different seasons, apples, oranges, pineapples, figs, coconuts, and peaches, it might have been supposed he would rest from his scientific labors. But Professor Jonkin was not that kind of a man.

He was continually striving to grow something new in the plant world. So it was no surprise to Bradley Adams, when calling on his friend the professor one afternoon, to find that scientist busy in his large conservatory.

"What are you up to now?" asked Adams. "Trying to make a rosebush produce violets, or a honeysuckle vine bring forth pumpkins?"

"Neither," replied Professor Jonkin a little stiffly, for he resented Adams' playful tone. "Not that either of those things would be difficult. But look at that."

He pointed to a small plant with bright, glossy green leaves mottled with red spots. The thing was growing in a large earthen pot.

395

It bore three flowers, about the size of morning glories, and not unlike that blossom in shape, save, near the top, there was a sort of lid, similar to the flap observed on a jack-in-the-pulpit plant.

"Look down one of those flowers," went on the professor, and Adams, wondering what was to come, did so.

He saw within a small tube, lined with fine, hairlike filaments, which seemed to be in motion. And the shaft or tube went down to the bottom of the morning-glory-shaped part of the flower. At the lower extremity was a little clear liquid.

"Kind of a queer blossom. What is it?" asked Adams.

"That," said the professor with a note of pride in his voice, "is a specimen of the *Sarracenia nepenthis*."

"What's that? French for sunflower, or Latin for sweet pea?" asked Adams irreverently.

"It is Latin for pitcher plant," responded the professor, drawing himself up to his full height of five-feet-three. "One of the most interesting of the South American flora."

"The name fits it pretty well," observed Adams. "I see there's water at the bottom. I suppose this isn't the pitcher that went to the well too often."

"The *Sarracenia nepenthis* is a most wonderful plant," went on the professor in his lecture voice, not heeding Adams's joking remarks. "It belongs to what Darwin calls the carnivorous family of flowers, and other varieties of the same species are the *Dionaea muscipula*, or Venus Flytrap, the *Darlingtonia*, the *Pinguicula*, and *Aldrovandra*, as well as—"

"Hold on, professor," pleaded Adams. "I'll take the rest on faith. Tell me about this pitcher plant, sounds interesting."

"It *is* interesting," said Professor Jonkin. "It eats insects."

"Eats insects?"

"Certainly. Watch."

The professor opened a small wire cage lying on a shelf and took from it several flies. These he liberated close to the queer plant.

The insects buzzed about a few seconds, dazed with their sudden liberty.

Then they began slowly to circle in the vicinity of the strange flowers. Nearer and nearer the blossoms they came, attracted by some subtle perfume, as well as by a sweet syrup that was on the edge of the petals, put there by nature for the very purpose of drawing hapless insects into the trap.

The flies settled down, some on the petals of all three blooms. Then a curious thing happened.

The little hairlike filaments in the tube within the petals suddenly reached out and wound themselves about the insects feeding on the sweet stuff, which seemed to intoxicate them. In an instant the flies were pulled to the top of the flower shaft by a contraction of the hairs, and then they went tumbling down the tube into the miniature pond below, where they were drowned after a brief struggle. Their crawling back was prevented by spines growing with points down, as the wires in some rat traps are fastened.

Meanwhile the cover of the plant closed down.

"Why, it's a regular flytrap, isn't it?" remarked Adams, much surprised.

"It is," replied the professor. "The plant lives off the insects it captures. It absorbs them, digests them, and, when it is hungry again, catches more."

"Where'd you get such an uncanny thing?" asked Adams, moving away from the plant as if he feared it might take a sample bite out of him.

"A friend sent it to me from Brazil."

"But you're not going to keep it, I hope."

"I certainly am," rejoined Professor Jonkin.

"Maybe you're going to train it to come to the table and eat like a human being," suggested Adams, with a laugh that nettled the professor.

"I wouldn't have to train it much to induce it to be polite," snapped back the owner of the pitcher plant.

And then, seeing that his jokes were not relished, Adams assumed an interest he did not feel, and listened to a long dissertation on botany in general and carnivorous plants in particular.

He would much rather have been eating some of the queer hybrid fruits the professor raised. He pleaded an engagement when he saw an opening in the talk, and went away.

It was some months after that before he saw the professor again. The botanist was busy in his conservatory in the meantime, and the gardener he hired to do rough work noticed that his master spent much time in that part of the glass house where the pitcher plant was growing.

For Professor Jonkin had become so much interested in his latest acquisition that he seemed to think of nothing else. His plan for increasing strawberries to the size of peaches was abandoned for a time, as was his pet scheme of raising apples without any core.

The gardener wondered what there was about the South American blossoms to require such close attention.

One day he thought he would find out, and he started to enter that part of the conservatory where the pitcher plant was growing. Professor Jonkin halted him before he had stepped inside and sternly bade him never to appear there again.

As the gardener, crestfallen, moved away after a glimpse into the forbidden region he muttered:

"My, that plant has certainly grown! And I wonder what the professor was doing so close to it. Looked as if he was feeding the thing."

As the days went by the conduct of Professor Jonkin became more and more curious. He scarcely left the southern end of the conservatory, save at night, when he entered his house to sleep.

He was a bachelor, and had no family cares to trouble him, so he could spend all his time among his plants. But hitherto he had divided his attention among his many experiments in the floral kingdom.

Now he was always with his mysterious pitcher plant. He even had his meals sent into the greenhouse.

"Be you keepin' boarders?" asked the butcher boy of the gardener one day, passing on his return to the store, his empty basket on his arm.

"No. Why?"

"The professor is orderin' so much meat lately. I thought you had company."

"No, there's only us two. Mr. Adams used to come to dinner once in a while, but not lately."

"Then you an' the professor must have big appetites."

"What makes you think so?"

"The number of beefsteaks you eat."

"Number of beefsteaks? Why, my lad, the professor and I are both vegetarians."

"What's them?"

"We neither of us eat a bit of meat. We don't believe it's healthy."

"Then what becomes of the three big porterhouse steaks I deliver to the professor in the greenhouse every day?"

"Porterhouse steaks?" questioned the gardener, amazed.

"Do you feed 'em to the dog?"

"We don't keep a dog."

But the butcher boy questioned no further, for he saw a chum and hastened off to join him.

"Three porterhouse steaks a day!" mused the gardener, shaking his head. "I do hope the professor has not ceased to be a vegetarian. Yet it looks mighty suspicious. And he's doing it on the sly, too, for there's been no meat cooked in the house, of that I'm sure."

And the gardener, sorely puzzled over the mystery, went off, shaking his head more solemnly than before.

He resolved to have a look in the place the professor guarded so carefully. He tried the door when he was sure his master was in another part of the conservatory, but it was locked, and no key the gardener had would unfasten it.

A month after the gardener had heard of the porterhouse steaks, Adams happened to drop in to see the professor again.

"He's in with the *Sarracenia nepenthis*," said the gardener in answer to the visitor's inquiry. "But I doubt if he will let you enter."

"Why won't he?"

"Because he's become mighty close-mouthed of late over that pitcher plant."

"Oh, I guess he'll see me," remarked Adams confidently, and he knocked on the door that shut off the locked section of the greenhouse from the main portion.

"Who's there?" called the professor.

"Adams."

"Oh," in a more conciliatory tone. "I was just wishing you'd come along. I have something to show you."

Professor Jonkin opened the door, and the sight that met Adams' gaze startled him.

The only plant in that part of the conservatory was a single specimen of the *Sarracenia nepenthis*. Yet it had attained such enormous proportions that at first Adams thought he must be dreaming.

"What do you think of that for an achievement in science?" asked the professor proudly.

"Do you mean to say that is the small, fly-catching plant your friend sent you from Brazil?"

"The same."

"But—but—"

"But how it's grown, that's what you want to say, isn't it?"

"It is. How did you do it?"

"By dieting the blossoms."

"You mean—?"

"I mean feeding them. Listen. I reasoned that if a small blossom of the plant would thrive on a few insects, by giving it larger meals I might get a bigger plant. So I made my plans.

"First I cut off all but one blossom, so that the strength of the plant would nourish that alone. Then I made out a bill of fare. I began feeding it on chopped beef. The plant took to it like a puppy. It seemed to beg

399

for more. From chopped meat I went to small pieces, cut up. I could fairly see the blossom increase in size. From that I went to choice mutton chops, and, after a week of them, with the plant becoming more gigantic all the while, I increased its meals to a porterhouse steak a day. And now—"

The professor paused to contemplate his botanical work.

"Well, now?" questioned Adams.

"Now," went on the professor proudly, "my pitcher plant takes three big beefsteaks every day—one for breakfast, one for dinner, and one for supper. And see the result."

Adams gazed at the immense plant. From a growth about as big as an Easter lily it had increased until the top was near the roof of the greenhouse, twenty-five feet above.

About fifteen feet up, or ten feet from the top, there branched out a great flower, about eight feet long and three feet across the bell-shaped mouth, which except for the cap or cover, was not unlike the opening of an immense morning glory.

The flower was heavy, and the stalk on which it grew was not strong enough to support it upright. So a rude scaffolding had been constructed of wood and boards, and on a frame the flower was held upright.

In order to see it to better advantage, and also that he might feed it, the professor had a ladder by which he could ascend to a small platform in front of the bell-shaped mouth of the blossom.

"It is time to give my pet its meal," he announced, as if he were speaking of some favorite horse. "Want to come up and watch it eat?"

"No, thank you," responded Adams. "It's too uncanny."

The professor took a large steak, one of the three the butcher boy had left that day. Holding it in his hand, he climbed up the ladder and was soon on the platform in front of the plant.

Adams watched him curiously. The professor leaned over to toss the steak into the yawning mouth of the flower.

Suddenly Adams saw him totter, throw his arms wildly in the air, and then, as if drawn by some overpowering force, he fell forward, lost his balance, and toppled into the maw of the pitcher plant!

There was a jar to the stalk and blossom as the professor fell within. He went head first into the tube, or eating apparatus of the strange plant, his legs sticking out for an instant, kicking wildly. Then he disappeared entirely.

Adams didn't know whether to laugh or be alarmed.

He mounted the ladder, and stood in amazement before the result of the professor's work as he looked down into the depth of the gigantic flower, increased a hundred times in size.

He was aware of a strange, sickish-sweet odor that seemed to steal over his senses. It was lulling him to sleep, and he fought against it. Then he looked down and saw that the huge hairs or filaments with which the tube was lined were in violent motion.

He could just discern the professor's feet about three feet below the rim of the flower. They were kicking, but with a force growing less every second. The filaments seemed to be winding about the professor's legs, holding him in a deadly embrace.

Then the top cover, or flap of the plant, closed down suddenly. The professor was a prisoner inside.

The plant had turned cannibal and eaten the man who had grown it!

For an instant, fear deprived Adams of reason. He did not know what to do. Then the awful plight of his friend brought back his senses.

"Professor!" he shouted. "Are you alive? Can you hear me?"

"Yes," came back in faint and muffled tones. "This beast has me, all right."

Then followed a series of violent struggles that shook the plant.

"I'll get you out. Where's an ax? I'll chop the cursed plant to pieces!" cried Adams.

"Don't! Don't" came in almost pleading tones from the imprisoned professor.

"Don't what?"

"Don't hurt my pet!"

"Your pet!" snorted Adams angrily. "Nice kind of a pet you have! One that tries to eat you alive! But I've got to do something if I want to save you. Where's the ax?"

"No! No!" begged the professor, his voice becoming more and more muffled. "Use chloroform."

"Use what?"

"Chloroform! You'll find some in the closet."

Then Adams saw what the professor's idea was. The plant could be made insensible, and the imprisoned man released with no harm to the blossom.

He raced down the ladder, ran to a closet where he had seen the professor's stock of drugs and chemicals stowed away on the occasion of former visits, and grabbed a big bottle of chloroform. He caught up a towel and ran back up the ladder.

Not a sign of the professor could be seen. The plant had swallowed him up, but by the motion and swaying of the flower Adams knew his friend was yet alive.

He was in some doubt as to the success of this method, and would rather have taken an ax and chopped a hole in the side of the blossom, thus releasing the captive. But he decided to obey the professor.

Saturating the towel well with the chloroform, and holding his nose away from it, he pressed the wet cloth over the top of the blossom where the lid touched the edge of the bloom.

There was a slight opening at one point, and Adams poured some of the chloroform down this. He feared lest the fumes of the anesthetic might overpower the professor also, but he knew they would soon pass away if this happened.

For several minutes he waited anxiously. Would the plan succeed? Would the plant be overcome before it had killed the professor inside?

Adams was in a fever of terror. Again and again he saturated the towel with the powerful drug. Then he had the satisfaction of seeing the lid of the pitcher plant relax.

It slowly lifted and fell over to one side, making a good-sized opening. The strong filaments, not unlike the arms of a devil fish, Adams thought, were no longer in uneasy motion. They had released their grip on the professor's legs and body.

The spines that had pointed downward, holding the plant's prey, now became limber.

Adams leaned over. He reached down, grasped the professor by the feet, and, being a strong man, while his friend was small and light, he pulled him from the tube of the flower, a little dazed from the fumes of the chloroform the plant had breathed in, but otherwise not much the worse for his adventure.

He had not reached the water at the bottom of the tube, which fact saved him from drowning.

"Well, you certainly had a narrow squeak," observed Adams as he helped the professor down the ladder.

"I did," admitted the botanist. "If you had not been on hand I don't know what would have happened. I suppose I would have been eaten alive."

"Unless you could have cut yourself out of the side of the flower with your knife," observed Adams.

"What! And killed the plant I raised with such pains?" ejaculated the professor. "Spoil the largest *Sarracenia nepenthis* in the world? I guess not. I would rather have let it eat me."

"I think you ought to call it the cannibal plant instead of the pitcher plant," suggested Adams.

"Oh, no," responded the professor dreamily, examining the flower from a distance to see if any harm had come to it. "But to punish it, I will not give it any supper or breakfast. That's what it gets for being naughty," he added as if the plant were a child.

"And I suggest that when you feed it hereafter," said Adams, "you pass the beefsteaks in on a pitch-fork. You won't run so much danger then."

"That's a good idea. I'll do it," answered the professor heartily.

And he has followed that plan ever since.

THE QUARE GANDER

J. SHERIDAN LE FANU

As I rode at a slow walk, one soft autumn evening, from the once noted and noticeable town of Emly, now a squalid village, toward the no less remarkable town of Tipperary, I fell into a meditative mood.

My eye wandered over a glorious landscape; a broad sea of cornfields, that might have gladdened even a golden age, was waving before me; groups of little cabins, with their poplars, osiers, and light mountain ashes clustered sheltering around them, were scattered over the plain; the thin blue smoke arose floating through their boughs in the still evening air. And far away with all their broad lights and shades, softened with the haze of approaching twilight, stood the bold wild Galties.

As I gazed on this scene, whose richness was deepened by the melancholy glow of the setting sun, the tears rose to my eyes, and I said:

"Alas, my country! what a mournful beauty is thine. Dressed in loveliness and laughter, there is mortal decay at thy heart: sorrow, sin, and shame have mingled thy cup of misery. Strange rulers have bruised thee, and laughed thee to scorn, and they have made all thy sweetness bitter. Thy shames and sins are the austere fruits of thy miseries, and thy miseries have been poured out upon thee by foreign hands. Alas, my stricken country! clothed with this most pity-moving smile, with this most unutterably mournful loveliness, thou sore-grieved, thou desperately beloved! Is there for thee, my country, a resurrection?''

I know not how long I might have continued to rhapsodize in this strain, had not my wandering thoughts been suddenly recalled to my own immediate neighborhood by the monotonous clatter of a horse's hoofs upon the road, evidently moving at that peculiar pace that is neither a walk nor a trot, and yet partakes of both, so much in vogue among the southern farmers.

In a moment my pursuer was up with me, and checking his steed into a walk he saluted me with much respect. The cavalier was a light-built fellow, with good-humored sunburnt features, a shrewd and lively black eye, and a head covered with a crop of close curly black hair, and surmounted with a turf-colored caubeen, in the pack-thread band of which was stuck a short pipe, which had evidently seen much service.

My companion was a dealer in all kinds of local lore, and soon took occasion to let me see that he was so.

After two or three short stories, in which the scandalous and supernatural were happily blended, we happened to arrive at a narrow road or bohreen leading to a snug-looking farmhouse.

"That's a comfortable bit iv a farm," observed my comrade, pointing toward the dwelling with his thumb; "a shnug spot, and belongs to the Mooneys this long time. 'Tis a noted place for what happened wid the famous gandher there in former times."

"And what was that?" inquired I.

"What was it happened wid the gandher!" ejaculated my companion in a tone of indignant surprise; "the gandher iv Ballymacrucker, the gandher! Your raverance must be a stranger in these parts. Sure every fool knows all about the gandher, and Terence Mooney, that was, rest his sowl. Begorra, 'tis surprisin' to me how in the world you didn't hear iv the gandher; and may be it's funnin' me ye are, your raverance."

I assured him to the contrary, and conjured him to narrate to me the facts, an unacquaintance with which was sufficient it appeared to stamp me as an ignoramus of the first magnitude.

It did not require much entreaty to induce my communicative friend to relate the circumstance, in nearly the following words:

"Terence Mooney was an honest boy and well to do; an' he rinted the biggest farm on this side iv the Galties; an' bein' mighty cute an' a sevare worker, it was small wonder he turned a good penny every harvest. But unluckily he was blessed with an ilegant large family iv daughters, an' iv coorse his heart was allamost bruck, striving to make up fortunes for the whole of them. An' there wasn't a conthrivance iv any soart or description for makin' money out iv the farm, but he was up to.

"Well, among the other ways he had iv gettin' up in the world, he always kep a power iv turkeys, and all soarts iv poultrey; an' he was out iv all rason partial to geese—an' small blame to him for that same—for twice't a year you can pluck them as bare as my hand—an' get a fine price for the feathers, an' plenty of rale sizable eggs—an' when they are too ould to lay any more, you can kill them, an' sell them to the gintlemen for goslings, d'ye see, let alone that a goose is the most manly bird that is out.

"Well, it happened in the coorse iv time that one ould gandher tuck a wondherful likin' to Terence, an' divil a place he could go serenadin' about the farm, or lookin' afther the men, but the gandher id be at his heels, an' rubbin' himself agin his legs, an' lookin' up in his face jist like any other Christian id do; an' begorra, the likes iv it was never seen— Terence Mooney an' the gandher wor so great.

"An' at last the bird was so engagin' that Terence would not allow it to be plucked any more, an' kep' it from that time out for love an' affection—jist all as one like one iv his childer.

"But happiness in perfection never lasts long, an' the neighbors begin'd to suspect the nathur an' intentions iv the gandher, an' some iv them said it was the divil, an' more iv them that it was a fairy.

"Well, Terence could not but hear something of what was sayin', an' you may be sure he was not altogether asy in his mind about it, an' from one day to another he was gettin' more ancomfortable in himself, until he determined to sind for Jer Garvan, the fairy docthor in Garryowen, an' it's he was the ilegant hand at the business, an' divil a sperit id say a crass word to him, no more nor a priest. An' moreover he was very great wid ould Terence Mooney—this man's father that was.

"So without more about it he was sint for, an' sure enough the divil a long he was about it, for he kem back that very evenin' along wid the boy that was sint for him, an' as soon as he was there, an' tuck his supper, an' was done talkin' for a while, he begined of coorse to look into the gandher.

"Well, he turned it this away an' that away, to the right an' to the left, an' straightways an' upside-down, an' when he was tired handlin' it, says he to Terence Mooney:

"'Terence,' says he, 'you must remove the bird into the next room,' says he, 'an' put a petticoat,' says he, 'or anny other convaynience round his head,' says he.

"'An' why so?' says Terence.

405

" 'Becase,' says Jer, says he.

" 'Becase what?' says Terence.

" 'Becase,' says Jer, 'if it isn't done you'll never be asy again,' says he, 'or pusilanimous in your mind,' says he; 'so ax no more questions, but do my biddin',' says he.

" 'Well,' says Terence, 'have your own way,' says he.

"An' wid that he tuck the ould gandher, an' giv' it to one iv the gossoons.

" 'An' take care,' says he, 'don't smother the crathur,' says he.

"Well, as soon as the bird was gone, says Jer Garvan says he:

" 'Do you know what that ould gandher *is*, Terence Mooney?'

" 'Divil a taste,' says Terence.

" 'Well then,' says Jer, 'the gandher is your own father,' says he.

" 'It's jokin' you are,' says Terence, turnin' mighty pale; 'how can an ould gandher be my father?' says he.

" 'I'm not funnin' you at all,' says Jer; 'it's thrue what I tell you, it's your father's wandhrin' sowl,' says he, 'that's naturally tuck pissession iv the ould gandher's body,' says he. 'I know him many ways, and I wondher,' says he, 'you do not know the cock iv his eye yourself,' says he.

" 'Oh blur an' ages!' says Terence, 'what the divil will I ever do at all at all,' says he; 'it's all over wid me, for I plucked him twelve times at the laste,' says he.

" 'That can't be helped now,' says Jer; 'it was a sevare act surely,' says he. 'but it's too late to lamint for it now,' says he; 'the only way to prevint what's past,' says he, 'is to put a stop to it before it happens,' says he.

" 'Thrue for you,' says Terence, 'but how the divil did you come to the knowledge iv my father's sowl,' says he, 'bein' in the ould gandher,' says he.

" 'If I tould you,' says Jer, 'you would not undherstand me,' says he, 'without book-larnin' an' gasthronomy,' says he; 'so ax me no questions,' says he, 'an' I'll tell you no lies. But blieve me in this much,' says he, 'it's your father that's in it,' says he; 'an' if I don't make him spake tomorrow mornin',' says he, 'I'll give you lave to call me a fool,' says he.

" 'Say no more,' says Terence, 'that settles the business,' says he; 'an' oh! blur and ages is it not a quare thing,' says he, 'for a dacent respictable man,' says he, 'to be walkin' about the counthry in the shape iv an ould gandher,' says he; 'and oh, murdher, murdher! is not it often I plucked him,' says he, 'an' tundher and ouns might not I have ate him,'

406

says he; and wid that he fell into a cold parspiration, savin' your prisince, an' was on the pint iv faintin' wid the bare notions iv it.

"Well, whin he was come to himself agin, says Jerry to him quite an' asy:

"'Terence,' says he, 'don't be aggravatin' yourself,' says he; 'for I have a plan composed that 'ill make him spake out,' says he, 'an' tell what it is in the world he's wantin',' says he; 'an' mind an' don't be comin' in wid your gosther, an' to say agin anything I tell you,' says he, 'but jist purtind, as soon as the bird is brought back,' says he, 'how that we're goin' to sind him tomorrow mornin' to market,' says he. 'An' if he don't spake tonight,' says he, 'or gother himself out iv the place,' says he, 'put him into the hamper airly, and sind him in the cart,' says he, 'straight to Tipperary, to be sould for ating,' says he, 'along wid the two gossoons,' says he, 'an' my name isn't Jer Garvan,' says he, 'if he doesn't spake out before he's halfway,' says he. 'An' mind,' says he, 'as soon as iver he says the first word,' says he, 'that very minute bring him aff to Father Crotty,' says he; 'an' if his raverince doesn't make him ratire,' says he, 'like the rest iv his parishioners, glory be to God,' says he, 'into the siclusion iv the flames iv purgathory,' says he, 'there's no vartue in my charums,' says he.

"Well, wid that the ould gandher was let into the room agin, an' they all begined to talk iv sindin' him the nixt mornin' to be sould for roastin' in Tipperary, jist as if it was a thing andoubtingly settled. But divil a notice the gandher tuck, no more nor if they wor spaking iv the Lord-Liftinant; an' Terence desired the boys to get ready the kish for the poultry, an' to 'settle it out wid hay soft an' shnug,' says he, 'for it's the last jauntin' the poor ould gandher 'ill get in this world,' says he.

"Well, as the night was gettin' late, Terence was growin' mighty sorrowful an' down-hearted in himself entirely wid the notions iv what was goin' to happen. An' as soon as the wife an' the crathurs war fairly in bed, he brought out some illigint potteen, an' himself an' Jer Garvan sot down to it; an' begorra, the more anasy Terence got, the more he dhrank, an' himself an' Jer Garvan finished a quart betune them. It wasn't an imparial though, an' more's the pity, for them wasn't anvinted antil short since; but divil a much matther it signifies any longer if a pint could hould two quarts, let alone what it does, sinst Father Mathew — the Lord purloin his raverence — begin'd to give the pledge, an' wid the blessin' iv timperance to deginerate Ireland.

"An' begorra, I have the medle myself; an' it's proud I am iv that same, for abstamiousness is a fine thing, although it's mighty dhry.

"Well, whin Terence finished his pint, he thought he might as well stop; 'for enough is as good as a faste,' says he; 'an' I pity the vagabond,' says he, 'that is not able to conthroul his licquor,' says he, 'an' to keep constantly inside iv a pint measure,' said he; an' wid that he wished Jer Garvan a good-night an' walked out iv the room.

"But he wint out the wrong door, bein' a thrifle hearty in himself, an' not rightly knowin' whether he was standin' on his head or his heels, or both iv them at the same time, an' in place iv gettin' into bed, where did he thrun himself but into the poultry hamper, that the boys had settled out ready for the gandher in the mornin'. An' sure enough he sank down soft an' complate through the hay to the bottom; an' wid the burnin' and roulin' about in the night, the divil a bit iv him but was covered up as shnug as a lumper in a pittaty furrow before mornin'.

"So wid the first light, up gets the two boys, that war to take the sperit, as they consaved, to Tipperary; an' they cotched the ould gandher, an' put him in the hamper, and clapped a good wisp iv hay an' the top iv him, and tied it down sthrong wid a bit iv a coard, and med the sign iv the crass over him, in dhread iv any harum, an' put the hamper up an the car, wontherin' all the while what in the world was makin' the ould burd so surprisin' heavy.

"Well, they wint along quite anasy towards Tipperary, wishin' every minute that some iv the neighbors bound the same way id happen to fall in with them, for they didn't half like the notions iv havin' no company but the bewitched gandher, an' small blame to them for that same.

"But although they wor shaking in their skhins in dhread iv the ould bird beginnin' to converse them every minute, they did not let an' to one another, bud kep singin' an' whistlin' like mad, to keep the dread out iv their hearts.

"Well, afther they war on the road betther nor half an hour, they kem to the bad bit close by Father Crotty's, an' there was one divil of a rut three feet deep at the laste; an' the car got sich a wondherful chuck goin' through it, that it wakened Terence widin in the basket.

" 'Bad luck to ye,' says he, 'my bones is bruck wid yer thricks; what the divil are ye doin' wid me?'

" 'Did ye hear anything quare, Thady?' says the boy that was next to the car, turnin' as white as the top iv a musharoon; 'did ye hear anything quare soundin' out iv the hamper?' says he.

" 'No, nor you,' says Thady, turnin' as pale as himself, 'it's the ould gandher that's gruntin' wid the shakin' he's gettin',' says he.

" 'Where the divil have ye put me into,' says Terence inside, 'bad luck to your sowls,' says he, 'let me out, or I'll be smothered this minute,' says he.

408

" 'There's no use in purtending,' says the boy, 'the gandher's spakin', glory be to God,' says he.

" 'Let me out, you murdherers,' says Terence.

" 'In the name iv the blessed Vargin,' says Thady, 'an' iv all the holy saints, hould yer tongue, you unnatheral gandher,' says he.

" 'Who's that, that dar to call me nicknames?' says Terence inside, roaring wid the fair passion, 'let me out, you blasphamious infiddles,' says he, 'or by this crass I'll stretch ye,' says he.

" 'In the name iv all the blessed saints in heaven,' says Thady, 'who the divil are ye?'

" 'Who the divil would I be, but Terence Mooney,' says he. 'It's myself that's in it, you unmerciful bliggards,' says he, 'let me out, or by the holy, I'll get out in spite iv yes,' says he, 'an' by jaburs, I'll wallop yes in arnest,' says he.

" 'It's ould Terence, sure enough,' says Thady, 'isn't it cute the fairy docthor found him out,' says he.

" 'I'm an the pint iv snuffication,' says Terence, 'let me out, I tell you, an' wait till I get at ye,' says he, 'for begorra, the divil a bone in your body but I'll powdher,' says he.

"An' wid that, he biginned kickin' and flingin' inside the hamper, and dhrivin' his legs agin the sides iv it, that it was a wonder he did not knock it to pieces.

"Well, as soon as the boys seen that, they skelped the ould horse into a gallop as hard as he could peg toward the priest's house, through the ruts, an' over the stones; an' you'd see the hamper fairly flyin' three feet up in the air with the joultin'; glory be to God.

"So it was small wondher, by the time they got to his Raverince's door, the breath was fairly knocked out of poor Terence, so that he was lyin' speechless in the bottom iv the hamper.

"Well, whin his Raverince kem down, they up an' they tould him all that happened, an' how they put the gandher into the hamper, an' how he beginned to spake, an' how he confissed that he was ould Terence Mooney; an' they axed his honor to advise them how to get rid iv the spirit for good an' all.

"So says his Raverince, says he:

" 'I'll take my booke,' says he, 'an' I'll read some rale sthrong holy bits out iv it,' says he, 'an' do you get a rope and put it round the hamper,' says he, 'an' let it swing over the runnin' wather at the bridge,' says he, 'an' it's no matther if I don't make the spirit come out iv it,' says he.

"Well, wid that, the priest got his horse, and tuck his booke in undher

409

his arum, an' the boys follied his Raverince, ladin' the horse down to the bridge, an' divil a word out iv Terence all the way, for he seen it was no use spakin', an' he was afeard if he med any noise they might thrait him to another gallop an' finish him intirely.

"Well, as soon as they war all come to the bridge, the boys tuck the rope they had with them, an' med it fast to the top iv the hamper an' swung it fairly over the bridge, lettin' it hang in the air about twelve feet out iv the wather.

"An' his Raverince rode down to the bank of the river, close by, an' beginned to read mighty loud and bould intirely.

"An' when he was goin' on about five minutes, all at onst the bottom iv the hamper kem out, an' down wint Terence, falling splash dash into the wather, an' the ould gandher atop iv him. Down they both went to the bottom, wid a souse you'd hear half a mile off.

"An' before they had time to rise agin, his Raverince, wid the fair astonishment, giv his horse one dig iv the spurs, an' before he knew where he was, in he went, horse an' all, atop iv them, an' down to the bottom.

"Up they all kem agin together, gaspin' and puffin', and off down wid the current wid them, like shot in under the arch iv the bridge till they kem to the shallow wather.

"The ould gandher was the first out, and the priest and Terence kem next, pantin' an' blowin' an' more than half dhrounded, an' his Raverince was so freckened wid the droundin' he got, and wid the sights iv the sperit, as he consaved, that he wasn't the better of it for a month.

"An' as soon as Terence could spake, he swore he'd have the life of the two gossoons; but Father Crotty would not give him his will. An' as soon as he was got quiter, they all endivoured to explain it; but Terence consaved he went raly to bed the night before, and his wife said the same to shilter him from the suspicion for havin' th' dthrop taken. An' his Raverince said it was a mysthery, an' swore if he cotched anyone laughin' at the accident, he'd lay the horsewhip across their shouldhers.

"An' Terence grew fonder an' fonder iv the gandher every day, until at last he died in a wondherful old age, lavin' the gandher afther him an' a large family iv childher.

"An' to this day the farm is rinted by one iv Terence Mooney's lenial and legitimate postariors."

The Real Wolf

Thomas Ligotti

Tonight shall be the first time we—that is, I—take the life of a human being. Can you read my thoughts, Moon, so full you're about to spill your whiteness all over the sky like a clumsy child? Can you see into my heart with your big pearly eye? That's how I love to see you, Moon, doming out of the blackness. And what do you think of how I look when you become all round up there? Oh, you're shining very nicely down into my alley hideaway, garnished as it is with winter's frozen spume. See how my blemished flesh flowers into perfectly silver-white fur; see how my flat face pushes itself into an elegant snout; see my eyes get bright and keen; see my legs go lean! From tooth to tail: a wolf. Not simply a werewolf; I am more than a split personality. I am now whole, undivided—one solid piece of walking wolf. Not merely *a* wolf, not even *the* wolf. But just Wolf. We are—I *am*—Wolf. Hear my howl

Shine, Moon, shine on your moonchild.

Ah, there it is, there's what I've been waiting for. The music, that Great Concert I always hear playing whenever I take this form. Do ordinary animals detect the sound of this distant symphony, I wonder? Perhaps only the ones whose ears are acute little points that prick up at the faintest tingling. Like mine do. The music is indefinite in a very definite way, vague but with all the clarity of the stars. To my ears it is powerful enough to drown out the sound of nearby traffic and other earthly noises, though it is so curiously quiet, quiet and steady as one's own heartbeat, the music seems to be throbbing and humming through the hollows of space: a fine bow singing across the invisible paths of planets, a needlelike vibration ringing the silver bells of galaxies, golden tones sent up into the towering pipes of infinity. A triad, innumerable systems of triads, all calling down to me with one tremulous voice. It is like no music I have ever heard as a human being. And I hope you, Moon, can hear it too!

The music inspires and encourages me to kill a human tonight. Their senses are too gross to perceive the music, and for this reason alone they

411

should be slaughtered. They are slaves to the moral miseries of their humanness—they are all deliberation and no liberation! Idiots, they mourn the extinction of their beauties and their loves—their pitiful vices —as if these were anything but futile illusions. And such illusions only breed other, more horrible, fantasies: pain, isolation, and ultimate annihilation. These things only happen to those who do not understand the Divine Mania, the animating force whose voice is that spine-freezing music—the Great Concert—and whose face is all things. This mania bids me kill and I obey, because *I am it*. It can never die, though it loves playing death, playing possum, rabbit, pouncing cat . . . prowling wolf! It loves to die, lives to die. It is invincible. You understand perfectly, don't you Moon? With icy brightness you yourself radiate the mania, the moon-mania that visits me whenever you reach the phase of fullness.

For you, then, I will kill my first human. Not that this is such an exceptional gift to bestow. A human is nothing special, merely another two-legged creature that bleeds. And as you know, Moon, I have already tasted their blood. You knew about my little escapades in the park even before they were reported in the newspapers: how I mauled a few strollers down by the frozen pond. To confess the truth, it was my intention to finish them off, but for some reason I didn't. Something about the taste of their blood when I opened one of their arms or legs. It is not like the blood of mice, of birds, or even of cats. These humans have bad blood, like some kind of poison, it seems. But that is ridiculous, for blood is blood. Their bodies run with the same singing river that flows in other animals. And I shall drink from it tonight I promise you, Moon.

Perhaps, though, I should work toward the human river by way of the beast's. There, I hear something rattling around the snow-stiffened debris back in the depths of this blind alley. A rat. An alley rat for an alley wolf. Where are you, nice little rat? Sweet little rat. I'm here to liberate you from your lowly rattiness. In a few moments you shall find ecstacy in my jaws. Listen to the Great Concert; it's calling you home, Rat. There it goes, scurrying, scrambling, scuttling—Got it! Well, Rat, you can make music of your own as my teeth play on your flesh. But now you grow quiet, and I can detect the strains of the Great Concert swelling a little louder as another being goes to join in that orchestral unity. I will have to find other things to play with, once I emerge from my alley lair.

I know, I know, Moon; I'm keeping to the back streets, where it's

412

safe and lonely for a lone wolf. There's no one around here who can do me any harm. Do you really think the humans who live in these dilapidated shacks are clever enough to threaten a creature that can change its shape and nature the way you go through your phases, the way the year shifts its seasons, the way this world spins from day to darkness? And how much more swiftly can I perform my transformation! Besides, in the snow-encrusted gloom of this slum I look just like a big dog.

And just as the thought of dogs crosses my mind, what breed of four-footed silhouette is that up there crossing the street in the distance? It looks like a half-starved stray; I've seen them before around here. Easy prey for a strong strutter of the streets. Why is it trotting faster now? Doesn't it know I only want to free its spirit from that pathetically bony frame? Listen to the music, my dear Dog. The Divine Mania is now conducting the band, which is about to reach one of those countless little crescendos of death. Don't bother to look behind you as you pace faster and faster down the street; you will only see your own image in a mirror. For the Divine Mania is not *murder* but self-slaughter, suicide. And suicide needs mirrors. We are much more than mere cousin-creatures, Dog and Wolf. We are two tiny shards of a mirror that has been shattered infinitely and is always looking at itself. Isn't that wonderful, dear Dog? And I see that you understand, because now you are slowing down to take a good look in the mirror, falling exhausted against this filthy snowdrift and staring up into my eyes. No, my twin, take a good look! It's too bad you cannot see how beautiful your red blood glistens on the white snow in the moonlight. This is one of your better moments, Moon. You can create marvelous effects with a beast's blood. But now this moonchild is ready for higher things.

The gates at the north end are open, all pearled with white ice. Nice to be welcomed to this island of wilderness beyond which loom the prison towers of the city. I hate them. Especially that horribly massive building called the library, where one of the lowest creatures in all the city's human population is incarcerated by day in a prison of books. Ah, but didn't some of those books locked in a special basement vault help him to become what he is now. And now he roams by night! A liberated moonchild.

I vow to you, Moon, I shall liberate more human hearts this night. They congregate like bugs by that light in the distance where night-skaters glide mindlessly across the frozen pond. I have drawn blood here before, so let them be warned: I am back and am burning with the Divine Mania. I want to take life from these miserable and arrogant

413

creatures; they do not deserve it. They are in bondage to their beauties and their loves, but they do not even love death and do not see how beautiful it is. They cannot even hear the Great Concert! They are afraid of its savage music, its icy liberation, its lyrical purity. For such creatures, living is only a dead end, and now I will chase a few of them to the *very* end of that blind alley.

Oh, what perfection. I can't believe my undeceiveable eyes. There stands my first victim, alone in the frosty clearing. With that outfit she is begging for harm: bright red coat, bright red cap, and bright red boots. Soon the sparkling snow will be spread with red. This is the essence of all my dreams. The moon is shining gloriously on the scene, the trees are heavy with diamond ice, and all is stillness. I am in fairyland.

Closer. (Why doesn't she run?) Closer. (Why doesn't she scream?) Closer. (Why does she not even move?) The only stirring thing is her red scarf flapping in the chill wind.

Closer, closer, closer—Spring on her. Now!

What are those noises, why have I fallen into the snow, and why do I feel this terrible pain? Run, Wolf, run. I can't, I can't. Oh, I have delivered myself to deception. The child hasn't moved, only her clothes flutter in the cruel breath of this winter night. How could I have been fooled by this false image? A real wolf would not have been deceived. A real wolf would have seen those hunters hiding among the trees. I shouldn't have tried to kill in the same place twice.

Now my beautiful silver fur is stained with hideous red, and I am beautiful no more. I am not even a real wolf. A real wolf would not feel so sad for itself. Oh, why do I have to die like this. I don't want to die; there's only *one* of me. I can feel myself changing back into my original form. How wide their eyes grow, those gazing groundward upon my transfigured shape. How pleased they are to see me perish, humbled at the feet of brute humanity. My heart is slowing down, and the music . . . the music is gone.

Here, Moon, here is the life I promised you.

The Sacrifice

Miroslaw Lipinski

The rightful goal of writing should be one and the same as the quest of any sensitive and intelligent person: either everlasting life (still clearly not within any grasp, including that of the written word) or pioneerings in new terrains where the multitudes, because of their mental inertia and misguided emotions, do not tread. The horror genre fits snugly into this prescription, for here theme and subject matter are not restricted; and darkness, the true final frontier, is explored by the bold mind of the fantasist, even if his hand is cold and shaking, even if his mind becomes undone in the process.

Yet which horror writer has kept to this noble goal? Which one, I say, has retained this pure intention foremost in his mind? Furthermore, which author of the eerie and the uncommon has visited the graveyard to sleep beside some troubled soul tortured under the canopy of a moonless night? Which one has roamed the land in search of genuine Satanic covens with their bestial, incestuous rites? Which one has taken a chance and partaken of ceraceous crawling food that ancient necromancers foretold would possess, if mixed with the gastric juices of modern man, potent insights and viable illusions? Which horror traveler has taken his work seriously, plunging bravely into the emptiness everyone feels at those revealing moments when all about is quiet and nothing moves and the mind panics, leaving us alone with the awesome fact that, somehow, we live? Which explorer of the damned and the demonic, faced with the opposite reality, has said: "Alright, so we eventually die. Let me outlive in acts my peers; let me break the terrible bond that adheres my spirit to my implacable and repressive humanness; let me make a mockery of habit and tradition; let me justify my life—let me not be just a horror fiction writer but a horror *nonfiction* writer"?

With these concerns and the credo that instigated them troubling my mind, I set out to R——, that unmapped and scattered town on the Hudson, to seek out T. Mordant. His works have never, to my knowledge, appeared in any national publication; but if one were a collector of

415

obscure small press releases, his name would not be unknown. From the first moment that I had read a story of his, I recognized the power, truth, and dedication he gave to the genre that was in his heart and a part of his breath. I was nineteen then, and his piece gave me hope that for one like myself, who trembled at the potential majesty of the printed word, near perfect in evoking a deeper reality than we experience generally, there was a method, an avenue, an achievement. Nevertheless, I was too distracted by school and primal sexual impulses to actively pursue the path I saw glimmering before me; and later, after college, in the midst of a tedious job, I was stricken by severe, debilitating phobias and could only, in the arena of the written word, manage to translate terror stories from the Slavic languages I was familiar with. These tales, ironically, were my saviors, for they were the only base of reality I possessed at the time. Everything else had crumbled; false gods were in the process of being destroyed.

Eventually I began to understand the anxieties that had overwhelmed me, and slowly, laboriously, I started on my own work, building on the vague but supportable foundation of my experiences—therefore, developing a unique manner of expression—wombed in a more ancient style, perhaps, but nevertheless of my own choosing, an attack against the university-mandated Hemingwayesque style that has hampered full emotional expression in writers, who must not laugh or cry too loudly, and who must be careful not to step into the forbidden zone of "purple prose." Some of my writings, glowingly purple and full of spleen, finally saw publication in prestigious though low-paying magazines. I reacquainted myself with Mordant's work, and while his stories were appearing with far less frequency than before, they were more impacting, intellectually developed and frightening than ever before. Mordant was delving into the ultimate darkness, and was coming back out with shreds of truths than hinted at even greater terrors and salvations than could have been previously hoped for.

Depressed by the inadequacy of my own work, bitter at continually falling short of touching that emptiness about and inside me, so I could finally hug it and call it friend, I determined to track down Mordant. Maybe a meeting with him would prove eventful in my artistic and spiritual journey.

I will not relate how I found the home of T. Mordant, for I respect his privacy, even though I am almost certain that he has passed away by now; but after months of research I finally stood in the ravine cradling his house—a simple Yankee cottage oppressed by dead yet forceful vines, and by a perpetual gray hue in the air induced by a respiring vegetation growing on the sides of the encompassing mountains. The whole effect of the quiet habitat was a shuddering warning to stay away.

I hesitated but briefly before I advanced along the little-worn path to knock on his door.

He was very Wellesian—tall, bulky, impressive. But unlike that innovative director, his face was not at all pleasant. The nose had been broken a couple of times, and one nostril was smashed permanently flat. His brows were bristly, erratic in their direction, and peculiarly long, while the eyes underneath were dull, dreamy, and incapable of steady focus. A craggy scar twisted and puckered his left cheek. The growth on his severely blotched face seemed almost an aftereffect—sparse, sickly, unkempt. To me, his physical appearance was just a noble symbol of the artistic battles he had waged in his many mind-dangerous years. Who knows with what demons he had actually fought?

I introduced myself, and when he answered me I received a surprise. His voice was a blatant contradiction of his fierce, rugged look. It was gentle, soft, and warm, and it bade me entrance.

Among the lit candles, oak beams, wooden stools and table, and the two walls filled with food provisions and dried, hanging meats, there was only one modern component: a battery-operated tape recorder of extraordinary excellence that I soon learned Mordant used to record all sorts of sounds—especially steady silence, the volume of which in replay he would turn up to a feverish pitch of intense nothingness.

Sitting down on an offered seat by the table, I gave Mordant a brief biography of myself and told him of my reasons for coming to see him. Meanwhile, he prepared some herb tea in a kettle.

As I watched him I saw that his mannerisms were slow, careful; and I also noticed that both his hands had brown gloves of smooth leather on them, though it wasn't at all cold in his cottage. I ascribed this to some individual sensitivity the man had; and having been subject to a few eccentricities in my lifetime, I thought nothing further of the matter. The minutes went by; the tea in the kettle was filling the room with a sharp, minty scent. I found Mordant eager to talk, courteous, and overly friendly—symptoms, I realized, of a person who is intelligent but lives alone, rarely interacting with another human being. I was reminded of a similar consciousness in my phobia days and felt deeply moved and an instant affection for this writing master.

"I am familiar with your work," Mordant said, placing an aromatic cup of tea before me. "And I am impressed with your sincerity."

"My necessity for dealing with the world," I admitted; then I asked: "Do you read much of the genre?"

"What I can. I'm on a vast number of subscriber lists under various aliases. I'm always interested in knowing who the partisans are in the war against the trivialities of the human condition, and what these partisans have to say. Nevertheless, my experiments take up much of my time. That is where my energies lie."

He related what he was doing with the tape recorder, and sitting close by, on a stool at the corner of the table, his own tea in hand, he described in loving detail certain sounds of nothing he found particularly interesting. The language he used was flavorful—subtle, moderate, or poundingly strong, depending on the need. Like myself, he was trying to find a source of life and hope beyond the boundaries of predictability and death, boundaries guarded by fear and an internal self-loathing that doesn't want to consider Godhood as a viable alternate life-style.

Yes, I could almost hear the nothing, and I distinctly felt the fear it provoked. Little had I suspected how much silence—genuine silence—was the seed of that omnipresent terror we all try to sublimate because we are afraid of reaching the other side. As Mordant talked on, I became hypnotized by the spell of his words, pulled as if by a bewitching magnet into a giddy, fascinating depth. When he stopped talking, I could not say anything or comprehend where I was, so stunned had I been by the mammoth journey on which I had been taken. When I regained clarity of mind, I wondered, in a moment of human weakness, if we were both mad.

"What made you come to this place?" I questioned, trying to adjust to base reality.

"The terror of the surroundings. You have seen the ugly, gray hue, and you have noticed the quiet. And I came for the Breachae."

"The Breachae?"

A sinister smile crept to T. Mordant's puffed, massively discolored face.

"They intrigued me immensely—to the point of fanaticism. I saw in them a living symbol of the Evil that underscores life. Evil is, of course, the brother of the Dark, and the Dark is the first and final ruler of man. Hence, the more we know of Evil, the more we are connected with the Cosmos, which is, after all, only infinite blackness doted with dying flashes of light. The study of one leads to the revelation of the other. And once we fully understand the Evil and the Dark, once we know them emotionally and physically, then, and only then, can we transcend our humanness and become eternal masters of a domain that knows no end.

"So it was important, you see, to study these Breachae, and this area was teeming with them. They are leeches, desperate bloodsuckers who will stop at nothing to draw the life force out of the healthy. I had to examine and understand them, perform experiments that made even me faint. Steel pins I used to trap their slimy bodies, razors to cut their shiny skin. . . . I studied their gruesome mating habits, even bred some of them. I did *everything* I could."

I glanced around me.

"No, no," Mordant said in a calming voice. "They are not out here. My experiments nearly eliminated them from this area."

Suddenly, as T. Mordant was raising his cup to his mouth, his expression became acutely sad. His bent arm stopped in midair. He was gazing at his gloved hand. Slowly the arm relaxed, went down to the table. At that moment I witnessed a defeated man, wrecked at a high point in the plot of his life. Embarrassed at seeing a giant so shaken, I attempted a diverting comment: "This tea is quite delicious. What is it made up of?"

Mordant's voice was a humiliating monotone. "It doesn't matter. . . . My herbs keep me alive. . . . They contain properties which stop *the bleeding*. . . ."

A chill coursed through me at those last words, but the overwhelming feeling within me was compassion—compassion for this noble journeyer who was now so very much alone with his mind and his honorable existence. As I watched his silent, bowed form, his hugeness heaving in melancholia, I realized the irony of my presence here. I had been seeking an uplift, a spark, a stimulus. Undoubtedly I found a part of what I had sought. Mordant's world was intoxicating. But more than that, I now began to see a magnificent, tremulous role in *his* destiny. In some lives direction is sharpened and made more potent by witnessing the dejection of others. The sight of a pathetic tragedy awakens in the sensitive the instinct of rising above defeat and conquering the natural downward course of the spirit.

Mordant was now the one who needed the uplift, the spark, the stimulus. I saw my humble place. Didn't we, after all, share the same philosophy—the same dreams? Yes, I would work with him. Together, we, the loners, the suffering travelers in a land few dare tread, could dispel the disillusion that tags along with every dedicated, original artist, the loneliness that eventually bastardizes any developed mind. But was I being hasty? No! How can one be hasty when faced with a glimpse of a macabre paradise! For a moment I felt like laying my hand on top of Mordant's gloved one in consolation, encouragement. Instead, I spoke:

"Mordant, I want to stay here with you. I want to help you. You've done wonderful things. Your writings are pure wisdom of the genre;

they will stand as landmarks and guideposts for future generations. And from what you've told me of your experiments, you have smashed the confines of commonplace existence. Mordant, I want to stay here. I *need* to stay here!"

His reaction was shockingly unexpected. He turned on me, his eyes glittering like a trapped animal's. "You must not stay!" he said in a voice that edged toward a scream. "This can only be a brief visit for you!"

I was taken aback, but realizing that I was not dealing with an average intelligence or an ordinary passion, and therefore was dealing with someone who was continually close to "insanity," I pressed on. "No, listen! You can help me, and I don't want to sound presumptuous, but I think I can help you—at least in moral support. I—"

"No!" he shot out. "No, no!" And he got up and began to pace madly about the room, all the time keeping his gloved hands limply by his side, as if they were weights.

I went on: "I have searched for a long time. Much of my life has been misspent; I dread future failures. That is why I need to stay here!"

"You cannot stay!" he boomed out, stopping a few paces before me, his awful blotched face registering unfathomable anger and fear.

"Why?" I challenged.

"The sacrifice!"

"I am prepared for it," I said boldly and naively, though I sensed disaster around the corner.

In the midst of his turmoil, I thought I saw tears welling up in his glowing eyes. He grabbed his head with both hands and moaned, as if hit with a sudden migraine. But he let down both hands almost instantly, gazed at the brown gloves on them, and then spat out at me:

"What do you know of my sacrifice? Who are you to suppose that you can stay here? Young fool! Young, idiotic fool!"

Noticing that I was about to protest, he continued—and how can I ever forget the emotional pain that made his expression a mask of titanic suffering and sorrow?

"You may be prepared for some sacrifice, some *other* one, but not for this—"

He tore away a glove from one hand with the ease of peeling off cheap paper. I saw the yellow, scabby pustules—no, boils—spread over it, the ill mounds seemingly pulsating. With a quick, savage slap against the edge of the table, he shocked, shattered, and splattered one boil. . . .

And then I understood—oh, how I understood.

The reason he was so huge, so round, the reason for the blotched face, the reason he *had* to drink this peculiar herb tea was that his body was full of Breachae! They were speedily gushing out of the gnashed boil, aided by its flowing sap, and like black, slimy flower petals from some horrid hybrid, they fell to the floor one right after the other, immediately slithering in frenzied hunger and instinct toward me!

To this day I regret my fear—but what else could I do? I was then, as now, a human being, full of faults and a singular lack of courage when faced with ugly reality.

Frightened, sickened, I rushed out of that monstrous cottage, from which I heard lonely wailing. . . .

I now remember T. Mordant's words to me. He had said that I might be prepared for another sacrifice, but not for his. Maybe, justly, each one of us has our own individual cross to bear in accordance with our psyche and life. As I write this by the intimate light of an antique lamp, terrified of the darkness around me (yes, my panic attacks have returned—and with a vengeance), I wonder what *my* sacrifice will be.

I reach over into the womb of the lamp and grasp the sizzling bulb. The stinging pain shooting up my arm confirms that I am, thankfully, still alive—and still have time to figure it all out before the Evil and the Dark have a chance to consume me forever.

The Seeds from Outside

EDMOND HAMILTON

Standifer found the seeds the morning after the meteor fell on the hill above his cottage. On that night he had been sitting in the scented darkness of his little garden when he had glimpsed the vertical flash of light and heard the whiz and crash of that falling visitor from outer space. And all that night he had lain awake, eager for morning and the chance to find and examine the meteor.

Standifer knew little of meteors, for he was not a scientist. He was a painter whose canvases hung in many impressive halls in great cities, and were appropriately admired and denounced and gabbled about by those who liked such things. Standifer had grown weary of such people and of their cities, and had come to this lonely little cottage in the hills to paint and dream.

For it was not cities or people that Standifer wished to paint, but the green growing life of earth that he loved so deeply. There was no growing thing in wood or field that he did not know. The slim white sycamores that whispered together along the streams, and the sturdy little sumacs that were like small, jovial plant-gnomes, and the innocent wild roses that bloomed and swiftly died in their shady cover—he had toiled to transfix and preserve their subtle beauty for ever in his oils and colors and cloths.

The spring had murmured by in a drifting dream as Standifer had lived and worked alone. And now suddenly into the hushed quiet of his green, blossoming world had rudely crashed this visitant from distant realms. It strangely stirred Standifer's imagination, so that through the night he lay wondering, and gazing up through his casement at the white stars from which the meteor had come.

It was hardly dawn, and a chill and drenching dew silvered the grass and bent the poplar leaves, when Standifer excitedly climbed the hill in search of the meteor. The thing was not hard to find. It had smashed savagely into the spring-green woods, and had torn a great raw gouge out of the earth as it had crashed and shattered.

For the meteor had shattered into chunks of jagged, dark metal that lay all about that new, gaping hole. Those ragged lumps were still faintly warm to the touch, and Standifer went from one to another, turning them over and examining them with marveling curiosity. It was when he was about to leave the place that he glimpsed amid this meteoric debris the little square tan case.

It lay half imbedded still in one of the jagged metal chunks. The case was no more than two inches square, and was made of some kind of stiff tan fiber that was very tough and apparently impervious to heat. It was quite evident that the case had been inside the heart of the shattered meteor, and that it was the product of intelligence.

Standifer was vastly excited. He dug the tiny case out of the meteoric fragment, and then tried to tear it open. But neither his fingers nor sharp stones could make any impression on the tough fiber. So he hurried back down to his cottage with the case clutched in his hand, his head suddenly filled with ideas of messages sent from other worlds or stars.

But at the cottage, he was amazed to find that neither steel knives nor drills nor chisels could make the slightest impression upon this astounding material. It seemed to the eye to be just stiff tan fiber, yet he knew that it was a far different kind of material, as refractory as diamond and as flexibly tough as steel.

It was several hours before he thought of pouring water upon the enigmatic little container. When he did so, the fiberlike stuff instantly softened. It was evident that the material had been designed to withstand the tremendous heat and shock of alighting on another world, but to soften up and open when it fell upon a moist, warm world.

Standifer carefully cut open the softened case. Then he stared, puzzled, at its contents, a frown upon his sensitive face. There was nothing inside the case but two withered-looking brown seeds, each of them about an inch long.

He was disappointed, at first. He had expected writing of some kind, perhaps even a tiny model or machine. But after a while his interest rose again, for it occurred to him that these could be no ordinary seeds that the people of some far planet had tried to sow broadcast upon other worlds.

So he planted the two seeds in a carefully weeded corner of his flower garden, about ten feet apart. And in the days that followed, he scrupulously watered and watched them, and waited eagerly to see what kind of strange plants might spring from them.

His interest was so great, indeed, that he forgot all about his unfinished canvases, the work that had brought him to the seclusion of these quiet hills. Yet he did not tell anyone of his strange find, for he felt that if he did, excited scientists would come and take the seeds away to study and dissect, and he did not want that.

In two weeks he was vastly excited to see the first little shoots of dark green come up through the soil at the places where he had planted the two seeds. They were like stiff little green rods and they did not look very unusual to Standifer. Yet he continued to water them carefully, and to wait tensely for their development.

The two shoots came up fast, after that. Within a month they had become green pillars almost six feet tall, each of them covered with a tight-wrapped sheath of green sepals. They were a little thicker at the middle than at the top or bottom, and one of them was a little slenderer than the other, and its color a lighter green. Altogether, they looked like no plants ever before seen on earth.

Standifer saw that the sheathing sepals were now beginning to unfold, to curl back from the tops of the plants. He waited almost breathlessly for their further development, and every night before he retired he looked last at the plants, and every morning when he awoke they were his first thought.

Then early one June morning he found that the sepals had curled back enough from the tips to let him see the tops of the true plants inside. And he stood for many minutes there, staring in strange wonder at that which the unfolding of the sepals was beginning to reveal.

For where they had curled back at the tips, they disclosed what looked strangely like the tops of two human heads. It was as though two people were enclosed in those sheathing sepals, two people the hair of whose heads was becoming visible as masses of fine green threads, more animal than plant in appearance.

One looked very much like the top of a girl's head, a mass of fluffy, light-green hair only the upper part of which was visible. The other head was of shorter, coarser and darker green hair, as though it was that of a man.

Standifer went through that day in a stupefied daze. He was almost tempted to unfold the sepals further by force, so intense was his curiosity, but he restrained himself and waited. And the next few days brought him further confirmation of his astounding suspicion.

The sepals of both plants had by then unfolded almost completely. And inside one was a green man-plant—and in the other a girl! Their bodies were strangely human in shape, living, breathing bodies of weird, soft, green plant-flesh, with tendrillike arms and tendril limbs too that were still rooted and hidden down in the calyxes. Their heads and faces were very human indeed, with green-pupiled eyes through which they could see.

Standifer stared and stared at the plant girl, for she was beautiful beyond the artist's dreams, her slim green body rising proudly straight from the cup of her calyx. Her shining, green-pupiled eyes saw him as he stood by her, and she raised a tendrillike arm and softly touched him. And her tendrils stirred with a soft rustling that was like a voice speaking to him.

Then Standifer heard a deeper, angry rustling behind him, and turned. It was the man-plant, his big tendril arms reaching furiously to grasp the artist, jealousy and rage in his eyes. Hastily the painter stepped away from him.

In the days that followed, Standifer was like one living in a dream. For he had fallen in love with the shining slim plant girl, and he spent almost all his waking hours sitting in his garden looking into her eyes, listening to the strange rustling that was her speech.

It seemed to his artist's soul that the beauty of no animal-descended earth woman could match the slender grace of this plant girl. He would stand beside her and wish passionately that he could understand her rustling whisper, as her tendrils softly touched and caressed him.

The man-plant hated him, he knew, and would try to strike at him. And the man hated the girl too, in time. He would reach raging tendrils out toward her to clutch her, but was too far separated from her ever to reach her.

Standifer saw that these two strange creatures were still developing, and that their feet would soon come free of their roots. He knew that these were beings of a kind of life utterly unlike anything terrestrial, that they began their life cycle as seeds and rooted plants, and that they developed then into free and moving plant-people such as were unknown on this world.

He knew too that on whatever far world was their home, creatures like these must have reached a great degree of civilization and science, to send out broadcast into space the seeds that would sow their race upon other planets. But of their distant origin he thought little, as he waited impatiently for the day when his shining plant girl would be free of her roots.

He felt that that day was very near, and he did not like to leave the garden even for a minute, now. But on one morning Standifer had to leave, to go to the village for necessary supplies; since for two days there had been no food in the cottage and he felt himself growing weak with hunger.

It hurt him to part from the plant girl even for those few hours, and he stood for minutes caressing her fluffy green hair and listening to her happy rustling before he took himself off.

When he returned, he heard as soon as he entered his garden a sound that chilled the blood in his veins. It was the plant girl's voice—a mere agonized whisper that spoke dreadful things. He rushed wildly into the garden and stood a moment aghast at what he saw.

The final development had taken place in his absence. Both creatures had come free of their roots—and the man-plant had in his jealousy and hate broken and torn the shining green body of the girl. She lay, her tendrils stirring feebly, while the other looked down at her in satisfied hate.

Standifer madly seized a scythe and ran across the garden. In two terrific strokes, he cut down the man-plant into a dead thing oozing dark green blood. Then he dropped the weapon and wildly stooped over his dying plant girl.

She looked up at him through pain-filled, wide eyes as her life oozed away. A green tendril arm lifted slowly to touch his face, and he heard a last rustling whisper from this creature whom he had loved and who had loved him across the vast gulf of world-differing species. Then he knew that she was dead.

That was long ago, and the garden by the little cottage is weed-grown now and holds no memory of those two strange creatures from the great outside who grew and lived and died there. Standifer does not dwell there any more, but lives far away in the burning, barren Arizona desert. For never, since then, can he bear the sight of green growing things.

Seeing the World

RAMSEY CAMPBELL

At first Angela thought it was a shadow. The car was through the gates before she wondered how a shadow could surround a house. She craned over the garden wall as Richard parked the car. It was a ditch, no doubt some trick the Hodges had picked up in Italy, something to do with their gardening. "They're back," she murmured when Richard had pulled down the door of the garage.

"Saints preserve us, another dead evening," he said, and she had to hush him, for the Hodges were sitting in their lounge and had grinned out at the clatter of the door.

All the same, the Hodges seemed to have even less regard than usual for other people's feelings. During the night she was wakened by Mozart's 40th, to which the conductor had added the rhythm section Mozart had forgotten to include. Richard mumbled and thrashed in slow motion as she went to the window. An August dawn glimmered on the Hodges' gnomes, and beyond them in the lounge the Hodges were sitting quite as stonily. She might have shouted but for waking Richard. Stiff with the dawn chill, she limped back to bed.

She listened to the silence between movements and wondered if this time they might give the rest of the symphony a chance. No, here came

426

the first movement again, reminding her of the night the Hodges had come over, when she and Richard had performed a Haydn sonata. "I haven't gone into Haydn," Harry Hodge had declared, wriggling his eyebrows. "Get it? Gone into hidin'." She sighed and turned over and remembered the week she and Richard had just spent on the waterways, fields, and grassy banks flowing by like Delius, a landscape they had hardly boarded all week, preferring to let the villages remain untouched images of villages. Before the Mozart had played through a third time she was asleep.

Most of the next day was given over to violin lessons, her pupils making up for the lost week. By the time Richard came home from lecturing, she had dinner almost ready. Afterward they sat sipping the last of the wine as evening settled on the long gardens. Richard went to the piano and played *La Cathedrale Engloutie*, and the last tolling of the drowned cathedral was fading when someone knocked slowly at the front door.

It was Harry Hodge. He looked less bronzed by the Mediterranean sun than made up, rather patchily. "The slides are ready," he said through his fixed smile. "Can you come now?"

"Right now? It really is quite late." Richard wasn't hiding his resentment that he need only call for them to come—not so much an invitation anymore as a summons or at the way Hodge must have waited outside until he thought the Debussy had gone on long enough. "Oh, very well," Richard said. "Provided there aren't too many."

He must have shared Angela's thought: best to get it over with, the sooner the better. None of their neighbors bothered with the Hodges. Harry Hodge looked stiff, and thinner than when he'd gone away. "Aren't you feeling well?" she asked, concerned.

"Just all that walking and pushing the mother-in-law."

He was wearing stained outdoor clothes. He must have been gardening; he always was. He looked ready to wait for them to join him, until Richard said firmly, "We won't be long."

They had another drink first, since the Hodges never offered.

"Don't wake me unless I snore," Richard muttered as they ventured up the Hodges' path, past gnomes of several nations, souvenirs of previous holidays. It must be the gathering night that made the ditch appear deeper and wider. The ditch reminded her of the basement where Harry developed his slides. She was glad their house had no basement: she didn't like dark places.

When Harry opened the door, he looked as if he hadn't stopped smiling. "Glad you could come," he said, so tonelessly that at first Angela heard it as a question she was tempted to answer truthfully. If he was exhausted, he shouldn't have been so eager to have them round. They followed him down the dark hall into the lounge.

Only the wall lights were on. Most of the light surrounded souvenirs —a pink Notre Dame with a clock in place of a rose window on the mantelpiece, a plaster bull on top of the gas fire, matches stuck in its back like picadors' lances—and Deirdre Hodge and her mother. The women sat facing the screen on the wall, and Angela faltered in the doorway, wondering what was wrong. Of course, they must have been gardening too; they were still wearing outdoor clothes, and she could smell earth. Deirdre's mother must rather have been supervising, since much of the time she had to be pushed in a wheelchair.

"There you are," Deirdre said in greeting, and after some thought her mother said, "Aye, there they are all right." Their smiles looked even more determined than Harry's. Richard and Angela took their places on the settee, smiling; Angela for one felt as if she was expected to smile rather than talk. Eventually, Richard said, "How was Italy?"

By now that form of question was a private joke, a way of making their visits to the Hodges less burdensome: half the joke consisted of anticipating the answer. Germany had been "like dolls' houses"; Spain was summed up by "good fish and chips"; France had prompted only "They'll eat anything." Now Deirdre smiled and smiled and eventually said, "Nice ice creams."

"And how did you like it, Mrs. . . . Mrs. . . ." They had never learned the mother's name, and she was too busy smiling and nodding to tell them now. Smiling must be less exhausting than speaking. Perhaps at least that meant the visitors wouldn't be expected to reply to every remark—they always were, everything would stop until they had—but Angela was wondering what else besides exhaustion was wrong with the two women, what else she'd noticed and couldn't now recall, when Harry switched off the lights.

A sound distracted her from trying to recall, in the silence that seemed part of the dark. A crowd or a choir on television, she decided quickly it sounded unreal enough—and went back to straining her memory. Harry limped behind the women and started the slide projector.

Its humming blotted out the other sound. She didn't think that was on television after all; the nearest houses were too distant for their sets to be heard. Perhaps a whim of the wind was carrying sounds of a football match or a fair, except that there was no wind, but in any case what did it matter? "Here we are in Italy," Harry said.

He pronounces it "eyetally," lingeringly. They could just about de-

428

duce that it was, from one random word of a notice in the airport terminal where the Hodges were posing stiffly, smiling, out of focus, while a porter with a baggage trolley tried to gesticulate them out of the way. Presumably his Italian had failed, since they understood hardly a word of the language. After a few minutes Richard sighed, realizing that nothing but a comment would get rid of the slide. "One day we'd like to go. We're very fond of Italian opera."

"You'd like it," Deirdre said, and the visitors steeled themselves for Harry's automatic rejoinder: "It you'd like." "Ooh, he's a one," Deirdre's mother squealed, as she always did, and began to sing "Funiculi Funicula." She seemed to know only the title, to which she applied various melodies for several minutes. "You never go anywhere much, do you?" Deirdre said.

"I'd hardly say that," Richard retorted, so sharply that Angela squeezed his hand.

"You couldn't say you've seen the world. Nowhere outside England. It's a good thing you came tonight," Deirdre said.

Angela wouldn't have called the slides seeing the world, nor seeing much of anything. A pale blob she assumed to be a scoopful of the nice ice cream proved to be St. Peter's at night; Venice was light glaring from a canal and blinding the lens. "That's impressionistic," she had to say to move St. Peter's and "Was it very sunny?" to shift Venice. She felt as if she were sinking under the weight of so much banality, the Hodges' and now hers. Here were the Hodges posing against a flaking life-size fresco, Deirdre couldn't remember where, and here was the Tower of Pisa, righted at last by the camera angle. Angela thought that joke was intentional until Deirdre said, "Oh, it hasn't come out. Get on to the proper ones."

If she called the next slide proper, Angela couldn't see why. It was so dark that at first she thought there was no slide at all. Gradually, she made out Deirdre, wheeling her mother down what appeared to be a tunnel. "That's us in the catacombs," Deirdre said with what sounded like pride.

For some reason the darkness emphasized the smell of earth. In the projector's glow, most of which nestled under Harry's chin, Angela could just make out the women in front of the screen. Something about the way they were sitting: that was what she'd noticed subconsciously, but again the sound beneath the projector's hum distracted her, now that it was audible once more. "Now we go down," Deirdre said.

Harry changed the slide at once. At least they were no longer waiting for responses. The next slide was even darker, and both Angela and Richard were leaning forward, trying to distinguish who the figure with the outstretched arms was and whether it was shouting or grimacing, when Harry said, "What do you do when the cat starts molting?"

They sat back, for he'd removed the slide. "I've no idea," Richard said.

"Give the cat a comb."

"Ooh, he's a one, isn't he." Deirdre's mother shrieked, then made a sound to greet the next slide. "This is where we thought we were lost." Deirdre said.

This time Angela could have wished the slide were darker. There was no mistaking the fear in Deirdre's face and her mother's as they turned to stare back beyond Harry and the camera. Was somebody behind him, holding the torch that cast Harry's malformed shadow over them? "Get it?" he said. "Cat a comb."

Angela wondered if there was any experience they wouldn't reduce to banality. At least there weren't many more slides in the magazine. She glanced at the floor to rest her eyes, and thought she knew where the sound of many voices was coming from. "Did you leave a radio on in the basement?"

"No." All the same, Harry seemed suddenly distracted. "Quick," Deirdre said, "or we won't have time."

Time before what? If they were ready for bed, they had only to say. The next slide jerked into view, so shakily that for a moment Angela thought the street beyond the gap in the curtains had jerked. All three Hodges were on this slide, between two ranks of figures. "They're just like us really," Deirdre said, "when you get to know them."

She must mean Italians, Angela thought, not the ranks of leathery figures baring their teeth and their ribs. Their guide must have taken the photograph, of course. "You managed to make yourself understood enough to be shown the way out then," she said.

"Once you go deep enough," Harry said, "it comes out wherever you want it to."

It was the manner—offhand, unimpressed—as much as his words that made her feel she'd misheard him. "When you've been down there long enough," Deirdre corrected him as if that helped.

Before Angela could demand to know what they were talking about, the last slide clicked into place. She sucked in her breath but managed not to cry out, for the figure could scarcely be posing for the camera,

430

reaching out the stumps of its fingers; it could hardly do anything other than grin with what remained of its face. "There he is. We didn't take as long as him," Deirdre said with an embarrassed giggle. "You don't need to. Just long enough to make your exit," she explained, and the slide left the screen a moment before Harry switched off the projector.

In the dark Angela could still see the fixed grin breaking through the face. She knew without being able to see that the Hodges hadn't stopped smiling since Harry had opened the door. At last she realized what she'd seen: Deirdre and her mother, she was certain, were sitting exactly as they had been when their record had wakened her—as they had been when she and Richard had come home. "We thought of you." Harry said. "We knew you couldn't afford to go places. That's why we came back."

She found Richard's hand in the dark and tugged at it, trying to tell him both to leave quickly and to say nothing. "You'll like it," Deirdre said.

"It you'll like," Harry agreed, and as Angela pulled Richard to his feet and put her free hand over his mouth to stifle his protests, Deirdre's mother said, "Takes a bit of getting used to, that's all."

For a moment Angela thought, in the midst of her struggle with panic, that Harry had put on another slide, then that the street had jerked. It was neither: of course the street hadn't moved. "I hope you'll excuse us if we go now," Richard said, pulling her hand away from his mouth, but it didn't matter, the Hodges couldn't move fast, she was sure of that much. She'd dragged him as far as the hall when the chanting under the house swelled up triumphantly, and so did the smell of earth from the ditch that was more than a ditch. Without further ado, the house began to sink.

Seven Drops of Blood

H. F. Jamison

The scourge of Death—the parting of loved ones forever—has been the one great sorrow of the ages. Saint and sinner alike have shared its devastating power. Men of science have sought to conquer the destroyer but have hopelessly failed. Superstition, in an array of mystic rites and ceremonies that included the slaying of goats and bullocks, the beating of tom-toms in weird devil-dances, the laying on of hands and the sprinkling of holy water, has promised immunity from death. Human puppets have crossed continents and seas, braving every known peril of the wilderness and jungle in search of the fabled Fountain of Youth in which they might bathe and be young again; but at last that insatiable monster—the Rider of the Pale Horse—has stretched forth his talons of bone and has dragged them down—down—into his endless embrace!

Life is but a vapor: a few days here and a man is gone, and in multitudinous cases, even his memory, after a moment of time compared to eternity, is obliterated entirely.

Whence came Man? Why was he created? What is his purpose? Why such a short and feeble existence? Is life worth the misery entailed upon him? Why a "Somewhere beyond this vale of tears?" Why not a perpetual existence here? Why look forward after his passing to a chimerical and doubtful resurrection of the dead?

These and many similar thoughts surged through the brain of Stanton J. Eldon, millionaire, dreamer, and master of weird experiments, as he sat alone in his private laboratory.

Somewhere in this world—he believed it with all his being—there was a force mighty enough to scoff at death and the grave if one could only find it. Was that force in chemistry? Was it electro-magnetic? What? Where?

Why should man let the motor of the body—the human heart—stop at all? And, in the event that it did stop, why not start it again?

He wondered if the experiment of the great scientists of which he had just been reading—where vitality had been momentarily reestablished in the human body after death had been in undisputed possession of it for twenty-nine hours—was really a success. Was it a forecast of greater things to come? Or was it merely a case of the use of a high-pressure drug so potent that even lifeless clay could not withstand the terrific onslaught; for example, an effect similar to that produced upon the muscles of a frog when salt is placed upon them? He did not know.

From another standpoint he reasoned: If the believers in what he termed superstition—the so-called Bible myths—were correct, even they had not taken advantage of their alleged unlimited possibilities; for had not Jesus broken the bonds of death and declared: "He that believeth in me shall never die," and "Death shall have no more dominion over you"?

What was the secret of the Nazarene's power? The fools! After seeing his actual demonstration—a return from the tomb—they mocked him, and didn't even attempt to learn the truth; so, for that reason, he let them "go their way."

But after a careful reading and rereading of their traditions, Eldon saw beneath the surface a startling ray of light—through lightning, and serpent's venom, and blood!

"I saw Satan, as lightning, fall from Heaven," the sacred writer declares. Satan is still here, Eldon reasoned: invisible, all-powerful—still here. All adherents to the sacred scriptures freely admit this regardless of their respective creeds. They acknowledge that His Satanic Majesty is the one great foe of humanity, for he is supposed to control death—infernal nemesis of mankind.

Again: Satan is the original Serpent of Eden's Garden, and the Creator had said that the seed of the woman should bruise the Serpent's head: therefore, any man who could conquer death, even momentarily, would fulfil that prophecy. Satan being lightning, personified, and virgin blood being a cleanser from the Adamic sin, why not make use of one of the fallen Archangel's own weapons—fight fire with fire, so to speak—and bring about a perpetual existence here?

Seven—mystic number! The golden candlesticks were seven upon the altar; there were seven lean and seven plenteous years of King Pharaoh's reign; the seven-word vow of eternal celibacy must be chanted by a novitiate of twice seven years with one hand upon a crucifix, the other upraised toward the Seven Stars; the seven drops of blood must be taken from the virgin's side—electrify those precious drops of consecrated blood with a voltage, the middle number of which must be seven—God! He saw it all as clearly as he could see the sun at noonday!

News item—Artificial lightning has just been produced; anywhere from 250,000 to one million volts.

Eldon smiled in a pitying way as he mused, "They are making a great to-do over their 'new' discovery. That is a year-old successful experiment with me, else I would not now attempt this demonstration.

The morgue—cold, cruel repository of silent forms.

"How long has this man been dead?" Eldon inquired, indicating a glass-topped refrigerating case.

"About thirty hours, sir," the keeper answered. "Unidentified, too, as you see by the blue tag. Guess the county will have him to bury. Looks like suicide to me."

"Not embalmed yet, of course, or he wouldn't be under refrigeration."

"No. Nobody in sight to pay the bill. If the county gets him, he'll go in 'cold,'" the keeper replied grimly.

Eldon leaned over and placed a bill in the other's hand. "Lay off the embalming and send the body to my laboratory. I'll fix it with Mr. Rothe."

"Yes, sir, coming up, sir." The keeper already knew the color of Eldon's money. It was always yellow.

Once more Stanton J. Eldon was in his element. He was nearly ready for the greatest experiment of his career.

The body of the unknown had been electrically heated to 77 degrees; the seven drops of virgin blood had been injected, together with the venom of the species of serpent by which the Israelites were bitten and later healed by the serpent of brass upon the pole; and the scientist stood with his hand upon a controlling rheostat from which led four high-tension wires: one of them to an ankle of the corpse, another to the top of his head, and the others directly into a dynamic aerial-fluid generator capable of producing artificial lightning up to one million volts!

A greenish-blue light enshrouded the silent subject. Now, if Eldon's preposterous formula to offset the terrible voltage—yet to be applied—was correct, all would be well; if not, an electrical cremation would result instead of a prospective resurrection.

Gruesome? Stanton J. Eldon knew no such word. Why should the dead body of a man excite any emotions different from those which might be occasioned by the sight of a fowl slain for dinner? It was all in the state of mind. Ghosts, spooks, and hobgoblins held no terrors for him. He had never known of the presence of an ogre at the advent of a human being into this world; why should there be any at one's exit? The fear of death, he said to himself, has been fostered by religious fanatics since the dawn of Creation, and civilization has paid dearly for it—is still paying.

One of Eldon's friends had told him that if there was any such thing as spirit return, if Eldon would go and sit on his friend's grave at midnight on the day following his demise, he would make himself manifest if possible. The instructions had been carried out, not only once, but for seven successive nights, and nothing had happened; so Eldon had smoked his black cigars in vain.

If there was anything on the Other Side, he wanted first-hand information concerning it. In his heart of hearts he might consider the possibility of another life; but scoffed at the idea of a spirit's return from that life to this mundane sphere. (Secretly, he may have been like the old negro, Hambone, who said: "No, sah. I don't bleeb in ghosts, but I don't want no truck wid 'em.")

Eldon turned the knob of the rheostat slowly, almost imperceptibly, and, familiar though he was with nearly every sort of crazy experiment, he gave a little grunt of approval as the body before him moved slightly according to his imagined schedule, when the voltmeter showed the 257,000 mark.

Was there any merit to words of incantation? Well—they were supposed to be the very foundation of all hocus-pocus, exorcism, magic, and mystery; so they must form a part of his own conjury in this case.

"Peace, be still," the Supreme Magician of the Universe had commanded, and the winds and the waves had obeyed. He could have calmed them just as easily with never a word.

"In the name of Jesus Christ of Nazareth, rise up and walk," said his Apostle, and a cripple, lame from his mother's womb, arose and began leaping and praising.

Furthermore, the Supreme Magician had promised: "If ye believe, greater things than these ye shall do."

Well—Eldon never doubted the Master's ability to do those things, but he was just a little skeptical regarding his own personal powers. However, he wouldn't dispute the Master's word; so his fingers clutched the rheostat knob a little tighter, and he intoned a sacred formula from

435

the Old Testament that he had selected as best suited for the occasion: "Thou of the Valley of Dry Bones, rise up and salute."

A long pause. Once more he chanted: "As I passed by Thee . . . I said while Thou wast in thy blood; yea, I said while Thou wast in thy blood, live."

The clammy thing upon the table slowly opened its eyes, its tongue moistened its lips; a smacking sound followed, and it spoke in ghastly unnatural tones such as might have come forth from the tomb itself!

"Gladys, you're all I've ever cared for, and now to think that you would betray me—would be unfaithful. . . . See this gun? I've always said that no wife of mine could ever betray me and get away with it! No! I won't let go of your arm. I don't give a damn if I do break it, for I'm going to send your cheating soul to Hell anyway. . . .

"Oh, my God! Gladys—I didn't intend to do that! Gladys! Gladys! speak to me!"

The frightful guttural cry which came from the living-dead Frankenstein-monster before Eldon was music to his scientific ears: For he had bruised the Serpent's head! He had conquered death!

The horrid spokesman upon the table continued: "Why, hello, Jim. Yes; I shot her and then killed myself! . . . What a beautiful grove of trees! . . . And over there is the River of Life and the Sea of Glass! . . . Where is that music coming from? . . . Gee, I'm thirsty! That was certainly a glorious drink. Is one's slightest wish gratified here? I wish I could see Gladys. . . . Why, there she is now! How radiantly beautiful she appears! . . . But she deceived me, Jim. . . . I wish I knew the truth! . . . Oh, Jim! I do know the truth! Gladys is coming toward me. I worship her, Jim. Then I 'saw through a glass, darkly,' but now I see 'face to face.' . . . She's gone! . . . She was tempted. . . . I understand. . . . The Master forgave her as he forgave the woman they would have stoned. . . . And now—*look! Look!* Those two are together! See, they embrace! . . . The Magdalene came to meet Gladys to tell her she need have no fears. . . . Gladys will be transformed, too; made pure and holy. . . . And I will join Gladys after I go through a slight purgatorial fire. . . . Jim! Jim! tell me more! . . . Quick! Jim —I've started back to earth and I don't want to go! The world is such a hell! Nothing there but misery and woe. . . . Heaven much better than even this? . . . This only Paradise, you say? . . . Oh, Jim! I'm going back. . . . Yes, yes—I see who is doing it! I know many things now. Death, which I dreaded so much, I find to be but the open door to complete happiness. . . . Yes, yes, I'll make that scientist——"

❊ ❊ ❊

436

The hideous form half arose from the table and turning, looked straight at Eldon with a gaze so all-seeing in those dead yet living orbs, that for a moment the scientist ceased chewing his black cigar.

"You fool!" The words burned the very air. "You miserable, contemptible, experimenting fool! Interfering with the plans of the gods! Why, I wouldn't be back on your accursed planet if you were to deed me the worthless thing! If a murderer, even as I, has a chance over Yonder, what will it mean to one who has always played square! . . . *Open that switch!*"

Eldon shifted the cigar to the other side of his mouth and chewed vigorously upon it for several seconds. Then he spoke:

"Not so fast, Brother. It's been some time since I've conversed with anybody with one foot over the Borderline, so to speak; and, as this will doubtless be my last opportunity to do so, I would like to ask a few questions. The first one is: 'Is your corporeal body suffering any pain?' "

"The torture is intolerable!" the other cried vehemently.

"One truth!" Eldon ejaculated. "There has been some doubt as to whether restored dead flesh has any feeling. That point is settled. Now I want to slip just a little more current to you. Perhaps I can be able to give you the eternal life possessed by the Fallen Archangel. How's that?" He shot the needle around to the 500,000 mark!

The monster was jerked violently backward a distance of eighteen inches, then sat bolt upright. A moment in that position and one foot was lifted outward and downward to the floor. The other followed, and the indescribable cadaver arose from the table, and with short, jerky steps—its progress impeded by the heavy copper electrodes and the large insulated wires—it started toward Eldon, pointing a curved, rigid finger into his face! The scientist backed away. One touch from the tips of those fingers of destruction and he would be in possession of full information regarding the Other Shore.

An ear-blighting shriek came from the lips of the walking remains.

"You fiend! You damnable hellion! Look at my hands—the flesh is beginning to roast! You are destroying my body and soul! My body will be consumed to ashes, and my soul consigned to oblivion! *Open that switch!*"

Eldon saw—heard—and smelled the diabolical scene of his own making; saw the flesh beginning to shrivel like cracklings; heard the blood seething; his nostrils were filled with the nauseating odor, and he knew that the virgin blood was being overcome by the terrible voltage—an improper mixture somewhere! He couldn't reach the rheostat for the

437

death-dealing fingers before him, so he ran to the master switch and kicked it open.

The burning carcass wavered back and forth, then laughed—a hideous, vultural croak which came from melting vocal chords!

"Has-iss—heiss—awk! Great news for you—Eldon." The spark of life still talked, though going fast. "You'll join me—May 21st—1930—ten A.M.—auto wreck—awk-hiss-hiss!" The uncanny volcanic manikin slumped down, sacklike. . . . Eldon wiped the cold sweat from his brow.

Two hours later he entered the morgue. "Heard anything yet about our unknown?" he inquired.

"Yes; I was just going to phone you. We have learned his name. He's a guy from up Slayton way. Killed himself after croakin' his wife. I think they said her name was Gladys. They were found out on a country road by the side of an old Ford car. . . . Why, what's the matter—you sick?"

Eldon had swallowed his cigar stub at the sudden confirmatory words of his experiment!

"No need to embalm the body when I return it," he said. His voice was weak and he was very pale. "It has been electrically embalmed. You may charge them for the job, however, if they want embalming done, and keep the money."

The keeper rubbed his chin in a thoughtful way. "Embalmed by electricity. That's a new one. Must be your latest, eh?"

Eldon walked slowly toward the front. "Yes," he replied, "and I think it will be my last."

When he reached the door he turned and called back: "Say, by the way; do you want to buy a good automobile, cheap?"

438

Short and Nasty

Darrell Schweitzer

My friend, who will never read this, I'm writing this for you. I want to tell you about the sound of the rats on the metal stairs. You'd appreciate that. Once, that would have been your sort of touch.

The rats. I heard them skittering after me as I descended into the darkness from the El platform at Ruan Street. At times the sound they made suggested not many creatures, but one, and not a rat either, but some sort of crippled, twisted dwarf: scrape-scrape, *thunk!* Scrape-scrape, *thunk!*

Ridiculous, *then.*

In the old days, we would have started this together like some collaborative Gothic novel, telling how we traveled comfortably by coach for some days in the winter of 182—while composing our thoughts in separate diaries with enviable elegance (alternating passages from such diaries forming the opening section of the novel) before reaching London and calling our old friend Sir Archibald Blank, with whom we had enjoyed cordial business and personal relations, lo these many years. That way the three of us could at least look forward to a cozy evening's chat by the fire, gently sipping brandy, our glasses unobtrusively kept full by the taciturn, enigmatic butler, who would figure hugely in the subsequent plot once the requisite weirdness began to manifest itself.

That was the old way, Henry, when we were young. Remember? When we two were in college together, when everybody else was reading Hermann Hesse, we were heavily "into" Gothic novels—Monk Lewis, Mrs. Radcliffe, and the ever prolific Anonymous—the early Romantics, De Quincey, Byron, Keats, Mary Shelley—in short anybody who seemed suitably exquisite, melancholy, and doomed for Art's sake.

Remember how we used to try to top each other's affectations, just for the fun of it, the outrageous, frilly clothes, the sweeping gestures, the dialogue never heard outside of a bad costume flick: "I say, old chap, I think I shall take up opium. It's so *frightfully* decadent."

"I much prefer laudanum, old bean. The visions of Hell are much more vivid that way—"

Neither of us could have fooled a real Briton for a minute, by the way. Our accents were pure college theater. I suppose most of our classmates just thought we were gay.

Ah, with a sweeping sigh. We had joy; we had fun; we had seasons in the crypt.

I try to be funny, Henry, to take the edge off the pain. We laugh to avoid weeping. There is no other way. It is hard to go on.

This isn't even London. It's merely Philadelphia. And I don't have much time.

Henry, the years have a way of taking the glitter off our dreams. Think of some piece of a Mummer's costume, soggy in the gutter the day after New Year's.

Rats on the stairway. I walked down, into the darkness as the train rumbled away above me, into the rain-slicked street of boarded-up storefronts and rubbish, past the occasional furtive late-night pedestrian; no longer the would-be Romantic fop but a worn-out man huddled in a worn-out trench coat against the bitter wind and drizzle, not exactly young either, but slouching into middle age gray-haired and forty pounds heavier.

Now I was there because Gretta, your wife, had called me. She said you were dying.

"Shouldn't you call an ambulance, then?" I'd asked.

"He's—crazy. It's too late. He says, no. You have to come. *Now.* Please." She was sobbing then.

Rats on the stairway, amid the trash on the street. Scrape-scrape, *thunk*.

I came because I was afraid, for you Henry, yes, and *of* you in a way, but mostly out of an even harder to define *fascination*, which brought me there at such an hour on such a night despite everything, despite even the souring of our friendship and the ostensible strangeness of Gretta's —and your—request that I, of all people, should be with you in your final hour.

Remember? The last time we'd seen one another there were a lot of obscenities. I think you started it. It hardly matters. Maybe it was me.

I came because I wanted to know how much you *knew*, Henry. That was what I was really afraid of. You'd found out a good deal about me, of course. And I'd found out that you'd found out. But I still had my own secrets. Yes.

I came because I had dreamed of you, and in my dream Gretta called on the phone and spoke exactly those same words in the same tone of voice. "Paul, you have to come. *Now*. Please."

Then I rode the elevated train, in my dream, and there were rats scraping on the metal stairway above me as I descended from the platform; and I walked in the cold January rain; and Gretta stood white-faced and wide-eyed at the door. She ushered me in without a word, without a sound; up to the dingy bedroom where you lay in the darkness, oblivious to the flickering TV in one corner. The place was crammed with books on leaning shelves, and odd statues and metal devices: pendants and symbols and a single, staring metal mask above the bed. The whole house smelled of dust and mildew and decay. The ceiling had cracked and sagged dangerously.

I leaned over the bed, in my dream, and you struggled to raise yourself on your elbows. At last you got a hand on my shoulder and pulled yourself up. You tried to whisper something—and out of your mouth came the sound of the telephone ringing, and Gretta's distant voice begging me to come, and her sobbing followed by the rattle of the train, and muttered words in my own voice, and the scrape-scrape-*thunk* of the rats.

Then I was at the door again, and once more Gretta ushered me upstairs, and you tried to rise, only this time you were visibly *smaller* as you lay there, fully two feet shorter than before.

You tried to speak, and the sound of the phone came out of your mouth.

And for a third time I reached the door, and Gretta met me, and your voice was no more than a faint croaking. You had shrunk to the size of a dwarf, or a malformed child.

And again, and again, until you were no more than a white lump of flesh like a beached and dying fish flopping among the bedclothes, still trying to speak, your face distorted almost beyond recognition.

You squeaked and wheezed. I couldn't make out any words. The noise was like rats, scratching.

I awoke with a start, sweating, my sleep interrupted by the sound of the phone ringing.

It was Gretta.

When I saw her standing at the door, where I somehow knew she would be, I didn't say anything. But I remembered a lot. I remembered what it had been like when both of us were young. I remembered one night in particular, when she had leaned dreamily out the window of my car as we drove along slowly somewhere out in the country, and the wind and the moonlight made her hair seem like flowing gold.

That was one of my little secrets. You hadn't been along that night. We'd never told you about it. It was only a few weeks before your wedding. I thought of it as my hopeless, impossible last chance then, and I suppose it was.

Now her face was lined, and her hair wasn't yet gray entirely, but it was stringy. It had been a long time since the moonlight.

I nodded to her and walked slowly up the stairs, certain of what I was going to see.

There you were in the semidarkness. I can't begin to describe what I felt, what I feared, confronting you at your pathetic end.

I don't think you were even aware of me as I leaned over and switched off the TV. You lay still, your breathing labored. Then, suddenly, you tried to raise yourself. I sat down beside the bed, leaned over, and you caught hold of my shoulder.

That was the worst part, you touching me, just then.

You struggled to speak.

"*You bastard—*"

I pulled away. You dropped back.

"Now, now, my dear Henry old chap, old bean, that's no way to talk to—"

"*You slime-sucking bastard—*"

"Ah, Henry, we had such dreams in the old days. Remember? We were going to be great poets, novelists, playwrights, actors, and now it has come to this."

"*Fuck you—*"

"Henry, at the very least, you always had a more impressive vocabulary than that."

"*I know—*"

God, Henry, I felt all the rage pouring out of me then, all the useless words pent up for years. "Shit. What do you know? That I stole money from the firm? That I took it from *you,* my esteemed partner in the second-rate, second-hand costume rental business? You can't prove a thing, Henry, for all the hurtful things you've said, for all you have ruined our friendship with your own paranoia. I never took more than my due. Not a cent more."

Even then I couldn't say everything I wanted to. There was so, so much. Could I tell you how you'd been the millstone around my neck for so many years, how every time I looked in the mirror and saw myself a little grayer, a little more rumpled, I thought of you? Yes, you, and I told myself that I could have taken another path, walked another road in life other than the one Henry Fisher led me on with his promises and his absurdities and his so-called ambitions. You wasted the best part of my life, Henry. You, somehow, you dragged me down, and I blame you for it. You made me part of the mediocrity we are today. I cannot forgive you.

One more joke, Henry, the knife twisting in my gut. You accused *me*. "I don't give a shit about the money. *I know what you did*—"

I leaned forward and whispered, "You know that I went to see Laura Howard? Yes, I did. She's very good. I thank you for recommending her to me."

I indulged in a little untruth, my friend. You merely mentioned that you'd run into her after so many years. You gave me the address of her shop. That was enough.

I never got over Laura any more than I ever got over Gretta. She was *very* special, more than another old college chum, Miss Occult 1970, whose burning ambition at nineteen had been to conjure up the ghost of Aleister Crowley so it could possess her and make her the greatest magician in the world. Now she ran a magic shop along Frankford Avenue, not far from your present hovel, behind one of those boarded-up storefronts. As your mind had gone progressively softer, as you babbled more and more about auras and past lives and all that New Age crap, you became rather a disciple of our old friend Laura Howard, didn't you?

I attended one of her, ah, sessions. At first it was all I could do that night to contain my laughter.

But no—

Afterward, when all the suckers were gone, with visions of Atlantean past lives dancing in their pointy little heads, she just stared at me, like a snake, her gaze inscrutable and implacable. Something deep inside me told me that it was time to leave, that it was time to *run,* that my entire soul was laid bare.

"Hello Paul," she said softly. I couldn't make any sense out of her tones, her words, her gestures. They seemed a mixture of surprise and fondness and hatred and almost robotic apathy, all blended together.

We talked for a long time, about the old days, about you, and about

Gretta, and sometimes she was almost like a confessor, someone I *could* lay my soul bare before, and at other times she was an inquisitor and I her helpless captive.

We went out for something to eat, not to a fancy restaurant, no, not in that neighborhood, but to this ridiculous hole-in-the-wall Japanese place that, in deference to the sophistication of the customers, served sukiyaki on a hoagie bun.

Then we came back, talked some more, and had sex. That, I think, was part of the spell she worked on me, something magical.

Afterward she stared into my face in the semidarkness—her eyes as impenetrable as a cat's—and she said, "You want something, Paul. You want it very much."

And I did. I was afraid to say it. But I did, just then, want a way to go back and reweave the strands of my life, to make everything better, to be rid of *you*, Henry.

Then she told me. She told me the secret of your death.

"I know what you did—"

You surprised me again by actually sitting up of your own accord. I could tell how gaunt and wasted you had become, like a ninety-year-old man with both feet and half your legs in the grave. I thought you were going to fall apart then and there into a mass of bones and squishy goo. But you were determined to have your say.

"I know about my *death*," you said. How you ranted just then, Henry. How your face was twisted with—was it simple hatred or elementary fear? "It has been growing within me like a seed, ever since I was born. Laura told me that. All that lives must die. *Death* is built in. When we're young, it's small, dormant, like a pinhead-sized tumor nobody's found yet. But it's there, slowly growing larger as we age, as our living tissue diminishes, until by the time we're old we carry around a great load of *death*, with little life remaining. Sometimes very old people can look in a mirror and see *death* staring back, *death* wearing an old man's face like a tissue-thin mask."

"She told me its name," I said. "I can make it come and go fetch, like a dog. All I had to do was whisper that name each night for a week, and I woke it up. So I did, every night before I said my prayers, thinking of you."

"Why?"

That took me aback. Suddenly it was I who dangled there on the edge of the abyss. I fumbled for words.

"Why? Because you deserved it."

"No, why did Laura Howard do it?"

That was exquisite, my friend. Your deft touch from the old days. Artistic and agonizing. Just then you seemed pleading with me, despairing not that your death was devouring you from the inside out even as we spoke, or that I seemingly hated you, but because you had lost Laura Howard's friendship, because *she* had turned on you for some inexplicable reason.

I really wanted to comfort you then. My own hatred started to unwind. I wanted to make it easier for you.

"I don't know," I said. "I paid her for her, ah, professional services— I mean the secret, the name, the spell, what have you—but I don't think she cared about the fee. It's part of some machination of hers, probably. God knows what she is trying to do. We're just tools to her, puppets."

I felt helpless then. I rose to leave.

"I don't understand," I said. "Why *did* you ask me to come here tonight if you knew all this? Just to confront me? What good would that do?" I was angry at you again. "You were always a bit of an idiot, Henry."

"Yes, I was, but not this last time. I went to Laura too, once I understood what was happening."

I paused in the doorway.

"She was as you described her, Paul, like an inscrutable snake, neither horrified that her old friends were murdering one another, nor pitying, nor anything at all. I don't think she's quite human anymore—"

"Henry, she's got more humanity left than you do just now, or I—"

"Shut up and let me finish. She told me something important. Something I found very comforting, all things considered. I think it's part of her scheme that you know this, so Goddamn you, Paul, you're going to hear it. She told me that my *death* was indeed like a little doggie out in the backyard that would come running after it had finished its business, after it had dropped the gigantic turd that is my rotting corpse. Then it comes running. Home to Papa. *You.* And it's hungry."

I turned back into the room, ready to—I don't know what—ready to throttle you then and there with my own hands, for the satisfaction, so I could deny, negate everything, so I could shout in your face as you died, *No, no, you snivelling moron, it's all your fault—*

But you were too quick for me. You died even you as sat there, eyes suddenly rolling up white, jaw dropping, and out of your mouth came the sound of the phone, of Gretta's voice, the rumble of the El, the scratching on the metal stairs.

And there was something more, something crawling *inside you* under

445

your skin, not like a dog at all, but more like a huge spider scratching to get out.

I screamed then and ran out of the room, down the stairs, colliding with Gretta. I hardly realized she was in my arms. We stumbled together to the base of the stairwell, bouncing off the wall, grabbing the railing, never quite off our feet. It was a weird kind of dance, and I was crazy then, as if the record needle in my mind were skipping and scratching all over the record, and everything was a jumble, a bit of that, a screech of this—and before I knew what I was doing I kissed her hard, passionately, not because I desired her anymore, but to *deny* it all, Henry, to fling one last defiance in the sanctimonious face of time; as if for just an instant you'd never existed and she and I had been married all these years but we weren't old and poor and everything had turned out differently; as if, no, that wasn't it at all—as if somehow the three of us were still together and you were still my friend and we both loved Gretta and she loved both of us equally and the end we came to was beautiful and romantic and not just sordid—

She broke away, frightened.

"What's happened?" she said.

"I can't talk about it. I'll call you later—"

I think she thought the look on my face and the tone of my voice bespoke grief.

She was sobbing behind me as I ran out of the house, down the street in the cold rain, toward the rusty elevated platform.

Scrape-scrape, *thunk!*

It was waiting for me. I saw it once, wriggling between the steps almost at my feet. I caught a glimpse of it as it dropped down into the darkness below: something like a fleshy, scaleless fish with a human face, and with crab legs and claws.

I ran the rest of the way up the stairs, onto the platform.

A black man sat at the far end of the furthest bench, smoking and reading a newspaper. He glanced up once, then resumed his reading.

Scrape-scrape.

I gazed down the steps in growing horror as I saw something moving on the landing below where the stairway turned. Something dwarfish and misshapen, but more human now, with arms and legs.

I wanted to run to the black man. But what could I have told him? What could he have done?

Down there on the landing, the thing stepped out of the shadows, into the half-light, and I saw that it had my face, hugely out of proportion to the body. Our eyes met. It spoke, clearly, with your voice, my friend.

"I'm all yours now."

I would have run then. I would have scrambled across the tracks risking getting fried on the third rail. But just then I saw that the train was coming. It was all I could do to remain where I was, clinging to a pillar and watching as the thing on the stairs ascended painfully, inexorably the steps much too large for its stunted legs.

It was all I could do to hang on as the train's light got brighter and brighter, as I could hear the rattling cars draw nearer, blessedly nearer.

Then I was aboard. The black man sat at the far end of the otherwise empty car, still reading his paper as if he hadn't noticed a thing. Just as the doors wheezed shut I saw the creature at the top of the stairs, glaring at me, croaking something I couldn't make out.

I think it had grown taller by then.

Of course there was no such easy escape. Your *death* at the very least knew where I lived, either from your memory or instructions, or from some inevitable homing instinct.

When I got off the train at 69th Street in Upper Darby, I heard the same scrape-scrape *thunk!* on the stairs behind me. I glanced back once across the nearly deserted station and saw something shuffle furtively behind a locked-up newsstand. I heard it scraping on the concrete floor.

A cop stared at me strangely, but only at me.

There was a cab outside, thank God, but just as I closed the door something struck hard against it, tearing metal, and I looked out; and there, inches from my face was *my face* or a distorted parody of it, filled with hate, mouthing words, the body behind it hunched and powerful.

"Drive!" I shrieked at the cabby.

"Where to? I said, *where too?*" he demanded. He hadn't seen, heard anything. I managed to give him my address correctly. He shrugged and muttered, "Jeez," and must have taken me for a drunk.

Not that my continued flight did any good. How the thing travels is something of a puzzle, alternately fast and slow if undeniably relentless. Did it hang onto the outside of the El train? Possibly it doesn't travel at all, but merely gathers itself together nearby like a cloud of guilt each time I come to a halt.

Somehow the cab ride confused it, and bought me a little time, so that, in the approved Gothic manner, this document serves as my confession and the tale shall end with my demise.

You would have appreciated that. If only we could go back, be young again; if only we — I — could find the strength within ourselves to go on, to shape our own lives. Hatred is a mere admission of failure. If only we could still be friends and talk about this in Sir Archibald Blank's cozy study and feel that last, delicious *frisson*. Then, it would all fit. I wouldn't be afraid of dying then. If it fit.

Then I might tell one final joke. I might speculate that the footsteps I hear on the stairs outside, that shuffling and thudding and crashing, could very well be two gigantic furniture movers delivering a grand piano to the apartment upstairs at four o'clock in the morning.

But, that would wreck the ending.

Scrape-scrape, *thunk*.

This story is for you, old friend. It's the least I can offer.——

The Silver Knife

RALPH ALLEN LANG

When Ross Nagel returned in less than a fortnight from his first manhunt in the uniform of a Northwest Mounted policeman it was a matter of surprise to all who witnessed his return to barracks. It was not that any one doubted his ability, for he came to the Mounties with an enviable service record in His Majesty's troops in the Far East. The surprise was due to the fact that he had been assigned to the trail of Wolf Dahlgren, a veritable wolf of the North, whose familiar ground constituted no less than a thousand square miles of frozen waste.

Still more surprised was the post commander when Nagel, in making his report, laid before him a package containing two curious articles.

The first of these was well calculated to inspire the astonishment with which the inspector regarded it. It was a knife of falchion shape, with a wicked curve at the point that suggested the purpose for which it had originally been made: a sacrificial knife. In the eyes of the inspector this impression was further confirmed by the material of which it was made —beaten silver—and by the pair of great twin rubies that ornamented the hilt. He had once seen a knife almost exactly similar to it while attached as guard to an expedition excavating the ruins of an ancient temple of Dagon. But what could such a knife, with its priceless inset gems, be doing here in the arctic wastes of North America? Only one explanation presented itself to the puzzled mind of the inspector; that it had been brought by an immigrating Old World tribe in some dim period of history when the continents were still connected by a strip of land. A remnant of this tribe might conceivably still exist in the unexplored regions of the north, the sacred knife having been handed down from generation to generation. How had Wolf Dahlgren gained possession of it while under pursuit by the Mounties on a murder charge? He turned his attention to the other article on the desk, a small leather-bound notebook, in hopes that it might furnish an explanation. It was in good condition except for blood stains on the cover, legibly written, and the inspector leaned back to read. The first entry was dated two weeks previously:

Dec. 3rd.

With this entry I begin another diary, one of a long series, written to be destroyed, that have solaced the loneliness of three years spent on arctic trails. It is lonely here in camp tonight, with the nearest white settlement two hundred miles away, and a hard day's trailing from the native village where I passed the last week. If luck stays with me this will be my last trek through this bitter, accursed country, and luck at last is coming my way. After three years of freezing, starving, and murdering miserable creatures for contemptible amounts, luck puts me in possession of a treasure more valuable than any gold mine in the North. The simple Indian fools who used the silver knife in their sacrificial service could have no idea of the value of the great rubies in its hilt. To them it is merely a religious relic handed down from long-forgotten ancestors; to me it is freedom, life, luxury, the silver key of desire. It is right and just that I should have the knife, who have so much better use for it than any the old sachem ever put it to. They will not have missed it until twilight tonight, and no Indians will cover as much trail in two days as the one I have left behind me today. In less than two weeks I will hit the sea coast; then for a ship to the States, and the Mounties can have their North.

Another good day's trailing, bettering perhaps the distance made yesterday. Nothing of interest has occurred and I have seen no living thing
except a skulking timber wolf. It is remarkable in that it is the largest I
have ever seen, a great shaggy brute standing inches higher than any of
my huskies, and it seems to be following me. Doubtless it is beginning to
feel the pinch of winter hunger.

An astounding thing occurred last night, unparalleled in all of my
experience in the North; an attack by a wolf or wolves on a camp
protected by an open fire. It was well after midnight and, due to the fact
that I was sleeping more soundly than usual, the fire had subsided
almost into a bed of coals when I was jarred awake by a sharp yelp from
the dogs, followed by the snarling fury of a fight. It could not be called a
fight, either, for the wolf or wolves were gone again into the night as
swiftly as they had come, and I had only a brief glimpse of one shaggy
giant as he faded into the obscurity of the darkness. But brief as the
engagement was, its effect was devastating to my team; the lead dog
having been literally torn to ribbons and another slashed on the shoulder. As a consequence I was able to make but poor time today and I had
trouble constantly with the dogs, so demoralized is their condition.
What puzzles me is that the attackers seemed to make no effort to obtain
food, but I suppose that my awakening frightened them away. I have
seen the lone wolf several times today, dogging my trail at an uncom-
fortably close distance. On one occasion I was close enough to see
his devilish fangs as he stood and snarled his hatred. Two clear shots I
had at him before he retreated and I am unable to explain how I could
have missed him. I have seen no other wolves at any time and am
almost forced to believe that it was he alone who made the attack last
night, although it seems impossible that one wolf could wreak such
havoc. Tonight I will keep a sharp watch to prevent a repetition of
it.

The wolf was back last night and despite all of my precautions took
toll of another of my dogs. I was sleeping lightly with my rifle at the
ready and was up at the first sound, getting my first close sight of him as

he raised his bloody fangs from the husky's throat and turned to face me. He must have stood nearly three feet high, but it was the ghoulish fury in his yellow eyes that unnerved me more than his great stature. I fired point-blank at the hideous head, but still he stood there fixing me with that baleful glare, and it was not until the pack closed in on his flank that he turned and loped away. Three dogs only are left of my original five, and these are so demoralized with terror that I can make but poor headway. I, too, own myself a victim of intense nervousness, and am weighted down by an uncanny, unreasonable feeling of dread. If I were more susceptible to superstitious beliefs I might find myself imagining all sorts of weird explanations of my failure to drop him at point-blank with a rifle that has brought down moose. As it is, though I take no stock in werewolf tales, my mental condition is such that I would not be above trying a silver bullet on him if I had one, merely to relieve my nerves.

Dec. 7th.

The Thing was back again last night, but this time he appeared in a different manner. He is bold now, and appeared as soon as dusk had fallen, skulking in the shadows just outside the circle of firelight. Three hours I sat there under the spell of those hellish yellow eyes, now appearing on one side of the circle, now on the other, compelling me frequently to change my position in order to watch him. I fired again and again with no result except that the eyes moved to another position. Then it happened. Before I knew what had occurred I was pouring shot after shot into the charging beast, until the hammer clicked on an empty chamber. He was so close that the hateful eyes seemed burning through my brain, and in desperate agony I grasped the only weapon my hand fell upon, the silver knife. What happened then I do not clearly know, but he swerved away from me and in some unexplainable way I sensed fear in his snarl. Then he was among the dogs, ripping and slashing, and a third victim was torn to ribbons. My nerve is shattered and I scarcely know what to believe. Bullets have no effect on the Thing and I am here in the wilderness a hundred miles from civilization with no protection against him. I have one hope, founded on the manner in which he avoided me last night. For some reason he fears me, although I am absolutely helpless before him. My only hope now is to push on to the coast with the two dogs I have left, praying that these, too, may not fall victims before I reach there.

I am writing this now not to dispel loneliness or even nervousness, but in sheer terror, and to take my mind off the horror that is prowling outside. It may be the last page of this ghastly tale, for the Thing has grown desperate now and apparently has submerged its fear of me in the greater fear of my reaching civilization and escaping it. Since early morning I have pushed forward at a killing pace, with the Thing growing steadily in confidence or in desperation and drawing closer to me with every mile. At noon I reached this abandoned miner's cabin and was able to gain its shelter in just the nick of time. The Thing evidently can think, for at sight of the cabin it threw all caution to the winds and charged, straining me to the utmost to reach the door, and forcing me to abandon the dogs. Their cries were pitiful, for so greatly had the terror grown upon them that they did not even try to fight. Watching from a small high window on the north side of the cabin I was sickened at the savage rending of their bodies and at the ghastly aspect of its bloody snout as it raised its head and gave vent to a blood-chilling howl, the first sound I have heard it utter. I can not describe the nightmare of horror that closed down on my brain as it rang through the silence and which has left me completely unmanned. It was minutes before I could pull myself together enough to make a search of the cabin for any means of defense, and then at last luck smiled and gave me a glimmer of hope. Among a collection of useless odds and ends left by the miners I found an old bullet-mold, and the thought has come to me that I may be able to melt enough silver from the knife to run a bullet. Weird and ridiculous as the idea seems, I am convinced that the thing outside can be nothing else than a werewolf, and my only hope is to try a silver bullet, to which alone they are said to be vulnerable. I have pried all of the loose wood obtainable off of the studding and wait now for the fire to burn into coals hot enough to melt the silver. It is almost ready and I stop now to break a piece from the guard of the knife.

All hope of killing the Thing is now gone. The wood I have is too dry and lifeless to make a fire hot enough to melt the silver. I must play a waiting game now, for as long as the provisions in my shoulder knapsack hold out I am safe. In its wolf form the Thing can not open the door, although I have no way of barring it, and if it assumes human shape I will kill it with a bullet. It is whining now, and scratching against the wall in an effort to rear up high enough to look in the window. . . . Now it is padding back and forth, back and forth, before the door; trying, doubtless, to work up courage to assume its human form and—there, now, is a hand on the latch!

It has been three minutes now since the latch was raised. Fear is doubtless holding him back. At any moment he may conquer it, but I am ready. Hounds of Hell! can it be possible that he is changing back into a wolf again? . . .

There was a strange look on inspector Moore's face as he raised his eyes in a questioning glance to the face of the constable, who still waited.

"Just how did you come into possession of these?" he asked.

Nagel's face showed plainly that he too had perused the contents of the diary.

"I found them in an abandoned miner's cabin beyond Bitter Creek," he answered slowly. "Wolf Dahlgren was in there dead, his throat torn as though by the fangs of a wolf. I found this diary on the table beside him. There was another corpse in there too, a wrinkled old Indian whose weird ceremonial garb marked him as some kind of medicine man or sachem. It was in his breast that I found the silver knife."

THE SKY GARDEN

PETER CANNON

Late on a hot, humid, and noisy day in Manhattan, during the most oppressive summer in recent memory, I had been riding uptown with hundreds of other sweating, long-suffering commuters on the Lexington Avenue subway, until at length I disembarked at 96th Street. I might have been heading home on the opposite side of the island but for a call that morning from an old college friend who had importuned me to join him for a drink after work at his parents' place on Fifth Avenue. I had been looking forward to spending the evening alone with a good book, but I could not resist such an unexpected summons to a part of town to which I was rarely invited, from someone I had greatly esteemed and had, if the sad truth be known, not heard from in ages. I confess that

Christopher Seabright and I had not been intimates at the small, elite eastern institution where we had moved in the same aesthetic circles, though I like to think that our relations had been cordial, especially during our senior year when he had edited the campus literary magazine and I had enjoyed the privilege of serving as his assistant. I say we were out of touch; however, on occasion I did experience the thrill of seeing him on the society page of the newspaper, usually depicted at some charity gala, escorting one or another debutante of model-perfect beauty.

The address proved to be one of the finest on the East Side, a stately high rise adjacent to a major museum. I could not help but be impressed; if not a gale then certainly a brisk, steady wind of material prosperity had borne Christopher Seabright from the cradle into early manhood. I gave my name to the doorman, a beak-nosed gentleman in a long-tailed green coat, who chirruped into an intercom and then, after a considerable pause for a reply, directed me to a gilded elevator, which I took up to the penthouse. At the top the elevator opened to reveal, not a common corridor, but a large, wooden-paneled door with an iron ring for a handle. This swung open onto a hallway with a bare marble floor, upon which I cautiously trod with all the humility appropriate to a mere mortal entering some temple of the demigods.

I do not make the classical reference frivolously, for the lofty passage in which I found myself was practically denuded of furniture and decoration, while along the plain white walls stretched a profusion of potted green houseplants, giving the scene a decidedly Arcadian air. I stood and gazed about in awe, though a closer inspection of the ceiling showed the paint to be cracked, peeling, and patched; eloquent testimony to how troublesome it was in even the best of these old buildings to maintain their crumbling roofs.

I was beginning to wonder about the absence of my host, when from a distance I heard a familiar voice call my name. "I'm out on the terrace —be with you in a moment." Not too long after there emerged from somewhere down the hall to my right the tall, weedy form of my friend, dressed in an Oxford shirt, khakis, and tassel loafers without socks, clutching a watering can. With his free hand, like a character out of one of those British TV series on PBS, Christopher Seabright swept the shank of fair hair falling in controlled disarray from off his patrician forehead and clasped my hand in a moist, limp grip. I recalled having overheard coeds of our mutual acquaintance remarking that he was handsome if a bit of a pretty boy, and I have no doubt they would not have altered this judgment today. His manner, never effusive, struck me as definitely more languid than before, though an unmistakable glimmer in his eyes betrayed his gladness to see me.

"Well, it's been a while, hasn't it?" he said in the understated tones that one associates with members of America's older families. "Funny how some people just slip out of your life without your really noticing it, and then suddenly you wonder whatever became of good old so-and-so. I can't wait to find out what you've been up to, but first let's get something cold to drink."

I followed him down the hall into a spacious interior room, the kitchen, where he set down the watering can and extracted from the refrigerator a couple of beers. These in hand, he proceeded to give me a quick tour of the premises. The main rooms lay in a row off the long central passageway, on the park side. All were sparsely furnished, except again for large clumps of luxuriant green plants and shrubs, which seemed to thrive in the damp, heavy air. I detected no air-conditioning; indeed, the whole apartment had the feel of some sweltering greenhouse, but queerly enough without any pervading flowery fragrance.

My companion's bedroom was as bosky as the rest, with a bed, bureau, and bookshelves squeezed in as if to accomodate the plants rather than the reverse. On top of the bureau was a silver-framed photograph of an elderly couple, recognizable to me from the society notices: florid, corpulent Mr. Seabright, the wealthy international financier, and high-cheek-boned Mrs. Seabright, the well-born Anglo-American actress, from whom her son had clearly inherited his looks. "Mother and Dad are away—haven't seen them for weeks," said my host. He went on to explain that they had a flat in London and a house in Jamaica, but at the moment they were probably at their weekend place on "the island" (by which he meant Long Island; more specifically, the chic village of West Islip). "I rarely go out there these days," he sighed. "Too much to do to keep me here, I'm afraid."

I asked if he was ever lonely living in such a gigantic apartment by himself. "Lonely? Why no, what gave you that idea? As you'll see, I don't lack for companionship." He lead me into the corner room at the end of the hall, the master bedroom, where on the limb of a small tree perched the most enormous parrot I had ever seen. "This is Sylvester," said my friend, "but don't expect him to return your greeting—he's painfully shy in front of strangers." On the contrary, in all his green glory Sylvester seemed to regard me with an air of lordly disdain, more like the preternatural parrot in John Collier's "Bird of Prey," I felt, than, say, the benign bird of Algernon Blackwood's *Dudley & Gilderoy*. But then parrots are notorious for caring only for their owners, I assured myself, and it would be paranoid to imagine that I was being singled out for hostile, beady-eyed scrutiny.

"I take care of Sylvester," said my friend. "Or does Sylvester take care of me? Sometimes I'm not sure." He giggled. When I asked where Sylvester's cage was, he giggled again, a trifle louder but still in the enervated tone of an *ennuyé* man of the world. Although curious to learn such things as the creature's age and vocabulary range and the length of time they had had him, I dropped the subject, sensing that further questions about the family pet would not be welcomed.

Displaying no concern that Sylvester might try to fly after us, the scion of the Seabrights showed the way from the master bedroom through a set of French doors out onto a narrow, hedge-bordered walkway, which ran the length of the penthouse, until it widened into a proper terrace. Leaning across the chest-level hedge, I could look down all the dizzying stories below to Central Park, its foliage patched with yellow since the recent drought, and spy such landmarks as the reservoir and the tennis courts. I settled myself into a deck chair in the lee of a brightly striped awning, which fluttered faintly in the breezes that, according to my host, always stirred at this altitude no matter what the weather. While he went inside to retrieve more beverages, I looked up from my genial vantage point at the sky, which had grown increasingly thick and brown since my arrival. With any luck a thunderstorm would soon be upon us, bringing a real downpour and not just a brief shower.

Behind me, rising from the middle of the roof, was a square, pediment-crowned tower, an architectural feature common to buildings on Central Park West but rare if not nonexistent, I had always thought, on Fifth Avenue. Was it simply an ornate water tank, or did it connect somehow with the Seabright penthouse? A shuttered window suggested that it might have human access. Upon his return with the beers, my friend confirmed that the tower belonged to them. "I'll take you up there later," he said. "It has the most incredible view." For all the magnificence of the prospect from the terrace, he observed, it was limited by the dense shrubbery along the edge.

Increasingly relaxed and refreshed as we swallowed our second and then our third beers, we began to feel once again that easy undergraduate comraderie of the staff of the college magazine that had seemed to us at the time the center of the universe. The nostalgia that my friend evinced, however, had a melancholy tinge. I could tell from certain elliptical remarks and cynical asides that he was discontent in his current career, that he had somehow gotten off track, that he was still far from fulfilling the brilliant promise of his youthful literary triumphs; and now, with the utmost delicacy, fearful that I might be touching on a sensitive issue, uncertain that he even had one, I finally asked him about his job.

He laughed, as if reacting to an especially bad pun or feeble joke. "Job? You want to know about my job? How shall I put it. You've heard of editors of special projects? Well, I'm editor of 'special events' at — — —," he said, naming a fashionable quarterly. "I organize the parties. Fortunately, it doesn't require my coming in from nine to five every day. But then, as I probably said before, there's plenty to keep me busy here at home." Like gardening? I was bold to suggest.

"Yes, like gardening. To be perfectly frank, I spend much of my free time looking after the plants—watering, pruning, transplanting—it's a lot of work. Of course, we could hire someone to come in, someone who could also feed Sylvester, but Sylvester is—is so particular. . . . At any rate, in due course I've turned into a devotee of landscape—or should I say 'rooftop'?—gardening." My host proceeded to launch into a somewhat technical lecture on the horticultural art, which clearly had become more than just a pastime; in fact, it constituted a passion that had virtually displaced all other interests. He scarcely had time, he proudly confessed, for the social life that had once been integral to his existence. Yet was not his enthusiasm for this new pursuit a bit forced? Did I not detect a certain ruefulness in his soft, fruity voice, as if he recognized but dared not admit that underlying the whole business was an element almost alarmingly unnatural?

Before I could offer any hint of criticism, however, he changed the subject. "Forgive me for boring you," my friend said at last. "I do tend to run on. So now, what have *you* been up to? I see you at least have succeeded in becoming a genuine editor." I responded that I was a junior editor of how-to and self-help books at one of the less prestigious midtown publishers, making no effort in my beery mood of self-pity to conceal my shame at having so far not edited any literary fiction.

"Hmm, maybe I can help in that department," said my host. "Despite all my gardening duties, I have been able to get started on a 'novel'—which I'd really appreciate your looking at. Since it's far from finished, you'd just have to give me your initial impressions. Of course, there're others I could've asked—some quite distinguished editors at major houses—but I always valued your opinion in the old days on the magazine and believe you're the one person I can trust to render a truly impartial evaluation. So if you wouldn't mind, I'll take you up to my study and show it to you right away." As we could now feel scattered drops of rain from the low, brown-black clouds and could hear the distant rumble of thunder, it was time in any event to retreat indoors. The wind rose up and rustled the shrubbery at our backs.

Through what I would have assumed was a closet door off the central corridor, Christopher Seabright conducted me up a short, winding stairway to the chamber contained within the tower I had noticed from the terrace. Dim light from a Tiffany lamp revealed a Mission-style chair and table with a manuscript on top in the middle of the room, while along the walls clustered huge potted plants, whose tendrils and branches shot up some fifteen or more feet to the arched ceiling, from which hung festoons of old paint. In truth, I felt as if I were in a tropical arboretum, not the refuge of a writer. Other signs suggested that the place was a favorite roost of Sylvester's. To one side another small stairway led up to a landing and perhaps beyond.

Ushering me into the chair at the table, my friend announced that he was going to leave me undisturbed; he would return after a while with some sandwiches and more brew. Reading conditions were far from ideal in that hot, dank, airless room, with the muffled sound of driving rain on all sides and the towering plants casting fantastic shadows in the gloom; yet I fixed my attention on the text before me, confident that it would prove more absorbing than any book I could have read that night at home. Typed on the first page was the title: "The Sky Garden: A True Story."

I can do no better than summarize the contents of this extraordinary narrative, for in my present situation I, alas, have no copy of the manuscript, nor do I have much hope of setting eyes on one again. Having a fondness for imaginative fiction, I was delighted to discover that the novel fell into that genre that might best be classified as heroic fantasy. In the opening chapter the bumptious protagonist, Budd Whitley, enters (whether as an act of free will or by accident is left unclear) an airy realm known simply as the "sky garden," located in some plane or dimension *above* our own. The Narnia-like inhabitants of this paradise, animals and elves and centaurs and satyrs, welcome this human interloper, so seldom do "children of apes" pass into their world. After proclaiming Whitley their king, they persuade him to finance a scheme to transform a vast tract of formal garden after the French or Italian manner into a ruder, more "natural" countryside of crags and tarns and hidden grottoes and moss-covered ruins. Despite the astronomical cost (yes, even in fairyland) of such a public works project, our hero cheerfully writes out a sizeable check, enough to allow the relandscaping to begin. Both in the scope of its vision and the exquisite beauty of its style, this early section resembled, without suffering from the comparison, Poe's "Domain of Arnheim."

Up to this point, I must say though, I saw little commercial potential in the work, since I knew from experience that my editor-in-chief was on the whole unsympathetic to this kind of stuff—unless it bore the name Tolkien or King. But then the plot took an unexpected turn. A new race of beings arrives on the scene: bald, spindly-limbed humanoids, with large, black, fathomless eyes, who evidently get their kicks from abducting people from earth and subjecting them to undignified physical examinations. The Xlom, as they are called, not sharing the same aesthetic tastes as the other denizens of the sky garden, object to the changes they notice underway. Insults are exchanged, an overzealous warrior strikes the first blow, and a wholesale war breaks out that devastates the land, leaving it, ironically enough, close to the state that Whitley and his allies were trying originally to achieve. Obviously my friend, while building upon precedents set by Hopkins in *Invaders* and Streiber in *Communion*, was venturing far beyond their puerile conceptions. Here, I realized in my excitement, was bestseller material, if only I could convince the author to market the story as nonfiction!

Totally hooked on the narrative by this juncture, I hardly heeded the storm raging outside, though a clap of thunder would on occasion shake my eyrie enough to send fine particles of paint down from the ceiling to settle like stardust on the page. I felt neither thirsty nor hungry, notwithstanding a certain lightheadedness from drinking on an empty stomach. Fresh air, possibly seeping in through minute cracks in the tower masonry, brought some relief from the humidity.

The battle for mastery of the sky garden concludes indecisively upon the sudden appearance of an entity who is utterly unhumanoid in aspect, Brotogeris, Lord of Most of Creation. Surveying the destruction, Brotogeris holds Whitley, as king and the most mature being involved, chiefly responsible. (The childish Xlom are merely banished to their spacecraft to go back to pestering gullible earthlings.) While Whitley may pass back and forth between the world of men and the sky garden, he must perform a penance that entails a good deal of manual labor, a prospect he views ambivalently at best. His only hope of mitigation of his punishment depends on his finding other people from outside, willing or otherwise, to help him do the dirty work. He succeeds in luring an old man and woman into the garden, but they prove too feeble to be efficient; they end up in confinement, as Brotogeris's personal playthings.

I was now approaching the end of the manuscript, and was wondering where the story could possibly go from here, when my host returned, curiously empty-handed. Food and drink, however, were the last things on my mind, so eager was I to discuss the novel, to clear up a few fuzzy points. Did the sky garden have any objective reality or did it exist only in the protagonist's dreams? How in particular did one get in and out of this fantasy world? There should be some sort of concrete entrance, like a wardrobe, I thought. My first impulse was to express my admiration for the work, but the storm was now at the height of its fury, and I could make myself understood only by shouting. Even so, my friend seemed barely to acknowledge my compliments; indeed, his responses verged on the inarticulate.

"Contact with unknown spheres . . . the beating of emerald wings . . . the scratching of outside shapes on the universe's utmost rim" were among the odd phrases he mumbled in what, it dawned on me, must be a state of extreme intoxication. I feared that all the while I had been reading my friend had been drinking. At this point I could do no more than humor him.

Swinging a comradely arm around my shoulder, Christopher Seabright proceeded to guide me, at the same time I leant him support, up the little side stairs, which turned at a right angle past a landing and came to an end before a pair of French doors, shuttered on the outside. "I said I'd show you the view, old pal," my friend cried above the roar of the storm as he fumbled at the latch. "I promise you, you won't be disappointed." I protested that we would hardly be able to see anything in this weather, but he persisted and at last succeeded in overcoming the force of the wind and flinging wide the shutters. My heart leapt as for a moment the inebriate teetered on the brink of the sill then recovered some semblance of balance.

At first I could make nothing out in the blackness as I squinted against the torrents of rain. Then a flash of lightning illuminated the sky and the terrace immediately below, which in that second appeared—if I could believe my eyes—to stretch, a sodden expanse of earth and undergrowth, all the way to the horizon! I had scarcely time to react to this titanic vision, for in another instant a tremendous crack of thunder shook the tower, and now it was I who, from that shockingly less than vertiginous height, was in danger of losing my grip. From behind my friend must have staggered against me. My head swimming, I reeled—I fell. But in the next lightning flash there arose in my pathway, breaking my descent, an avian figure, very far larger in its proportions than any dweller of the jungle. And the hue of the feathers of the figure was of the greenness of the summer grass.

Note

I discovered the above account while cleaning out the desk of my cubicle mate at Throne Publishers, part of the Throne Publishing Group, several days after his abrupt firing. (Or did he, as one rumor has it, simply walk out of the office one afternoon and never come back?) I have heard nothing of or from him in the weeks since — nor has anyone else to my knowledge. The text is in my coworker's handwriting, and the narrator is pretty clearly autobiographical, yet I cannot ascribe authorship to him beyond a shadow of a doubt. One might suppose that it had been resting in his drawer before his disappearance, though I suspect that it somehow found its way there afterward. The condition of the manuscript itself raises as many questions as the content, for stuck in between its tattered and soiled pages is a great deal of downy fluff, together with one long, perfectly formed, blue-green feather.

SMOKE FANTASY

THOMAS R. JORDAN

The hour hand was close on to one o'clock, and Sanderson was still working on his latest story. His reading lamp was the only light burning in the lonely house, and shadows clustered in the corners of the library waiting for their chance to be rulers of the night.

Something had happened to Sanderson's power of imagination. In the past, it had never been difficult to describe his characters, regardless of their position in the plot. He now found himself unable to describe the man who was to be the central figure of his tale; a man of cruel and wanton deeds, black of soul and hard of heart, a man of unnatural and sadistic desires, capable of a multitude of evils. But the appearance and build of this man still eluded him, and his features seemed only a blur in the mind's eye of the writer.

461

It might be because he had written so many stories of a similar nature that his mind was unable to produce an original description and he found himself facing a blank wall. Always his stories had been grotesque and weird, woven around men and women possessing strange and terrible qualities.

Sanderson was confronted with a frenzied thought. Perhaps he had lost the knack of twisting words and phrases so that the reader would get a clear picture of the characters described. If such a thing had happened he would have to find some way to help him restore that faculty.

He paced to the window and looked out into the night, watching the rain patter gently on the ground outside, seeking for an inspiration. The darkness yielded nothing and only seemed to mock him as he strained for a suitable picture of the man he was trying to visualize.

The smoke from his cigarette on the ashtray drifted idly into a corner and formed into a billowy cloud. As he stared at it he suddenly thought that here was a way to reach his goal. If he could imagine that his character was sitting there, hidden by the smoke, perhaps he could materialize a picture of him from the mist, as one imagines visions and palaces in the clouds on a windy day.

Sanderson seated himself in his chair and peered into the blue billows. A ragged wisp of smoke jutting out from the thick mist could be his hair, unkempt and tangled, like that of a madman. One section was dividing from the rest in a long angular streamer to the right, forming an imaginary arm, and he could almost make out two indistinct legs at the foot, with another arm making itself manifest on the other side.

But his attempts at conjuring a face and body from the vapors were difficult. In vain he concentrated on the upper portion of the fog in an attempt to create in his imagination the lines and expressions of a countenance. Suddenly, success began to reward his efforts.

He could barely discern a pair of eyes, wild and inflamed, staring from the mist, while whirls of smoke eddied around them, wider and wider, until a long evil nose was revealed.

The face was beginning to disclose itself more clearly when he became aware that the body had taken a definite form, long and lean with a sinuous strength to it that reminded Sanderson of a great cat. It sat in the chair in a tensed forward position as if ready to spring. One long arm hung at his side while the other gripped the back of the chair for support.

Sanderson's delighted gaze returned to the face. Clear and evil it now stood out, the mouth vicious and hard, leering at him with diabolical cunning, while sharp deep lines ran up from the corners of its mouth. Similar lines creased the uncouth forehead into a permanent scowl and the bulging eyes still stared crazily.

The vision was perfect, and the writer closed his eyes for a moment, phrasing sentences of description and feeling a surge of confidence flow through him. His character was perfect in every detail and now he could go ahead on his story with a new confidence in his powers of imagination.

He opened his eyes to find that the vision had not left. It sat there in the corner, clearer than ever, and it seemed to him that the mouth was working in a grimace of hate. A wave of fear swept through Sanderson and he wondered if his mind had deserted him. The figure was now rising, eddies of smoke still clinging to it, and an evil vitality made itself manifest to the writer, for it was now striding toward him with quick, catlike movements.

It had all happened so quickly that Sanderson was unable to get out of his chair before the thing was on him. The long clawlike hands reached for his throat and the air was instantly cut off. He made a frantic, futile struggle to loosen that relentless grasp, and all the time those mad eyes stared mercilessly into his own.

The last thing that Sanderson sensed before pain-pierced blackness enveloped him was the faint odor of his cigarette, still burning in the ashtray.

Smudge Makes a New Best Friend

PETER CANNON

Before Fran opened her apartment door, she warned Paul that there was someone else in her life. Uh oh, he thought. Was the old boyfriend whom she hadn't quite gotten over still in residence, or worse yet did she have a small child in dire need of a daddy? To his relief, Fran's great love turned out to be neither of the above, though the object of her affections was nowhere to be seen when she switched on the light just inside her entryway/dining room/living room. (Fran lived in a fashionable postwar highrise, in one of those low-ceilinged boxlike spaces that so many Manhattanites are proud to call home.)

"I'm afraid Smudge is on the shy side," Fran said by way of apology. "She probably ran into the closet as soon as she realized I was coming home with a stranger."

"Smudge?"

"My cat. When I got her at the shelter as a kitten, she was covered with newsprint from the newspaper in her cage. She's actually black and white."

"Kind of like a cow."

"Yes, like a cow. Would you like a drink? Maybe a saucer . . ." Fran giggled. "Sorry, Freudian slip. A glass of milk?"

"Are you offering any other dairy products this evening? Ice cream perhaps?"

"Sure. Vanilla Swiss almond okay with you?"

"My favorite."

Fran suggested Paul sit on the couch while she went into the kitchen. Haven't exactly cleaned up the place for guests, thought Paul, as he picked his way to the couch, careful to step over the paper bags, cardboard boxes, Ping-Pong balls, tennis balls, and wads of aluminum foil that littered the living room floor. It dawned on him while he waited that these were all cat toys.

"You take pretty good care of Smudge, don't you?" said Paul when his hostess returned with the bowls of ice cream.

"I do my best," said Fran, taking a seat next to him on the couch. "It's not easy, though. Because I often work late and on weekends, she spends a lot of time by herself."

"Ever consider getting her a companion?"

"Well, there was Tabitha." Fran took a deep breath. "But about a year ago Tabitha got lymphoma and had to be put to sleep right away. Smudge was left alone, at just three months old, since I had to leave on a ten-day business trip. The only company she had was the lady next door who came in once a day to feed her. I felt so guilty. Smudge was really traumatized."

"Did you get professional help?"

"Yes, fortunately I knew enough to call Miss Purrfecto, the psychic psychia*cat*rist. She lives on the West Coast and specializes in phone consultations. If necessary she'll send you things like crystals and herbs, the types of medicines that veterinarians don't know about. I must say therapy has been a big help to Smudge."

At this point, as if on cue, the patient herself emerged warily from the direction of the bedroom. She did indeed resemble a small cow, a small fat cow, her stomach sagging like an udder nearly to the carpet. At first she poked her head into a bag or two, then waddled to the coffee table, where she raised herself on her front paws and sniffed at the now empty ice cream bowls.

"Vanilla Swiss almond is Smudge's favorite, too."

"You feed her ice cream?"

"From time to time I let her lick the bowl, but otherwise she eats only diet catfood."

When Paul reached over to pet the animal, Smudge jumped down and skittered back toward the bedroom, with surprising speed given her girth.

"Kind of nervous, isn't she?"

"Like I said, she's shy of new people, but over time I bet you and she could become the best of friends."

"You think so?" said Paul, slipping an arm around Fran's shoulder.

Later, in the bedroom, Paul was on the verge of falling asleep when he felt something furry leap on his pillow. Soon he heard an odd slurping sound by his ear. In the dim light from the window he could see that Smudge was working her front paws up and down against—was it Fran's hair? No, there was some other object, a piece of underwear perhaps?

"I should have told you," said Fran, as if reading his thoughts. "Because Smudge was weaned too early, she has this infantile urge to knead."

"What does she need?"

"She kneads an old pair of pantyhose I keep on the bed. In kittens kneading helps the mother's milk to run. Smudge really gets off on it. You can tell because she slobbers a lot."

Yuck, thought Paul as he drifted off to dreamland.

In the months that followed, Paul became a regular overnight guest. To his relief, Fran didn't seem to mind that they always stayed at her place, which was far cozier than his own bachelor quarters farther uptown. This arrangement suited him perfectly. As a self-employed freelancer with an income supplemented by a modest if not insubstantial inheritance from his late parents, Paul valued his freedom. Fortunately, Fran respected this. Not the least of her charms was the store she set on her own independence. Unlike virtually every other single woman in her late thirties he had dated in New York, Fran never even hinted that she was in a rush to get married and have children. A demanding job as a senior vice-president at a prestigious Wall Street firm appeared to be sufficiently fulfilling.

The nature of his work allowed Paul to spend all the time he wanted at home. Since more often than not he was already there in the morning, he began staying later and later into the day at Fran's apartment. As a result, he couldn't avoid getting better acquainted with Smudge. Paul had never kept a pet in the city. In his view, the affection and companionship weren't worth the bother and responsibility. On the other hand, he wasn't averse to looking after someone else's animal on occasion. He willingly enough fell into the routine of feeding Smudge while Fran was out of town on business, which happened every third week or so.

Fran encouraged the relationship, though at first Paul could do little since Smudge tended to hide in the bedroom closet whenever he was around. Gradually, however, she warmed up to him in her own undemonstrative if teasing way, especially after he started feeding her the local cat food she greedily gobbled up as soon as it was served. Afterward she would roll on her back, raise her paws in a seductive pose, and give him a come-hither look. But if he reached down to touch her she would immediately turn over and scamper off. She would regard the Ping-Pong balls he rolled at her with indifference if not outright disdain. At best she would permit him to sit next to her on the couch, where she liked to doze during the day.

Paul liked the couch, too. He preferred to do his work there as well as read the *New Yorker* and fill in the Sunday *Times* crossword or, on alternate weeks, the acrostic puzzle. In the evenings he would turn on the TV and watch the news or maybe a ball game if Fran wasn't getting home until late, which was frequently the case. Paul didn't have a lot of friends, and those few he did have he began to lose touch with as he settled in more and more comfortably at Fran's. Smudge wasn't such bad company, he eventually decided, boring though she was. Fran didn't dispute this assessment, claiming that her personality had been totally flattened by her trauma as a kitten.

If after a while Paul grew almost as fond of Smudge as he was of her mistress, he did, however, remain disgusted by the cat's performance in bed, to wit, the pathetic kneading and worrying of the drool-soaked pantyhose, which somehow never got thrown in the wash as often as its condition warranted. To his horror, he shortly discovered that this was a nightly ritual with the animal, who as soon as the lights were off leaped up on his side of the bed and began to nuzzle the vile garment that Fran took care to place between their two pillows.

Since Paul hated arguments, and Fran was always so agreeable, he held off any protest. Finally, however, the moment came when he had to say something.

"I hope you won't be offended if I bring it up, honey," he murmured to Fran in bed one midnight. "But do you think anything can be done to cure Smudge of her kneading habit?"

"I'm sorry, sweetie," answered Fran a trifle defensively. "I know it's sort of gross, but if you'd gone through a childhood as trying as Smudge's I'm sure you'd understand."

"Don't you think maybe that cat therapist of yours could do something to break her of this regressive behavior pattern?"

"Well, I suppose it'd do no harm to call Miss Purrfecto," Fran conceded.

"I'd really appreciate it, honey."

"Okay, sweetie. I promise."

In any event, as she later reported to Paul, Fran did have a series of phone consultations with Miss Purrfecto about Smudge's health, both physical and emotional. These, alas, produced no apparent results, even though at one point Fran sent Miss Purrfecto a saliva sample to analyze. Smudge continued to knead the old pair of pantyhose just as before. Even when Paul stayed overnight in the apartment while Fran was away, the animal would meow until he provided her with her bedtime fetish.

At last another, unexpected breakthrough was achieved: Paul discovered that he could stroke Smudge while she was in the act of kneading. It may have been that the cat was simply oblivious, high on her fix, but the next day while sitting next to Smudge on the couch Paul found he could put a hand on her without scaring her off. Fran was delighted when he later told her this happy news.

It was probably no coincidence that things came together for Fran and Paul at this time. They agreed to make the setup that suited them both so well more permanent. By giving up his own apartment, Paul could save significantly on expenses. Best of all, from his standpoint, Fran never once mentioned the word "commitment." It was understood that they'd shack up, play it by ear, and see how it went, no conditions attached.

On the evening Paul officially moved in, Fran broke out a bottle of champagne to celebrate. Brimming glasses in hand, they sat down on either side of Smudge on the couch, where she lay curled, contented as a cow.

"To you, dear," said Fran, clinking her glass against his.

467

"And to you, dear," said Paul. "Oh, yes, and let's not forget Smudge."

The cat, seemingly recognizing her name, rolled over and lifted her paws. Paul reached down to scratch her stomach. While he was thus distracted, Fran poured a dose of fine powder into his champagne glass.

"To Smudge." Fran drained her glass in one gulp.

"To Smudge." Paul followed suit.

"If Smudge could talk, sweetie," said Fran as she refilled their glasses, "I'm sure she'd tell you how pleased she is to have you as her new friend."

"Yes, we certainly do get along all right, I guess—and someday I'm sure she'll get over her need to knead, as it were, heh heh." Paul took a break from patting Smudge and sipped his second glass cautiously. Already he felt the liquor going to his head. It was putting him in a queer, confessional mood, he realized. "You know, honey, to be honest I have to wonder what you see in a guy like me. I mean—"

Over time Paul adjusted satisfactorily enough to his new regime. He had plenty of oversized bags and boxes to crawl into and balls to bat around the floor. As for Fran, she was so glad she had taken Miss Purrfecto's advice and sent her that saliva sample from which the psychic therapist concocted her "magic medicine." A few grains in Paul's water dish each morning keeps him fit, if not always serene. When visitors come over, he does tend to run and hide in his own roomy closet. On the other hand, life has its rewards. Sometimes before going to bed she lets him lick her ice cream dish. (Vanilla Swiss almond remains a special treat.) And oh yes, Paul now has his own pair of pantyhose—well, in truth an old leotard—which every night he mouths to his heart's content, side by side with his new best friend.

Snail Ghost

WILL MURRAY

The moon rose blue and I sensed a shift, not only in the night, but in my own mind. I approached the door, which was neither gray nor blue, and no other possible color, either.

I opened the door.

A hand, four-digited and of the hue and texture of unpolished blue jade, darted out and grasped my wrist. The hand was like a vise. It possessed two pair of digits, each pair in opposition to the other. There were two thumbs.

A tall, silent form inched forward.

The creature had no face, only a domed head, unfeatured but for two blank white eye patches. The head devolved into the shoulders the way a bullet fits a cartridge. There was no neck. The trunk was normal, but the waist spread out into a skirtlike fall that ended in a round, fleshy pad on which the entity stood. A shiny, sticky film extruded from the pad, producing locomotion. Like a snail, then, it advanced.

I stood firm, and waited unresisting.

My real name does not matter, for I was not then in my real body, but in the demi-shell that enables me to traverse the undimensioned spaces as Goblin X, the unknown. My outward form must have been as bizarre to this creature from beyond the door as he was to me. To his white eyes, I was a biped with death-white head and hands. My head is featureless, too, except for the single froglike orb, and my hands possess three snakey appendages, each tipped with a small hard ball. I was dressed in a shagreen tunic and short cloak, with red pants tightly fit and covered with black lines like frenzied-brushstrokes. Electrum ornaments dotted my tunic, which is gray.

As I said, I am Goblin X, the unknown.

I was in Tibet, in a cave whose entrance was filling with snow while the wind outside howled and somewhere a lama played a signaling instrument deeply. The moon outside was blue, and the door whose color

469

defies naming was where the crystal had said it would be. Of the crystal, I will not speak, but what I learned from it brought me to Tibet in search of the gateway to a world no literature had named before this.

The interlocking hand of the ghostly snail creature withdrew, and I passed beyond the door, which closed of itself. There was no sound, no sensation, although my many senses were attuned by enhancement and habit to register all aspects of dimensional travel. There was none.

There was a Mobius Road, which turned in on itself like a twisted ribbon. It gave the appearance of going nowhere, but I knew otherwise. I was dragged once around the road, and we sank into its pale surface — one of its surfaces.

We emerged in a black space, in which a door floated. The door was neither red nor orange, but it was no other possible color, either. The snail entity dragged me behind the door, and I saw that from behind, the door could not be seen, nor did it exist. The entity led me back around and pointed to the door in a gesture that partly commanded, partly implored. I opened my eye to the fullest and peered into his mind. I almost fell in.

There were gray-blue clouds, a fog, dust, and age. Inchoate thoughts roiled wordlessly. Confusion. Lostness and a single thought: *H-e-l-p*.

I lidded my eye just in time. And I understood. The creature needed help. But with what? The door clearly led toward the answer.

I opened the door, and passed through it alone. The snail creature did not follow. I knew he could not follow; I knew he desired to follow; but I did not know why. I only knew that it was not a spell keeping him out.

Beyond the door, which rolled shut, was a square room. It was large, with bone walls, and empty of furnishings. I stood facing another blue snail creature. He might have been identical with the one who conducted me to this place — except he stood immobile, as if dead. I opened my eye to its fullest and encountered a black blankness in its mind. Perhaps it was dead.

If so, the others were dead, too. For there were almost a score of the blue entities, equally motionless. They stood about in various positions, and I wended my way around them, searching their minds. All were empty. I noticed only one thing: these creatures — all indistinguishable from one another — were arrayed in a winding, confused train, as if they had all died or been suspended while following one another about the room. Seeking an exit? Perhaps. But perhaps this was a burial chamber for their dead. Or a travel chamber in which its occupants were placed in suspended animation. I could tell nothing.

I left the room.

When the door had reclosed, the snail creature vised my wrist once more, fearful of being deserted. I peered into its mind again, but there was only chaos. The creature turned its bullet head to me, and I saw nothing in its blank white eyes.

It gestured back to the door. This time it pushed me. I thought of breaking away, but my curiosity was strongly aroused—and curiosity is my most powerful emotion. Perhaps the only one I possess as Goblin X.

The room had changed. The blue creatures were still there. But so were others. They were all single-orbed entities who looked exactly like myself. They were immobile, and arrayed in a chain, each single form distinguished only by a gesture or positioning of limbs. Some of these frozen images were locked in attitudes of examination of the blue entities. I examined them closely, and found them to be solid. But I did not understand.

This time I left the room at great speed and floated past the blue snail creature, back toward the far door that led back to Tibet. But when I got there, I could not open the door. I was trapped, and I understood that I was trapped in just the same way the blue creature had been trapped until I had opened that door. I had been its only hope, but who was mine?

The snail was beside me again. This time he only approached and did not touch me. He knew I understood my plight. Our plight.

There was an answer here. Perhaps not a solution, but an answer. I set out to discover it.

The mind of my fellow prisoner was of no help. Whatever held him held also his mind, except for the single impulse to seek help. I knew that somehow I had left behind afterimages of my examination of that room, just as the snail ghost had—but our images were solid. Thus, they were not merely images. But there was something else. My sensation as I first entered this area of blackness through the first door—or my lack of sensation. I had traveled through many dimensions, and I knew the sensations of each, just as a seasoned earthly sailor knows which sea he is sailing just by its smell. I recognized no sensation, not even analogous sensations. Could this mean something? It must—and as I thought those thoughts, a partial answer came to me. There was but one dimension through which I had never traveled, and that was *time*.

In all the arcane books I had ever read, it had been written that one could not travel ahead in time any faster than one lived, and that traveling back through time was impossible. The past was gone. One could not return to a time before one's own, nor to a time one had already passed through. How could an entity meet itself? One does not leave duplicates of one's self behind as one journeys through life and through space, like footprints in dirt. Certainly not living footprints, endlessly reenacting one's past actions. Perhaps the ghostly images could be viewed once more, but their substance is forever gone. A building may exist seemingly unchanged from year to year, or a rock might, but they are changed, and creatures not only change, but move and age and evolve.

Yet in the room beyond existed solid but unliving remnants of my past actions within that room—and of the snail of the ghostly movements.

I opened that door again, and tried to enter. This time I could not. Something barred me. And there was an extra image of myself exactly where I had stood the second time I had entered that bone-white room.

I shut my single eye and left my body. The room did not resist me then. I floated freely, adjusting my vision. The room vibrated, the images vibrated. They possessed some thwarted atomic motion, immobile as they were. I entered the shell of my most recent entrance into the room and took possession of it. I hastily left the room, solid once more.

When I had returned to the black outer chamber my fellow prisoner in time was there. My body was not. I left this body and reentered the room, claiming another. When I returned in its shell, my previous host was gone. Strange. But I felt normal in the body I possessed. What would happen if I tried to possess one of the snail creature's frozen afterimages?

I left my host and entered one of the snail ghosts. It was a weird creature to inhabit. I felt heavy and thick, as if composed of organless tendonous tissues. My brain felt dull. I slid slowly from the room.

When I emerged, the blue snail creature saw me, and I recognized, through eyes like its own, a shocking horror I would not have been able to read had I been in my own body.

I never knew what really happened to this creature. There was that blank, mindless expression, and it suddenly imploded into a blue ball. The ball compressed rapidly and was gone in the blackness. Vanished? Shrunken to subatomic size? Had it ceased to exist? I did not know, nor did I care, for my own body was likewise gone.

No matter. I left my host and traveled back into the frozen-time chamber in search of another Goblin X host. There were many to chose from.

But they were all gone. The room was devoid of objects!

Hastily, I reclaimed my snaillike host.

I had no time to consider the cosmic irony of the conceit that I had assumed the identical position of the one who had dragged me into this timeless chamber, when the door leading back to the Tibetan cave slowly opened. I glided toward it.

Framed in the opening, I saw the hooded amber eye of Goblin X, the crimson spiderspark dancing deep within it. I was seeing myself as I had first sought to enter the door that was neither gray nor blue. I reached out with my double set of opposable fingers and caught the wrist nearest to me. Goblin X froze unresisting. In the dangerous moment (I know not how I knew it was dangerous) when we touched, I left this body and reclaimed my own. Before I could be dragged beyond the door, I spoke the words that brought the Black Fire of Isirus to consume invisibly the four-digited hand vising my wrist. It shriveled and withdrew.

As the door closed on me, I saw the snail ghost recede into the blackness, its blank eyes holding some alien light. Then it was gone.

I stood in the howling snow, under a blue moon slowly whitening as if in death and there was only one cold thought in my brain: *Whose soul had possessed the snail ghost?*

SOMETHING NASTY

WILLIAM F. NOLAN

Have you had your shower yet, Janey?"

Her mother's voice from below stairs, drifting smokily up to her, barely audible where she lay in her bed.

Louder now; insistent. "Janey! Will you *answer* me!"

She got up, cat-stretched, walked into the hall, to the landing, where her mother could hear her. "I've been reading."

"But I *told* you that Uncle Gus was coming over this afternoon."

"I hate him," said Janey softly.

"You're muttering. I can't understand you." Frustration. Anger and frustration. "Come down here at once."

When Janey reached the bottom of the stairs her mother's image was rippled. The little girl blinked rapidly, trying to clear her watering eyes.

Janey's mother stood tall and ample-fleshed and fresh-smelling above her in a satiny summer dress.

Mommy always looks nice when Uncle Gus is coming.

"Why are you crying?" Anger had given way to concern.

"Because," said Janey.

"Because why?"

"Because I don't want to talk to Uncle Gus."

"But he *adores* you! He comes over especially to see you."

"No, he doesn't," said Janey, scrubbing at her cheek with a small fist. "He doesn't adore me and he doesn't come specially to see me. He comes to get money from Daddy."

Her mother was shocked. "That's a terrible thing to say!"

"But it's true. *Isn't* it true?"

"Your Uncle Gus was hurt in the war. He can't hold down an ordinary job. We just do what we can to help him."

"He never liked me," said Janey. "He says I make too much noise. And he never lets me play with Whiskers when he's here."

"That's because cats bother him. He's not used to them. He doesn't like furry things." Her mother touched at Janey's hair. Soft gold. "Remember that mouse you got last Christmas, how nervous it made him . . . remember?"

"Pete was smart," said Janey. "He didn't like Uncle Gus, same as me."

"Mice neither like nor dislike people," Janey's mother told her. "They're not intelligent enough for that."

Janey shook her head stubbornly. "Pete was *very* intelligent. He could find cheese anywhere in my room, no matter where I hid it."

"That has to do with a basic sense of smell, not intelligence," her mother said. "But we're wasting time here, Janey. You run upstairs, take your shower and then put on your pretty new dress. The one with red polka dots."

"They're strawberries. It has little red strawberries on it."

"Fine. Now just do as I say. Gus will be here soon and I want my brother to be *proud* of his niece."

Blonde head down, her small heels dragging at the top of each step, Janey went back upstairs.

"I'm not going to report this to your father," Janey's mother was saying, her voice dimming as the little girl continued upward. "I'll just tell him you overslept."

"I don't care what you tell Daddy," murmured Janey. The words were smothered in hallway distance as she moved toward her room.

Daddy would believe anything Mommy told him. He always did. Sometimes it was true, about oversleeping. It was hard to wake up from her afternoon nap. *Because I put off going to sleep. Because I hate it.* Along with eating broccoli, and taking colored vitamin pills in little animal shapes and seeing the dentist and going on roller coasters.

Uncle Gus had taken her on a high, scary roller coaster ride last summer at the park, and it had made her vomit. He liked to upset her, frighten her. Mommy didn't know about all the times Uncle Gus said scary things to her, or played mean tricks on her, or took her places she didn't want to go.

Mommy would leave her with him while she went shopping, and Janey absolutely *hated* being there in his dark old house. He knew the dark frightened her. He'd sit there in front of her with all the lights out, telling spooky stories, with sick, awful things in them, his voice oily and horrible. She'd get so scared, listening to him, that sometimes she'd cry.

And that made him smile.

"Gus. Always so *good* to see you!"

"Hi, Sis."

"C'mon inside. Jim's puttering around out back somewhere. I've fixed us a nice lunch. Sliced turkey. And I made some cornbread."

"So where's my favorite niece?"

"Janey's due down here any second. She'll be wearing her new dress —just for you."

"Well, now, isn't that nice."

She was watching from the top of the stairs, lying flat on her stomach so she wouldn't be seen. It made her sick, watching Mommy hug Uncle Gus that way, each time he came over, as if it had been *years* between visits. Why couldn't Mommy see how mean Uncle Gus was? All of her friends in class saw he was a bad person the first day he took her to school. Kids can tell right away about a person. Like that mean ole Mr. Kruger in geography, who made Janey stay after class when she forgot to do her homework. All the kids knew that Mr. Kruger was *awful*. Why does it take grown-ups so long to know things?

Janey slid backward into the hall shadows. Stood up. Time to go downstairs. In her playclothes. Probably meant she'd get a spanking after Uncle Gus left, but it would be worth it not to have to put on her new dress for him. Spankings don't hurt *too* much. Worth it.

"Well, *here's* my little princess!" Uncle Gus was lifting her hard into the air, to make her dizzy. He knew how much she hated being swung around in the air. He set her down with a thump. Looked at her with his big cruel eyes. "And where's that pretty new dress your Mommy told me about?"

"It got torn," Janey said, staring at the carpet. "I can't wear it today."

Her mother was angry again. "That is *not* true, young lady, and you know it! I ironed that dress this morning and it is perfect." She pointed upward. "You march right back upstairs to your room and put on that dress!"

"No, Maggie." Gus shook his head. "Let the child stay as she is. She looks fine. Let's just have lunch." He prodded Janey in the stomach. "Bet that little tummy of yours is starved for some turkey."

And Uncle Gus pretended to laugh. Janey was never fooled; she knew real laughs from pretend laughs. But Mommy and Daddy never seemed to know the difference.

Janey's mother sighed and smiled at Gus. "All right, I'll let it go this time—but I really think you spoil her."

"Nonsense. Janey and I understand each other." He stared down at her. "Don't we, sweetie?"

Lunch was no fun. Janey couldn't finish her mashed potatoes, and she'd just nibbled at her turkey. She could never enjoy eating with her uncle there. As usual, her father barely noticed she was at the table. *He* didn't care if she wore her new dress or not. Mommy took care of her and Daddy took care of business, whatever that was. Janey could never figure out what he did, but he left every day for some office she'd never seen and he made enough money there so that he always had some to give to Uncle Gus when Mommy asked him for a check.

Today was Sunday so Daddy was home with his big newspaper to read and the car to wax and the grass to trim. He did the same things every Sunday.

Does Daddy love me? I know that Mommy does, even though she spanks me sometimes. But she always hugs me after. Daddy never hugs me. He buys me ice cream, and he takes me to the movies on Saturday afternoon, but I don't think he loves me.

Which is why she could never tell him the truth about Uncle Gus. He'd never listen.

And Mommy just didn't understand.

After lunch, Uncle Gus grabbed Janey firmly by the hand and took her into the backyard. Then he sat her down next to him on the big wooden swing.

"I'll bet your new dress is *ugly*," he said in a cold voice.

"Is not. It's pretty!"

Her discomfort pleased him. He leaned over, close to her right ear. "Want to know a secret?"

Janey shook her head. "I want to go back with Mommy. I don't like being out here."

She started away, but he grabbed her, pulling her roughly back onto the swing. "You *listen* to me when I talk to you." His eyes glittered. "I'm going to tell you a secret. About yourself."

"Then tell me."

He grinned. "You've got something inside."

"What's that mean?"

"It means there's something deep down inside your rotten little belly. And it's *alive!*"

"Huh?" She blinked, beginning to get scared.

"A creature. That lives off what you eat and breathes the air you breathe and can see out of your eyes." He pulled her face close to his. "Open your mouth, Janey, so I can look in and see what's living down there!"

"No, I *won't.*" She attempted to twist away, but he was too strong. "You're lying! You're just telling me an awful *lie!* You *are!*"

"Open wide." And he applied pressure to her jaw with the fingers of his right hand. Her mouth opened. "Ah, that's better. Let's have a look. . . ." He peered into her mouth. "Yes, *there.* I can see it now."

She drew back, eyes wide, really alarmed. "What's it like?"

"Nasty! Horrid. With very sharp teeth. A *rat,* I'd say. Or something *like* a rat. Long and gray and plump."

"I don't have it! I *don't!*"

"Oh, but you do, Janey." His voice was oily. "I saw its red eyes shining and its long snaky tail. It's down there all right. Something nasty."

And he laughed. Real, this time. No pretend laugh. Uncle Gus was having himself some fun.

Janey knew he was just trying to scare her again—but she wasn't absolutely one hundred percent sure about the thing inside. Maybe he *had* seen something.

"Do . . . any other people have . . . creatures . . . living in them?"

"Depends," said Uncle Gus. "Bad things live inside bad people. Nice little girls don't have them."

"I'm nice!"

"Well now, that's a matter of opinion, isn't it?" His voice was soft and unpleasant. "If you *were* nice, you wouldn't have something nasty living inside."

"I don't believe you," said Janey, breathing fast. "How could it be real?"

"Things are real when people believe in them." He lit a long black cigarette, drew in the smoke, exhaled it slowly. "Have you ever heard of voodoo, Janey?"

She shook her head.

"The way it works is—this witch doctor puts a curse on someone by making a doll and sticking a needle into the doll's heart. Then he leaves the doll at the house of the man he's cursed. When the man sees it he becomes very frightened. He makes the curse real by *believing* in it."

"And then what happens?"

"His heart stops and he dies."

Janey felt her own heart beating very rapidly.

"You're afraid, aren't you, Janey?"

"Maybe . . . a little."

"You're afraid, all right." He chuckled. "And you should be—with a thing like that inside you!"

"You're a very bad and wicked man!" she told him, tears misting her eyes.

And she ran swiftly back to the house.

That night, in her room, Janey sat rigid in bed, hugging Whiskers. He liked to come in late after dark and curl up on the coverlet just under her feet and snooze there until dawn. He was an easy-going, gray-and-black housecat who never complained about anything and always delivered a small "meep" of contentment whenever Janey picked him up for some stroking. Then he would begin to purr.

Tonight Whiskers was not purring. He sensed the harsh vibrations in the room, sensed how upset Janey was. He quivered uneasily in her arms.

"Uncle Gus lied to me, didn't he, Whiskers?" The little girl's voice was strained, uncertain. "See . . ." She hugged the cat closer. "Nothing's down there, huh?"

And she yawned her mouth wide to show her friend that no rat-thing lived there. If one did, ole Whiskers would be sticking a paw inside to get it. But the cat didn't react. Just blinked slitted green eyes at her.

"I knew it," Janey said, vastly relieved. "If I just don't believe it's in there, then it *isn't*."

She slowly relaxed her tensed body muscles—and Whiskers, sensing a change, began to purr—a tiny, soothing motorized sound in the night.

Everything was all right now. No red-eyed creature existed in her tummy. Suddenly she felt exhausted. It was late, and she had school tomorrow.

Janey slid down under the covers and closed her eyes, releasing Whiskers, who padded to his usual spot on the bed.

She had a lot to tell her friends.

It was Thursday, a day Janey usually hated. Every other Thursday her mother went shopping and left her to have lunch with Uncle Gus in his big spooky house with the shutters closed tight against the sun and shadows filling every hallway.

But *this* Thursday would be all different, so Janey didn't mind when her mother drove off and left her alone with her uncle. *This* time, she told herself, she wouldn't be afraid. A giggle.

She might even have fun!

When Uncle Gus put Janey's soup plate in front of her he asked her how she was feeling.

"Fine," said Janey quietly, eyes down.

"Then you'll be able to appreciate the soup." He smiled, trying to look pleasant. "It's a special recipe. Try it."

She spooned some into her mouth.

"How does it taste?"

"Kinda sour."

Gus shook his head, trying some for himself. "Ummm . . . delicious." He paused. "Know what's in it?"

She shook her head.

He grinned, leaning toward her across the table. "It's owl-eye soup.

479

Made from the dead eyes of an owl. All mashed up fresh, just for you."

She looked at him steadily. "You want me to upchuck, don't you, Uncle Gus?"

"My goodness no, Janey." There was oiled delight in his voice. "I just thought you'd like to know what you swallowed."

Janey pushed her plate away. "I'm not going to be sick because I don't believe you. And when you don't believe in something then it's not real."

Gus scowled at her, finishing his soup.

Janey knew he planned to tell her another awful spook story after lunch, but she wasn't upset about that. Because.

Because there wouldn't *be* any after lunch for Uncle Gus.

It was time for her surprise.

"I got something to tell you, Uncle Gus."

"So tell me." His voice was sharp and ugly.

"All my friends at school know about the thing inside. We talked about it a lot and now we all believe in it. It has red eyes and it's furry and it smells bad. And it's got lots of very sharp teeth."

"You *bet* it has," Gus said, brightening at her words. "And it's always hungry."

"But guess what," said Janey. "Surprise! It's not inside me, Uncle Gus . . . it's inside *you!*"

He glared at her. "That's not funny, you little bitch. Don't try to turn this around and pretend that—"

He stopped in midsentence, spoon clattering to the floor as he stood up abruptly. His face was flushed. He made strangling sounds.

"It wants out," said Janey.

Gus doubled over the table, hands clawing at his stomach. "Call . . . call a . . . doctor!" he gasped.

"A doctor won't help," said Janey in satisfaction. "Nothing can stop it now."

Janey followed him calmly, munching on an apple. She watched him stagger and fall in the doorway, rolling over on his back, eyes wild with panic.

She stood over him, looking down at her uncle's stomach under the white shirt.

Something *bulged* there.

Gus screamed.

*   *   *

480

Late that night, alone in her room, Janey held Whiskers tight against her chest and whispered into her pet's quivering ear. "Mommy's been crying," she told the cat. "She's real upset about what happened to Uncle Gus. Are *you* upset, Whiskers?"

The cat yawned, revealing sharp white teeth.

"I didn't think so. That's because you didn't like Uncle Gus any more than me, did you?"

She hugged him. "Wanta hear a *secret*, Whiskers?"

The cat blinked lazily at her, beginning to purr.

"You know that mean ole Mr. Kruger at school. . . . Well, guess what?" She smiled. "Me an' the other kids are gonna talk to him tomorrow about something he's got inside him." Janey shuddered deliciously. "Something nasty!"

And she giggled.

The Specter Spiders

WILLIAM J. WINTLE

The fog hung thickly over London one morning in late autumn. It was not the dense compound of smoke and moisture, pea-souplike in color and pungent to eyes and nose, that is known as a "London peculiar"; but a fairly clean and white mist that arose from the river and lay about the streets and squares in great wisps and wreaths and banks.

The passing crowd shivered and thought of approaching winter; while a few optimistic souls looked upward to the invisible sky and predicted a warm day when the sun had grown in strength. A little child remarked to a companion that it smelled like washing day: and the comparison was not without its point. It was as if the motor machinery of the metropolis had blown off steam in preparation for a fresh start.

People passed one another in the mist like sheeted ghosts and did not speak. Friend failed to recognize friend; or, if he did, he took for granted that the other did not. Apart from the steady rumble of the traffic and the long deep note that the great city gives forth to hearing ears all the day long, the world seemed strangely silent and unfriendly.

Certainly this applied with truth to one member of the passing crowd whose business brought abroad that misty morning when home and the fireside gained an added attraction. Ephraim Goldstein was silent by nature and unfriendly by profession. For him language was an ingenious device for the concealment of thought; and when there was no special reason for such concealment, why should he trouble to speak?

It was not as if people were over desirous to hear him speak. He was naturally unattractive: and where nature had failed to complete her task, Ephraim had brought it to perfection. A habit of scowling had effectually removed any trace of amiability that might have survived the handicap of evil eyes and unpleasing features. When strangers saw Ephraim for the first time, they looked quickly around for a pleasant face to act by way of antidote.

We have said that he was unfriendly by profession. But the unwary and innocent would never have suspected this from his professional announcements in the personal column of the morning papers. The gentleman of fortune who was wishful, without security or inquiry, to advance goodly sums of money to his less fortunate fellow creatures on nominal terms and in the most delicate manner possible, was surely giving the best of all proofs of a soul entirely immersed in the milk of human kindness.

Yet those who had done business with Ephraim spoke of him in terms not usual in the drawing room: men of affairs who knew the world of finance called him a blood-sucking spider, and Scotland Yard had him noted down as emphatically a wrong 'un. Ephraim was not popular with those who knew him. He had in fact only one point of character that could be commended. He had never changed his name to Edward Gordon or even to Edwin Goldsmith: he was born Ephraim Goldstein — and Ephraim Goldstein he was content to remain to the end. A rose by any other name smells just as sweet — but people did not express it quite like that when Ephraim was under discussion.

He had not always been a gentleman of fortune, nor had he always been wishful to share his fortune with others. People with inconveniently long memories recalled a youth of like name who got into trouble at Whitechapel for selling Kosher fowls judiciously weighted with sand: and there was also a story about a young man who manipulated three thimbles and a pea on Epsom Downs.

But why drag in these scandals of the past? In the case of any man it is unfair to thus search the record of his youth for evidence against him; and in the case of Ephraim it was quite unnecessary. He was a perennial plant: however lurid the past, he blossomed forth afresh every year in renewed vigor and in equally glowing colors.

How fortune had come to him seemed to be known by no one save himself; but certainly it had come, for it is difficult to lend money if you do not possess it. And with its coming Ephraim had migrated from Whitechapel to Haggerston, then to Kilburn, and finally to Maida Vale, where he now had his abode. But it must not be supposed that he indulged in either ambition or luxury. He was content with very modest comfort, and lived a simple bachelor existence; but he found a detached villa with some garden behind it more convenient for his purposes than a house in a terrace with an inquisitive neighbor on either side. His visitors came on business and by no means for pleasure: and privacy was as congenial to them as it was to him.

The business that had brought him out on this foggy morning was of an unusual character in that it had nothing to do with money making. It in fact involved spending money to the extent of two guineas now, with a probability of further sums; and he did not at all relish it. Ephraim was on his way to Cavendish Square to consult a noted oculist.

For some weeks past, he had been troubled with a curious affliction of his sight. He was still on the sunny side of fifty, and hitherto he had been very sharp-sighted in more senses than one. But now something seemed to be going wrong. His vision was perfect during the day, and usually through the evening as well; but twice recently he had been bothered with a curious optical delusion. On each occasion he had been sitting quietly reading after dinner, when something had made him uneasy. It was the same sort of disquiet that he always felt if a cat came into the room. So strong had been this feeling that he had sprung out of his chair without quite knowing why he did it; and each time had fancied that a number of shadows streamed forth from his chair and ran across the carpet to the walls, where they vanished. They were evidently nothing but shadows, for he could see the carpet through them; but they were fairly clear and distinct. They seemed to be about the size of a cricket ball. Though he attached no meaning to the coincidence, it was a little odd that on each occasion he had been reluctantly compelled during the day to insist upon his pound of flesh from a client. And when Ephraim insisted, he did not stick at a trifle. But obviously this could have nothing to do with a defect of vision.

The great specialist made a thorough examination of Ephraim's eyes, but could find nothing wrong with them. So he explored further and investigated the state of his patient's nervous and digestive systems; but found that these were perfectly sound.

Then he embarked upon more delicate matters, and sought to learn something of the habits of Ephraim. A bachelor in the forties may be addicted to the cup that cheers and occasionally inebriates as well: he may be fond of the pleasures of the table: he may be attracted by the excitement of gambling: in fact he may do a great many things that a man of his years should not do. The physician was a man of tact and diplomacy. He asked no injudicious questions; but he had the valuable gift of inducing conversation in others. Not for years had Ephraim talked so freely and frankly to any man. The result was that the doctor could find no reason for suggesting that the trouble was due to any kind of dietary or other indiscretion.

So he fell back on the last refuge of the baffled physician. "Rest, my dear Sir," he said; "that is the best prescription. I am happy to say that I find no serious lesion or even functional disturbance; but there is evidence of fatigue affecting the brain and the optic nerve. There is no reason to anticipate any further or more serious trouble; but a wise man always takes precautions. My advice is that you drop all business for a few weeks and spend the time in golf or other out-of-door amusement — say at Cromer or on the Surrey Downs. In that case you may be pretty confident that no further disturbance of this kind will occur."

Ephraim paid his two guineas with a rather wry face. He had the feeling that he was not getting much for his money; still it was reassuring to find that there was nothing the matter. Rest! Rubbish! He was not overworked. Surrey Downs indeed! Hampstead Heath was just as good and a great deal cheaper: he might take a turn there on Sunday mornings. Golf? You would not catch him making a fool of himself in tramping after a ridiculous ball! So he simply went on much the same as before, and hoped that all would be well.

Yet, somehow, things did not seem to be quite right with him. Business was prosperous, if you can speak of business in connection with the pleasant work of sharing your fortune with the less fortunate — always on the most reasonable terms possible. Ephraim would have told you that he lost terribly through the dishonesty of people who died or went abroad or whose expectations did not turn out as well as they should; and yet, in some mysterious way, he had more money to lend than ever. But he was worried.

One evening, after an unusually profitable day, he was sitting in his garden, smoking a cigar that had been given him by a grateful client who was under the mistaken impression that Ephraim's five per cent was to be reckoned per year, whereas it was really per week. It was a good cigar; and the smoker knew how to appreciate good tobacco. He was lying back in a hammock chair, and idly watching the rings of smoke as they rose on the quiet air and floated away.

Then he suddenly started and stared. The rings were behaving in a very odd fashion. They seemed to form themselves into globes of smoke; and from each of them protruded eight waving filaments that turned and bent like the legs of some uncanny creature. And it seemed as if these trailing limbs of smoke turned and reached toward him. It was curious and not altogether pleasant. But it was no case of an optical delusion. The evening light was good, and the thing was seen clearly enough. It must have been the result of some unusual state of the atmosphere at the time.

He was aroused by hearing conversation on the other side of the wall. The occupant of the next-door house was in his garden with a friend, and their talk was of matters horticultural. It did not interest Ephraim, who paid a jobbing gardener the smallest possible amount to keep the place tidy, and concerned himself no further about it. He did not want to hear of the respective virtues of different local seed vendors. But the talk was insistent, and he presently found himself listening against his will. They were talking about spiders; and his neighbor was saying that he had never known such a plague of them or such large-sized specimens. And he went on to say that they all seemed to come over the wall from Ephraim's side! The listener discovered that his cigar had gone out; and he went indoors in disgust.

It was only a few days later when the next thing happened. Ephraim had gone to bed rather earlier than usual, being somewhat tired, but was unable to sleep. For some hours he tossed about wearily and angrily— for he usually slept well—and then came a spell of disturbed and restless slumber. Dream after dream passed through his mind; and somehow they all seemed to have something to do with spiders. He thought that he fought his way through dense jungles of web; he walked on masses of soft and yielding bodies that crushed and squished beneath his tread; multitudinous hairy legs waved to and fro and clung to him; fanged jaws bit him with the sting of fiery fluids; and gleaming eyes were everywhere staring at him with a gaze of unutterable malignancy. He fell, and the webs wrapped him round in an embrace of death; great woolly creatures flung themselves upon him and suffocated him with their foul stink; unspeakable things had him in their ghastly grip; he was sinking in an ocean of unimaginable horror.

He awoke screaming, and sprang out of bed. Something caught him in the face and clung round his head. He groped for the switch and turned on the light. Then he tore off the bandage that blinded him, and found that it was a mass of silky threads like the web that a giant spider might have spun. And, as he got it clear of his eyes, he saw great shadows run up the walls and vanish. They had grown since he saw them first on the carpet; they were now the size of footballs.

Ephraim was appalled by the horror of it. Unrestful sleep and persistent nightmare were bad enough; but here was something worse. The silky wisps that still clung about his head were not such stuff as dreams are made of. He wondered if he was going mad. Was the whole thing a hallucination? Could he pull himself together and shake it off? He tried; but the bits of web that waved from his fingers and face were real enough. No dream spider could have spun them; mere imagination could not have created them. Moreover, he was not a man of imagination. Quite the opposite. He dealt in realities: real estate was the security he preferred.

A stiff glass of brandy and soda pulled him together. He was not addicted to stimulants—it did not pay in his profession—but this was a case that called for special measures. He shook off the obsession, and thought there might be something in the golf suggestion after all. And when a client called during the morning to negotiate a little loan, Ephraim drove a shrewd bargain that surprised even himself.

The next incident that caused considerable disquiet to the gentleman of fortune seems to have occurred about a month later. He was no lover of animals, but he tolerated the presence of a Scots terrier in the house. It occasionally happened that he had large sums of money on the premises—not often, but sometimes it could not be helped—and the alert little dog was a good protection against the intrusive burglar. So he treated the animal as a sort of confidential servant, and was, after his fashion, attached to it. If he did not exactly love it, he at any rate appreciated and valued it. He did not even grudge the veterinarian's charges when it was ill.

At night the terrier had the run of the house, but usually slept on a mat outside Ephraim's door. On this particular occasion Ephraim dreamed that he had fallen over the dog, and that it gave a loud yelp of pain. So vivid was the impression that it woke him, and the cry of the animal seemed to still linger on his ear. It was as if the terrier outside the door had really cried out. He listened, but all was quiet save for a curious clicking and sucking sound that he heard at intervals. It seemed to come from just outside the door; but that could not be, for the dog would have been roused and would have given the alarm if anything was wrong.

So he presently went to sleep again, and did not wake until his usual time for rising. As he dressed, it struck him as unusual that he heard nothing of the dog, which was accustomed to greet the first sounds of movement with a welcoming bark or two. When he opened his door, the terrier lay dead on the mat.

Ephraim was first shocked, then grieved, and next alarmed. He was shocked because it was simply natural to be shocked under the circumstances; he was grieved because it then dawned upon him that he was more fond of the animal than he could have believed possible; and he was alarmed because he knew that the mysterious death of a watch dog is often the preliminary to a burglary.

He hurried downstairs and made a hasty examination of the doors and windows, and particularly of a safe that was hidden in the wall behind what looked like a solid piece of furniture. But everything was in good order, and there was no sign of any attempt on the premises. Then he went upstairs to remove the body of the dog, wondering the while if it would be worth the expense to have a post mortem. Ephraim disliked mysteries, especially when they happened in the house.

He picked up the dead terrier, and at once met with a bad shock. It was a mere featherweight, and collapsed in his hands! It was little more than a skeleton, rattling loose in a bag of skin. It had been simply sucked dry!

He dropped it in horror, and as he did so he found some silky threads clinging to his hands. And there were threads waving in the air, for one of them twined itself about his head and clung stickily to his face. And then something fell with a soft thud on the floor behind him, and he turned just in time to see a shadow dart to the wall and disappear. He had seen that shadow form before; but it somehow seemed to be less shadowy and more substantial now.

It seems to have been about this time that a rumor circulated in Maida Vale that a monkey had escaped from the Zoological Gardens in Regent's Park and had been seen climbing on Ephraim's house.

It was first seen early in the morning by a milkman, who mentioned it to a policeman, and soon afterward by a housemaid who was cleaning the steps of a house opposite. It was a rather dark and misty morning, which doubtless accounts for a certain vagueness in the descriptions of the animal. But, so far as they went, all the descriptions agreed.

The monkey was described as a very fat specimen, almost like a football in size and rotundity, with very long arms. It was covered with thick, glossy, black hair, and was seen to climb up the front of the house and enter by an open window. The milkman, who was fond of reading, said that he thought it was a spider monkey; but his only reason for this seems to have been some fancied resemblance to a very large spider.

Later in the morning, the policeman called on Ephraim to mention the matter, and to ask if the monkey was still there. His reception was not polite; and he retired in disorder. Then he rang up the Zoological Gardens, but was informed that no monkeys were missing. The incident was duly recorded at the police station, and there it ended, for no more was ever heard of it.

But another occurrence in the following week gave rise to much more talk, especially among the ladies of the neighborhood. The empty skin of a valuable Persian cat was found in the shrubbery of the house next to Ephraim's—empty, that is, except for the bones of the animal. The skin was quite fresh; as it well might be, for the cat had been seen alive the evening before. The mystery formed a nine days' wonder, and was never solved until an even more shocking mystery came to keep it company. The cat's skin had been sucked dry and the local theory was that a stoat or other beast of prey had escaped from the zoo and done the dire deed. But it was proved that no such escape had occurred, and there the matter had to stop.

Although it seems to have no significance, it may be well to place on record a trifling incident that happened a week or two later. A collector for some charitable institution called upon Ephraim under the mistaken impression that he was a person who wanted to get rid of his money. He was speedily undeceived, and was only in the house for a few minutes. But he told his wife afterward that Mr. Goldstein was evidently a great cat fancier, for he had noticed several fine black Persians curled up asleep in the house. But it was curious that they were all in the darkest and most obscure corners, where they could not be seen very clearly. He had made some passing reference to them to Mr. Goldstein, who did not seem to understand him. Indeed he stared at him as if he thought him the worse for drink!

Another incident at this time was made the subject of remark among Ephraim's neighbors. For reasons best known to himself, he had long been in the habit of sleeping with a loaded revolver at his bedside; and one morning, about daybreak, the sound of a shot was heard. The police were quickly on the spot and insisted upon entering the house. Ephraim assured them that the weapon had been accidentally discharged through being dropped on the floor; and, after asking to see his gun licence, the police departed.

But what had really happened was much more interesting. Ephraim had woke up without apparent cause, but with a vague sense of danger;

and was just in time to see a round black body, covered with a dense coat of hair, climb up the foot of his bed and make its way cautiously toward his face. It was a gigantic spider; and its eight gleaming eyes blazed with lambent green light like a cluster of sinister opals.

He was paralysed with horror; then, summoning all his force of will, he snatched up the revolver and fired. The flash and the noise of the report dazed him for a moment; and when he saw clearly again the spider was gone. He must have hit it, for he fired point blank; but it had left no sign. It was just as well, for otherwise his tale would not have passed muster with the police. But, later in the morning, he found a trail of silky threads running across the carpet from the bed to the wall.

But the end was now very near. Only a few days later, the police were again in the house. This time they had been called in by the gardener, who said that he could not make Mr. Goldstein hear when he knocked at his door, and that he thought he must be ill. The door was locked, and had to be forced.

What the police found had better not be described. At the funeral, the undertaker's men said that they had never carried a man who weighed so little for his size.

The Spider of Guyana

EMILE ERCKMANN AND ALEXANDRE CHATRIAN

The mineral waters of Spinbronn, in Hundsruck, a few leagues from Pirmesans, formerly enjoyed an excellent reputation, for Spinbronn was the rendezvous of all the gouty and rheumatic members of the German aristocracy. The wild nature of the surrounding country did not deter the visitors, for they were lodged in charming villas at the foot of the mountain. They bathed in the cascade that fell in large sheets of foam from the summit of the rocks, and drank two or three pints of the water every day. Dr. Daniel Haselnoss, who prescribed for the sick and those who thought they were, received his patients in a large wig, brown coat, and ruffles, and was rapidly making his fortune.

Today, however, Spinbronn is no longer a favorite watering place.

The fashionable visitors have disappeared; Dr. Haselnoss has given up his practice; and the town is only inhabited by a few poor, miserable woodcutters. All this is the result of a succession of strange and unprecedented catastrophes, which Councillor Bremen, of Pirmesans, recounted to me the other evening.

"You know, Mr. Fritz," he said, "that the source of the Spinbronn flows from a sort of cavern about 5 feet high, and from 10 feet to 15 feet across; the water, which has a temperature of 67 degrees centigrade, is salt. The front of the cavern is half hidden by moss, ivy, and low shrubs, and it is impossible to find out the depth of it, because of the thermal exhalations that prevent any entrance.

"In spite of that, it had been remarked for a century that the birds of the locality—hawks, thrushes, and turtledoves—were engulfed in full flight, and no one knew of what mysterious influence it was the result. During the season of 1801, for some unexplained reason, the source became more abundant, and the visitors one evening, taking their constitutional promenade on the lawns at the foot of the rocks, saw a human skeleton descend from the cascade.

"You can imagine the general alarm, Mr. Fritz. It was naturally supposed that a murder had been committed at Spinbronn some years before, and that the victim had been thrown into the source. But the skeleton, which was blanched as white as snow, only weighed twelve pounds; and Dr. Haselnoss concluded that, in all probability, it had been in the sand more than three centuries to have arrived at that state of desiccation.

"Plausible as his reasoning was, it did not prevent many visitors leaving that same day, horrified to have drunk the waters. The really gouty and rheumatic ones, however, stayed on, and consoled themselves with the doctor's version. But the following days the cavern disgorged all that it contained of detritus; and a veritable ossuary descended the mountain—skeletons of animals of all sorts, quadrupeds, birds, reptiles. In fact, all the most horrible things that could be imagined.

"Then Haselnoss wrote and published a pamphlet to prove that all these bones were relics of the antediluvian world, that they were fossil skeletons, accumulated there in a sort of funnel during the universal Deluge, that is to say, four thousand years before Christ; and, consequently, could only be regarded as stones, and not as anything repulsive.

"But his work had barely reassured the gouty ones, when one fine morning the corpse of a fox, and then of a hawk, with all its plumage, fell from the cascade. Impossible to maintain that these had existed before the Deluge, and the exodus became general.

" 'How horrible!' cried the ladies. 'That is where the so-called virtue of mineral waters springs from. Better die of rheumatism than continue such a remedy.'

"At the end of a week the only visitor left was a stout Englishman, Commodore Sir Thomas Hawerbrook, who lived on a grand scale, as most Englishmen do. He was tall and very stout, and of a florid complexion. His hands were literally knotted with gout, and he would have drunk no matter what if he thought it would cure him. He laughed loudly at the desertion of the sufferers, installed himself in the best of the villas, and announced his intention of spending the winter at Spinbronn."

Here Councillor Bremen leisurely took a large pinch of snuff to refresh his memory, and with the tips of his fingers shook off the tiny particles, which fell on his delicate lace jabot. Then he went on.

"Five or six years before the revolution of 1789, a young doctor of Pirmesans, called Christian Weber, went to St. Domingo to seek his fortune. He had been very successful, and was about to retire, when the revolt of the negroes occurred. Happily he escaped the massacre, and was able to save part of his fortune. He traveled for a time in South America, and about the period of which I speak, returned to Pirmesans, and bought the house and what remained of the practice of Dr. Haselnoss.

"Dr. Christian Weber brought with him an old negress called Agatha; a very ugly old woman, with a flat nose, and enormous lips. She always enveloped her head in a sort of turban of the most startling colors; and wore rings in her ears that reached to her shoulders. Altogether she was such a singular-looking creature that the mountaineers came from miles around just to look at her.

"The doctor himself was a tall, thin man, invariably dressed in a blue swallow-tailed coat and leather breeches. He talked very little, his laugh was dry and nervous, and his habits most eccentric. During his wanderings he had collected a number of insects of almost every species, and seemed to be much more interested in them than in his patients. In his daily rambles among the mountains he often found butterflies to add to his collection, and these he brought home pinned to the lining of his hat.

"Dr. Weber, Mr. Fritz, was my cousin and my guardian, and directly he returned to Germany he took me from school, and settled me with him at Spinbronn. Agatha was a great friend of mine, though at first she

491

frightened me, but she was a good creature, knew how to make the most delicious sweets, and could sing the most charming songs.

"Sir Thomas and Dr. Weber were on friendly terms, and spent long hours together talking of subjects beyond my comprehension — of transmission of fluids, and mysterious things they had observed in their travels. Another mystery to me was the singular influence that the doctor appeared to have over the negress, for though she was generally particularly lively, ready to be amused at the slightest thing, yet she trembled like a leaf if she encountered her master's eyes fixed upon her.

"I have told you that birds, and even large animals, were engulfed in the cavern. After the disappearance of the visitors, some of the old inhabitants remembered that about fifty years before a young girl, Loisa Muller, who lived with her grandmother in a cottage near the source, had suddenly disappeared. She had gone out one morning to gather herbs, and was never seen or heard of again, but her apron had been found a few days later near the mouth of the cavern. From that it was evident to all that the skeleton about which Dr. Haselnoss had written so eloquently was that of the poor girl, who had, no doubt, been drawn into the cavern by the mysterious influence that almost daily acted upon more feeble creatures. What that influence was nobody could tell. The superstitious mountaineers believed that the devil inhabited the cavern, and terror spread throughout the district.

"One afternoon, in the month of July, my cousin was occupied in classifying his insects and rearranging them in their cases. He had found some curious ones the night before, at which he was highly delighted. I was helping by making a needle red-hot in the flame of a candle.

"Sir Thomas, lying back in a chair near the window and smoking a big cigar, was regarding us with a dreamy air. The commodore was very fond of me. He often took me driving with him, and used to like to hear me chatter in English. When the doctor had labeled all his butterflies, he opened the box of larger insects.

" 'I caught a magnificent horn-beetle yesterday,' he said, 'the *lucanus cervus* of the Hartz oaks. It is a rare kind.'

"As he spoke I gave him the hot needle, which he passed through the insect preparatory to fixing it on the cork. Sir Thomas, who had taken no notice till then, rose and came to the table on which the case of specimens stood. He looked at the spider of Guyana, and an expression of horror passed over his rubicund features.

" 'There,' he said, 'is the most hideous work of the Creator. I tremble only to look at it.'

"And, sure enough, a sudden pallor spread over his face.

" 'Bah!' said my guardian, 'all that is childish nonsense. You heard your nurse scream at a spider, you were frightened, and the impression has remained. But if you regard the creature with a strong microscope, you would be astonished at the delicacy of its organs, at their admirable arrangement, and even at their beauty.'

" 'It disgusts me,' said the commodore, brusquely. 'Pouff!'

"And he walked away.

" 'I don't know why,' he continued, 'but a spider always freezes my blood.'

"Dr. Weber burst out laughing, but I felt the same as Sir Thomas, and sympathized with him.

" 'Yes, cousin, take away that horrid creature,' I cried. 'It is frightful, and spoils all the others.'

" 'Little stupid,' said he, while his eyes flashed, 'nobody compels you to look at them. If you are not pleased you can go.'

"Evidently he was angry, and Sir Thomas, who was standing by the window regarding the mountains, turned suddenly round, and took me by the hand.

" 'Your guardian loves his spiders, Frantz,' he said, kindly. 'We prefer the trees and the grass. Come with me for a drive.'

" 'Yes, go,' returned the doctor, 'and be back to dinner at six.' Then, raising his voice, 'No offense, Sir Thomas,' he said.

"Sir Thomas turned and laughed, and we went out to the carriage.

"The commodore decided to drive himself, and sent back his servant. He placed me on the seat beside him, and we started for Rothalps. While the carriage slowly mounted the sandy hill, I was quiet and sad. Sir Thomas, too, was grave, but my silence seemed to strike him.

" 'You don't like the spiders, Frantz; neither do I. But, thank Heaven! there are no dangerous ones in this country. The spider your cousin has in his box is found in the swampy forests of Guyana, which is always full of hot vapors and burning exhalations, for it needs a high temperature to support its existence. Its immense web, or rather its net, would surround an ordinary thicket, and birds are caught in it, the same as flies in our spiders' webs. But do not think any more about it; let us drink a glass of Burgundy.'

"As he spoke he lifted the cover of the seat, and, taking out a flask of wine, poured me out a full leathern goblet.

"I felt better when I had drunk it, and we continued our way. The carriage was drawn by a little Ardennes pony, which climbed the steep incline as lightly and actively as a goat. The air was full of the murmur of myriads of insects. At our right was the forest of Rothalps. At our left was the cascade of Spinbronn; and the higher we mounted, the bluer became the silver sheets of water foaming in the distance, and the more musical the sound as the water passed over the rocks.

"Both Sir Thomas and I were captivated by the spectacle, and, lost in a reverie, allowed the pony to go on as he would. Soon we were within a hundred paces of the cavern of Spinbronn. The shrubs around the entrance were remarkably green. The water, as it flowed from the cavern, passed over the top of the rock, which was slightly hollowed, and there formed a small lake, from which it again burst forth and descended into the valley below. This lake was shallow, the bottom of it composed of sand and black pebbles, and, although covered with a slight vapor, the water was clear and limpid as crystal.

"The pony stopped to breathe. Sir Thomas got out and walked about for a few seconds.

" 'How calm it is,' he said.

"Then, after a minute's silence, he continued: 'Frantz, if you were not here, I should have a bathe in that lake.'

" 'Well, why not?' I answered. 'I will take a walk the while. There are numbers of strawberries to be found a little way up that mountain. I can go and get some, and be back in an hour.'

" 'Capital idea, Frantz. Dr. Weber pretends that I drink too much Burgundy; we must counteract that with mineral water. This little lake looks inviting.'

"Then he fastened the pony to the trunk of a tree, and waved his hand in adieu. Sitting down on the moss, he commenced to take off his boots, and, as I walked away, he called after me: " 'In an hour, Frantz.'

"They were his last words.

"An hour after I returned. The pony, the carriage, and Sir Thomas's clothes were all that I could see. The sun was going down and the shadows were lengthening. Not a sound of bird or of insect, and a silence as of death filled the solitude. This silence frightened me. I climbed on to the rock above the cavern, and looked right and left. There was nobody to be seen. I called; no one responded. The sound of my voice repeated by the echoes filled me with terror. Night was coming on. All of a sudden I remembered the disappearance of Loisa Muller, and I hurried down to the front of the cavern. There I stopped in affright, and glancing toward the entrance, I saw two red, motionless points.

"A second later I distinguished some dark, moving object farther back in the cavern, farther perhaps than human eye had ever before penetrated; for fear had sharpened my sight, and given all my senses an acuteness of perception that I had never before experienced.

"During the next minute I distinctly heard the chirp, chirp of a grass-hopper, and the bark of a dog in the distant village. Then my heart, which had been frozen with terror, commenced to beat furiously, and I heard nothing more. With a wild cry I fled, leaving pony and carriage.

"In less than twenty minutes, bounding over rocks and shrubs, I reached my cousin's door.

" 'Run, run,' I cried, in a choking tone, as I burst into the room where Dr. Weber and some invited friends were waiting for us. 'Run, run; Sir Thomas is dead; Sir Thomas is in the cavern,' and I fell fainting on the floor.

"All the village turned out to search for the commodore. At ten o'clock they returned, bringing back Sir Thomas's clothes, the pony, and carriage. They had found nothing, seen nothing, and it was impossible to go ten paces into the cavern.

"During their absence Agatha and I remained in the chimney-corner, I still trembling with fear, she, with wide-open eyes, going from time to time to the window, from which we could see the torches passing to and fro on the mountain, and hear the searchers shout to one another in the still night air.

"At her master's approach Agatha began to tremble. The doctor entered brusquely, pale, with set lips. He was followed by about twenty woodcutters, shaking out the last remnants of their nearly extinguished torches.

"He had barely entered before, with flashing eyes, he glanced round the room, as if in search of something. His eyes fell on the negress, and without a word being exchanged between them the poor woman began to cry.

" 'No, no, I will not,' she shrieked.

" 'But I will,' returned the doctor, in a hard tone.

"The negress shook from head to foot, as though seized by some invisible power. The doctor pointed to a seat, and she sat down as rigid as a corpse.

"The woodcutters, good, simple people, full of pious sentiments, crossed themselves, and I, who had never yet heard of the hypnotic force, began to tremble, thinking Agatha was dead.

"Dr. Weber approached the negress, and passed his hands over her forehead.

" 'Are you ready?' he said.

" 'Yes, sir.'

" 'Sir Thomas Hawerbrook.'

"At these words she shivered again.

" 'Do you see him?'

" 'Yes, yes,' she answered, in a gasping voice, 'I see him.'

" 'Where is he?'

" 'Up there, in the depths of the cavern—dead!'

" 'Dead!' said the doctor; 'how?'

" 'The spider! oh, the spider!'

" 'Calm yourself,' said the doctor, who was very pale. 'Tell us clearly.'

" 'The spider holds him by the throat—in the depths of the cavern—under the rock—enveloped in its web—Ah!'

"Dr. Weber glanced round on the people, who, bending forward, with eyes starting out of their heads, listened in horror.

"Then he continued: 'You see him?'

" 'I see him.'

" 'And the spider. Is it a big one?'

" 'O Master, never, never, have I seen such a big one. Neither on the banks of the Mocaris, nor in the swamps of Konanama. It is as large as my body.'

"There was a long silence. Everybody waited with livid face and hair on end. Only the doctor kept calm. Passing his hand two or three times over the woman's forehead, he recommenced his questions. Agatha described how Sir Thomas's death happened.

" 'He was bathing in the lake of the source. The spider saw his bare back from behind. It had been fasting for a long time, and was hungry. Then it saw Sir Thomas's arm on the water. All of a sudden it rushed out, put its claws round the commodore's neck. He cried out, "Mon Dieu, Mon Dieu." The spider stung him and went back, and Sir Thomas fell into the water and died. Then the spider returned, spun its web round him, and swam slowly, gently back to the extremity of the cavern; drawing Sir Thomas after it by the thread attached to its own body.'

"I was still sitting in the chimney-corner, overwhelmed with fright. The doctor turned to me.

" 'Is it true, Frantz, that the commodore was going to bathe?'

" 'Yes, cousin.'

" 'At what time?'

" 'At four o'clock.'

" 'At four o'clock? It was very hot then, was it not?'

" 'Yes; oh, yes.'

" 'That's it. The monster was not afraid to come out then.'

"He spoke a few unintelligible words, and turned to the peasants.

" 'My friends,' he cried, 'that is where the mass of debris and those skeletons come from. It is the spider that has frightened away your visitors and ruined you all. It is there hidden in its web, entrapping its prey into the depths of the cavern. Who can say the number of its victims?'

"He rushed impetuously from the house, and all the woodcutters hurried after him.

" 'Bring fagots, bring fagots!' he cried.

"Ten minutes later two immense carts, laden with fagots, slowly mounted the hill; a long file of woodcutters followed, with hatchets on their shoulders. My guardian and I walked in front, holding the horses by the bridle; while the moon lent a vague, melancholy light to the funereal procession.

"At the entrance of the cavern the cortege stopped. The torches were lighted and the crowd advanced. The limpid water flowed over the sand, reflecting the blue light of the resinous torches, the rays of which illuminated the tops of the dark, overhanging pines on the rocks above us.

" 'It is here you must unload,' said the doctor. 'We must block up the entrance of the cavern.'

"It was not without a feeling of dread that they commenced to execute his order. The fagots fell from the tops of the carts, and the men piled them up before the opening, placing some stakes against them to prevent their being carried away by the water. Toward midnight the opening was literally closed by the fagots. The hissing water below them flowed right and left over the moss, but those on the top were perfectly dry.

"Then Dr. Weber took a lighted torch, and himself set fire to the pile. The flames spread from twig to twig, and rose toward the sky, preceded by dense clouds of smoke. It was a wild, strange sight, and the woods lighted by the crackling flames had a weird effect. Thick volumes of smoke proceeded from the cavern, while the men standing round, gloomy and motionless, waited with their eyes fixed on the opening. As for me, though I trembled from head to foot, I could not withdraw my gaze.

"We waited quite a quarter of an hour, and Dr. Weber began to be impatient, when a black object, with long, crooked claws, suddenly approached in the shadow, and then threw itself forward toward the opening. One of the men, fearing that it would leap over the fire, threw his hatchet, and aimed at the creature so well that, for an instant, the blood that flowed from its wound half quenched the fire, but soon the flame revived, and the horrible insect was consumed.

"Evidently driven by the heat, the spider had taken refuge in its den. Then, suffocated by the smoke, it had returned to the charge, and rushed into the middle of the flames. The body of the horrible creature was as large as a man's, reddish violet in color, and most repulsive in appearance.

"That, Mr. Fritz, is the strange event that destroyed the reputation of Spinbronn. I can swear to the exactitude of my story, but it would be impossible for me to give you an explanation. Nevertheless, admitting that the high temperature of certain thermal springs furnishes the same conditions of existence as the burning climate of Africa and South America, it is not unreasonable to suppose that insects, subject to its influences, can attain an enormous development.

"Whatever may have been the cause, my guardian decided that it would be useless to attempt to resuscitate the waters of Spinbronn; so he sold his house, and returned to America with his negress and his collection."

SPIDERTALK

STEVE RASNIC TEM

Really . . . there's nothing to be afraid of, Amie."

The child curled into the corner, making herself as small as possible. Her thin arms were so rigid Liz couldn't pry them away, even using all her strength. The child seemed paralyzed, in shock, as if she'd been bitten by something poisonous.

"Amie, it's all right. They're not going to hurt you."

Amie turned her head stiffly and looked up through a mop of thick, black hair. "Everybody's always talking spidertalk! Always trying to make me afraid. I can't stand it, Miss Malloy!"

Liz thought that a strange way to put it. But then Amie was a highly nervous, anxious little girl; the tension in her often made her word choices, and even her tone of voice, sound strange. They'd been studying spiders this month in school, and Liz had gone to the trouble of setting up a terrarium with two tarantulas in the classroom. Today the other kids had been teasing Amie—Amie was terrified of spiders, even when they were just talking about them. When Liz lectured the class Amie would lay her head on the desk. Of course, most of the other children were a bit nervous around the terrarium, but Amie had always been an easy target, and she served ably to help the others forget their own fears.

"It's okay, Amie. The other kids are gone now; it's just you and me. Your mother will be here to pick you up soon. Let's get up and wait for her. Okay?"

"Okay. . . ." Amie said into her arms. With a great deal of effort she unwound herself and stood up unsteadily. Liz moved her gently by the shoulders, maneuvering her around the table with the terrarium, to the windows beyond. Amie pressed against her firmly as they passed the table, both arms wrapped tight and monkeylike around Liz's thighs. For some reason the desperation in the child's grip, the completeness of the child's embrace, gave Liz the creeps. Liz suppressed a tremor until they reached the windows, then delicately but forcefully removed the child's arms.

Liz would normally be home by now, but since Amie's parents had undergone a rather messy divorce she was under strict instructions from Amie's mother, and her principal, that she was to wait until Amie's mother picked her up. Amie's father wasn't permitted on the school grounds. Liz wasn't aware of all the details, but she did know that the father had been denied visitation rights, which was unusual in their small community.

"He hurt me sometimes," Amie had told her once, out of the blue, in response to some question Liz had asked her totally off that subject. The child did that at times when she was really agitated; you had to make her slow down and think before you could follow what she was talking about. Liz had never met such a high-strung, fearful little girl. She wanted to reach out to the child while, at the same time, she was vaguely repelled by her. Perhaps she reminded her somewhat of herself—as a girl Liz had been painfully thin, and afraid of almost everything. No wonder the other children didn't like Amie. They hadn't liked Liz either.

"That's not my mommy's car." The child's voice was so unusually flat, so emotionless, that Liz at first couldn't understand what she was saying. Then the child was suddenly screaming, "It's not! It's not her car!"

"Amie! Calm down!" Liz looked out the window. It was near dusk, the sun had just begun to set, the worse time of the day for visibility.

Especially from these windows facing the sun, filling with red and orange light. Trying to see through these windows into the gray-filled space between the school and the trees beyond was almost impossible in the late afternoons.

But she could just barely make out something today: a squat black car, a Volkswagen, she thought, slowly circling the visitors' parking lot. It stopped about ten yards away from their window. A tall, thin figure stepped out dressed in gray sweat pants and a stained, darker sweat shirt. She couldn't make out the face. The figure stood very still, staring at the window.

"Daddy," Amie gasped.

The figure walked slowly forward. Again, Amie began to scream.

The girl's rising screams panicked Liz. She turned and ran out the door, the strength of the little girl's voice terrifying her, spurring her on. There were only two entrances to the small school building. In a few minutes Liz had locked both and returned to the classroom. She locked her classroom door and returned to the window. Amie was silent now, staring out the window, her forehead pressed against the glass.

And then Liz had to stop and wonder why she herself had become so frightened. She'd never met the man personally, and she certainly had no evidence that he might harm either one of them.

The black car was gone. Liz started to pull away, to go to the other side of the building and look there, but she hesitated to leave Amie alone. She felt like a fool—she'd gotten so scared when Amie screamed, and hadn't realized she could have called the police from the principal's office.

"Come on, Amie. I'm taking you to another room." Liz pushed her past the terrarium, noting how agitated the normally placid tarantulas seemed. She watched their legs rising and falling in the still air of the terrarium, so many legs it seemed, many more than eight she might have thought. She found herself pulling away from them as she passed. She'd always been frightened of spiders herself—one of the many unreasoning fears that still clung from her childhood. That was the main reason that every school year she'd done this lesson on spiders. Although the fear was still there under the surface, the lesson helped her control it. And yet now, with that black Volkswagen moving slowly through the dusk out there, perhaps even now circling the building searching for a way in, she could not believe she had so calmly held one of these creatures in her hand that very afternoon.

They reached the door, opened it, and Liz pushed Amie out into the hall. Amie began to scream. When Liz rushed to the girl's side, she found her staring at the end of the hallway, at the glass entrance doors there, which were now filled with the glare of headlights. A car had pulled up head-on against the door, only a few inches away. The glare obscured its form.

Liz expected the car to come crashing through those doors at any moment. She grabbed Amie and pulled her back into the classroom, again locking the door. Once inside, she shoved one of the work tables against the door, as well as several of the children's desks. She grabbed the table holding the terrarium, began to shove it, then saw the glass case begin to rock simultaneously with Amie's loud sobs.

She stopped. The terrarium settled into place. Amie flew into her arms, trying to wrap wiry legs around her thighs, both bony arms around her neck. Suddenly Liz couldn't breathe—she felt attacked by the child's small limbs, trapped. "Amie!" she gasped, and struggled to pull her off. The girl was crying. "Amie, please!" She slipped her arms around the girl's shoulders and jerked down. Amie fell at Liz's feet, almost hysterical now, her hands clenching and unclenching, needing something to hold.

Liz picked her up and carried her to a bench by her desk, and sat down with her, holding her, stroking her dark hair. She stared at the tarantulas, now calm behind their walls of glass. She felt exhausted by her own fear, and drained by this fearful little girl. She remembered she had a date with Roger tonight, Roger with the sure hands and fierce embraces, who wanted to marry her, to—as he often said—*make her his forever*. It didn't bother her that he might be worried; she wasn't even sure why she continued to see him. She had thought she loved him. But somehow he made her afraid. Chilled, Liz began to speak slowly, softly, trying to think of lullabies as she talked about the spiders. She held Amie tight as the child began to pull away from her spidertalk.

"No, Amie. It helps to know about what you're afraid of. No . . . please, Amie. They can't hurt you—we've fixed them so they can't bite. Besides, even in the wild their bite won't kill you. That's just a story. People are afraid of them just because they look so ugly. We're all afraid of ugly things, things with lots of legs that grab and hold on.

"All spiders are like that. And when you're afraid of them, it seems like you see them everywhere. . . ."

They were standing by the terrarium now, Amie transfixed, gripping Liz's hand. Liz opened the lid and inserted a long rod beneath one of the tarantulas, turning it over. It immediately righted itself, making unbroken progress in its cage-crawl, inexorable, driven, mindless in its movements. Liz found that appalling. "See how it rights itself? It wants to be left alone, not bothered, just like we do." She removed the rod, careful not to touch the end that had touched the spider. "The smaller one there is the female. See how she crouches in the dirt, Amie? There's a tunnel under there where she keeps her babies." Amie looked up at her. "Yes . . . you never thought about spiders having babies, did you?" Amie shook her head.

"Can I see them . . . the babies?" Amie asked.

"No, not now—we wouldn't want to disturb them. But we will later in the class. I promise." The talk about babies seemed to have done it. Amie looked much more relaxed. She didn't even glance at the windows anymore. Liz, however, continued to stare at the larger male spider, its hairy, bristly legs, the too-rapid way it moved. Spiders were damn fertile things, and they wove such beautiful webs. To trap insects, to kill them. It seemed as if they produced life only in order to bring about death. But wasn't that the terrible truth about all life and birth? Maybe that was the real reason they appalled and frightened her so. They were a perverted reminder of the human condition.

When she was a girl in Texas, some of the neighborhood kids had doused a tarantula with lighter fluid, and set it on fire. The enormous spider had staggered a minute, blazing brightly. Finally the legs gave out, it collapsed on the ground, and then the fire went out. The other kids poked it—and the shell broke. It had burned from the inside out, all the softness melting away, leaving just that terrible mask.

"They eat birds, small mice sometimes. . . ." she continued. "But they're not dangerous to people. There's no reason to be afraid, Amie. No reason at all."

But her fear was a living thing with a mind of its own, that would not respond to her own sense of reason. She was afraid of these spiders, as she was afraid of Roger, afraid of little Amie, afraid of the black Volkswagen outside circling the building so slowly, penning her in, trapping her, wrapping its long bristly dark legs around her thighs and shoulders, embracing her so roughly, needing her so much. She'd always been afraid as a small child, and as she had grown so had her fear. Now it was bigger than these spiders. No one had been much help to her with it; most of her friends just made fun of her. Or made it worse, talking spidertalk all the time, spidertalk about spiders, snakes, the dark, and withered old men with ugly eyes and rough hands. Hideous talk.

She could sense the small gray spiders in all corners of the room, building their webs, listening, all these small fears lying in wait for her wherever she went. Once you're afraid of them, they seem to pop up everywhere. It was true.

She'd behaved illogically, irresponsibly, this afternoon, and she'd always prided herself on being a responsible teacher. It was because she had been so afraid. Her fear had paralyzed her, as if she'd been bitten.

She went to the window. The sun was setting rapidly. Broad threads of silk were floating down out of the darkening sky, the setting sun making them glisten a blood-red color, thousands of them, each silk-strand bearing a spider. When Liz was a child they called it gossamer.

Amie's father stood in front of the black Volkswagen, his dark figure hard to see because of all the spidersilk. He had raised his hand; a red and green scarf hung from it like a trophy. Liz had seen that scarf many times: Amie's mother wore it often when she picked up Amie in her old Chevy convertible.

The scarf floated to the ground. Then Liz saw the convertible parked nearby, the shadowed form sprawling half out the door, the door light on, the bright red interior rapidly filling with silk, the spiders, traveling.

The tall, narrow shape of Amie's father, draped with silk, was strolling toward the building. Crushing hundreds of the quick-legged spiders beneath his feet. Everywhere.

"Look! Miss Malloy, look at the spiders!"

Liz turned to Amie to reassure her, ready to deny her own vision of the spiders floating down from the skies, when she saw that Amie wasn't looking out the window, but into the terrarium containing the two tarantulas. Liz stumbled against several desks in her haste.

The female tarantula was moving slowly, as if reluctantly. "The babies!" Amie cried gleefully, as all the glass in the room began to break, the terrarium, the windows, the cupboard, as the hundreds of bone-white infants spilled from the cocooned cavity in the dirt, each wearing a mask of Liz's fear.

The Tabernacle

Henry S. Whitehead

AUTHOR'S NOTE: *This is a very ancient tale, running back far into the early history of religion in Europe. It has cropped up, traditionally, in many lands and in various periods. Members of the older religions will understand its implications without explanations. To those unversed in the traditional belief concerning the* Sanctissimum *(the consecrated bread of Holy Communion among the older, Catholic, religions), it may be mentioned that this bread, known as the Host, is, after consecration at the hands of a validly ordained priest, understood to be "really" the Body of the Lord. The type of this "reality" varies among different theologians, but the belief in the essential identity of the consecrated Host with the True Body, with all the implications that follow this belief, is general. As the Lord (Jesus) is Lord of the Universe according to ancient Christian belief, His Body should be sacred to all His creatures. Hence this very ancient tradition that is here told in a modern setting.*

Kazmir Strod knelt very low in his seat in the pine pew of St. Stanislas's Church just after he had come back from the altar rail, so low, by purpose, that no one up there at the altar, not Father Gregoreff nor any of the acolytes, could possibly see him. The clean handkerchief he had taken to church, unfolded, was still in his left hand where he had put it, somewhat damp because of his emotion and the fact that it was a warm April day. It was, indeed, so warm that his bees had swarmed the evening before and he had got them, successfully, into the new hive.

The Holy Host remained intact, between his teeth, held lightly. He felt sure that It was not even damp, because he had carefully wiped his lips and teeth, in that same low-kneeling posture, with the clean handkerchief just before rising, genuflecting, proceeding to the altar.

He placed the handkerchief over his mouth now and to the accompaniment of several brief prayers took the Host from his mouth. He held It, very gently, the Sanctissimum, in the clean handkerchief. He felt very strange. He had never done such a thing before.

Bending now, very low, he felt for the small, thin wafer inside the clean handkerchief's folds, broke off a tiny piece, and placed It in his mouth. He must receive Holy Communion or it would be further sacrilege. He swallowed It, with difficulty, for his mouth, under this stress, had remained very dry. He said the prayers of Reception with his mind on them, but as rapidly as he could. He did not leave out a word of those prayers.

Then, and only then, he slipped the handkerchief into his pocket. He was kneeling upright, like the rest of the congregation, the men with shining newly shaved faces, the women, on the other side of the central alleyway, with multicolored shawls over their sleek heads, when Father Gregoreff was turning toward the congregation at the end of the Mass.

"Ite, missa est," boomed Father Gregoreff, and turned to the altar's end for the Last Gospel.

Kazmir spoke to nobody on the way home. That, too, he imagined, would be sacrilegious, for, like a priest, he was carrying the Sanctissimum upon him.

He went straight to the new hive. There were almost no flowers out at this time of year. On the broad landing board, several dozen bees were lined up in rows, like little soldiers, finishing the sugar-and-water honey he had placed for them to keep them in the hive where he had placed them last night. He was sure the new queen was within. She would be, of course, in the center of the swarm, and he had lifted them, very carefully, off the bush where they had swarmed, into the new hive. It had been an unusually large swarm. He had worn his high rubber boots, his bricklayer's gloves, and a folded net about his head over his cap. Even so, he had had a few stings.

He was going to make this hive the greatest hive there was! He was going to use old, old "magic," the way it had been done in the Old Country, for luck and for the success of a vegetable garden, and for many other good purposes, even though it was, good purpose and all, sacrilege. God didn't mind such things. It was only the priests who objected. A little bit of the Host placed inside the hive. That was all. That would make the bees prosper, bring luck to the new hive. Over here, in America, you didn't hear so much about doing things like that. But Kazmir knew what to do for bees. Those old-time ways were good ways. They worked. The Holy Host had many virtues. Along with garlic-flowers it was a sure safeguard from vampires. Placed in a coffin, he had heard, It kept the body from decay. With even a tiny crumb of It, wrapped tightly in a piece of clean linen, sewed into your clothes, It was sure proof against the Bad-Eye.

There was practically no sound inside the hive. The bees on the landing board moved slowly, lethargically. If this heat held, there would be flowers soon, and he could discontinue the sugar-and-water honey. Too much of that and the bees laid off working! Bees were like humans, very much like humans, only dumber! They never took a rest, had no relaxations.

He raised the hive's top, carefully, leaned it against the side of the packing box on which the hive itself stood. There were the frames, just as he had placed them yesterday, a little old comb, for the bees to build onto, near the middle. That was all right. He removed the crushed bodies of several bees that had got caught when he had placed the top on the hive in yesterday's dusk of evening. The new queen would be down inside there, somewhere, surrounded by her eager, devoted workers, the swarm that had accompanied her out of the older hive yesterday.

Kazmir crossed himself, furtively, and glanced around. Nobody was looking; indeed nobody was, at the moment, in sight. He took the handkerchief out of his pocket, touched his right thumb and the index finger to his lips reverently, extracted the Sanctissimum and dropped It into the open hive between the frames. Then he replaced the top and went into the house. The bees should prosper now, according to all the old rules. Kazmir had never heard of putting such a charm on bees before. That was his own idea. But—if it worked as the old tales said it worked, for horses and cows and the increase of a flock of goats, why not for bees?

It was a quarter past six by the kitchen clock. Time for the woman and kids to be getting up for seven o'clock Mass. He went up the rough stairs to awaken his wife and their two children. This done, he returned to the kitchen to boil four eggs for his breakfast.

It turned out to be a very quiet hive, the new one. Its bees, too, seemed to be stingers. He received many stings during the summer, more stings than usual, it seemed to him. He had to warn Anna and the children to keep away from it. "They got a lotta pep, them bees," he said, and smiled to himself. It was he, applying an old idea with true American progressiveness, who had "pepped them up." He gave the process this phrase, mentally, without the least thought of incongruity, of irreverence. The efficacy of the Sanctissimum was the last, the very last thing that Kazmir Strod would have doubted, in the entire scheme of the world's regulations and principles.

It was only occasionally nowadays that Kazmir worked at bricklaying. Ten years before, in the Old Country, he had learned that trade. Always a willful, strong-headed youth, independent of mind, he had flown in the face of his family custom to learn a trade like that. All his family, near Kovno, had been market-gardeners. That strong-headedness had been responsible for his emigration, too. There had been many disputes between him and his father and older brothers. The strong-headedness and the trade! There were great openings for a good brick-layer in America.

But, since he had married—rather late in life, to this Americanized Anna of his, at twenty-two; he was twenty-seven now—with enough money to buy this place, earned at the bricklaying, he had reverted to his gardening. There wasn't as much in gardening, even with good land like this, and sometimes Anna would nag him to take a job when a contractor offered one, but there were all the deep-rooted satisfactions of the soil; the love of it was bred deep in his blood and bones, and he had a way with tomatoes and early peas and even humdrum potatoes.

This devotion to the soil, he felt, triumphantly, had been amply justi-fied that August. He had an offer to go and be gardener on a great estate, a millionaire's, eighteen miles away. The offer included a house, and the use of what vegetables he needed for his family. He accepted it, and told Anna afterward.

Anna was delighted. He had not been sure of how she would take it, and her delight pleased him enormously. For several days it was like a new honeymoon. He spread it all over the community that he wanted to sell his place.

He got six hundred dollars, cash, more than he had paid for it. There was a couple of thousand dollars worth of improvement he had dug into its earth, but six hundred dollars was six hundred dollars! The title passed, after a day and a night's wrangling with the purchaser, Tony Dvorcznik, a compatriot. Kazmir and Anna and the children moved their possessions in a borrowed motor-truck.

It was in October that Tony Dvorcznik killed off the bees. Tony did not understand bees, and his wife was afraid of them. He hired Stanislas Bodinski, who was one of Father Gregoreff's acolytes, to do the job for him, for a quarter-share of what honey might be discovered within the four hives. Stanislas Bodinski arrived, with sulfur and netting. Tony and his wife stood at a little distance, watching interestedly; telling each other to watch out for stings; marveling at Stanislas Bodinski's noncha-lance, deftly placing his sulfur-candles, rapidly stuffing the horizontal opening above the landing boards, the edges all around the hive tops.

Stanislas joined them, removing his head-net, and stood with them while the sulfur fumes did their deadly work inside the hives. Later, they all walked over to the hives, Stanislas reassuring Tony's wife. "They ain't no danger now. They're all dead by now. Anyhow, they die after they sting you, but you needn't worry none. Jus' the same, you better keep away a little. They's some bees was out the hives when I stopped up them cracks. They'll be flyin' around, kinda puzzled, now."

The comb was lifted out, to exclamations on the part of Tony's wife, into a row of borrowed milk pans. It piled up, enormously, honey covering the bottoms of the pans viscidly.

"You'd wonder where it all come from," said Tony's wife, again and again, "outa them little hives! You wouldn't think they'd hold that much stuff, would ya?"

Stanislas Bodinski arrived at the last hive, with two remaining milk pans, and proceeded to lift the top away from the hive. They saw him look in. Then he stopped and looked close. Then he stepped back, raised his arms in an amazing gesture of wonderment, sank to his knees beside the hive, and made the sign of the cross on his breast many times.

Wonderingly, they approached, Tony's wife murmuring:

"What's *bitin'* him? Is he gone loony, huh?" Then: "Hey, Tony, they mus' be somethin' awful strange in that-there hive, huh—for Stan to ac' that way!"

There was indeed something strange in the hive, although there was very little honey in it. They did not dare touch it, and, after Stanislas had somewhat recovered himself, and put back the top with hands shaking, the three of them, just as they stood, Tony's wife not even taking off her apron, started for the rectory, to get Father Gregoreff.

The priest came, rather grumblingly, Stanislas following half a block behind the other three. He had run into the sacristy to get the priest's cope and a stole, and something that he had to hold onto, in his pocket, to keep it quiet! He hoped Father Gregoreff would not look behind him and see what he was carrying. He was a bit of a mystic, this Stanislas; otherwise he would not, perhaps, have continued to be an acolyte after he was nineteen. He, too, had come from near Kovno, like Kazmir Strod. Stanislas had listened to strange tales in his earlier boyhood, back there in the Old Country.

He came in through Tony Dvorcznik's gate well behind the rest, furtively. They were all standing, looking at the hive, when he came around the corner of the house. He walked around them, knelt before his priest, seized and kissed his hand. He handed the amazed Father Gregoreff his stole, and the priest put it on mechanically, murmuring, "What's this? what's all this?" Stanislas rose, hastily invested his pastor with the white cope, and stepped over to the hive. He knelt, and turning to the others, motioned them, authoritatively, to kneel also. They did so, all three, the priest's cope trailing on the ground, a few feet behind Stanislas.

Stanislas, making the sign of the cross, reached his arms into the hive. Carefully, the sweat running down his face, he lifted out a shining yellow, new-wax structure, intact, with infinite care. He turned, still on his knees, and placed what he had lifted in the priest's hands. It was a little church, made of wax, made by the bees whose dead bodies, suffocated by sulfur fumes, now littered the dead hive.

Then Stanislas took the sacring bell from his left-hand pocket, and, his head on the ground, rang it to indicate to all who might be within earshot that they should prostrate themselves before the Sanctissimum.

Take Me, for Instance

Hugh B. Cave

Four of us heard the thing, it turned out later.

Arthur Pottle, who lives alone, was in his yard calling to his dog. "It was pretty dark, you recall," he said, "and when I heard the humming I thought it was old man Sheldon's bees. But it wasn't. It was too high up."

Moddy Williams was in bed with his missus and she'd just told him for heaven's sake leave her alone, it was too hot for nonsense. It *was* a hot night, so he got up to open the window. "That damn window sticks all the time," he said. "It let go with a clap of thunder, and I thought the other noise was just an echo. It wasn't, though. It kept on for a good half minute more."

At Jeff Watley's place it was Margaret, Jeff's daughter, that heard the thing. To tell the truth, Jeff had been at the bottle again and was in no fit condition to hear anything. "I was in the kitchen making him some coffee," Margaret said. "I opened the back door to let some air in, and what came in was the humming. The thing was right over the house, whatever it was."

I couldn't find anyone else who'd heard it, though I did a lot of asking around the village. So the four of us held a meeting at my house, finally, and I got out a map.

"Take a good look at this," I said. "Arthur's house is here, Moddy's here, Margaret's here, and mine right here. Now we don't know which way the thing came because none of us knows who heard it first. But it came one way or the other in a straight line, right over us."

They couldn't argue with that. But Margaret, who's a real smart girl in spite of her sotted pa, made a point I hadn't thought of.

"We don't know it was landing," she said. "You couldn't tell from the sound. At least, I couldn't."

The others said exactly the same, and I had to agree with them.

"Of course, it *could* have been landing," Margaret admitted, studying the map again. "If it came from the west, it could have been making for Fenley Thompson's big field here. There's no better place to land in these parts."

We decided we ought to go out to Fenley Thompson's and have a look. Fenley would probably laugh at us—he was the schoolmaster and a bit of a snob—but he wouldn't laugh too loud. Margaret was engaged to him.

We went in my old car and stopped at the house first, of course. Fenley wouldn't take kindly to us prowling around without permission. Sitting in his study, which was just about walled with books, we told him what we'd heard and what we suspected.

He looked at us as if we were daft.

"Never in all my days have I heard such utter nonsense," he said. "What do you expect to find? A ship from space? Little green men running around?"

"Now, Fenley," Margaret said, "we heard this thing and we just want to have a look, that's all."

"I didn't hear anything," he said.

"You weren't home. You were visiting your sister."

That stopped him. He'd forgotten. "Very well, I shan't stop you," he said. "Go and look your heads off. But it's ridiculous, and I am shocked that you, Margaret, are mixed up in this."

We thanked him and went into the field, and we looked. And he was right: we didn't find anything. The grass was straight up everywhere, none of it singed or flattened, not even a daisy out of place.

When we got back to the house, Fenley gave us the kind of treatment we expected.

"It's lack of schooling that makes people behave the way you do," he said. "I don't exclude you either, Margaret. Now take me, for instance. I don't believe in this nonsense because I'm well enough read to know better."

"We know what we heard," I argued.

"Fiddlesticks! What you heard was an airplane or the wind."

We let it go at that. But on the way home Moddy Williams gave a snort. "For Mr. Fenley Thompson's information—no offense to you, Margaret—there wasn't no plane within a hundred miles of here at that hour. Nor there wasn't a birdbreath o' wind that night neither. 'Take me, for instance' indeed! The only way to take him is for a fool!"

For a week or so, nothing more happened. Nothing we could be certain of, at any rate. I got the feeling I was being watched a time or two, and the others said they did too, but it wasn't a thing we could be sure about.

When matters did come to a head, there was no doubting them. We *knew*.

There were three of us in the pub that evening—Moddy, me, and young Jeremy Bliss—along with Bessie Barnett, the proprietress. Jeremy was a nice young lad, a carpenter; he was sweet on Margaret Watley, though of course it didn't do him any good, with her engaged to the schoolmaster. We were sitting there in the pub having a pint or two, when all three of us heard the humming at the same time. Only this time it wasn't in the sky or so loud; it was just a whispery sort of humming right there in the pub with us.

It was Bessie Barnett—she's a big, no-nonsense kind of woman—who figured it out. With her hands jammed on to her hips, she peered up at the ceiling and said, "Now what in thunderation is that?"

That's where the sound was, up close to the ceiling as though there were bees up there, only it was not quite the same.

"All right," I said out loud. "Who are you and what do you want?"

"What does 'thunderation' mean?" a kind of squeaky voice answered.

"What?"

"We are sorry. Your language so many words has, it for us is hard. You new ones keep using."

"What the devil language do you speak?" Moddy asked.

"You not could it learn," the voice said. "You not could manage the sounds. We must yours learn."

"Well, you seem to be doin' pretty good," young Jeremy Bliss said, "except you don't put things in very good order yet. Just keep tryin' and you'll get it right. How many of you are up there?"

"Oh, many."

"How'd you get here?"

"You do not a word for it have," another voice said. "But you it heard."

"Well, I'm glad that's settled," I said. "But if we heard it, where is it?"

"We do not think that is wise to tell that," the first voice said. "You might it try to harm."

"Is it in Fenley's field?"

"Indeed yes, in a manner of speaking. But you not can it see."

"Invisible, eh?" Jeremy said. "Like you up there. Can you make yourselves visible just for a second or two maybe, so we'll know who we're talking to?"

"Some of us can," the voice said. "Wait."

Anyone walking into the pub would have thought we were crazy, I guess, the three of us and Bessie gazing at the ceiling like that, waiting. It took a long time, too. And even then we couldn't be sure we saw anything.

It seemed to me—and afterward the others said the same—that little blue lights began to come on after a while. Not bright, mind you—just glowy things, drifting about under the ceiling in slow motion. If they were real, they were only just. I got an idea that I could catch one maybe, if I was sly about it, so I climbed up on a stool slowly and deliberately, then shot my hand out.

All the lights went out—if they'd ever been on in the first place.

"You not should have that done," the voice said. "We not do mean *you* any harm."

"What do you want with us then?" Moddy demanded, reasonably enough.

"We want to take one of you back us with, for study," the voice said. "But not his will against, of course. That not would right be."

"Back where?" I said.

The name of the place sounded like Sutaurus.

I didn't have any idea where Sutaurus was, or what, and neither did Moddy or Jeremy or Bessie Barnett. We looked at each other and shook our heads. Then we looked at the ceiling again and I said, "Well, if you fellers got any idea that one of us is going to volunteer, we ain't. Moddy and me learned that in the army, and Jeremy here is too smart. We're staying right here." "And if you think you can *take* us any place, you just try it," Bessie said grabbing a broom.

"Oh, we lots of time have," the voice said. "We can wait."

"Wait all you like," Bessie said, "but just wait someplace else."

"Very well," the voice said. "But we watching be will."

When Moddy and Jeremy and I left the pub, we held a conference. What we ought to do, we decided, was go out to Fenley Thompson's place and look for the vehicle again. "We can talk all we like," I said, "even with Bessie backing us up, but people won't believe any of this until we find the thing those fellers came in. We *got* to find it to save our reputations."

"Fenley won't like it," Jeremy said. "He's still annoyed with Margaret about your last visit."

"I don't see how she can stand that man," Moddy said. "A sweet, simple girl like her."

"Well he reads books and I don't. Not many, at any rate."

"There's things a lot more comforting than books on a winter night," Moddy grumbled. "You ask me, she ought to chuck—"

"Now, Moddy, it's none of our business," I said, and he buttoned up.

Jeremy was right about Fenley not wanting to see us, though. He was busy with school work and grudged us the time, and when we got through telling him what'd happened to us at the pub, he just about exploded.

"You're intoxicated, the three of you!" he shouted. "You ought to be put away to sober up instead of disturbing an honest man's work with your hallucinations!"

"We're as sober as you are, Fenley," I said. "If you'd come out from under them big words and look at us, you'd see it."

"Well, you're not going into my field again!" he said. "You've had *something* to drink, and that's enough. Responsible people don't indulge at all. Now you take me. In all my life I haven't found it necessary to imbibe a single drop. And have *I* seen those crazy blue lights and heard this idiotic humming you talk about? I have not!"

"We won't hurt your precious field just walking through it," I said.

"You've already walked through it, and that's that!"

"We got to find this vehicle, Fenley," I said, but Jeremy Bliss gave me a look and I shut up.

"It'll be near to the full o' moon tonight," Jeremy said, as we drove home, "and he's taking Margaret to a do at the school. A play or something like that. We'll have our look at his field, all right. Just be patient."

What we did, we stole up to the schoolmaster's place on foot and waited for him to drive off in his car. That was about eight o'clock. Then we went to the field and got in a line, holding hands, and walked up and down to cover every inch of it.

There were four of us. Bessie wouldn't come—she wasn't going to break the law for any queer foreigners, she said; let 'em mind their own business and she'd mind hers. And Margaret was at the school with Fenley, so there was just me and Moddy and Arthur Pottle and Jeremy Bliss.

It took us a long time to walk that big field, I can tell you. And what did we find for our trouble? Nothing. We didn't hope to see anything, mind you—just to walk into it and feel it. But if anything was there, it was so small we walked right over it or past it.

"Course," Moddy said, "they might've moved it. I mean after they landed here, they might have run it off into the woods. We'd never find anything invisible in those woods."

"Or it could be sort of floating, the same as they do," Jeremy said. "Up there off the ground a bit maybe, just out of reach. We might've walked under it."

"Anyway," I said, "we're finished and that's a fact. Nobody's going to believe us without proof, so we'd better forget the whole thing."

But I'd reckoned without the strangers. Those things were watching us all the time, and inside of a week the whole village was talking about it. In our homes, in the shops, on the road—everywhere we went they were watching. We could feel it.

"We've got to hold a meeting," Bessie Barnett said. "We got to decide what to do." It ought to be at my house on Saturday, she said, because mine was handiest. "I'll put up a notice in the pub," she said.

Just about everybody came. Everybody but Fenley Thompson, that is. We didn't expect him to know about any notice in the pub, of course, or to come on account of it, if he did know. Nor was it likely, living out so far, he'd felt the strangers watching the way we had.

But we had a crowd, I can tell you. By the time we were ready to talk, it was so big we had to move out of the house into the yard.

I put a good sturdy table out there under my oak tree, and we got up on it, one after another, to tell what we knew. First there was me and Arthur Pottle and Moddy Williams and Margaret, telling how we'd heard the vehicle that first night. Then Bessie Barnett and young Jeremy Bliss, telling what happened at the pub. Then a lot of others, one by one, telling how they'd heard the humming sounds at this time or that, or felt they were being watched.

Finally I got up on the table again to give a brief summing up.

"What it seems to amount to is this," I said. "These strangers don't mean us no real harm—they told us so in the pub—but they want one of us to go back with 'em. What they're hanging around us for is to learn our language well enough to convince one of us to go off with them.

They've got this vehicle hid somewhere, either in the woods or floating there over Fenley Thompson's field and—"

Just then Fenley Thompson pushed through the crowd and said in a thundering voice, "There is absolutely nothing floating over my field, and you know it! Stop talking this incredible nonsense!"

"How do we know it?" I said, when I got over the shock of seeing him there.

"Because it would cast a shadow in the moonlight, of course!" he said.

"Not if it was transparent, it wouldn't," Jeremy Bliss chimed up. "The light would go right through it. Them little blue things in the pub didn't cast no shadows on the ceiling, I noticed."

Fenley Thompson got mad then. He was the schoolmaster, and no simple carpenter boy like Jeremy was going to talk to him that way in front of the whole village. "Stand aside, sir," he said, and climbed up on the table. "Now you listen to what I say, all of you!" he shouted, standing up there stiff as a post and belittling the lot of us with a grand look of contempt. "You listen and pay attention to words of wisdom, and then you'll go home and forget this idiocy!

"What you're suffering from at this point is hysteria," Fenley said. "That's the name of it: mass hysteria. And the reason you are caught up in it is because you're all of a kind, all ignorant and foolish, and when I say that, I don't make any exceptions."

"That's a fine way to talk about your own fiancée," Jeremy Bliss yelled back at him.

"Hold your tongue!" Fenley shouted. "I speak only the truth, and you know it. Mass hysteria, that's what it is. Sheer idiocy born of ignorance. Now then, take me. Take *me*, I say. None of this can touch me because I—"

Well, it was a good thing, I guess. They were bound to take someone sooner or later, and nobody could have been less missed. And you've got to admit he asked for it. Spouting all those schoolmaster's words, getting the creatures all mixed up with stuff they never heard before—when he thundered two simple words like "Take me," what else did he expect?

Anyway, before you could even be sure it happened, Fenley Thompson was just a shimmering bit of blue light, there one second and gone the next.

"You might say he volunteered," Moddy Williams said, shaking his head. "Yes, sir, that's what he did, he volunteered. But I don't think he meant to."

That Only a Mother Could Love

Mollie L. Burleson

The contraction shook her, heaved at her, tore her in two. She felt a warm gush between her legs and, suddenly, a sense of ease. She lifted herself up on two weak arms, hair falling damply forward, and fumbled at the bloody mess between her thighs. Something moved. Sally tore at the membrane, ripping at it with her long, pointed nails. With a cry of frustration she attacked the tough skin, tearing at it until like a ripe melon it popped open. Her fingers brailled their way frantically through the tissue and pulled out a moving lump of flesh. Her baby! Blind with tears, she clutched the little form to her breast and fell back exhausted, sending the tears streaming into her hair.

It was all right. There had been nothing to the fears and half-remembered dreams she had experienced all through her pregnancy. Dreams of squat and misshapen little people dancing, dancing on her swollen belly.

She thought about Ted. Their wedding had been bridal-magazine perfect, Sally radiant in old white lace, Ted handsome and shy in his blue tux. Their marriage was the proverbial made-in-heaven union. Only one thing had marred their happiness during those first years: her inability to bear a child. She had always loved children, from the time she played with her first doll, through the years babysitting five younger brothers and sisters. Sally had been an unusual teenager; she had truly enjoyed being a little mother. Grown up, she had wanted a baby of her own.

She had gone to specialists, *he* had gone to specialists. They had done exercises, taken health cures, had even resorted to her grandmother's old-wives'-tales remedies. But nothing had worked. She was still barren after five years of trying, trying so hard she felt empty and dry. So Ted had suggested a vacation, a trip to get away, to give them both a new perspective on life. A long-postponed vacation to bring back a little of what they had lost throughout the years. And it had worked.

She remembered it now, the long flight over the Atlantic, the landing

516

at Shannon Airport, the detour through customs. She and Ted had boarded the bus and started their once-in-a-lifetime trip they had dreamed about ever since they had discovered their love for each other.

In the little town of Kilderry, with its cottages so charming in their thatched crowns, Sally and Ted had stayed, mingling with the friendly people, eating the plain but good Irish fare, drinking maybe just a little too much Irish ale, and loving. Oh yes, the loving! There were mornings when they'd lie in the soft, white-sheeted bed afterward, letting the sun from the latticed windows play upon their naked bodies. Yes, it had been good.

Except for that peculiar experience in the woods nearby when Sally had wandered off alone, walking for what had seemed hours upon the soft and spongy turf.

Ted had felt tired that day and decided to stay in bed. "Why don't you go for a walk?" he said, yawning widely. "It's a beautiful day. I'll just grab a few winks and when you get back we'll go down to the pub and hoist a few. Guess I'm getting old, love."

So Sally kissed him goodbye, grabbed her sweater, and took the road that ran past the lovely and ancient woods. She was walking and thinking soft and tranquil thoughts when a small and strangely dressed child ran across the road directly in front of her and disappeared into the thorny thickets on the other side. She called after him, and when he didn't answer she ran into the woods searching for him beneath low hanging branches and under bushes, but no child was to be found. What a strange child that was. Where did he go? Not finding him, she shrugged her shoulders and turned around to discover that she was lost. She wasn't afraid, really, for what was there to fear in this shadow-dappled forest? She'd find her way out quickly enough. But she wandered deeper and deeper into the dark interior, the leaves above her growing thicker and thicker and the branches seeming to lock their fingers together above her head, imprisoning her.

Coming upon a deep pool, where the darkness seemed not fearful but strangely calming, she stopped to sit down, taking off her shoes and stockings, and bathing her aching feet in the limpid coolness. Finding herself growing very sleepy she leaned against the bark of a gnarled and venerable tree. And slept. And dreamed.

The dreams were wild and distorted, of diminutive people cavorting madly about on the emerald grass before a row of standing gray stones. Little men in funny feather-topped hats and pointed shoes. Suddenly, in the middle of a complex and somehow darkly charming movement, they stopped, looking frenziedly about, and scattered into the woods.

Scuttling upon the scene came a creature horrible in its grotesqueness, a little taller than the tiny dancers but gnarled and twisted and humped. Although the little people had been strange, they were nonetheless humanlike; but this creature was an abomination.

He had huge flopping ears, a hooked and warty nose, and beady reptilian eyes that leered at her from under beetling brows. He waddled over to her and ran his twisted hand under her dress, caressing her. She screamed then, and woke to find her clothes crumpled and her face hotly flushed.

My God, what an awful dream, she thought, brushing at her dress in an attempt to press out the wrinkles, and combing her fingers through her hair. I've got to find my way out of here. Looking at her watch, she was amazed to find that over two hours had elapsed since she had started off on her walk. I can't believe I slept that long. What a weird day this has been. God, I wonder what Ted's thinking. Turning back the way she felt she had come, she found the road with surprising ease, and headed back toward the inn and Ted.

The vacation, as vacations will do, had ended all too soon, and they had gone home, picking up their skein of life where they had left off, with one big difference. After all those nights of lovemaking under the quaintly thatched roof in Kilderry, Sally was pregnant. How they had celebrated after the doctor confirmed her suspicions! Drunk and amorous, they had made love that night slowly and deliciously.

Her pregnancy had not been an easy one; she had experienced days of horrible nausea and miserable headaches. Early in her third month, arms hugging the toilet bowl, vomit sour on her lips, Sally had almost hated the life within her, hated what she had begun to call the "parasite." But then things began to change; she started feeling better, and by her sixth month she felt fine.

This morning she had awakened bright and fresh and waddled clumsily into the bathroom, rubbing her lower back. She stripped and stood naked in front of the full-length mirror, stroking her watermelon stomach, patting it and crooning to the child within. It won't be long now, Mama's little darling. Soon Mommy will hold you and rock you and love you.

Finished with her shower and dressed in what she liked to call her "tent," she made her laborious way to the kitchen where Ted already had coffee brewing and bacon sizzling. "Looks like we may have some snow, Sal," he said, pouring coffee into Ma and Pa mugs.

"You'll be back tonight, though, won't you?"

"I'll do my best, babe. Not to worry; you're not due for another couple of weeks anyhow."

Sally bit hungrily into her toast. "Yeah, I know, but I still hate to have you go so far."

"Hey, honey, listen, with luck I'll be back by eight. This load's gonna bring us some extra dough. We'll need it now with little Teddy coming."

"You mean Cassandra, don't you?" Grinning, she punched him in the ribs.

"Sure. Cassandra. Theodore Cassandra O'Malley."

"Quit that, you big lug, and don't squeeze me so hard. Baby doesn't like it. Feel him kick!"

"Sorry, Teddy old boy," Ted said as he patted her belly.

He had kissed her hard then, bundling up and going out into the driving wind.

She had been sitting by the window in her favorite chair knitting and watching the snow fall ever harder. God, I'm worried. What if Ted can't make it back tonight? He will, you ninny, her sensible side replied; relax, already. And she did.

By four o'clock the lawn birdfeeder was buried in snow and the drifts had begun to climb the sides of her Dodge Colt. The weather bureau predicted a heavy snowfall amounting to a possible twenty inches or more by morning. Omigod, she thought, he'll never make it.

That was when the first contraction hit.

And now she lay here in the gloom, tired but happy. I've done it, I've really done it. I've delivered my own baby. My baby . . .

Coming out of her exhausted stupor, she jerked awake. The baby! My God, I haven't even *looked* at him. Or her. She sat up weakly and lifted him with wobbly arms. Wow, he's a heavy one. And lusty. Gotta be a boy. Oh, Ted, where *are* you? Squinting to see him better in the near darkness, she laid the kicking baby down carefully on the bed and reached over to turn on the bedside lamp.

Baby looked at her with beady eyes that lay prunelike in a pastry-dough face. His thick dark hair hung in spikes around his misshapen head. He grinned at her, revealing blackened stumps of teeth. Chattering to her in a strange tongue, he raised his grotesquely twisted arms to her in supplication. "Mma-mma," he guttered. "Mma-mma."

"Mama's here, darling," Sally crooned, reaching out to take his gnarled little hands. "Mama's here." She was here, Baby was here. Suddenly she had begun to realize that that was all that mattered.

519

There was Soot on the Cat

SUZANNE PICKETT

A chill wind bristled through the trees and tugged at my hat as I walked through the cold, brooding air. Good to get out after four weeks of feverish cutting, revising, and polishing on what I hoped would be the "great American novel."

Back to the office tomorrow. I smiled at the thought. But I would have smiled at anything. A cold wind always exhilarated me. Something in me seemed kin to the fierceness of the wind.

Coming to an old, deserted-looking road I turned into it, walked a few feet, then slackened my pace and looked up in surprise. Queer that the air should feel so strange all at once. The road seemed lost between old, gnarled oaks, tall pines, and thick underbrush. The actual thick, murky feel of horror seemed to emanate from it.

"This is what comes of too hard concentration," I muttered. But a minute ago I had been happy, exhilarated—I shivered in the gloom and listened to the ceaseless murmur of the pines and the dismal creaking of the oaks. Impelled onward by some strange force in spite of my frantic desire to go back I stepped over rocks and gullies in the road, hesitated, shivered, and walked on again until I came to an old house set back from the road. The horror jumped at me as I looked at the house; yet it was pleasant to the eyes, situated on a small hill, picturesque with its gables and high windows.

Unable to move, I stood still a minute. Then I heard a car behind me, looked back, and saw a jeep bounding over the ditches and rocks.

Caught by a movement on the roof my eyes returned to the house. Scrabbling and clawing, a huge, tiger-striped cat clambered down the roof and bounded to the road at my feet. Crouching before me, he looked at me with almost human eyes; large, yellow-green, with a dark rim around the iris.

His yellow coat was covered with soot!

There was knowledge in those eyes and a look—but don't let me speak of that look. Then he, too, noticed the jeep. With a cry that ended in a squeal, he tried to escape it. I shuddered as his life was crunched out beneath the wheels.

The jeep swerved, roared, and stopped. I knew the driver, a nearby farmer, Mase Oliver. He climbed to the ground. In spite of the chill in the air, drops of sweat stood on his face. His hand trembled as he mopped his upper lip. "I don't like cats," he said to me, his eyes almost the color of the iron gray of his hair. "I am glad when I kill one, but that cat—" He looked at the animal and his lips tightened. "Did you see his eyes?"

We stood silent, both looking at the cat, just a dead beast now, then he turned to me. "By the way," he remarked. "Seen Henson lately?"

"Who?" I asked.

"Jude Henson."

"Never heard of him."

"He lives here. Thought you might be going there." His eyes had a worried look. "Want to go with me?"

"Well—" I hesitated. I wasn't in the mood to meet a strange man.

"I wish you would," Oliver said. He looked at me as if I might be some sort of new species. "You a writer, ain't you?"

"Well—yes." I wondered what that had to do with it.

"Him too," Oliver pointed to the house. "Raised here. Paw used to own this place. Always was a queer kid. He come to me about a month back, asked to rent the old place, said he wanted to write." There was the contempt of the man who works in the good honest soil for anyone who would waste his time on words. Then the worry was back in Oliver's voice again. "Henson got milk and butter at my house, we ain't seen him for a week, so I come down to ask was anything wrong."

"Gone somewhere," I suggested. I didn't want to enter that house. "There's no smoke."

"Heats with oil."

"Well—I'll go with you," I said quickly. At least I'd meet the man.

Oliver rapped on the door and waited a minute. The house seemed to wait too. He knocked again, this time louder. Still no sound within. Suddenly he shook the knob. It turned and the door moved slightly. It wasn't locked, but something, a bar or latch, held it.

"He must be there," Oliver said. "Door's barred on the inside." He was a big man with thick, ruddy skin. I noticed that he had paled. We looked at each other. "Let's try the back," I said. I felt pale too. There was something about that house. We must get inside.

The back door was barred too.

We tried the windows. They were locked, the shades drawn. "Something wrong inside." Oliver mopped his face.

"Yes," I answered.

"I'm going." I held the screen wide and he hurled himself at the door. It creaked and gave. He stumbled inside and I followed.

The living room and large kitchen were empty. Dirty dishes littered the table, a greasy skillet, egg shells, and empty milk bottles.

"Not very neat," I remarked.

We crossed the hall into the front bedroom. It was empty. Oliver looked at me as I glanced his way. "Well," his voice shook, "there's one more room."

"Yes," I muttered and looked at the door. I knew, and he knew. Something was in that room.

Finally, he opened the door. He jerked to a stop, then stumbled back, his soundless lips moving.

"What is it?" I asked holding his arm. He tried to control his lips and speak, but still no sound came. Finally he pointed to the door.

As a "Sob Sister," I have covered fire, theft, murder, disaster, but nothing could prepare me for the "thing" I beheld. The sunken eyes, the pitifully clawing outstretched hands, the horror in the eyes of the grinning corpse on the floor.

I was worse than Oliver. I couldn't even move. I could only stand and stare. The room was a wreck. The curtains torn, a chair overturned, some crockery broken. But, gentlemen, there was not a sign of violence on the face of the man. Not a scratch, not a bruise. Later, when the body was examined, there was not found anywhere any evidence of injury. That he had died of terror was evident. What had caused the terror was unknown. "He must have gone mad," was the verdict of the doctors.

Perhaps I did wrong. Well, I'll let you decide. But I alone saw the diary lying open. I read the last page, picked it up and put it in my pocketbook.

That night I read it.

It has been a month now.

Perhaps I am going mad. The boys at the office can't understand my sudden fear of cats. Before my vacation it was I who brought milk to the office cat, I who gave him cheese, rubbed his back in the way he loved. Now if he comes near me — But I'm getting away from the diary. This is what I read:

Well, it began, the perfect crime at last. Nice-looking man too from his pictures, Fey (what a name for a man) — Fey Brandon. Dead by person or persons unknown, shot once through the heart on a lonely country road. Yes, the gun was found and identified. It was stolen a few days before from a pawnshop in Birmingham. The theft had been reported, but neither the owner of the shop nor the customer who looked at the gun could describe the man who came in as they crossed the aisle to look at a watch. When they came back, the man was gone; so was the gun.

I don't know what there was about Brandon. Irene Sharp was — well almost the prettiest girl I ever saw. I was crazy about her and thought she loved me. But one day I ran across her in the park with a strange man. From behind an azalea bush I watched them. If I had been a dog my bristles would have risen. There was something about the fellow's eyes — they were large, yellow-green with a dark rim around the iris. His hair was a tawny yellow, streaked by the sun. I noticed the ripple of smooth muscles under his thin, sport shirt, and his walk was beautiful, graceful, catlike.

As they moved away he looked down at her and laughed. I could have killed them both — and I never spoke to Irene again. She called me a few times, wondered what was wrong, but I wouldn't give her the satisfaction of knowing that I cared.

And then I didn't want Brandon, yes, it was Brandon with her, I didn't want him to gloat over me. I hated his eyes, I could have cut them out. When I saw him — and I was always running into him, I shuddered as I looked at him.

He pretended that I was a stranger, never seemed to notice me. But I knew, all the time I knew he was laughing inside.

I hadn't gone with Ruth Clearwell a month until she mentioned the new man in town, Fey Brandon. We never had so much fun before. I spent every penny I had, and Ruth was gay, bright. "You know," her voice was husky as I kissed her good night. "I didn't know that you could be so — so sweet and so nice."

I never spoke to her again.

And then I met Margot and learned why God made us male and female. Little she was, gay and golden. Like sunshine, and as pure, with the clear blue eyes of an angel.

Margot loved me too, then suddenly she changed. She wouldn't see me, wouldn't talk over the telephone. I didn't know what was wrong. One day I cornered her in the library, and for some reason I glanced at the book she was reading. "Fey," she had written. "Fey Brandon."

"Margot!" I said, trying to whisper above the rage in my heart. "Margot, do you know this man?"

"Yes," she said dreamily. "You know, Jude, there's something about him. He has the strangest eyes —"

I tried to reason with her. She laughed at me, then grew angry.

When she left me I was exhausted. Somehow, I managed to get home. I was sick for a month, couldn't eat and couldn't sleep.

Then one afternoon Margot's picture stared at me from the paper. Oh God! it couldn't be! But she was — Margot was dead! She and Fey Brandon had been riding down the Montgomery Highway. Margot was driving, the paper said, and Brandon was thrown from the car. Except for a bruise or two he was unhurt, but Margot — I closed my eyes. This is what Brandon had done for her.

I can't remember anything for three days. I must have acted all right as no one said anything later. I was able to go to work the day after Margot's funeral. No one knew that I had loved her or that I had ever seen Brandon. I didn't dare ask about him, but that is when I stole the gun.

Fate has been kind to me. I was driving a few miles from town one day when I saw and recognized that tawny head, that feline walk. I pulled into the side road he had just taken and followed slowly until out of sight of the main road, then I eased up behind him and stopped the car. "I'd like to speak to you a minute," I addressed Brandon. I knew enough to avoid his eyes.

"Of course," he answered. I drew the gun and pointed it at him.

"My God!" he said harshly. "What do you mean?"

"This is for Irene and Ruth and Margot," I said calmly feeling neither tremor nor excitement.

"But you can't do it." His voice was calm now, purring, and my hand began to shake.

"I'm going to do it." I tried to keep my voice as calm as his.

"But you can't kill me," he insisted. "I've done nothing to you, I don't even know you. Look at me, man!"

I kept my eyes over the spot that covered his treacherous heart.

"You know," he said, his voice growling in his throat. "Surely you know what will happen to you if you do this thing."

As I pulled the trigger I looked at his eyes. They blazed at me and glowed. Green fire darted from them. It was too late to stop my hand, I saw his eyes as the bullet hit. Two demons from the darkest hell looked at me from them, then they grew blank as he sank to the ground.

I had not seen it before, but as he fell a large, tawny, tiger-striped cat came down the road. Suddenly the cat screamed, arched his back and enlarged his tail. For one paralyzing minute he looked at me with large, blazing, yellow-green eyes. Eyes whose irises wore a dark ring. Two demons looked at me from those eyes as I jumped into my car and roared away.

The cat sprang and missed me by less than an inch.

I traveled a mile, took a road that turned back to the highway and came home.

A month has passed. There's only occasional mention of the murder (they call it murder) but my nerves are growing bad. Oh no, it's not

524

him! Every day I grow more glad that I killed him. The gun was found the day that Brandon was found. Fortunately, I had presence of mind to wipe it carefully before I hurled it into the woods. Also it rained that day and there were no car tracks on the gravel road.

Now, every time I see a beautiful girl I think, perhaps you owe me a lot. Perhaps you would have been his next victim. So I'm not sorry I killed him. I'd be almost glad if they found me, but fate who delivered him to me seems to will otherwise. It's only these devil-begotten cats. These green-eyed demons from hell that pursue me. I never knew before there were so many large, tawny, tiger-striped cats. Everywhere I go I see one.

I am afraid to be alone.

I have decided to leave the city. There is a farm where I lived as a boy. Perhaps I can rent it and get away from these damned cats.

Three weeks of warm, pure beauty, spring almost here. Three weeks of rest. The hills are beautiful, and the trees are beginning to show tiny signs of spring. My walk to farmer Oliver's twice a week is pleasant. I think I'll go home tomorrow. My nerves are calm, everything is wonderful. I haven't seen a cat here.

Later . . . Let me see again if the windows are all barred.

Yes, they are fastened! Nothing can get in! Nothing, I tell you! What was that? It's that—that cat. Yes, he has found me. This morning when I started out for Oliver's he sprang at me. His green eyes blazed and he just missed me. I managed to slam the screen as he hit the floor, but I dropped my key outside. One of his paws was inside the screen before I could latch it. Oh God, he is strong! He almost tore open the door, yelling and spitting at me horribly, then his eyes caught mine.

Yes, I'll admit it at last. They are Fey's exactly. And I—I still shudder to think of it—I almost opened the door to him. Somehow I managed to close and bar it and then I barred all of the windows.

But he has stalked me all day. Whichever room I am in he is outside the window, mewing and scrabbling to enter.

Next day . . . What a horrible night! I'm weak and tired—I ate nothing all day yesterday. My shade will not stay down and every time it raises to the top there are those demon-possessed eyes gleaming at me.

Two days later . . . I thought I almost escaped today. I saw him enter the woods across the road, and cautiously opened the door only to spring back. A coiled rattlesnake darted his fangs at me. (It had been warm, he must have left his den. It is raining and turning cold now.) I had heard Fey . . . the cat . . . dragging the rattler onto the porch. There had been a peculiar whipping and slithering noise mixed with low growls. Were they conversing? Are all the demons in league with him? As I slammed the door the monster came bounding across the road to renew his efforts to get in.

Next night . . . I'm going mad. I know he can't get in. He can't!

525

Yet he continues to scrabble and howl at my window. Why can't I eat? He can't get in. . . . Why don't I go out and face him?

But I have no gun. I threw it away.

If he should touch me! I can't face him.

Oh my God! Oh Margot!

He is outside my window. But he can't get in I tell you. He can't!

He is quiet now. Am I to get some sleep? He has been prowling the yard but he is quiet now. And I am writing. . . . But tired. . . . So tired.

What was that?

Soot! Falling down the chimney!

He can't get in I tell you!

But he is! He's coming down the chimney!

Oh my God! He's coming down the chimney!

There's No Such Thing as Monsters

STEVE RASNIC TEM

There's nothing to be afraid of," he said. "There's no such thing as monsters."

Eddie looked up hesitantly. He obviously wasn't so sure. His father smiled; he remembered very well what it had been like at Eddie's age. "Tell you what, sport." He lifted the boy into the bed and slipped the heavy comforter with the Winnie-the-Pooh pattern up to his neck. "I'll make a magic pass over your room."

"Fairy magic, Dad?"

"Sure. Fairy magic."

He'd started reading the stories to his son early in the evening, and had gone on several hours. They weren't the stories his son requested — the easy-to-read books about small cars and trucks and puppies and kittens — but the old books with the fine bindings the father had saved from childhood. Inside these old books were the stories from another world — the ones about trolls and fairy kings, adventuring sons and talking cats. And monsters of all kinds.

He stood over his son's bed and began to gesture slowly with narrow, long-fingered hands, hands good at everything from designing kites to fixing automobiles to making magic passes.

"Make it a good one. I hate bad dreams."

"I will, Eddie. I hate the bad dreams, too."

First the hands were fish, backs turning silver as they maneuvered through the dark air. Then they opened into pale yellow birds, winging their way over the bed posts. The boy's eyes filled with the wings, his mouth curling with pleasure. It made his father smile as he allowed his too-delicate hands to pass, to turn, and drift through the crowded corners and brightly rugged open spaces of his son's room, the hands ancient toys and prehistoric beasts, the hands futuristic fighting machines and angels' feet walking the boy into his sleep. Finally the eyes shut down, and the magic hands pulled the covers a little closer around the sleeping form, and closed the door as the father left.

The old books with the even older stories lay sprawled across the living room cushions where they'd been left. He sat down among them and closed them carefully, as if for sleep. Then he stacked them precisely, all edges together.

He'd read them for himself, not for the boy. He'd read them because he'd wanted to enter that world again. But his son also was attracted to that world, and turned the pages hungrily.

And had been frightened by the monsters they found. The shadows that moved with intention. And had to have a magic pass, a fairy pass, before falling down to sleep.

"There's no such thing as monsters," he said quietly to no one, and wondered why he'd done this to his son, taken the risk. "But some get lost, some get trapped there and cannot find their way back," he said to the night, and could not understand why he hadn't said this to his son, told him this part of the stories. "And some grow up there, all alone," the father said quietly to the dark.

He sat there for hours, hours past the time the outside world had gone quiet and dark. Then as he did every night, he opened his son's door and slipped inside. To check and to touch, to fix the entangled and discarded covers, to pray in his way.

The boy was well into sleep. He confirmed it with a pat and a stroke. With hands now downed in silver, fingers gone wiry, nails gone sharp. His teeth bit into his lower lip, and he gasped softly at the quick taste of blood. He forced the trembling hands to continue their tucking, his thoughts to continue their praying. And when the bloody flashes of insight came—the boy's neck breaking, the small face painted in reds and blues, the small limbs splintered under the force of old anger—he stopped, and let the beast's hands rise awkwardly to move in magical passes through the air.

"There's no such thing as monsters," he whispered, a magical chant to retrieve a boy lost too long in the woods.

THE THROWBACK

ORLIN FREDERICK

Heinz was a corporal in our own battery. None of his buddies ever thought about him, or if they did it was only to wonder why he had been "made." He was extremely round-shouldered, heavy-set, awkwardly muscular. His hands were large and broad, his hair dark, his face cruel; but it is almost impossible to describe his eyes. They were tiny, black disks, shallow and yet too deep to penetrate, shifting yet darting queer glances directly at one. At times they seemed quiet (never gentle or kind, but docile like those of a great beast raised in captivity); but how they flashed when that madness was aroused!

There was a peculiar brute insanity that so entwined itself with his nature that it was inseparable. His eyes flashed with the venom of the pacing tiger when his will was crossed, and their glance sent shivers of dread, of unspeakable horror, up and down one's spine. It was not the ordinary fear of danger—I am too accustomed to facing death to notice that—but an intangible loathing, a horror that paralyzed all motion, a voice from ages past that spoke and held one in its grip while some great terror approached. No definite form of dread took precedence, yet there was all the grinding torture of crunching bones, the sound of ripping flesh, the smell of warm blood.

Time and again I have thanked my lucky stars that I never met Heinz alone on the open prairie in the dead of night. His eyes held a power of hypnotism that would have made me powerless even to shriek. I avoided him as I would the beasts of the jungle if unarmed. He was of the species that strikes for the love of cruelty, and that devastated Belgium.

Somehow Heinz made friends of a few. I suppose they were satellites of his stronger will. Perhaps they were drawn to him by that blood tie of their kind that ages had not broken—love of cruelty. His parents emigrated from Prussia in 1895, actuated no doubt by the same restlessness that caused the throwback of centuries in their first-born. What irony that he was to fight against the very land that lent asylum to his forbears!

We were stationed at a Western post when an incident occurred that I have never forgotten. The mystery of the affair has never been solved officially, but to me it is as clear as the noonday sun. Perhaps I am wrong—but I think not. I have no evidence other than my eyes and that strange fourth sense that held me in Heinz's power when his spells came on.

He had gone out somewhere in the afternoon. It was Sunday. He returned before 11 and turned in. I saw him as he entered the tent. His eyes flamed at that moment with a greenish light, like those of a wolverine in the shadows of the woods. His hands trembled as he reached for the flap, to draw it back, and his lips parted like a dog snarling over a bone. Then he grinned. That grin haunts me yet. He was like a lynx hard put for food when it has smelled fresh blood.

The following morning we learned that there had been a murder, supposedly by some maddened beast. A man's body was found on the open plain a mile from the nearest habitation. No one had heard any sound of struggle during the night, but the body was torn apart, ripped open by great cruel claws (or was it hands?). There were marks of teeth upon the neck where it (or he) had sucked the warm blood. The flesh was bruised from head to foot as if beaten mercilessly with a club.

Heinz was there with the rest of the boys to help if need be. But he seemed uninterested. He watched the distant hills more intently than he did the helpers. When he gazed at the blood-spattered earth he seemed neither surprised nor sympathetic but (or did I imagine it?) seemed rather to gloat over the carnage. It was as if he had seen it all before.

He was exceedingly docile that day, and during the next two months he seemed content. But gradually the old rumbling growl came back to his throat and the murderous look to his eyes. He took to wandering alone again at night. The beast was stalking its prey.

Weeks later the sheriff (he told me with the utmost horror) found a coyote killed fiendishly and left on the mountainside. It was in the same condition as the body had been, but no one ever connected the two incidents.

It was the blood lust again, but as it was satiated it left him quiescent for a time. He had no soul. He died in France; and were I to guess, he was grinning when he died, for he lay in a pool of blood upon the battlefield in the Argonne.

The Toad Idol

Kirk W. Mashburn

The thing—the toad—comes from a small, ruined Aztec temple in Central Mexico. My standing as an archeologist has not come unearned, and I know that none of the Aztec gods was represented by a toad; nor does evidence exist that the reptile had any other sacred significance in their religious symbolism. Yet this one occupied the place of honor in the temple; and except for it, there was no image in the ruins.

The thing struck me with an odd loathing, a sense of dread and oppression, almost at sight. As for my Indian workmen, they were persuaded to enter the temple only with difficulty. No explanation was obtainable, but their terror of the place was manifest.

When I removed the toad from its pedestal overlooking a small altar, they groveled on the ground in abject misery, frantically beseeching me to leave the image undisturbed. It was nothing but a small, curved piece of obsidian stone (though I have already admitted the malignant impression I received from it); yet I strongly suspect that, had I not been formidably armed, the Indians would have forcibly compelled me to leave it untouched. I would to God they had done so!

Overcome by a perverse fascination for the thing, notwithstanding my dislike of toads and reptiles in any form, to say nothing of my steadily mounting (if then unreasoning) repugnance for the thing, I smuggled out the amphibian idol upon my return to this country, circumventing the Mexican laws that prohibit exportation of archeological objects.

Who has not experienced similar attraction for some very thing that repels and disgusts, even while it fascinates? So, in my case, with this toad. Instead of turning it over to the museum, I placed it upon the writing desk in my study. Each passing day has added to my repugnance; but now, finally, something of the horror and terror of those Indians has succeeded my former mere loathing.

For the toad has come *alive!* It deserts my desk, by night, to sit upon the floor, looking at the windows, waiting—for God alone knows what.

As I write, I feel the beady eyes of the accursed reptile, the loathsome, mottled toad, burning into my back from where it squats behind me in a corner of this room. It is but a common, ordinary toad, to all appearances; and that is what lends it the significance of a small but horrific monster out of hell—for it should be a thing of carved volcanic obsidian, lifeless upon my desk. I have not even the power to touch it, cast it with loathing through the open window. I have tried, once, and failed. . . .

Whether I am mad, or the victim of hallucinations induced by some tropic fever hitherto dormant in my blood—whether I have, in violating the Temple of the Toad, brought upon my head some dread, nameless curse, I do not know. I am aware, only, that the figurine monster upon the floor has become an obsession of torment and dread. More than anything else, it is the thing's attitude of *waiting.* . . .

I have lived and worked alone in this house for years; the one servant who attends my scant wants stays only through the day. Thus, as usual, I was alone in my study, resting wearily at my desk, upon the evening when the toad first moved. It was dusk; but there was yet enough light for shadowy visibility. Something intruded upon my tired thoughts; some indistinct prompting impelled me to raise my head and look down to the floor in the nearest corner of the room.

It was then that I saw the toad, removed from its place upon my desk —and alive. What I saw was not of itself alarming, to other eyes than mine. But I knew the toad, huddled in the corner with its beady eyes meeting my own, for the idol that should have rested upon my desk—the idol come alive.

I am naturally neurotic, and the apparition stabbed at every taut nerve in my body. I determined to evict the thing; to throw it out and have done with it, once and for all. I rose and, taking a section of newspaper in order to avoid contact of my bare hand with the reptile's loathsome hide (I was convinced the thing was clammily alive), I stooped to take it from the floor and cast it out the window.

The toad made no effort to escape as the paper descended, and I gathered it up. I could not feel my captive beneath the several thicknesses of paper; but I had no doubt of its being wrapped in the wad of newsprint I tossed through the window. I turned with a feeling of relief and satisfaction—and there in the corner the toad squatted as before.

With an exclamation of annoyance, I again moved to enfold the reptile in paper, using a small, thin piece. Again it appeared that I had secured the thing; but this time I turned my hand over, to make certain. Expecting to see the bloated belly of the creature exposed, I beheld, instead, nothing but the wadded newspaper! The toad blinked balefully up, from the floor at my feet!

Stupidly, I stared from the paper in my hand to the toad upon the floor. A third time I essayed to seize the elusive monstrosity, in the same manner as before—and with the same result. I moved then to turn on the lights, as dusk had deepened into night. My hand trembled so violently that I pressed the switch with difficulty.

I decided to dispense with the paper and, overcoming my natural repugnance, grasp the toad with my naked hand. Determinedly, I bent down; my fingers swooped to snatch the thing. With a gasp I straightened, stepped back uncertainly. I had thought to scoop up the toad, but my hand had clutched nothing more than empty air!

I laughed. Even in my own ears, the sound possessed a startling quality. The thing had been a carven stone toad upon my desk, and had become alive. And now, to my touch, there was *no* toad!

"Hallucination," I muttered; "I am seeing things that do not exist."

The implications of that conclusion were far from comforting, however. And whatever I might think—or whatever else than a stone idol it might be—there it sat upon the floor, its sardonic eyes unswerving from my face, blinking . . . *waiting.* . . .

I sat down at the desk, stared back, baffled—and afraid—into those cold, glittering eyes. Gradually, sullen rage possessed me. I sprang up, furiously, and stamped upon the small monster. I fell upon my knees, sought to seize it with my hands, to tear and rend it into nothingness. Each time I lifted my grinding heel, each time I drew back my clawing fingers, the thing was there: gloating up at me with its cold, demon's eyes.

Finally, I staggered again to my chair, and fell forward across the desk, burying my head in my arms. I awoke in that position, in the chill, gray dawn that succeeded. My first coherent thought moved me to rouse, groaning with misery, and look toward that corner where the accursed toad had huddled the night before. Even in abjection, I found heart to rejoice, for the living creature that had been upon the floor was gone with the night; and the small idol rested in its accustomed place atop my desk—clearly, a carved, lifeless piece of obsidian.

But chill dread awoke with the sudden thought that life might return with another night. All through that day, the apprehension lay like a somber shadow upon my mind. I left the house, returning after nightfall. When I came to the door of my workroom, I hesitated for long minutes before entering.

Groping through the darkness, I switched on the lights. After one fearful, revealing glance, I sank into my chair, utterly abject with terror and despair. For, settled in the same corner it had occupied the night before, the toad regarded me with bright, malevolent eyes.

If I am mad, I have every reason to be. Night after night, for so many nights that it wearies me to number them, I have been stared out of countenance by a fiend in the shape of a malformed toad. Hoping that its manifestations were confined to this room, I have fled the house more than once at night. But wherever I seek to hide, my familiar demon appears with darkness. Seemingly, it has been ages since I have known sleep that was not induced either by drunkenness or soporific drugs; more often than not, neither of these suffices to bring merciful oblivion.

Tomorrow, I shall leave this country forever; I have already completed my arrangements. Perhaps if, as I intend, the end of my flight places half the world between us, I shall elude my tormenter.

That I am not mad, I have established to my satisfaction, by writing this account. Obviously, the effort and orderly thought required for a coherent narrative of this length is outside the scope of a deranged mind. And in the course of this exercise, there remains but one further item to be set down.

This has to do with the pebbles that have accompanied the idol's latter nightly transformations. I noticed the first of them, a little longer than a fortnight ago. Upon each succeeding night, there has been one more pebble, each about the size of a small walnut, added to the growing pile beside the creature. These appear only at night, like the living reptile that squats beside them; they are not on the desk with the lifeless, obsidian toad in the daytime.

What this addition to the toad's nocturnal animation may portend, I have sought to fathom, with growing unease. I have lately recalled that there was a pile of just such pebbles, heaped at the foot of the altar in the ancient temple, from which—may God forgive the stupid act!—I took the vile toad. . . .

❊　❊　❊

Something very dreadful has occurred since I wrote the preceding words. I am impelled to write the few remaining lines that will be necessary—or possible—by some power, some gleeful and *triumphantly* malignant force outside of me:

While I was writing, I felt a blow upon the back of my head. It was more as if I had been hit forcibly, *inside,* upon my uncovered brain, by an object thrown from behind my back. For a moment, I was unable to move, so great was the pain. Partly recovering, I turned to discover the source of the missile with which I had been struck. Then my blood chilled, seemed truly to freeze in my veins. . . .

The toad has moved out of its usual squatting position. About it there is an unfathomable impression of unholy joyousness; I know without understanding, that the thing no longer is waiting—its hour has struck!

I wrote that the toad has moved. It stands erect, upon its deformed and twisted rear members. Grotesque and unnatural as that is, the circumstance that constricts my heart is that, raised above its head in the act of casting as I turned—the frightful little monster gripped a pebble in its tiny, handlike forefeet! Even as I saw and gasped, the missile hurtled through the air, struck *inside* my forehead with stunning impact.

The pile of pebbles—those pebbles, the purpose of which I *now* know! —probably is diminished by more than half. At intervals, one of them crashes into the back of my brain. I am paralyzed now, all except, oddly, this arm with which I write. I can not move aside, seek to evade the battering pebble hail. But I feel that I should not escape, though the power to move, to cry out, still remained to me.

All about this room, there are intangible rustlings and scurryings. There are things around me, unseen but present, that have come to watch with grim, unhallowed satisfaction as the toad hurls pebbles into my brain.

My death, beyond doubt, will be attributed to cerebral hemorrhage. My head, to all outward appearances, will be whole and unmutilated; for the toad's missiles pass unscathing through my skull, by some unholy means, and batter only upon my brain.

I shall die—very soon, now—beneath the barrage of pebbles cast by the paws of that thing in the corner behind me. I shall die as, in all likelihood, no man ever met death before: stoned to death by a foul, loathsome *toad!* . . .

Tzo-Lin's Nightingales

Ben Belitt

All that day it had been raining; a swift, violent onslaught of long drops, slashing sharply upon the face, pelting against the body, seeping down past muffler and topcoat, into the very marrow of one's bones. I have no great affection for autumn rains, especially when they are inclined to spout into malicious pools and overflow into one's overshoes—that is, for me, the last of the proverbial straws. Accordingly, I sought shelter in the building nearest at hand—a small, unostentatious little shop wedged in securely between two rather dubious "hotels." A meager patch of windowglass constituted its front, upon which were painted in red several Chinese characters, and the name Tzo-Lin. My plight had made me desperate and so, throwing caution and several drops of rainwater from my dripping umbrella to the winds, I turned the carved brass doorknob and entered.

Could a snap of my fingers, a mere gesture of my head, have summoned some Nubian genii, ear-ringed and bewhiskered, from the depths of my vestcoat pocket, I should have been no whit more startled. I stood with my mouth agape and with the rainwater trickling from my forehead down my cheek, beading in little drops at my chin, and dropping slowly to the floor—staring dumbly ahead and trying to distinguish between the thousand different objects that confused my vision.

At first I was aware only of a rich, Oriental pungency, so acutely sweet and so heavy as to seem almost tangible. It swept through my brain like a fire. I reeled. Then, gradually, my eyes became accustomed to the gloom and I could make out the innumerable objects arrayed before me.

I could discern that the rectangular walls of the shop were lined with long, dark shelves bearing a fragile burden of curios and *chefs-d'oeuvre* of every type and variety imaginable. Here and there, I could detect the mellowed lambency of bronze and beaten brass and copper—shallow serviettes, long, slim vases, fat and contented-looking pots, little clapperless bells hung in ebony belfries. There were rack after rack of figurines wrought in jade and ivory and green marble, upon whose highly polished glaze the light, subdued as it was, flickered in sharp contrasts of oily highlights and smooth, deep-purple shadows. There were pewter mugs and slender mirrors and metallic tapestries; there were scimitars and black telescopes with bands of gold encircling their tips. Everything one could think of, or dream of, and even more was laid away upon those dusty, shadowed shelves. It was as though every people had, in passing, bequeathed some memento to adorn the shop of Tzo-Lin; to help fill his endless rows, and stack them more solidly from floor to ceiling; to dream in the warm silence and peace and grow old, hearing the chiming of the many clocks—slowly, sedately, mysteriously old. . . .

For despite the overwhelming reek of incense, there was everywhere an odor of age . . . incalculable age; of must and decay and mystery. I found myself somehow recalling the picture of a ruined Aztec city I had once explored by night—recalling the gray chillness of the moonlight upon those moldered stones; the horrible heaviness of the black shadows, unmoving as though they had been frozen into that parched soil; and oddly enough, the very same odor of age unfathomable clinging to those bat-infested ruins that now pervaded the shop of Tzo-Lin. And recalling this, I shuddered.

By this time, every detail of the shop had grown quite visible, and I could penetrate into the darkest corners. Along the entire extent of the shop, hung from the ceiling with golden cords, placed upon low, lacquered tables, suspended from every available support, every nook and corner, I could see tiers of bird cages. Within them were discernible little gray shapes—shapes that seemed to be nightingales with their wings tightly pressed to their bodies and their heads drooped on their bosoms. "Artificial birds," I told myself. "Very clever imitation, though."

However, my observations were brought to a sudden end, for, somewhere in the darkness, I heard a soft, slow whisper of slippered feet. I turned my head; the rather emaciated figure of a man in a robe was making its way toward me. "This," I hazarded, "is Tzo-Lin!" And my surmise was correct, for, almost before I was aware of it, I found myself staring full into the face of the aged Chinaman.

Tzo-Lin was an old man—a gnarled, ancient patriarch with the infinite look of one who had lived a million years—and lived them all in vain. Indeed, at my first glimpse of that shrunken, parchmentlike face, those unwinking eyes of inexorable learning and wisdom, that yellowed mustache depending in long, fine wisps from either corner of his upper lip, below his meager shoulders and upon his breast, I wondered if Time had not been negligent with his hourglass, and Death with his scythe; if they had not, for all their punctilious thoroughness, forgotten one mortal—and forgotten him for a long time. Perhaps the startling contrast of the brilliance of his silken robes with the faded colorlessness of his skin might have exaggerated the man's age. Perhaps . . .

All this occupied my mind for only an instant, and before I could recover sufficient equanimity to murmur an apologetic excuse, Tzo-Lin spoke. The clear freedom of his voice amazed me. I had anticipated a more or less unintelligible mumbling, cracked and thrown out of pitch by the unbelievable senility of the man. Instead, in richest and almost gonglike tones, Tzo-Lin accosted me. "Ten thousand greetings on your head, in the name of Confucius, the many-eyed! Perhaps this most despicable of men may be of service to your so-enlightened self?"

I could not have repressed a smile at this naïve flow of eloquence, had not there been a distinctly ironic and ingratiating edge to his voice. Immediately I was on my guard, combatting fire with fire. I bowed deeply and countered by asking his hospitality in the lengthiest and most sonorous diction I could muster.

A ghost of a smile hovered for a moment about Tzo-Lin's lips and vanished. He returned my bow with imperturbable dignity, and indicated the little fireplace at the rear of his shop with a slow nod of his head. I made my way thence, through the dim aisles of dusty bric-a-brac. Behind me walked Tzo-Lin, serenely, lightly as a girl, fluttering his ivory fan.

I found the fire, for all its minuteness, to be quite satisfying and congenial. I sat on one side of it, luxuriously toasting my chilled knees before its pleasant warmth. Tzo-Lin sat on the opposite side on a little lacquered bench and stared into the fire, as oblivious of my presence as though I had not been there. For a time we both remained thus, hearing the flames crackle, the fresh wood hiss and splutter, the clocks ticking off the seconds, and the rain pattering softly, monotonously, unceasingly upon the roof. In the end, several questions that had been rankling in my mind forced me to break the silence.

"I could not help noticing how very natural those artificial nightingales are that you have all around. You made them yourself, I suppose?"

Tzo-Lin smiled and shook his head. A sort of contemplative dreaminess crept into his voice. He said: "No. How could I? The birds—the nightingales are not artificial. . . ." And he resumed his revery.

I laughed his words aside. "Come, come, my dear man, I am no prospective customer. You can be perfectly frank with me—and quite truthful."

The old Chinaman seemed to be speaking in a dream. "I said they were real nightingales, and I repeat what I said. They are as much alive as you and I. Only—they have been—sleeping."

I strove to conceal my contempt for what I knew to be an untruth. "Sleeping?" I asked. "And pray, for how long?"

The man's lips scarcely moved. "Three hundred years ago, they were my wife's betrothal-gift from her husband. . . ."

I drew my breath sharply. What pleasure did this man derive in doling me out such preposterous nonsense? I took no pains to repress my contempt now. "And when, dear sir, will they awake?"

"They will awake on the night—of the full moon . . . on the night when my bride—will return to me for an hour—from the Purple Halls of the—Dead." His voice sank into a whisper.

It was quite enough. I arose from my seat and grasped the Chinaman by the shoulder. "What sort of a fool do you take me for?" I began. "Perhaps—"

Tzo-Lin cut me short with a steady glance. Very slowly he rose, as if in a daze, removed my hand from his person, and spoke with a keen deliberateness. "I will not have—doubted—my friend! If it is your pleasure, you may come and see for yourself—on the night of the full moon. Meanwhile—it will please me to have you—leave."

Again he sank down into his seat, opened his fan, and stared into the fire as though he saw—what?

Despite my resentment of this indignity, I had sufficient presence of mind to do as I was bid. I left—clanging the door shut with a reverberating report that set the brassware trembling and made the china tinkle, leaving the silence and the warmth and the solitude of the shop for Tzo-Lin's sole enjoyment. . . .

That month the full moon came with a vivid silverness that dominated the entire length and breadth of the sky. It came floating up out of the darkness of the city, and hung in space like a vast bubble of ice just about to burst, with a transparent mist of cloud scud clustered about it. On the ground the snow, soft as a new-shorn fleece, lay several inches thick, stretching away on every hand to a wilderness of pearl and diamond, and a low sky flushed to a dull mauve, as though it had been afire. . . .

There were a few flakes tumbling about in a rather lazy fashion when I first set out, but when I had finally reached the tiny lozenge of a shop bearing Tzo-Lin's name, I found myself shouldering through nothing less than a blizzard. My coat flapped and cracked in the wind like a banner, and my umbrella was blown inside out. Hurling the tattered wreckage of the latter into the darkness, I opened the narrow door and entered. I was fairly catapulted inside by the violence of a savage gust that lifted the innumerable rugs and carpets from the floors and blew out the tapestries upon the walls like sails. I shook the snowflakes from my person and made my way back into the rear of the little shop to where the cheerful fire snapped on the hearth. There was a little recess I had not before noticed adjoining the rear compartments; a sort of niche sheltering a gilded idol mounted on a low pedestal of ebony, and lighted on either side by a pair of smoking joss sticks.

As I stood, silently looking on, the overwhelming reek of a composite incense smote my nostrils again, this time more heavy and nauseating than ever. I coughed. The old Chinaman looked up from his devotions, motioned me to be seated, and then resumed his prayers.

Having no other alternative, I obeyed and soon gave myself up to the magic of watching the yellow flames that leaped and fell, and shod in pale blue slippers, ran swift little races across the brown logs. And in the small alcove, Tzo-Lin went on praying to his pagan gods, tearing into bits the scarlet prayer paper. And so the minutes passed on. . . .

Then, when I had almost drowsed off into sleep, the hour struck — slowly, deliberately, portentously. The heavy silence that followed lay like a weight upon my brain; seemed to pour, a tide of whirring sound-lessness, into my ears. I gasped for breath, and waited for whatever might happen, my glance riveted upon the little cages that thronged the shop.

At first, all I saw was the quivering of a cage, and then of many cages. Then I could hear the brushing and thrashing of innumerable wings. And finally, to climax the entire inexplicable occurrence, a clear, shrill chirp cut the air like a tiny knife thrust, soared upward, a silver sky-rocket of sound, burst into a sudden confusion of trills, and spent itself, gradually, softly, like a shower of many-colored sparks. Almost immedi-ately, before I could force myself to realize it, before I was even aware of it, the hundreds of little cages all about were swinging violently to and fro with their tassels waving frantically, like yellow hands. And of a sudden there arose such a burst of song, such a passion of mad, sweet music, that I felt my very body must crumble like a liquid beneath it and melt and be lost, quietly, into the turning vortices of that consecrated air. It seemed impossible that such perfect, rounded harmony could come from the throat of any bird in such rapid and faultless succession. Fascinated and half reeling, I watched the nightingales. Their entire bodies seemed to shimmer and tremble in the ecstasy of their music. Each tiny throat so swelled and puffed and quivered that I marveled how like some bubble overweighted with air, they did not suddenly burst.

The whole shop was afire with their singing. The room seemed somehow to grow a hundred times more sweeping and spacious. Each wall seemed to have been thrust back and the ceiling cloven from its supports by some gigantic hand, leaving nothing but the broad and open blueness of heaven about it. The shop, strangely, unaccountably, seemed to fill with mist and vague vapors, twisting and rolling upward, with all the grotesque quietness of a nightmare.

Dimly, then, was borne to my ears the tireless chanting of Tzo-Lin. . . . And his voice, triumphant and exalted into something as beautiful and intolerable as the nightingales' flood of song, was full of love, as though he spoke to someone immeasurably dear to him . . . as though he addressed a—*bride*. I gave a great cry and rose to my feet. . . .

I shall never know what took place in the few moments that followed. A blackness, like the shadow of an enormous arm, seemed suddenly to creep out of the corners, to mount steadily like a flow of dark water, while down from the roof and ceiling fell silence, fold on fold, loop on loop, stilling the crying of the birds, choking the loud surge of my own pulsebeats. . . . More I cannot remember.

But the horror, the incredible madness of the waking hour—that will be with me always. I think it was the cold that first aroused me. I recall shuddering with an extreme violence that made my teeth knock; then my shoulder struck something sharp, and I awoke. A single glance above me, ahead of me, over my shoulder, and I leaped to my feet, shaking and shrieking for terror with all the strength of my lungs.

Where once shelf upon shelf had borne up a thousand odds and ends of brasses and statuary, many compartments layered with dust and cobwebs glowered emptily out of the darkness. The ceiling had fallen through at irregular intervals, and six or seven of the blackened beams strewed the floor, straddling the breadth of the room diagonally, like prone colossi. On every joint and cornice the spiders had woven heavily, and, as if to reinforce their workmanship, a dust, like pumice-powder, had settled on every thread, and clotted. But more than this, more than

540

the horror of dust and spiders, it was the swift glimpse of the two figures in the rear of the room that left me weak and tortured with a terrible unrest for so many months after.

Two figures. And I saw them just at the moment the trapdoor over my head was lifted, in response to my insane pummelings (I had heard the scrape of feet somewhere above me and guessed myself to be in a cellar of some sort). Two figures. One a man, the other a woman; both in glittering, flower-painted robes, lying with phosphorescent pallor and green horror on their faces, arms interlocked and veiled over three times with cobwebs, while cage after cage, each holding a single brown figure like a bird within it, glimmered silently in a wide circle above their heads. . . .

The Unnamable

H. P. LOVECRAFT

We were sitting on a dilapidated seventeenth-century tomb in the late afternoon of an autumn day at the old burying ground in Arkham, and speculating about the unnamable. Looking toward the giant willow in the center of the cemetery, whose trunk has nearly engulfed an ancient, illegible slab, I had made a fantastic remark about the spectral and unmentionable nourishment which the colossal roots must be sucking in from that hoary, charnel earth; when my friend chided me for such nonsense and told me that since no interments had occurred there for over a century, nothing could possibly exist to nourish the tree in other than an ordinary manner. Besides, he added, my constant talk about "unnamable" and "unmentionable" things was a very puerile device, quite in keeping with my lowly standing as an author. I was too fond of ending my stories with sights or sounds which paralysed my heroes' faculties and left them without courage, words, or associations to tell what they had experienced. We know things, he said, only through our five senses or our religious intuitions; wherefore it is quite impossible to refer to any object or spectacle which cannot be clearly depicted by the solid definitions of fact or the correct doctrines of theology—preferably those of the Congregationalists, with whatever modifications tradition and Sir Arthur Conan Doyle may supply.

With this friend, Joel Manton, I had often languidly disputed. He was principal of the East High School, born and bred in Boston and sharing New England's self-satisfied deafness to the delicate overtones of life. It was his view that only our normal, objective experiences possess any aesthetic significance, and that it is the province of the artist not so much to rouse strong emotion by action, ecstasy, and astonishment as to maintain a placid interest and appreciation by accurate, detailed transcripts of everyday affairs. Especially did he object to my preoccupation with the mystical and the unexplained; for although believing in the supernatural much more fully than I, he would not admit that it is sufficiently commonplace for literary treatment. That a mind can find its greatest pleasure in escapes from the daily treadmill, and in original and dramatic recombinations of images usually thrown by habit and fatigue into the hackneyed patterns of actual existence, was something virtually incredible to his clear, practical, and logical intellect. With him all things and feelings had fixed dimensions, properties, causes, and effects; and although he vaguely knew that the mind sometimes holds visions and sensations of far less geometrical, classifiable, and workable nature, he believed himself justified in drawing an arbitrary line and ruling out of court all that cannot be experienced and understood by the average citizen. Besides, he was almost sure that nothing can be really "unnamable." It didn't sound sensible to him.

Though I well realized the futility of imaginative and metaphysical arguments against the complacency of an orthodox sun-dweller, something in the scene of this afternoon colloquy moved me to more than usual contentiousness. The crumbling slate slabs, the patriarchal trees, and the centuried gambrel roofs of the witch-haunted old town that stretched around, all combined to rouse my spirit in defense of my work; and I was soon carrying my thrusts into the enemy's own country. It was not, indeed, difficult to begin a counterattack, for I knew that Joel Manton actually half clung to many old-wives' superstitions which sophisticated people had long outgrown; beliefs in the appearance of dying persons at distant places, and in the impressions left by old faces on the windows through which they had gazed all their lives. To credit these whisperings of rural grandmothers, I now insisted, argued a faith in the existence of spectral substances on the earth apart from and subsequent to their material counterparts. It argued a capability of believing in phenomena beyond all normal notions; for if a dead man can transmit his visible or tangible image half across the world, or down the stretch of the centuries, how can it be absurd to suppose that deserted houses are full of queer sentient things, or that old graveyards teem with the terrible, unbodied intelligence of generations? And since spirit, in order to cause all the manifestations attributed to it, cannot be limited by any of the laws of matter; why is it extravagant to imagine psychically living dead things in shapes—or absences of shapes—which must for human spectators be utterly and appallingly "unnamable?" "Common sense" in reflecting on these subjects, I assured my friend with some warmth, is merely a stupid absence of imagination and mental flexibility.

Twilight had now approached, but neither of us felt any wish to cease speaking. Manton seemed unimpressed by my arguments, and eager to refute them, having that confidence in his own opinions which had doubtless caused his success as a teacher; whilst I was too sure of my ground to fear defeat. The dusk fell, and lights faintly gleamed in some of the distant windows, but we did not move. Our seat on the tomb was very comfortable, and I knew that my prosaic friend would not mind the cavernous rift in the ancient, root-disturbed brickwork close behind us, or the utter blackness of the spot brought by the intervention of a tottering, deserted seventeenth-century house between us and the nearest lighted road. There in the dark, upon that riven tomb by the deserted house, we talked on about the "unnamable," and after my friend had finished his scoffing I told him of the awful evidence behind the story at which he had scoffed the most.

My tale had been called "The Attic Window," and appeared in the January 1922 issue of *Whispers*. In a good many places, especially the South and the Pacific coast, they took the magazines off the stands at the complaints of silly milksops; but New England didn't get the thrill and merely shrugged its shoulders at my extravagance. The thing, it was averred, was biologically impossible to start with; merely another of those crazy country mutterings which Cotton Mather had been gullible enough to dump into his chaotic *Magnalia Christi Americana*, and so poorly authenticated that even he had not ventured to name the locality where the horror occurred. And as to the way I amplified the bare jotting of the old mystic—that was quite impossible, and characteristic of a flighty and notional scribbler! Mather had indeed told of the thing as being born, but nobody but a cheap sensationalist would think of having it grow up, look into people's windows at night, and be hidden in the attic of a house, in flesh and in spirit, till someone saw it at the window centuries later and couldn't describe what it was that turned his hair gray. All this was flagrant trashiness, and my friend Manton was not slow to insist on that fact. Then I told him what I had found in an old diary kept between 1706 and 1723, unearthed among family papers not a mile from where we were sitting; that, and the certain reality of the scars on my ancestor's chest and back which the diary described. I told him, too, of the fears of others in that region, and how they were whispered down for generations; and how no mythical madness came to the boy who in 1793 entered an abandoned house to examine certain traces suspected to be there.

It had been an eldritch thing—no wonder sensitive students shudder at the Puritan age in Massachusetts. So little is known of what went on beneath the surface—so little, yet such a ghastly festering as it bubbles up putrescently in occasional ghoulish glimpses. The witchcraft terror is a horrible ray of light on what was stewing in men's crushed brains, but even that is a trifle. There was no beauty; no freedom—we can see that from the architectural and household remains, and the poisonous sermons of the cramped divines. And inside that rusted iron straitjacket lurked gibbering hideousness, perversion, and diabolism. Here, truly, was the apotheosis of the unnamable.

Cotton Mather, in that daemoniac sixth book which no one should read after dark, minced no words as he flung forth his anathema. Stern as a Jewish prophet, and laconically unamazed as none since his day could be, he told of the beast that had brought forth what was more than beast but less than man—the thing with the blemished eye—and of the screaming drunken wretch that they hanged for having such an eye. This much he baldly told, yet without a hint of what came after. Perhaps he did not know, or perhaps he knew and did not dare to tell. Others knew, but did not dare to tell—there is no public hint of why they whispered about the lock on the door to the attic stairs in the house of a childless, broken, embittered old man who had put up a blank slate slab by an avoided grave, although one may trace enough evasive legends to curdle the thinnest blood.

It is all in that ancestral diary I found; all the hushed innuendoes and furtive tales of things with a blemished eye seen at windows in the night or in deserted meadows near the woods. Something had caught my ancestor on a dark valley road, leaving him with marks of horns on his chest and of apelike claws on his back; and when they looked for prints in the trampled dust they found the mixed marks of split hooves and vaguely anthropoid paws. Once a postrider said he saw an old man chasing and calling to a frightful loping, nameless thing on Meadow Hill in the thinly moonlit hours before dawn, and many believed him. Certainly, there was strange talk one night in 1710 when the childless, broken old man was buried in the crypt behind his own house in sight of the blank slate slab. They never unlocked that attic door, but left the whole house as it was, dreaded and deserted. When noises came from it, they whispered and shivered; and hoped that the lock on that attic door was strong. Then they stopped hoping when the horror occurred at the parsonage, leaving not a soul alive or in one piece. With the years the legends take on a spectral character—I suppose the thing, if it was a living thing, must have died. The memory had lingered hideously—all the more hideous because it was so secret.

During this narration my friend Manton had become very silent, and I saw that my words had impressed him. He did not laugh as I paused, but asked quite seriously about the boy who went mad in 1793, and who had presumably been the hero of my fiction. I told him why the boy had gone to that shunned, deserted house, and remarked that he ought to be interested, since he believed that windows retained latent images of those who had sat at them. The boy had gone to look at the windows of that horrible attic, because of tales of things seen behind them, and had come back screaming maniacally.

Manton remained thoughtful as I said this, but gradually reverted to his analytical mood. He granted for the sake of argument that some unnatural monster had really existed, but reminded me that even the most morbid perversion of Nature need not be *unnamable* or scientifically indescribable. I admired his clearness and persistence, and added some further revelations I had collected among the old people. Those later spectral legends, I made plain, related to monstrous apparitions more frightful than anything organic could be; apparitions of gigantic bestial forms sometimes visible and sometimes only tangible, which floated about on moonless nights and haunted the old house, the crypt behind it, and the grave where a sapling had sprouted beside an illegible slab. Whether or not such apparitions had ever gored or smothered people to death, as told in uncorroborated traditions, they had produced a strong and consistent impression; and were yet darkly feared by very aged natives, though largely forgotten by the last two generations— perhaps dying for lack of being thought about. Moreover, so far as aesthetic theory was involved, if the psychic emanations of human creatures be grotesque distortions, what coherent representation could express or portray so gibbous and infamous a nebulosity as the spectre of a malign, chaotic perversion, itself a morbid blasphemy against Nature? Moulded by the dead brain of a hybrid nightmare, would not such a vaporous terror constitute in all loathsome truth the exquisitely, the shriekingly *unnamable?*

The hour must now have grown very late. A singularly noiseless bat brushed by me, and I believe it touched Manton also, for although I could not see him I felt him raise his arm. Presently he spoke.

"But is that house with the attic window still standing and deserted?"

"Yes," I answered. "I have seen it."

"And did you find anything there—in the attic or anywhere else?"

"There were some bones up under the eaves. They may have been what that boy saw—if he was sensitive he wouldn't have needed anything in the window glass to unhinge him. If they all came from the same object it must have been a hysterical, delirious monstrosity. It would have been blasphemous to leave such bones in the world, so I went back with a sack and took them to the tomb behind the house. There was an opening where I could dump them in. Don't think I was a fool—you ought to have seen that skull. It had four-inch horns, but a face and jaw something like yours and mine."

At last I could feel a real shiver run through Manton, who had moved very near. But his curiosity was undeterred.

"And what about the windowpanes?"

"They were all gone. One window had lost its entire frame, and in the other there was not a trace of glass in the little diamond apertures. They were that kind—the old lattice windows that went out of use before 1700. I don't believe they've had any glass for a hundred years or more —maybe the boy broke 'em if he got that far; the legend doesn't say."

Manton was reflecting again.

"I'd like to see that house, Carter. Where is it? Glass or no glass, I must explore it a little. And the tomb where you put those bones, and the other grave without an inscription—the whole thing must be a bit terrible."

"You did see it—until it got dark."

My friend was more wrought upon than I had suspected, for at this touch of harmless theatricalism he started neurotically away from me and actually cried out with a sort of gulping gasp which released a strain of previous repression. It was an odd cry, and all the more terrible because it was answered. For as it was still echoing, I heard a creaking sound through the pitchy blackness, and knew that a lattice window was opening in that accursed old house beside us. And because all the other frames were long since fallen, I knew that it was the grisly glassless frame of that daemoniac attic window.

Then came a noxious rush of noisome, frigid air from that same dreaded direction, followed by a piercing shriek just beside me on that shocking rifted tomb of man and monster. In another instant I was knocked from my gruesome bench by the devilish threshing of some unseen entity of titanic size but undetermined nature; knocked sprawling on the root-clutched mold of that abhorrent graveyard, while from the tomb came such a stifled uproar of gasping and whirring that my fancy peopled the rayless gloom with Miltonic legions of the misshapen damned. There was a vortex of withering, ice-cold wind, and then the rattle of loose bricks and plaster; but I had mercifully fainted before I could learn what it meant.

Manton, though smaller than I, is more resilient; for we opened our eyes at almost the same instant, despite his greater injuries. Our couches were side by side, and we knew in a few seconds that we were in St. Mary's Hospital. Attendants were grouped about in tense curiosity, eager to aid our memory by telling us how we came there, and we soon heard of the farmer who had found us at noon in a lonely field beyond Meadow Hill, a mile from the old burying-ground, on a spot where an ancient slaughterhouse is reputed to have stood. Manton had two malignant wounds in the chest, and some less severe cuts or gougings in the back. I was not so seriously hurt, but was covered with welts and contusions of the most bewildering character, including the print of a split hoof. It was plain that Manton knew more than I, but he told nothing to the puzzled and interested physicians till he had learned what our injuries were. Then he said we were the victims of a vicious bull — though the animal was a difficult thing to place and account for.

After the doctors and nurses had left, I whispered an awestruck question:

"Good God, Manton, but *what was it?* Those scars — *was it like that?*"

And I was too dazed to exult when he whispered back a thing I had half expected —

"*No — it wasn't that way at all.* It was everywhere — a gelatin — a slime — yet it had shapes, a thousand shapes of horror beyond all memory. There were eyes — and a blemish. It was the pit — the maelstrom — the ultimate abomination. Carter, *it was the unnamable!*"

The Vampire Maid

Hume Nisbet

It was the exact kind of abode that I had been looking after for weeks, for I was in that condition of mind when absolute renunciation of society was a necessity. I had become diffident of myself, and wearied of my kind. A strange unrest was in my blood; a barren dearth in my brains. Familiar objects and faces had grown distasteful to me. I wanted to be alone.

This is the mood that comes upon every sensitive and artistic mind when the possessor has been overworked or living too long in one groove. It is Nature's hint for him to seek pastures new; the sign that a retreat has become needful.

If he does not yield, he breaks down and becomes whimsical and hypochondriacal, as well as hypercritical. It is always a bad sign when a man becomes overcritical and censorious about his own or other people's work, for it means that he is losing the vital portions of work, freshness, and enthusiasm.

Before I arrived at the dismal stage of criticism I hastily packed up my knapsack, and taking the train to Westmorland I began my tramp in search of solitude, bracing air, and romantic surroundings.

Many places I came upon during that early summer wandering that appeared to have almost the required conditions, yet some petty drawback prevented me from deciding. Sometimes it was the scenery that I did not take kindly to. At other places I took sudden antipathies to the landlady or landlord, and felt I would abhor them before a week was spent under their charge. Other places that might have suited me I could not have, as they did not want a lodger. Fate was driving me to this Cottage on the Moor, and no one can resist destiny.

One day I found myself on a wide and pathless moor near the sea. I had slept the night before at a small hamlet, but that was already eight miles in my rear, and since I had turned my back upon it I had not seen any signs of humanity; I was alone with a fair sky above me, a balmy ozone-filled wind blowing over the stony and heather-clad mounds, and nothing to disturb my meditations.

How far the moor stretched I had no knowledge; I only knew that by keeping in a straight line I would come to the ocean cliffs, then perhaps after a time arrive at some fishing village.

I had provisions in my knapsack, and being young did not fear a night under the stars. I was inhaling the delicious summer air and once more getting back the vigor and happiness I had lost; my city-dried brains were again becoming juicy.

Thus hour after hour slid past me, with the paces, until I had covered about fifteen miles since morning, when I saw before me in the distance a solitary stone-built cottage with roughly slated roof. "I'll camp there if possible," I said to myself as I quickened my steps toward it.

To one in search of a quiet, free life, nothing could have possibly been more suitable than this cottage. It stood on the edge of lofty cliffs, with its front door facing the moor and the backyard wall overlooking the ocean. The sound of the dancing waves struck upon my ears like a lullaby as I drew near; how they would thunder when the autumn gales came on and the seabirds fled shrieking to the shelter of the sedges.

A small garden spread in front, surrounded by a dry-stone wall just high enough for one to lean lazily upon when inclined. This garden was a flame of color, scarlet predominating, with those other soft shades that cultivated poppies take on in their blooming, for this was all that the garden grew.

As I approached, taking notice of this singular assortment of poppies, and the orderly cleanness of the windows, the front door opened and a woman appeared who impressed me at once favorably as she leisurely came along the pathway to the gate, and drew it back as if to welcome me.

She was of middle age, and when young must have been remarkably good-looking. She was tall and still shapely, with smooth clear skin, regular features, and a calm expression that at once gave me a sensation of rest.

To my inquiries she said that she could give me both a sitting room and bedroom, and invited me inside to see them. As I looked at her smooth black hair and cool brown eyes, I felt that I would not be too particular about the accommodation. With such a landlady, I was sure to find what I was after here.

The rooms surpassed my expectation, dainty white curtains and bedding with the perfume of lavender about them, a sitting room homely yet cosy without being crowded. With a sigh of infinite relief I flung down my knapsack and clinched the bargain.

She was a widow with one daughter, whom I did not see the first day, as she was unwell and confined to her own room, but on the next day she was somewhat better, and then we met.

The fare was simple, yet it suited me exactly for the time, delicious milk and butter with homemade scones, fresh eggs, and bacon; after a hearty tea I went early to bed in a condition of perfect content with my quarters.

Yet happy and tired out as I was I had by no means a comfortable night. This I put down to the strange bed. I slept certainly, but my sleep was filled with dreams so that I woke late and unrefreshed; a good walk on the moor, however, restored me, and I returned with a fine appetite for breakfast.

Certain conditions of mind, with aggravating circumstances, are required before even a young man can fall in love at first sight, as Shakespeare has shown in his Romeo and Juliet. In the city, where many fair faces passed me every hour, I had remained like a stoic, yet no sooner did I enter the cottage after that morning walk than I succumbed instantly before the weird charms of my landlady's daughter, Ariadne Brunnell.

She was somewhat better this morning and able to meet me at breakfast, for we had our meals together while I was their lodger. Ariadne was not beautiful in the strictly classical sense, her complexion being too lividly white and her expression too set to be quite pleasant at first sight; yet, as her mother had informed me, she had been ill for some time, which accounted for that defect. Her features were not regular, her hair and eyes seemed too black with that strangely white skin, and her lips too red for any except the decadent harmonies of an Aubrey Beardsley.

Yet my fantastic dreams of the preceding night, with my morning walk, had prepared me to be enthralled by this modern posterlike invalid.

The loneliness of the moor, with the singing of the ocean, had gripped my heart with a wistful longing. The incongruity of those flaunting and evanescent poppy flowers, dashing their giddy tints in the face of that sober heath, touched me with a shiver as I approached the cottage, and lastly that weird embodiment of startling contrasts completed my subjugation.

She rose from her chair as her mother introduced her, and smiled while she held out her hand. I clasped that soft snowflake, and as I did so a faint thrill tingled over me and rested on my heart, stopping for the moment its beating.

This contact seemed also to have affected her as it did me; a clear flush, like a white flame, lighted up her face, so that it glowed as if an alabaster lamp had been lit; her black eyes became softer and more humid as our glances crossed, and her scarlet lips grew moist. She was a living woman now, while before she had seemed half a corpse.

She permitted her white slender hand to remain in mine longer than most people do at an introduction, and then she slowly withdrew it, still regarding me with steadfast eyes for a second or two afterward.

Fathomless velvety eyes these were, yet before they were shifted from mine they appeared to have absorbed all my willpower and made me her abject slave. They looked like deep, dark pools of clear water, yet they filled me with fire and deprived me of strength. I sank into my chair almost as languidly as I had risen from my bed that morning.

Yet I made a good breakfast, and although she hardly tasted anything, this strange girl rose much refreshed and with a slight glow of color on her cheeks, which improved her so greatly that she appeared younger and almost beautiful.

I had come here seeking solitude, but since I had seen Ariadne it seemed as if I had come for her only. She was not very lively; indeed, thinking back, I cannot recall any spontaneous remark of hers; she answered my questions by monosyllables and left me to lead in words; yet she was insinuating and appeared to lead my thoughts in her direction and speak to me with her eyes. I cannot describe her minutely, I only know that from the first glance and touch she gave me I was bewitched and could think of nothing else.

It was a rapid, distracting, and devouring infatuation that possessed me; all day long I followed her about like a dog, every night I dreamed of that white glowing face, those steadfast black eyes, those moist scarlet lips, and each morning I rose more languid than I had been the day before. Sometimes I dreamed that she was kissing me with those red lips, while I shivered at the contact of her silky black tresses as they covered my throat; sometimes that we were floating in the air, her arms about me and her long hair enveloping us both like an inky cloud, while I lay supine and helpless.

She went with me after breakfast on that first day to the moor, and before we came back I had spoken my love and received her assent. I held her in my arms and had taken her kisses in answer to mine, nor did I think it strange that all this had happened so quickly. She was mine, or rather I was hers, without a pause. I told her it was fate that had sent me

551

to her, for I had no doubts about my love, and she replied that I had restored her to life.

Acting upon Ariadne's advice, and also from a natural shyness, I did not inform her mother how quickly matters had progressed between us, yet although we both acted as circumspectly as possible, I had no doubt Mrs. Brunnell could see how engrossed we were in each other. Lovers are not unlike ostriches in their modes of concealment. I was not afraid of asking Mrs. Brunnell for her daughter, for she already showed her partiality towards me, and had bestowed upon me some confidences regarding her own position in life, and I therefore knew that, so far as social position was concerned, there could be no real objection to our marriage. They lived in this lonely spot for the sake of their health, and kept no servant because they could not get any to take service so far away from other humanity. My coming had been opportune and welcome to both mother and daughter.

For the sake of decorum, however, I resolved to delay my confession for a week or two and trust to some favorable opportunity of doing it discreetly.

Meantime Ariadne and I passed our time in a thoroughly idle and lotus-eating style. Each night I retired to bed meditating starting work next day, each morning I rose languid from those disturbing dreams with no thought for anything outside my love. She grew stronger every day, while I appeared to be taking her place as the invalid, yet I was more frantically in love than ever, and only happy when with her. She was my lodestar, my only joy—my life.

We did not go great distances, for I liked best to lie on the dry heath and watch her glowing face and intense eyes while I listened to the surging of the distant waves. It was love made me lazy, I thought, for unless a man has all he longs for beside him, he is apt to copy the domestic cat and bask in the sunshine.

I had been enchanted quickly. My disenchantment came as rapidly, although it was long before the poison left my blood.

One night, about a couple of weeks after my coming to the cottage, I had returned after a delicious moonlight walk with Ariadne. The night was warm and the moon at the full, therefore I left my bedroom window open to let in what little air there was.

I was more than usually fagged out, so that I had only strength enough to remove my boots and coat before I flung myself wearily on the coverlet and fell almost instantly asleep without tasting the nightcap draught that was constantly placed on the table, and which I had always drained thirstily.

I had a ghastly dream this night. I thought I saw a monster bat, with the face and tresses of Ariadne, fly into the open window and fasten its white teeth and scarlet lips on my arm. I tried to beat the horror away, but could not, for I seemed chained down and thralled also with drowsy delight as the beast sucked my blood with a gruesome rapture.

I looked out dreamily and saw a line of dead bodies of young men lying on the floor, each with a red mark on their arms, on the same part where the vampire was then sucking me, and I remembered having seen and wondered at such a mark on my own arm for the past fortnight. In a flash I understood the reason for my strange weakness, and at the same moment a sudden prick of pain roused me from my dreamy pleasure.

The vampire in her eagerness had bitten a little too deeply that night, unaware that I had not tasted the drugged draught. As I woke I saw her fully revealed by the midnight moon, with her black tresses flowing loosely, and with her red lips glued to my arm. With a shriek of horror I dashed her backward, getting one last glimpse of her savage eyes, glowing white face, and blood-stained red lips; then I rushed out to the night, moved on by my fear and hatred, nor did I pause in my mad flight until I had left miles between me and that accursed Cottage on the Moor.

The Werewolf Howls

CLIFFORD BALL

Twilight had come upon the slopes of the vineyards, and a gentle, caressing breeze drifted through the open casement to stir into further disorder the papers upon the desk where Monsieur Etienne Delacroix was diligently applying himself. He raised his leonine head, the hair of which had in his later years turned to gray, and stared vacantly from beneath bushy brows at the formation of a wind-driven cloud as if he thought that the passive elements of the heavens could, if they so desired, aid him in some momentous decision.

There was a light but firm tap on the door that led to the hall of the château. Monsieur Delacroix blinked as his thoughts were dispersed and, in some haste, gathered various documents together and thrust them into the maw of a large envelope before bidding the knocker to enter.

Pierre, his eldest son, came quietly into the room. The father felt a touch of the pride he could never quite subdue when Pierre approached, for he had a great faith in his son's probity, as well as an admiration for the straight carriage and clear eye he, at his own age, could no longer achieve. Of late he had been resting a great many matters pertaining to the management of the Château Doré and the business of its vineyards, which supported the estate, on the broad shoulders poised before him.

But Etienne Delacroix had been born in a strict household and his habits fashioned in a stern school, and was the lineal descendant of ancestors who had planted their peasants' feet, reverently but independently, deep into the soil of France; so visible emotions were to him a betrayal of weakness. There was no trace of the deep regard he felt for his son evident when he addressed the younger man.

"Where are your brothers? Did I not ask you to return with them?"

"They are here, Father. I entered first, to be certain that you were ready to receive us."

"Bid them enter."

Jacques and François came in to stand with their elder brother and were careful to remain a few inches in his rear; he was the acknowledged spokesman. Their greetings were spoken simultaneously; Jacques's voice breaking off on a high note which caused him obvious embarrassment, for he was adolescent. Together, thought Monsieur Delacroix, they represented three important steps in his life, three payments on account to posterity. He was glad his issue had all been males; since the early death of his wife he had neither cared for any woman nor taken interest in anything feminine.

"I have here, my son, some papers of importance," he announced, addressing Pierre. "As you observe, I am placing them here where you may easily obtain them in the event of my absence." Suiting the action to the word, he removed the bulky envelope to a drawer in the desk and turned its key, allowing the tiny piece of metal to remain in its lock. "I am growing older"—his fierce, challenging eyes swept the trio as if he dared a possible contradiction—"and it is best that you are aware of these accounts, which are relative to the business of the château."

"*Non, non!*" chorused all three. "You are as young as ever, papa!"

"*Sacre bleu!* Do you name me a liar, my children? Attend, Pierre!"

"Yes, Papa."

"I have work for you this night."

The elder son's forehead wrinkled. "But the work, it is over. Our tasks are completed. The workers have been checked, the last cart is in the shed—"

"This is a special task, one that requires the utmost diligence of you all. It is of the wolf."

"The werewolf!" exclaimed Jacques, crossing himself.

The other brothers remained silent, but mingled expressions of wonder and dislike passed across their features. Ever since the coming of the wolf the topic of its depredations had been an unwelcome one in the household of the Château Doré.

"Mon Dieu, Jacques!" exploded the head of the house. "Have you, too, been listening to the old wives' tales? Must you be such an imbecile, and I your father? Rubbish! There can be no werewolves; has not the most excellent Father Cromecq flouted such stories ten thousand times? It is a common wolf; a large one, true, but nevertheless a common mongrel, a beast from the distant mountain. Of its ferocity we are unfortunately well aware; so it must be dispatched with the utmost alacrity."

"But, the workers say, Papa, that there have been no wolves in the fields for more than a hundred—"

"Peste! The ever verbose workers! The animal is patently a vagrant, a stray beast driven from the mountains by the lash of its hunger. And I, Etienne Delacroix, have pronounced that it must die!"

The father passed a heavy hand across his forehead, for he was weary from his unaccustomed labor over the accounts. His hands trembled slightly, the result of an old nervous disorder. The fingers were thick, and blunt from the hardy toil of earlier years; the blue veins were still corded from the strength he had once possessed.

"It is well," said Pierre in his own level tones. "Since the wolf came upon and destroyed poor little Marguerite D'Estourie, tearing her throat to shreds, and the gendarmes who almost cornered it were unable to slap it because they could not shoot straight, and it persists in—"

"It slashed the shoulder of old Gavroche who is so feeble he cannot walk without two canes!" interrupted François, excitedly.

"—ravaging our ewes," concluded the single-minded Pierre, who was not to be sidetracked once he had chosen his way, whether in speech or action. "The damage to our flocks has been great, papa. It is just that we should take action, since the police have failed. I have thought this wolf strange, too, although I place no faith in demons. If it but seeks food, why must it slay so wantonly and feed so little? It is indeed like a great, gray demon in appearance. Twice have I viewed it, leaping across the meadows in the moonlight, its long, gray legs hurling it an unbelievable distance at every bound. And Marie Polydore, of the kitchens, found its tracks only yesterday at the very gates of the château!"

"I have been told," revealed Jacques, flinging his hands about in adolescent earnestness, "that the wolf is the beast-soul of one who has been stricken by the moon demons. By day he is as other men, but by night, though he has the qualities of a saint he cannot help himself. Perhaps he is one with whom we walk and talk, little guessing his dreadful affliction."

"Silence!" roared Monsieur Delacroix. One of his clenched fists struck the desk a powerful blow and the sons were immediately quieted. "Must I listen to the ranting and raving and driveling of fools and imbeciles? Am I not still the master of the Château Doré? I will tend to the accursed matter as I have always, will I not? I have always seen to the welfare of the dwellers in the shadow of the Château Doré! And with the help of the good God I shall continue to do so, until the last drop of my blood has dried away from my bones. You comprehend?"

In a quieter tone, after the enforced silence, he continued: "I have given orders to both the foreman and Monsieur the Mayor that this night, the night of the full moon by which we may detect the marauder, all the people of the vineyards and of the town beyond must remain behind locked windows and barred doors. If they have obeyed my orders—and may the good God look after those who have not—they are even now secure in the safety of their respective homes. Let me discover but one demented idiot peeking from behind his shutter and I promise you he shall have cause to remember his disobedience!"

Pierre nodded without speaking, knowing he was being instructed to punish a possible, but improbable, offender.

"Now, we are four intelligent men, I trust," said Monsieur Delacroix, pretending not to notice the glow of pleasure that suffused Jacques's features at being included in their number. "We are the Delacroixes, which is sufficient. And as leaders we must, from time to time, grant certain concessions to the inferior mentalities of the unfortunate who dwell in ignorance; so I have this day promised the good foremen, who petitioned me regarding the activities of this wolf, to perform certain things. They firmly believe the gray wolf is a demon, an inhuman atrocity visited upon us by the Evil One. And also, according to their ancient but childish witchlore, that it may only be destroyed by a silver weapon."

Monsieur Delacroix reached beneath his chair and drew forth a small but apparently heavy sack. Upending it on the surface of the desk, he scattered in every direction a double dozen glittering cylindrical objects.

"Bullets!" exclaimed Jacques.

"*Silver* bullets!" amended Pierre.

"Yes, my son. Bullets of silver that I molded myself in the cellars, and that I have shown to the men, with the promise that they will be put to use."

"Expensive weapons," commented the thrifty François.

"It is the poor peasant's belief. If we slew this wolf with mere lead or iron they would still be frightened of their own shadows and consequently worthless at their work, as they have been for the past month. Here are the guns. Tonight you will go forth, my sons, and slay this fabulous werewolf, and cast its carcass upon the cartload of dry wood I have had piled by the vineyard road, and burn it until there is nothing left but the ash, for all to see and know."

"Yes, Papa," assented Pierre and François as one, but the boy Jacques cried: "What? So fine a skin? I would like it for the wall of my room! These who have seen the wolf say its pelt is like silver shaded into gray—"

"Jacques!" Etienne Delacroix's anger flooded his face with a great surge of red and bulging veins, and Pierre and François were stricken with awe at the sight of their father's wrath.

"If you do not burn this beast as I say, immediately after slaying it, I will forget you are my son, and almost a man! I will—"

His own temper choked him into incoherency.

"I crave your pardon, father," begged Jacques, humbled and alarmed. "I forgot myself."

"We will obey, Papa, as always," said François, quickly, and Pierre gravely nodded.

"The moon will soon be up," said Monsieur Delacroix, after a short silence. The room had grown dark while they talked; receiving a wordless signal from his father, Pierre struck a match and lit the blackened lamp on the desk. With the startling transition, as light leaped forth to dispel the murky shadows of the room, Pierre came near to exclaiming aloud at sight of the haggard lines in his father's face. For the first time in his life he realized that what his parent had said earlier in the evening about aging was not spoken jocularly, not the repeated jest Monsieur Delacroix had always allowed himself, but the truth. His father was old.

"You had better go," said Etienne Delacroix, as his keen eyes caught the fleeting expression on his son's face. His fingers drummed a muffled tattoo upon the fine edge of his desk, the only sign of his nervous condition that he could not entirely control. "Monsieur the Mayor's opinion is that the wolf is stronger when the moon is full. But it is mine that tonight it will be easier to discover."

The three turned to the door, but as they reached the threshold Monsieur Delacroix beckoned to the eldest. "An instant, Pierre. I speak to you alone."

The young man closed the door on his brothers' backs and returned to the desk, his steady eyes directed at his father.

Monsieur Delacroix, for the moment, seemed to have forgotten what he intended to say. His head was bowed on his chest and the long locks of his ashen hair had fallen forward over his brow. Suddenly he sat erect, as if it took an immense effort of his will to perform the simple action, and again Pierre was startled to perceive the emotions that twisted his father's features.

It was the first time he had ever seen tenderness there, or beheld love in the eyes he had sometimes, in secret, thought a little cruel.

"Have you a pocket crucifix, my son?"

"In my room."

"Take it with you tonight. And—you will stay close to Jacques, will you not?" His voice was hoarse with unaccustomed anxiety. "He is young, confident, and—careless. I would not wish to endanger your good mother's last child."

Pierre was amazed. It had been fifteen years since he had last heard his father mention his mother.

"You have been a good son, Pierre. Obey me now. Do not let the three of you separate, for I hear this beast is a savage one and unafraid even of armed men. Take care of yourself, and see to your brothers."

"Will you remain in the château for safety, Papa? You are not armed."

"I am armed by my faith in the good God and the walls of Château Doré. When you have lit the fire under the wolf's body—I will be there."

He lowered the leonine head once more, and Pierre, not without another curious look, departed.

For a long while Monsieur Delacroix sat immobile, his elbows resting on the padded arms of the chair, the palms of his hands pressing into his cheeks. Then he abruptly arose and, approaching the open casement, drew the curtains wide. Outside, the long, rolling slopes fell away toward a dim horizon already blanketed by the dragons of night, whose tiny, flickering eyes were winking into view one by one in the dark void above. Hurrying cloudlets scurried in little groups across the sky.

Lamps were being lit in the jumble of cottages that were the abodes of Monsieur Delacroix's workmen, but at the moment the sky was illuminated better than the earth; for the gathering darkness seemed to cling like an animate thing to the fields and meadows, and stretch ebony claws across the ribbon of the roadway.

It was time for the moon to rise.

Monsieur Delacroix turned away from the casement and with swift, certain steps went to the door, opening it. The hall was still, but from the direction of the dining room there came a clatter of dishes as the servants cleared the table. Quickly, with an unusual alacrity for a man of his years, he silently traversed the floor of the huge hall and passed through its outer portals. A narrow gravel lane led him along the side of the château until he reached the building's extreme corner, where he abandoned it to strike off across the closely clipped sward in the direction of a small clump of beech trees.

The night was warm and peaceful, with no threat of rain. A teasing zephyr tugged at the thick locks on his uncovered head; from somewhere near his feet came the chirp of a cricket.

In the grove it was darker until he came to its center, wending through and past the entangled thickets like one who had traveled the same path many times, and found the small glade that opened beneath the stars. Here there was more light again but no breeze at all. In the center of the glade was an oblong, grassy mound, and at one end of it a white stone, and on the stone the name of his wife.

Monsieur Delacroix stood for an instant beside the grave with lowered head, and then he sank to his knees and began to pray.

In the east the sky began to brighten as though some torch-bearing giant drew near, walking with great strides beyond the edge of the earth. The stars struggled feebly against the superior illumination, but their strength diminished as a narrow band of encroaching yellow fire appeared on the rim of the world.

With its arrival the low monotone of prayer was checked, to continue afterward with what seemed to be some difficulty. Monsieur Delacroix's throat was choked, either with grief for the unchangeable past or an indefinable apprehension for the inevitable future. His breath came in struggling gasps and tiny beads of perspiration formed on his face and hands. His prayers became mumbled, jerky utterances, holding no recognizable phrases of speech. Whispers, and they ceased altogether.

A small dark cloud danced across a far-off mountaintop, slid furtively over the border of the land, and for a minute erased the yellow gleam from the horizon. Then, as if in terror, shaken by its own temerity, it fled frantically into oblivion, and the great golden platter of the full moon issued from behind the darkness it had left to deluge the landscape with a ceaseless shower of illusive atoms; tiny motes that danced the pathways of space.

Monsieur Delacroix gave a low cry like a child in pain. His agonized eyes were fixed on the backs of his two hands as he held them pressed against the dew-dampened sward. His fingers had begun to stiffen and curl at their tips; he could see the long, coarse hairs sprouting from the pores of his flesh — as he had many times within the past month since the night he had fallen asleep by the grave of his wife and slept throughout the night under the baleful beams of the moon.

He flung back his head, whimpering because of the terrible pressure he could feel upon his skull, and its shape appeared to alter so that it seemed curiously elongated. His eyes were bloodshot, and as they sank into their sockets his lips began to twitch over the fangs in his mouth.

The three brothers, crouching nervously in the shadows of the vineyards, started violently.

Jacques, the younger, almost lost his grasp on the gun with the silver bullets that his father had given him.

From somewhere nearby there had arisen a great volume of sound, swirling and twisting and climbing to shatter itself into a hundred echoes against the vault of the heavens, rushing and dipping and sinking into the cores of all living hearts and the very souls of men — the hunting cry of the werewolf.

THE WEREWOLF'S HOWL

BROOKE BYRNE

The doctor walked briskly through the chill night, his cloak wrapped closely about him. The white light of a full moon showed him his way clearly, for all that on either side the forest was black with shadow, and full of vague cracklings and reports like pistol shots as the frost gripped the pine branches. His way ran through the forest of Martheim, up the steep slope that led to Schloss Martheim, his goal. Within that gloomy pile the old Baron Martheim was dying.

The thought of the great, shadowy room where, in a canopied carven bed, the old man waited for death, made the doctor quicken his pace. Ever since the young doctor had come to the little village that snuggled close to the river below the bluff where Schloss Martheim clung perilously, he had played chess once a week with the frail master of the castle, and a genuine friendship had sprung up between the two. He felt a poignant regret that the delicate ivory chessmen would never reappear from their inlaid box, to be set up carefully by the baron's white, fastidious fingers. More deeply he regretted the cutting off of their conversations over vintage wine, when the game was played out and the fire had lapsed to a bed of ruddy coals. Whatever village gossip said of the baron's early escapades, the doctor had found him, in his old age, a pleasant companion, full of a wise, calm knowledge of men and things. The reserve he maintained concerning his past erected no barrier in their friendship; his occasional fits of abstracted melancholy seldom marred their quiet evenings.

Musing thus upon the end of good things in a bitter world, the doctor came out of the forest and climbed a long flight of steps cut into solid rock. At the top he paused. He was on the terrace of Schloss Martheim; below him the river glittered in the moonlight, and a light or two showed the outskirts of the village. But all about him, barring all the approaches to the castle save the side that looked over the cliff, was the impenetrable black forest, seeming to crowd in upon the *schloss* eagerly, as if sensing an ultimate victory.

The doctor turned and struck the brazen bell that hung beside the oaken door. Before the clamorous echoes had died away, the lone servitor who tended the baron had opened the door to him. In one trembling hand he bore a lighted taper. His face, in the fitful gleam, was twisted with grief.

"Well, Hans? How is he?" questioned the doctor as he stripped off his cloak and gloves.

"He is very low, doctor. All day he has asked for you. He seems afraid. Come quickly; he does not like to be alone."

They hastened to the upper chamber where, in the light of a single candle and a leaping fire, the last Baron Martheim awaited death. The doctor, advancing swiftly to the bedside, read in the transparent waxen face the imminence of dissolution; yet, when his practiced fingers touched the blue-veined, fragile wrist, they felt a pulse beating spasmodically, almost tumultuously. As he bent to listen to the weary heart, the old man opened his eyes suddenly.

"Ah, God, is it time already? Have they come? No, not yet! Tell me they have not come!" Unreasoning terror burned in the shadowed, sunken eyes. The voice was a trembling wail.

"It is I, Doctor Gradnov," the doctor hastened to assure him. "No one has come. You must be quiet."

A long sigh lifted the breast beneath the cover. Slowly reason returned to the staring eyes. The baron spoke again.

"Ah, it is good you have come. I must share my secret now. I must tell you . . . you, my only friend." Something like peace came into the wasted features.

"You must not try to talk, Baron," the doctor soothed him. "I will give you a sedative."

He turned to his bag. Hans yet lingered in the background, murmuring prayers under his breath. The baron spoke clearly. "No, I must talk. It is better than thinking . . . waiting. . . . Listen to me, rather, and learn perhaps. I am very tired," he ended pathetically.

The doctor poured out a goblet of brandy from the decanter near by. He held the glass to the dying man's lips; after a few sips a faint tinge of color showed along the cheekbones. When he spoke again a new strength and purpose were in his shrill voice.

"That is better. You will hear me, then. These forty years I have been haunted, and now the end is drawing near. At last I shall know . . . I shall be rid of dread. . . . Listen. I shall tell you a strange thing, and you will believe."

His thin hands closed over an ebony crucifix that lay on the covers. With an effort he took a deep breath and began.

"When I was young, I was sent to the university, as you were. Like you I was proud of my learning—I was very young. I spent much time boasting in taverns, and I liked the girls. My first year I fell in love with a little girl who waited on us in a café. In this I stupidly crossed another student, an older man whom I disliked because of his loud scorn of my fine theories. I gloated over him one night because Hilda preferred me. He stalked away, but not before I had seen his eyes. . . . He hated me. From that time on we never spoke, but whenever I was near him, I felt his eyes on me. Thus passed two years, and then the third came, and still Ivan remembered. It was in his eyes always."

The doctor administered more brandy. He saw in the sunken sockets eyes that burned with terror and delirium, and his own skin tingled inexplicably.

Revived by the strong liquor, the old man went on, his words coming out in jerks, as though the effort were almost too much. Yet some obscure force drove him on, hurrying his tale as if he were in fear of interruption.

"One night, in deep winter, I lingered in a wine shop after my companions were gone. It was such a night as this outside, and I hesitated over my last drink. The innkeeper eyed me, for I was alone, and he wished to shut up his shop and go to bed. But as I was about to rise, the door was flung open and a student came in. The light fell across his features; I recognized Ivan.

"A flicker of hatred ran across his face when he saw me; yet he came to my table and asked permission to sit with me civilly enough. We ordered two drinks, and until the keeper had withdrawn yawning, we said nothing. But then Ivan leaned across the table and said softly, "Well met, little Konrad! This is well met."

"Something in his voice sent a chill through me, but I answered him curtly.

"'What do you mean?' I asked.

"'For a long time I have wished to ask you something,' he returned, with a little chuckle. 'May I speak with you, little Konrad?'

"'What is it?'

"'Do you still deny the existence of the soul?' he demanded earnestly.

"Puzzled, I stared at him. 'Yes, of course,' I replied. 'I have not returned to superstition.'

"Ah, I was young then, and the fine theories were new. I was very proud. . . .

"Ivan nodded at me. 'Then you do not think that one can—sell one's soul?' he asked, more softly still.

"'What nonsense is this?' I asked in return.

"'Konrad, I have sold my soul,' he whispered. 'And in return I have learned many things. How you would gasp if you knew! I am wiser than any of you in the classes, for I have learned the secrets of the old ones, the dark secrets. I could show you. . . . Konrad, would you like to see ghosts?'

"'You are mad,' I said, only half convinced that I spoke the truth. There was something in his eyes that held me listening.

"'No, learned little Konrad! I tell you it is true, that which I speak. Dare you come with me, and prove it? I will show you the undead,

Konrad! I will show you werewolves! Do you dare?' He leaned forward, and his breath was hot on my face.

"I tried to laugh, and could only shudder. He saw it, and laughed mockingly.

" 'Konrad is afraid,' he taunted. 'Konrad knows that I speak truth, and he is afraid. Poor little Konrad!'

"He laughed in my face, but his eyes did not laugh. They held me, fascinated.

" 'No! I am not afraid,' I told him harshly.

" 'Then come with me, now, and laugh at me when you are proved right,' he invited, rising.

"I felt my whole being revolt with nameless dread, but I rose with him. As if he held me chained, I followed him into the street. The inn door shut behind us sharply."

Once again the narrative broke off, and the room was silent save for the old man's gasping breath. The doctor moistened the dry lips with brandy again. Terror was a living flame in the eyes now, the only living thing in the wasted body, save the lips, which scarcely moved to allow the husky voice to go on. The chill presence of death, and something more horrible still, filled the room with vague, fantastic shapes of dream.

"For a long time we walked, so swiftly that I hardly managed to keep pace with Ivan. We followed an icy-rutted track into the forest that hedged the town, far into the dark deeps of it, where I had never penetrated before. Overhead the stars were bright as sparks, and the moonlight was white. Sometimes Ivan threw back his head and laughed up at the stars, silently, but he did not speak. As I hastened by his side and thought of flight, I sensed the presence of beasts near us. I heard little rustles in the brush, and a snapping of twigs, and even a muffled whine. A new fear seized me: the wolves were abroad in packs because of the deep cold. I dared not turn back. We went on, interminably.

"At last we reached a clearing, and I saw in the moonlight the dark pile of such a castle as this. But it was deserted, as this will be; it was falling into ruin. Against the bare stone walls the icy vines clattered sharply, like clicking bones. I heard Ivan curse as his skin was torn on the cold metal of the lock. Then the door opened, and we were inside, in the musty dark.

"Ivan led me, groping and stumbling, down many corridors to a room that had one casement, a glimmering dimness across the room. I stood with my back to the door, trying to conquer the fear that tore at my vitals. I was glad when Ivan managed to light a candle and set it in a sconce on the wall. By its light I made out the furnishings—a great chest, a rough table, and over all the dead dust of years.

"Ivan did not pause. From the chest he took out a brazier, a bronze bowl, and some little boxes and vials. Also he laid on the table a great old pistol that gleamed in the light. Then from a pocket he drew a folded parchment. This also he laid upon the table before he turned to me.

"'So, now we are ready,' he smiled evilly. 'No, not quite; we have forgotten.' He picked up the pistol and put it in my hand. 'Listen, now,' he said. 'You know the legend of the werewolf. A human may take shape as a wolf during life, but at his death he becomes one of the undead. He may be slain for ever only by a silver bullet blessed and marked with a cross. This you know?'

"I nodded, dumbly.

"'Here!' he said, and I stretched out my hand. He dropped a bullet into it. It was of silver, and graven into it was a cross.

"'You do not believe in souls,' he mocked. 'Yet it will kill a human as quickly as any other bullet. Load the pistol, little Konrad, and we shall begin. I would not take advantage of you. Yet remember—if you fire at a werewolf with such a bullet, and miss, your soul is forfeit to the undead! So it is written.' Abruptly he turned to the table and bent to his task.

"I do not remember all that he did; yet he mixed some powders and liquids from his store, and set the bowl of them over the brazier. The flame licked around the metal bluely; smoke began to rise thinly. As it thickened, Ivan took up the parchment and began to chant. A scent as of burning flesh filled the room. I could not move or speak; I was as if in the clutch of a hideous nightmare. The chant deepened and swelled; it was like some diabolic distortion of the Mass. And now a sinister accompaniment began to sound above and around the shuddering chant; I recognized it as the howl of a hungry wolf outside.

"With a swift movement Ivan flung open the casement; the candle guttered out in the draft. The room was full of stinging smoke. Ivan's chant ended in a deep quavering howl. The answer swelled from all the forest outside. For an interminable second I stood in the smoky dark, my nostrils choked with the vile odor, my eyes blinded, my limbs weak as water. And then I sensed that evil indescribable had entered the room, unearthly evil, perilous and near.

"I strove to pierce the gloom. Through the smoke I caught the gleam of green, baleful eyes. They came toward me slowly, crouching near the floor. I heard a snarl of hatred through the wild chorus outside. I knew, then. I was alone with a beast. . . .

"He sprang as I fired, and I felt his fangs in my flesh as the pistol kicked out of my hand in the recoil. . . . I do not remember anything else."

The old man's forehead was cold and wet with the death-sweat, but his desperate, inexorable voice went on, faltering now and weak, yet relentlessly driving to an end.

"I came to myself in the dawn, wandering the streets with a shirt caked with blood from a wound in my chest. I crept to my lodgings, packed my bags, and fled the town by the first coach. I came here, and besought my mother for money. Though her heart broke at the sight of me, and my decision never to return to school, she gave me all she had, and promised to send enough for me to live on. Thus I wandered across the earth for years, seeking the tropics and the sea. . . . In time my father died. I came home, but too late to find my mother waiting. They were both in the old chapel, together and asleep.

"I wandered again, seeking to forget. Useless; never have I told any man the terror that has dogged my footsteps all these years, that has lain down with me and risen with me, that even in sleep has returned to gibber at me through the nights. God, how long has been my penance! And now it comes to an end . . . an end! Ah, God, be merciful!"

He ended on a choked sob of fear. The doctor sought uselessly for words that might bring a decent peace to this fantastic deathbed.

"Here you are safe," he urged. "None can harm you. There are no werewolves, Baron. You are safe."

"Safe? God, that I might believe it! But I cannot know. . . . I can not tell. Listen!" he cried out.

Rigid with stark terror, his hands clutching at the doctor's arm, he pulled himself half erect. A bloody foam stained his pallid lips. They listened. Even Hans, shivering and crouching by the door, ceased his muttered prayers. There was no sound anywhere, within or without.

"There is nothing. Lie quiet," the doctor begged. The old man clung to him with maniacal strength.

"You do not understand!" he shrieked. "They will come. . . . They are coming . . . black shapes in the moonlight, with lolling tongues. . . . I see them. . . . I did not kill that night. . . . I fired . . . Ivan lives! He has come for my soul. . . . Pray for me, my friend . . . pray—"

A paroxysm shook the frail body in the doctor's arms. The old man's face twisted into a staring mask of horror, and his hands clawed at the coverings, as though he would fight off some unseen shape. His breath ended in a rattle. It was over.

The doctor lowered the baron's body back to the bed. For a full minute there was utter stillness in the room, as though the watchers had been stricken breathless. And then, from the forest outside, a long bitter howl lifted and swelled, the howl of a hungry wolf, sobbing with inhuman despair. Three times it shivered to the startled stars, filling the night with echoes of pulsing horror. Within the *schloss*, after the last echo had died for ever, there was only the sound of old Hans, sobbing, and the voice of the doctor muttering in unaccustomed prayer.

The Werewolf Snarls

MANLY WADE WELLMAN

I want you to meet Mr. Craw," prattled Lola Wurther to me. "He claims to be a werewolf."

And she turned—fluttery hands, fluttery white shoulders, fluttery blond curls, fluttery skirts of green silk—to lose herself in the crowd of noisy guests at the bar. Mr. Craw and I took two or three steps together, as though we both sought quiet.

"Sit down," I suggested, and we dropped upon a divan in the half-gloom behind Lola Wurther's big grand piano. Then we looked at each other.

He was a huge, high-shouldered creature in rather seedy dress clothes, with coarse black hair grown low on his forehead and around his flat-lying, pointed ears. His long anvil of a chin lay snugly between the wings of his collar, his long poniard of a nose lay upon his chin, and his mouth caught between was as tight and lipless as a slit in leather. The pallor of his face accentuated the wet-licorice black of his eyes. He made me feel my own physical frailty as a little, rheumatic old man half his volume.

"Well," he invited huskily, "do I look it?"

"You mean like a werewolf?" I suggested, and waited smiling for the witty retort. But he shook his head.

"It happens to be quite true," he assured me with the absolute solemnity of the very drunken or the very insane.

I jumped at that, although I was used to meeting bizarre figures in the Wurther parlor. Not knowing what to say, I kept my own nervous mouth shut. After a musing moment, Craw went on.

"I came here tonight looking for help in my desperate problem. Wurther and his wife are supposed to be experts in occultism."

"Mr. Craw," I could not help saying, "the Wurthers are unmitigated fakes."

"I was thinking that," he nodded glumly. "Apparently their only reason for letting me come was to make sport for their friends." A pause, awkward for me at least. "Well, then, shall I tell you?"

"Please do," I urged, feeling strangely foolish.

Craw hunched his shoulders, sank his head, and let his clasped hands slide down, down between his knees until the thick knuckles almost rested on the floor. There was something animallike in the attitude: his body and limbs seemed measured and joined according to an abnormal pattern. His licorice eyes sought mine, and at the moment they did not look exactly human, either. Too much gloomy iris for one thing, and too little rim of white for another. In their depths lurked a green light, feeble but hard.

"It began," said Craw, "when I experimented with the witch ointments."

"Witch ointments?"

"Yes. Supposed to be rubbed on for changes into animal forms— made and used by magicians according to Satanic formulas. They sound fantastic, I know, but I was a medical student, working on a paper about pre-Renaissance medicine. There were several recipes."

"Recipes?" I repeated. "Not really?"

"Yes, a dozen at least. The 1896 bulletin of Johns Hopkins Hospital printed one, in an article by Doctor Robert Fletcher. Several other modern scientists have offered others, wholly or in part. And let me tell you that there's more sound pharmacy in them than you'd think."

I thought, indeed hoped, that he was merely spoofing. But there was no bantering smile upon his thin lips, and his eyes looked drawn and haggard about the corners.

"Belladonna, for instance," he amplified. "It's a common ingredient. Makes you see visions, as you probably know. And monkshood, full of deadly aconite. Henbane, that Shakespeare called 'the insane root,' and hemlock. These and other things, made into a salve with the fat of an unbaptized child—"

"I say," I broke in again, not very politely, "you don't ask me to believe that you—"

"But I did." Again that melancholy nod of assurance. "There was a baby's body fetched to the dissecting room at school." He paused and his eyes narrowed, as though to gaze down a fearsome groove into the past. "Well, I mixed the stuff up. For a lark." His mouth slashed open in a rueful grin, revealing oversized, uneven teeth.

"You rubbed it on?" I prompted. Once more he nodded, and I pursued: "What happened?"

"Nothing." Craw sat up straight again and spoke more clearly. "I don't know what I expected to happen, or if in truth I expected anything. But I do remember feeling like a fool, and an unclean fool to boot. I started to clean the grease off, but it had absorbed into me somehow, like a vanishing cosmetic."

He shuddered slightly, briefly.

"As I say, nothing happened all that day, or that night, or the next day. But the next night," and his voice dropped suddenly to a breathy mutter, "was the night of the full moon."

On the instant I remembered a host of stories with which my childhood nurse had regaled me, stories about the full moon and its effect on the human soul and fate. Few of them had been pleasant. Craw was plunging ahead:

"Moonlight meant romance to me then, and nothing more. Collegian-like, I went on a riverside walk with a girl—a Liberal Arts sophomore. There was a sort of sandy jut out into the water, and we loitered there. Something I said made her laugh, with her face turned up to me in the moonlight. Then she stopped laughing, and her mouth twisted like a snake when you step on it."

"Whatever for?" I almost gasped.

"Her eyes—on my face—were frightened."

Craw leaned suddenly toward me. I caught, or fancied I caught, a whiff of musky odor as from an animal cage. In spite of myself I slid back and away from him on the cushions. I had just remembered that there was a full moon tonight.

Again Craw's tense voice: "She tried to scream and, frightened myself, I grasped her by the shoulder to calm her. When I touched her flesh, a new mood suddenly took possession of me. Of its own will my hand switched to her throat. Shaking her, I snarled at her to be silent. And she sagged down, in a faint. My thoughts and senses churned all up, as if in a new feeling of exultation at conquest. Then—"

He spread his great, spatulate fingers.

"In the morning they found her gnawed body. In the afternoon, while

I was still telling myself that it was a dream, the police came to my dormitory. They found blood on my clothing and under my nails."

"You were *that* Craw!" I exclaimed.

His smile was bitter and tight-lipped this time. "Oh, so you read the papers? 'Undergraduate beast-man' the headlines called me, and 'medico monster.' What I told the police—the solemn truth—was too much for them to believe. They called in alienists. So I was sent to the asylum, not to the electric chair."

"Look here," I ventured, in a voice that threatened to close up in my throat with every word, "I think you'd better talk about something else. You shouldn't have let yourself talk about this business in the first place."

But he shook his head so emphatically that the coarse locks stirred at his narrow temples. "I'm not crazy, old chap. You see, just two weeks ago I was officially certified normal." He sniffed. "How could they know the frenzy, the throttling rage and the blood thirst, that closed over me like water in my locked room—every month, on the night when the moon was full?"

His clenched hands lifted. I saw his nails, pointed and thick and opaque, like pieces of mussel-shell.

"I used to howl and shriek, so that the attendants came to pacify me. They got bitten for their pains; so there were barred cells and straitjackets. It was two years before a cunning sneaked in with the moon-madness, a cunning that whispered I must suffer in silence if ever I wanted to go free."

"And you were silent?"

"I was. At length the doctors had me up for another examination. They hammered at my knees for reflexes, asked a bunch of clever questions, and finally discharged me as cured." Once again a pause. "But I wasn't cured, of course."

"Surely," I mouthed in the most stupid fashion imaginable, "surely you wanted to be cured."

"Of course." Craw snapped his big teeth together after the two words, as though they needed emphasis. "So I turned to the Wurthers, as I said at the beginning. I'd heard somewhere that they knew devil and all about occultism and the night side of the soul. A week ago I hunted James Wurther out at his club and told him the whole cursed business."

"Told him what you've just told me?"

"Exactly. And he heard me out, then said nothing for a full five minutes. Finally he smiled and said, 'I'll help you. On the night of the full moon I'll be entertaining. Come to my place then, and we'll make everything all right.' "

He leaned against the cushions, as if his story was done. I wriggled nervously, wondering whether he was very clever, even cleverer than most of the bizarre Wurther guests, or whether he was dangerous. I weighed the chances of getting up and walking away without seeming too furtive. . . .

"Oh, there you are, Mr. Craw!" squealed Lola Wurther behind our shoulders. "Some new people have come—girls—and they're dying to meet—"

She swooped down upon him and bore him away toward three young women with vapid, painted smiles.

It was my chance to leave, and I took it. I crossed the room to the chairs where the hats and coats were piled. Glancing back, I saw Craw yet again, from behind.

His shoulders seemed strangely narrow, and humped in a fashion somehow hyenalike. His hair—perhaps it was not carefully combed at the back of his low skull—was shaggy. A first I had thought his ears flat, but I saw now that they inclined forward, as though involuntarily pricked up.

"He claims to be a werewolf," Lola Wurther was finishing her introduction, and a tinkle of laughter ascended all around.

I got my things and left without being noticed.

That was last night. Before me lies the morning paper, with an arresting headline:

4 TORN CORPSES
FOUND IN PARLOR

———

Police Baffled Over Murder
of James Wurther and
Guests

———

SEEK "BEAST MAN"

I have not yet forced myself to read the rest.

The White Dog

FEODOR SOLOGUB

Everything was irksome for Alexandra Ivanovna in the workship of this out-of-the-way town. It was the shop in which she had served as apprentice and now for several years as seamstress. Everything irritated Alexandra Ivanovna; she quarreled with everyone and abused the apprentices. Among others to suffer from her tantrums was Tanechka, the youngest of the seamstresses, who had only recently become an apprentice.

In the beginning Tanechka submitted to her abuse in silence. In the end she revolted, and, addressing her assailant, said quite calmly and affably, so that everyone laughed, "Alexandra Ivanovna, you are a dog!"

Alexandra Ivanovna scowled.

"You are a dog yourself!" she exclaimed.

Tanechka was sitting sewing. She paused now and then from her work and said, calmly and deliberately, "You always whine . . . you certainly are a dog. . . . You have a dog's snout . . . and a dog's ears . . . and a wagging tail. . . . The mistress will soon drive you out of doors, because you are the most detestable of dogs—a poodle."

Tanechka was a young, plump, rosy-cheeked girl with a good-natured face that revealed a trace of cunning. She sat there demurely, barefooted, still dressed in her apprentice clothes; her eyes were clear, and her brows were highly arched on her finely curved white forehead, framed by straight dark chestnut hair, which looked black in the distance. Tanechka's voice was clear, even, sweet, insinuating, and if one could have heard its sound only, and not given heed to the words, it would have given the impression that she was paying Alexandra Ivanovna compliments.

The other seamstresses laughed, the apprentices chuckled, they covered their faces with their black aprons and cast side glances at Alexandra Ivanovna, who was livid with rage.

"Wretch!" she exclaimed. "I will pull your ears for you! I won't leave a hair on your head!"

Tanechka replied in a gentle voice: "The paws are a bit short. . . . The poodle bites as well as barks. . . . It may be necessary to buy a muzzle."

Alexandra Ivanovna made a movement toward Tanechka. But before Tanechka had time to lay aside her work and get up, the mistress of the establishment entered.

"Alexandra Ivanovna," she said sternly, "what do you mean by making such a fuss?"

Alexandra Ivanovna, much agitated, replied, "Irina Petrovna, I wish you would forbid her to call me a dog!"

Tanechka in her turn complained: "She is always snarling at something or other."

But the mistress looked at her sternly and said, "Tanechka, I can see through you. Are you sure you didn't begin it? You needn't think that because you are a seamstress now you are an important person. If it weren't for your mother's sake—"

Tanechka grew red, but preserved her innocent and affable manner. She addressed her mistress in a subdued voice: "Forgive me, Irina Petrovna, I will not do it again. But it wasn't altogether my fault. . . ."

Alexandra Ivanovna returned home almost ill with rage. Tanechka had guessed her weakness.

"A dog! Well, then, I am a dog" thought Alexandra Ivanovna, "but it is none of her affair! Have I looked to see whether she is a serpent or a fox? It is easy to find one out, but why make a fuss about it? Is a dog worse than any other animal?"

The clear summer night languished and sighed. A soft breeze from the adjacent fields occasionally blew down the peaceful streets. The moon rose clear and full, that very same moon that rose long ago at another place, over the broad desolate steppe, the home of the wild, of those who ran free and whined in their ancient earthly travail.

And now, as then, glowed eyes sick with longing; and her heart, still wild, not forgetting in town the great spaciousness of the steppe, felt oppressed; her throat was troubled with a tormenting desire to howl.

She was about to undress, but what was the use? She could not sleep anyway. She went into the passage. The planks of the floor bent and creaked under her, and small shavings and sand that covered them tickled her feet not unpleasantly.

She went out on the doorstep. There sat the *babushka* Stepanida, a black figure in her black shawl, gaunt and shriveled. She sat with her head bent, and seemed to be warming herself in the rays of the cold moon.

Alexandra Ivanovna sat down beside her. She kept looking at the old woman sideways. The large curved nose of her companion seemed to her like the beak of an old bird.

"A crow?" Alexandra Ivanovna asked herself.

She smiled, forgetting for the moment her longing and her fears. Shrewd as the eyes of a dog, her own eyes lighted up with the joy of her discovery. In the pale green light of the moon the wrinkles of her faded face became altogether invisible, and she seemed once more young and merry and lighthearted, just as she was ten years ago, when the moon had not yet called upon her to bark and bay of nights before the windows of the dark bathhouse.

She moved closer to the old woman, and said affably, "*Babushka* Stepanida, there is something I have been wanting to ask you."

The old woman turned to her, her dark face furrowed with wrinkles, and asked in a sharp, oldish voice that sounded like a caw, "Well, my dear? Go ahead and ask."

Alexandra Ivanovna gave a repressed laugh; her thin shoulders suddenly trembled from a chill that ran down her spine.

She spoke very quietly: "*Babushka* Stepanida, it seems to me—tell me is it true?—I don't know exactly how to put it—but you, *babushka*, please don't take offense—it is not from malice that I—"

"Go on, my dear, say it," said the old woman, looking at Alexandra Ivanovna with glowing eyes.

"It seems to me, *babushka*—please, now, don't take offense—as if you, *babushka*, were a crow."

The old woman turned away. She nodded her head, and seemed like one who had recalled something. Her head, with its sharply outlined nose, bowed and nodded, and at last it seemed to Alexandra Ivanovna that the old woman was dozing. Dozing, and mumbling something under her nose—nodding and mumbling old forgotten words, old magic words.

An intense quiet reigned out of doors. It was neither light nor dark, and everything seemed bewitched with the inarticulate mumbling of old, forgotten words. Everything languished and seemed lost in apathy.

Again a longing oppressed her heart. And it was neither a dream nor an illusion. A thousand perfumes, imperceptible by day, became subtly distinguishable, and they recalled something ancient and primitive.

In a barely audible voice the old woman mumbled, "Yes, I am a crow.

Only I have no wings. But there are times when I caw, and I caw, and tell of woe. And I am given to forebodings, my dear; each time I have one I simply must caw. People are not particularly anxious to hear me. And when I see a doomed person I have such a strong desire to caw."

The old woman suddenly made a sweeping movement with her arms, and in a shrill voice cried out twice: "Kar-r, Kar-r!"

Alexandra Ivanovna shuddered, and asked, *"Babushka,* at whom are you cawing?"

"At you, my dear," the old woman answered. "I am cawing at you."

It had become too painful to sit with the old woman any longer. Alexandra Ivanovna went to her own room. She sat down before the open window and listened to two voices at the gate.

"It simply won't stop whining!" said a low and harsh voice.

"And uncle, did you see?" asked an agreeable young tenor.

Alexandra Ivanovna recognized in this last the voice of the curly-headed, freckled-faced lad who lived in the same court.

A brief and depressing silence followed. Then she heard a hoarse and harsh voice say suddenly, "Yes, I saw. It's very large—and white. It lies near the bathhouse, and bays at the moon."

The voice gave her an image of the man, of his shovel-shaped beard, his low, furrowed forehead, his small, piggish eyes, and his spread-out fat legs.

"And why does it bay, uncle?" asked the agreeable voice.

And again the hoarse voice did not reply at once.

"Certainly to no good purpose—and where it came from is more than I can say."

"Do you think, uncle, it may be a werewolf?" asked the agreeable voice.

"I should not advise you to investigate," replied the hoarse voice.

She could not quite understand what these words implied, nor did she wish to think of them. She did not feel inclined to listen further. What was the sound and significance of human words to her?

The moon looked straight into her face and persistently called her and tormented her. Her heart was restless with a dark longing, and she could not sit still.

Alexandra Ivanovna quickly undressed herself. Naked, all white, she silently stole through the passage she then opened the outer door (there was no one on the step or outside) and ran quickly across the court and the vegetable garden, and reached the bathhouse. The sharp contact of her body with the cold air and her feet with the cold ground gave her pleasure. But soon her body was warm.

She lay down in the grass, on her stomach. Then, raising herself on her elbows, she lifted her face toward the pale, brooding moon, and gave a long-drawn-out whine.

"Listen, uncle, it is whining," said the curly-haired lad at the gate. The agreeable tenor voice trembled perceptibly.

"Whining again, the accurst one!" said the hoarse, harsh voice slowly.

They rose from the bench. The gate latch clicked.

They went silently across the courtyard and the vegetable garden, the two of them. The older man, blackbearded and powerful, walked in front, a gun in his hand. The curly-headed lad followed tremblingly, and looked constantly behind.

Near the bathhouse, in the grass, lay a huge white dog, whining piteously. Its head, black on the crown, was raised to the moon, which pursued its way in the cold sky; its hind legs were strangely thrown backward, while the front ones, firm and straight, pressed hard against the ground.

In the pale green and unreal light of the moon it seemed enormous. So huge a dog was surely never seen on earth. It was thick and fat. The black spot, which began at the head and stretched in uneven strands down the entire spine, seemed like a woman's loosened hair. No tail was visible; presumably it was turned under. The fur on the body was so short that in the distance the dog seemed wholly naked, and its hide shone dimly in the moonlight, so that altogether it resembled the body of a nude woman, who lay in the grass and bayed at the moon.

The man with the black beard took aim. The curly-haired lad crossed himself and mumbled something.

The discharge of a rifle sounded in the night air. The dog gave a groan, jumped up on its hind legs, became a naked woman, who, her body covered with blood, started to run, all the while groaning, weeping, and raising cries of distress.

The black-bearded one and the curly-haired one threw themselves in the grass, and began to moan in wild terror.

The White Wyrak

Stefan Grabinski
(Translated by Miroslaw Lipinski)

I was a young journeyman at that time, like you, my dear boys, and I worked like a house on fire. Master Kalina—may the Lord shine on his worthy soul—frequently said I would be first in attaining mastership following him, and he spoke of me as the pride of our profession. I don't want to brag, but I had strong legs and could dig my elbows into a chimney like no one else. In the third year of my service, I received the assistance of two apprentices and became an instructor to my younger comrades.

In all, there were seven of us. We got along splendidly with one another. Even on holidays and Sundays our brotherhood would gather at the master's house for a chat by a beer or, when it was winter, by warm tea near the chimney, and we talked our fill, so that the evenings we spent together passed nicely, like a brush lowered into the mouth of a furnace.

Kalina—what can I say about him? The man was literate and intelligent. He had seen a lot of the world. As the saying goes, he cleaned out not just one chimney. He was a bit of a philosopher, and books he really liked. He apparently even wanted to put out a gazette for chimney sweepers. But in matters of faith he didn't play the philosopher; on the contrary, he had a particular devotion to St. Florian, our patron.

I felt closest to the master and, after him, to the young journeyman Jozek Biedron, a boy as pure as gold, whom I liked for his good heart and gentle soul. Unfortunately I wouldn't enjoy his friendship for long!

After Biedron, I most liked Antarek, a melancholic lad who usually kept to himself. He was a born worker, however, conscientious and strangely relentless in his job. Kalina valued him a lot and tried to get him to socialize with people, though without success. Nevertheless, Antarek gladly spent his evenings at the master's house, listening with interest from his dark corner to the master's stories, which he completely believed.

And no one could tell a story like our "old man." He drew out them out as if from a bag, one more interesting than the other. When he finished one, he would start a new one, then throw in a third one, and so on. And in each story one could detect some deeper thought hidden behind all those words. But one was still young and foolish then, and took from these stories only what amused one, for a laugh. Only Antarek looked at the master's tales in a different light, and managed to get to their core. The rest of us, however, called Kalina's stories balderdash. They were engrossing, sometimes horrible, until one's flesh crept and one's hair stood on end, but despite it all, only tales and balderdash. Yet life soon taught us a little differently. . . .

One day in the middle of summer, a comrade of ours was absent at our evening get-together: Antarek was not present at his usual dark corner beyond the cupboard.

"He must have gotten sidetracked with some girls," joked Biedron, though he knew that his friend was ill at ease with women and avoided their company.

"Stop talking nonsense," Kalina said. "He's probably very depressed and is sitting at home like a bear in the back woods."

The evening passed sadly and slowly, as it was without the presence of our most fervent listener.

There was no joking around the following morning, for Antarek did not show up for work at ten o'clock. The master thought he was sick and went to his home. He found only his mother there, an old woman much distressed by her son's absence. She reported that her son had left for the city at dawn of the previous day and had not yet returned.

Kalina decided to undertake the search himself.

"Antarek is a gloomy fellow; God knows what he's done. Maybe he's hiding out somewhere."

But he searched in vain. Finally, remembering that Antarek had to clean out a chimney in an old brewery beyond the city, he directed his investigation there.

At the brewery he was told that, indeed, yesterday morning a journeyman had reported to them to clean the chimney.

"At what time did he finish the job?" asked Kalina of some old man, gray like a pigeon, whom he met at the threshold of the one of the brewery's annexes.

"I don't know, Master. He left so imperceptibly that we even didn't know when. He must have been in a great hurry because he didn't even look in to us for payment."

"Hmm . . ." muttered Kalina, lost in thought. "A strange bird, that fellow. But did he clean out the chimney well? How is it working now? Is it drawing properly?"

"Not too well. This morning my daughter-in-law complained once again that it's smoking terribly. If it doesn't get better by tomorrow, we'll ask for another cleaning."

"It will be done," the master quickly retorted, angry that here they were not satisfied with his worker, and very worried about the lack of more specific information concerning him.

That evening we gathered together in sorrow at our supper and parted early. The following day the same thing: neither sight nor sound of Antarek—he had disappeared like a stone in water.

In the early afternoon the brewery sent a boy with the request to clean the chimney because it was "smoking for all it's worth."

Biedron went around four and didn't return. I wasn't there when Kalina sent him out, so I knew nothing about it. But I got a bad feeling when, later that evening, I saw the downcast faces of the master and the other sweeps.

"Where's Jozek?" I asked, looking for him about the room.

"He hasn't returned from the brewery," answered Kalina gloomily.

I jumped up from my seat. But the master forcibly stopped me:

"I won't let you go alone. I've had enough of this! Tomorrow morning both of us will go. An evil spirit, not a brewery! I'll clean out their chimney for them!"

That night I didn't sleep a wink. At daybreak I put on my climbing gear, and throwing over my shoulder my brushes with their attachments, I went out and in a short while presented myself at the master's door.

Kalina was already waiting for me.

"Take this," he said, handing me a hatchet that appeared to be newly whetted. "This could be more of use to you than a broom or a scraper."

Without a word I took the hatchet, and we started at a quick pace toward the brewery.

The August morning was beautiful and tranquil. The city still slept. In silence we passed through the marketplace, went over the bridge, and turned left, along the river embankment, onto a road that wound its way through poplar trees.

It was a long walk to the brewery. After a strenuous pace of fifteen minutes, we got off the road and took a shortcut through a hayfield. In the distance, beyond an alder forest, the coppery slices of the brewery roofs were visible.

Kalina removed the cap from his head, crossed himself, and began silently to move his lips. I walked next to him, not interrupting his prayers. After a while the master covered his head again, gripped his hatchet tighter, and starting talking in a soft voice:

"An evil spirit, not a brewery. There's beer there and for at least ten years it hasn't been brewed. An old ruin and nothing more. The last brewer, someone named Rozban, went bankrupt and hanged himself out of despair. His family sold the buildings and the entire inventory dirt-cheap to the city, and moved away somewhere. No one has lived there since. The boilers and machines are supposed to be evil. They're of an old system. No one wants to take the financial risk of replacing it with a new one."

"Then who exactly wanted the chimney cleaned?" I asked, glad that the conversation had interrupted the morose silence.

"Some gardener, who a month ago, for practically nothing, moved into the empty brewery with his wife and his father. They have many rooms and enough space for several families. For sure they moved into the center rooms, which are in the best state, and they are living there for very little money. Now their chimneys are smoking, because they are old and heavily packed with soot. They haven't been cleaned for ages." He added after a thoughtful pause: "I don't like these old chimneys."

"Why? Because there's more work with them?"

"Don't be silly, my dear boy. I'm afraid of them, do you understand? I'm afraid of old flues that haven't been touched for years by a brush or scraper. It's better to demolish such a chimney and put up a new one than to have someone clean it."

I glanced at Kalina's face at that moment. It was strangely altered by fear and aversion.

"What's the matter, Master?"

And he, as if he hadn't heard, continued on, staring somewhere ahead:

"Soot is dangerous, particularly when it accumulates in narrow, dark spaces unreachable by the rays of the sun. And not just because it can easily catch fire. No, not just because of that. Consider this, we chimney sweeps battle our entire lives with soot, we prevent its excessive accumulation, and so prevent an explosion. But soot is treacherous, my boy, soot lays dormant inside dark smoke chambers and stuffy furnaces, and it lies in wait—for an opportunity. Something vindictive resides in soot, something evil lurks there. You never know what will emerge from it, or when."

He became silent and glanced at me. Even though I didn't understand what he had said, his words, uttered with such strong conviction, had their effect on me. But he smiled his good, kindhearted smile, and added soothingly:

"Maybe I'm wrong, maybe something completely different has happened here. Cheer up! We'll find out everything in a moment. We've arrived at our destination."

Indeed, we had reached the brewery. Through the open entrance gate, I followed the master to the wide courtyard, from which a multitude of doors led to the various buildings of the brewery. At the threshold of one door sat the gardener's wife, a child at her breast; while beyond her, leaning against the door sill, stood her husband. Seeing us, the man became confused and with visible uneasiness came out to greet us:

"You've come to see us about the chimney?"

"Of course, you," the master answered coldly, "but not because of the chimney, but because of the two people I sent to clean it."

The gardener's uneasiness increased; his eyes shifted continually.

"My men haven't yet returned from this brewery!" cried out Kalina passionately, glaring at him. "What happened to them? You're responsible for them!"

"But, sir," the gardener mumbled, "I really don't know what happened to them. We thought that the first one had already turned up, and as for the second one—I just don't know. Yesterday afternoon, in my presence, he entered the chimney through the door in the kitchen wall; for some time I clearly heard him scraping the soot away. I would have remained to the end of the operation if I hadn't been called out to the courtyard. Afterward, I left my home for a couple of hours, and when I returned, nothing was said about the chimney or your man. I thought that he had done his job and returned to the city, so we closed the ventilation door for the night. Only now, when I saw the both of you entering our courtyard, did I become troubled. It suddenly occurred to me that something terrible has been happening here for the last two days. I see that I am right. But what is going on, Master Kalina? What can be done?" He spread out his hands in a sign of innocence. "I'm not to blame."

"At least you shouldn't have closed the door to the chimney, fool!" Kalina cried out angrily. "After me, Peter!" he shouted, pulling me by the arm. "We don't have a second to lose." And to the gardener: "Take us to the chimney!"

The terrified gardener led us inside. We soon found ourselves in the kitchen.

"Here, in the corner," said the gardener, pointing to the rectangular chimney door.

Kalina took a step toward it, but, anticipating him, I moved quickly and opened the small door.

A smell of smoke blew over us, and a little soot fell to the floor.

Before the master could interfere, I was already kneeling at the inlet, my arms stretched upward in preparation for a climb.

"Are you crazy?" Kalina's angry voice responded. "Let me go up! This is my affair. You set up the ladder to the roof and get on top to guard the outlet."

For the first time in my life I did not listen to him. A mad stubbornness and a desire to uncover the truth possessed me completely.

"Why don't you go to the roof yourself, Master!" I responded. "I promise to wait here until you give me the signal."

Kalina uttered an ugly curse, and whether he liked it or not, he had to surrender to my command. Soon I heard his distancing steps. Then I tied a silk mask tightly over my mouth and nose, adjusted the straps at my belt, and gripped the hatchet. Before you could say two Hail Marys I heard the knocking of the ball that had been lowered down the chimney: Kalina was already on the roof and was giving me the agreed-upon signal.

I crawled on all fours into the throat of the chimney and, groping about, found the ball. I pulled on it three times in a sign that I had received the signal and was commencing my journey.

After passing the turn in the chimney, I straightened up, instinctively protecting my head with the hatchet.

The chimney was wide, navigable with ridges, and thickly packed with soot. Here at the bottom, right beside the door, layers of easily flammable "enamel" glowed with a cold metallic luster in the faint light coming from the top of the chimney.

I threw a glance upward—and shuddered.

Above me, several feet beyond the blade of my hatchet, I saw in the half-light of the flue a snow-white being staring at me with a pair of huge, owlish yellow eyes.

The creature—part monkey, part large frog—was holding in his front claws what seemed like a human arm, which hung limply from a corpse, vaguely outlined in a twisted shape next to the neighboring wall.

Drenched in cold sweat, I propped myself against the sides of the chimney with my legs and raised myself up slightly. Then, from the creature's long mouth came a savage predatory sound, and he ground his teeth menacingly. My movement seemed to have alarmed him, and he apparently changed position, for at that moment a wider shaft of light rushed into the depths of the chimney and lit up the horrible picture more clearly.

Attached through some miracle, as if stuck to the wall with the bottom of his toes, the creature held Biedron tightly with his arms. His rear limbs, covered with white, downy fur, wrapped in a crosswise grip the legs of his victim, while the greedy proboscis of his elongated snout now adhered to the temple of the unfortunate man.

A rage enveloped me, and overcoming my fear, I climbed up a couple more feet. The white creature, apparently upset, turned to me again and started to prick his spoonlike ears and grind his teeth ever more loudly, but he didn't move from his place.

I saw his vain endeavors as he wanted to spring down on me or escape up the chimney. But his movements were unusually awkward and ponderous; it seemed that he had grown torpid, as a snake does after swallowing a victim, or that he had become drunk on an overabundance of sucked blood; only his bulging eyes, round like plates, buried themselves into me with increasing severity, and he threatened me with his look and sound. . . .

But my anger predominated over my terror. I drew back the hatchet swiftly and with all my might let it go on the horrible white skull.

The blow was strong and accurate. In one moment the light in his large eyes died out, something brushed by me, and I heard a dull groan below; the strange being had fallen to the bottom of the chimney, pulling down his victim in the process.

A shudder of disgust shook me to the core; I didn't have courage to go down and check the result of my blow. The only thing left for me to do was to go up to the roof. Besides, I was already at the halfway point in the chimney, from whose outlet I heard Kalina's voice.

I began a quick climb to the top, using all my strength to dig into the sides of the chimney with my elbows and legs. But who can relate my horror when a couple of feet higher I saw, hanging on a hook sticking out of the wall, the carcass of Antarek?

The body of the poor man was in a terrible state—incredibly gaunt and shriveled up to a sliver—almost skin and bones. It seemed half-cured by exposure to smoke, and was stretched out like a string, and dry and hard like a piece of wood.

With trembling hands I unhooked the carcass, and winding its middle a few times with the rope from the ball, I pulled twice on the cord as a signal to Kalina.

A couple of minutes later, I found myself on the roof, where the master was waiting for me, Antarek's body by his side. He greeted me sullenly, with knitted brows.

"Where's Biedron?" he asked tersely.

In a few words I told him everything.

After we had carefully lowered Antarek to the ground along the ladder, he said calmly:

"The White Wyrak. That was him. I had a feeling it would be him."

In silence we went through the hall and two rooms, and returned to the kitchen. There wasn't a living soul here; the gardener and his family had slunk away to some wing of the building.

Placing Antarek's body by the wall, we advanced to the opening of the chimney. Sticking out of it were a pair of stiff, naked legs.

We pulled out Biedron and placed him on the floor by his comrade.

"See those two small wounds they have on their temples?" asked Kalina in a subdued voice. "That is his sign. He cuts into his victims there and consumes them." And he repeated a couple of times: "The White Wyrak! The White Wyrak!"

"I have to finish him off," I replied stubbornly. "Maybe he isn't dead yet."

"I doubt it. Apparently he can't stand light. Let's take a look, though."

And we gazed into the depths of the opening.

Deep inside we vaguely saw something white. Kalina glanced about the kitchen and spotted a long pole with an iron hook at its end. He picked up the pole and shoved it into the chimney opening. Then he started to draw it out. . . .

Slowly a white mass began to emerge from the darkness, a sort of snowy, downy fleece that came closer and closer to the ventilator.

But along the way, the Wyrak's corpse seemed to melt and contract. When Kalina finally drew out the entire pole, there hung from its iron tip only a small, milk-white substance; it was flaky and disarranged, and resembled a soft hide or fluff.

Suddenly this substance slid off the hook and fell to the ground. And then a strange change occurred in it; in the twinkling of an eye, the white material turned a coallike color, and at our feet lay a large mass of soot—glittering and black like tar.

"That's all that remains of him," whispered Kalina, plunged in thought.

And after a moment he added, as if to himself:

"From soot you came, and to soot you shall return."

584

And placing our unfortunate comrades on a stretcher, we carried off their bodies to the city.

Shortly afterward, the master and I got a peculiar outbreak on our skins. Over our entire bodies appeared large white pimples, resembling pearly grits. After several weeks, these pimples disappeared as quickly and as unexpectedly as they had arrived, leaving not a trace of their repulsive presence.